Take One
Take Two

TWO BOOKS IN ONE

WHAT READERS ARE SAYING ABOUT KAREN KINGSBURY'S BOOKS

Karen's book *Oceans Apart* changed my life. She has an amazing gift of bringing a reader into her stories. I can only pray she never stops writing.

Susan L.

Everyone should have the opportunity to read or listen to a book by Karen Kingsbury. It should be in the *Bill of Rights*.

Rachel S.

I want to thank Karen Kingsbury for what she is doing with the power of her storytelling—touching hearts like mine and letting God use her to change the world for Him.

Brittney N.

Karen Kingsbury's books are filled with the unshakable, remarkable, miraculous fact that God's grace is greater than our suffering. There are no words for Ms. Kingsbury's writing.

Wendie K.

Because I loaned these books to my mother, she BECAME a Christian! Thank you for a richer life here and in heaven!

Jennifer E.

When I read my first Karen Kingsbury book, I couldn't stop.... I read thirteen more in one summer!

Jamie B.

I have never read anything so uplifting and entertaining. I'm shocked as I read each new release because it's always better than the last one.

                                            Bonnie S.

I am unable to put your books down, and I plan to read many more of them. What a wonderful spiritual message I find in each one!

                                            Rhonda T.

I love the way Karen Kingsbury writes, and the topics she chooses to write about! Thank you so much for sharing your talent with us, your readers!

                                            Barbara S.

My husband is equally hooked on your books. It is a family affair for us now! Can't wait for the next one.

                                            Angie

I can't even begin to tell you what your books mean to me.... Thank you for your wonderful books and the way they touch my life again and again.

                                            Martje L.

Every time our school buys your next new book, everybody goes crazy trying to read it first!

                                            Roxanne

Recently I made an effort to find GOOD Christian writers, and I've hit the jackpot with Karen Kingsbury!

                                            Linda

When Karen Kingsbury calls her books "Life-Changing Fiction," she's merely telling the unvarnished truth. I'm still sorting through the changes in my life that have come from reading just a few of her books!

                                            Robert M.

I must admit that I wish I was a much slower reader ... or you were a much faster writer. Either way, I can't seem to get enough of Karen Kingsbury's books!

Jillian B.

I was offered $50 one time in the airport for the fourth book in the Redemption Series. The lady's husband just couldn't understand why I wasn't interested in selling it. Through sharing Karen's books with my friends, many have decided that contemporary Christian fiction is the next best thing to the Bible. Thank you so much, Karen. It is truly a God-thing that you write the way you do.

Sue Ellen H.

Karen Kingsbury's books have made me see things in ways that I had never thought about before. I have to force myself to put them down and come up for air!

Tabitha H.

Other Life-Changing Fiction™ by Karen Kingsbury

9/11 Series
- One Tuesday Morning
- Beyond Tuesday Morning
- Every Now and Then

Lost Love Series
- Even Now
- Ever After

Above the Line Series
- Above the Line: Take One
- Above the Line: Take Two
- Above the Line: Take Three (spring 2010)
- Above the Line: Take Four (summer 2010)

Red Glove Series
- Gideon's Gift
- Maggie's Miracle
- Sarah's Song
- Hannah's Hope

Stand-Alone Titles
- Oceans Apart
- Between Sundays
- When Joy Came to Stay
- On Every Side
- Divine
- Like Dandelion Dust
- Where Yesterday Lives
- Shades of Blue

Redemption Series
- Redemption
- Remember
- Return
- Rejoice
- Reunion

Sunrise Series
- Sunrise
- Summer
- Someday
- Sunset

Firstborn Series
- Fame
- Forgiven
- Found
- Family
- Forever

Cody Gunner Series
- A Thousand Tomorrows
- Just Beyond the Clouds

Women of Faith Fiction Series
- A Time to Dance
- A Time to Embrace

Forever Faithful Series
- Waiting for Morning
- Moment of Weakness
- Halfway to Forever

Children's Titles
- Let Me Hold You Longer
- Let's Go on a Mommy Date
- We Believe in Christmas

Miracle Collections
- A Treasury of Christmas Miracles
- A Treasury of Miracles for Women
- A Treasury of Miracles for Teens
- A Treasury of Miracles for Friends
- A Treasury of Adoption Miracles

Gift Books
- Stay Close Little Girl
- Be Safe Little Boy
- Forever Young: Ten Gifts of Faith for the Graduate

www.KarenKingsbury.com

KAREN KINGSBURY

#1 BESTSELLING AUTHOR

Take One

TWO BOOKS IN ONE

Take Two

ZONDERVAN

ZONDERVAN.com/
AUTHORTRACKER
follow your favorite authors

ZONDERVAN

Take One /Take Two Compilation
Copyright © 2009 by Karen Kingsbury

Take One
Copyright © 2009 by Karen Kingsbury

Take Two
Copyright © 2009 by Karen Kingsbury

This title is also available as a Zondervan ebook.
Visit www.zondervan.com/ebooks.

This title is also available in a Zondervan audio edition.
Visit www.zondervan.fm.

Requests for information should be addressed to:

Zondervan, *Grand Rapids, Michigan* 49530

ISBN-10: 031062021x
ISBN-13: 9780310620211

All Scripture quotations, unless otherwise indicated, are taken from the Holy Bible, *New International Version®, NIV®.* Copyright © 1973, 1978, 1984 by Biblica, Inc.™ Used by permission of Zondervan. All rights reserved worldwide.

Any Internet addresses (websites, blogs, etc.) and telephone numbers printed in this book are offered as a resource. They are not intended in any way to be or imply an endorsement by Zondervan, nor does Zondervan vouch for the content of these sites and numbers for the life of this book.

All rights reserved. No part of this publication may be reproduced, stored in a retrieval system, or transmitted in any form or by any means — electronic, mechanical, photocopy, recording, or any other — except for brief quotations in printed reviews, without the prior permission of the publisher.

Published in association with the literary agency of Alive Communications, Inc., 7680 Goddard Street, Suite 200, Colorado Springs, CO 80920. www.alivecommunications.com

Interior design: Michelle Espinoza

Printed in the United States of America

11 12 13 14 15 16 17 18 /DCI/ 20 19 18 17 16 15 14 13 12 11 10 9 8 7 6 5 4 3 2 1

DEDICATION

To Donald, my Prince Charming...

How I rejoice to see you coaching again, sharing your gift of teaching and your uncanny basketball ability with another generation of kids—and best yet, now our boys are part of the mix. Isn't this what we always dreamed of? I love sitting back this time and letting you and God figure it out. I'll always be here—cheering for you and the team from the bleachers. But God's taught me a thing or two about being a coach's wife. He's so good that way. It's fitting that you would find varsity coaching again now—after twenty years of marriage. Hard to believe that as you read this, our twentieth anniversary has come and gone. I look at you and I still see the blond, blue-eyed guy who would ride his bike to my house and read the Bible with me before a movie date. You stuck with me back then and you stand by me now—when I need you more than ever. I love you, my husband, my best friend, my Prince Charming. Stay with me, by my side, and let's watch our children take wing, savoring every memory and each day gone by. Always and always ... The ride is breathtakingly beautiful, my love. I pray it lasts far into our twilight years. Until then, I'll enjoy not always knowing where I end and you begin. I love you always and forever.

To Kelsey, my precious daughter...

You are nineteen now, a young woman, and my heart soars with joy when I see all that you are, all you've become. This year is a precious one for us because you're still home, attending junior college and spending nearly every day in the dance studio.

When you're not dancing, you're helping out with the business and ministry of Life-Changing Fiction™—so we have many precious hours together. I know this time is short and won't last, but I'm enjoying it so much—you, no longer the high school girl, a young woman and in every way my daughter, my friend. That part will always stay, but you, my sweet girl, will go where your dreams lead, soaring through the future doors God opens. Honey, you grow more beautiful—inside and out—every day. And always I treasure the way you talk to me, telling me your hopes and dreams and everything in between. I can almost sense the plans God has for you, the very good plans. I pray you keep holding on to His hand as He walks you toward them. I love you, sweetheart.

To Tyler, my lasting song ...

I can hardly wait to see what this school year brings you, my precious son. Last year you were one of Joseph's brothers, and you were Troy Bolton, and Captain Hook—becoming a stronger singer and stage actor with every role. This year you'll be at a new high school, where I believe God will continue to shape you as the leader He wants you to be. Your straight A's last year were a sign of things to come, and I couldn't be prouder, Ty. I know it was hard watching Kelsey graduate, knowing that your time with your best friend is running short. But you'll be fine, and no matter where God leads you in the future, the deep and lasting relationships you've begun here in your childhood will remain. Thank you for the hours of music and song. As you finish up your sophomore year, I am mindful that the time is rushing past, and I make a point to stop and listen a little longer when I hear you singing. I'm proud of you, Ty, of the young man you've become. I'm proud of your talent and your compassion for people and your place in our family. However your dreams unfold, I'll be in the front row to watch them happen. Hold on to Jesus, Ty. I love you.

Take One   *11*

To Sean, my happy sunshine...

   What a thrill it was watching you play tackle football for the first time this past school year. No question you were the fastest receiver on the field, always open and ready for a touchdown catch. Your papa would've loved watching you and Josh play under the lights, but I still believe he has a window, that somewhere in heaven he has a great seat with a perfect view. New things are just around the corner for you, Sean. I can hardly believe you are starting high school in the fall, taking on a host of new adventures in the process. Always remember who you are and whose you are as you venture into that next step. One of the things I love most about you, Sean, is your beautiful smile and the way your eyes light up when we're together as a family. Keep that always. You are a bright sunbeam, bringing warmth to everyone around you.

   One thing that will stand out about this past year is your crazy ping-pong skills. I absolutely love playing against you, Sean. You're quick as lightning and it makes me a better player. Of course ... I never really thought I'd be hoping for a win against my little boy. But then, you're not all that little anymore. I'm proud of you, Sean. I love you more than you know. I pray God will use your positive spirit to always make a difference in the lives around you. You're a precious gift, Son. Keep smiling and keep seeking God's best for your life.

To Josh, my tenderhearted perfectionist...

   The weeks of this past school year have flown by, and you have grown right along with them, my precious son. So many memories will remind me of your eighth grade year, but some will always stand out. The week, for instance, when you scored five touchdowns in your team's city championship—three rushing, two on interception returns. Then that same week you turned around and scored a total of eight goals in two intense soccer games against the top teams in our state. Amazing. No wonder I'm always seeking to make our devotions about staying humble!

Seriously, sweetheart, God has given you tremendous talent in sports. I have no doubt that someday we will see your name in headlines and that—if God allows it—you'll make it to the pros. You're that good, and everyone around you says so. Now flashback to that single moment in a broken-down Haitian orphanage. There I was meeting Sean and EJ for the first time when you walked up, reached up with your small fingers and brushed back my bangs, and said, "Hi, Mommy. I love you." It might've taken six months, but I knew as you said those words that you belonged with us. The picture becomes clearer all the time. Keep being a leader on the field and off. One day people will say, "Hmmm. Karen Kingsbury? Isn't she Josh's mom?" I can't wait for the day. You have an unlimited future ahead of you, Josh, and I'll forever be cheering on the sidelines. Keep God first in your life. I love you always.

To EJ, my chosen one ...

Here you are in the last few months of seventh grade, and I can barely recognize the student athlete you've become. Those two years of homeschooling with Dad continue to reap a harvest a hundred times bigger than what was sown, and we couldn't be prouder of you. But even beyond your grades, we are blessed to have you in our family for so many reasons. You are wonderful with our pets—always the first to feed them and pet them and look out for them—and you are a willing worker when it comes to chores.

Besides all that, you make us laugh—oftentimes right out loud. I've always believed that getting through life's little difficulties and challenges requires a lot of laughter—and I thank you for bringing that to our home. You're a wonderful boy, Son, a child with such potential. Clearly, that's what you displayed the other day when you came out of nowhere in your soccer qualifiers and scored three goals. I'm amazed because you're so talented in so many ways, but all of them pale in comparison to your desire to truly live for the Lord. I'm so excited about the future, EJ, because God has great plans for you, and we want to be the first to congratulate you as you work to discover those. Thanks for your giving heart, EJ. I love you so.

To Austin, my miracle boy ...

Here it is, baseball season again, and once more I smile when I see you up to bat. You take your sports so seriously, but even more than that, you take your role as our son seriously. The other day we were driving somewhere and you said that your friend Karter made an observation. "Austin," he said, "I think you're going to grow up to be just exactly like your dad." You shared that story proudly and beamed at us from the backseat. And up in the front seat, your dad had tears in his eyes.

Yes, Austin, you are growing up to be like your daddy. There could be no greater compliment, because your dad is the most amazing man. The bittersweet of knowing that every morning you stand a little taller is juxtaposed with the joy of knowing that Karter is right. You're a little more like your dad every day. I love your tender heart, Austin, the times late at night when you come to me, tears in your eyes, and tell me you're missing Papa. The other kids miss him too, but I don't hear it from them as often as I hear it from you. Papa's still cheering for you, Son. As you soar toward your teenage years please don't forget that or him. You're my youngest, my last, Austin. I'm holding on to every moment, for sure. Thanks for giving me so many wonderful reasons to treasure today. I thank God for you, for the miracle of your life. I love you, Austin.

And to God Almighty, the Author of Life, who has — for now — blessed me with these.

Acknowledgments

No book comes together without a great and talented team of people making it happen. For that reason, a special thanks to my friends at Zondervan who combined efforts to make *Above the Line: Take One* all it could be. A special thanks to my dedicated editor, Sue Brower, and to my brilliant publicist Karen Campbell, and to Karwyn Bursma, whose creative marketing is unrivaled in the publishing business.

Also, thanks to my amazing agent, Rick Christian, president of Alive Communications. Rick, you've always believed only the best for me. When we talk about the highest possible goals, you see them as doable, reachable. You are a brilliant manager of my career, and I thank God for you. But even with all you do for my ministry of writing, I am doubly grateful for your encouragement and prayers. Every time I finish a book, you send me a letter that deserves to be framed, and when something big happens, yours is the first call I receive. Thank you for that. But even more, the fact that you and Debbie are praying for me and my family keeps me confident every morning that God will continue to breathe life into the stories in my heart. Thank you for being so much more than a brilliant agent.

A special thank-you to my husband, who puts up with me on deadline and doesn't mind driving through Taco Bell after a basketball game if I've been editing all day. This wild ride wouldn't be possible without you, Donald. Your love keeps me writing; your prayers keep me believing that God has a plan in this ministry of fiction. And thanks for the hours you put in working with the guestbook entries on my website. It's a full-time job, and I am grateful for your concern for my reader friends. I look forward to that time every day when you read through them, sharing them with me and releasing them to the public, lifting up the prayer requests. Thank you, honey, and thanks to all my kids, who pull together, bring me iced green tea, and understand my sometimes crazy schedule. I love that you know you're still first, before any deadline.

Thank you also to my mom, Anne Kingsbury, and to my sisters, Tricia, Sue, and Lynne. Mom, you are amazing as my assistant—working day and night sorting through the mail from my readers. I appreciate you more than you'll ever know.

Tricia, you are the best executive assistant I could ever hope to have. I treasure your loyalty and honesty, the way you include me in every decision and the daily exciting website changes. My site has been a different place since you stepped in, and the hits have grown tenfold. Along the way, the readers have so much more to help them in their faith, so much more than a story with this Life-Changing Fiction™. Please know that I pray for God's blessings on you always, for your dedication to helping me in this season of writing, and for your wonderful son, Andrew. And aren't we having such a good time too? God works all things to the good!

Sue, I believe you should've been a counselor! From your home far from mine, you get batches of reader letters every day, and you diligently answer them using God's wisdom and His Word. When readers get a response from "Karen's sister Susan," I hope they know how carefully you've prayed for them and for the responses you give. Thank you for truly loving what you do, Sue. You're gifted with people, and I'm blessed to have you aboard.

A special thanks also to Will Montgomery, my road manager. I was terrified to venture into the business of selling my books at events for a couple of reasons. First, I never wanted to profit from selling my books at speaking events, and second, because I would never have the time to handle such details. Monty, you came in and made it all come together. With a mission statement that reads, "To love and serve the readers," you have helped me supply books and free gifts to tens of thousands of readers at events across the country. More than that, you've become my friend, a very valuable part of the ministry of Life-Changing Fiction™. You are loyal and kind and fiercely protective of me, my family, and the work God has me doing. Thank you for everything you're doing, and will continue to do.

Thanks too, to Olga Kalachik, my office assistant, who helps organize my supplies and storage area, and who prepares our home for the marketing events and research gatherings that take place there on a regular basis. I appreciate all you're doing to make sure I have time to write. You're wonderful, Olga, and I pray God continues to bless you and your precious family.

I also want to thank my friends with Extraordinary Women — Roy Morgan, Tim and Julie Clinton, Beth Cleveland, Charles Billingsley, and so many others. How wonderful to be a part of what God is doing through all of you. Thank you for making me part of your family.

Thanks also to my forever friends and family, the ones who have been there and continue to be there. Your love has been a tangible source of comfort, pulling us through the tough times and making us know how very blessed we are to have you in our lives.

And the greatest thanks to God. The gift is Yours. I pray I might use it for years to come in a way that will bring You honor and glory.

FOREVER IN FICTION

WHENEVER I RECEIVE THE COMPLETED paperwork for a Forever in Fiction winner, I read through the details of the life being honored in fiction—whether the person is alive or dead—and I am touched by the real-life stories that come my way. That was especially true when I heard about Rachel Baugher.

Rachel was the third of four children born to Dan and Sharon Baugher in Chestertown, Maryland. She was kind and loyal, deeply responsible and intelligent. Rachel gave her life to the Lord at a young age and lived out her faith daily. She had an understanding of God and a relationship with Him that went beyond that normally seen in young people. Rachel had brown eyes and long shiny brown hair that fell in gentle layers around her pretty face. Everyone knew her for her smile.

During her high school days, Rachel attended Chestertown Christian Academy where she graduated with a 4.0 and was valedictorian of her class. Her classmates and teachers remember her as the perfect blend between the Bible's Mary and Martha, a young woman who could be serene and reflective while reading or studying the Bible, but who was the first to roll up her sleeves and help out when a project was due. She loved learning and reading, and I was her favorite author.

Rachel kept a quote book where she jotted down inspirational thoughts and words of wisdom—from teachers and her parents, from friends or politicians, from Scripture and from my books. Everyone who knew her, knew of her quote book—the carefully kept words that inspired her on a daily basis.

After graduating from high school, Rachel was accepted to the nursing program at Pensacola Christian College and completed one year—determined to someday be the best nurse ever, a nurse who would've spent her life serving her patients and showing them Christ's love.

Tragically, Rachel never had the chance to live out her dream here on earth. She was killed in a car accident on August 7, 2007, at the age of eighteen. Not long afterward, Dave and Sheila Smith of Chestertown, Maryland, came up with the idea to honor Rachel by having her placed in one of my novels—Forever in Fiction.

For those of you who are not familiar with Forever in Fiction, it is my way of involving you, the readers, in my stories, while raising money for charities. To date, Forever in Fiction has raised more than $100,000 at charity auctions across the country. Obviously, I am only able to donate a limited number of these each year. For that reason, I have set a fairly high minimum bid on this package so that the maximum funds are raised for charities.

Sheila, the development director at Chestertown Christian Academy, wanted to offer Forever in Fiction at the school's auction, but she was concerned that even if someone met the minimum bid, they would likely want to name their own friend or family member as a character in one of my upcoming books. So Sheila took a different approach. She offered the item at the auction in honor of Rachel, explaining that everyone who donated money toward the item—any money—would be mentioned in the front of one of my books, and that in the process they could meet the minimum bid, and the entire community could honor Rachel Forever in Fiction.

The community responded beyond Sheila's wildest imagination.

At the auction, the donations toward Rachel's name Forever in Fiction poured in and nearly $10,000 was raised for the school. Rachel's memory lives on in Chestertown, Maryland, and now her memory will live on in the pages of this novel, and the entire *Above the Line* Series.

I chose to mirror Rachel's life in her character in this novel, making her the deceased friend of one of my main characters—Andi Ellison. In *Above the Line: Take One*, Andi will be deeply hurt and troubled by Rachel's death. Rachel's character will have been a very genuine friend for Andi, and now Andi is questioning her faith in light of Rachel's accident. The actual quotes from Rachel's quote book—copies of which were handed out to all who attended her funeral—will be used occasionally in the *Above the Line* Series as a way of giving Andi a look back at the roots of her faith, a way of helping Andi find the answers that will often elude her through the early telling of this new series.

The death of a young person is difficult—especially the death of one with so much love and joy, so much potential and faith. I believe all of us will learn something about the value of life—however long or short—while traveling the pages of this novel alongside Andi as she processes the loss of Rachel, and the way Rachel's life truly did make a difference.

I pray that Dave and Sheila Smith, and the community of Rachel's family and friends in Chestertown, Maryland, will always see a bit of their precious Rachel when they read her name in the pages of this novel, where she will be Forever in Fiction. I also pray that her character in this series will deeply honor her memory, and the memory of all the lives she touched along the short journey of her life.

Rachel was survived by her parents, Dan and Sharon; her older sister Janet and brother-in-law Butch Singleton, and their children Grace and Luke; her older brother Daniel and sister-in-law Beth; and her younger sister, Rebekah.

A special thanks to the following people who helped place Rachel Forever in Fiction: Ron, Julie, Eddie, and Tricia Athey; Dolly and Robin Baker; Benjamin and Sarah Baugher; Dan and Sharon

Baugher (Dad and Mom of Rachel); Daniel and Beth Baugher; Joe and Katie Baugher; Joe and Debbie Baugher; John and Dianna Baugher; Rebekah Baugher (in memory of Stuart and Sara Baugher); Curtis, Derikka, Tatiana, Andrew, Quinn, Genevieve, and Aurora Baughman; Amber Beach; Lynn Beauchamp; Mark and Becky Botts; Shannon Boyle; Pete, Joyce, Jared, Sam, and Kenley Brice; David and Jamie Brindley; Jim, Susan, James, and Sam Brindley; Pastor, Jeannette, Bill, and Emily Brindley; Helen Bryden; Daniel, Angela, and Tyler Cerniglia.

Also Lee, Chris, and Shelby Clough; Lewis and Norma Clough; Gordon and Sue Collison; Nathan and Cindy Cronquist; Larry and Brenda Cryder; Frank, Becky, Catherine, Elizabeth, Lydia, Allison, George, and Elizabeth Davis; Mr. and Mrs. Joe DelCiotto; Kurt, Connie, Mason, and Megan Dill; Aunt Alice and Uncle Jack Douglas; Joe and Julie Dugan; Greg, Cyndi, Cody, and Caleb Eichler; Thomas and Helen Elville; Mommom Faulkner; Andrew and Stephanie Feehan; John, Lois, David, and Karyn Foxwell; Madison Gibson; Todd, Missy, Elizabeth, Amber, and Thomas Green; Ruth Haines; Lois Haines; Lyle Hammer and Melyn Rhodes; Carl, Jennifer, Carl-David, and LeAnna Hardin; Harry and Pam Harrison.

Also Ray and Anna Harrison; Ken and Edie Hearn, and James Bugaj; Esther Heatwole; Leonard and Jerry Herring; Ken and Jan Hibbs; John and Gale Holland; Uncle Sonny; Joe Holmes; Sandee Baugher Holmes and Alon Holmes; Mr. and Mrs. Henry Ingram; Marion and Marilyn Ireland; John and Deb Jones; Trenton Kersey; Larry and Judy Leonard; Diana Long; Dickie, Heidi, Ryan, and Logan Manning; Michael, Ruthie, and Elizabeth Marine; Don, Cindy, Kristen, David, and Brianna McFarland; Wayne and Barbara McFarland; Charlie Miller; Kelly Mills; John and Debra Mullens; Lesley Murray; Ken and Tammy Newton; Frank, Robin, Leah, and John Plummer; Lauren Plummer; Dolly Pratt and family; Marian Quick; Peter and Tracy Raymond; Vicki Rhodes; Dave and Cheryl Richardson; Rick and Diane Rokita; George Rust; Mr. and Mrs. Wayne Rust; Ben and Nancy Baugher Sauselein.

Also Jason, Brandi, Savannah, and Barron Scott; Norman and Donna Scott; Victor and Susie Shepard; Mike Singleton; Butch, Janet, Grace, and Luke Singleton; Barbara Smith and Gracie, Dave, and Sheila Smith; Al and Nikki Snover and Kathryn Shaw; Chris, Fiona, and Katrina St. Remy; Jonathan, Jennifer, Emma, Kendall, and Jonathan Stoltzfus; Richard, Marian, Allysa, and Dillon Stoltzfus; Thomas and Lourdes Suarez; Stephen Swift and family; Aunt Joanne and Uncle Carl Taton; Jennifer Todd and family; Matt, Torie, Austin, and Ashley Troyer; Tommy, Bonnie, Amanda, and Tommy Tucker; Taylor Walker; Frank and Linda Williams; Jen Wilson; John, Josie, and Jonathan Wiltbank and Dorothy; Grayson and Beilin Zia.

In addition, a special thanks to Jessica Bryant who won Forever in Fiction at the Christian Youth Theater auction in Washington State. Jessica chose to honor her deceased mother, Janetta Drake, by naming her Forever in Fiction. Janetta had blonde hair and blue eyes and an extraordinary love for God and the people He placed in her life.

She was married twenty-three years and raised three children—Jordan, Jason, and Jessica—all of whom are young adults. Janetta spent her younger married years traveling the country doing evangelism events for children. Later she became a nurse and spent time as the head of a nursing home. She loved playing the piano and writing, and once penned a children's book called *Jessica's Special Angel*. Janetta loved children, and was happiest when she spent time with her family—children and grandchildren. People often said of Janetta that she loved all children as if they were her own.

Janetta's character in *Above the Line: Take One* is that of an actress in the first movie being produced by my main characters.

In the fictional world of the actors and actresses that make up the cast of my producers' first film, there is much arrogance and self-indulgence, many difficult people. In that arena, Janetta's character is a bright light, a quiet example to others, and one of the main reasons the producers feel encouraged to continue in their work.

I pray that Jessica will see the memory of her mother deeply honored by her gift and by Janetta's placement in *Above the Line: Take One*, and that Jessica will always see a bit of her mom when she reads her name in the pages of this novel, and in subsequent novels that make up this series, where she will be Forever in Fiction.

If you are interested in having a Forever in Fiction package donated to your auction, contact my assistant, Tricia Kingsbury, at Kingsburydesk@aol.com. Please write *Forever in Fiction* in the subject line.

Take One

One

CHASE RYAN DOUBTED THERE WAS ENOUGH oxygen in the plane to get him from San Jose to Indianapolis. He took his window seat on the Boeing 737, slid his laptop bag onto the floor space in front of him, and closed his eyes. Deep breaths, he told himself. Stay calm. But nothing about the job ahead of him inspired even a single peaceful feeling. On Monday Chase and his best friend Keith Ellison would set up shop in Bloomington, Indiana, and start spending millions of dollars of other people's investment money to make a film they believed would change lives.

Even during the rare moments when that fact didn't terrify him, Chase could hear the quiet anxious voice of his wife, Kelly, splashing him with a cold bucket of reality. "Only two million dollars, Chase? Seriously?" She had brought it up again on the way to the airport. Her knuckles stayed white as she gripped the steering wheel. "What if you run out of money before you finish the film?"

"We won't." Chase had steeled his eyes straight ahead. "Keith and I know the budget."

"What if it doesn't go like you planned?" Her body was tense, her eyes fearful. She gave him quick, nervous glances. "If something happens, we'll spend the rest of our lives paying that off."

She was right, but he didn't want to say so. Not when it was too late to turn back. The actors were arriving on set in two days, and the entire film crew would be in Bloomington by tomorrow. Plans were in motion, and already bills needed to be paid. They had no choice but to move ahead and stick to their budget, trusting God that they could make this film for two million dollars, and illustrate a message of faith better and stronger than anything the industry had ever seen.

Failure wasn't an option.

They reached the airport, but before she dropped Chase off, Kelly turned to him, lines creasing the space between her eyebrows. She was only thirty-one, but lately she looked older. Maybe because she only seemed to smile when she was playing with their two little girls, Macy and Molly. Worry weighted her tone. "Four weeks?"

"Hopefully sooner." He refused to be anything but optimistic.

"You'll call?"

"Of course. Every day." Chase studied her, and the familiar love was there. But her anxiety was something he didn't recognize. The faith she'd shown back when they lived in Indonesia, that's what he needed from her now. "Relax, baby. Please."

"Okay." She let out a sigh and another one seemed right behind it. "Why am I so afraid?"

His heart went out to her. "Kelly ..." His words were softer than before, his tone desperate to convince her. "Believe in me ... believe in this movie. You don't know how much I need that."

"I'm trying." She looked down and it took awhile before she raised her eyes to his again. "It was easier in Indonesia. At least in the jungle the mission was simple."

"Simple?" He chuckled, but the sound lacked any real humor. "Indonesia was never easy. Any of us could've been arrested or killed. We could've caught malaria or a dozen different diseases. Every day held that kind of risk."

The lines on her face eased a little and a smile tugged at her lips. She touched her finger to his face. "At least we had each other." She looked deep into his eyes, to the places that belonged to only the two of them and she kissed him. "Come on, Chase ... you've gotta see why I'm worried. It's not just the money."

He caught a quick look at his watch. "You're afraid we won't finish on time and that'll put us over budget and—"

"No." She didn't raise her voice, but the fear in her eyes cut him short. "Don't you see?" Shame filled in the spaces between her words. "You're young and handsome and talented ..." Her smile was sad now. "You'll be working with beautiful actresses and movie professionals and ... I don't know, the whole thing scares me."

She didn't come out and admit her deeper feelings, those she'd shared with him a week before the trip. The fact that she didn't feel she could measure up to the Hollywood crowd. Chase ached for her, frustrated by her lack of confidence. "This isn't about the movie industry. It's about a bigger mission field than we ever had in Indonesia." He wove his fingers into her thick dark hair, drew her close, and kissed her once more. "Trust me, baby. Please."

This time she didn't refute him, but the worry in her eyes remained as he grabbed his bags and stepped away from the car. He texted her once he got through security, telling her again that he loved her and that she had nothing to worry about. But she didn't answer and now, no matter how badly he needed to sleep, he couldn't shake the look on her face or the tone of her voice. What if her fears were some sort of premonition about the movie? Maybe God was using her to tell Keith and him to pull out now—before they lost everything.

Once on the plane, he tightened his seatbelt and stared out the window. But then, Keith's wife was completely on board with their plans. Her father was one of the investors, after all. Besides that, Keith's daughter, Andi, was a freshman at Indiana University, so the shoot would give Keith a window to Andi's world—something he was grateful for. Andi wanted to be an actress, and apparently her roommate was a theater major. Both college girls would be extras in the film, so Keith's entire family could hardly wait to get started.

Chase bit the inside of his lip. From the beginning, all the worries about the movie came from him and Kelly, but now that he was on his way to Indiana, Chase had to focus not on his fears, but on the film.

He ignored the knots in his stomach as he leaned against the cold hard plastic that framed the airplane window. The movie they were making was called *The Last Letter*, the story of a college kid whose life is interrupted when his father suffers a sudden fatal heart attack. The kid isn't sure how to move on until his mother reveals to him a letter—one last letter from his father. That letter takes Braden on a quest of discovery in faith and family, and finally into a brilliant future Braden had known nothing about.

The story was a parable, an illustration of the verse in Jeremiah 29:11: "'For I know the plans I have for you,' declares the Lord, 'plans to prosper you and not to harm you, plans to give you hope and a future.'" The verse would be their mantra every day of the filming, Chase had no doubt.

He closed his eyes, and in a rush he could hear the music welling in his chest, feel the emotion as it filled a theater full of moviegoers. He could see the images as they danced across the big screen, and he could imagine all of it playing out beyond his wildest expectations.

But the way from here to there could easily be a million miles of rocky back roads and potholes.

They were still at the gate, still waiting for the plane to head out toward the runway. Chase blinked and stared out the window, beyond the airport to the blue sky. Every day this week had been blue, not a cloud in sight, something Chase and Keith both found fitting. Because no matter what Kelly feared, no matter what pressures came with this decision, here was the moment Chase and Keith had dreamed of and planned for, the culmination of a lifetime of believing that God wanted them to take part in saving the world—not on a mission field in Indonesia, but in packed movie houses across America. Oak River Films, they called themselves. The name came from their love of the first Psalm. Chase had long since memorized the first three verses:

> *Blessed is the man who does not walk in the counsel of the wicked or stand in the way of sinners or sit in the seat of mockers. But his delight is in the law of the Lord, and on his law he meditates day and night. He is like a tree planted by streams of water, which yields its fruit in season and whose leaf does not wither. Whatever he does prospers.*

Oak River Films. That everything he and Keith did would be rooted in a delight for the Lord, and a belief that if they planted their projects near the living water of Christ, they would flourish for Him. Chase shifted in his seat. He silently repeated the Scripture again. Why was he worried about what lay ahead? He believed God was sending them to make this movie, right? He pressed his body into the thinly padded seat. *Breathe. Settle down and breathe.*

In every way that mattered, this film would make or break them in the world of Hollywood movie production. Easy enough, he had told himself when they first began this venture. But as the trip to Bloomington, Indiana, neared, the pressure built. They received phone calls from well-meaning investors asking how the casting was going or confirming when the shoot date was. They weren't antsy or doubtful that Chase and Keith could bring a return for their investment, but they were curious.

The same way everyone surrounding the film was curious.

Keith handled these phone calls. He was the calmer of the two, the one whose faith knew no limits. It had been Keith's decision that they would make the film with money from investors rather than selling out too quickly to a studio. Producers who paid for their projects retained complete creative control—and the message of this first film was one Chase and Keith wouldn't let anyone change. No matter how much easy studio money might hang in the balance.

Moments like this Chase worried about all of it. His wife and little girls back home, and whether the production team could stick to the aggressive film schedule they'd set. Chase massaged his thumb into his brow. The concerns made up a long list. He had to manage a cast of egos that included an academy award winner and two household names — both of whom had reputations for being talented but difficult. He had to keep everyone working well together and stick to his four-week schedule — all while staying on budget. He worried about running out of money or running out of time, and whether this was really where God wanted them — working in a world as crazy as Hollywood.

Chase took a long breath and exhaled slowly. The white-haired woman next to him was reading a magazine, but she glanced his way now and then, probably looking for a conversation. Chase wasn't interested. He looked out the window again and a picture filled his mind, the picture of an apartment building surrounded by police tape. The image was from his high school days in the San Fernando Valley, when a major earthquake hit Southern California. The damage was considerable, but the Northridge Meadows apartment symbolized the worst of it. In a matter of seconds, the three-story apartment building collapsed and became one — the weight of the top two floors too great for the shaken foundation.

A shudder ran its way through Chase.

That could be them in a few months if the filming didn't go well, if the foundation of their budget didn't hold the weight of all that was happening on top of it. Chase could already feel the weight pressing in along his shoulders.

"Excuse me." The woman beside him tapped his arm. "Does your seatback have a copy of the *SkyMall* magazine? Mine's missing."

Chase checked and found what the woman wanted. He smiled as he handed it to her. "Helps pass the time."

"Yes." She had kind blue eyes. "Especially during takeoff. I can usually find something for my precious little Max. He's a cockapoo. Cute as a button."

"I'm sure." Chase nodded and looked out the window once more. Pressure came with the job, he'd known that from the beginning. He and Keith were producers; with that came a certain sense of thrill and awe, terror and anxiety, because for every dollar they'd raised toward this movie, for every chance an investor took on their film, there was a coinciding possibility that something could go wrong.

"You ever wonder," Chase had asked Keith a few days ago over a Subway sandwich, "whether we should've just stayed in Indonesia?"

Keith only smiled that slow smile, the one that morphed across his face when his confidence came from someplace otherworldly. "This is where we're supposed to be." He took a bite of his sandwich and waited until he'd swallowed. He looked deep into Chase's eyes. "I feel it in the center of my bones."

Truth and integrity. That's what Keith worried about. The truth of the message when the film was finally wrapped and they brought it to the public, and integrity with the cast and crew, the investors and the studios. For Keith, every day was a test because God was watching.

Chase agreed, but the pressure he felt didn't come from being under the watchful eye of the Lord. That mattered a great deal, but God would accept them whether they returned home having completed their movie mission or not. Rather Chase worried because the whole world was watching to see what sort of movie the two of them could make on such a limited budget. And if they failed, the world would know that too.

They were in the air now and the woman beside him closed the *SkyMall* magazine and handed it back to him. "I've seen it all before. Nothing new for Max." She shrugged one thin shoulder. "I've been making this trip a lot lately. Trying to sell my house in Indiana."

Chase still didn't want to talk, but the woman reminded him of his grandmother. She had a warmth about her, and something else ... a sadness maybe. Whatever it was he felt compelled to give her at least a little time. "Moving to San Jose?"

"Yes. It's time, I guess." She looked straight ahead at nothing in particular. "Lived in Indiana all my life." Light from the window fell on her soft wrinkled skin, and for a few seconds her smile faded. She had to be eighty at least, but she seemed a decade younger. Then, as if she suddenly remembered she'd begun a conversation with a stranger, she grinned at Chase again. "What about you? Heading home?"

"No." He angled himself so his back was against the window. "Going to Bloomington for business."

She looked delighted that he was talking to her. "Business!" She raised an eyebrow. "My husband was a businessman. What line of work?"

"I'm a producer." Chase fought with the sense of privilege and headiness that came with the title. "We'll be on location four weeks."

"Produce! Isn't that wonderful." She folded her hands in her lap. "My great nephew works in produce. Got a job at the grocer not too far from his parents' house and now he unpacks tomatoes and cabbage all day long."

Chase opened his mouth to tell her he was a producer, and not in produce, but she wasn't finished.

"He's only been at it a few months, but I don't think he'll end up in produce long term. He wants to finish school." She angled her head sweetly. "Did you finish college, young man?"

"Yes, ma'am. But—"

"Well, of course you did." She laughed lightly at herself. "You must be a produce manager, heading to the farms of Bloomington for harvest season, making sure the crop's coming up good and going out to stores across the country." She gave as hearty a nod as she could muster. "That's a mighty important job." Her finger gave a quick jab in his direction. "The public takes it for granted, the way we need produce managers. We walk into a store and just assume we can buy a pound of red apples or Vidalia onions." She settled back in her seat, but she looked straight at him. "Farming's the American way." Her grin held a level of admiration. "Thanks for what you do for this great nation ... what'd you say your name was?"

"Chase. Chase Ryan."

"Matilda Ewing. Mattie."

"Nice to meet you, ma'am."

"Well, Mr. Ryan," she held out her bony fingers. "It's a pleasure to meet you too. But what about your family back home? Four weeks is an awful long time to be apart. My son nearly lost his marriage once because of that. He was in sales ... had to figure out a different territory to save his family." She barely paused. "You do have a family, right?"

"Yes, ma'am. It's hard to be away." He was touched by the woman's transparency. "My wife, Kelly, is home with our little girls. They're four and two."

She sucked in a surprised breath. "And you'll be gone four weeks! You must have a peach for a wife. That's a long time to tend to a family by yourself."

"Yes, ma'am." Chase wondered if the woman was slightly confused. Seconds ago she was singing his praise, claiming the virtues of his being a produce manager, and now she was practically chastising him for daring to take such a long trip.

"Don't get me wrong," she was saying. "Farming's a good thing. But be careful. Fences pop up when you're away from each other that long. Nothing on the other side of the fence is ever as green as it seems." She chuckled softly. "Even in produce."

The flight attendant peered into their row. "Something to drink?"

Matilda ordered ginger ale, and in the process she fell into a conversation with the person on the aisle. The diversion gave Chase the chance to stare out the window again and think about the old woman and her wisdom. Never mind that her hearing was a little off, Chase almost liked the idea that the kind woman thought he worked producing vegetables and not movies. But more than that, her words were dead on when it came to his family back home. Especially the part about fences.

With all his concerns and worries, he hadn't thought about how the four weeks away would feel to Kelly and their girls.

He must've fallen asleep as he thought about his conversation with Matilda, because in no time she was tapping him on the arm again. "Mr. Ryan, we're landing. Your seatback needs to be up."

He stretched his legs out on either side of his laptop bag and did as he was told. "Thank you."

"My pleasure." She adjusted the vent above her seat. "You were sleeping pretty hard. You'll need that rest when you hit the fields."

"Yes, ma'am." Chase rubbed his eyes and ran his fingers through his hair. When he was more awake he turned toward her again. "So ... why are you moving to San Jose?"

At first she didn't seem like she intended to answer his question. She pursed her lips and stared down at her hands, at a slender gold wedding band that looked worn with age. When she looked up, the sadness was there again. "My husband and I were married fifty-eight years." She wrung her hands as the words found their way to her lips. "He passed away this last January. My girls want me to live closer to them." She smiled, but it stopped short of her eyes. "We're looking for an apartment at one of those ... senior facilities. Somewhere that'll take Max and me, both." Her expression told him she was uncomfortable with the idea, but she wasn't fighting it. "I can get a little forgetful, and, well, sometimes I don't hear as well as I used to. It's a good idea, really." A depth shone from deep inside her. "Don't you think?"

"I do." He wanted to hug the woman. Poor dear.

"My girls say I'm dragging my feet." She shifted her gaze straight ahead once more. "And maybe I am. When I close up that house and shut the door for the last time, that'll be that." She looked at him through a layer of tears. "We spent five decades in that house. Every square inch holds a hundred memories."

"Leaving won't be easy."

"No." Matilda sniffed. "That's why I'm saying," her composure gradually returned, "look out for fences, Mr. Ryan. Produce or no produce, home's the better place. Kids grow up and God only gives us so many days with our loved ones."

"Yes, ma'am."

The captain came on, advising them that they'd be landing soon, and the announcement stalled the conversation with Matilda. She started talking to the passenger on her left once more, and not until they were at the end of the jetway did she turn and flash her twinkling eyes his way. "Good luck with the produce, Mr. Ryan. And remember what I said about fences. The greenest grass is back at home."

Chase thanked her again, and then she was gone; between the gate and baggage claim he didn't see her again. He rented a Chevy Tahoe and headed for Bloomington. Once he arrived, the first thing he did was call Kelly.

"Hello?"

"Honey ... it's me." Chase felt a sense of relief. His words spilled out far faster than usual. "There's something I should've said, back at the airport when we were saying goodbye. I mean, we stood there all those minutes, but I never really told you what I should have, so that's why I'm calling."

She laughed. "Someone's had too much coffee."

"No." He exhaled and slowed himself. "What I mean is, I appreciate you, Kelly. You have to handle the house and the girls for a very long time, and I never ... I never thanked you."

For a few beats there was no response. "You really feel that way?" A tentative joy warmed her tone.

"I do." Another picture flashed on the screen of his heart. The two of them holding hands in front of a church full of family and friends, and Chase knowing that in all the world he could never love anyone as much as he loved the beautiful bride standing before him. "I love you, Kelly. Don't ever forget that, okay?"

"Okay." She laughed and the sound was wind chimes and summer breeze, the way it hadn't been for a while. "You don't know how much it means ... that you'd call like this."

"I miss you already. Give the girls a kiss for me."

"Okay. Oh, and Chase ... one more thing." She laughed again. "Go get 'em tomorrow ... I know you can do it. I've been praying since you left and I feel like God cleared some things up for me. This is going to be bigger than Keith and you ever dreamed."

Her confidence breathed new life into his dreams. "Seriously?"

"Yes." The sound of the girls singing about Old McDonald's Farm came across the lines from the background. "I believe in you, Chase. I promise I'll keep believing."

"Thank you." He thought about old Matilda and how she would smile if she could see the conversation Chase was having with his wife. "Okay, then ... I guess I'm off to the harvest."

"The harvest?" Kelly still had a laugh in her voice. "What on earth?"

"Nothing." He chuckled. He told her again that he loved her, and he promised to call that evening to tell the girls goodnight.

After he hung up, he caught himself once more drawn back to the sweet woman's words. In some ways he really was headed out to the fields, out to a crop that needed harvesting—the crop of human hearts and souls that might only be found if they created the best movie possible. But more than that, he thought about the fences.

With Keith and him producing, the months ahead figured to be crazy at times. But no matter how bumpy the ride, he vowed to stay on the same side of the fence as Kelly and the girls. Because Matilda was right.

God only gave a person so many days with their family.

Two

IT WAS AFTER MIDNIGHT, AND THE house was quiet when Keith Ellison finished packing and headed into the small study off the kitchen in their two-story tract home in south San Jose. The study was the only room that gave any indication of the world they'd left behind, the villages and tribal people from the different regions of Indonesia where Keith and Lisa and their daughter, Andi, lived for more than a decade.

Keith flipped on the standing lamp, the one that cast just enough light across the small room to see the pictures that hung on the wall. He stopped at the first one, always a favorite, and smiled as he let it take him back. The picture was from their first month on the mission field. On the left side an eight-year-old Andi stood boldly next to Lisa, hands on her hips ready to tell the entire tribe about Jesus. Lisa's eyes were a little less lively. She'd been sick that week, but more sure than ever that Indonesia was where they were supposed to be.

Chase and Kelly—newly married—were on the right side of the picture. Determination shone in both their faces, as brightly as the love they had for each other. And in the middle, more than a foot shorter, were three leaders of the tribe. Keith laughed quietly to himself as he remembered the conversation they'd had just before the pictures were taken.

Through a translator from Mission Aviation Fellowship, the leaders explained why they hadn't beheaded the missionaries on their first visit into the bush. "You came off the plane," the chief leader explained, "and we knew you wouldn't go back home alive.

But then …" his eyes grew big, "your guards came off the plane behind you. Big men. Ten feet tall with shining golden hair and long swords. You were our honored guests after that."

Both Lisa and Kelly had lost a few shades of color in their face as the full meaning of the story became clear. They brought no ten-foot guards with them. The tribal leaders could only have seen angels, heavenly protection visible only to the tribal leaders and sent by God so that Keith and Chase and their families might get the job done. After that, Keith never once felt concerned for their safety. Like the Bible said, if God was for them, who could be against them?

Even now. When the mission field was no longer Indonesia, but the hard and mostly dried ground of Hollywood.

"Hey."

Keith turned to see his wife's silhouette in the doorway. "I thought you were asleep."

"No." She came to him and eased her arms around his waist. "I'm too excited for you. I can't believe it's finally here."

"Me either." He leaned down and kissed her forehead. "You sure you can't come with me tomorrow?"

"I want to." She swayed with him, her eyes never leaving his. "I'll be there Wednesday."

"And you'll stay for the entire shoot?"

"Most of it." She touched her lips to his, and for a while their eyes did all the talking. "I'm so proud of you, taking this step." She eased away from him and turned to the same photo he'd been looking at, the first one on the study wall. With her fingertips, she brushed off some of the dust that had accumulated on the frame. "I loved every minute we spent with those people. But even back then I used to ask God how we wound up in Indonesia when you were born to make movies." She looked over her shoulder at him. "I don't think there's another producer out there like you, Keith. I mean that."

"Babe, there are lots of producers." He put his arm easily around her shoulders.

"Not like you." She leaned her head on his shoulder. "I've seen what you can do. You're amazing, Keith. The films you made in college blew everyone away, remember?"

"Not everyone."

"Your professors." She pulled away just enough to make eye contact. "They wanted you to submit a couple of those films to Sundance."

"I guess." Those days felt like they'd happened to someone else, a lifetime ago at least.

She slipped her arm around his waist and snuggled close to him again. "No one has your talent and passion for a life-changing message. I can't wait to see what God's going to do over the next month."

"Remind me of that." He smiled at her, at the fierce belief she had in him. "Remind me when I feel like giving up, okay?"

"God brought us this far." She had nothing but utter confidence in her voice. "He won't let you give up now. Neither will I."

They were quiet a moment, studying the other photos on the wall, the pictures of Andi at age twelve, sitting in the cockpit ready to fly the bush plane on her own, and the one of Lisa holding two babies born to village women who had given their lives to Christ. Chase and Kelly performing minor surgery on a man whose leg had been cut open, and a photo of two tribes who had come together for a Bible study after decades of warring against each other.

"The job we had to do, it was all so black and white back then." He removed his arm from her shoulders and lifted a framed photograph of their daughter from the cluttered desk. "I worry about Andi ... if she'll make the transition well."

They'd been home from Indonesia for almost two years, and Andi had finished her high school education at Chestertown Christian Academy, fifteen minutes from their new home. As always, she'd been a bright light, but sometimes her enthusiasm and zest for each day crossed the line from exuberance to daring. Something wild and adventurous shone in Andi's eyes, and more than once Keith and Lisa had prayed fervently for their daughter, begging God to protect her and to use her charisma and curiosity for good.

"She loves life." Lisa smiled. "She can't get enough."

"But she needs to love the life God wants for her."

"She will." The strength in Lisa's eyes was unwavering. "And if it takes a little time, we'll just love her through it."

"Right."

Lisa kissed him once more. "See you upstairs."

After she left, Keith stared a little longer at the picture of their only child, their precious daughter. As a young girl, Andi's unbridled love for God had led countless people into a relationship with Jesus. The tribal people were drawn by her blonde hair and blue eyes and the innocent full-hearted way she sang songs of praise and raised her hands in prayer.

From the time she could walk, Andi had been fearless around strangers, showing them unrestrained attention and concern and making friends as easily as she breathed. One time when she was thirteen, she hadn't shown up for dinner so they quickly formed a search party. Half an hour later they found Andi talking about her faith with the women of the neighboring tribe, telling them in their native tongue about the grace and mercy of Christ.

But as she neared sixteen, Keith and Lisa had to admit that their daughter might not be safe in the bush. She was willowy and long-legged, her straight blonde hair hanging in a single sheath halfway down her back. So much time outdoors had given her a honey-colored complexion, and rather than seeing her as the delightful pixie she'd been as a child, the village people began treating her differently—like there was something almost mystical or special about her. The men especially took extra notice of her wherever she went.

Keith and Lisa directed her to wear men's pants and baggy shirts, but even so, Andi had a way of making people catch their breath when she walked up. Now, dressed in fitted jeans and stylish sweaters, Andi was a stunning, fresh-faced beauty, wide-eyed and innocent, afraid of nothing. Keith could only imagine the impact she was having on the freshmen boys at Indiana University.

And what about her interest in acting? Ever since he and Chase determined to come back to the States and make movies that might influence the culture, Andi had been driven to appear on the big screen. Keith and Chase had met at USC's film school, and both of them had been around enough young actors to recognize talent. There was an "it" factor that was absolutely essential for young people looking to make it in the movies. That indefinable something.

Whatever that something was, Andi had it. Keith and Chase both agreed. But so what? She could be the next Reese Witherspoon or Kate Hudson, but how would that make a difference for eternity? And what about Andi's faith? Could it survive the movie industry, the fame and attention, the ridiculous scrutiny?

Keith set the photo back on the desk. Sometimes he wished they could all move back to Indonesia, back where life truly was simpler, and the activities of their days were clear-cut and singly focused. Before the contemporary American culture could change Andi. But there was no turning back now. This was where she wanted to be, and Keith and Lisa had no choice but to let her follow her dreams — including her desire to embrace all of life — to experience it.

Whatever the lessons involved might cost.

Keith was grateful he'd have the next four weeks to interact with her, to meet her roommate, and see how she was settling in at college. But even so he felt a heaviness in his heart. *Keep her safe, Lord ... please. She has to grow up, and we have to let her ... but keep her on the right path. Please.*

A line from last week's sermon sounded again in his heart. "Don't worry about your children," the pastor had said. "Raise them in the way they should go, pray for them, and trust them to Jesus. He loves them even more than you do."

Yes, Keith told himself. *That's true.* He and Lisa had done that, hadn't they? They'd raised Andi in the way she should go, and they'd prayed for her. Now, in her first year of college at Indiana University, they had to trust her to Jesus. That meant they had to believe that the roommate she'd been assigned to was exactly the right person for this new season in both their lives. They knew the girl's name now, and Keith had been praying for her as often as he prayed for Andi. She was a local girl, the daughter of an NFL coach and the oldest of six kids. A theater major like Andi, whose faith was important enough to list on her housing application.

A girl Keith believed would not only be a great roommate for Andi, but something far more than that.

An answer to their prayers.

Three

THE WEEKEND HAD BEEN WONDERFUL, BUT now it was Sunday night and the first full week of classes at Indiana University would begin in the morning. Bailey Flanigan stood in her family's driveway and hugged each of her younger brothers, saving her goodbye to Connor for last. She was only three years older than Connor, and the two of them had always been close — especially because of their involvement in the town's Christian Kids Theater group.

Connor was taller than her now, so she stood on her tiptoes and hugged him around his neck. "It's not like I'm going across the country."

"I know." Connor smiled, but his eyes stayed glum. "But you're not down the hall." He raised a single shoulder. "It's not the same."

Bailey felt her heart sink. "Things are never the same when you grow up."

"Right." He found a grin for her. "Just come back next weekend, okay?"

"I will." She moved on to her dad, and then to her mom.

Connor and the other boys headed back inside, talking about their coming football season and the homework their teachers were already handing out even though it was just the first week of school. Bailey loved the familiarity of their voices mingled together. This was why she hadn't chosen a college farther away. She loved her family and these weekends home were something she would look forward to. Still, the time on campus would be good for her. She smiled at her parents. "It was the right decision, moving onto campus."

Her dad put his hand on her shoulder. "I agree with you, honey." His eyes filled with pride for all she was doing. "You're ready for this. If you want to experience college life, you have to be there."

Her mom nodded. "Even if the college is only fifteen minutes away."

"Right." Bailey smiled, grateful for their understanding. She'd earned nearly a full scholarship based on her grades and her audition for the drama department. Now that she was living on campus she could handle a full load of courses and still participate in school plays and get involved in student activities. She could practically feel her eyes sparkling with all that lay ahead. "I'm excited about Campus Crusade too. The first Cru meeting is Thursday night."

"You'll love it." Her dad put his arm around her mom. "It's a great way to meet other kids."

"And keep your focus." Her mom's look went deeper than her dad's, the way it often did. Bailey had always considered her mom her best friend, and these early days of college life hadn't changed that. "I have a feeling you'll be a very bright light for Campus Crusade."

"Me too." She hugged her mom once more. "I better get going. Andi will be looking for me."

"You have auditions this week, right?" Her mom wasn't stalling, just getting every last bit of conversation in before Bailey had to leave.

"On Tuesday, for the whole season." Bailey raised her eyebrows. "First show is *Scrooge*." She made a nervous face. "Pray for me. I've always wanted to play Isabel."

"You'd be perfect for the part." Her dad leaned in and kissed her forehead. "You certainly have the talent and experience for it.

After all those CKT shows. The director'll probably beg you to take the part."

"Dad." Bailey laughed and shook her head.

"I'm serious. Indiana University doesn't know how lucky it is to have you."

"Not yet, anyway." Her mom joined in. "Seriously, sweetheart. You'll be amazing." She hugged Bailey once more. "Are you babysitting for Ashley this week?"

"Wednesday and Friday." Bailey didn't have time for a real job, but a few times a week she watched the three kids of Ashley Baxter Blake and her husband, Landon. Ashley was an amazing artist, and she'd even helped out with sets for a number of CKT shows. These days she was painting landscapes again, and two afternoons a week she needed a few quiet hours to work. Her kids were great—Cole and Devin, and their baby sister, Janessa. The family lived in Ashley's old house, the one where Bailey and her family had joined the Baxter family for a number of celebrations.

Someday when God brought the right person into her life, she hoped she had a marriage like her parents or a marriage like Ashley and Landon's. In some ways, Ashley was like an older sister, always willing to listen or spend an extra few minutes talking. For now, Bailey figured babysitting the Blake kids wasn't only a job, it was one of the best ways to pay back Ashley's kindness.

She walked to her car and her parents followed. "Drive safely," her mom folded her arms against the cool night breeze. The smell of burning leaves and damp grass mixed in the air the way it did every fall.

"Call us when you're in your room." Her dad winked at her. "Bring down the house at the audition."

Bailey laughed. They said another round of goodbyes and then she was on the road. She checked the time on her car radio. It was just after nine. Her roommate Andi should be back in the dorm by now. Her dad had flown in today for the movie he was filming in town and on campus over the next few weeks. The two of them were supposed to have dinner, and then Andi needed to get back to finish setting up her side of their dorm room.

An easy smile lifted the corners of her lips. She'd only met Andi Ellison a week ago, but already she could see the two of them becoming good friends. Andi was striking, but she wasn't into herself or stuck up like she could've been. Instead, she was anxious to connect with Bailey and quick to share her own experiences on the mission field and in her final few years in high school. And she was always wanting to know more about Bailey's life in Bloomington.

"What about love?" Andi had asked after they turned out the lights their second night together. Her bed was beneath the window, and Bailey's was near the door, but the room was so small they could easily talk in whispers and hear each other. "You ever been in love?"

Bailey's heart beat a little quicker at the question. "Well ... you know, I'm sort of dating Tim Reed. I told you about him. The guy I did Christian Kids Theater with all those years."

"Yeah, I know." Andi kept her voice low since the walls were thin. "But you didn't say you were in love with him. So ... have you ever been in love?"

Bailey sighed because this was exactly what she wrestled with at least once a day. Was she in love with Tim, or were the two of them only following some script that their CKT friends had practically written out for them? Tim was the natural choice for her, right? Wasn't that what she'd always believed? But if so, then how come she didn't see his face in her mind as she lay there in the dark?

Instead, the face that took over her thoughts belonged to Cody Coleman, the boy she still couldn't forget—no matter how hard he tried to convince her to move on. Cody was two years older than her. He'd lived with their family when she was a sophomore and junior, and though he'd had his struggles, in the end he'd learned much about life from his high school football coach — Bailey's dad. More than a year ago Cody joined the army, but after a few months in Iraq he'd been captured by enemy forces. During his escape, he was shot, and when he returned this past summer, he was missing his lower left leg.

Bailey didn't think him any less for his injuries. But despite her feelings for him, Cody had been adamant when he stopped by her house his first day back in town. It was the Fourth of July, and even though his eyes had told her his real feelings for her, his words said something else. "You deserve better than me, Bailey." He had hugged her close, and clearly neither of them wanted to let go. "Tim's good for you. The sort of guy you deserve. You and I ... we can be friends, nothing more."

Cody had stuck to his determination, keeping his visits to the Flanigan house brief and rare, and maintaining a distance with Bailey. But no matter how hard he worked at it, Bailey knew better. Because there was something else he'd told her that day when he returned home from war. Something that would always stay with her.

"Bailey?" When the silence lasted too long, Andi giggled. But her whispered tone was sharp with impatience. "Come on. Tell me if you've ever been in love."

"I'm not sure." Bailey answered quicker, because she wasn't ready to talk about Cody. Maybe one day she'd tell Andi. If they became close enough. But for now only her mom knew about her feelings for Cody. "What about you?"

"Nah." Andi laughed again. "There were no guys in Indonesia, and once I came home everyone had their friends and cliques. It was all I could do to finish school with decent grades."

"Really?" Bailey was surprised. A girl as pretty as Andi, and she'd never been in love? "So you didn't date or anything?"

"A couple times. No one special." She sighed, and there was a dreamy sound in her voice. "I have a feeling I'll meet him here. Like somewhere out there on the big campus of Indiana University is my own Prince Charming." She yawned. "Now all I have to do is meet him." She hesitated. "Has Tim kissed you?"

"Just once. After prom back in June."

"Was it amazing? I mean, I haven't had my first kiss so I'm scared to death about it," she giggled. "But still ... I know it'll be amazing. So was it?"

Amazing? Bailey let the question drift slowly through her mind and into her heart. She enjoyed being with Tim, and that night at the prom they'd had a great time laughing and dancing. The kiss left her with butterflies, and she'd never forget it as long as she lived. But amazing? "I don't know." Bailey stared at the ceiling, searching for the right words. "It was my only kiss, so I guess."

"Hmmm." Andi rolled over onto her side and peered at Bailey through the dark shadows. "If you have to think about it that hard, it couldn't have been too amazing."

After that, Bailey had found a way to change the subject, and though they talked every night, true love didn't come up again. Bailey was glad. Now she could hardly wait to get back to her dorm and hear the details of the movie Andi's father was about to film.

She stuck to the speed limit, but she pulled her cell phone from her purse. Her dad had installed the hands-free unit in her car so she'd be safe. A conversation would make the drive feel shorter. She thought for a few seconds about who to call, and a wild idea came to mind. Cody Coleman. She should call Cody, just so he'd know he couldn't hide from her forever. But before she could hit the first number, her phone rang. It was a song by Taylor Swift — "Teardrops on My Guitar." The song was about a girl who loved a guy she could never have. Tim Reed must've heard her ring tone a dozen times when they'd hung out, but he hadn't made the connection.

She kept her eyes on the road and slid her phone open. As she did, she caught Tim's name in the caller ID. With one hand, she pressed the hands-free button. "Hey ..." her tone softened. She cared for Tim, really she did. Sometimes she thought she might be in love with him. He'd been around as long as she could remember, and for years she had dreamed of dating him. He was the theater group's leading man, the best singer and actor, the guy every girl in CKT dreamed of dating. He was comfortable. And now Tim was calling her. That had to mean something. She leaned back in her seat. "You're up late."

"Finished my homework in music comp." He released a long breath. "No mercy. Especially in music."

"I know. I mean, it's the first week."

"You driving?"

"How'd you know?" She liked the easy way they had with each other, how every time they talked on the phone, she felt like they were in the same room.

"You have me on speaker, for one thing." He laughed. "And I called your dorm. Andi told me. She said you should be home anytime. I sorta hoped I'd catch you before you got back." He paused. "You know, so I can have you to myself for a few minutes."

Bailey smiled. "You have me that way when I'm in my dorm. Andi's always doing her own thing—homework or texting friends back home."

"Yeah," he drew out the word. "I guess this is just better. You and me. Hey, so did you hear?" His tone was instantly more upbeat. "Auditions for this year's musicals are Tuesday."

"I know." Bailey could hardly wait. "Andi's going to audition too."

They talked for a few minutes about *Scrooge*, and how the leading roles were fairly small. "Which is good," Bailey stifled a yawn. She was almost back to campus. The thought of Tim and Andi and her joining a bunch of college kids from all over the country in daily rehearsals for an actual Indiana University production was more than she could imagine. The competition was bound to be intense. "Smaller leads give a lot of kids the chance to make the adjustment to college theater. Anyway, I'm not worried about a lead. I just hope we all get in."

"Come on." A smile hung in Tim's voice. "We'll get in. You know that."

"Not really. This isn't CKT."

"Yeah, but you and me? We're ready for this." He sounded more intense than before. "And you're right about the smaller leads, but there is one main role. I hope they'll at least consider underclassmen."

Something about Tim's competitiveness, or maybe the direction of the conversation, shot a blast of cold air over the moment. "So ... you want Scrooge? The main role?"

"I'm gonna try." Tim laughed but the sound felt a little awkward. "It'd be great on a résumé. It's all I've been thinking about."

Bailey pulled into the dorm parking lot and found a spot. She suddenly wanted to get off the phone. "Hey, so I'll see you at auditions."

"Pray for me."

"Yeah." She hesitated. "For all of us, right?"

"Right. Of course." Tim's laugh sounded forced. "That's what I meant."

As Bailey hung up she took a last look at her phone and shook her head. That was the trouble with Tim. He was more about himself than anyone else, and at times like this she wondered if she was wasting her time dating him. She sighed and slipped her phone into her jacket pocket. The call to Cody would have to wait since she didn't want Andi asking about him. Her roommate knew about Tim, but Cody ... Cody wasn't someone Bailey was willing to talk about yet. What could she say? Right now things with Cody were weird. They hardly saw each other, so Bailey couldn't even say he was her friend.

She walked quickly through the well-lit parking lot, past the security guard who was always on duty, and up the stairs to her building. Cody was living off campus with a few friends he'd played football with at Clear Creek High. Bailey saw him last week on campus, but their paths didn't exactly cross. Cody seemed like he kept things that way on purpose.

He would probably not admit that. He'd tell her he was busy with class and his newest thing—training for a local triathlon. He wore a prosthetic beneath his jeans and no one could've guessed about his injury. Bailey wasn't surprised that Cody was going all out to become once more the athlete he'd been before going to war. Years ago Cody had nearly died from alcohol poisoning. The ordeal changed his life and made him determined to make the most of every day he'd been given. Whether on a battlefield in Iraq or recovering from his battle wounds, his quiet determination was one of the reasons Bailey was so drawn to him.

A group of girls from the dorms across the hall from Bailey and Andi were sitting on the couches just inside the front door, and Bailey talked to them for a few minutes.

"Hey ... some really cute guy came by earlier asking for you." The girl with the news sat on the arm of one of the sofas. She was tall and thin—a freshman forward for the IU women's basketball team. She raised her eyebrow. "I mean, really cute."

The other girls nodded their agreement, and one of them giggled at the others and then at Bailey. "Seriously. He was hot."

Bailey thought back to her conversation with Tim. He'd been studying all night, so then who? "He asked for me?"

"Definitely." One of the girls elbowed a cute blonde sitting on her right side. "Bimbo here tried to convince him she was you."

The blonde shrugged. "He wasn't interested. He only wanted you."

"It wasn't that dark-haired guy who comes around now and then. What's his name? Tim something?"

Bailey was almost afraid to ask, as if it might be better to privately hope that the guy who'd come by was Cody, rather than to find out it had only been some classmate looking to exchange notes on their history class. "Did he say his name?"

"Nope." The tall girl stood and stretched. "Believe me, we tried to get it out of him. He said it didn't matter. Not much of a sense of humor. Very intense."

The blonde rolled her eyes. "Yeah, and when you weren't here, he just left."

"Hmmm." Bailey wasn't even sure about the names of the girls. She was hardly going to give any hints about who she hoped the guy might be. "Maybe he'll come back."

"We hope." Several of the girls giggled again.

Bailey laughed too, and she waved at the group as she headed down the hall to her dorm. So far, attending Indiana University was everything Bailey had dreamed. Her classes were interesting—even when she disagreed with her professors. Her classmates were outgoing and easily engaged, the dorm life felt a little like a giant slumber party, and the freedom of planning her own daily schedule was making her feel more grown up. She thought about the mystery guy and figured he couldn't have been Cody. Not when Cody was determined to stay out of her way, to give her a life without him. No, only one thing about college wasn't how she dreamed it would be.

She wasn't experiencing it with Cody Coleman. He wasn't her boyfriend the way she'd once dreamed, and he wasn't even her friend. No matter how often she thought of him, she had to be honest with herself.

Cody was nothing more than a stranger now.

Four

ANDI ELLISON KNELT ON HER NARROW dormitory bed and positioned a nail just left of the small boxy window that overlooked a pretty courtyard. The girls across the hall had asked her to come hang out later, but first she wanted to finish setting up her room. With the hammer she'd borrowed from the RA, she tapped the nail into place. She had nearly all her photos hung on the wall, but she'd forgotten this one.

The picture of her with Rachel Baugher.

Andi studied their faces as she straightened the framed photograph on the wall. Graduation day. They both wore blue caps and gowns, their grins stretched across their faces, arms around each other's necks, happier than they'd ever been. Rachel and Andi. Two best friends, all of life laid out before them.

"We're really going to do it," Rachel had shouted that night over the noise of a hundred celebrating graduates. "God's going to help us make all our dreams come true!"

"It's going to be a wild ride, Rach ... you'll be a nurse and I'll be an actress."

The two joined their friends for an all-night grad party in the high school gym, and when their energy ran low, they sat in the bleachers and talked about the future, about their hopes and dreams and the kinds of men they wanted to marry someday. With Rachel, Andi could talk about anything at all, because Rachel had a gift of listening that few people had.

The picture looked great on that part of the wall, and it took Andi back to that night, to the joy and sorrow the girls both felt at graduation. Andi stared at the photo. Rachel was the first friend Andi made when she and her family returned home from the mission field of Indonesia. They shared a passion for life and a faith in God that meant everything to them, and together they pushed each other to a senior year of straight A's. Rachel was valedictorian, and Andi was runner-up—the two girls an inspiration to their friends at Chestertown Christian Academy.

Their hard work paid off, and when it came time for college, Andi's top choice was Indiana University because of their theater department. Rachel was accepted to Pensacola Christian College's nursing program, and though they wouldn't be at the same university, they would stay in touch and travel to Europe the first summer they had enough money, and one day they planned to be in each other's weddings. Rachel was organized and responsible, and as loyal as a friend could be. But she was also a dreamer, a girl who saw the deeper side of life and longed to be the best at whatever she attempted.

Andi ran her fingers over the image of Rachel's smiling face, her long brown hair and bright hope-filled eyes. Once in a while Andi would do this, search deeply into her friend's expression for some sort of sign. But there was none, no indication that in only a few months she would be gone. The car accident was fast, Rachel's death, instant. And just like that heaven gained one of the most brilliant, unforgettable lights Andi had ever been around.

Heaven's gain, and Andi's loss.

She smiled at the picture the two of them made on that happy day. "I miss you, Rach ... every day."

She set the hammer down on her nightstand and stared out the open window into the dark night. Her smile faded. All her life she'd been taught that God was faithful, that He had plans for His people. Good plans. But what about Rachel? She had wanted to be a nurse so badly, she could hardly wait to get through school. So why hadn't God been faithful to her?

Andi wasn't sure what to make of herself when her feelings led her down this path. If God wasn't faithful to Rachel, then maybe God wasn't faithful at all. She felt terrible, totally guilty for thinking such a thing, but she couldn't stop herself. Maybe everything they'd taught the people in Indonesia was only one glorious and great-sounding story. A fairy tale like the kind her daddy used to tell her before bedtime when she was a little girl. She could almost hear her father's voice telling her the story of God as she'd always believed it. Only instead of the words sounding true and right, the way they did from the pulpit, they sounded silly and sing-song. Like one more bedtime story. The words ran flippantly through her mind. *There is a God. He made you and the whole world. Love Him and live for Him, and He'll rescue you from your sins. Your life will be special because He has good plans for you, and then one day you'll die and go to heaven.*

"And everyone lived happily ever after," she muttered against the window screen. Unless you're sitting in the passenger seat of a friend's car one sunny August day and you die in a sudden car accident. Or unless you get murdered or sick or lose your job and have to live on the streets. Unless you're born in Kenya and both your parents die of AIDS before you're two years old. "What about those people, huh, God?" She lifted her eyes to the sky, but it was too dark to make out any stars, and the moon was nowhere in sight.

She hated when her thoughts went this way. Her stomach hurt and her heart beat faster than usual. Every breath felt tighter than the one before it. Because this was her very deep, dark secret — the thing no one knew about her.

Andi Ellison had doubts now. Her perfect faith in God was riddled with subtle cracks and shifts.

Her elbows pressed harder into the windowsill and she remembered once when she was eight or nine in Indonesia, waiting for a Mission Aviation Fellowship plane to fly in with supplies for the village. She loved the old runway, because it was the most open stretch of land anywhere, and she and the village kids would run along it, racing each other and watching the sky for the first sign of the plane.

But that day one of the kids discovered a snake on the runway, and in no time Andi and the others gathered around and watched it, amazed. The snake was shedding its skin. Gradually, it moved and writhed and eased itself free of the old dead skin and moved on into the brush—sleek and beautiful and brand new.

Andi felt a little like that now, like the faith that had clothed her all these years was dried up and old. Like it didn't fit anymore. She could almost feel herself making her way free of it, ready to move on with a sleek, new exterior of her own design. The feeling was one more thing she couldn't tell anyone. She was Andi Ellison, missionary kid, after all. Everyone expected her to be the perfect Christian, the girl with the unwavering faith. No one could've guessed how she was really feeling.

Voices sounded outside and she watched two guys make their way into view and head down the path toward the dorm building. At first Andi couldn't hear what they were saying, but as they came into view she saw something that still shocked her. The guys were holding hands.

"You need to tell your dad," the one on the outside of the path sounded frustrated. His voice was the louder of the two.

The quieter one said something Andi couldn't quite understand.

"It doesn't matter." The first one stopped, his tone frustrated. "We love each other, and love is a beautiful thing. People have to get over their old-fashioned views of homosexuality and embrace us the way we are."

Another couple—a guy and a girl—were walking in the opposite direction, and the two pairs passed each other just as the one guy made his statement about people getting over their old views. The second couple gave the first a thumbs-up sign and the girl said, "Preach it, brother. Live and let live!"

Live and let live. That sounded pretty good, right? As long as no one was hurting anyone else? Her sociology teacher had said basically the same thing Friday during class discussion on the signs of a healthy culture. More love than hate—whatever form love happened to take wasn't important. Just more love than hate. The two couples had stopped and they were talking to each other, laughing and making easy conversation.

Andi didn't want to be caught watching them, so she slid back down onto the end of her bed and leaned against the wall. She'd been taught to believe the Bible, and the Bible was clear that homosexuality was wrong. But was it? Was it really so bad for two people of the same sex to love each other? There had to be worse things. Like anger and hatred and racism, right? Murder and the harming of little children?

She closed her eyes and tried to organize the whirling thoughts in her mind. No one loved God more than Rachel Baugher. If she could be killed without reaching her dreams, then maybe God wasn't really there at all. And then what would it matter how a person lived, as long as they were treating others with kindness? All around her—on TV and across campus—people were coming out in favor of gay relationships. Not only that, but celebrities rarely got married, choosing to have babies and live together instead. Christians were the only ones who seemed to have a problem with the change in morals, which made people of faith seem old-fashioned and out of style. Worse, it sometimes made Christians seem narrow-minded and judgmental.

Andi liked guys, but in these first few days of school she'd seen several same-sex couples. In her science class she sat next to a guy named Julian who talked nonstop about his attraction to other guys. Andi even found herself agreeing with him over which guys were hot and which guys weren't. Julian was kind and funny and interesting. He gave her his cell number and promised to take notes for her when she missed class. He fussed over her pretty hair and was—by far—the nicest person she'd met on campus besides Bailey Flanigan.

Was he going to hell just because he liked guys?

She breathed in deep, and the smell of old leaves and fresh-cut grass mixed in with the cool air. Across the hall she heard a group of girls laughing and someone running from one room to another yelling about free pizza. She kept her eyes closed. *Dear God, I'm so confused. How can I know what's real and what's not? Show me that You're there, that You care about me ... please, God.*

"You praying or sleeping?" The voice was Bailey's.

Andi's eyes flew open and she shot forward, her back suddenly straight, slightly breathless from the surprise. She'd been so caught up in her thoughts that she hadn't heard Bailey enter the room, and the timing ... how weird was that? She asked God for a sign, for proof that He was there, and just at that moment Bailey mentions prayer?

A chill ran down her arms. She'd have to analyze later whether God was trying to tell her something. Bailey looked sort of funny at her as she tossed her bag on her bed and peeled off her jacket. "Seriously ... were you praying?"

"Uh ..." Andi could feel the heat in her cheeks. Could her friend see how great her doubts were becoming? She cleared her voice. "Sort of." She raised up onto her knees once more and adjusted the picture of Rachel a final time. "Lots on my mind, I guess. Still unpacking the last of my stuff."

"More pictures?"

"Just one." Andi set the hammer down on her nightstand. She studied the photograph again. "Rachel was my best friend once we came back from Indonesia."

Bailey set her bag down on her bed and came closer. "You haven't talked about her."

"It takes me awhile." Andi sat back on her heels. "She was killed in a car accident in August."

Shock changed Bailey's expression, and she looked again at the photo. "That's terrible."

"I know. She was with another friend of ours. He was driving." Andi recited what she knew about the accident, but the details were never enough, never what any of them needed to make sense of it. "Sunny day, middle of the afternoon. For some reason he lost control and hit a tree. He lived, but Rachel ... she died at the scene."

Bailey looked at the picture a little longer and then backed up until she dropped slowly to the edge of her bed. "Wow, Andi. That's so sad."

Andi thought about being honest, telling Bailey about her new struggles with faith, but she couldn't bring herself to voice them. Not yet, anyway. She looked at the picture of Rachel. "She left behind a quote book." Andi opened the second drawer in her nightstand and pulled out a small spiral-bound notebook. Rachel's photo was on the front. "Everyone got one of these at her memorial service. A copy of her exact quote book, written in her own printing and everything."

"A quote book." Bailey leaned back on her elbows. "That's such a cool idea."

"Here." Andi sat on the edge of her bed and flipped the book open. She hadn't looked through Rachel's quote book since she arrived in Bloomington, but she was glad she kept it close by. Reading the things that meant something to Rachel made Andi feel like the two of them could still be friends. Even if Rachel was in heaven. If there was a heaven, anyway. She stopped when she found what she was looking for. "Here's one of my favorites: 'God is more concerned about our character than our comfort. His goal is not to pamper us physically, but to perfect us spiritually.'" She glanced beneath the quote. "That came from some guy named Paul Powell."

"Hmmm." Bailey positioned her pillow against the wall and slid back against it. "God is more concerned with our character than our comfort." She smiled. "I can definitely relate to that."

Andi pictured Rachel so full of life, so excited about the future. Suddenly she didn't want to spend another minute remembering her friend or looking through her quote book. Not another second thinking about God or His concerns for people or somehow attaining a perfect sort of spirituality. She set the collection back in her drawer and took a quick breath. "Enough of that." She pulled one knee up and hugged it to her chest. "How was your weekend at home?"

"Great." Bailey smiled, though some of the sadness about Rachel remained. "We went to my dad's game this morning, and they won. So that was good. They're doing better than last year."

"Yeah, I heard on the news." She bounced up off the bed and flipped on the radio. She didn't want to sit around feeling sad. God or no God, Rachel never would've wanted that. "What about your cute little brothers? They had soccer, right?"

"They won. BJ scored a goal and Justin scored two. Shawn was named defensive player of the game." Bailey laughed. "Just another day on the soccer field for those three." She jabbed her finger in the air. "And don't forget about Ricky, our little football player. He's only eleven, but he threw for two touchdowns."

"Maybe he'll play for your dad one day."

"That's all he talks about. Being a Colt and playing for my dad." Bailey laughed. "It's like a circus at my house. Always something going on." Her smile was genuine. "You have to come home with me one of these weekends. See for yourself how crazy it is." The kindness in her eyes was genuine. "What about you? What did you do over the weekend?"

"My dad and I met for dinner. He's excited about his movie. A lot riding on it, that's for sure." She felt her eyes light up. "He said we could both be extras. He might even have a line or two for us, depending on how it goes."

"I can't wait." Bailey angled her head. "So come home with me, okay? Maybe next weekend?"

"I'd probably never leave." Andi grabbed a water bottle from a case on the floor beneath their desk. "I always wanted a bunch of sisters and brothers. It wasn't so bad in Indonesia, because all the kids felt like my family." She twisted off the bottle cap and took a swig of water. "But back here it's boring being an only child."

"Speaking of not being bored ..." Bailey jumped up and took a bottle of water for herself. "I grabbed a flyer from the Campus Crusade booth before I left for the weekend." She sorted through a stack of papers on her nightstand and then held up a blue piece of paper. "Here. Every Thursday they have CRU at eight o'clock. Singing and a message. I guess a couple hundred kids go."

"Really?" Andi took the flyer and looked over the details. She pushed her doubts as far down as they would go. "Yeah, I meant to find out about that last week. You wanna check it out?"

"Definitely. The guy I talked to said it's great. They have small group Bible studies too."

Andi nodded. "I'd love that." When it came to matters of faith, the dialogue came so easily she might as well have been reading a script. No matter how she was feeling inside. "Monday night would work for a small group. For you too, right?"

"Definitely."

"Depending on the auditions and whether we make it into *Scrooge*." Andi felt a batch of butterflies zip through her middle. "I'm scared to death for Tuesday. I can't believe you talked me into it."

Bailey laughed. "You're tall, thin, and gorgeous. You have a personality bigger than the IU campus and you want to be an actress." She took a long sip of water. "What're you afraid of?"

"I want to act, not sing!" Andi stared at herself in the small mirror that hung near their bathroom door. "I hope they don't laugh me off the stage."

"We'll pray about it before we go." Bailey heaved her backpack onto her bed and dug through it until she pulled out an advanced algebra book. "You have your song yet?"

"I found the music for "Tale As Old As Time" from *Beauty and the Beast*."

"That's perfect." She sat cross-legged on her bed and pulled out her binder. "Ugh ... I have about a hundred math problems to finish."

"That stinks." Andi turned away from the mirror. "What about you? What are you singing?"

"I don't know." Bailey's blue eyes looked deep and innocent. "Probably something from *Last Five Years*. Every song in that play's so emotional." She released a long breath. "Don't you have homework?"

"I did it already." Andi remembered her earlier invitation from the girls across the hall. They were going to watch the latest Reese Witherspoon movie, just out on DVD, and they asked her to join them. Andi finished her water and tossed the empty bottle in a recycling bin. "I'll be across the hall. That way you can get your work done."

"Okay." Bailey smiled. "I can't wait for CRU." She raised her eyebrows. "Maybe that's where you'll meet him."

"Who?" Andi blinked.

"Your Prince Charming." Bailey laughed. "Remember? You said he's somewhere on this campus."

"Oh, him." Andi let her own laughter mix with her roommate's. "I guess we'll see on Thursday."

Andi left, but not until she was alone in the hallway did she realize how phony she felt, talking to Bailey about Campus Crusade and small group Bible studies, and agreeing that there was a good chance she'd meet her Prince Charming come Thursday night. Andi liked Bailey, and she hoped with all her heart that the two of them could become best friends. But if so, then one of these days Andi would have to be honest about her doubts.

As she opened the dorm room across the hall and joined the half dozen girls who had gathered there, she still couldn't get a handle on her thoughts or the desperate prayer she'd uttered before Bailey came home. She wanted to live life to the fullest — the way Rachel always wanted to live it. But no matter how strongly she'd once believed, she was no longer sure about God or the reason for praying or the need for Bible study. Truth seemed like something gray without lines or definition, and she could no longer clearly state what she did and didn't believe. But when it came to her Prince Charming, she was pretty sure about this much.

She didn't expect to find him at a Campus Crusade meeting.

Five

THE CAST AND CREW WERE SET up in and around an old corner house in downtown Bloomington, ready for the first day of shooting. The actors involved in the first scenes had done their read-throughs, grips and techs were ready, and the cameras and lighting were in perfect position. The set dresser had scoured every inch of the house, even replacing photos that had been on the fireplace mantle with new photos of the movie's key characters. Every detail had been addressed.

Keith had made sure of it, and Chase had double-checked that every person, every position, was ready for filming to begin. Call was at seven that morning, but most of the cast and crew reported half an hour early, checking in at base camp where the cast trailers were set up alongside a tent-covered outdoor dining area and the oversized food truck that would service meals for the shoot.

It was a few minutes before seven and Keith watched the cast and crew file over from base camp and take their places. He lifted his eyes beyond the orange and yellow tops of the trees that lined the neighborhood. *It's really happening, God ... we dreamed about making this movie and now here we are. You are faithful beyond all—*

"Somebody better tell me what's going on!"

The loud angry words stopped Keith short. He turned to see Rita Reynolds—their lead actress—storming toward the set, her face red, her footsteps angry and purposeful. But before he could intercept her, she launched into a tirade like nothing Keith had ever seen. He watched her huff her way over to Chase, who was sitting with the director of photography a few yards away from where Keith was set up.

"Are you kidding me?" she screeched the question as she came up to Chase. Her tone made everyone in shouting distance turn to see what was wrong.

"Rita?" Chase stood, his expression blank. "Something wrong?"

"Yes, something is very wrong." She tossed her hands in the air and moved closer to Chase. "I asked for salmon, and it's not here!"

Whatever she said next, Keith couldn't quite make out, but she remained animated and angry—something none of them could mistake. Keith studied her, their leading lady. She'd already been to makeup and wardrobe, so she wore a pale blue silk cover-up and a matching scarf tied loosely over her platinum blonde hair—a getup that meant no one could mistake her for anything but the star she was. The dark sunglasses had to be at least partly for dramatic effect, because the sky was completely overcast.

Chase was saying something about making a few phone calls, trying to get salmon on the set by dinnertime. Rita shook her head and took three angry steps away from Chase before turning back to him. "Look," she was yelling again, "I'm supposed to have a filet of salmon every morning. Every single morning." She flipped her hand toward the food truck. "But the guy in the truck tells me he knows nothing about it." She put her hands on her hips. "Wild Alaskan salmon, Chase. Does that ring a bell?"

Keith wasn't sure whether to move closer and rescue his friend, or watch from a distance. He decided on the latter. He knew nothing about the salmon request, and he doubted Chase did either.

"For breakfast?" Chase kept his tone calm. He set his clipboard down on his director's chair and faced her squarely. "You want wild Alaskan salmon for breakfast?"

"Yes!" The word came out as a shriek. "Check my contract! Wild Alaskan sockeye salmon. Every morning. Every day I'm on the set." She made an exasperated sound and then realized how many eyes were watching her. She glared at a group of grips. "What're you looking at?"

Keith felt the hair on his neck rise. Rita Reynolds was one of the finest actresses in Hollywood, but the casting director had warned them. "She's a handful. Be ready to wait on her."

Given their budget and the lack of A-list actresses interested in a lesser paycheck, Keith and Chase had told the casting director no problem. "We'll wash her feet if it comes to that."

"You might have to," they were told. "Don't say I didn't warn you."

Keith took a deep breath and held it for a beat. As he exhaled, he resolved that he would find a way to serve Rita—even if it meant cooking her salmon every morning himself. They needed her in this picture. She would play the young mother of the college boy whose story they were about to tell through film, a significant part with featured scenes in every act. But if this was how she handled herself on day one, he could hardly imagine the rollercoaster ride she would put them through over the next four weeks. He picked up his megaphone. "Everyone take five. We'll start up after that."

The forty-some people who made up the crew didn't have to be told twice. They formed cliques of twos and threes and milled across the street to the second truck, the one that would be set up all day with water, coffee, and snacks. Keith didn't tell them not to watch Rita Reynolds, but clearly they knew. Like with any temperamental actress, if Rita wasn't working, no one was working. A few of the electricians glanced over their shoulders at Keith, and one of them raised an eyebrow. The message was unmistakable. Whatever the trouble about the salmon, the producers better get things fixed.

Keith drew a steadying breath. *Is this how it's going to be, God? The whole time?* He checked his watch. Ten minutes. They hadn't started filming and already they were ten minutes behind schedule. *We're using other people's money for this movie, Father ... we can't get behind or we won't have enough to finish.* A verse flashed in his mind, one he'd read early that morning before leaving his hotel room for the set: "In this world you will have trouble. But take heart! I have overcome the world." The verse came like a direct answer from God. Of course there would be trouble. He didn't need to panic, he needed to rest in the greater truth. God was in control. He joined his friend and gave a look that dismissed the director of photography.

Chase locked eyes with him, casting him a baffled look that cried for help.

But before Keith could add any perspective to the conversation, Rita turned her tirade on him. "Tell me you didn't know about this! I mean, I come down here completely ready because I'm a professional, expecting that everyone else is just as ready for day one. But no one, not one person, has told the guy in the truck about my salmon breakfast." She used both hands to point to her pretty cheeks. "I'm not a teenager, guys. I need my omega threes every morning if I'm going to keep this skin. Botox can only do so much. I need Alaskan salmon. Every morning. No exceptions." She made a dramatic attempt to calm herself down. When she spoke again, she was no longer yelling but her eyes and tone still screamed with anger. "Greasy eggs are not good for my face. Do I make myself clear?"

"Yes, Rita." Keith sounded apologetic, but not guilty. He thought about reminding her that anger couldn't be good for her face either, but he decided against it.

"Now listen," Chase crossed his arms, his own frustrations beginning to sound in his voice. "This isn't our fault. If your agent would've made it clear, then maybe we could—"

"Hold on." Keith held his hand up and shot a look of empathy at Chase. Keith had always been the easier going of the two, and now he needed to keep his friend in check or the issue could blow up in their faces. Calm, he told himself. Keep things calm. Keith put his hand gently on his star actress's arm. "Rita, we'll find you some salmon. It'll be here every morning after today." He managed to maintain a stance of authority despite giving in to her demands. "But Chase is right. I can promise you, we knew nothing about this. The two of us went over every line of your contract and there was nothing about a daily salmon breakfast. The issue never once came up in negotiations with your agent."

"Are you serious?" She made an exasperated sound. "Great. If this is his fault, I'll fire him today." She rolled her eyes. For a few seconds it seemed she might reel herself in, reflect a little on her temper tantrum and the unflattering light it put her in. But then she unleashed another wave at Keith. "Here's how it is." Her hands were on her hips again. "Someone gets my salmon here in the next hour, or I walk."

"We'll find something." Keith's look told Chase to keep quiet.

She tossed her head. "I won't ask for broccoli. That'd be too much for you people." A loud sigh rattled in her throat. "I'll be in my trailer. Let me know when my breakfast is here." With that she took hard fast steps toward the trailers at base camp, set up around the corner in an empty field.

Chase hung his head and rubbed the back of his neck, his breathing fast and jagged. "This is ridiculous." He hissed. He kept his voice low, but his words sounded like they were forced through clenched teeth. "It's seven in the morning. Where are we supposed to find salmon at this hour?"

"Let me think." Keith could still feel the rest of the cast and crew watching them from across the street. He knew what they were thinking. He and Chase were the producers, and whatever problem came up, the solution had to be theirs. Even the task of finding wild Alaskan sockeye salmon at seven in the morning. Suddenly an idea hit him. "Wait ... I just remembered something."

"It better be good. If our star walks on the first day because of a fish, we might as well just pack our bags and go back to the jungle." Chase twisted his face in absolute confusion. "I mean, salmon? For breakfast?"

"Okay, listen." Keith kept his voice down. "Yesterday I was talking with a few of the locals and a guy comes up. Tells me he runs the best restaurant in town and that he's always wanted to be in a movie. He said he'd treat the cast to steak and lobster if I'd get him or his restaurant in a few scenes. I didn't think about him until now."

"If he has lobster, he's bound to have salmon." A disbelieving smile worked its way up Chase's face. "This might work ..."

"Right." Keith glanced at the table. The crew was looking restless, ready to get back to the set and start working. He pulled his wallet from his back jeans pocket and sorted through a small group of business cards until he found the one with the lobster on it. "Here it is. Indiana's finest lobster," he read from the card.

"You got his card?" The shock on Chase's face grew. "No one would believe any of this."

Keith slipped his wallet back in his pocket, picked up Chase's clipboard from the nearest chair, and took a quick look at the scene list. Rita was in just about every scene scheduled to be filmed at the house, but there had to be something Chase could get started with. The clock was ticking. If the solution was at hand, good, but they needed to get everyone else busy. "Jake Olson's ready, right?"

"He is. I saw him way before Rita showed up."

Jake was the main lead, a good-looking twenty-four-year-old, recently discovered by the tabloids. The camera loved him, and girls across America were just finding out about him. After this movie, he was slated to star opposite Will Smith. The investors figured they were lucky to be getting Jake Olson now while they could still afford him. Keith ran his finger over the list of scenes. "There it is." He held up the sheet so Chase could see it. "Switch the order, and start with Jake taking the letter outside to the front porch and reading it. Also the scene where he's in his room looking at the letter a second time, going through photos of his father." Keith studied the business card in his hand. "I'll call the lobster guy and see what he can do."

"Okay." Doubt darkened Chase's eyes. He took the clipboard and lifted his own megaphone toward the milling cast and crew. "Jake Olson, I need you." He scribbled something on the call sheet. "Everyone else, break's up. We're shooting scenes four and six. Get to your places, and thanks for your patience."

Keith had his cell phone out as he crossed the street to base camp. He placed the call as soon as he stepped into their trailer—a no-frills single-wide with a simple table and two bench seats on either side of it. He sat down and waited while the phone rang.

"Bloomington's finest steaks and lobster, JR McDowell, how can I help you?"

The reason for his phone call would've been laughable at any other time but now. "This is Keith from the movie set down the street. We talked yesterday."

"Oh, yes." JR chuckled. "You ready to take me up on that swap. Gonna get me in the movies, are you?"

Keith winced. "Actually, let me explain what we need..." Five minutes later when he got off the phone, they had the promise of a hot filet of Alaskan salmon every morning for the next four weeks—starting with the piece he was putting in the broiler even as they spoke. After this morning, JR would even deliver the cooked fish to the set each day at seven. He would deliver it to the food services truck, where it would be kept warm until Rita reported for breakfast. In turn, Keith had promised the guy he could be a professor walking in the background on one of the scenes set to be shot on campus next week.

The salmon wasn't free, of course. At twenty-five and change per filet, they'd just added more than five hundred dollars to the budget. Keith had no choice. They'd have to find the money somewhere. He climbed into his rental car and headed toward Town's Square. As he drove, he found a reason to be grateful. Yesterday when they were setting up, dozens of townspeople approached him to ask questions about the film. Be kind to the locals, that's what they'd learned in the mission field. In the two years since then, he and Chase had worked on the set of a new hit reality show, and they'd produced a few direct-to-DVD films for the Christian market.

With each project, Keith had only become more convinced about his philosophy regarding the locals—they'd get a lot farther in their goals if they were extraordinarily nice from the get-go. Loving people the way Jesus loved them. Not only did kindness foster good will among the neighbors and make them more agreeable to the disruption of a film crew taking over their street, but oftentimes producers needed a certain car in a shot, or some yard furniture moved to create a different look. Any of a hundred strange requests, and always the neighbors were more inclined to work with the producers if they'd been shown kindness and respect.

Now they could take the next step toward their goals all because he'd been nice to a local. Keith bounded up the steps of the restaurant, and after only a few minutes, JR handed him a plastic plate with a great-smelling piece of salmon and a heap of fresh steamed broccoli. Keith shook the man's hand. "I might have to get you in two scenes for this."

"No problem." The man tipped his baseball cap. "Glad to be of service."

Keith pulled up on the set and hurried the hot plate to Rita's trailer door. He knocked and waited a full minute before she opened it. She was still in her pale blue wrap, and she scowled at him, ready for a fight until she saw the plate in his hand. "Here," Keith gave it to her. "Salmon and broccoli. The same thing will be here for you every morning from now on."

Rita studied the plate and her expression softened. "Thank you." She smelled the plate and a quiet, nervous-sounding laugh came from her. "I don't mean to be any trouble, Keith. You know that. I didn't think you'd find salmon this morning, and, well ... I wouldn't really have walked. It's just ... someone dropped the ball—not you and Chase—but someone, and ..." another laugh, "I can't work without salmon." She smiled again. "You understand, right?"

"Of course." Keith took a step back and checked his watch. "When can we expect you on set?"

"How about twenty minutes?" Again she looked sheepish. "Sorry if I made a scene. I can be a little ... overdramatic at times."

"We want you happy, Rita." He tried to see her as a vulnerable human being, not as a spoiled actress wasting precious money and making unreasonable demands. His smile felt genuine as he took a few steps away from her trailer. "We'll do whatever we can. See you in twenty."

On the short walk back to the set, Keith thought about the change in his star actress. What if he'd fought with her and chastised her for her demands? This would've been the beginning of an adversarial relationship, and everyone on the set would've suffered as a result. Instead, she'd actually apologized. *This is a mission field, too, isn't it God? But is it always going to be this difficult?*

My son, consider it pure joy whenever you face trials of many kinds. For you know that the testing of your faith develops perseverance ...

The answer was a quiet whisper, one that danced in the breeze and soothed his soul. He would've preferred some kind of assurance that the filming could only get easier from here, but he had a better promise instead. One that was tried and true, straight from the Bible.

He stepped up onto the curb and walked up to the house, but again nothing was being shot. He'd been gone forty minutes, so he could only hope they'd finished at least one of the two scenes with Jake Olson. The electricians hovered over a section of wires off to the right side of the house, and Chase appeared to be deep in conversation with the director of photography and the assistant director.

Keith stopped a grip along the way. "What's going on?"

"Cameras aren't getting power." He motioned to the group working on the side of the house. "Took awhile, but they finally figured out where the problem was. Looks like a cat chewed through a handful of wires."

For a long moment, Keith stared at the guy as if maybe the man might laugh out loud and admit he was only kidding. Certainly this sort of trouble wasn't a normal part of shooting on location. At least it hadn't been for the smaller projects Keith had worked on. He thanked the guy and went to Chase, who confirmed the trouble and the fact that the damage had been done by a cat.

"We patched the wires and the cameras are working again. But the cord to the main light is damaged in several areas." Chase raked his fingers through his hair and shook his head. "The university doesn't have one that big, so I have one coming from Indianapolis. It'll be here in an hour."

Keith allowed the news to fully register. Then once more he took the clipboard from Chase and scrutinized the scene list. "Ask the DP if we can use two smaller lights and get a few outdoor scenes shot. There are three here that we can work on. One of them doesn't include Rita. Let's start there."

By the time they broke for dinner at five, they had captured just five of the eight scenes slated for day one. Keith wanted to lock himself in the trailer and cry out to God, because this pace would never do. They would have to add another three weeks to their film schedule if they crawled along at this rate. Chase seemed discouraged too, but they wouldn't have time to talk until they were back at the hotel. He longed for Wednesday, when Lisa would be here and he'd have her arms to look forward to at the end of a day like this.

He was climbing into his car, leaving for the day, when he practically heard an audible reminder of the verse from earlier. *Consider it pure joy whenever you face trials of many kinds...* He stopped and braced himself against his car. *Pure joy...* had day one on the set been so bad that he could forget what God was clearly trying to tell him? Ministry of any kind came at a price, and trials were part of the cost. He filled his lungs with fresh air and did one more walk around the base camp, thanking whatever cast and crew were still around and assuring them that tomorrow would be better for everyone.

"You guys are really different," one of the grips told him when Keith was almost finished making his final rounds. "We're not on the same team, you and us." He removed his baseball cap and scratched his head. "But you and Chase, you're different. It's like you really care, you know? Ain't never seen anything like it."

"Thanks." Keith grinned at the guy. "And you're wrong. No matter what the union reps say, as long as we're making this film, we *are* on the same team. All of us."

As Keith drove back to the hotel, he felt a new, deeper joy filling his heart, giving him strength for whatever the next day held. His father used to tell him that when hard times came, they had all the more reason to be excited about the future. "The bigger the mountain, the greater the view on the other side," he would say. Keith smiled to himself. The mission field in this new venture of filmmaking wasn't only the audience who would see the movie. It was every cast and crew member who had reported for duty this morning. And if every day was going to bring the sort of mountains that cropped up today, he could only be certain of one thing.

The view on the other side must be breathtaking.

Six

CHASE LIKED THE ANALOGY ABOUT THE mountains and the vistas, but he had a copy of their bank statement in front of him when he and Keith met up in the hotel room. "We can't do it," he slid the piece of paper across the small table. "We have enough in the budget for a few days overage, but at this rate?" He released a defeated chuckle. A few delays midway through the shoot was one thing, but this early? "We'll run out of money before the third act."

"I'm still making phone calls, contacting people about investing." Keith kept his tone upbeat.

"What about the investors who've already committed? Have you talked to them?" Chase still hoped more money might come from the familiar sources. If they'd already put up five hundred thousand or a million, they might be willing to put up more.

"You know the answer." Keith sounded like he was trying to be patient.

"Sorry. You're doing everything you can." The two of them had been best friends for nearly ten years, and when it came to producing movies, Keith was by the far the more experienced. Chase leaned back in his chair, and with his free hand he tried to rub out the tension in his neck.

"I sent them all letters three weeks ago, suggesting they might want to invest more, increase their returns down the road." He tossed his hands. "Not one bite."

"What's our accountant say?"

"I called him after lunch. He thinks we're in trouble. Everyone expected at least one of the investors to come up with a few hundred thousand more, but people are nervous. The market's shaky and investors are playing it safe."

Chase tried not to look nervous. "Okay ... then what are the options?" This was ministry, they'd agreed on that. But if they ran out of money, they'd not only fail in their mission, but they'd be in trouble with their investors. Chase took the paper from Keith again and stared at it for a long moment.

Keith's tone bordered on dire. "There's only one option. We find another investor. Someone who can pad us with another three hundred at least. Ten days of on-location filming. Otherwise we're irresponsible to move forward."

"I agree." Chase leaned forward on his elbows. "Our accountant's looking for someone, right? I thought he had a lead last week."

"He had four leads. I'm following up on them, but no one's returning my calls." Keith massaged his temples with his thumb and fingers. "I've got a dozen copies of our portfolio, detailed information on the movie and its distribution channels, the breakdown on how investors will be repaid first and how they'll benefit from the sale of DVDs. The package is enticing, but in this market no one's sure of anything. I need to get the packets into the hands of the people who can help."

"Exactly." Chase felt the beginning of a headache. "We only have enough in the account if we stick to the schedule."

For what felt like a solid minute, neither of them said a word. Then Keith sat up straighter and sucked in a full breath. "Well, then ... until I can get a hold of one of these potential investors, we'll have to stick to the schedule."

"Come on." Chase could feel his defeated attitude dragging both of them down, but he couldn't help himself. They couldn't make a movie without some kind of cushion in the bank. "That's crazy, and you know it."

Keith leveled his gaze across the table. "There we were in Indonesia, trapped on the wrong side of a rising river." His voice was low and intense, every word hitting its mark. "Three women and twelve tribal children surrounded us, screaming for help. Rain flooding down from the skies." He didn't blink. "Can you see us, Chase? Remember how it was?"

Chase felt goose bumps rise along his arms, felt again the nausea that had swept over him at the certain death they all faced in that single moment. He swallowed hard. "We ... we cried out to God." He closed his eyes and he could hear the rushing water, feel the spray against his face. "At the top of our lungs we cried out."

"And from nowhere a barge sailed up and rescued us."

"Later, no one knew where the thing had come from or who had sent it."

Keith exhaled and folded his arms across his chest. "Are you kidding me, Chase, buddy? You're worried about a little funding for a Hollywood movie?" He lifted his chin, his confidence and faith so strong it dispelled the darkness from the room. "God brought us here. He will see us through to the end. Until then, we can plan and act and take all the prudent steps. But we can't give way to fear and worry." He smiled. "We have to believe, same as we did in that storm."

"Man." Chase clenched his teeth, flexing the muscles in his jaw. "I beg God to give me a faith like yours."

"He will. Days like this can only make us stronger." Keith stood and headed for the door. "Enough doom and gloom. Come with me. There's fresh coffee in the lobby."

Chase wasn't sure about the coffee. It was after eight and call was at seven again tomorrow. He still needed to talk to Kelly about things back home, how she and the girls were doing. But right now he needed time with Keith more than anything. Every hour with his friend made the mountain they were facing seem less formidable.

They sat at a table in the lobby not far from a roaring fireplace. The atmosphere was more open, less oppressive than it had been back in the hotel room. Chase made himself a cup of hot cider and sat opposite his friend. "Doesn't anything scare you?" He'd seen Keith show fear before. The time in Indonesia when Andi went missing, and another season when it looked like Lisa might be sick. But most of the time the guy was rock solid. Chase breathed in the steam from his sweet-smelling drink. "Don't you ever wonder why we're doing this?"

"No." He grinned over the top of his coffee cup. "I know why we're doing this. But sure ... I get scared sometimes. Scared for our culture, our country. Scared that Andi and your girls will have to grow up in a world where the lines between right and wrong have vanished for good." He was quiet for a minute, thoughtful. "When I think about all this, about the purpose in making movies with a message, I guess it comes down to conveying one thing."

"One?"

"Pretty much." He took a slow sip of his coffee. "We need to tell the world the truth."

"Not everyone's lost the truth. Andi has her head on straight. The kids she went to high school with, they seemed pretty strong."

"For now." Keith narrowed his eyes. "Sometimes I'm not so sure about Andi. Once in a while she'll say something and I'll know she didn't get that from Lisa and me, and certainly not from anything she learned in the Bible." He gave a slow, sure nod. "The culture's a powerful thing. And the culture pays attention to movies." He stared for a while into the dancing fire. "Everywhere you look, nearly every movie out there has a lie at its core. I want so much more for Andi, for the kids of her generation."

"And we can help with that?"

"We could." Keith's smile was easy. "A couple of willing guys looking to change the world ... God's used less than that in the past. A stuttering recluse to change the mind of the Pharoah of Egypt ... a scrawny kid with a stone and a slingshot to bring down the Philistine army." His eyes shone brighter than before. "A group of fishermen to bring the message of hope to an entire world."

"They didn't even have a movie screen."

"Exactly."

Chase raised his eyebrows and waited. Keith's assessment of the culture was bleak, but it was right on. "Truth. The foundations that used to hold up our culture. If we can resurrect those, then the next generation might find the direction it's missing." Chase gave a low whistle. "Pretty big mission."

"Pretty big God." Again Keith smiled. A couple of electricians from the set walked by and nodded in their direction. When they'd passed, Keith's expression became more intense. "Here's the deal. I don't want to make even one movie unless the message at the core helps our culture find its way to daylight again. Back to truth."

Chase thought about the film they were making, *The Last Letter*. Jake Olson's character was like a lot of college guys, given over to a wrong relationship with his girlfriend and drifting along in a shallow stream of activity without purpose or passion. He had no connection to family, no faith, and no reason to believe in his future. But after his father dies, he receives a letter advising him that he's the last of the men in his family's line, the last one who can restore a sense of character and godly principles for future generations. Chase had always seen the movie as good and wholesome.

But until now, he hadn't seen it as restoring truth. He took a long drink from his cider and studied his friend. "That's why you're so passionate about this one."

"Exactly." Keith finished his coffee and stood. "I'm turning in. I need to call Lisa and give her the update. She's been praying all day."

"You sure?" Chase laughed lightly. "Maybe she got distracted."

Another easy smile lifted Keith's lips. "We found the salmon, didn't we? And the new light came in from Indianapolis."

"Yeah. I guess." Chase was tired of his cider. He pushed it toward the center of the table and crossed his arms. No point reminding Keith about the three scenes they didn't shoot, or how far they'd fall behind tomorrow if they couldn't keep up with the schedule. "Thanks for the talk." Chase sat at the table with his cider, thinking about what Keith had said. They'd come through much to get where they were, and they'd done it all for one reason—to bring change to the current culture. Keith was right. God had seen them through dire situations in the past. He would see them through this.

He was about to turn in when Rita Reynolds walked through the front door of the lobby, fixing her hair and pulling her sweater tight around her middle. She was headed for the elevator when she spotted him and stopped. Her expression became humble and apologetic, and for a few seconds she only stood there. Then she released her hold on her sweater and let it open to reveal a white tank top, tight against her middle. Chase crossed one leg over the other and nodded at her, same as he would to any of the cast or crew who might pass by.

But clearly Rita had something to say. She came closer, pulled out the chair where Keith had been sitting, and lifted one eyebrow cautiously. "You got a minute?"

"Sure." Chase had no idea what she wanted to talk about, but here in the public lobby he had no reason to fear her intentions. After her earlier tirade, she was probably only checking on her breakfast order. "What's on your mind?"

"You, I guess. You and Keith." She sat down and rested her forearms easily on the table between them. "I had no right blowing up this morning." She made a face that suggested she was embarrassed by her actions. "Yes, I like salmon, but the scene I made? Really?" She wrinkled her nose. "I'm sorry, Chase. I was out of line."

Something in Rita's tone kept Chase on his guard. She was volatile and difficult, just like they'd been warned. If this was a true apology, it would likely be followed by some other request, something she still wanted and hadn't gotten. He remained unmoved except for a polite smile. "Apology accepted."

"Really?" In the shadows near the fireplace she looked younger than her thirty-seven years, more like a school girl seeking attention. "I felt bad all day."

"Let it go." It hit Chase that he was sitting across the table talking to one of the country's favorite movie stars. Rita was blonde and willowy with the ability to play a decade younger or older than her age—depending on the role. She'd won an Academy Award for supporting actress in her teens, and she'd raised the bar in every movie she'd been in since. Chase still wasn't sure what she wanted. "Tomorrow's a new day for all of us."

Rita tapped her fingers lightly on the table, her eyes searching his as if she was trying to see past his position as producer. "So who are you, Chase Ryan? You're awfully young to be making movies."

"I'm more the director on this one." He felt his guard drop a little. Maybe she only wanted to make small talk to repair the damage from earlier. "Keith and I are a team." He gave a look that said he couldn't be sure about anything. "We hope this is the first of many movies to come. Our dreams are pretty big."

She hesitated, and her eyes found the ring on his left hand. "You're married, of course." A grin eased the embarrassment that had colored her expression since she sat down. "The best looking ones always are."

It took Chase a few heartbeats to register what she'd said. Even then he figured she was still only looking to make a connection, trying to erase the impression she'd made at breakfast. "Making points, huh?" He laughed and leaned his head back, trying to read her intentions. On the handful of movies he and Keith had worked over the past few years, he'd been hit on here and there. He couldn't tell about Rita.

When he didn't say anything else, she leaned a little closer across the table. "So tell me about Chase ... what's behind those deep brown eyes?"

"You had it right." He kept his tone easy, but he had no intention of letting her see past his professional exterior. "I'm happily married to Kelly. We have two little girls — Molly and Macy, four and two. Other than missing my family? I love God and my wife and the idea of making movies that pack a message." He felt his smile cool some. "That's about it."

"You know why I took this movie?" She seemed anxious to move on. "I mean, I get a lot of offers."

"I'm sure." Chase was curious. They'd put the script out to twenty-some actresses, and all of them turned the part down because of the budget or because Keith and he were untested. Then one day when they were running out of time, a call came into their small office from Rita Reynolds' agent. She wanted a shot at the lead role. At the time, the phone call and the interest from Rita was one more miracle allowing them to move forward with a movie that would hopefully wind up on the big screen. But they never really knew why Rita had sought them out. "Tell me why."

"I research the unknown people in this business. Through IMDB's website and on a handful of blogs and chat groups I check up on."

Chase remembered the first time he saw their work on the Internet Movie Database, and the thrill that came with feeling like that made them legitimate producers. The warmth from the fire felt good and lent a slow pace to the conversation. "We didn't have many credits."

"No, but I caught a few people agreeing that you and Keith could be the next big thing—a pair of producers with talent in directing that was fresh and cutting edge in the industry." She'd backed off on the flirty eyes and body language. Now she seemed intent only on telling her story. "I got a hold of your direct-to-DVD movie—*Finding Mercy*. Watched it alone in my house one night, and you know what?"

Chase raised his eyebrows subtly, waiting.

"I was blown away. The quality and camera work, the music and acting. The direction." She angled her head. "You couldn't have had much of a budget, but one thing was clear. You and Keith hadn't compromised on quality." Her eyes sparkled. "I called my agent the next morning and asked him to find out what you were working on next." She lifted her hands a few inches off the table and lowered them again. "Just like that, here I am."

"Well." He gave a slight nod in her direction. "You did your homework."

"I get tired of working with the same people, hearing the same names." Her eyes tried to find a deeper connection, and even when she didn't find one she didn't look away. "You and Keith are going places. I saw it in your work, and then today ... watching you with the cast and crew. The two of you are different, somehow." The embarrassed look flashed on her face again. "Even after my tirade."

Her compliment hit its mark. Especially after a day when they'd finished little more than half of what they intended to get done, and when their finances were so dire there was no guarantee they could finish the film. He clasped his hands and studied her, choosing his words carefully. He didn't dare tell her how much he needed her kind words. Not when to say so would be an open invitation for whatever else she might have in mind. "I appreciate your feedback. Keith and I have big dreams."

"You'll reach them. I can feel it." Admiration filled her tone. "Three years from now, I have a feeling the whole world will know." She reached out and patted his hand. "Just remember I told you first."

Chase almost couldn't believe this was the same woman who had threatened to walk off the set earlier. He stood and smiled at her. "I'm expecting great things from you too." He pushed in his chair. He allowed a hint of teasing in his voice. "Especially now that you'll have your salmon every morning."

She fell in beside him as they walked to the elevators and waited when Chase pushed the button. "I'm not really tired." Her smile seemed intentionally innocent-looking. "Do you want to watch a movie in my room? There's a drama showing and I'd love your feedback."

"No thanks. Gotta call my wife and turn in." Chase didn't let his surprise show. She really was coming on to him, and if he didn't have his faith, if he didn't love his wife, then tonight he could make choices that would ruin him. He felt sick at the thought. They stepped into the elevator together. "What floor?"

"Six." She didn't look disappointed, but almost humored.

He pushed the six, and the four. Before he stepped off, she gave him a smile that left no guessing at her intentions. "Maybe some other night. We have four weeks to get to know each other."

"Goodbye, Rita." Chase smiled, but his tone was cool and impersonal. "Thanks again for the apology."

"I enjoyed it."

The last thing he saw as the doors closed behind him was a smile that told him she believed one thing about their time together. He might not be willing to accept an invitation to her room tonight. But he would change his mind.

Chase put the entire conversation out of his mind and hurried into his hotel room for the call to Kelly. They were using a video chat system, one that allowed them to talk through their laptop computers and see each other at the same time. Skyping, it was called. Almost as if they were looking through a window, or sitting across from each other.

The call from Chase was supposed to come half an hour earlier, but the talk with Rita had sidetracked him. Even so, Kelly wasn't angry. She didn't even mention it. "I love this." She must've been looking straight into the built-in camera at the top of her computer screen, because her eyes looked deep into his. She'd done herself up for the conversation. Her hair was curled, and she wore enough makeup that her green eyes looked gorgeous—even on his laptop screen.

"You look beautiful." He longed to reach out and touch her, feel her soft hair beneath his fingers and take her into his arms. "I wish you were here."

"Me too." The intimacy between them was far stronger than it had been when he left. "The girls have been talking about this call all afternoon." Kelly smiled. "We all miss you." She stood and her orange sweater came into view. "I'll get them. They're upstairs."

Chase waited, glad that the offer from Rita hadn't even been tempting. He and Kelly were doing better than ever, and this was the only way he wanted to spend his late nights. He couldn't imagine living like so many in Hollywood, where every movie, every location, brought with it a different affair, a different set of people sneaking into each other's hotel rooms.

The squeal of his little girls' voices sounded in the distance, followed by the staccato taps of their feet racing across the floor toward the computer. All at once their faces appeared, each of them vying for a better position as their voices ran together. "Hi, Daddy ... love you, Daddy ..."

Again Chase's heart ached that he couldn't lift them up in his arms and swing them around, the way he would if he were there in person. A lump formed in his throat, but he found his voice anyway. "Hey, girls ... you being good for Mommy?"

"Yes, Daddy ... yes." Molly, the older of the two, pushed her way to the center of the screen. "I made you a card today. It has the best ballerina on it, Daddy. The best ever."

"Me too." Macy wouldn't be outdone. She might be only two, but she did everything in her power to keep up with her sister.

"How did the movie go?" Molly blinked her big eyes. "We prayed for you." She looked up at Kelly, who was almost entirely out of the picture. "Right, Mommy? We prayed, right?"

"We did." She tilted her face so that only her eyes joined the crowded picture. "Was it a good day?"

"Very good." Chase laughed at the picture they made, crowding in around the laptop. "I can't wait to see your card, Molly."

"Yeah, me too." She reached out and touched the screen. "I like seeing you, Daddy. I wish you could give hugs through this thing."

"I know, baby." The ache in his heart spread. "Me too."

They talked a few more minutes, and then Kelly asked the girls to go back upstairs. "Bedtime in ten minutes," she told them. "Brush your teeth, and I'll be up in a little bit."

When the girls were gone, Kelly took her place in front of the screen once more. "Really, Chase? How was it?"

He sighed, and in it he heard how worn out the day had left him. "Tough. Rita Reynolds needed salmon before she would work, and then a neighborhood cat chewed up our lighting wires."

"Salmon?" Kelly looked baffled. "For breakfast?"

"Yep." He ran his hand over his hair. "Supposed to be in her contract. Salmon every morning or she doesn't work."

"Yuck." Kelly laughed and wrinkled her nose at the same time. "Did you make your goal?"

"Not even close." He didn't want to end the day worrying about the budget, but the reality remained. "We need to make up time tomorrow."

For an instant, worry darkened her eyes, but then she let it pass. "You will. The girls and I will keep praying." Her smile was genuine and warm. This was where they'd struggled far too often, and Kelly seemed determined to be an encouragement now — however difficult day one had been. "You look tired."

"I am." He considered telling her about the conversation with Rita, but he changed his mind. He wasn't taken by her interest. No need to worry Kelly about it. "Listen, babe. I need some sleep. Let's talk longer tomorrow."

"Okay." Again if she was disappointed by the shorter call, she didn't show it. "I'm proud of you, Chase. You're doing what God wants you to do." She reached out and put her fingers against the screen. "I can't wait to see you in person."

"Me either. If we get on track, I wanna come home over the weekend — not this one, but maybe the next."

"Okay. Until then I'm here for you." Her eyes looked shinier than before, and she blinked a few times. "I love you."

"Love you too."

The call ended and Chase shut down his laptop. As he brushed his teeth, he studied his look in the mirror and celebrated the great feeling of knowing he wasn't open to compromise. Sure, he and Kelly had struggled at times. But they loved each other, and no movie shoot was going to change that. Not for him, and definitely not for Keith. They would show the world that a couple of married men could go on location for a month and not be swayed into having an affair. God had given them strength; Chase had felt it keenly in his earlier talk with Rita. He might not be sure about tomorrow's film schedule, or whether they'd have enough money to complete the project. But no one was going to make him compromise the vows he'd made to Kelly.

He was sure about that.

Seven

TWO HOURS INTO THE MORNING, KEITH was thrilled with how much ground they'd covered. Already they were a scene ahead of where he'd wanted to be at this time today, so maybe they really could make up lost time. This was why he hadn't wanted Chase to worry last night. God knew how much money they had and how many days they could afford to be on location. All morning things had been going right, with Chase moving people in and out of the house and celebrating the quality of acting they were getting on only a few takes.

Before arriving on set, Keith had placed a call to Ben Adams on the West Coast. Word around town was that the billionaire was looking to help fund movies with a moral message, and Keith had the feeling Ben was the answer to their problems. The trouble was, he and Chase weren't on Ben's radar, and though Keith had called the man four times in the past two weeks, there'd been no return call.

"May I take a message?" Ben's secretary sounded almost bored with the process. She probably took phone calls from a hundred would-be producers every day.

"Yes, I've called before. My name's Keith Ellison. I'm working with Chase Ryan, and the two of us are already on the set of a movie we're making called *The Last Letter*. I think Mr. Adams would be interested in helping finance the film."

The secretary sounded a little more interested. "Mr. Adams is out of the country until the end of the month. I'll give him the message."

Out of the country. Keith had worked to keep his frustration at bay. The one man who might help them wasn't in town and so he couldn't help if he wanted to. Keith was still thinking up ways to get word to him overseas, ways that the message might become urgent enough to pass along to Ben Adams regardless of where he was or what he was doing.

Now it was a five-minute break and Keith was looking over his notes for the next few scenes when Rita Reynolds walked up. There wasn't a cloud in the sky, but the trees provided enough shade that she didn't have on her sunglasses. "Hey," she came up against his elbow and looked at the clipboard. "We're making good time, huh?"

"We are." He felt his guard go up. After her temper tantrum over the salmon, Keith wasn't sure what his star was going to do next. "Want some coffee?"

"No thanks." She turned slightly so she was facing him. "I talked to Chase yesterday. Told him I was sorry. I owe you the same."

Keith lowered his clipboard. "It's okay. You have a right to whatever breakfast you want. It wasn't your fault someone dropped the ball."

"Yeah, but ... still." She looked up at the clear blue overhead and took a deep breath. "I'm just glad that's behind us."

"Me too." He smiled at her in a fatherly sort of way. "I was watching the monitors on those scenes this morning. You're very good, Rita. We're getting some great stuff."

"Thanks." She rocked slightly onto her toes, and her expression told him she had something she wanted to say. "Hey, tell me something."

Keith glanced at his watch. They had just three minutes left in the break. "Walk with me. I need a bottle of water."

"Okay." She kept to his pace as they crossed the street toward the snack table. "Tell me about Chase. We talked for a long time last night, and I can't stop thinking about him."

She might as well have kicked Keith in the stomach. He stopped and looked straight at her. It was all he could do to keep his tone in check. "He's your director and he's married. Not much else matters."

"I know." She waved her hand around in front of her face, as if the notion of Chase being married was nothing more than a troublesome buzzing insect. "Of course he's married, but ... I mean, is he happy? He and his wife?"

"Rita ... I find this discussion very awkward." Keith shifted his weight. "Let's pretend you never brought it up." He started walking again. "And yes, Chase is very happily married."

"Don't be offended." Rita laughed, and the sound was just short of condescending. "I figured if he wasn't that happy you'd tell me. If he is, then fine." She flipped her hair. "It was just a question." She patted Keith on the shoulder. "Don't look too deep into it."

"Like I said, I'll forget you ever brought it up."

She laughed and then turned toward a group of actors gathered near the coffee station. Keith watched her a moment longer, and then moved in the opposite direction and grabbed a cold water bottle from a cooler. He was shocked at Rita's brazen behavior. And what about her conversation with Chase? How come he hadn't mentioned it?

Keith snatched a second water bottle and walked quickly back to the set. Chase was still inside, talking over a camera angle with the DP. He looked up when he saw Keith and grinned. "I should've listened to you. Today's been amazing."

He stuffed the anger churning inside him and tossed Chase a water bottle. "You have a sec?"

"Sure." Chase's expression changed. He followed Keith outside to the back of the house. People were walking back from their break, but for now they had a few seconds of privacy. Chase twisted the bottle open, but his eyes were suddenly filled with anxiety. "Don't tell me something's wrong. Not now."

Keith reigned in his emotions. He couldn't accuse his friend, not without hearing his side of the story. "Did you and Rita talk last night?"

"She sat down with me after you left." He looked baffled. "We talked about the movie and why she took the part."

"That's it?"

"I don't know." He shrugged, but there was nothing guilty about his tone or expression. "I thought maybe she was coming on to me. She asked me to watch a movie in her room. I almost laughed at her."

"You didn't go, right?"

"Of course not." Irritation flooded Chase's voice. "Are you kidding? You honestly think I'd go in some woman's room to watch a movie?"

"Rita's used to getting her way." Keith could feel his heart trying to find its normal rhythm again. He hadn't considered what could happen if one of them compromised their integrity. Even innocently. "Be careful of her, Chase. A scandal would ruin us."

"A scandal?" Chase laughed, but it sounded more angry than humorous. "I love my wife, you know that. I'm not interested in Rita Reynolds or any other woman."

"Okay." Keith paced a few steps out into the grassy backyard, and then turned and walked back to his friend. He exhaled, trying to find the composure he'd had before the break. "She just asked me about you, said she couldn't stop thinking about you." He didn't hide his disgust. "Wanted to know how happily married you were."

"That's ridiculous. I made the answer to that question clear last night."

"Apparently she wasn't listening."

Chase groaned and ran his hand along the back of his neck. "Thanks for telling me. I'll make sure not to give her a reason to think I'd be interested."

The situation was awkward, because Chase was still her director. He would need to work closely with her until the shoot was finished.

"Good." Keith gave his friend a solid pat on his shoulder. "Keep your guard up. A guy with your pretty boy looks could get into a lot of trouble on the road."

"Listen to you." Chase laughed, and the sound told Keith he was still baffled by the ordeal. "A couple of the actors say you're a dead ringer for Kevin Costner."

"Right." Keith rolled his eyes as they headed back into the house.

"I'm just saying..." Chase was teasing him now. "As long as you're watching out for me, I'll keep an eye your way too."

By the sounds of it, most of the cast and crew were gathered in front of the house, and as the two producers made their way that direction, they heard a few sharp barks and then the sound of a shrill scream.

"What in the..." Keith took the lead, racing to the front door and flinging it open in time to see Jake Olson grab his arm. At the same time, the dog they were using for the movie scurried to the nearest tree, cowering low to the ground.

Rita's face was a twist of fear, and she motioned to Keith. "Quick. Someone help him!" A number of actors followed Jake toward the curb, and from the side yard the dog handler ran up to the dog and chained him. Chase flew down the stairs and motioned to a police car parked across the street. "We need a medic. Right away."

As was normal for a location shoot, an ambulance was parked at the other end of the street, out of the way but ready in case they ran into a medical emergency. The police officer took hold of his radio, shouted something into it, and in seconds the ambulance wheeled into view.

"What happened?" Keith walked quickly toward Jake.

"Jake picked the dog up." Rita was breathing fast, fighting tears. "He was being a little rough with him, and then all of a sudden the dog ripped into his arm. I mean, there was no warning or anything."

Keith held his hand up to her. "Thank you. I'll take it from here." He cupped his hands around his mouth. "Okay everyone, take another ten. We need to make room for the paramedics."

As the cast and crew cleared the area, Keith and Chase moved in close to Jake. Someone had wrapped an old T-shirt around his arm, but even so, blood was seeping through. Jake cussed softly under his breath. "It was my fault."

"What were you doing?" Chase pulled tighter on the T-shirt, creating more of a tourniquet effect over the wound. The paramedics were walking up now, carrying a medical bag and looking concerned.

Jake winced. "I'm a method actor. First half of the film I'm a jerk, you know ... always storming off."

Keith had no idea where their male lead was headed with this story. "How did that involve the dog?"

"I wanted to make him a little afraid of me." He exhaled and the sound was heavy with pain. "You know, so that when I walked into the room, the dog sort of looked nervous. The way I make everyone feel before the letter."

"So you picked the dog up in your arms?" Chase looked slightly pale, probably thinking ahead to where this would all wind up.

"Yeah." Jake tucked his wounded arm in close to his body. "Like I said, I wanted to intimidate him a little." He looked up at Chase, and then at Keith. "It was my fault. Don't blame the dog."

The medics moved in then and one of them unwrapped the T-shirt from Jake's arm. The few teeth marks weren't very big, just deep. So deep Keith wondered if the dog had nicked an artery. What else could explain the heavy bleeding? One of the medics tended to the wound, while the other took Jake's blood pressure and started an IV. Once the needle was in place, he turned a knowing look to Keith. "He needs to get to a hospital."

"There's one a few miles from here," Keith said. "I'll ride with you, if that's okay." He turned to Chase. "See if you can get everyone back on track. There are still a few scenes here without Jake."

Chase nodded. He looked worried sick, but whatever was going through his mind, he didn't express it. "Keep us posted."

"We will."

The ride to the hospital took almost no time, and by then the paramedic riding in the back had settled Jake onto a stretcher and used a combination of gauze and pressure to slow the bleeding. Keith turned to the driver. "You think an artery's involved?"

"Could be. If so, he'll need surgery. He needs stitches, for sure. Might be dealing with shock too. His blood pressure's a little low."

They parked out front at the emergency doors. Keith watched while the medics wheeled Jake in on a stretcher, and inside the hospital they were met by a nurse who led them to an examination room. "You're lucky you came in early. Dr. John Baxter's on duty—he's the best in Bloomington."

Keith silently thanked God for the single piece of good news. He waited off to the side, and in a matter of seconds, a kind man with mostly white hair entered the room and moved up alongside Jake's bed. Something about the doctor looked familiar. He introduced himself and then peered at the wound on Jake's arm. "He definitely got you good." He studied Jake's eyes for a moment. "How're you feeling?"

"Not so good." Jake looked a little greener than before. "But it was my fault." He was still on his back, still on the stretcher. He covered his eyes with his uninjured arm. "I'm a method actor."

"Is that right?" Dr. Baxter smiled. "My son is too."

His son? Keith began putting the pieces together, and suddenly he wondered if the reason Dr. Baxter looked familiar was ... "Your son isn't Dayne Matthews, is he?"

"He is." Dr. Baxter lifted his eyes to Keith's. "You're one of the producers?"

"Yes, sir. Keith Ellison." No wonder the man had looked familiar. Dayne Matthews was the most recognized actor in the world. Only recently had he stepped down from acting to live here in Bloomington with his wife and baby daughter. Everyone expected that at some time in the future he'd act again, but for now he and his wife ran a kids' theater group in town. Keith didn't know Dayne, but he wondered if maybe they'd run into each other during the location shoot.

Dr. Baxter gave him a look as if to say they would talk about their movie connection in a minute. Jake clearly needed the doctor's help first. He directed the nurse to get a suture tray, and he glanced at Keith again. "What about the dog? Can someone get his current shot record? We need to rule out rabies."

"Definitely." Keith stepped into the hall and dialed Chase.

"How is he? We're filming, but everyone's worried."

"The doctor's working on him. I don't know anything yet." Keith explained who the doctor was and that they needed the dog's shot record.

"The handler already showed it to me. I'll send him right over."

"Great. And pray Jake doesn't need surgery." Keith didn't come right out and explain what he was thinking. Surgery would not only be bad for Jake, but if the doctor had to operate, they were bound to lose a few days in the recovery process. He didn't need to spell out the possibilities. Chase certainly knew the dire situation they faced.

When Keith returned to the exam room, Dr. Baxter was asking Jake when he'd gotten his last tetanus shot.

Jake moved his arm from his face and thought for a moment. "High school, I think."

"Get me a tetanus booster too, please," Dr. Baxter told the nurse. "Stat. I want to get him cleaned up and stitched." He pulled a large magnifying glass down from a machine near the ceiling and positioned it over the dog bite. "I see your concerns about the artery," he told the medic still in the room. "He nicked it all right, but just barely." He smiled at Jake. "No surgery this time."

Jake exhaled long and slow. "I'm so stupid. I was just trying to get into character." He lifted his head off the pillow and looked at Keith. "Don't take it out on the dog. He can stay. He won't bite anyone else."

Keith didn't want to upset Jake further, but he was pretty sure the dog would have to be replaced. For now, though, Keith only nodded. "We'll take care of everything."

They made small talk while Dr. Baxter worked on Jake. At one point, the young actor grinned at Keith. "Hey, I hear you have a real pretty daughter, Ellison."

"Oh, yeah." Keith's defenses shot up at the mention of Andi. Jake Olson was a wonderful actor, but at twenty-four he'd already left a trail of broken hearts. "Where did you hear that?"

"Some of the grips saw the two of you at dinner last weekend." He smiled, but it looked more like a wince as the doctor kept stitching. "When do I get to meet her?"

Keith tried to keep his answer serious and light all at the same time. Especially because Jake was probably only making conversation. "She'll be out at the shoot Friday." He made a face. "But she's not your type. Way too young for you." He tossed his hands. "Sorry about that, Jake."

Jake laughed, careful to keep his eyes from the repair work being done on his arm. "I'd still like to meet her."

Half an hour later Jake was cleaned up and stitched, ready to be dismissed. Dr. Baxter gave him instructions to keep his wrapped arm clean and come back immediately at the first sign of infection. "You should be fine. You're young." Dr. Baxter put his hand on Jake's shoulder. "You'll heal quickly. It could've been a lot worse." The doctor went over a few other details, advising Jake to take ibuprofen only if the pain got worse. "I'm not a fan of pain medication for something like this."

"Nah." Jake's color was back. He looked like he was feeling a lot better. "I hate pain meds. People get messed up bad with those things."

"Exactly." Dr. Baxter took a few steps back. "You think you can walk out of here?"

"Definitely." Jake shook his head. "I still can't believe I'm so stupid." He shot Keith an apologetic look. "Sorry about the trouble. I'll be more careful next time."

"I'm glad you're okay."

The nurse was in the room, clearing away the suture table. "I told you Dr. Baxter was the best." She smiled at them as she headed back into the hallway.

"I'll walk you out to the ambulance." The medic took firm hold of Jake's good arm and helped him to his feet. "Just in case you're still a little dizzy."

When they'd left the room, Dr. Baxter leaned against the nearest wall and looked at Keith. "We've been following your story, how you want to make movies that bring glory to God."

"Yes." Keith was amazed that this tremendously talented doctor was also Dayne Matthews' father, and more, that he knew about Keith and Chase and their intentions with the film. "We were missionaries until two years ago. We believe God wants this to be our next mission field."

"Dayne and I were talking about that same thing last night. We need more films that will express core values, stories that will help restore character where so much has eroded away." He allowed a slow nod. "We're praying for you. My whole family's praying."

Keith was touched deeply by the doctor's kindness, and the fact that God had allowed this man to be working at the emergency room exactly at this time—when Keith needed more than a good doctor, but someone who would tell him what he told Chase last night. That everything was going to be okay. They talked for a few minutes longer. Dr. Baxter had six kids living in and around Bloomington—a daughter and son-in-law who were both doctors, and another who was a lawyer—and a dead ringer for Dayne.

"I think I saw his picture in the tabloids a year or so ago."

Dr. Baxter allowed a wry smile. "That was him. We've been through a lot to get to where we are. All of us know the hard road ahead for you and Chase." He looked like he had a dozen amazing stories playing in his mind. "Maybe we'll get the chance to talk before you leave town." The doctor pulled a business card from his pocket, flipped it over, and wrote something on the back before handing it to Keith. "My home number's there for you. We have Sunday dinner just about every week at my daughter Ashley's house. You and Chase can join us anytime. It might help to have a few friends on your side."

Keith thought about all that had happened since they started filming yesterday morning. "Definitely." Again he was struck by John Baxter's kindness. "My wife comes into town later this week. I'm sure she'd love a Sunday dinner with your family."

"You might not have time. I know how these things go." They moved toward the door together. "Look for Dayne on the set. He told me he was going to stop by and encourage you."

"Great." Keith reached out and shook the doctor's hand. "Not the best circumstances, but I'm glad we met. It helps to know someone else is praying."

Keith and Jake arrived back on set just before lunchtime, and by then Chase and the others had knocked off a couple more scenes—enough that they were still ahead of the day's schedule. Keith and Chase were walking across the side street to base camp and the lunch truck when Keith heard a few grips laughing about something directly behind them. One of them was telling a funny story, and at that moment he let out a loud string of swear words—all of which were intended to get a laugh.

"Hey." Keith stopped and turned around. "Watch your language."

The offender's eyes grew wide and he chuckled a few more times. "You talking to me?"

"Absolutely." Keith wasn't one to lose his temper. But he didn't want his cast and crew exposed to that kind of language. Not on the set of a movie with such a great message. "Find a better word choice."

The guy laughed again, and this time he elbowed the man next to him. "D'ya hear that? Find a better word choice?" He took a step closer and sneered at Keith. "I'll use whatever words I feel like using."

"Listen." Keith held his hands up. "I'm only asking if you'd watch your language."

The guy held his ground for a few seconds longer, and then backed down. "Whatever, man." Under his breath he muttered, "Stick to producing and mind your own business."

Chase had kept quiet throughout the exchange, but he put his hand on Keith's shoulder. "Come on. We need to eat."

As they walked on, they heard the guy talking to his friends, cussing every other word and speaking loud enough for Keith and Chase to hear as they walked away. They dished themselves chicken and rice and bowls of salad. Chase directed them to the production trailer. "Come on. We can eat in here."

Inside, Keith pushed his plate aside and leaned back in his metal folding chair, his eyes staring at the spot where the wall and ceiling met. "Do you feel it?"

"The battle?" Chase whistled low. "I can feel it, all right."

"I mean, come on." Keith uttered a desperate sort of laugh. "Our lead actor gets bitten by a dog?"

"And then the below-the-line guys. The guy you were talking to is Steve Jenkins. He could've handled himself better."

"Yeah." Keith thought about the Scripture verse again, the one he'd drawn on yesterday. *Consider it pure joy ...* He sighed and found his smile. "All in a day's work, right?"

"At least we're actually getting a day's work in today." Chase took a big bite of his chicken. "I need to check with Jake before lunch is over, see if wardrobe has something that'll cover his bandage."

"He can switch to a smaller one tomorrow." Keith was still composing himself. As they finished eating, he told Chase about Dr. Baxter and his offer for a Sunday dinner.

"I remember their story, how Dayne was raised by a set of adoptive parents who were killed when he was just out of high school."

"Right. And when he first found the Baxters, the paparazzi were all over the story."

"It's nice to know they're aware of us."

"And that they're praying." Keith took the last bite of rice and dragged his napkin across his mouth. "He said Dayne might come by."

"That'd be great." Chase grinned. "For us and the whole cast and crew." Chase stood and headed for the door. "I'll see you outside." He stopped. "Don't get down about today. Jake'll heal, and grips are gonna cuss. There's not much we can do about that."

"Jenkins could at least show a little respect. I mean, I was polite about asking." Keith pushed his plate back from where he was sitting. "You imagine what would've happened if that dog had gotten Rita Reynolds?"

Chase's expression darkened. "Thought about it the whole time you were at the hospital. She would've called her agent and been on the next plane back to Hollywood." He snapped his fingers. "Just like that, we could've called it a day. No lead actress, no movie. Nothing to repay the investors."

The enormity of the possibility rested squarely on Keith's shoulders. "I left another message with Ben Adams. Apparently he's out of the country. I need to find a way to get on his radar." He sighed. "Oh, and I talked to the handler. We'll have a different dog here early this afternoon. The other one will take a week off before he works again."

"Amazing." Chase shook his head and left the trailer.

Alone with only the slight buzzing of the air conditioning, Keith stared out the small window at the trees that lined the street where they were filming. *God ... that was close ... we could've lost everything.*

I'm with you, my son ... don't be discouraged, don't lose heart. The battle is mine ...

Like a gentle breeze on the most stifling summer day, the answer from the Holy Spirit breathed life into Keith's soul. He thought about Steve Jenkins and the other grips. The crew, everyone who worked behind the scenes, was considered "below the line." An ongoing strike in Hollywood worked to their advantage this time, since they couldn't afford union workers for the below-the-line jobs. Every one of the grips and techs and set guys were working for less pay than usual, but because there were no other jobs to take, they were grateful for any work at all. Each of them had signed an agreement attesting to the fact that they wouldn't receive union wages, and that they understood this wasn't a union film—at least not for anyone below the line.

The cast, though, was considered above the line, and everyone who would appear on camera was working with union wages and conditions. It was the part of making movies Keith liked least of all—the separation between above and below the line, and the way both cast and crew expected an adversarial relationship between themselves and the producers. The cast and crew wanted an excellent picture, however long it took. The producers needed to keep everyone on track, and make sure that in the quest for excellence, the budget and timeline weren't compromised.

He pictured Jenkins again, the sneer on his face when he told Keith he'd use whatever words he wanted. How could God want them in an environment where He was mocked, in the quest of making a product where He was marveled at? The contradiction was unsettling, and it rattled the core of everything Keith believed about his decision to leave Indonesia for filmmaking.

They were Davids in an entire industry of Goliaths, true. But Keith couldn't settle for mediocrity—not in any area of making a movie. It wasn't enough to make an unforgettable life-changing film. He and Chase needed to be a bright light along the way, pointing people to Christ, to a life different than the one they'd come to know in Hollywood. The goal had to be that the cast and crew no longer saw the distinction between union and nonunion, on-screen talent or behind-the-scenes workers. So that no one on their set for a minute saw themselves as *below the line*, somehow lesser. Keith wanted every single person's actions and attitudes, their character and commitment—on or off the screen until they wrapped the film—to be one place and one place only.

Above the line.

Period.

Eight

AUDITIONS WERE NOTHING LIKE WHAT BAILEY Flanigan was used to. At CKT, a hundred or more kids would gather in a room and watch one after another as their friends took the stage and struggled through a one-minute song. At Indiana University, they'd been allowed to sign up in time blocks, with groups of three other students.

Bailey signed up Tim and Andi to join her for the afternoon audition at 2:10. She and Andi were already there, leaning against a cold brick wall and looking for Tim. Two groups were in line ahead of them, and though they could hear the faint sounds of someone singing in the auditorium, there was no way to tell whether any of the auditions had been great, or what sort of act they were going to follow.

"CKT's auditions were more fun." Bailey had her hair pulled back in a ponytail. She'd talked to her mom last night for a long time, telling her the assignments and essays already due in her classes over the next few weeks. That, and how she planned to get involved with Campus Crusade at the first meeting later this week.

"You sure you want to do a play on top of everything else?" her mom hadn't sounded doubtful, just curious. "It's a lot for your first quarter."

But that was why Bailey had moved on campus, and she reminded her mother of the fact. She would get through this busy season, as long as she stayed organized. By the end of the phone call, her mom agreed.

Andi shifted, restless beside her. "What if I throw up?"

"Come on," Bailey laughed. "You won't throw up."

"I might. I want to act, not sing."

"You'll do great. You could sound like a dying cat with your looks and you'd still get a part."

"Thanks." Andi made a funny face. "I think, anyway."

They heard footsteps on the stairs and turned to see Tim bounding in their direction. He'd seen a picture of Andi, and she of him, but the two had never really met. Bailey watched him register Andi's presence, and then turn his attention to her. He was out of breath as he hugged her. "I thought I'd be late."

"Nah." Bailey kept her arm loosely around Tim's waist. "We still have fifteen minutes." She motioned to her roommate. "This is Andi Ellison. Andi ... Tim Reed."

Andi wasn't a flirt, but she carried with her a charisma that took over a room. She grinned at Tim. "I've heard a lot about you. Lead roles in a dozen plays, killer singing voice, you know ... all the juicy details."

Tim blushed slightly beneath her gaze, and then he seemed to remember Bailey. "She exaggerates." He tucked his arm around her waist and turned his attention completely to her. "What're you singing?"

Bailey didn't mind that Tim was flustered by Andi's presence. She and Andi were quickly becoming good friends, and Bailey could hold her own around her roommate. Andi couldn't help the effect she had on guys, and at least she didn't flaunt herself around them the way some girls did. She eased away from Tim, pulled her piano music from her bag, and handed it to him. "'I'm Still Hurting,' from *Last Five Years*."

"That's perfect. Something Isabel would sing, for sure."

"I heard her practice." Andi linked arms with Bailey. "She's amazing. She'll get Isabel for sure." She played with a lock of her pale blonde hair. "What about you? There are lots of good parts for guys."

"He wants Scrooge." Bailey gave Tim a teasing look. "Only the best for Tim Reed, right?"

"Well..." Again Tim looked slightly embarrassed. "I'd be happy with any part, but... yeah, sure. Scrooge would be amazing."

The group ahead of them was called in and Bailey peered down the hallway. "Looks like our fourth person didn't show."

"Great. I'll probably have to sing first." Andi grinned at the two of them. "Don't make me laugh, okay? I mean, no matter how bad I am, don't make me laugh."

They kept the conversation light until it was their turn. Once inside the auditorium, there were six director types sitting in the front row. One man seemed to be in charge, and he waved them up onto the stage where there were four chairs on the far side. On the opposite side, an older woman sat at an oversized grand piano. "Present your music to our pianist, and let's have you sing in order. Please keep your audition to no more than two minutes." He looked at his paper. "Bailey Flanigan, you go first."

Bailey was more nervous than she'd expected herself to be. She handed her music to the pianist and took a spot near the microphone at center stage. The director didn't have to tell her to introduce herself and her musical selection. After years performing with CKT, that much went without saying. She quietly cleared her throat. "My name is Bailey Flanigan. I'm nineteen, and I'm a freshman." She explained the song she'd be singing, and then she nodded to the woman at the piano.

Okay, God ... please help me do my best. She felt a strength and peace that wasn't her own as she began. The section she'd chosen was just over a minute and a half, and Bailey sang it as well as she ever had. Along the way, she caught admiration in Tim's eyes, and surprise in Andi's. When she finished, she was filled with an exhilaration that came only from performing.

The director thanked her, and then called Tim onto the stage. As Bailey took her spot in one of the chairs, Andi gave her hand a squeeze. "That was unbelievable," she whispered. "Seriously, I can barely breathe, it was so good."

Tim was introducing himself, so they turned their attention to him. He sang *This Moment* from Jeckyl and Hyde, and as the song built and grew, Bailey was reminded again of just how much they'd grown as actors because of their time with CKT. She was glad the theater group was still helping kids, still under the direction of Katy Hart, and her husband, Dayne Matthews. The kids in Bloomington were blessed to have the program here.

When Tim was finished, he took a chair beside Bailey, and Andi flashed them both an anxious look. "Pray for me. I'll probably trip on my way up to the microphone."

"Andi Ellison." The director's tone was completely void of any humor. "You're up, please."

Andi didn't trip, and she didn't get sick all over the stage as she took her place. She introduced herself and her music, and then she began to sing. From the moment she opened her mouth, Bailey could only sit back and stare. Andi hadn't once rehearsed in front of her, insisting that she couldn't sing, and didn't want to sing. But here, as she launched into the theme from *Beauty and the Beast*, her voice sounded like something from an angel.

"She's good," Tim whispered beside her.

"So good." Bailey couldn't stop watching her. Combined with her looks and grace, and that certain something that couldn't quite be defined, Andi was bound to get a lead role. Maybe even the part of Isabel. A shadow of jealousy cast itself over the moment, and Bailey fought against it. At the same time, she understood now why Andi was a theater major, why she pictured herself on the big screen one day. The way she commanded a stage, Bailey couldn't think of anything that would stop her. So strong was her audition, that when she finished, Bailey half expected the directors to burst into applause. They stopped short of that, but their smiles made it clear they had caught what Bailey and Tim had seen.

Andi Ellison was going to be a star.

As they left the auditorium and the next group filed in, Andi was slightly winded from her performance. But rather than wait for feedback from Bailey or Tim, she launched into a story about her dad and the filming they were doing in downtown Bloomington.

"It must be cool." Tim stuck his hands in his pockets. His look fell just short of adulation. "You know, having your dad be a producer."

"I don't know." The three of them grabbed their things and walked toward the stairs at the far end of the hall. Andi seemed to make sure she kept Bailey in the middle. "My dad's hard to please. He feels like people in Hollywood are pretty shady." She gave a look that said she understood where her father was coming from. "I think he'd rather me be a teacher or a writer. Something a little safer."

As they walked, Bailey could almost feel something sitting on her shoulder, whispering discouragement and making her resent Andi for ever coming to Bloomington and being assigned as her roommate. Was this how it would be, competing against Andi for the next four years? Bailey couldn't measure up to Andi in any area, so how great would that be? She stared at the floor while they walked, but as they reached the bottom of the stairs and headed out into the sunshine, she remembered that she hadn't commented on Andi's audition yet. "You have an unbelievable voice." She smiled at Andi, hoping it looked genuine.

Andi's mouth came open and she made an exaggerated sound of disbelief. "Not really. I mean, I sang in choir, but I'm not a singer. Acting is my strength—at least I've always thought so."

"If you can act half as good as you sing, you'll make it for sure." Tim's light laugh expressed his own appreciation for her audition. He peered around Bailey, his tone filled with awe and sincerity. "You were amazing, Andi. Where'd you learn to sing like that?"

"Like what?" She hugged her bag to her chest and kept her eyes straight ahead. "I grew up in the jungle, guys. Choir at my Christian school, and that's about it. Growing up, the only singing we did was worship songs around the campfire. I don't know the first thing about performing."

"You fooled everyone in that auditorium." Again Tim seemed to remember Bailey. He put his free hand around her shoulder. "I'm gonna go out on a limb here and say I think we'll all get cast." He gave Bailey a light squeeze. "You were amazing too."

"Thanks." Bailey was still silently fighting the jealousy welling inside her, but outside in the fresh air, she was recovering some. It wasn't Andi's fault she was born with a gifted voice. She grinned at her roommate. "How fun would that be, if we're all cast?"

"I don't know." Andi looked genuinely concerned. "I don't have your experience."

Bailey wanted to tell her that she clearly didn't have an accurate picture of her own abilities, but she let the moment pass.

"You know what I'd like to see?" As they walked, Tim made eye contact with Andi and then Bailey. "I'd like to see the two of you play Elphaba and Glinda, you know, if the school ever performs *Wicked*."

"Oh, I couldn't imagine it." Andi gasped. "That's the best show ever. Who would've thought to make a prequel to the *Wizard of Oz*?"

"It's a great show, for sure." Bailey tried to imagine the two of them cast as the leads in *Wicked*. "That'd be the best ever." But even as she kept up with her part of the conversation, she realized that with Andi's light blonde hair and striking looks, Tim had to be seeing her as Glinda. Which would make Bailey the green witch—Elphaba. It was the bigger part, sure, but not the glamorous one. After dreaming for years that someday she might be considered for Glinda, in Andi's shadow at IU, there was no way it would happen. Bailey would be lucky to be Elphaba.

"You okay?" Andi nudged her, concern lining her forehead. "You're too quiet."

"I'm fine." Bailey silently chastised herself. What point was there in imagining the casting decisions of a show that wasn't even on the docket. She drew a long breath and walked a little straighter. "Auditions take everything out of me." Again her heart warmed toward her friend. Somehow she would learn to shine brightly even next to Andi. Otherwise she'd miss out on the golden friendship God had for the two of them.

"Hey, I need to stop by the library before I go back to the room." Andi stopped and looked at Bailey and Tim. "You guys go ahead." She was about to wave goodbye when she sucked in a quick breath. "I almost forgot." She pulled an envelope from the side pocket of her backpack. "Some guy was looking for you after class today. You left early to get your music, remember?"

"After history?"

"Right." She handed the letter to Bailey. "He asked if I was your roommate. Told me to give you this."

Bailey felt her heart lurch as she took the envelope. "Thanks."

"Hey, and one more thing." Her face lit up. "My dad needs extras for Friday. They're filming on campus. You guys wanna do it?"

"Definitely." Tim's answer came first. He shot a questioning look at Bailey. "You too, right?"

"Of course." Again Bailey's smile felt stale. "We'll talk about it later."

"Okay. See you back at the room." Andi bid them both goodbye, her eyes dancing, cheeks pink and full of life as she turned and ran lightly down the path toward the library.

When she was out of earshot and they were walking across campus again, Tim gave a disbelieving shake of his head. "She has no idea the gift she's been given." He couldn't keep the admiration from his voice if he tried. "I mean, seriously. She has no idea."

Thanks, Tim. Rub it in, Bailey thought. "Yeah." She gave Tim a tired smile. She hated feeling this way. Jealousy was as foreign to her as Greek. She worked to sound genuine. "She's really talented, for sure."

"You know how people talk about the "it" factor, how a person needs to have that if they're going to make it as an actress?"

Bailey knew where he was headed, and she wanted to cut him off, finish his thought so she wouldn't have to listen to Tim spell it out. Instead she nodded absently and lifted the envelope up so she could read the face of it. If she'd wondered at first, she had no doubts now. The letter was from Cody. After a year of getting his letters from Iraq, she would've recognized his printing anywhere.

Tim didn't seem to notice her interest in the letter. He looked over his shoulder in the direction where Andi was still in sight, still heading for the library. He laughed again, clearly struck by what he'd seen in Andi. "All I can say is that girl has it ... the "it" factor, ten times over."

"Yeah." Bailey gave him a smile that didn't reach her eyes. "You should tell her. I'm sure she'd love to hear that from you."

"Bailey ..." Tim took hold of her arm and the two of them stopped, facing each other. A group of students passed them on either side, so Tim waited until they had a private moment. "What is it? Why are you acting like this?"

"Like what?"

"Bugged. I mean, come on. You and I both thought she'd fall flat on her face—if not literally then figuratively—as soon as she opened her mouth. You have to admit she was good."

"Very good." Bailey shrugged. "I don't know, I guess I'm just ready to talk about something else."

His expression changed, and it was clear in his eyes that he knew what was wrong. "You're jealous."

"I am not. I've never been jealous of other girls." Bailey was telling the truth. She shared her thoughts and feelings with her mom, and whenever another girl had come across prettier or smarter or better somehow, her mother always convinced her that God had only made one Bailey Flanigan, one girl exactly like her, and that no one could ever compare with the perfect way she was — no matter who else came along. That's why her feelings now were so foreign. "I'm not jealous. It's just ... I'm not sure how to compete around Andi."

"Silly." He leaned in and kissed her forehead. "You're one in a million, Bailey. You're gorgeous and talented, and your love for God shines in your eyes. Andi's eyes are more ... I don't know, more ready to take on the world." He started walking again. "She can sing, that's all."

Bailey slipped the letter into her back jeans pocket and stared at the path in front of them. She wasn't about to read something from Cody here, with Tim walking beside her. She would save it for later when she was alone, after she'd had time to work through her strange and unattractive feelings.

"Who's the letter from?"

"Cody."

Tim let that sink in for a minute. They walked past a group of students chatting on a bench and crossed a narrow service street before he gave her a brief glance. "You two have talked?"

"No. Not at all." Bailey was able to find a more upbeat tone. Never mind about Andi. She had no reason to be down. She'd given the directors one of her best auditions ever. She checked Tim's expression and saw something familiar. The same jealousy she'd been feeling since Andi's audition. "Once in a while Cody and I will see each other across campus between classes. That's about it."

"I thought he wanted the two of you to be friends."

"He did. At least that's what he said." Bailey didn't want to talk about Cody with Tim.

"You know why he keeps his distance, right?" Tim kept his tone casual, trying not to let the jealousy in his eyes reach his voice.

"Why?" Bailey felt a fresh smile tug at her lips.

"Because he's in love with you, Bailey. He can't stand to see you dating someone else."

"Hmmm." Bailey looked straight ahead. She didn't let it show in her face that she thought he was right. "Now you're an expert on Cody?"

"I don't know." He sighed and slipped his hands into the front pockets of his jeans. "I've seen the way he looks at you." He turned his eyes to her again. "You going to read it?"

"Later. Cody hasn't made any effort. If he's in love with me, he has a fine way of showing it." She kept her tone purposefully plain. "He probably figured he should apologize for being so distant." She shrugged one shoulder. "I'll read it later."

"Okay." The news didn't seem to settle well with Tim. He put his arm around her shoulders again. "So how was your babysitting job? You worked two hours, right?"

"I did." She liked that she could fluster Tim. It meant he still cared about her, no matter how wonderful Andi was. "Ashley's working on a painting of her three children. She's using a photo her dad took."

"So she was upstairs?"

"The whole time. Cole was at school, so I only had Devin and Janessa. They were great. They might come by the set Friday when they're filming on campus. Ashley said she'd seen it in the paper that they'd be on location here."

They reached Bailey's dorm, and suddenly the air between them felt awkward. Tim looped his arm around her waist and pulled her close. "You sure everything's okay?"

"Of course."

"With us, I mean." Tim looked deep into her eyes. "You're not mad at me."

This was the worst part about the jealous feelings that had come over her, the fact that they left her scrambling to explain herself. "I'm fine." This time her smile came from her heart. "I'll call you later."

"Okay." He looked like he wanted to kiss her, but there were students milling about headed one way or another, and a kiss here in the open would be out of character for both of them. Besides, even when they went to dinner or a movie and they were alone in his car, Tim hadn't kissed her again, not the way he'd done after prom. They didn't talk about it, but she could only figure that he was trying to respect her. That or his feelings for her weren't that strong. "I like this," he'd told her one day last week, "how you and I are like best friends. It's good for now."

She agreed, but the idea of being Tim's good buddy didn't exactly send chills down her spine or make her long for their next meeting. Either way, Bailey was happy with where things were. She wasn't sure how she really felt about Tim. Better that they didn't kiss more often. She wasn't ready for that. Not while the letter from Cody was practically all she could think about.

Tim left her with a final hug and then headed off to the parking lot. He tried to park in the same place each day, because by now, like most of the students, he'd fallen into a routine—even if part of his routine was driving home each day. When he was gone, Bailey ran up the steps and down the hallway to her dorm. Andi was still bound to be a half hour behind her, which meant she had time by herself to read the letter.

She sat on the edge of her bed, her heart pounding, and carefully slid her finger beneath the flap at the back of the envelope. The letter inside was written on a plain piece of white typing paper, folded in fourths. She opened it and saw that it wasn't long, not nearly as long as some of his letters from war.

Her eyes found the beginning.

Bailey,

I never seem to run into you on campus, and when I do you're always far away or in a hurry. So I'm sitting here in lab, finished with my work, and I thought I'd take a minute and write to you. Okay, so where do I start? With the truth, I guess. I just wish you were sitting beside me and I could tell you this in person. It might make more sense, but oh well.

Okay, so here it is. I think about you all the time, you probably didn't know that. But every time I do, I go back to the Fourth of July, that day at your house when I first got back in town. About a thousand times I've played those few minutes over again in my mind, and I always think that I blew it somehow. Like I didn't make myself clear.

I don't know, Bailey. I meant what I said. You deserve someone better than me. Someone like Tim. He's great for you. I see you guys around campus sometimes when you don't see me. I'm happy for you, really I am.

Out in the hallway a group of laughing kids ran by and the noise pulled her from the letter. She felt her heart beating in her throat. What was this, this admission he was making? She wanted to savor his words, but she couldn't wait to read the rest, to get to the point of his letter. She picked up where she left off.

But here's the deal ... somehow things have gotten awkward between us, because now we're not even friends.

See... I meant what I said about my time in Iraq. Thinking about you, about how close we'd gotten that last summer before I left... that's what kept me going. But now I'm back and we don't even talk. I'm not sure who's avoiding who here, but it has to stop. I miss you too much. Even now I have to write this lousy letter because I can't find you long enough to tell you what I'm feeling.

Again ... I don't want to get in the way of you and Tim. That's great, and I really mean it. But you don't know what it's like walking across campus looking for your best friend, and knowing that even if you see her you might as well be half a world away. Because at least back then you used to write to each other, but now ... well, you get what I'm saying, right?

So that brings me to the real point of this letter. I heard about Campus Crusade. Their Cru meeting is this Thursday at eight. You probably know about it already, being that you're Bailey Flanigan and all. But just to let you know, I'll be there, and I'll be looking for you. If you're with Tim, I'll let him sit beside you. But I won't be far away, because this is crazy. I feel like we've lost everything we had, and I feel like it's my own fault. Okay, so there it is. I hope this makes sense.

See you Thursday, Bailey.
Finally.

Love ya, Cody.

Bailey sucked in her breath and held it, her eyes locked on that last part. The love ya part. Her entire junior year, Cody was one of her closest friends, and all that summer they'd been inseparable. Yes, he'd lived with her family, and he'd been very careful not to cross lines between friendship and something more. But that didn't stop the way he looked at her, or the way she felt when she was with him. Now, with his voice echoing in her heart and his words etched across the page, she could only be grateful he'd made this move.

Because she missed him more than she'd admitted to anyone, even herself. She read the letter again, slower this time. When she reached the part about finally, she felt tears in her eyes. He was right about everything. After their brief reunion that July fourth just inside her family's front door, things had changed between them. His adamant refusal to consider anything other than a friendship—whether or not she was dating Tim—made her feel rejected, as if maybe he wasn't interested in her. Then knowing they were both on the IU campus, but that the two of them never did more than glance at each other in passing... she had to think he had moved on in every possible way.

Until this. She held the letter close against her face and convinced herself she could smell his cologne, ever so slightly, mixed in with the fibers of the paper. Cody cared about her! Enough that he'd taken the time to write her a letter and wait for her after class. Enough that he knew where to find her. She carefully folded the letter, placed it back in the envelope, and tucked it safely in the top drawer of her nightstand. *Thank you, God ... for letting me know how Cody really feels. I don't know what'll happen after this, but at least I know he cares. Please ... let us find the friendship we once had.* As she finished praying, she breathed in deeply and realized that every jealous feeling she'd been plagued with was gone. She was happy for Andi, happy about the auditions, and thrilled beyond words about the letter from Cody.

Now if she could only survive until Thursday.

Nine

ANDI COULD HARDLY CONTAIN HER EXCITEMENT. She filed into the Campus Crusade meeting room along with a dozen other kids and surveyed the auditorium. Already there had to be three hundred students, all milling about and talking, finding various flyers on the information table and grabbing cookies from a snack area. Andi smiled to herself. She might have her doubts about God, but she had a feeling she was going to love these Thursday evening Cru meetings.

For now she had to find Bailey. She scanned the room but didn't see her.

"Hi." A tall guy with red hair and freckles held out his hand. "I'm Daniel. Welcome to Cru."

"Thanks." Andi flashed a smile at the guy. "You're in my world history class, right?"

"I am. But I'm a junior. That's a tough class for a freshman."

"I took a lot of history in high school." She shrugged. "Plus I was homeschooled. History interests me."

"How'd you do on the quiz?"

She made a see saw motion with her hand. "Eighty-nine. I need to study more, but I think I'm getting it."

Daniel led her to the table that held ten different flyers on upcoming events and small groups. "IU has one of the most active Campus Crusade chapters anywhere. I'm a small group leader. Been involved since my freshman year." He picked up an orange flyer and handed it to her. "I'm in charge of the Halloween party.

You definitely need to come. We're actually bobbing for apples this time."

The noise level in the room was rising, so Andi had to work to hear him. She took a step closer so she didn't have to yell. "I haven't been to a Halloween party before."

"What?" Daniel looked shocked, but his eyes told her he was teasing. "You haven't lived until you've been to a Halloween party. Especially with a group like Cru."

"Yeah, well I was a missionary kid. Grew up in the jungle." This was one more time when she felt sheltered and different because of her past. The feeling made her anxious to shed the image. She gave him a look that said she couldn't help the obvious. "Not a lot of pumpkins out there in the jungle."

"Hmmm. I can imagine." He laughed. "Hey, you're here now. That's what matters."

Andi was ready to move on, back to the door so she wouldn't miss Bailey. She had to tell her what she'd found out about the auditions, and about her father's offer for tomorrow. The news was practically bursting from her. Not only would they get to be extras on the film, but they'd get to work with Jake Olson. Jake Olson! The guy was gorgeous, and so talented Andi could hardly wait for tomorrow. She'd sit Daniel down and tell *him* if Bailey didn't get here soon. She scanned the group of kids once more. People were finding their places in the auditorium. "I better get a seat. I'm waiting for a few friends."

"Don't forget the Halloween party." He winked at her.

"How could I?" She thanked him for his help and found a seat in a half-empty row near the back of the room, not far from the door. Daniel had moved to the center up front and appeared ready to start the meeting. At the same time, seven musicians had taken their places on the stage. Mostly musicians, but a few vocalists. Andi looked back at the door. *Come on, Bailey ... get here.*

But instead of her roommate, through the door walked the tall, handsome guy who'd given her the envelope for Bailey. He hadn't said his name, so she couldn't call out to him, but she didn't need to. He looked around, and after a few seconds, he saw her and nodded his head in her direction. Daniel was tapping on his microphone, grinning at the crowd. "This is great. Best fall turnout I've seen." He beamed at the crowd, his voice loud and excited. Behind him, the music kicked in, the beginning of *From the Inside Out*, a worship song Andi loved. The leader said, "Okay, let's rock this place. Everyone get on your feet!"

As Andi stood with the others in her row, Cody slipped in and took the seat beside her. "Hey ... you seen Bailey?"

"No." Andi had to lean in to make herself heard. The smell of Cody's cologne filled her senses. "She's supposed to be here by now." Andi moved a little closer to him so he could hear her over the music. "I have good news for her."

Cody looked only slightly interested. He still had one eye on the door and the rest of his attention focused on the front of the room. "What?"

"About our audition the other day. All three of us got callbacks."

"Callbacks?" Cody angled his head toward Andi. "Is that what you said, callbacks?"

"Right." She giggled. Clearly this friend of Bailey's knew nothing about theater. "We auditioned for the school's play season the other day. A callback means we made it to the next level, and we have a good chance of being cast." She looked around to make sure she wasn't bothering anyone by talking. No one seemed to notice. The music was too loud for their voices to be heard above the sound. She spoke near Cody's ear again. "We're all trying to get into *Scrooge*." Andi tried not to stare. The boy had beautiful eyes. "I can't wait to tell her."

Cody looked like he wanted to focus on the music, but he leaned close once more. "Who else auditioned? You said three of you got callbacks."

"Me and Bailey, of course. And her boyfriend, Tim." She assumed this friend knew about Bailey's boyfriend. "You know Tim, right?"

"Sort of." Cody smiled, but something in his eyes shut off a little. He leaned in again. "I'm Cody Coleman." He had to tilt his head close to hers every time he spoke. "Bailey and I've been friends for years. I used to live with her family."

Andi nodded and turned her attention back to the front of the room. The guy next to her used to live with Bailey's family? Why hadn't Bailey said anything about him? She tried to think of a reason, but all she could come up with was the obvious. He and Bailey were only friends, so why would she have thought to mention him? Still, he'd acted sort of funny when Tim's name came up. Andi sang a few lines from the song and tried to focus on the words. But it wasn't easy with Cody beside her.

The song ended and Daniel told everyone to sit for a few minutes while he went over the announcements. Cody's arm brushed against hers as they sat, and once more he leaned in close. "Tim and Bailey are still pretty serious?"

Andi thought the question strange coming from someone who was supposed to know Bailey so well. "I think so." She gave him a look that said she wasn't sure of all the details. "They're together a lot, and they talk on the phone." Andi remembered Bailey's words, about not knowing whether she was in love, and not being completely sure of her feelings for Tim. But she kept that information to herself. It wasn't her place to give Cody all the details, right? Either that or she didn't want Cody thinking Bailey was anything but happy in her current relationship. Andi didn't like thinking of her motives that way, so she tuned in once more to the front of the room.

Daniel talked about each of the flyers, the different opportunities to get closer to God and each other. "This is a great campus, a great school." His smile remained through everything he said. "But these days we need each other more than ever." A roar of hoots and hollers and applause came from the crowd. "That's right," the leader laughed. "Two weeks on campus and I see you know what I'm talking about!" More appreciative noise from the crowd.

Andi tried to focus, because it was rude talking while Daniel was still going over announcements, but she was still stuck on that last exchange with Cody. Did he have feelings for Bailey that went beyond friendship? Was that why he wanted to know about Tim? Or was he only a big brother type, interested in the details? Andi hoped it was the latter, because out of all the guys she'd met on campus, none had captured her attention as quickly and completely as Cody.

Up front the leader was holding up the last flyer. "Finally, is Andi Ellison in the room?" He gave an appreciative grin to a group of guys near the front. "I met Andi before Cru. I just put her together with this last announcement. Andi's dad is producer Keith Ellison. You might've read about him in the newspaper this week. He'll be on campus with his film crew tomorrow and they're looking for a few hundred extras." Another roar of enthusiasm from the crowd. "That's right. We're all going to be famous. We got a call about this just a few days ago. Andi, can you stand up?"

In a heartbeat she remembered that her dad had contacted Campus Crusade to let the kids know about tomorrow's filming. She stood and gave a slightly awkward wave to the rest of the room. Then just as quickly she sat back down. Whether she wanted to be an actress or not, she was uncomfortable with all eyes on her.

"You and I'll have to talk later, Andi. You didn't tell me your dad was a producer." He raised his eyebrows up a couple times. "Maybe you can get me a speaking role." He laughed at himself.

"Seriously, guys. Any questions about tomorrow's filming, talk to Andi."

Cody smiled at her, and Andi realized it was the first time he'd done that. "Your dad's a producer?"

"Yeah. He and the crew are in town for a month or so."

"Big screen?"

"They hope so. It depends on the studio interest after the movie's made." She wondered if he felt even some of the attraction she was feeling. Even so she kept herself in check, not wanting to flirt or appear overeager. He had come looking for Bailey, after all. Without her approval, she would never really consider the boy beside her. Up front the band was launching into another song, pushing Andi closer again to Cody. "It's an independent film for now. My dad and the other producer want creative control. So no one can change the message."

Cody looked interested, but he didn't add anything else. Instead he looked again toward the back door, and then turned his attention toward the music at the front of the room.

Andi sang along with the words. The song was "Mighty to Save," another favorite of hers. It was easiest to believe the way she used to when she sang songs like this. But even still she was only half engaged in the music. Instead she tried to remember the walk from auditions across campus the other day, and how Bailey had reacted when she handed her the note from Cody. She'd been hand-in-hand with Tim, and she hadn't seemed more than slightly interested by the letter, right? Because if somehow Bailey had feelings for Cody, Andi would be sick at the thought of letting herself be attracted to him. But Bailey hadn't talked about him at all, so that could only mean one thing.

She didn't have feelings for him, not that way at least. Andi had all but convinced herself of the fact, when from the corner of her eye, she saw a blur at the back doorway. Bailey appeared, completely out of breath. But as flustered as she looked, she had clearly gone to the trouble of dressing nice. She had on skinny jeans and a tailored blouse, along with a pretty jacket. Her hair still had curl in it from earlier in the day, and she'd pinned part of it up around her face.

"Hey!" She mouthed the word as she spotted Andi, and at the same time she must've noticed Cody beside her, because for what felt like a long moment, Bailey froze.

Andi might've lived most of her life in a jungle on the other side of the world, but she could spot attraction between two people same as any other girl. As Cody caught Bailey's stare, their eyes held and Andi had the feeling that for those few seconds they were the only two in the room. She willfully and discreetly moved one seat over from Cody and motioned for Bailey to join them.

"Hi." She spoke to both of them as she sat down between them, rolling her eyes at herself. "I needed a blue book from the campus store and I locked my keys in my car. Some security guy had to help me." She tossed her hands and grinned as she took her seat. "At least he was there when I needed him. It's pitch dark and freezing out there." She crossed her arms and rubbed her hands along her jacket sleeves, trying to warm up. "I thought I'd miss the whole meeting."

"It just started." Andi wouldn't let herself look at Cody, not while she was still trying to figure things out. "Hey," she leaned in close to Bailey. "Where's Tim? He'd love this."

"He had a meeting with his science professor." Bailey gave Andi a quick side hug. "He'll be here next week. Hey, thanks for saving me a seat." She said nothing about Cody, didn't raise an eyebrow or cast even a curious glance about what had led her two friends to sit by each other. If Bailey was bothered by Andi's nearness to Cody, she didn't let on even a little. But that didn't change one very clear and unsettling fact.

The adoring way she'd looked at Cody from the moment she spotted him.

Ten

BAILEY WAS STILL CATCHING HER BREATH, still trying to assess what might have been happening between Cody and Andi, when Cody leaned over and hugged her, the same way she'd hugged Andi a few seconds earlier. It wasn't a long hug, or one that could be misinterpreted in any way. But for the few seconds it lasted, his arms felt wonderful around her shoulders. He smiled, and in his eyes was a familiarity Bailey missed. "You still have my number?"

"Of course." Heat spread through her cheeks. How long since she'd been this close to Cody, since the two of them had sat together close enough to touch? The answer resonated through her heart immediately. Not since that July afternoon at her parents' house. Cody was right in his letter. The two of them had practically avoided each other since then.

"So why didn't you text me?" His teasing look said he was mildly upset with her. "I could've met you in the parking lot at least. That's no place for a pretty girl like you to be hanging out looking for a security guard."

Bailey glanced down at her lap, because it was impossible to draw a full breath while she was lost in Cody Coleman's eyes. She nodded, in full agreement. The parking lot had been scary, and even with the occasional security guard, she would've been smarter to have someone with her. She lifted her eyes to his again. "Next time."

He patted her knee and both of them focused on the music at the front of the room. The sound was full and rich, filling the auditorium. Bailey glanced over at Andi, and the two exchanged a smile. But something didn't seem quite right with her. She hadn't wanted to look too deeply into the fact that her two friends were sitting next to each other. Andi and Cody had only met for the first time the other day—when Cody asked Andi to deliver the note. But tonight, in the first few seconds after Bailey reached the doorway of the meeting room, she saw something she couldn't mistake. An attraction—at least from Andi to Cody.

Bailey's mind raced with the possibilities. Of course Andi would've been attracted to Cody. Who wouldn't be? And Andi wouldn't have any idea that Bailey had feelings for Cody that went beyond friendship. Every time the subject of love and relationships came up, Bailey had steadfastly avoided talking about Cody. Her feelings for him were too deep, too private to share right away. Private and complicated. Especially in light of the fact that she was supposed to be dating Tim Reed. Bailey could hardly blame Andi if—in the course of fifteen minutes—she'd fallen for Cody.

But she couldn't stand for it either.

With all that Andi had going for her, Bailey would have to find another college if Cody and Andi began dating. A situation like that would be more than Bailey could handle. Her heartbeat came fast and uneven, shouting at her that she needed to find a way to fix the problem. If there was a problem. *Breathe, Bailey... focus on the music and breathe.* The song was "Step by Step," and Bailey directed all her attention to the words: "Step by step, you'll lead me ... and I will follow you all of my days."

Slowly, gradually, the panic building inside her faded a little. They'd only spent a few minutes together. It wasn't like Cody had asked Andi to marry him, or even out on a date. He probably slipped into the room late, saw Andi, and joined her so he'd have an easier time finding Bailey whenever she got there.

"You okay?" Cody brought his face close to hers again. "You're quiet."

She elbowed him lightly in the ribs and felt her eyes dance as she looked at him. "I'm hardly quiet. We're singing, remember?"

He laughed and shielded his eyes for a moment, embarrassed. When he looked up, his cheeks were flushed. "Okay, not that kind of quiet. You know what I mean."

"We'll talk later." She leaned against his arm for a moment. "It's good to see you."

"You read my letter?"

"Yes." Her eyes locked on his. "We need to talk."

Cody checked the door again. "Is Tim coming?" His question seemed loaded, especially because his eyes seemed to want more information than whether Tim was joining them for the meeting.

Bailey tried to find the right words, but the job took a moment longer than she intended. She wanted to tell him that she and Tim were figuring things out, that she wasn't sure she had romantic feelings for him, and that sometimes she wondered if she weren't acting out a part — the one everyone expected of her. But with the music playing loud, and the kids around them trying to focus on praising God, Bailey settled for a simple answer. "Not tonight."

Cody nodded. Again he patted her knee, and this time his hand seemed to linger a little longer than before. The band up front sang one more song, and then a red-headed tall guy took over.

Andi whispered in her direction, "That's Daniel. I met him before Cru."

"Looks like he's funny."

"He is." Her smile seemed intended to convey a deeper message to Bailey — that she was happy and completely uninterested in Cody. In case Bailey wondered. "I can't believe so many kids turned out."

"I know." Bailey gave her roommate an enthusiastic look. "I'm so glad we heard about this."

Daniel took the microphone from the lead singer, and when the band had taken their seats, he welcomed everyone again and reminded them about the flyers. "You gotta check into all these upcoming events. This is going to be our best year ever." The crowd responded in agreement. When the room quieted down again, Daniel moved closer to the front row and searched out the faces around him. "So why are we here? I mean ... why are we really here?"

Bailey squirmed in her seat, and when her shoulder came up against Cody's, she didn't move away.

His eyes were kind, his smile a permanent part of his face. "You're here because you love God, and this might be the only place you feel comfortable talking about Him." He paused, his delivery easy and direct. "There are definitely some pretty girls here tonight." Another series of laughter.

Naturally, Bailey thought. Daniel only just met her, but he has a thing for Andi too. She looked beside her, but Andi didn't seem to notice. Her attention was fully on wherever Daniel was headed with his message.

"We're here because we need each other." Daniel's smile faded a little. "Coming to Cru is like coming to a family reunion. We belong to the same family and we have a lot in common. That and we're here to help each other throughout the school year."

Bailey thought about how true that was. Her first two weeks at college had been amazing, and a lot of that was because of Andi. Having a roommate who shared her faith was like having a sister — for the first time ever. A bit of guilt spread through her. She couldn't blame Andi for sitting next to Cody or even for being attracted to him. If Cody didn't want anything but a friendship, then why couldn't he and Andi have a thing for each other?

The idea felt like sandpaper against her soul, and she hugged her arms to her chest, suddenly colder than before.

"Here's what I'm going to ask you. When you come to Cru, come with an open heart and leave all that other stuff at the door. This isn't the place to gossip about the "emo" girl in your chem class, or laugh about a cheerleader who fell doing the splits at the last home game. At Cru let's come wanting the best for each other as we grow in our friendships and in our bond with Jesus. Assume nothing but the best of the people sitting on either side of you." His grin got big again. "That way we'll have a great time, and we'll have a lot more energy to focus on the message." His eyes moved slowly around the room. "Make sense?"

The sea of kids nodded and muttered their agreement.

At various times in her life, Bailey had sat through a message where she wondered if her parents or her brother had cued the speaker ahead of time about exactly what words she needed. Without question, this was one of those times. Here she'd come to Cru excited more about seeing Cody than hearing a message. And then when she arrived and saw Andi sitting with him, her heart had done strange flip-flops wondering what she'd missed between the two of them. She was acting practically paranoid, and not once through the worship had her focus really been on anything other than Cody and Andi.

She stifled a long sigh and stared at the floor near her feet.

Daniel was finishing. "We won't go long tonight. There's a snack table set up and lots to talk about. It's important you get to know each other. But keep in mind what I said. In this environment, we're going to expect the best *of* each other and want the best *for* each other. We're going to practice all the one-anothering we can. We'll serve one another and love one another and encourage one another, and at the end of the day we'll be tight with God and ..." he gave the roomful of kids an expectant look. "Tight with ..."

Bailey looked up as the crowd finished for him, shouting in unison, "... one another!"

"Exactly."

Wow, God ... that got my attention. Bailey bit the inside of her lip. In light of the message, she felt convinced about what she needed to do next. As long as she was dating Tim, she couldn't lay claim to Cody—not in any possible way. If he ended up liking Andi—and what guy wouldn't—then she'd have to get used to the idea. If that was part of God's plan, she couldn't fight it or try to change it. After all, long before Andi came into the picture, Cody had made up his mind. He wouldn't consider dating Bailey. So what point was there in worrying about Andi and an attraction she might have to Cody? If there was one, she needed to rejoice with her roommate and be grateful that two of her closest friends had found their way to each other. Bailey's brain could agree with all of that completely. She wondered how many more messages like this she'd need before her heart felt the same way.

Daniel prayed to close the meeting, and as everyone stood and began talking and milling about, Bailey found her happiest smile. "So ..." she looked at her friends. "Cody ... you met Andi?"

"I did." Cody gave a polite nod in Andi's direction. Bailey tried not to look too deeply into the moment, but nothing in his eyes or expression revealed any interest in Andi beyond what was polite.

Andi, though ... Bailey already knew her well enough to catch the sparkle in her eyes, the way she kept her attention on Cody a little longer than she needed to. "Cody was asking about Tim." Andi turned to Bailey. "He's coming next week, right?"

"Yes. He should definitely make it." Bailey looked at her roommate. Was she trying to remind Cody that Bailey had a boyfriend? So Cody would know where not to put his attention? Bailey willed herself to remember tonight's message, to think the best of Andi. Besides, Andi didn't have any idea about Bailey's real feelings for Cody.

"Bailey, wait! I didn't tell you the news!" Andi took hold of her arm, her entire face lit up. "You and Tim and I ... we all got callbacks for *Scrooge*! Monday after school! Isn't that great?"

"Really? That's incredible!" Bailey wanted to be excited, but all she could think about was Cody, and how badly she wanted a few minutes alone with him so they could talk. "I hope we all get cast!"

"We will, I can feel it." Andi's eyes lit up even more. "Oh, and tomorrow's the filming! My dad said that the two of us might have a line or so. He was looking over the script, and the lead stops to talk to a couple girls. He thought we'd be great for that!"

That last news really was amazing. "We could get into the Screen Actors Guild with those parts."

"I know. Imagine having our SAG cards already. We could get summer jobs acting in LA if we wanted to."

Cody was listening to the conversation, but every time Bailey looked at him, his eyes seemed to say the same thing. That he, too, wanted to get away somewhere so the two of them could catch up.

"You're coming to the shoot, right?" Andi took hold of Cody's elbow and gave him an irresistibly adorable look. "You have to come. Maybe you'll get discovered!"

Cody gave a halfhearted laugh. "Hollywood's not for me." He let his eyes find Bailey's again. "I might come by to watch. That's about it."

"Okay. You'll change your mind once you get on set. There's something about the draw of the cameras. You'll see."

"Maybe." He looked at his watch, and as he did he shifted just enough that Andi released his elbow. He turned to Bailey. "Hey ... what time's your first class tomorrow?"

"Eight." She made a face. "Pretty early, you?"

"Not till nine." He slipped his hands in his jeans pocket. His expression said he was feeling awkward about what to say next.

Before Bailey could rescue him and state something blunt, like that the two of them were going to go outside for a while so they could talk, the Cru leader, Daniel, walked up. "A lot of kids are talking about the movie shoot tomorrow." He stood next to Andi, his attention fully on her. "Looks like your dad will have a good turnout."

"Great." Andi smiled politely at Daniel. "Thanks for saying something."

Bailey silently thanked Daniel for his distraction. She briefly touched Andi's shoulder. "Hey, Cody and I'll be outside. We haven't caught up since school started."

"Okay." Andi sounded hesitant. "Wait for me to walk back?"

"Which dorm are you in?" Daniel didn't sound pushy, just willing to help.

Andi told him, and he assured her he'd be happy to walk her back. "I have to go that way too."

"I'll wait." Bailey was quick with her offer. She didn't want Andi feeling like she had to walk back with a guy she'd just met. "Seriously, Andi. We'll be right outside."

"No." Andi seemed to think the situation over. She looked from Bailey to Cody and back. She showed a flicker of what looked like hurt feelings, but then her smile took over. If she was upset, her tone didn't give her away. "It's okay." She brushed off the idea. "You guys go. I'll be all right with Daniel." She turned her attention to him.

Daniel looked more than happy to help. When Bailey was sure Andi was okay with the plan, she nodded at Cody and the two of them headed for the door. "Nice to meet you," Cody told Andi as they left.

"You too." There was a coolness in Andi's tone, but Cody didn't seem to catch it.

Outside, Cody drew a long breath and let it out slowly. "I thought we'd never get this chance." The path outside the building was dark and crisscrossed with shadows, but there was enough light that Cody could make eye contact with her as they walked.

"I know." Bailey hugged her bag to her chest. "Great meeting, though. I'm glad we went."

"Me too. I needed something like that."

Bailey wasn't sure where to start. They had so much to catch up on, so much about the new school year that neither of them had talked about. Bailey opened her mouth to ask how things were working out with Cody's roommates, but at the same time he asked if Bailey was liking rooming with Andi.

They both laughed and Cody led her by her arm to an alcove just off the pathway. "C'mere." He took her bag from her and set it down near their feet. Then he pulled her into a hug and held her for a long time. "Maybe we should start here."

Bailey hoped he couldn't feel her heart pounding beneath her jacket, but if he could she wouldn't have pulled away. She'd longed for a moment like this since the last time she and Cody were together back in July. Now, with a cool wind in the trees overhead and autumn leaves sifting down around them, Bailey wanted nothing but to stay that way, warm in his arms, the stars dancing above them.

"There." He eased back and searched her eyes. "I missed you, Bailey. You don't know how much."

She wanted only to enjoy the moment, not analyze it. But the emotions in his eyes, his tone, seemed to go way beyond a desire for friendship. She swallowed, not sure what to say except the obvious. "I missed you too."

"The way things are," he looked off to the side, as if he could see his frustrations hanging from the trees nearby, "this was never how I wanted it." He ran his hand over the back of her head. "We pass each other and it's like ... I don't know, it's like we're strangers."

Bailey thought about the nights she'd longed for Cody's voice, his presence. All the months when he was in Iraq, and even after he came home. She would rely on his letters, believing that someday they'd find more than the friendship they'd started. "I guess," she let herself get lost in his eyes, "I thought you were ending things that day, when you first got back in town. I figured you'd have to set the pace, and then ... I never heard from you."

He looked like he wanted to kiss her, but then he drew back. His hands were still looped around her lower back, but there was more space between them now. "Remember," he gave a subtle raise of one eyebrow, "you have a boyfriend. It's a little awkward for me to call and ask you to lunch."

Bailey nodded. "I know." She wanted to clear things up, that Tim might be her boyfriend, sort of. But that didn't mean she was in love with him. "About Tim ... he and I ..."

"It's okay." Cody released his hold on her. He put his finger to her lips and shook his head. "Don't tell me. I don't need the details." His smile didn't hide the sudden sadness in his eyes. "You're happy, Bailey. That's all that matters. It's just ... you and I shared something very special. If Tim's okay with it ... and if you're okay, I want to stay in your life. See you more often."

Confusion clouded Bailey's heart. She still wanted to tell him about Tim, but now to do so felt wrong, like a betrayal. And that wasn't fair to anyone, least of all Tim. All she could do was take Cody's words at face value. If she wanted to cut things off with Tim, that had to happen in a separate conversation—not here with Cody. She wanted to hug him again, but she folded her arms in front of herself instead. "Tim won't have a problem with that. He knows we're friends."

Cody's eyes warmed. "Not lately." His eyes sparkled as she walked close to him again. "But that's going to change. I promise."

"Good." She was tempted to ask what he thought about Andi, but she didn't want to encourage her own jealousy. Not when she'd worked so hard to get over her feelings of envy toward her roommate after the auditions. She picked up her bag and they started walking again, their pace easy, not too fast. "Tell me about your apartment. Are the guys working out?"

"They're great. Most of them." He gave her a wry look. "I told Stan he needed to find another place. He keeps buying beer and having buddies over to drink on the weekend. No drinking at our place, that's the rule."

Bailey looked into the shadows ahead and remembered seeing Cody passed out on the floor of their guestroom, nearly dead from the effects of alcohol poisoning. "You've come a long way."

"With God alone." He narrowed his eyes and lifted them to the dark sky. "Every day I have to admit I'm powerless over alcohol. And every day Jesus gets me through on His strength. It'll be that way the rest of my life."

They walked in quiet for a minute or so. "You ever tempted?"

"Honestly? Not at all. I was pretty sick the last time I drank. I feel nauseous just thinking about alcohol."

"Good. I'm glad for you." She kicked lightly at a pile of yellow and red leaves. They were halfway to her dorm already. She sort of expected they'd see Andi walking home. But then a number of paths led to the dorms. She and Daniel could've taken any of them. Another question burned in Bailey's heart, one she wasn't sure she wanted an answer to. "You seeing anyone?"

Cody hesitated, and for a few seconds he only stared at her, as if there were things he wanted to say that he simply couldn't voice. Not now. Finally he shrugged one shoulder and looked ahead. "No one."

Bailey laughed. "I remember when there was a different girl every week. Back when you played ball for my dad."

"I was such a jerk." He shook his head. "I guess I had my fix of easy girls, easy dates. Now I'd rather get home and hit the books."

A grin lifted the corners of his lips and his eyes sparkled. "Did I tell you my plan?"

"What?" Her stomach did somersaults under his gaze, and she had to remind herself to breathe.

"I want to be a doctor. I'm thinking of doing my internship in the mission field somewhere. The Philippines, maybe, or India. Something like that."

"Really?" Bailey was amazed. "I thought you wanted to coach."

"I do. My own kids someday. By then I'll have my own practice and I can set my hours around their activities."

Admiration coursed through her. She slowed her pace, stretching out their time together as long as she could. "What brought all this on?"

His answer took awhile. "War, I guess." The look in his eyes was haunting, unforgettable. "I lost my leg, but I gained a lot while I was there. More wisdom and direction than I would've if I'd stayed here."

She realized that she hadn't thought about his leg the whole time they'd been together. His prosthesis was completely hidden with his tennis shoe and jeans, and he walked without a trace of a limp. She allowed her shoulder to stay close to his as they walked, closer than before. "In what way?"

"I like helping people, for one thing. Helping them keep their freedom or get well again, either way it feels right. Like that's what God created me to do."

"Which means you have a lot of school ahead of you."

"Exactly." His quiet laugh filled her senses. "I guess that answers the question about girls. I want to get through school as fast as possible. Doesn't leave a lot of time." He nudged her with his elbow. "Except for the people I really care about." His grin grew more shy than before. "You know?"

Bailey loved this, the way they'd fallen back into the camaraderie they'd shared before Cody went to war. There were times after he came back when she didn't think they'd ever find this again, especially after feeling like he'd purposefully ignored her these last two weeks. But now ... now her heart was alive with the familiar ways Cody made her feel.

They talked about her auditions, and when Andi came up, Bailey was quick to say she was wonderful. "I'm still getting to know her, but we're already close, like the two of us could be best friends."

He gave a single shake of his head. "She's got a ton of charisma, that's for sure."

"She does." Bailey didn't want to ask him what he meant. She didn't want to hear Cody say he was attracted to her, or find out that he had even a little interest in her. For now it was enough that they had this time together, without anything dimming the bright light in her soul.

Too soon they were back at her dorm, and once more Cody easily took her in his arms. "I pray for you every day, Bailey. That God will keep you close to Him, and that you'll grow in all the right ways while you're here." He no longer looked like he might kiss her, but only glad that the two of them had found each other again. "This night ... I needed it."

"Me too. I'm sorry we let so much time pass." She grinned and angled her face. "It won't happen again."

"I'll call you or text you. Maybe we can have coffee together once in a while. And you'll tell me if Tim gets upset." His look grew more serious. "Whatever happens, I don't want to come between the two of you."

Bailey felt her heart sink fast. She wouldn't let his comment ruin the moment, but there was no denying the effect it had on her mood. They said goodnight and promised to talk soon, but once she was back in her dorm, she wanted to open the window and yell back at him. Why didn't he want to come between the two of them? If he had feelings for her the way she had feelings for him, then shouldn't he want to come between them?

There was only one reason he'd end the night with a comment like that. Because when he looked down the pathway of life, when he saw himself finishing years of school and becoming a doctor and doing an internship on a mission field, he must not have seen her by his side. That's where Tim was different. Even though he didn't make her heart take flight the way Cody did, he was kind and steady and a wonderful guy in every possible way. More than that, he'd told her the one thing Cody never had.

That he was in love with her.

Eleven

THE SOUND WAS LIKE AN ALARM, screaming at him, pushing him from the deepest sleep. It took what felt like five minutes before Chase sat up in bed and looked around, not sure where he was or why he was in a strange room with bells going off. Then, gradually, it all came back to him. He was in a hotel room in Bloomington, Indiana, and he'd been asleep, and the screaming sound was only his iPhone. He looked at the red glowing numbers on the small alarm clock by his bed. Four fifty in the morning. No wonder he was asleep.

He picked up his phone, but the caller ID showed a blocked number. He slid the unlock bar across the phone and forced himself to be clearheaded. "Hello? Chase Ryan, here."

"Sorry to wake you, Chase. You won't believe this." The voice was only vaguely familiar.

Chase rubbed his eyes. It was Friday, day five on the filming, and even after the progress they'd made Tuesday, they'd since fallen further behind. If they didn't fall behind another hour, they'd still have to add at least two days to the schedule. The last thing he needed was more bad news. He squinted toward the window of the dark hotel room. "Who is this?"

"Gary. From catering."

Chase made the connection. Gary was the guy intercepting Rita's salmon every morning, the one in charge of getting meals to the cast. "Okay, Gary, what's up?"

"Like I said, you won't believe it." He sounded shaken. "I was coming back from headquarters this morning, driving in from

Indianapolis like I do every day, and suddenly people are flashing their brights and honking at me. That's when I saw the smoke."

"Smoke?" Chase's heart kicked into a higher gear.

"Pouring out from my kitchen trailer. I pulled over, but by the time I climbed out of the cab, the whole thing was in flames. I mean, completely engulfed."

"Your food truck?" Chase had to be dreaming. He wanted to close his eyes and find his way out of this nightmare and back to sleep.

"It's gone, Chase. Now don't worry, I mean, not too much, anyway. The truck's insured, and I called headquarters. They can have another one ready by this afternoon. You might need to sign some papers, but I think you can count on me for dinner. It's just ... I'm not sure what to do about breakfast and lunch."

Chase swung his legs over the edge of the bed. It wasn't a nightmare. Not this or the salmon or the dog bite. Just part of making a movie. He groaned. "You're serious, your food truck burned up?"

"To the ground. Nothing but a small pile of debris." He uttered a nervous laugh. "Firemen said I was lucky to get out alive. A few more miles and the thing could've blown up with me in it."

Words escaped him. Chase stood and paced to the window. He was bare-chested with just his pajama bottoms, and now that he was out of bed, he shivered a little from the chill in the air. "What you're saying is, I need to come up with a breakfast plan."

"And lunch. I'm sorry, Chase. Really. Things like this don't happen."

Chase wanted to tell him that actually they do happen — to Keith and him, at least. "Okay, Gary. Don't worry about it. I'll figure something out." He grabbed a T-shirt from the top dresser drawer and slipped it over his head. It wasn't even six. Way too early to call around for a breakfast plan. But then he remembered JR at the Lobster house. Keith had given him the guy's card, and he easily found it in his bag. Maybe together they could think of something that would work.

He got up and showered, and for a minute or so, he considered passing on his Bible study. The matter at hand was far more pressing. But then he remembered something Kelly had told him last night. She said in her Bible time she'd come to the conclusion once more that even on the most busy days there wasn't time *not* to read the Bible, not to study God's Word. "The busy days are when I need Him most," she'd said.

Chase easily agreed, and now here he was with the chance to put the theory to work. He knew right where he wanted to read — the section of Scripture Keith had talked about the other day. James, chapter 1. He'd read it over enough times, he practically knew it by heart, but this time he wanted to find something else, something deeper that would help him handle yet another crisis on the set. He started at the beginning and worked his way past the part about considering it pure joy whenever he faced trials of many kinds.

Not until he reached verse 11 did he see something that stopped him cold. He read it over again:

> *For the sun rises with scorching heat and withers the plant; its blossom falls and its beauty is destroyed. In the same way, the rich man will fade away even while he goes about his business.*

Wasn't that exactly what had happened to Gary's food truck? It had perished even while Gary went about his work. The point wasn't that Gary had done something wrong, but that the work of a man's hands was temporary. Only what was wrought for eternity would last. That meant that a hundred years from now, most likely no one would remember a movie called *The Last Letter*. Certainly no one would remember the trials Keith and Chase had survived as they shot the film.

But generations to come would remember the impact those actions had on the souls of men. Chase would find breakfast and lunch for the cast and crew, and he would do so with his eye on the eternal — on the sharpening of his faith and the message that could change lives for Christ. Everything else would fade away in the end anyway.

Gary's food truck had proved that much.

By the time Chase called JR's cell number at six that morning, he felt almost excited about the challenges that lay ahead. Each of them had a purpose, even in this. JR sounded fully awake when he answered the phone. "Hey, how's my buddy Keith doing?"

"Great." Chase realized he hadn't told his friend about the food truck yet. "Keith says you can get it done when it comes to food, is that right?"

"You bet. Best steak and lobster in town." JR's confidence rang across the phone lines. "If you're looking for a nice dinner for the cast, you called the right guy."

"Actually," Chase held his breath. "I was thinking more about eggs and turkey sandwiches. Not at the same time."

Chase explained the situation, and together he and JR came up with a plan. The nearby grocery store was already open, so Chase drove there first and picked up twelve dozen eggs, ten loaves of bread, fifty blueberry muffins, eleven pounds of sliced turkey, and a cartful of sandwich fixings, chips, and salads. The rest of the ingredients JR had at his restaurant.

The shopping happened quickly, and Chase and JR worked feverishly in his kitchen so that by seven o'clock they had a massive container of scrambled eggs and cheese, fresh pico de gallo, warm muffins, a variety of jams and juices, and one filet of salmon. Together they delivered the food to the set. By then, most of the cast and crew had gathered at the tables and were looking around for the food truck.

"Breakfast," Chase announced as he and JR hurried out of the car. "Come and get it!"

Keith walked up to him, clearly baffled. "What in the world's happening?"

"I didn't tell you?" Chase laughed, all signs of frustration gone. "Gary's food truck burned to the ground this morning. I'm in charge of breakfast and lunch today."

For a moment, Keith stood there, his mouth slightly open. Then he nodded slowly, saluted Chase, and headed for the back of the line. Chase and JR stayed just long enough to make sure everyone was satisfied. When word spread about the burned up food truck, several cast members came up to Chase and patted him on the back or shook his hand. "You take producing to a new level every day," one actor told him.

Janetta Drake, the lone Christian among the cast, sat down across from Chase and gave his hand a gentle squeeze. "You have no idea the example you're giving to everyone on this set." She kept her words soft, her tone intense. "People know something's different about the two of you." She grinned at him before she stood and made her way to the next table. "I know you want to change the world with your movies, Chase. But it's good to know you're getting a start right here."

Chase and JR returned to the restaurant to work on lunch. An hour later they had a hundred turkey sandwiches spread across five platters, fruit and vegetable trays, and eight bowls of chips. Chase returned to the set and stored everything in a couple of refrigerators in their trailer, and then hurried out to find Keith. They were doing location shots on the campus of IU today, and his friend was bound to need his help. Whatever the day brought, Chase was ready for it. He made a mental note that later when he and Kelly pulled out their laptops for one of their much-needed talks, he would tell her how right she was. Some days there simply wasn't time to miss out on reading the Bible. Days like this one. Never mind that short of a miracle they didn't have enough money to finish the film, or that Ben Adams still hadn't returned Keith's calls, or that they were only a week into the shoot and there was no telling what troubles next week would bring.

For now, none of that mattered. Lives were being changed, no matter how crazy the movie shoot was playing out. The message would stay with Chase forever.

Food trucks were temporary. People, the souls of people, were eternal.

Twelve

KEITH WASN'T SURE HOW CHASE HANDLED the food truck disaster, but everyone was happy with the meals at breakfast and lunch, and by two that afternoon the new truck was in place, Gary and his guys working on the dinner meal. Now most of the cast and crew were gathered in a shady grass area on the Indiana campus waiting for the next scene. Chase had shown up, and he and Keith needed to meet before they started filming. Meanwhile, Keith's wife, Lisa, was trying to reign in a couple hundred students who had descended upon them to be extras. Keith gave her a knowing look as he headed off with Chase. She had flown in a few days ago, and Keith was grateful. She'd helped out on Keith's shoots before. She seemed to know just what to do, how to keep things moving.

"You ready?" Chase was breathless, but he looked happier than he had all week. The story about his meal-making would have to come later.

"Ready. Jake's here, and he's been completely on for every scene." Keith shook his head, amazed that they'd landed a talent like Jake Olson. "The kid's got chops, that's for sure. He's giving us his best work yet."

"Great." Chase looked over the clipboard. "You knocked out four scenes this morning. That's amazing."

"Without my director." Keith gave him a wry smile. "We could write a book about this when we're all finished." He looked at his notes. "Obviously this is the part of the movie where Jake's character does the most soul-searching. He's arrogant and self-centered, and that comes painfully to light while he's talking to his friends on campus. Especially in light of the letter he's just received from his father."

"Andi's in these next few scenes, right?" Chase looked over the list and then peered at the group of college kids gathered around Lisa.

Keith followed his gaze, and only then did he see Andi and a girl who must've been her roommate, Bailey, set apart from the other kids, talking to Jake Olson. He frowned. "Great."

"Hmmm." Chase saw it too. For the first time that day, he looked concerned. "Not exactly the guy I'd want my nineteen-year-old daughter talking to."

A sigh escaped from Keith. Lisa didn't see what was happening with Andi, because she was too busy organizing the other extras. Keith set his notes on his chair. "I'll be right back." He crossed the grassy lawn, his eyes on Andi the entire time. Her body language wasn't suggestive but it was flirty. No question about that. The way she held her shoulders and her chin, the toss of her hair that could be seen forty yards away. This was what he'd been worried about all along with Andi, that here at IU she'd fall headlong in love with the world. Not that she'd given him a reason to doubt her faith and commitment to living right. But the world had a way of drawing in girls like Andi, girls with a voracious appetite for life. As naïve as Andi was, she wouldn't know trouble like Jake Olson until it was too late.

"Andi ..." he called to her, and she turned immediately, her sunshiny smile all his.

"Daddy, hi!" She grabbed hold of her friend's hand and the two of them ran up, laughing and giddy with excitement. "I told Bailey about the couple lines we might get to say and—" she stopped herself. "Wait, I haven't introduced you." She laughed at herself. "Dad, this is my roommate, Bailey Flanigan."

"Hi, Bailey. I've heard a lot about you." Keith felt his concerns for his daughter cool some. Maybe Andi was only being friendly. Certainly she knew better than to show interest to a guy like Jake Olson. "You ready for a few lines today?"

"Definitely. Thank you, sir."

Keith was relieved that this girl was Andi's roommate. Bailey's eyes shone with an unmistakable light. There seemed to be nothing flirtatious or pretentious about her, and Keith had the strong sense she was the real deal. Not just a roommate, but hopefully a lifelong friend for his daughter. Yesterday when they talked on the phone, Andi had told him how neither of them had been lucky enough to have had a sister.

"But now we have each other," she'd said before they hung up. "Isn't that wonderful, Daddy?"

It was indeed. Maybe Bailey would help add a voice of reason to Andi if she started letting herself wander toward Jake or any other actor on the set. He was about to address the issue of Jake, and his thought that Andi should keep her distance, when Chase came jogging up.

"Keith, we need you." He nodded at the girls. "Sorry, something's come up."

"We'll be over here." Andi pointed to the place where they'd been standing before. "Just tell us when you want us."

Keith nodded, distracted. Then he turned to Chase, concern already tightening his stomach. "What happened?"

"Some rumor on the set." Chase raked his fingers through his dark hair. His words came fast, his mouth dry from this most recent sudden problem. "I guess the actress playing Jake's girlfriend started telling everyone we're marketing this movie only to the Christian market. She's already walked, told the DP she wanted nothing to do with some sort of God movie." Chase's face had lost a few shades of color. The Director of Photography wasn't bound to care for the rumor either. "Now Rita Reynolds is locked in her trailer talking to her agent, threatening to do the same thing. The DP's worried that Jake'll walk too. He wants one of us to stand up at break in half an hour and make an announcement, telling the cast and crew not to worry, that this isn't being marketed as a Christian film."

Keith ordered himself to exhale. In a matter of minutes everything they'd worked toward, every bit of fund-raising and convincing investors, the time spent with the screenwriter and getting everyone out here on location, all of it was on the brink of destruction. If the cast walked, their movie would become little more than a mention in *Variety* magazine, another independent filmmaker having failed royally. He put his hand on Chase's shoulder. "Pray with me. Right now. God knows the answers even if we can't see them."

Chase bowed his head, neither of them even the slightest bit concerned that they were praying publicly about an accusation of making a Christian film. There was no time for irony or scrutiny or doubt. They needed a miracle, and they needed it now.

"Lord, we don't know the enemy we're up against. Give us wisdom, give us words ... give us a movie. Please, Father, let us remain in this mission field, and we promise to make it all for You, through You ... to Your glory, amen."

"Amen." Chase looked doubtful. "You're going to do it, right? I mean, what are our options?"

"What, stand up at dinner and make an announcement that this isn't being marketed as a Christian film?" His nerves were stretched, but not so far that this was a tough question. "Watch me, Chase. Then you'll know."

"Come on, Keith. I want this movie to change lives just like you do. But it isn't a Christian film. Not the way they're worried it'll be — playing only to the church crowd."

Break wasn't for thirty minutes, and they had at least one scene to shoot in the meantime. Keith started walking toward

Lisa and the group of extras. "I'll handle it," he looked at Chase over his shoulder. "Don't worry."

The first campus scene was a simple one, and Keith was able to spend much of the time mentally rehearsing how he would handle the coming announcement. The scene had Jake, distant and distraught, walking across campus ignoring everyone he passed by. After crossing a section of pathway, he dropped to a bench and pulled out the letter—not to read it again, but to remember the words he'd just received, the news that had changed his life. The extras were wonderful, great kids who cooperated and didn't pull anything funny. Keith and Chase got the cut on the second take.

"Great work," Chase used his megaphone to get the word out to the crowd. Then he lowered it and turned to the DP. "Check the gate."

Keith waited while the director of photography did as he was asked. All film ran through a small metal gate in the camera, and when they got a take they liked, the last thing they needed to do was check the gate for stray fuzz or hairs, anything that would mar the footage.

"Gate's clean." The DP raised his fist. "Good stuff, guys. Good stuff all the way around."

Keith didn't let his anxiety show. If the director of photography was worried about the rumor, he wasn't showing it. The fact gave Keith at least one reason to hope that his cast and crew weren't on the verge of mass panic. Even so, the meeting was essential and Keith was only going to do this once. He picked up Chase's megaphone. "Okay, extras take twenty and meet back here. I need the rest of the cast and crew to meet at the tent near the food truck. I have something to share with everyone."

His tone was ominous, which he intended. He wanted everyone to take what he was about to say seriously. He walked alongside Chase, saying nothing. If he were honest with himself, he was disappointed in Chase's reaction. They needed faith to stand up to moments like this, or they might as well pack it up and head back to Indonesia.

"You're mad at me." Chase seemed like he was working to keep up. They'd moved the tent and food truck to a field across the street. It'd remain there a few days, as long as they were filming on campus.

"Not mad." Keith smiled at his friend the way he might smile at a younger brother. "As long as one of us keeps our focus, we'll get through this. Today it's me. Next time it might be you seeing clearly when I'm ready to throw in the towel."

"I'm not ready to—"

"Chase." Keith stopped and leveled his look right at his friend's eyes. "If you're even for a minute thinking about standing in front of our cast and crew and telling them this isn't a Christian film, then you've lost something." He held up his hand. "Now I know you've had a long day."

"A good day."

"Right, a good day. I can't wait to hear about it back at the hotel. But how we handle the next fifteen minutes will define us from here on out. It's that important." He put his arm around Chase's shoulders and the two started walking again. "Pray God gives me the words."

Chase sighed, his eyes downcast. "I'll pray. I'm sorry."

Keith met quietly with Lisa before he walked to the center of the eating area and waited. Gradually the tables in front and on the sides of him filled up until everyone was present. Gary and the other cooks were barbecuing ribs out back, and the smell wafted in, lending promise to Keith that they'd all still be there three hours later for dinner—whatever the reaction to this announcement. Keith thought about using the megaphone, but he knew how to project his voice. Under the tent, he was sure he could talk loud enough for everyone to hear. He took his place and noticed where people were sitting, who they'd grouped together with. At one table sat Rita Reynolds, whispering to Jake Olson and three other leads. Keith could tell from the looks on the faces of his key grips and electricians, his lighting and cameramen, that word had gotten around to them too. This was the moment when the producer was going to banish the thought of this film being marketed as a Christian movie. A hush fell over the cast and crew.

"Okay, most of you know why we're having this meeting." Keith silently asked God for direction. He caught Chase standing next to Lisa at the far side of the tent. Chase's arms were crossed, his head bowed. He was praying, he had to be. Lisa, too. Keith raised his voice, encouraged. "Apparently our young actress has left the set because she doesn't want to work on a Christian film." Keith felt a calm come over him. With each set of eyes he looked into he prayed that calm would be contagious, that levelheaded behavior would rule the moment for all of them. He looked around the entire seating area. "How many of you read the script before taking on this assignment? I'd like a show of hands."

Hands slowly came up around the tented area until every single person had theirs high in the air. Keith nodded. "That's what I thought." He felt God breathing strength into him. "Now another show of hands. How many of you read the script and thought that this movie was exclusively a Christian movie—whatever that means?"

One at a time every hand came down. Keith stood a little straighter than before. Across the area, Chase had his head up now, and he seemed less afraid than before. Keith felt pride building in his chest. "Now let me be very clear about one thing. I am a Christian. Make no mistake." He kept his tone warm, the confidence in his voice warm and unwavering. "My co-producer and the director of this film, Chase Ryan, is also a Christian. For those who don't know it, Chase and I spent seven years in the mission fields of Indonesia, telling people about Jesus Christ." He lifted his hands in an unaffected manner. "If you want to know about going to heaven or having a life-changing relationship with God, please ... by all means come see one of us."

Around the eating area a few chuckles rose from the crowd. Keith saw only a few people squirm in discomfort at the direction of the talk. He looked directly at key people, the ones he was most concerned about. "You want to know my dream for this movie? I hope people walk out of theaters changed forever because they saw our film. I hope this movie makes them want to improve their character and deepen their love for this country. I hope it makes them stronger in their commitment to faith in God, and in their commitment to family."

A few of them nodded their agreement. Keith smiled his thanks in their direction. "I hope that as Jake experiences the change the letter brings, millions of viewers experience that same change." He took a step closer to them. "But with all that, I wouldn't want anyone to limit or label this film as a Christian-only film. We've added nothing to the script—it's the same one each of you read and agreed to make. *The Last Letter* isn't going to be marketed as a Christian film, it's a film made by people like you and me—some of us Christians, some of us not. People who believe that moviegoers have a right to more inspiring films than some of the garbage that's out there on the big screen."

Chase and Lisa were beaming now, both of them silently cheering him on. Keith was almost finished. "This film is one that has the chance to win awards because of the depth of professionalism you all are bringing to it every day. Don't think about walking out now, not when we're on the brink of something great." He took a step back and lowered his voice just a little. "I hope that clears things up for everyone."

For a moment, no one moved or spoke, and all eyes remained on Keith. Then from the back corner, actress Janetta Drake stood and slowly, loudly, she began to clap. Keith felt tears gather in his eyes, but he resisted them. *Thank You, Lord, for Janetta.* She was playing the role of nurse in this movie, the one who shares critical insights with Jake, insights that help him change for the better and fully grasp the power of his father's letter. She was the lone Christian among the cast, a woman in her mid-forties, tall, blonde, and beautiful on the inside and out. She was a mother and a grandmother, and before her acting career she was an avid horseback rider and the head of a nursing home. Compassion was something that came easily to Janetta, and it showed every time she was in front of the camera.

Now, despite the risk of alienation among her peers and fellow cast members, she was taking a stand in support of Keith's explanation. And her support was all the cast and crew needed. The director of photography stood next, adding his applause to that of Janetta's, and after that came the lead grip and three cameramen. A few of the minor actors crossed the room and stood with Janetta, lending not only support but solidarity in their decision to stay and work with Keith and Chase.

Seconds ticked away, and one at a time everyone seated stood and clapped for the courage of Keith Ellison, for taking a stand that was far from popular in an arena where no one had the guts to declare truth for what it was. Finally when Jake Olson and Rita Reynolds rose and began clapping, Janetta's emotions got the better of her. Tears streamed down her face and Lisa came up alongside her, placing an arm around her shoulders. The two women rested their heads on each other as Keith added his applause to that of his cast and crew. "This is for you!" he shouted above the noise. "Now let's go make a movie that will change the world."

As the crowd disbursed and headed back to the set, Keith caught Chase staring at him from across the eating area. The look they exchanged said everything Keith knew his friend was feeling. Chase was sorry — angry at himself for nearly giving in to the pressures at hand. But more than that, he understood that Keith forgave him. The two men were best friends, on the same team. The way they would always be.

Keith nodded at Chase, and there was more understanding — they would talk about this later, back at the hotel. For now Keith walked up to his wife and wrapped his arms around her. "Thanks for praying." He whispered against her hair. "I felt it every second."

She lifted her face to his and kissed him lightly on the lips. They had loved each other since they were in high school, and the look in her eyes told him that the feelings between them now were as strong as they'd ever been. "You were brilliant."

"God won." The tent was nearly empty now, and he returned her kiss. "Let's go knock out some scenes."

As they walked back to the set, Keith registered the victory, the enormity of it. What had happened this afternoon wasn't going to earn them an Academy Award, and it wouldn't put more money in the bank account. There were still towering mountains ahead. But they'd gotten around this one. Keith put his arm around Lisa and crossed the street, watching his cast and crew busy themselves around the set. As he did, he smiled to himself.

Because sure enough, the view on this side of the mountain was breathtaking.

Thirteen

ANDI AND BAILEY DIDN'T ATTEND THE afternoon meeting. They weren't really part of the cast and crew, and none of the other extras had attended. Whatever had happened during break, Andi knew only that the people who answered to her dad were returning to the set fired up and ready to work.

The next scene involved Janetta Drake, an actress people in Hollywood were talking about. She'd gotten a late start on her acting career, but she brought emotion to the screen that few actors could pull off. This scene involved her and a professor, both of whom were aware of the letter that had been given to Jake's character. The extras were still needed, but Andi's dad had asked if Bailey and Andi could sit this one out.

"Is that a good thing?" she asked her mom when they returned from base camp.

"It is." Her mom kissed her forehead. "If you and Bailey get speaking lines, we can't have you milling about in the background of other scenes."

"Of course." Andi could've shouted at the good news. She hurried across the grassy lawn to share the details with Bailey, who was talking to a couple young moms and little kids near the edge of the crowd.

The police had set up tape to keep the public from spilling into the area where they'd be filming. Bailey was on the inside of the tape, talking with a few young moms and their children gathered on the other side. Andi had almost reached her, when she felt a hand on her shoulder. She expected it to be her mom, but when she spun around, she was looking straight into the eyes of Jake Olson.

His grin was slow and easy. "Hey." He lowered his hand, his eyes never breaking from hers. "We didn't finish our conversation earlier."

Andi wasn't sure it had been an actual conversation. More like an introduction. She forced herself to be calm, not to think about the fact that this was Jake Olson, America's newest heartthrob. She laughed as a way of catching her breath. "You're right. I guess we didn't."

"I have a few minutes." He glanced toward the place where Janetta was filming her scene. "Fifteen at least." He nodded for her to follow him. "Come on, stand with me over here ... out of the way."

"Okay." Andi shot a quick look around to see if her father was watching them. But he and Chase were gathered around a small monitor close to the action, and her mother was working with the extras on the campus pathway behind where Janetta was set up. Bailey was still busy talking near the police tape. Andi tried not to appear overanxious. She kept her pace even with his, and when they reached a grouping of trees, Jake leaned against one of them, lifting up one foot and bracing it against a different tree trunk.

"So you're a missionary kid, is that right?" His eyes were more gorgeous in person, or at least in the lighting beneath the trees.

Andi had no idea how he knew about her background, but she had nothing to hide. "I was. I spent seven years in the jungle." She could feel her eyes come to life. "It was amazing." A shyness came over her, though she didn't look away. "But now I'm ready to experience life here in the States, you know?"

He raised one eyebrow. "There's a lot to experience." A smooth bit of laughter tickled his throat. "You have no idea, Miss Andi. I'll bet you haven't done much yet."

"Not really." She felt the conversation slipping precariously toward something suggestive. In a hurry, she brought it back. "I should tell you about Indonesia sometime."

"Yeah." His expression grew less flirty, more serious. "I've always wanted to do something like that." He looked across the street toward the food tent and the trailers that had been moved there. "I took some great pictures when I was in Africa shooting my last movie." He thought for a couple seconds. "Hey, a few of them are in my trailer ... wanna see them?"

"Really?" Andi looked around, but no one seemed to be paying them any attention. "All right, I guess. We'll be right back?"

"Of course." He grinned at her and the two of them fell into a quick pace, headed toward base camp and the trailers lining the parking lot near the food tent.

As they walked, warning bells sounded in Andi's heart. Her parents would never approve of her going to base camp alone with Jake Olson, taking a look at something in his trailer. They'd be horrified to think she'd even consider the offer. But she let the warning bells fade against the backdrop of her beating heart. She was an adult, after all. If her dad wasn't filming his movie here, she wouldn't have her parents around to give their opinions about her decisions. It was broad daylight, and Jake needed to be back on set as soon as the current scene was shot. There wasn't enough time to get in any real trouble. What could happen if she walked across the street and looked at some pictures?

"What are you thinking about?"

"The movie," she lied. "My dad's giving me and my friend a few lines."

"Hmmm," he gave her a light bump with his shoulder. "Another pretty girl who wants to be an actress."

"I'm serious." Andi liked the diversion. "I had the chance to do a few projects at my high school last year. That and a class I took in California. There's something about being in front of the camera, allowing yourself to become the part." She felt magical just talking about it. "I love it."

"Me too." They reached the other side of the street and walked through the food tent toward the trailers. "Except for the paparazzi."

"Seems like they just found you this year." She gave him a sympathetic look. "Can't be easy having everyone watching."

"Especially when you fall for a girl." He slowed his pace and looked at her an extra beat. "It makes dating weird, you know?"

Andi couldn't begin to imagine. She felt more nervous the closer they got to his trailer, and by the time they stepped inside, she wondered if he could hear her heart thudding hard against her chest.

He crossed the small floor and true to his word he reached for a framed picture on a shelf near the window. In it was a picture of Jake and a small black boy with a torn white T-shirt. "That's JJ." Jake grinned at the photo. "I can't say his Nigerian name, so JJ's what I call him."

"He's cute."

"Our location shot wasn't far from where he lived. I had the chance to buy him a mattress before we left."

Andi felt a sense of admiration for Jake. "Most people wouldn't think about that, making sure the child has a bed."

"It wasn't fair he had to sleep on the ground."

The trailer was quiet inside, and suddenly Andi felt strangely awkward. What was she doing alone with Jake Olson in his trailer? She took a step back toward the door, just as her cell phone rang. She pulled it from her pocket and made a nervous face as she held it up. "My dad."

"Oops." Jake laughed as a way of showing empathy to Andi. But it came across as cavalier. Clearly he didn't care whether she was in trouble. "Forgot you needed to check in."

"No, I don't—he probably just wants to tell me when they're doing the scene I'm in." She clicked her phone open. "Hi, Dad."

"Where are you?" He sounded more worried than irritated. "I talked to Bailey. No one saw you leave."

"I'm at base camp with Jake. He wanted to show me something." She gave Jake a sheepish smile. "We're on our way back."

Her father's silence said more than his words ever could've. "I'll be watching for you."

"Okay." Andi snapped her phone shut and let it fall easily to her side. "Thanks for showing me the picture." She was shaking, she was so nervous. "I guess we should get back."

Jake didn't look like he was in a hurry to leave. He was as cool and collected as she was anxious. Then without warning, he reached for her hand and she gave a light gasp, jerking back as if she'd been burned.

"Hey, it's all right." Jake held up his hands in a show of innocence. "I was just reaching for your phone." His smile told her he thought she was very young and inexperienced. But even so he seemed interested. "I wanted to give you my number. That's all."

She was breathing fast, still terrified about the time she'd spent alone with him and ready to get back. Her dad was waiting for her, probably watching for her even now. But still she felt silly for thinking he intended to touch her.

"Well?" Jake's expression turned utterly harmless. "Can I give you my number?"

"Sure." Andi laughed at herself. "Sorry. It's a little weird being here."

"I know. I should've asked first." He took her phone and programmed his number into her contacts. "My turn ... can I have yours?"

Was this really happening? Jake Olson programming his number into her phone, and now asking for hers? She blinked twice. "Sure. Of course."

He handed her phone back and pulled his from his pocket. "Shoot."

She rattled off the number and then took a few steps toward the door. "They're probably looking for us."

"One thing." He leaned against the doorframe of the small trailer and searched her eyes. "The actress playing my girlfriend walked off the set today. They'll need a replacement." He took a step closer. "You should ask your dad if you can read for the part."

Andi was speechless at the thought. She only nodded and bit her lip. "Thanks ... I'll ... I'll ask him." She hadn't heard about the young actress, and now she couldn't feel her feet on the ground. The idea of getting the part was more than she could've dreamed.

On the way back, a quote from Rachel Baugher's book came to mind, one Andi had read a number of times: "God is more concerned with our character than our comfort." The words played over in Andi's head several times as she and Jake headed for the set. She wasn't sure how they applied in this situation, except that whatever acting God allowed her to do, she had to be careful of one thing.

That she didn't lose her character in the process.

Jake let his eyes find hers again as they neared the others. "It was nice spending time with you. Maybe we can take a trip to Lake Monroe one of these days. When they don't need me on the set as much."

"I'd like that." Her answer came without giving the situation even a moment's thought. She could feel her father's eyes watching her from fifty yards away. She smiled at Jake. "Talk to you later."

"I'll text you."

She gave him one last smile and then turned and ran lightly toward Bailey, who was still by the police tape talking with the group of spectators. Bailey flashed her a concerned look. "Where were you?" she whispered. "Your father was looking everywhere for you."

"I went with Jake." She could hear the excitement in her voice, and she allowed a quiet squeal. "I'll tell you about it later."

For now she didn't want to talk to her parents. They were still very much the missionaries they'd always been, very protective and old-fashioned in their views. They wouldn't for one minute understand her attraction to Jake. Besides, they were busy with the scenes taking place. Andi worked her way closer to the action so she could watch when Jake took his turn opposite Janetta Drake. His work was amazing, brilliant, even. He better get used to the paparazzi because he was going to be making powerful movies for decades to come.

When the take was finished, Andi looked across the field to Bailey. She liked her new roommate. Maybe this was the friend she'd always longed for, the one who would be like the sister she'd never had. She cared enough for Bailey that right now she didn't dare consider mentioning the attraction she'd had to Cody Coleman. There was something between Bailey and him, even if Bailey wouldn't admit it.

She angled her head and studied Bailey another few minutes. What was it about Bailey that made Andi feel jealous? Jealousy wasn't a feeling she was used to, whether that was because she'd grown up without peers to compare herself to, or because she'd never felt intimidated by another girl. Andi wasn't sure, but Bailey's eyes held something sweet and indescribable, something Andi had never seen in her own. A depth and confidence, a faith that knew no bounds. Whatever it was, the result made Bailey far more beautiful than she knew.

Andi was glad the situation with Cody never really came up. It didn't matter now. Her interest was no longer in Bailey's handsome friend, but in Jake Olson. *The* Jake Olson! She and Bailey were in the scene second from last that afternoon. The scene wasn't very long. The two of them would sit on a bench making idle conversation until Jake walked up and asked if they were in a certain math class. Andi would tell him yes, and he would ask if they'd seen the professor passing by a few minutes earlier. Bailey would say no, but that they weren't really looking, and that would be it. End of scene. Even so, being on the same set as Jake gave Andi chills every time their eyes met. The day couldn't have been any dreamier.

At least not until her dad pulled her aside as everyone was headed back to base camp. "Is it true?" Disappointment ran deep in his eyes.

"What?" She hadn't done anything wrong, so it was easy to keep her tone light.

"You went into Jake's trailer? The two of you by yourselves?"

Andi felt her cheeks growing hot. "Yes. Nothing happened." She made a dramatic sound, as if she couldn't believe he was even suggesting she'd behaved poorly. "He showed me a picture of a little Nigerian boy he met on his last movie shoot." She raised her brow so he'd know he'd overstepped his bounds by suspecting anything. "What'd you think we were doing, Daddy?"

"Listen, baby." He stopped and put his hands tenderly on either side of her face. "Jake's very experienced with girls. There's no other way to say it." He studied her eyes, her expression. "It's flattering, getting attention like that. But honey, please ... please be careful. You're a one-in-a-million girl. Jake isn't your type."

"Yes, Daddy." She nodded her agreement. "I'm sorry. I ... I didn't mean to worry you." She meant her apology, only because of the deep concern in his voice. They hugged, and then her dad went off to find her mom—who had walked back with Janetta Drake. Only after they were gone did Andi let herself experience the concern that came with having a crush on Jake Olson. Her father was right. Jake was used to getting his way with girls, which meant the two of them had nothing in common. But did she have to go through her whole life avoiding any type of temptation? Always staying on the safe side of the street?

She sighed and scrolled through her phone numbers until she saw his. She'd do well to ignore his calls or texts — if he even followed up with her. But while her common sense took charge, she felt an unfamiliar thrill taking root deep in her heart. The thrill of being inches away from a guy like Jake. Maybe he would be different with her. No matter what her common sense had to say, or however hard her faith tried to hold her back, she had a feeling about that strange and new thrill. A feeling that wasn't altogether bad.

That if she let it, this intoxicating thrill could consume her.

THE FILMING WAS FINISHED FOR THE day, and Bailey returned to her friends near the tape, the ones who had come out to watch. There was Ashley, the young mom she babysat for, and Ashley's sisters, Kari, Erin, and Brooke, and all their kids. Also Katy Hart Matthews, Dayne's wife. Katy had brought a few of the new CKT kids, so they'd have the chance to see an actual movie being filmed.

The whole thing took Bailey back. Just a few years ago, she, her mom, her brother, Connor, and Tim Reed were the ones on the other side of the tape while Dayne filmed a movie here.

"You did great today." Ashley put an arm around her shoulders and hugged her. "I still say we'll see you on the big screen someday."

"Not the big screen." Bailey made a polite face and then grinned at Katy. "I've seen how hard that life is. But maybe on a Broadway stage. That would be the best."

"Not so much scrutiny." Katy gave Bailey a hug too. "But Ashley's right. You were amazing. You have a gift, something that can't be taught."

"You really think so?" Bailey loved her time on the set.

"Thanks for introducing us to Lisa Ellison." Brooke was holding hands with her two little girls, Hayley and Maddie. "I guess our dad met her husband, Keith, at the hospital the other day."

"Everyone knows Dad from the hospital." Kari had her baby girl on her hip. "He's more famous than anyone in town."

"That's for sure." Erin grinned at her sisters.

"I heard something about that." Bailey nodded. "Is that what you were talking about with Lisa?"

"Yes." Ashley had Cole by her side, and she tousled his blond hair. "We invited them to join us for a Baxter dinner one of these Sundays while they're in town. I think it'd be good for them. Knowing people are praying for their success, and that they've got new friends in Bloomington."

"Definitely." Bailey loved the idea. "You should include Andi, so she'll have someone else to connect with once her parents return to Los Angeles."

"You'll have to come too." Katy smiled at her. "We don't see enough of you now that you're on campus."

The Baxter sisters and their sister-in-law Katy were so close. The group of them reminded Bailey of her own family, the way everyone around the dinner table was best friends with each other. She hoped she and her brothers were this close when they were married and raising kids of their own.

The Baxter girls rounded up their kids and bid their goodbyes. As they were leaving, Tim Reed drove up, climbed out of his car, and headed toward Bailey. "Don't tell me I missed it."

She giggled at the picture he made, hurrying toward her, disappointment shading his face. "Seriously? I hurried over here so I could see your big-screen debut and now I'm too late."

"They wrapped earlier than they expected." Bailey hugged him as he reached her. "You could feel God bringing things together today. Everything the producers tried to capture they got on the first or second take, and at a quality that everyone was talking about."

Most of the people had gone their own way by then, and though the police tape was still up, the scene was no longer something from a movie, but just another section of campus. Tim motioned to a bench nearby. "Can we sit there? I mean, since they're not filming."

"Of course." Bailey laughed as they moved to the spot and sat next to each other. "How was your day?"

"Honestly?" He looked troubled, like he had something very deep and important on his mind. "Something hit me today. I couldn't wait to talk to you."

She looked into his eyes, and she felt the confusion that had become a regular part of her life. Last night with Cody was amazing, but here ... with Tim beside her, she wasn't ready to let him go. What if Cody was right, and Tim really was better for her? Maybe Cody could see something about Tim's character, the way they were when they were together, that she hadn't quite figured out.

Tim took her hand, holding it the way he might hold a precious treasure. Without saying a word, he lifted her fingers to his lips, and with the lightest touch, he kissed them.

"Wow." She wasn't sure what to say. Butterflies filled her stomach, and she felt unsure of her next breath. "What's this all about?"

"I was in science and it hit me. I wasn't sure you really know how I feel about you." He took hold of her other hand too and slid closer so their knees were touching. "I always think there's time down the road for things to get serious, but then I thought about last night. There you were at Cru without me, and ... well, I talked to Daniel, the group leader."

"Daniel?" Bailey was baffled. "How do you know him?"

"He sits next to me in science."

Bailey had a feeling where this was going. "He told you I was there?"

"You and Cody Coleman." Tim let himself get lost in her eyes. "Cody walked you back to your dorm, right?"

"Right." She smiled sympathetically at him, but she didn't feel guilty. Their dating relationship wasn't exclusive, no parameters or boundaries. "We hadn't seen each other in a while."

"And that's fine, it's just ... I don't know, I guess I realized that if I'm not careful I could lose you." He hadn't shown this much emotion toward her since prom. He released one of her hands and brought his fingers to the side of her face. "I might not tell you often enough, but I care, Bailey. I care a lot. You're on my mind more than you know."

Bailey thought of all the times when she would've thought she was dreaming, hearing Tim Reed share his feelings this way. So where did that leave her? She searched his eyes, looking straight to the place in his heart that he was laying out for her. "I do wonder," her voice was softer than before, and she leaned in, her face inches from his. "Most of the time I'm not really sure how you feel. I mean ... you haven't kissed me since prom."

"Because I respect you." He smoothed his fingers down the side of her face and caught one of her long curls in his hands. "If I let myself get too physical with you, I won't want to stop. So I try to keep it light. Keep the pressure off for both of us."

Not only was that the right answer, it was an answer that acted like a road map to her undecided heart. Cody wasn't looking for more than a friendship, and here was Tim telling her that he cared enough to keep his distance. Wasn't that what she had prayed for in a guy all along?

"So ... you do care? I mean, really?" Bailey wanted to hear him tell her one more time. So she could convince herself later when she was alone and doubting that this moment ever happened.

"Of course I care. Bailey, you and me ... we grew up together. We shared the same stage and all the while I had feelings for you. There was always a reason I had to wait—either we were in the same show, or I was one of the directors. But now ... I can't let you go another day wondering how I feel." He leaned in, and for a long moment he touched his lips to hers. When he pulled away, his voice was different, his feelings for her wonderfully clear. "You're everything I've ever wanted in a girl, Bailey. Please know that."

"Thank you." His kiss still burned on her lips, and she wanted more than anything for him to kiss her again. But she wouldn't push the issue. If he was trying to respect her she could hardly make things more difficult for them. And now that she knew how much he wanted to kiss her, it made his kiss that much more meaningful.

"See ..." He looked dizzy, the same way she probably did. "I'd kiss you like that all the time, but," he sat up straighter and took a slow breath, "you deserve better than that."

Again her heart turned quiet somersaults. She didn't say anything, but she didn't have to. She had a feeling her eyes were doing all the talking for her. She could've guessed that Tim felt this way, but there was nothing more satisfying than having him tell her here, in this moment that would stay with her always.

Tim stood and helped her to her feet. "You have to go."

"I do." She was staying with her family again this weekend, and her mom was expecting her help for dinner. Slowly she came into his arms, easing her hands around his waist. Sometimes with Tim, she felt like her heart was never fully engaged. But that wasn't the case here, now.

Tim slipped his hands around her waist and pulled her close. "Be patient with me, okay. I want this to work."

"I know." She whispered against his face. "We're young. We need to take things slow."

"Exactly." He brushed a strand of hair off her cheek with his thumb. "I'll bet you were wonderful today. In your scene."

"Katy and the Baxter girls were here. They all said I did well." She grinned. "It wasn't even a full minute. I mean, big deal."

"It is a big deal." He kissed her again, this time not as long as before. "You're a big deal wherever you are, Bailey. But especially to me." He took a step back and walked with her toward the path that led to the parking lot where her car was. "Don't ever forget it, okay."

Bailey was telling him okay, that she would never again doubt his feelings, when on the distant path she spotted a guy who looked an awful lot like Cody. Yes, it was him. She was sure of it. His build and his hair color. She couldn't quite make out his face, but it was him, and he had clearly been watching them. Now that she was looking his way, he turned and kept walking without so much as a wave or a smile or a shout-out. Seeing him made Bailey's heart skip a beat, and because of her distraction, the goodbye she shared with Tim was brief and anticlimactic. Why couldn't she get Cody out of her heart?

The whole way home to her parents' house she was frustrated with herself. Here Tim had just bared his heart, telling her his true feelings and making her feel like a princess. Why then did it take just one glance at Cody to pull her from the moment? Now that she'd seen him she couldn't stop thinking of him, which made no sense whatsoever. She could tell herself that her feelings for Cody were different, more of a deep friendship, but then why was her reaction so strong at seeing him? Or maybe the truth was something she wasn't ready to admit even to herself.

That no matter how wonderful things were with Tim, a part of her would always be in love with Cody Coleman.

Fourteen

KEITH AND CHASE WERE WATCHING DAILIES in Chase's hotel room, amazed at what they were seeing. Word was getting out that *The Last Letter* was going to be a powerful film, and the producers were beside themselves with what the future might hold for their moviemaking. A reporter from *Entertainment Tonight* had even contacted them requesting a possible interview.

"I wish Lisa wasn't already asleep. I can't believe this stuff." Keith rewound a section and played it again. "This is crazy good."

"No wonder none of it has come easily." Chase's laugh revealed the weariness they both felt after such a long day.

Keith surveyed the list of scenes they'd wrapped and felt the gratitude overwhelm him. "All this and a whole day where no one else has threatened to walk off the set? It's enough to make me believe God's going to come through with the financing."

Chase gave a wary look. "Our best bet is to keep making up time. That'd be miracle enough."

It was the end of their first full week on location, and without question it was the best day so far. Never mind that the food truck had burned up, the guys were the happiest they'd been since they'd started filming. They made up lost ground by covering three additional scenes that afternoon, and the quality was truly magnificent. They still had a few details to work through, and now that they'd admired the day's work, Keith turned to his friend. "We need someone to replace Penny."

"I still can't believe she walked because she heard we were marketing this as a Christian film."

"It's just as well. Her attitude would've hurt the shoot." He realized as he had a number of times since the midday break, that the meeting he'd had with the cast and crew just might've brought about a solidarity among everyone, that had in turn caused them to give their best performances ever. "God works all things to the good for those who love Him, that's what I read this morning. If Penny's gone, she's gone. But we need to think about having the casting director send a few local choices in for a read sometime Monday morning."

"I hate starting over." Chase crossed his arms. "Any other ideas?"

"The part isn't that big, but still we need someone who knows what they're doing. The other actors deserve that much."

"Hey!" Chase's face lit up. "What about Andi or Bailey, her roommate? They're the right age."

The idea wasn't something Keith would've brought up. Andi had mentioned it to Lisa, but that didn't mean the idea was to be taken seriously. "I guess Jake Olson suggested as much to Andi this afternoon." He clicked on the scene with Bailey and Andi on the bench talking to Jake about his professor. They'd have to reshoot this piece if one of the girls won the part of Jake's girlfriend. But that would be a lesser problem than recasting the role at this late date.

Keith played the short scene three times through, and when he clicked the stop button after the third time, he wasn't sure he wanted to voice what he saw. Instead he looked at Chase. "Well... what'd you see?"

"Truthfully? I kept being drawn to Andi's roommate, Bailey."

That was exactly how Keith felt, but he hadn't wanted to say so. Especially when he felt like he was betraying his own daughter by feeling this way. "I saw it too." He rewound the clip one more time. "She's how I picture the part."

"Exactly." Chase scrutinized the scene. "Andi's gorgeous. She lights up the camera and everyone notices her when she walks in a room. Her day's coming. But Bailey ... there's a depth in her eyes that we need for this role."

"That's what it is, depth." Keith hid his disappointment that the girl with what looked like the greater depth, the greater internal makeup, was Bailey Flanigan and not his daughter. But he wasn't altogether surprised. Since Andi had made the decision to attend Indiana University, she hadn't been the same. Not that she'd crossed any lines, but he wasn't sure she was always making the wisest choices. It was why she had allowed herself to follow Jake Olson into his trailer when no one else was around.

"Should we give Bailey a read?" Chase stood and took the chair across from the bed. He crossed one leg over the other. "I think it's worth a shot."

"Definitely." Keith still had his concerns. "We'll need to pray about a few things, though."

"What's that?"

"That Jake keeps his distance from both girls, and that once I place the call tomorrow, Andi will forgive me."

"You're right." Chase sighed and ran his hand along the back of his neck. "We'll have to add those to the list."

Keith closed up his computer and stood. "Any word from the below-the-line union?"

"Not a word. The union should know better than to bug us now. With strikes in Hollywood and other problems, their people have to work, otherwise they won't be able to afford their dues." Chase's tone was a little sarcastic. "The union should be handling bigger issues. I'm guessing we're too small for them to mess around with."

"I hope so. As long as none of the crew tells someone from the union, they might not even be aware we're here filming."

"We're not doing anything illegal." Chase sounded frustrated. "The guys agreed to the contracts we gave them."

"The union wouldn't see it that way."

"Yeah, well ... God's got our back in that area. He knows we can only take so much." Chase put his hands behind his head and stretched out. "Did Lisa have a good day?"

"Great, actually." Keith was so glad she was here with him. Countless times today he'd drawn on her presence to help him. "I guess she met the family of that Dr. Baxter, the one who stitched up Jake. They convinced her we need to join them for a Sunday dinner before we leave town." He stretched his side one way and then the other. He hadn't gotten in his usual run for the past three days, and with everything so volatile on the set, he was missing the chance to unwind. "Hey, before I go ..." his tone was more serious than before. "Any other attempts by Rita? Or is she keeping her distance?"

"She's given up." Chase shook his head. "I made it pretty clear I wasn't interested."

"Just be careful. The devil wants to dance all over this movie. Every day it's something."

"Like we talked about, with mountains this big we can't even imagine the vistas on the other side." Chase smiled and pointed to Keith's computer. "Just look at the view He's already giving us."

Keith laughed. "It was a good day. Let's gain more ground tomorrow." He bid Chase goodnight and headed down the hall to his room. Along the way he started praying about tomorrow. For the cast and crew, for their safety and integrity, and for the pace they were keeping—that they'd continue to make progress. And most of all he prayed for his precious daughter.

That the news she was going to get in the morning wouldn't make her doubt herself or how very much he loved her. But that she'd let the experience and disappointment grow her so that one day soon, the girl with the deep eyes and breathtaking inner beauty wouldn't be someone else.

But rather his own sweet Andi.

CHASE WASN'T QUITE READY TO TURN in for the night. It was still only nine o'clock back home and he wanted to tell Kelly about the events of the day, the great way the week had ended even with everything that had gone wrong. He grabbed his hotel key and cell phone and took the elevator down to the lobby.

He poured a cup of coffee and took the familiar spot by the fireplace. Kelly picked up on the second ring. "What, no video chat this time?" She sounded relaxed and grateful for his call.

"I'm having coffee in the lobby." He settled back in a leather armchair on the other side of the fireplace. "I couldn't wait to hear your voice. You won't believe the day we've had." He told her everything, from the burned up food truck to the meeting Keith had with the cast and crew. "You should've heard him, boldly telling everyone that the movie wasn't Christian, but we were, and how he hoped the message of the film would change lives around the world."

"Lisa was there, right?"

"She was. I wish you were here too. There was Keith, smiling at everyone, facing a walkout by half his cast, and he tells them that if they want to know more about a relationship with Jesus Christ, they know where to come."

"A walkout?" Kelly was clearly trying to keep fear from her voice, but she seemed to have just understood the gravity of the situation.

"The buzz was that if the movie was a Christian project, several of the key actors were going to leave. One of them — a supporting actress — left before the meeting. We're looking to replace her with Andi's roommate."

"My goodness, Chase." She laughed, but she sounded more dazed than amused. "You're right. That's some day."

Chase took a drink from his coffee and stared into the fire. "But Kelly ... you should see what we got today. The actors outdid themselves the last half of the day. Especially Janetta Drake and Jake Olson. Amazing work."

Their conversation shifted to Kelly and the girls. Molly had a cold and Macy had tripped and skinned her knee. "We all miss you." Kelly's voice was upbeat again. "You still thinking about coming home next weekend? For a day or so?"

Chase didn't see how he could—not with their schedule being what it was, but he wanted to try. "I'll let you know the closer we get." They talked a few more minutes about life back home, and Chase finished his coffee. "I better turn in. Call's early again tomorrow. Seven a.m." He told her he loved her and asked her to give the girls hugs and kisses for him.

When he hung up, he sat by the fire a few more minutes, thanking God for the truth from James that morning, and how the message had impacted everything about the day, how the theme kept recurring—only what was eternal lasted. He smiled at the goodness of God, tossed his cup in the trash can, and headed for his room. He yawned as he slid the key in the door, but as he opened it he jerked back. It took a few seconds to register what he was seeing, but there, sitting in the chair near his bed, was Rita Reynolds.

"How'd you get in here?" Chase's heart was beating hard. He'd never opened a hotel room to find someone had broken in like this.

Rita wore tight workout pants and a tank top. She held up a key. "Keys are easy to get, Chase. Much easier than you are." She tossed it on the table and smiled. "Night managers believe anything."

The situation was so outrageous, Chase wasn't sure what to say. "You don't belong here." He held open the door and waited. "Get out."

"Hold on." She crossed her arms, her expression a little more tame. "I have a question about tomorrow's shoot. This seemed like a good place to talk."

Chase didn't believe her for a minute. "We can talk tomorrow. Over breakfast on the set."

Rita studied him. "You're really not going to shut the door and come here? You won't let me stay and talk with you?"

"No." Chase was still trying to believe she'd actually done this, that she'd gotten a copy of his key from the manager and was sitting here in his room. "I'm married, Rita. I don't entertain women in my hotel room." He allowed his tone to relax some. "I know you'll be shocked by this, but not even you."

She stood and stretched. "I had a good workout. The weight room here is good for a hotel." Once more she stretched, and as she did her tan flat stomach became visible below her tank top.

Chase refused to stare. "Rita. I'm serious." He pointed out the door. "Leave."

She walked toward him on her way out. When she was only inches from him, she stopped and looked deep into his eyes. "You don't know what you're missing, Chase. Good Christian boy that you are." She put her hand loosely on his waist. "I watch you all day, Chase. You're the hottest producer I've ever been around. What's wrong with a little time getting to know each other?"

There was no temptation for Chase when it came to Rita Reynolds. But here, with her so close, he could smell the mint on her breath, see how it could happen, how a guy with the strongest convictions and faith could make a series of small compromises and wind up with a giant moral failure. He swallowed and pressed himself back against the wall. "The only woman I want to know that well is my wife." He smiled, unwavering, his words clear and purposeful. "Goodnight, Rita."

She stood on her tiptoes and kissed him on the cheek. "Goodnight, handsome." She shrugged one shoulder as if to say the loss was his. "I'll look for you tomorrow at breakfast."

He held out his hand. "My key?"

A bit of laughter sounded between her lips. "Okay." She dropped the key card in his hand. "But there are more where that came from."

"Listen," he wanted to make himself very clear. "I'm serious, Rita. Don't do this again. My room's off limits."

Her smile told him she wasn't exactly dissuaded by his request. "Let me know if you change your mind. I think we'd both enjoy getting to know each other better."

She finally left and he shut the door quickly, sliding the chain lock across and walking slowly to the edge of the bed. Was she that used to having her way with men, any man she wanted? Or was that the way things played out on most movie sets? He'd heard of starring actors finding their way into a relationship on the set — married or not. But for Rita to sneak into the room of her producer? That had to happen about as often as a food truck burning to the ground.

He pulled his Bible from the nightstand and read once more from James, chapter 1. No doubt they'd had more than their share of trials and temptations thrown at them. This last one was almost laughable. But God's Word was true, and Chase clung to that as he brushed his teeth and settled in. *Consider it pure joy whenever you face trials of many kinds ...* He could be angry at Rita and frustrated by the delays that morning. Fear could've dominated his night, knowing that the cast had even considered walking out. But given the events of the day, the trials of many kinds, and the wisdom in the book of James, there was only one emotion Chase allowed himself to feel as he fell asleep that night.

Pure joy.

ANDI DROVE OUT TO BAILEY'S HOUSE Saturday morning in the pouring rain so the two of them could study for a few hours. That and she wanted to meet Bailey's family, all those brothers she talked about. As she pulled up, she slowed her car and stared. If this was Bailey's house, then no wonder she wanted to come home for the weekend. Andi couldn't understand why she ever would've wanted to live on campus if she had the option of living here.

She turned into the driveway and came slowly past a series of manicured trees and bushes to the circular drive in front of a long covered porch. Three porch swings dotted the stretch on the right side of the front door, and Andi could imagine sitting out here on summer nights watching the sunset. She parked and came to the door.

Bailey answered it, her eyes sparkling. "You're in time! Dad made his famous pancakes!" Bailey's father coached the Indianapolis Colts, but the team was home this weekend and next. "The whole family loves when Dad's here for the weekend. Come on in."

"Wow." Andi walked through the door and stopped, taking in the chandelier and sweeping staircase. "You didn't tell me you lived in a resort."

"It's just a house." Bailey laughed as she took hold of Andi's hand and led her down a short hallway into the largest kitchen ever. "Come meet everyone else."

Sitting around the kitchen bar were Bailey's brothers — Connor, who was at least six-foot-two, Shawn, BJ, Justin, and Ricky. Three of the boys — Shawn, BJ, and Justin — were adopted from Haiti. Andi already knew that about Bailey's family from pictures she had in the dorm. But it was great meeting all the boys in person. In no time Andi and the Flanigans were caught up in conversations about college life, the movie Andi's dad was shooting, and the boys' football season.

"Justin scored five touchdowns last week," said Ricky. He was the youngest, with light blond hair and big blue eyes. "You shoulda' seen him, Andi." He tried to squeeze in between Andi and Bailey, anxious for her to hear the details. "It was the middle school championship game and on the second play Justin gets an interception and runs it all the way back." Ricky held up three fingers. "Three rushing touchdowns, and two interceptions run back for scores. Unbelievable, huh?"

Andi raised her eyebrows at thirteen-year-old Justin. "I wish I could've seen it."

He shrugged, embarrassed over the big deal his little brother had made. "That's okay. It's just middle school."

Ricky pumped his fist in the air. "Yeah, but wait till next year. You have to come to a game, okay?"

The boys continued to share stories and questions, and after Bailey's parents came down, Andi understood even better why Bailey wanted to be home over the weekends. Her family was amazing, her parents kind and strong in their faith, and clearly in love with each other. Bailey had said that her mother was her best friend, and after sitting near her at breakfast, Andi could see the bond the two of them had. The size of the house was long forgotten.

Andi was happy for her friend, for the life she had here with her family. But being with the Flanigans underlined Andi's restlessness, her desire to be something other than a missionary's daughter. If her parents had held normal jobs, they might've had other kids and Andi would've had siblings — a big family like this, even. Instead she'd missed out on every kind of traditional family time they might've had. It was one more reason she wanted to find her own way now, so that she could branch out and maybe discover aspects of life that she'd missed out on.

"You want to be an actress, is that right?" Jenny Flanigan's smile was warm and understanding, and it drew her from her wandering thoughts.

"Yes, ma'am. I'd like that." Andi remembered what Jake had said about her reading for the part of his girlfriend. "There might be an opportunity for me to have an actual role in my dad's film." She flashed excited eyes at Bailey. "We'll find out this weekend."

"Katy Hart lived here when she was an actress." BJ had just taken a full bite of pancakes and his words weren't close to clear.

"Finish your food first." Jim Flanigan was flipping another batch, but he looked over his shoulder at his son. "This isn't men's town."

"Sorry." BJ covered his mouth and kept chewing.

Andi giggled and gave Bailey a curious look. "Men's town?"

"That's when mom and I are gone." Bailey plugged her nose. "You don't want to know what goes on in men's town."

The boys all chuckled and Ricky giggled until his cheeks turned red. "Men's town isn't for girls."

"No." Andi grinned at Jenny. "Be sure to let me know when it's men's town around here. I'll stay at the dorm."

"Anyway," BJ's mouth was empty now, "Katy Hart lived here when she was an actress."

Andi was still putting the pieces of Bailey's life together. "Katy Hart, the one who's married to Dayne Matthews?"

"Right." Bailey smiled.

"I watched a lot of it play out in the tabloids. Not that I read them, but in the supermarket, you know, the headlines tell you a lot."

"A lot of lies for the most part." Jenny exchanged a look with Jim. "It's a miracle Katy and Dayne survived the way the press treated them."

The breakfast continued, with so much laughter and conversation, Andi again found herself wishing for a family like this one. Her parents were wonderful, but being an only child had never felt so lonely. By the time they moved into the living room to do their homework, Andi was sure of one thing. After this she was going to spend as much time at Bailey's house on the weekends as she could.

They set up in front of an oversized fireplace in a room that had floor-to-ceiling windows along one entire wall. Bailey flipped a switch that brought the gas flames to life, and then settled into the corner of a cushy-looking sofa. Andi sat on the floor so she could spread out her history notes. She and Bailey were the only two freshmen in the class, and they needed to put in a few hours to catch up.

Before they started, Andi looked around. "I can't believe this is where Dayne Matthews fell in love with Katy Hart. That's so cool."

Bailey shrugged. "They're just normal people like you and me."

"Still ... I mean, how great that Katy was just this small-town drama director and next thing you know she's married to America's most popular actor." She lowered her voice, the excitement in her heart building. "It'd be like me marrying Jake Olson."

"Except Dayne was a changed guy by the time he started dating Katy." She gave Andi a wary look. "Jake ... he seems a little wild for you, don't you think?"

"Not at all. He was nice yesterday. I mean, Bailey, like you said, you can't believe everything you read." She wanted her friend to feel good about her attraction to Jake. "Anyway, I think I could fall for him. I guess we'll see if he calls."

Bailey was scouring her history book, but she nodded absently. "The test is on all of chapter 5, right?"

"And part of 6." Andi had her book too, and she found the same section Bailey was opened to.

"Hey, so have you seen Cody again? Since Thursday's Cru meeting?"

"Nope." Andi hadn't thought much about Cody since meeting Jake, but now that Bailey brought him up she wanted to get to the bottom of her friend's feelings for the guy. Andi leaned her elbow on the edge of the sofa and peered at Bailey. "Why do you ask?"

"Just wondered. You two seemed like you were getting along pretty well when I showed up."

Andi tried to discern even a little jealousy in Bailey's tone, but there was none. She let her guard down some. "He's very good looking, I'll give him that." Andi looked off into the fire. "I sort of thought maybe you liked him."

"I'm dating Tim." Bailey's answer was quick. She lifted smiling eyes toward Andi. "Cody and I are only friends. That's all we'll ever be."

"Really? I mean, you and Tim are doing that great?"

Bailey's eyes danced in the light of the fire. The rain was coming down harder outside, and the sky was so dark with clouds, it almost felt like nightfall. "We had an intense talk yesterday. If things keep going this way, then I'll have to say yes."

"Yes?" Andi kept her voice low, despite the thrill in her tone. "Yes to what?"

"To your question, goofy." Bailey giggled. "You know, the one about how Tim and I are doing. And maybe yes to your other question." Bailey raised her brow. "You know, the one about being in love."

"Oh, that." Andi made an exaggerated wipe of her hand across her forehead. "I thought you were making some sort of announcement."

"Not hardly. That's forever away." Bailey tapped her open book. "Okay, we better get serious here."

They were fifteen minutes into outlining chapter 5 when Andi's phone rang. She pulled it from her pocket and flashed a quick look at the caller ID. Her dad! "Okay, here goes." She sat up on her knees and fought the nervousness that had suddenly come over her. "My parents have been in a meeting all morning deciding if I can read for the part of Jake's girlfriend." She took a quick breath and snapped open her phone. "Hi, Dad ... so what's the verdict? Can I have a shot?"

Her father's hesitation told her that whatever they'd decided, the news couldn't be good. "Listen, honey, Chase and I talked it over last night and again this morning. Your mom was in on today's talk, and all of us agree with our decision." He paused.

"Which is what?" Andi lowered her head close to her knees, desperate for the news.

"Well, we watched the dailies from yesterday. A dozen times at least, and we've decided we're going to let Bailey read for the part."

Slowly Andi rose up onto her knees again. Her eyes found Bailey's and she shook her head, clearly conveying that she wasn't going to read for the part. Bailey shot her a quick look of sympathy, and Andi appreciated the genuine way she cared. Not for a minute did Bailey think the reason Andi wasn't going to read for the part was because the producers wanted her instead. Her reaction was that of a true friend, and Andi had never cared more for her than she did right now.

Her father was going on, trying to explain himself. "God has great plans for you, Andi. We all know that. You have something very special, and that will come across on the big screen someday if that's God's will for your life. There'll be other opportunities. But right now ... I don't know honey, I can only tell you to keep God first. That way He'll open those doors when the time is right."

"Okay."

"You're disappointed, I know. But try to understand. We had to think of the movie first, and Bailey ... she has something we're looking for in this character."

"It's all right." Andi could hear in her father's voice that this was as hard for him as it was for her. She didn't want him to feel bad, so she kept her tone as understanding as she could. "Don't worry about it, Daddy. It's just one part. Like you said, there'll be others."

Again her father hesitated. "Are you at the Flanigans' house right now?"

"I am." She gave Bailey another sad smile. "Her dad made us pancakes and we're about to study history."

"Would you mind too much, honey, if I talked with Bailey for a minute? We'd like to see her later today, so that if she's going to work out we can film her scenes Monday afternoon."

Andi fought hard against the urge to be jealous of Bailey. She had that beautiful confidence, that strong sense of knowing who she was, a wonderful family, and connections in the movie industry, and now this — the part Andi had dreamed of having. Even so, she couldn't be mad at Bailey. None of this was her fault, and anyway, they were already too close for that. Andi thanked her dad for trying. She told him she loved him and asked him to hold on.

Then she looked at Bailey and tried to feel happy for her. "Here. My dad wants to talk to you." And as she passed the phone over, Andi felt the beginning of real happiness for Bailey. Because Bailey was her new best friend, and best friends didn't get jealous of each other or begrudge the other for finding success. They celebrated every victory together.

And this was only the first of many Andi hoped they shared.

Fifteen

CHASE COULD FEEL GOD'S COVERING, HIS protection as they breezed through the first two days of the next week. Bailey's reading went brilliantly, and Chase and Keith marveled at how natural she was in front of a camera. Not that they were completely surprised. She'd been trained by Katy Hart, after all—another very natural acting talent. Bailey would do her scenes Friday, and possibly one or two days the following week. Chase and Keith had shuffled the order of the scenes to streamline their production some. So far the move was working. They were only a day behind now, instead of two or more. Every day cost tens of thousands of dollars, and though Keith kept working his contact list, especially trying to contact investor Ben Adams, nothing had come through yet. It was imperative that they get as much done every day as possible.

They were just wrapping up a scene between Rita and Jake, and a few of the grips were whispering close to Chase, agreeing that there was something special happening with this movie. The takes they were getting were the sort of stuff that showed up at big-time award shows. Chase couldn't think about the possibility. All he could ask for was that God would get them through the filming before they ran out of money.

The scenes today were at a restaurant and across the street at a park. Chase watched the scene underway, and when his assistant director yelled, "Cut," Chase was the first to clap. "Beautiful work, guys. Check the gate."

Rita and Jake came out of the restaurant, laughing with each other and looking slightly worn out. Someone handed Rita a hand towel and she ran it along the back of her neck. "It's like a sauna in there," she announced to the crew standing around. She winked at Jake. "Either that, or Mr. Olson here's a little too hot."

He chuckled again and patted her back. "You were amazing." He nodded toward the snack table across the street. "I'll get you a bottle of water."

Chase watched the two of them and concern bubbled to the surface. Rita was in her mid-thirties. Certainly she wasn't interested in her twenty-four-year-old co-star. He made a mental note to talk to Keith about the two of them, just to make sure everyone stayed above board. He smiled to himself. Above the line, the way he and Keith were determined things on their shoot would be.

Rita caught his eye as she walked by. Her eyes flirted with him and mocked him at the same time. "You missed your chance, Chase."

"Come on, Rita. Leave Jake alone. He's a kid." Chase kept his tone easygoing. He had no authority to tell Rita who she could and couldn't be interested in. "Let's keep character a priority, okay?"

She stopped and positioned herself as close to him as she could. "I'm a professional, don't worry." She started to walk away, but she tossed a final eyebrow raise at Chase. "I'll say this. Jake's definitely not a kid." She laughed as she walked toward the snack table. Chase released an exasperated sigh and tried not to let her attitude bother him. As long as she didn't create a scandal, she was right—her decisions were her own.

Keith came up beside him, talking low so that only Chase could hear him. "She's hitting on Jake now, huh?"

"I don't know. If she steps out of line, maybe you could talk to her. With me, she thinks it's personal."

"I'll take care of it if things get out of hand."

"Thanks." Chase was about to ask whether Keith thought they could get one or two more scenes shot before lunch, when around the corner a caravan of three shiny black Suburbans pulled into view and came to a screeching stop on the road in front of the restaurant. "What's this?" Chase moved a few steps closer to the vehicles. Panic quickly closed in around him as he stared at the Suburbans. "They've got picket signs."

"I don't like the looks of it." Keith crossed his arms, stationed right next to Chase. Neither of them mentioned the below-the-line union, and whether this could be their representatives coming to attack their filming. But as two dozen men spilled out of the Suburbans, shouting about unfair working conditions and waving a variety of different-sized picket signs, there was no need to guess what was happening. This was their worst nightmare come true.

The union had come to shut them down.

A stunned sense of shock came over the set, but as the below-the-line guys realized what was happening, they gathered grumbling around Chase and Keith. One of the more outspoken cameramen turned to his co-workers and pointed at picketers, anger flashing in his eyes. "Who called them? Don't be a coward, step forward so we can all see who did it."

No one came forward.

The twenty-some men from the union marched like a group of bullies toward the front of the restaurant and made a line that blocked the doorway. Chase couldn't believe what was happening. "They can't do this," he hissed at Keith, who was still at his side, still just as disbelieving.

"It looks like they already have." Keith seemed to know more about the union. But before he could share any information with Chase, a guy who must've been the leader came forward.

He was a thin guy, not how Chase would've pictured him. But what he lacked in stature, he made up for in attitude. "I assume you're the producers?"

Keith reached out to shake the man's hand. "I'm Keith Ellison. This is my co-producer, Chase Ryan."

The guy stared at Keith's hand and chuckled. "Save your handshake." He crossed his arms. "I'm Larry Fields, president of the Indiana chapter of the below-the-line union. It's come to our attention that you're making a movie here, paying our below-the-line guys less than union wages."

"This is an independent film with a very limited budget." Keith waved at the group of crew members gathered around him. "These men agreed to work for a fair wage, if slightly less than what union work would usually pay."

"Working conditions here are great," one of the grips yelled at the union boss. "Get lost and let us work!"

A chorus of shouts followed, with a number of the crew reiterating the sentiment, telling the union guy he wasn't wanted or needed. "Go resolve Hollywood's problems if you want something to do. We need work," an electrician yelled.

"Yeah, leave us alone!"

"This isn't about us!"

"Get out of here."

The ruckus grew, the crew practically ready to force the picketers back to their vehicles. Chase felt his emotions swell. They were in trouble this time, big trouble. But at least the crew was on their side. He studied the group and wondered which of them had made the call. It had to be someone, otherwise the union wouldn't have found out about the film in the first place.

Larry Fields sneered at them and waited for the crowd to quiet. "You might want to check your union handbooks, friends. When you join, you agree to let us handle the working conditions." He chuckled, and the sound was just short of sinister. "That's what we're about to do here. Handle the working conditions."

Chase started to say something, but Keith held his hand up, stopping him. Instead he directed a kind, quieter voice to the union boss. "This isn't a union job. The crew knew that when they signed on." He smiled as if maybe that might be all it would take to clear up the problem and send the union reps back to wherever they'd come from.

Again Larry chuckled. "Well then, my friend, you've got yourself a problem. Because the crew you picked for your little low-budget picture is a union crew. Every one of them." He raised his voice and directed this next part to the grumbling crew members. "Let me make one thing very clear. We've set up a picket line against any further production of this movie. If you choose to cross the picket line and work, you'll lose your union cards." He pointed harshly at them. "And I'll personally see to it that you don't work another day in this business."

Chase was horrified. This wasn't representation. It was blackmail. Strong-armed bullying tactics designed entirely to benefit the union — not the workers. As long as the job was non-union, the leaders couldn't take a cut of the crew's wages. If it became a union film, these men would benefit financially. That had to be the only reason they were here. That, and because one crew member had felt the need to place a phone call to the union.

The cast had joined the group gathered around Keith and Chase, and Jake Olson shouted at the union leader. "No one's unhappy, go away!"

"You're happy." Larry volleyed right back. "You're making union wages."

"Below-the-line's on strike because of you clowns." Jake thrust out his chest, not willing to back down. "How're they supposed to eat if you won't let them work?"

Larry laughed again. "Throw a fit, Mr. Movie Star. We're not going anywhere." His smile was proud and arrogant as he turned and crossed the parking lot toward the restaurant to join the others. The place had been closed down for the day because Keith and Chase had paid for the privilege to have it all to themselves.

Now it wasn't quite noon and the union had given them an ultimatum they couldn't do anything about.

Chase started walking toward the picket line, but Keith grabbed hold of his arm. "Be careful. If we get through this, it'll be because we reach common ground. Remember that."

"Thank you." Chase wanted to scream at his friend. Of course he knew they needed to find common ground, but he refused to let a bunch of union thugs intimidate him. "Come with me. So I don't lose it." He held his head high, and together with Keith, they walked to the middle of the picket line where Larry Fields was now holding a sign of his own. The sign read, "Producers of *The Last Letter* use unfair work conditions!" Chase was blown away by the thoroughness of their attack. When had they had time to make up signs specific to this movie set? He glanced at a few of the other signs. Two read, "Unfair Conditions," and several said simply, "STRIKE!"

Chase stood facing Larry, hating everything about this. "What do you want, Fields? What're your demands?"

"Like we said," Keith added. "We're a low-budget production. If it weren't for strikes in Hollywood, we couldn't have offered this job to these guys. But you heard them. They want to work. They're very happy and they're getting paid."

Larry ignored that. Instead he directed his words to Chase. "We want every below-the-line guy at union pay starting today, and we want back wages paid by Friday. On top of that, we want you to increase your medical insurance in case of an accident."

Chase might as well have run straight into a tree. He struggled to take a full breath, because what Larry was telling them was better said this way: The movie was finished. Paying the crew union wages and back pay would reach a six-figure number in no time, money they didn't have and couldn't raise. They'd already proved that this past week with every closed door Keith ran into. No one was investing in their film, and unless they continued to make up time, they would run out of money before they finished shooting.

The union boss was waiting, but there wasn't anything Chase or Keith could say in response to the demands. Chase worked to keep a wrap on his temper. "Very well then, you'll be hearing from our attorney." It was some way to save face in the sense that, like it or not, negotiations for the ransom of their film had already begun. But as Chase and Keith walked back to the nervous-looking cast and crew, neither of them had a clue what sort of announcement to make. Chase nodded to Keith. If anyone could keep panic from breaking out, it was him. He'd already proved that once on this set.

"Okay, listen up." Keith cupped his hands around his mouth. "The union doesn't have a right to shut us down like this, but we're going to need a lawyer to get things back on track." The only sign that he was nervous was the pace of his words. Of course no one could blame him for talking fast. The minutes were ticking away with the entire production at a sudden and sickening standstill. "Everyone go to lunch and we'll update you as soon as we know something."

The faces among the cast and crew reflected the emotions exploding inside Chase. Anger and fear, sorrow and frustration. All of them seemed grateful for a reason to turn their backs on the picketers and head across the parking lot to their base camp. Chase kept his pace even with Keith's. "Okay, so what lawyer? The last time we talked to a lawyer we were writing up contracts."

"I have an idea." He was sorting through his wallet, looking for a business card. "I'm calling Dr. Baxter."

"The guy who treated Jake?" Chase wanted a solution immediately. He didn't see where this would get them.

"Yeah, and Dayne Matthews' father." Keith stopped and motioned for Chase to stay close. The cast and crew passed by them, talking in small groups of three and four, their anger over the incident evident in their tone and body language. When they had more privacy, Keith pulled out his cell phone and dialed a number from the back of the business card. A quick conversation and explanation ensued, and Keith was making a second call, this one to Dayne. Again the call didn't last long, but when Keith hung up he was smiling. "Dayne's on his way down. He wants to encourage the cast and crew."

"What else?" Chase tapped his foot on the asphalt. The sun was out, and he squinted at his friend. "Did he know of an attorney?"

"Yes." Keith was already making the call. "His brother Luke's an entertainment attorney. Dayne said he'll cover his fee, whatever it is."

Chase paced a few feet away and stared into the clear blue. He drew his first full breath since the Suburbans pulled up. *God ... You're with us ... we can feel You. Please, get us through this nightmare. We're in way over our heads.*

I am with you, my son ... I know the plans I have for you ... plans to prosper you and not to harm you, plans to give you hope and a future.

God's mercy so overcame him that he nearly fell to his knees. Tears filled his eyes and he blinked them back. This was their key Scripture verse, the one that the movie was supposed to illustrate. God had good plans for His people. But here, with the insanity that was playing out across the street, Chase had all but forgotten the truth. He breathed another thank-you toward heaven and turned to see Keith in a serious conversation.

When he hung up, his tone was the most confident it had been in the past half hour. "Luke Baxter feels very strongly about this. He can help us, but he works out of Indianapolis and he's in court today. The soonest he can be here is three o'clock. In the meantime, he doesn't want us talking to the union, not without representation."

Chase exhaled and felt his shoulders slump forward. "We'll lose the whole day."

"At least." Keith slung his arm around Chase's shoulders and the two headed toward base camp. "God is with us, we have to believe it now just like we did back in the jungle."

"I know." Chase remembered the verse again. "It'll be okay. Somehow it'll work out."

Dayne Matthews pulled up in a Dodge truck not long after Chase and Keith reached the lunch area. He said hello to a few of the actors, people he obviously knew. His presence caused a buzz among the cast and crew and lent a general positive feeling to the afternoon.

He found Chase and Keith and introduced himself. "I'm sorry I didn't make it out sooner. We're getting things going for our fall production at CKT." They talked about kids and Bloomington and Dayne's decision to take time away from making movies. "But I want you both to know we completely support what you're doing. My wife and I, my family, we've been praying for you, believing that God will work mighty things out of this movie."

"Until this." Chase didn't want to sound defeated, but the tick of the clock in his mind was so loud he could barely think. "Have you seen this happen before?"

"I've heard about it." Dayne's look was more concerned than before. "It depends on their goal. If they just want more money, usually you and your lawyer find the funds somewhere and they walk away, happy. But if they're trying to make an example out of you, teach you a lesson for using union workers in a non-union film, they can be pretty mean." His smile was filled with empathy. "I can tell you this — you've got the best lawyer in the business."

Chase and Keith thanked him for his help and Dayne promised to check back in as the ordeal played out. When he was gone, Keith dismissed the cast and crew and told everyone to be on call for the morning. Just in case. After that, he and Chase withdrew to the production trailer to do the only thing they could do until Luke Baxter arrived.

Beg God for a miracle.

NEGOTIATIONS STARTED AT FOUR O'CLOCK THAT day and broke at ten for the night. As far as Keith could tell, they hadn't made much progress, but Luke Baxter was staying overnight at his father's house, committed to stick with the process until they reached a breakthrough.

The issue was simple, for as complex and heated as the arguments in the production trailer had become. Larry and three of his cronies from the union were unmoved in their demands, insisting on full union wages and complete back pay. Luke had gone round and round with them, trying to talk reason into the situation. Keith and Chase had given him full access to their accounts and financing, so they could dispel what Larry had already suggested—that this was in fact a big-budget film because of Rita Reynolds and Jake Olson. The books told the real story. For very minimal union pay, the two actors had agreed to star in this project because they believed in it.

"Everything is not dependent on money," Luke eloquently told the union reps. "Even in Hollywood."

Larry and his team looked over the finances, but still they were skeptical. "There's more money somewhere. There always is." He leaned back and tried to assume a friendly air. "I only want what's coming to my people. Fair wages, nothing more."

Of course, he really wanted more than that—the additional insurance and back pay. But all of his demands were irrelevant, because the truth was, they didn't have the money.

When they were on a break, Luke pulled Keith and Chase aside. "To be honest, I talked with Dayne about putting in money as an investment, but his funds are tied up until March."

Keith was touched that Luke would even ask his brother. It wasn't something he or Chase would've considered.

"Dayne told me he would've offered when he met you in person, but his financial advisor saw the unstable market looming and had him invest in some longer term savings. By the time March comes, it'll be too late for you."

"We need more money, that's for sure. But even then it isn't right that we pay these guys what the union wants. This crew agreed to their contract, and they're good wages."

Luke whistled. "Very high for a non-union job."

"And they weren't working anyway." Chase looked beat, defeated by the hours of talks. Already he'd told the cast and crew they wouldn't be needed until lunchtime tomorrow. And that was if everything went very well in the morning. "What time do we start up again?"

"Let's be here at eight. That's the earliest the union reps are willing to meet."

The night was a restless one, with Keith's wife, Lisa, up at different times, unable to sleep. "I need to pray more than I need to sleep," she told Keith. "Don't worry about me."

At eight the next morning they were gathered around the table again and Larry started the dialogue. "We're not going anywhere. I have twenty guys willing to picket around the clock if they have to. Those are union workers and they should get union wages."

"That's not what they agreed to ..." Luke had a copy of the below-the-line contracts for each of the crew in a large folder. He slid it across the table. "Take a look, Mr. Fields. A producer can't ask for more than a worker's word. And they each gave their word in writing — agreeing to work for the pay being offered."

"They never checked with us." He swapped a look with his men. "Union workers take union jobs. Every one of them stands to lose their card at this point, and that means they're finished in this industry."

Keith hated when Larry talked about pulling the union cards of the crew. There weren't enough non-union films around for the cameramen and electricians and grips to make a living. Larry was right. Without their cards, they were finished. He felt his stomach twist in knots and he leaned back in his seat, helpless to do anything but listen and pray.

The hours passed slowly, and after lunch Keith made one more call, giving the cast and crew the rest of the day off and again telling them to be ready for a morning shoot. This time the DP had a request. "Tomorrow's Friday. The cast wants to know if they should just take a three-day weekend—unpaid—and show up again on Monday."

"No." Keith was slightly tempted by the unpaid offer, but once his cast spread out and left town, the chances of getting everyone back together again Monday would be very small. "We have to work this through. Something will give today, I promise you. Tell everyone we'll shoot tomorrow and Saturday, so we can catch up. They all agreed to work two Saturdays—so this will be one of them."

Even as he said the words, Keith had no idea how they would make up the time they were losing, or how working Saturday would help even a little. They could afford to pay the crew this week and next, but after that? He came back into the room of negotiations and struggled to keep his head up. All he wanted to do was find a quiet place in the woods somewhere and cry out to God, beg Him for a miracle meeting of the minds between Luke Baxter and Larry Fields.

Instead he sat down next to Chase and watched the hours slip away. Sometime around five o'clock, both sides broke for dinner, with plans to talk all through the night if that's what it took. Larry and his team wanted to go over each individual contract and the entire set of financials. "It could take us all night," Luke warned them. "We'll need lots of coffee."

Before they met back for what figured to be a marathon session of negotiations, Keith placed a call to Lisa. "I feel drugged, like I'm playing the role in some bad movie without any sign of resolution."

"Honey, I'm so sorry." Lisa sounded like she'd been crying. "I want to help, but there's nothing I can do except pray."

"That's exactly what we need, baby. God knows what's happening here."

"But you've been talking with these people all day and all last night. What more could there be to say?"

"Luke's handling it. He's amazing, and to think Dayne's covering his fees. We're in great hands, but meanwhile our cast is losing interest hanging out in Bloomington. We need to reach an agreement tonight."

Lisa was quiet for a moment, and then she drew a sharp breath. "I have an idea. There's power in numbers, especially when it comes to praying. I think I'll call my new friends—and see if any of them would like to meet me somewhere to pray. If we raise enough voices to heaven, God's bound to have mercy on us, right?"

Keith pictured a town of strangers surrounding his wife, gathering with her to pray about this crisis. He was sure Dr. Baxter's married daughters and other family members would rise to the challenge before them, and he wanted to say so. Lisa was waiting for an answer, after all. But he couldn't say a word.

The tears choking his throat wouldn't let him.

Sixteen

THE PHONE CHAIN STARTED IMMEDIATELY. LISA called Ashley, the one who had given her number as the Baxter family contact, and though she tried to talk with a clear voice, her composure cracked and she started crying.

"Lisa, what is it? What happened?" In the background at Ashley's house, there was the sound of a baby crying.

Lisa felt terrible for troubling her new friend, but she had no choice. Her husband was out of options. She struggled and finally found her voice. "The union for the crew is in town. They've stopped all filming, and they're picketing the set."

Ashley didn't understand, and Lisa took a few minutes to explain the situation. "So Luke's helping with negotiations?"

"Yes, but ... the union leaders are being very difficult. Your brother's afraid they might be trying to make an example out of our movie. Prove that they have the power to take down a film if they want to."

"That's terrible!"

"Yes." Lisa didn't let Ashley hear her sniff. She drew a steadying breath. "The talks tonight are crucial. I told Keith I'd see if there was a place where we could pray."

Ashley thought for a few seconds. "The theater! I'll call Dayne and Katy. I'm sure they'd be okay with it. Classes meet there tonight, but they're over by seven. We could meet there and lock up whenever we're done."

Lisa caught Ashley's enthusiasm. "Really? You think we can do that?"

"Definitely. Let me make a few calls, but plan to meet me and my family at the theater at seven tonight. Even if it's just us, we'll pray together."

The next hours passed slowly, and at seven o'clock Lisa parked her car across the street from the Bloomington Community Theater and headed inside. Katy Matthews met her just inside. "Classes are over, come on in. Ashley told us about the prayer meeting. We can stay here all night if we need to." She hugged Lisa. "Whatever it takes."

Lisa could hardly believe the kindness of these people. They barely knew each other, and yet Katy and Dayne, Ashley and her family, were all willing to stop what they were doing and pray about her husband's movie. Lisa followed Katy into the theater, and though classes had just been dismissed, dozens of kids still sat in the rows of seats. Every few seconds another parent or set of parents entered the theater, but instead of collecting their kids and leaving, they took seats with their children.

"What's happening?" Lisa found Ashley, baffled at the crowd that was starting to fill up the theater.

"CKT is a pretty tight group. They understand the kind of film your husband's trying to make. We need to stick together. We got word to the parents. Most of them asked if they could stay and pray too."

Tears sprang to Lisa's eyes, and she put her fingers to her mouth. "I ... I don't know how to thank you, Ashley."

"Don't worry about it." Ashley touched Lisa's shoulder. "I know what it feels like to have half the town praying for me. There's something very powerful in that kind of love."

"Yes." Lisa wasn't sure she could say anything else. She took a seat next to Ashley and her husband, Landon, and their three kids, and over the next ten minutes Ashley's sisters and their families arrived. Erin, the youngest of Ashley's sisters, explained that her husband was at home with their little girls. "If we're still here in an hour, I'll take the other kids to my house. That way the rest of you can stay here and pray."

"Stay?" Again Lisa was baffled.

"We have to stay." Cole, Ashley's fifth-grade son, held up his arm and showed Lisa a bracelet that read, "P.U.S.H." He grinned at her. "Know what that means?"

"Not really." Lisa's heart was beating hard. She had the thrilling feeling that God was going to work a miracle tonight. The people still pouring through the front doors were living proof.

"It means, 'Pray Until Something Happens.'" He grinned big. "That's what we're going to do tonight, the whole team of us. Pray until something happens."

Lisa looked quickly from Cole to Ashley. "I ... I don't understand."

"We're not putting an end time on this prayer meeting." Ashley patted Lisa's hand. "You'll keep in contact with your husband, and we'll keep praying."

"Yeah." Cole looked thrilled with the idea. "Until something happens."

There was no easy way to comprehend the love of this family, of these people who until a week ago were strangers. This was how the family of God was supposed to operate, and Lisa could only silently thank Him. A few more minutes passed, and still people were coming in and taking seats and again Lisa was confused. All these people couldn't be CKT families. Once more she asked Ashley what was happening.

"Our pastor at church put it on the emergency prayer chain. People are calling each other and getting the word out."

This time Lisa only hugged Ashley. As she drew back she looked long into the eyes of her new friend. "Time will take us from this place, and we'll go back to our separate lives soon. But as long as I live, I'll never forget this."

"It's nothing." Ashley returned the hug. "Now let's get this group praying."

Just as Dayne walked up to start the impromptu meeting, Bailey Flanigan and her family and Andi Ellison entered the theater. By then the place was so full they had to take a spot standing along the wall. Lisa waved to them, silently expressing her thanks as Dayne took hold of the microphone at center stage. "Thanks for coming, everyone. The Bible tells us to pray without ceasing, and that where two or more are gathered, there He is also." He smiled at the group, his expression tender. "That's definitely the case tonight."

A round of hearty applause came from the crowd, and Dayne continued. "Friends of ours—Keith Ellison and Chase Ryan—are making a movie they hope will glorify God. Their story has been covered by the local press, and many of you are aware of their presence in town. I've met with the producers, and they're the real deal. They were missionaries before deciding to make movies." He paused. "Tonight Keith Ellison's wife, Lisa, has asked us to pray because her husband and his co-producer face a dire situation. Very dire." Dayne explained in simple terms what was happening on the set.

"And so, like my nephew Cole likes to say, tonight we will pray until something happens. We'll give you updates as we hear anything, and please feel free to leave whenever you need to. We realize it's a school night."

With that, he suggested a pattern whereby he would start the praying, and then anyone who wanted to could take a turn and come up on stage to lead the prayer. Lisa watched, disbelieving. The faith of the people in Bloomington was enough to make her want to flee their home in San Jose and move here tomorrow. Andi was fortunate to be connected to this group. Lisa would never again worry about her having a support group.

Dayne began the prayer, and even when an occasional baby cried out or a bit of whispering came from one or more of the kids, the focus remained. One after another they lifted fervent, heartfelt prayers up to God on behalf of Keith and Chase and the battle they were waging against the union.

At eight o'clock, Lisa texted Keith, looking for some sign of improvement, but there was none. By nine she stepped outside the theater and placed a call directly to him. "You can't believe what's happening here. The whole town showed up to pray, Keith. Something's going to break through, I have to believe it."

"I hope so." He sounded beaten and weary. "They're going over every document line by line. So far we haven't made even a step in the right direction. Luke's relentless, though. Keep praying."

By ten o'clock, many of the families with young kids had to leave, and Erin made good on her offer, taking the little kids, except for Cole and Maddie, home so they could get some sleep. The two cousins who stayed were intent on making good on their promise. Praying until some sort of answer came along. As eleven neared, Lisa found Ashley and conveyed her concerns. "Really, you all need sleep. You don't have to stay."

"It's fine." She didn't look tired whatsoever. "This is what we're supposed to do. We'll keep praying. God's not finished with this night yet."

One of the CKT dads was at the microphone, and as he stepped down Lisa realized she hadn't taken a turn. Her voice was steadier now, God giving her strength for a battle they never intended to fight. She made her way up the stairs and spoke clearly, confidently.

"God, we beseech You, give us a miracle tonight. Speak to the hearts of those men who have come against this movie, and let a breakthrough happen even this very moment. We need You, Lord ... we can't fight this battle alone. Thank You for all ..." her voice cracked and she blinked back tears as she looked out at the still fifty or so people who remained. She stared at the stage floor and managed to regain her composure. "Thank You for all our new friends. In Christ's name, amen."

Cole had already been up to the microphone a number of times, but he was quick to follow her. Lisa found him adorable, the sort of boy she had once hoped for back when she thought they'd have a houseful of children one day. Before getting word from her doctor that she couldn't possibly have more children, Lisa had three late miscarriages. All three babies were boys.

She smiled at Cole as he started to pray. "You're a very big God, because we've seen You do all sorts of miracles. My baby sister, my dad, our old Baxter house. Hayley's bike-riding." He gave an adorable shrug. "Too many to count, God. So we know for sure You can get this movie back on track. I'm not even going to ask You again. Instead, I'm just going to thank You because I know You'll get this done. In Jesus' name."

And so it went.

Eleven became midnight, and though people began to yawn, still twenty-three people remained, committed to pray through the night. The breakthrough didn't happen until two thirty that morning, just when Lisa was feeling horribly guilty for having cost these wonderful friends a perfectly good night of sleep. Her cell phone vibrated in her pocket, and she slipped outside to take the call.

"We're back in business." Keith was on the other line, tears in his voice. "It's a long story, but somehow the news station got hold of what was happening and a reporter from the Indianapolis paper began calling Larry Fields. Everything that happened next was so that he could save face." Keith sighed, and the relief in his voice was thick and heartrending.

"So what's the compromise?"

"We pay union wages from here out. It's a few thousand more per crew member, per week, but Luke was brilliant. Because this means we're union, he recognized that we were giving the crew a hundred dollars a day for location spending money. Union rules don't require that, so starting tomorrow we save that much. The difference isn't going to break us."

Lisa wanted to point out the obvious, that even before agreeing to union wages they didn't have enough money to finish the film. Now that they were behind two full days, they would still need an investor to come through. But they could wage that battle later. For now all that mattered was that she get word to the praying people inside. God had won; the producers could begin filming again tomorrow.

When she stepped back inside the theater, all eyes were on her. "It's over!" she raised her hands in the air. "They've reached an agreement. Filming starts again in the morning!"

The crowd came instantly to life, people standing and hugging and raising their hands to a God who loved them no matter what the size of the problem they were facing. Lisa caught Ashley's eyes across the room and she mouthed a silent thank you. What she'd said earlier was so true. A night of praying together had bound them as friends for life—whether they ever had a time like this again or not.

Before they left, Cole came up and flung his arms around her middle. "I told you." He flashed his bracelet once more. "I knew God would get it done."

They were words Lisa took with her on the drive back to the hotel room, and as she crawled alone into their bed. Keith and Chase would work with Luke the rest of the night writing up the new contracts for each crew member and making sure everything was in order for their seven o'clock call time. They hadn't slept at all, but God would see them through tomorrow. In the meantime, she would hold tight to the wisdom from young Cole—no matter what problem they faced through the rest of the shoot. She would pray until something happened.

The way a town of believers and friends had prayed tonight.

Seventeen

ANDI AND BAILEY WERE TOGETHER WHEN they read the *Scrooge* cast list Friday after school.

"I can't believe it!" Andi braced herself against the hallway and stared at the list. "Isabel? I never thought in my wildest dreams I'd be Isabel!"

Bailey's hug came quickly and solidly. "See, God had it all figured out. We each won big parts this week."

They scanned the list a little further and saw that Bailey had been named the Ghost of Christmas Past. "That'll be fun. She's really dry ... I like that." At the same time, Bailey's eyes flew to the top of the list and she gasped. "Look at that! Tim's Scrooge!" She grabbed hold of Andi's arms and they danced in a tight circle. "I can't believe it! Tim's gonna flip!"

Both of them needed to be on the movie set in half an hour, and now that they'd seen the cast list, they started walking across campus to the movie location for the day—the same auditorium on the west side of the school where Campus Crusade held its meetings. Bailey's scene was on the list for this afternoon, and if things went well she could get her part done in one day.

As they walked, Bailey tried Tim's cell phone, but she only reached his voicemail. "I can't leave a message telling him something this big." She slipped her phone back in her pocket and hurried along beside Andi. "What a week!"

Andi loved that there was no tension between them. Whatever ways either of them were tempted to be jealous of the other, they'd worked past that. But there were still things Andi hadn't shared with Bailey. The walk ahead of them would take a good fifteen minutes or so, and as the excitement over the cast list died down, Andi took a deep breath. "You ever wonder ... if everything isn't just sort of random?"

Bailey shot her a funny look. "Random how?"

"I don't know. My friend Rachel dying before she had a chance to really live ... my dad struggling to make this movie." She narrowed her eyes against the glare of the afternoon sun. "Just random. Like God isn't really part of everything that happens."

"Hmmm." Bailey slowed her pace. Worry sounded in her tone. "You mean like you wonder if God isn't real?"

"No, not exactly." Andi wasn't sure how to voice her feelings. "Just the whole way the world is, you know? I mean there's a gay couple in my science class, and I really like them. They're the nicest guys there." She lifted one shoulder and dropped it again. "Are they really going to hell just because they love someone of the same sex?"

"Well," Bailey raised her eyebrows, but kept her eyes focused on the pathway ahead of them. Her tone was kind, but firm. "The Bible's pretty clear about it. I mean, the people can be nice and everything, but it's not okay just to give in to our own desires, you know ... do our own thing."

"That's the right answer." Andi felt her confusion like two hands pressing down on her shoulders. "Believe me, with my parents, I know the right answers." She smiled. "Sometimes it's hard to just believe it because the Bible says so. What if it's all one big hoax? I guess I have to figure it out on my own."

"Yeah." Bailey looped her arm through Andi's. "And you will. You know the truth; it'll always be there inside you."

Andi leaned her head on Bailey's shoulder and then suddenly she stopped walking. "My phone. I can hear it." The ring tone was something from Usher, and Andi was almost positive that it was Jake Olson. She crouched down and began tearing through her backpack until finally she held it up and clicked it open at the same time. "Hello?"

"Hey." His voice was smooth and easy. "I thought you were ignoring my call."

"Of course not." She covered the speaker and whispered, "It's Jake!" Then she cleared her throat and put the phone to her ear as she swung her backpack over her shoulder once more. They started walking, slower this time. "I thought you'd never call."

"Your parents probably wouldn't like it that I was doing this."

"They wouldn't care. My parents are great, they let me make my own choices now that I'm in college." Andi sent a nervous look in Bailey's direction. Clearly her parents would care that she was talking with Jake. Of course they would. She and Bailey both knew that much.

"So ... in case we don't talk on the set today, I just wondered if you wanna go to Lake Monroe when we wrap tonight."

Andi felt the same thrill she'd experienced the first time she was with Jake. "Who would go?" She didn't want to look at Bailey, didn't want to feel any sense of disapproval.

Jake laughed softly. "Just us. If that's okay."

"Sure, I mean ... sounds great."

"Can we take your car?"

"Definitely. It's parked close to where we're shooting this afternoon."

"Great." Again his voice was low and sexy, enough to make her dizzy. "You can show me this lake I keep hearing about and, well ... maybe we can find something else to do. Ya know?"

"Okay." Andi felt her face grow hot, and she was certain Bailey could tell she was flustered. They made a plan to meet near his trailer when they finished for the day, and then the call ended. Andi slipped her phone in the outside pocket of her backpack and flashed a thrilled look at her roommate. "Seriously, Bailey ... you won't believe it. He wants to go with me to Lake Monroe tonight.

Just the two of us!" She let out a quiet scream. "This day keeps getting better!"

Bailey made a face that wasn't nearly as happy as Andi's. "Just the two of you? I don't know. He's got a pretty wild reputation."

"He won't try anything. He knows better." She brushed her hand in Bailey's direction. She didn't mention the part about Jake's promise to show her a few things too. "My dad's the director."

"What if he tries to kiss you?"

Andi let the question sit for a few seconds, and then she stopped and frustration filled her tone. "Then maybe I'll let him. I mean, I've never been kissed. Would that be so bad if my first kiss came from Jake Olson?" She started walking again, her irritation showing in her increased pace. "You have Tim, right? I mean you said so yourself, that you think you're in love with him."

"I feel that way lately, yes."

"So everything's fine for you. But when's it going to be my turn, Bailey? Tell me that."

Bailey didn't try to come up with a quick and perfect answer. No Scripture or preaching, like Andi was afraid of. Instead she kept her voice soft. "It's hard. I'm sure it is."

They were quiet for a few minutes, and then Andi released a a loud sigh. "I mean, everyone in church is always talking about being rescued from this or being saved from that. People have their testimonies, about how they lived these terrible lives and then God swept in and changed everything." She still gripped her backpack with one hand, but now she lifted her free hand and let it fall to her side. "It seems like I've always had God in my life. Sometimes I want to know what that feels like, the feeling of being rescued. Like maybe I have to live a little on the other side before I can really appreciate God and what He's done for me."

Bailey seemed pensive at that, as though she had a lot to say and wasn't sure where to begin.

"Go ahead." Andi wasn't mad, just not exactly sure of anything she was supposed to be sure of. The feeling put a shadow over everything else good about the day. "Go on, I know you're thinking something. Just say it."

"I was going to tell you about my high school friends."

"What?" Andi realized she didn't sound very open to Bailey's story, but she turned toward her as they walked. "Seriously, tell me."

"It's just, well, I didn't go to a Christian school. Back in eighth and ninth grade I had a whole group of really close friends, but as we got older they sort of felt like you, I think. They wanted to experience life, walk a little on the dangerous side of things."

"I don't want too much danger." Andi protested, but she stopped herself long enough to hear the rest of what Bailey had to say.

"I know, neither did they." Bailey looked up through the almost barren branches of a tree they were passing by. "But one by one they got sucked in. Drinking and then drugs, sex with one guy and then another. Pretty soon they were different, like life had changed them. We didn't have anything in common anymore, and so ... I don't know, my senior year was pretty lonely."

Andi could imagine how weird it would be to be caught up in partying and boyfriends and still spend time with someone as innocent as Bailey. At the same time, it wasn't Bailey's fault her friends changed. "So ... you think the thrills ruined them."

"It's never what you think it's going to be. None of my friends from school who went that way ended up happy." She gave Andi a sympathetic look. "My mom always says if those girls could have their purity back, if they could do it all over again, they would every time. She says God has special plans for girls like you and me, girls who do things God's way."

"Yeah, well ... what if God doesn't really care?" The question came out quickly and carelessly. "I mean, how come God took

Rachel? And if He wants me to have a good guy in my life, then how come the only one who's shown any interest is Jake Olson?"

"You have to be patient. God has someone for you, Andi. Don't make yourself easy for Jake tonight—if you decide to go. He probably expects everything to go his way. But girls like you ... like us ... we're special. Your first kiss should be with someone like you."

Andi blinked back a sudden layer of tears, because that was one of the nicest things any friend had ever said to her. "You know what I hate?"

"What?" The air between them felt suddenly lighter.

"I hate when people expect so much of me. Just because I'm ... I don't know, whatever I am. A missionary's kid, a producer's kid ..."

"Beautiful and talented and completely pure." Bailey raised her brow. "I get that a ton from my old friends. I hate it too. They think I'm perfect, when that's not even close to true."

"My dad says it's because girls like me and you are sort of a bright white sheet of paper. The other girls, like at your high school, are kind of beige white—not really bad, but they've compromised along the way."

Bailey laughed. "My mom's told me that one too. The beige color feels pretty good until she comes up against the pure white, right?"

"Right." Andi laughed and gave Bailey a side hug. As she did she wrinkled her nose and added one last thought. "But don't you ever think that pure white's a little boring?"

They had reached the set, and Bailey shook her head at her friend. Then she stopped and in a mock show of disappointment, she put her hands on Andi's shoulders and gave her a little shake. "Don't think like that. You have it all, Andi Ellison." Bailey lowered her hands and her eyes grew tender and serious. "You and I ... we both have it all. Don't sell yourself short for anything."

Andi looked long into Bailey's eyes. "Thanks." She hugged her friend. "I needed to hear that." She glanced across the set at the place where Jake Olson was talking to her father. "Especially tonight." They hugged once more, and then Bailey scrambled off to find out where she needed to be. Before she got too far, she turned around and grinned at Andi. "Hey, tonight's homecoming at Clear Creek High ... wanna go? Maybe skip the lake?"

"Uh ... if things fall through with Jake, maybe."

"Okay ... but you don't know what you're missing. Everyone'll be there!" She waved once more, her smile full of a deeper meaning. "Don't say you didn't have options on this beautiful Friday night!"

Andi laughed. "Look for me. I just might show up."

Bailey gave her the thumbs up, and then she ran off. A nervous feeling messed with Andi's stomach as she thought about her options. Hang out with Bailey at a safe high school football game, or take a drive to the lake with Jake. In almost every possible way, there really didn't seem to be any real decision to make. The safe bet was the game. But Andi had spent her whole life being safe.

Today Andi would reshoot the scene on one of the campus pathways, this time with another girl from IU. The speaking lines would only be Andi's though, a compromise her father had texted her earlier today. She headed toward her mom, who would again be in charge of the extras, and as she did she thought about Bailey's wisdom and whether later that night she'd still remember what her friend said.

Or if being beneath a full moon on the shores of Lake Monroe with Jake Olson would make her forget every bit of wisdom she'd ever known.

CODY HADN'T BEEN TO A CLEAR Creek High School football game since he came home from the war. Every time he thought about it, all he could see was himself, bigger than life, running the ball in for a touchdown, flying downfield under those Friday night lights. He could feel the pads rubbing against his shoulders, smell the sweat on his uniform, and hear the roar of the crowd all around him.

Going back now, without the pair of legs that had been so faithful to him all those years of playing for Clear Creek? The loss would never feel greater, and so he hadn't planned on making this trip. Another homecoming, maybe. Three, four years down the road when his prosthesis was as much a part of him as his leg once was. But now? When he still had to work to make his gait look normal? Cody hadn't planned on it.

But there was one thing that mattered more to him than avoiding the pain of watching the Clear Creek High football team play on the field where he once did some of his best work. Bailey Flanigan might be here.

More than a football game was taking place here tonight. The movie crew was getting B roll for their movie—at least that's what the newspaper had said. Besides that, Bailey's dad would be here. The Colts were home again this weekend, and with it being homecoming he would definitely be on the field—reminiscing with his former coaching staff about the dozens of great games they'd played here.

Cody parked his car in the side lot, the one where players used to park when they'd practice under the lights on occasion. He could hear the noise, see the lights long before he walked up the ramp to the stadium entrance. Don't think about it, he told himself. This is a new season, a new day. Help me see it as a new day, Lord. Please ... I can't be here if You don't get me through it.

My son, I will never leave you nor forsake you ... where you go, there I am.

The answer sounded in his soul louder than the noise coming from the stadium. God was with him, Cody anchored himself in the certainty of the fact. He'd gotten him home from Iraq, after all. He would get him through a homecoming game at Clear Creek High School. Cody went to pay his admission, but the woman selling tickets did a double take when she saw him.

"Wait ... you're Cody Coleman, right?" She was sitting in a little wooden booth, and she peered out into the light to see him better. "My son played ball with you three years ago." She introduced herself and then studied him for a moment. "I haven't seen you around since you got back from Iraq."

"Yes, ma'am." The newspaper had covered his homecoming. There weren't many people who had missed the fact that he was back from the war, and that he'd come home wounded.

"I won't take your money." The woman held out her fingers and shook Cody's hand. "Thank you for serving our country. You're the best and brightest we have, Cody. Stay that way."

Cody thanked the woman and then headed up the stairs to the stadium. Along the way he smiled. God had known just what he needed, and with a welcome like the one he'd just received, it was easy to see this as a fresh start, the beginning of his life as a fan of the Clear Creek High football team. He breathed in deep the cool autumn air, the crispness that always signaled football season. He found a quiet spot out of the way of the home crowd and studied the field.

There it was. Number 81 — his old jersey. Some tall skinny kid was wearing it. Cody sat down and dug his elbows into his knees, taken by the sight. Wasn't it just yesterday when that was him out there, patting his teammates on the back and firing up the bench, ready for another touchdown catch whenever his number was called? The lines blurred and for a few moments he tried to will himself back, back in time to that place where Friday night games seemed a given, like there would always be another season, another chance to suit up for Clear Creek.

He sat a little straighter and blinked. Just once, but in that blink the images cleared and he remembered who he was and where he was and how that wonderful time in his life would never come again. No matter how badly he still wanted to suit up, how much he still believed he could take a pass from the quarterback and run like the wind for the end-zone. He reached down and rubbed his hand against the hard plastic and metal that made up his lower left leg. Even with his prosthesis he would've loved the chance to feel the ball in his arms again.

He stood and scanned the crowd until he saw Bailey's mother and brothers. If Bailey was here, maybe she was getting something at the snack stand. He ambled down the stairs and over a few sections and came up behind them.

"Hey! Game just got started, huh?"

Jenny Flanigan turned around and her face lit up. "Cody! You came!" She turned around and hugged him. As she did, Bailey's brothers turned around and each of them hugged him or patted him hard on the shoulder.

"Good to see you." Connor was as tall as Cody now. "Bailey'll be here any minute."

"She's on her way. She's got a scene in the movie, and it went a little late." Jenny slid over and patted the spot beside her. "Sit here."

Cody was still processing what Bailey's mother had just said. "She ... has a scene in the movie?"

"Yes!" Jenny's smile filled her face. "I thought for sure she would've told you. It's a pretty big deal." She hesitated, confused. "When's the last time you saw her?"

"More than a week ago. At Campus Crusade."

"Right. She missed last night because of the prayer meeting."

Again Cody felt out of the loop, but this time he didn't say anything. Connor must've been able to read his blank expression, because he filled in the missing details, explaining that the producers had a crisis with their film, and half the town had gathered at the theater after CKT to pray for the producers. "Everything worked out," he grinned. "I guess it was a good thing they had so many people praying."

Cody nodded, then turned his attention to the game on the field. But inside he was thinking about last night's meeting and how he hadn't heard about it. He imagined Bailey was probably there with Tim, and where was he? At the Cru meeting, and then back sitting at his apartment doing homework and wondering why he'd lied about his feelings.

Twenty minutes passed and still Bailey hadn't shown up. Cody stood and smiled at her family. "I'm going down on the field."

"Yes, go." Jenny's smile told him how much she cared. "Jim would love to talk with you. He'll stay down there the whole game."

"Okay, well ... tell Bailey I said hi."

Her smile faded. "She'll want to see you." She looked toward the stadium gates, but there was no sign of Bailey. "You'll come back up, right?"

"Maybe. I still have a lot of homework." Cody leaned in and hugged Bailey's mother again. "It was good seeing you."

"You too." They had to yell above the noise from the crowd. "Come by more often, Cody. We miss you."

"Okay." Cody didn't mean it, but that was the only right answer for the moment. "I'll see what I can do."

He took the stairs better than he expected. There was no railing to lean on, nothing to steady himself. But he was getting familiar enough with the prosthesis, and the time he'd spent training for the local triathlon was helping.

As he walked, he thought about Bailey's mother and her offer for him to come by the house. When he didn't show up, the way he hadn't hardly at all since July, she probably figured he was busy. But that wasn't it at all. None of them could've known that he couldn't spend much time there with Bailey dating Tim. Every moment was a reminder of all he didn't have, all he would probably never have.

He reached the field and walked behind the bench to the place where Jim Flanigan stood with a few of the defensive coaches. He spotted Cody right away and grinned, waving at him to join them. Again the moment took Cody back, walking toward Coach Flanigan, feeling the turf beneath his feet, hearing the pulse of the game a few yards away.

Jim Flanigan pulled him into a big bear hug. "You've been a stranger." He gave Cody a light punch in the shoulder. "You're part of our family, Cody. You gotta come around more."

"I know. I was just talking to Jenny about that." Cody never had a dad growing up. Jim Flanigan was the closest he'd ever come, which made it even harder. It was one more reason he could only imagine what it would be like to actually date Bailey.

He let the thought pass. "The team looks good."

"I wish I could say the same about the Colts."

"You're not bad. You're winning half your games." Cody was proud of Jim, glad he'd gotten back into coaching in the NFL. He was too talented to keep out of that arena for long.

They talked about games gone by and the film crew shooting B roll at tonight's game, and how the boys were doing in their middle school sports. "That Justin," Jim made a face that said even he was surprised. "The kid can run. I think you'll see him getting some varsity time next year as a freshman."

The longer they talked, the more Cody felt at home. Standing on the field this way, he was almost part of the team again. But when halftime came, he didn't want to go in the locker room. Even after Jim invited him. "I have homework waiting for me. A research essay due Monday."

"Did you see Bailey? She was running a little late."

"Not yet." He squinted up at the home crowd. "Maybe on the way out." He was about to leave when the announcer came over the loudspeaker. "Ladies and gentlemen, most of you know it's homecoming tonight, and we'd like to give a big shout-out to the returning alumni from Clear Creek High, but especially to our veterans, the ones who left high school and went on to serve our country, fighting for our freedom and protection. And because he was a former Clear Creek High football player, I'd like everyone to give a special welcome to Cody Coleman."

Cody felt like a deer caught in the headlights of an entire community. A part of him wanted to run, take his place in the stands with the other anonymous people. But then something began to happen. The crowd rose to its feet, and an applause started across the stadium, celebrating Cody's safe return and telling him the best way they knew that they appreciated him. Not only for the touchdowns he once scored, but for putting his life on the line for the sake of every person in the stadium.

Jim put his arm around Cody's shoulders. "Soak it in, buddy. You deserve it."

And for one last moment, one more time, Cody Coleman stood on the twenty-yard-line under the Friday night lights and lifted his face to the view of thousands of screaming fans. He listened while the crowd cheered him on, while they clapped like crazy for him and for everything he stood for. Character, community, and country. Cody Coleman, Clear Creek football star, American hero. And Cody let the applause fall over him like water to his soul.

One last time.

Eighteen

ANDI LET JAKE DRIVE, NOT THAT he knew his way around, but their night out felt more like a date that way. Her parents had meetings back at the hotel with a few of the lead crew members, and neither of them had gotten much sleep in the past couple days. Andi figured they were too tired to look deeply into her plans for the evening.

Her mom had found her as the shooting wrapped for the evening. "You have plans tonight?"

Andi smiled and kept her tone casual. "Bailey asked me to go to her high school's homecoming game. I guess the whole town's supposed to show up."

"We're shooting B roll there. The assistant director's handling it so we can get some rest." Her mom touched the side of Andi's face. "I feel like we haven't spent much time together ... with all the drama on the set."

"It's okay." She kissed her mother's cheek. "We'll catch up this weekend."

As soon as her mom left the set, Andi headed for her meeting place with Jake near his trailer. As she walked, she comforted herself with the fact that she hadn't really lied. Bailey actually *had* asked her to come to the game. And she might go later, depending on how the night went.

They were ten minutes from Lake Monroe, and Andi couldn't help but notice how good Jake looked behind the wheel. He glanced her way. "Did your parents have a problem with us hanging out?"

Andi gave him a nervous smile. "I didn't see my dad, and I didn't exactly tell my mom."

"I'm hurt." He flashed her the teasing smile moviegoers everywhere were coming to know. "You're embarrassed to be with me?"

"Let's just say my parents and I don't see life through the same lens these days."

"Hmm. Nice alliteration." He raised his brow appreciatively. "I didn't know missionary kids were so smart."

"We're not all the same." She hated the way people wanted to stereotype her. She wanted to add that life was the only thing that had gotten more complicated lately. But she wasn't sure she wanted to have that conversation with him. He'd already made it clear that he had more experience than her. Now that they were alone, she didn't want to give him a reason to prove himself.

Andi didn't want to stare, but she caught another glance at him and her mind raced ahead to the lake. It would be sunset by the time they reached the water, so what exactly were they going to do? Talk about everything they didn't have in common? A tension began to build inside her, and no matter how relaxed Jake seemed, she thought about asking him to take her back to town. They could have coffee at the little shop near campus, something around other people.

"How much farther?" The sun was still out, but shadows covered much of the road. He peered ahead. "The last sign said two more miles."

"Right." Andi had only been out here once with Bailey. The two of them had hiked along the path at the edge of the lake after school one day. "The parking lot's on the right, after the next bend."

"Great." He turned on the radio and flipped the station until he found something rap. He moved to the beat, singing every word, including a few that made Andi blush.

She looked out the side window and pictured her mother's face, the sincerity in her voice when she'd worried that the two of them weren't spending enough time together. Back in Indonesia, she and her mom had been best friends—the way Bailey and her mother were. But in the last year or so—since Andi began doubting some of what she'd always believed—she and her mom had grown distant. Not in a bad way. They still got along when they were together. It was Andi's fault, really. She didn't tell her mom everything she was doing or feeling, didn't check in with her as often. If her mom knew her doubts and the desires she was feeling for nights like this, she would've wanted to talk with her. Her parents might even pull her from IU and make her attend a junior college near their house in San Jose.

She couldn't have that, so she kept her confusion and questions, her curiosity and temptations, to herself.

"You're quiet." Jake pulled the car into the parking lot and parked in one of the first spots. The only other vehicle was a Dodge Ram, parked close to the trailhead. He turned off the engine and angled himself toward her. "You okay?"

"Fine." Her answer was quick. She wanted to be here, right? A night with Jake Olson? How many girls across the country would die for a chance like this? She grasped for an explanation for her pensive behavior. "Just thinking about today's shoot."

"Let's talk out there." He climbed out of her car, and in a few easy steps he jogged around and opened her door. "We're losing daylight."

Andi liked the way he said that, as if he didn't want to be alone with her after dark anymore than she did. She let him take the lead and once they were on the path, she walked beside him. Andi was five-foot-eight, and she noted as they walked that Jake wasn't much taller. Five-ten maybe.

"So about the shoot." He held his head high and even with his lack of height he was bigger than life. "What did you think?"

"I liked it." She felt the purpose in her expression. "It's what I want to do — make feature films like this."

"I watched some of the dailies." His grin seemed genuine. "You look good on camera."

"Really?"

"Definitely." He looked deep into her eyes. "You're impossibly beautiful. Partly because you don't know it."

She looked at her feet, not sure what to do with the giddy way his compliment made her feel. "Thanks." She lifted her face again and she felt stars in her eyes. "That means a lot coming from you."

The lake was on their left, down a craggy embankment. The other side of the path was entirely shrouded by a canopy of trees, lending an intimacy to the experience that wasn't as uncomfortable as Andi had imagined it might be.

"We got a lot done today. Bailey was good." He gave a noncommittal look. "I mean, she's talented." He slowed his pace and then gradually came to a stop, his eyes locked on hers. "But you would've been better. I think your dad didn't want anyone accusing him of playing favorites."

Andi had never thought about that. Bailey was very talented, and she had more experience acting, but maybe Jake was right. Maybe she — and not Bailey — would've been better for the part, but her father was afraid of how the cast would react if he put his daughter in the role. She smiled at Jake, glad for his perspective. Her tension over being alone with him was fading fast.

"You believe me, right?" He moved closer so that there were only a few inches between them. "You're very talented, Andi Ellison." He brought his hand gently to the side of her face. "You're not afraid, are you?"

She swallowed, but she didn't look away. "Of what?"

"This." He looked around, registering the quiet solitude for both of them. His eyes melted into hers. "Being alone with me."

"No." She shook her head and felt her smile grow shyer than before. The ground beneath her feet felt suddenly unstable and her heart was racing within her. "I'm not afraid. I ... I wanted to come here with you."

"Good." He came closer still. "I wouldn't want you to be scared."

This close, he looked so good she wasn't sure she could move away from him if she wanted to. Like he'd captivated her, and she was powerless to change the fact.

"You're trembling." His voice fell to a whisper.

She could feel his sweet breath against her cheek, smell the faint remainder of the day's cologne. Cool air swirled lightly around their faces, and Andi was absolutely certain she would remember this moment as long as she lived. There was no reason for her knees to be trembling. Being here with Jake was a dream come true, because in all the world she was the girl he wanted to be with.

He searched her eyes, and something changed in his. The smile was gone, and in its place his eyes looked intense, layered in shadows of desire. He ran his fingers along her cheekbone. "Not a lot of guys out there in the jungle."

"No." Shame threw itself into the mix of emotions swirling in her heart. Because she should've wanted to run by now, but she couldn't. The feel of his touch against her skin was wildly intoxicating, like nothing she'd ever known before.

"So ... you're a virgin?" He was breathing differently, faster and more raspy. "Is that a safe assumption?"

"Of course." She lifted her chin, trying to remain proud of the fact the way she normally was. But somehow with Jake like this, her inexperience made her feel like a child, like a ten-year-old who hadn't yet learned to read. She grabbed for something to say, some untruth that would help her save face. She was a college freshman, after all. She put her hand lightly on his waist. "Not that I haven't had my chances."

"That," he leaned in and left a trail of light kisses along her neck, winding up with his lips nearly touching hers, "doesn't surprise me."

Her whole world was consumed by the way his lips felt against her throat, and suddenly she realized what was about to happen. She was going to be kissed for the first time here on a secluded path overlooking Lake Monroe with none other than Jake Olson. Even during the drive here she hadn't really thought he would kiss her. Being kissed at all felt far off and unreal, like this moment would never really happen to her.

Her heart slammed around inside her so loud the sound filled her senses. *What's happening to me?* He slipped his hands around her waist, to the small of her back. She had no time to analyze her feelings except to acknowledge the obvious—she couldn't stop him now if she wanted to. And she didn't want to. She needed a full breath in the worst way, but she couldn't get her lungs to keep up with her heart.

"Is it okay?" his words felt like velvet against her face. "Can I kiss you?"

She wasn't sure if she said yes, or if the sound came out that way as she tried to exhale, but at the same time he closed the distance between them. His lips pressed in softly against hers, and at first the sensation was so wonderful she felt weightless, carried away on the winds of a feeling better than anything she'd ever imagined.

But even while she was savoring the first-time emotions filling her senses, he eased her back a few feet, back against a tree. His kiss which had seemed like something from a fairy tale became aggressive and rough. She squirmed some, and fear placed its clammy fingers around her neck. What was she doing? How could she have come here with a boy she didn't even know? She'd heard stories of girls who went to places like this with guys who were little more than strangers.

"Jake ..." She put her hand against his chest and wiped her mouth with her other one. She was breathless. "Not so ... not so fast."

"There's nothing wrong with it. We're just enjoying each other." He kissed her again and one more time. "Being with you like this ... you drive me crazy, Andi. I can't stop."

He slid his hands up her sides, his kisses more intense, more consuming. He worked one hand up into her hair and pressed her closer still, while he put his lips against her earlobe. "I promised ... I'd show you a few things. Remember?"

In that moment Andi realized the impossible could actually happen. Already he was taking this beyond where she felt comfortable. She wanted her first kiss to be tender and romantic, and this was feeling like some cheap scene in a second-rate movie. Again she tried to put distance between the two of them, but before she could say anything, they heard voices coming their way from the opposite direction.

Jake drew back, his eyes wide and nervous, his breathing fast. "What was that?"

"I don't know." She silently thanked God for the distraction and adjusted her sweater. "Someone's coming."

At that moment, Dayne Matthews and his wife, Katy, came into view. They were holding hands, talking, lost in each other. Katy had their baby girl in a front pack carrier, her hand sheltering the back of the child's head. They looked up at the same time and noticed Andi and Jake. For a second they stopped, probably surprised to see anyone on the path ahead of them.

"Jake?" Dayne's look was both puzzled and knowing. "What're you doing?"

Andi was still breathless, and her face felt like it was on fire. She met eyes with Katy and then looked down at the ground, ashamed. Of course Dayne would know Jake. They'd probably been to the same red carpet events in Hollywood.

Jake released a nervous laugh. He put one hand in his pocket and with the other he reached out and shook Dayne's. "Hey, man ... didn't get to talk to you much the other day at the set."

The few beats of silence that followed made Andi look up. Dayne had one eyebrow raised, first toward Jake and then toward her. "You're Keith's daughter, right?"

"Yes, sir." Andi was shaking. She took a step closer to Jake and gave a polite nod to Dayne. "I've seen you a few times, but we haven't officially met."

"Nice to meet you." Dayne's words were hesitant. No question he knew what they had stumbled onto. He put his arm around his wife. "This is Katy and our little girl, Sophie." He aimed a direct look at Jake. "It's getting a little too dark to be out here, don't you think?"

"Yeah," Jake laughed again and reached for Andi's hand. "We were only staying a few more minutes at the most."

"Good." Dayne resumed his pace, motioning to Jake as he went. "Come on. You can walk back with us."

The relief that flooded Andi told her how frightened she'd been. Beside her she could feel Jake's resistance to the idea, but before he could protest, Andi slipped her hand free from Jake's, smiled at Katy and moved next to her as the group started walking. "Bailey Flanigan is my roommate." She was deeply embarrassed, but she could only move the conversation forward. "She thinks the world of you."

"Thanks." There was nothing critical in Katy's kind expression. "I think the world of her too."

Jake and Dayne made small talk as they walked back to the parking lot. The Dodge Ram was Dayne's — something Andi remembered now. It was the same truck he'd driven to the set earlier. Dayne shook Jake's hand again. "You living right, man?"

Again Jake's laugh sounded more nervous than funny. "Not like you. Family man and church and all."

"Best change I ever made." He eyed Jake. "Make good choices, Olson. This business'll eat you alive." He gave him a soft slap on the arm. "You ever want to talk about God ... the bigger picture ... you know where to reach me. Just leave a message at the Bloomington Community Theater."

"Okay." Jake looked more serious than he had before. "Thanks, man."

Andi hugged Katy. "Your baby is beautiful."

"She's feisty, that's for sure." Katy kissed the top of Sophie's head. "She's changing every day." Katy met Andi's eyes. This time she kept her voice low enough so the guys couldn't hear her. "Do your parents know you're here?"

She felt the shame from earlier come back stronger. A lie was forming in her mind, but she had the strong feeling Katy would see right through it. "No."

"I didn't think so." Katy put her hand on Andi's shoulder. "Jake's not ready for a girl like you, Andi. Don't sell yourself short."

The sky was nearly dark overhead, but she could still make out the sincerity in Katy's eyes. Andi bit her lip and nodded quickly. "Okay." She had her back to Jake and Dayne, who were still talking. Even still she kept her voice low. "I think ... you came along ... at just the right time."

Katy smiled. "Me too."

They said their goodbyes and climbed in their vehicles, and only after Dayne and Katy drove away did Jake release a frustrated sigh. "Great timing." He reached out and put his hand on her knee. With none of the sweet words or tender looks, he moved closer. "Now ... where were we?"

She moved back against the car door, just out of his reach. What was wrong with her? She felt cheap and easy and disappointed. What had she been thinking? And what if Katy and Dayne hadn't walked by just then? Her confidence was in place again as she aimed her answer straight at Jake. "We were headed back." Her lips still burned from his kiss, but she couldn't wait to get home and wash her face.

He clenched his jaw and turned away from her to stare out his side window. When he faced her again the charming mask was gone. "Are you kidding me? You let me kiss you like that, and we're just supposed to stop?"

The fear from earlier rose up. Dayne and Katy were gone, and if Jake wanted to have his own way, she couldn't think of a thing she could do to defend herself. It was nearly pitch dark now, so running back on her own was also out of the question. *Calm*, she told herself. *God, please help me be calm. Help me make sense.* She steadied herself with a slow breath. "Jake, we stopped a long time ago." She made a squeamish face. "I don't feel good. Seriously. I'd like to get back."

Jake frowned, his jaw set. But at her mention of being sick his shoulders slumped and he started the engine. "Fine." He peeled out of the parking spot and broke the speed limit all the way back to his hotel. The whole way he blasted the radio so there would be no need for small talk.

With every mile, Andi felt worse. She had told herself that going to the lake with Jake would be exciting, daring, the sort of thrill she'd been sheltered from all her life. Instead she couldn't wait to be rid of him. At the hotel he slammed the gearshift into park and studied her. His smile was almost mean. "You missed out tonight, sweetheart. I was willing to show you the ropes." He lifted his hands and cocked his head, as if to say she'd truly made a mistake. "We were having a good time."

"You know what?" Andi had just enough spunk left to be honest with him. It would probably be the last time he talked to her anyway. "That's not my idea of a good time."

He chuckled, his tone lacking any respect for her. "Coulda' fooled me." He patted her hand, as if in this final moment he was trying to make things right between them again. "Maybe you just have less experience than you think." He gave her a mock salute and he was gone. She didn't watch him go as she climbed out and went around to the driver's side of her car. The five-minute drive to the dorm she could do nothing but play the evening over in her head again and again. She'd been a fool, and worse, she'd almost been raped. So what if he was a movie star? That didn't mean he wouldn't have forced himself on her. She would've been too embarrassed to report him, which was something he probably figured before they ever left.

She felt sick to her stomach as she parked and headed up the stairs into her dorm building. A night guard was there, but he was reading so he didn't look up as she passed by. The world wouldn't have cared if she were coming home now having been accosted. She'd be just one more lonely college girl carrying a world of heartache.

In her room, she looked at the picture of Bailey and her family that hung near her bed. Bailey never would've done something so risky, so dangerous. She had warned Andi about Jake earlier today, so of course she'd seen this coming. Andi flopped down on her bed and stared at the ceiling. But she could never be as good as Bailey Flanigan. Or maybe after tonight she could be. She wasn't sure.

She pictured Jake mocking her, telling her he'd wanted to show her a few things. He was gross and disgusting, even if he was famous. Andi blinked, trying to imagine the night ending differently. If she were honest with herself, it was more Jake she disliked than what he wanted to do. If he'd been more romantic or tender with her, then she might not have cared if he didn't stop at kissing. His words came back to her. What was wrong with two people making out? They were only enjoying each other, right?

Wasn't that what Jake had said? If he'd been more of a gentleman, if he hadn't gone so fast, she might have been willing to explore that enjoyment a little more.

Her graduation photo with Rachel caught her attention and she looked long into her friend's eyes. *You were a good girl, Rach ... but where did it get you? What was the point?* In some ways she wanted to go out and get into worse trouble. Prove to Jake that she was plenty capable of going farther than kissing — regardless of her inexperience. But the thought of doing something that crazy didn't only trouble her. It sickened her.

What a waste of a first kiss.

Tears flooded her eyes and she thought about staying home the rest of the night and reading Rachel's quote book. Every time she looked through it she found something meaningful — as if God could speak straight to her soul through the lines of her friend's journal. She picked up her cell phone and checked the screen. It wasn't quite eight thirty. That meant they were probably just into the second half in the Clear Creek homecoming game.

She sat up and talked herself into going. Being with Bailey would help her forget the terrible night. She made up her mind and looked in the mirror on the way out, and for a few seconds she could only stare at her image. Something looked different, though she couldn't figure exactly what. Not until she turned and grabbed her purse from the desk chair did it occur to her why her reflection looked off, why she didn't have the same glow in her eyes that she'd always had. The one Bailey had. The reason weighed on Andi as she left for the football game because it was both obvious and sad.

Some of her innocence was gone.

Nineteen

CODY'S HEART SANK AS HE WATCHED Bailey join up with her mom and brothers at the end of halftime. She wasn't alone. She was with Tim Reed, and though they weren't holding hands, they looked happy. They sat down in front of Bailey's mother, the same place where Cody had been. He watched Bailey lean back and say something to her mom, and then turn quickly and shade her eyes, staring down at the Clear Creek sidelines.

If she was looking for him, he wasn't going to let her catch him watching. She was with her boyfriend, and now that halftime was over, he was ready to go. He found Jim Flanigan again and gave him a hug. They'd talked a little about Cody's decision to pursue a medical career, and how he'd been attending a new church not far from campus. Now he thanked the man who had been more of a father than anyone else in his life. "I wouldn't be doing any of this if it weren't for you." Cody didn't allow his tone to get too serious, but it was one of those nights when he didn't want to leave a compliment unsaid.

Jim returned his hug, holding onto him the way he did his own sons. "Come around. I mean it, Cody."

"I will." He smiled, but only to cover up the ache he was feeling. He missed the Flanigans more than he let on. He gave a last wave as he walked away. "Go win tomorrow."

"It'll be a tough one." Jim gave a familiar grin, the one Cody had known all those years playing for him and living at the Flanigan house. "We're proud of you, Cody. Call if you need anything."

Cody looked toward Bailey only twice as he walked up the stairs to the exit. Both times she wasn't caught in a conversation with Tim or lost in the thrill of a Friday night with the people she cared about most. Both times she was looking straight at him. Even from across the stadium sections he could see the hurt look in her eyes, a mixture of confusion and frustration, as if she couldn't understand why he would leave without talking to her.

He was being a jerk, but he couldn't help himself. He gave a slight wave of his fingers the second time he looked, and then he didn't turn his eyes to her again. He walked up the sloped path toward the parking lot, steeling himself against the now cold wind. Couldn't Bailey see why he didn't walk over to her? He could never casually hang around Bailey and Tim, acting like he was fine with the situation.

Not when he still hadn't learned how to stop loving her. Never mind that he truly believed someone like Tim Reed would be better for Bailey, more her type. That didn't stop him from feeling.

"Hey! Cody, is that you?"

He looked up, and there, hurrying down the hill, was Andi Ellison — Bailey's roommate. "Hey." He kept his tone upbeat. If he was going to have to live without Bailey, he might as well figure out a way to adjust. "The third quarter's half done."

"I know." She reached him, out of breath. "I couldn't get here until now."

"You're not missing much. Clear Creek's winning by three touchdowns."

"I was more looking for Bailey." She stopped and hugged herself, and in the spray of light from the stadium, her eyes looked like she'd been crying. "Did you see her?"

"She's sitting with Tim and her family, near the fifty-yard line."

"Oh ... she's with Tim." She tried to hide her disappointment, but she failed. Again something in her eyes looked deeply sad. "Maybe I'll just go back to the dorm then."

"Okay." He kept walking toward his car, and she turned and walked next to him. Cody wasn't sure he should ask. He didn't really know her, so he couldn't expect her to tell him how she was doing. Even if something was wrong. But the cold night and the closeness of her beside him gave him the courage to ask anyway. "Hey ... you all right?"

She angled her face but lifted her eyes to his. "Not really." Her teeth chattered softly as she walked. "It's a long story." They continued on another few yards, and then she met his eyes again. "So what's with you and Bailey?"

He laughed softly. "Another long story."

This time she slowed her pace and an idea seemed to come to her. "Maybe I'll wait out here for Bailey." Her tone was lighter than before. "You have to be somewhere?"

"No." He allowed a quiet laugh at the idea. "Not hardly. Just heading back to work on an essay."

She gave a half shrug. "Wanna talk? We could sit in my car." She pointed just ahead of them at the first row of cars. "I'm in front. That way I could see when Bailey walks by."

He thought for a minute. "Sure, I guess." There were no reasons why he couldn't sit for a while with Bailey's roommate. They walked together, plenty of space between them, and he slid into the passenger side of her ancient blue Jetta. In his high school days, Cody could easily tell if a girl was coming onto him or not. But Andi's voice, her body language, and the look in her eyes told him this wasn't one of those times. He actually liked the idea of getting to know Andi better. She was a nice girl, even if she wasn't Bailey. Besides, he hadn't had a good conversation since ... well, since his walk across campus after Cru more than a week ago. And Bailey was too busy to talk tonight.

"Okay," he positioned himself against the passenger door. "Tell me your long story."

Andi took a long breath and gripped the steering wheel. Her eyes stared straight ahead, but it was clear in the reflection of parking lot lights that she was seeing something else—maybe whatever had made her so sad. Finally she looked at him, an embarrassed frown on her face. "I went out with Jake Olson earlier tonight."

"Hmmm." Cody wasn't altogether surprised. Andi was a striking girl, and Jake had probably noticed her on the set a number of times this week. "Things didn't go so well?"

"No." She told him how they'd gone to Lake Monroe and how she'd been worried when they seemed to be the only people alone on the hiking trail around the edge of the lake. "But I don't know, at the same time I was okay with it. I've lived such a safe life. So predictable." She leaned her head back against the headrest. "Sometimes I'm tired of being so safe."

Cody wanted to tell her that he was exactly the other way around. His younger days, through much of his high school years, were as unsafe as they could've been. He gave her a sad smile. "Honestly? It's not all it's cracked up to be ... living dangerously."

"Still," Andi seemed restless, and he could sense in her an insatiable appetite for life—all life. "I guess I'm a little tired of the perfect missionary kid image." She brushed her hand in the air, like she didn't want to bore him with all the details. "Anyway, when we got out there he said all this nice stuff, and then before I knew what was happening he was kissing me."

Cody understood. There was a time in his life when he would've been Jake, taking whatever he could get from an innocent, willing girl like Andi. He listened and she looked slightly uncomfortable as she told him how the kissing grew more intense. Just when she started to feel afraid, Dayne Matthews and his wife walked up from the other direction.

"So maybe God was looking out for you." Cody felt like an older brother, the way he'd felt at the beginning when he and Bailey used to have talks like this one.

"Yeah. Or it was just good timing. Something." She closed her eyes. "I keep thinking my first kiss should've been more special than that. The way it was for Bailey and Tim."

Cody sucked in a quiet breath and kept his reaction to himself. But the blow couldn't have hurt worse if she'd pierced an arrow through his heart. He had guessed that Tim had given Bailey her first kiss, but he tried not to think about it. Now, though, the image was in his heart and soul, along with a river of regret. He needed to say something, otherwise she'd read into his silence. "So," he ran his tongue over his lower lip and tried to find his voice. "Bailey and Tim are doing great?"

"They are." Andi shifted so her back was against her door. "When school started, she wasn't sure. She liked him, but she wasn't sure she was in love with him. You know?"

"Mmmhmm." His heart was breaking, and there was no way he could show it. He didn't want to ask the next question but he couldn't stop himself. "And now?"

"I guess Tim got worried that he hadn't really told her how he felt. So after the shoot one day last week he met her and shared exactly how he's been feeling."

Again Cody felt sick. He knew what day Andi was talking about because he'd been walking by on a path a ways off, and he'd seen the two of them. They'd been sitting where the filming had taken place that day, lost in conversation. He was too far off to tell if Tim had kissed her that afternoon, but even if he hadn't, the two of them were very close, too caught up in each other and the moment to even notice him.

Andi was going on about how now that Bailey and Tim had talked, Bailey's feelings for him were stronger. She hesitated, and her look said she was trying to figure him out. "It's your turn."

"The long story?"

"Yep." She seemed comfortable with him, and less sad than before. "You used to live with Bailey's family, right?"

"They pretty much rescued me. I needed a lot of help back then." He remembered those early days with the Flanigans. He used to watch Bailey, the sweet way she had about her, the strong faith in God that was so much a part of who she was. He had told himself often that he would never be good enough for a girl like Bailey. He still told himself that.

"What happened to your family? Were they just, you know, okay with you leaving home?"

"It was only my mother, and she wasn't doing well, either. She spent some time in prison, so ... without the Flanigans, I would've been in foster care."

"Hmmm." She studied him, her tone understanding. "They're really nice. I was at their house last weekend."

"Very nice."

"You said you needed a lot of help ... were you in trouble?"

Cody wasn't afraid to tell her the truth. Part of the greatest joy in his life was the distance he'd come since those days. "I was into girls and drinking—pretty heavily on both accounts." He narrowed his eyes, seeing himself as he was. "When you talk about not wanting to live so safe and sheltered, it makes me cringe. I know what the other side's like. There's nothing good about it, no matter how it seems at the time."

She wanted to know more details, and he told her how he'd come home one night so drunk that he'd fallen unconscious. "I nearly died. If the Flanigans hadn't found me the next morning, I wouldn't be here." He gave a slow shake of his head. "It was close."

"Cody ... that's awful."

Her alarm told him that all of this was news to her. Bailey hadn't said a word about his background, and the truth about that made him smile to himself. Even on a night when he had more proof than ever that Bailey and Tim were getting very serious. Bailey still cared, because she hadn't casually talked about his background to her roommate.

"You and Bailey," she looked slightly uncomfortable this time. "Did the two of you ever, you know ... think about going out?"

"Not really." He couldn't say no, because the feelings they'd had for each other before he left for the war were real. No matter that nothing had come from them, they were real all the same. "We got close after my alcohol poisoning. She was having a hard time at high school, and I was there. We talked a lot, took walks, that sort of thing."

Andi's smile told him she was still waiting for an answer. "So ..."

"So she was still in high school and I had enlisted in the army. I wouldn't have dared cross that line with her back then, and ... I don't know, when I came back from the war things were different. A lot of time had passed."

"And she was dating Tim?"

"Right."

"You have feelings for her, though ... don't you? I mean, it seems like you do."

"I still care about her." He tried to look casual, hoped she couldn't see the arrow still sticking out of his side. "She'll always be like a sister to me, I guess. Tim was in her life even before I left for the war. He's good for her. Really. I'm happy for them."

Andi didn't look completely convinced, but she let the moment pass. They talked awhile longer, about their classes and Campus Crusade and the mission trip to the Philippines some of the kids were taking next summer. By then, the stadium crowd began emptying, and Andi started looking for Bailey.

"Tim usually turns in pretty early. He lives at home." Andi rested her chin on her steering wheel and searched the crowd.

"Maybe I'll go back with Bailey to her parents' house." She shot a quick smile at Cody. "It beats being alone."

Cody understood how she felt. If he had the chance he would've gone back to the Flanigan house tonight, too. No matter how much time passed, the place would always feel like home. He yawned and put his hand on the door. "Thanks for talking."

"Yeah, you're a good listener. And it was nice getting to know you better." Her eyes danced, more like they had the first time he sat by her at the Cru meeting. She held out her hand. "Give me your phone, and I'll give you my number. We can text that way."

"Sure." He pulled out his phone, and after a minute they both had each other's numbers. "Okay, well ... see you around." He opened the door and stepped out as she said a final goodbye.

"Hey," she leaned across the passenger seat so she could see him better. "You going to Cru this week? Bailey and I have rehearsals so we might be a little late."

"I'll be there."

"Sit near the back again and save us seats." She grinned. "It's more fun that way."

He agreed and after another minute of talk about Cru, they parted ways. As he stood and headed for his car, he scanned the crowd of fans, in case Bailey might be among them. But there was no sign of her.

As he reached his car, he realized he felt better than he had in a while. The conversation with Andi was nice, nicer than he'd expected. She was kind and pretty and though she maybe had a wild streak, he could see through it to the God-fearing girl she was deep inside. If it weren't for Bailey he might've been interested in a girl like Andi Ellison. But there were two problems that would keep anything from ever developing between him and Andi. First, because she was Bailey's roommate.

And second, because no matter how wonderful she was, she would never be the girl he really wanted.

A girl who could only be Bailey Flanigan.

Twenty

KELLY RYAN OPENED THE WINDOW OF their three-bedroom house and felt the warm autumn afternoon air move by her. Fall in San Jose was absolutely perfect. A hint of color in the trees, the distant mountains and hills clear against the blue sky, and the countryside dotted with fully ripe vineyards, ready for harvest season or "crush" as the locals called it. Kelly stared out the window and sighed. None of it looked as beautiful as usual this time around for one reason.

Chase was two thousand miles away.

Last night's talk hadn't ended well. He was exhausted from the showdown with the union, and he admitted that with the setback in filming, they didn't have enough money to finish the film.

"What?" She didn't want to sound alarmed. She'd done everything she could to support his decision to make this movie. She managed the house and the girls and their life back in San Jose by herself and tried to understand when he couldn't call until late each night. But this was exactly what she'd feared all along. If they ran out of money, they'd have to repay something to the investors. Bankruptcy was almost a certainty.

She felt her stomach tighten, something that had been happening often lately. *God ... is this really why you brought us here? To get caught up in the weirdness of Hollywood only to lose everything?*

An answer would've been nice, an assurance that if the Lord owned the cattle on a thousand hills, certainly He could send a few investors their way. But God hadn't been sending answers or investors—not lately. Kelly breathed in the warm air and tried to will away the heaviness in her heart. Nothing about herself or her life felt right, and she no longer had any idea how to escape the dark clouds around her.

"Mommy, come see my picture!" Molly's sing-song voice rang out through the house. "Hurry, Mommy. 'Fore Macy rips it up!"

She fought against the weariness as she headed toward the sound of her daughter's voice. "Coming, baby." She rounded the corner and there was Molly, sitting on her knees at their old wooden kitchen table. The surface wobbled as she worked her blue crayon across the top of the page.

"The table's breaking, I think." Molly pushed her straight blonde hair out of her face and tucked it behind her ear. Then she peered under the table and gave the nearest leg a shake. "Yep, it's breaking."

Kelly tried not to let the news discourage her. They'd bought the table at a garage sale when they first returned from Indonesia. Fifty bucks, including four chairs. She came closer and sat next to her four-year-old. "Daddy will fix it when he gets back."

She cocked her head, her big blue eyes wide with concern. "When does he get back again? Tomorrow?"

"No, baby. A few more weeks."

"Oh." She frowned and then turned her attention back to her drawing. "Weeks are a long time." She pointed to her drawing. "See this? I made it for Daddy."

Kelly studied the intricate picture. "Let's see ... that's you, right? With the long blonde hair?"

"Right." She pointed at the other stick figure, this one much taller, larger than life. "And this one's Daddy. It's a picture of when we see each other again." She pointed to the blue sky and bright yellow sun. "See? It's the happiest day ever!"

At that moment, Macy came tearing into the room, her baby doll high in the air. She had the toy stretched out in front of her, flying the doll around the house. While she ran, she made a low rumbling sound like a jet, and when she reached Molly, she swept the doll in low over her paper.

"Don't!" Molly shielded her artwork with her body and glared at her sister. "See, Mommy. I told you Macy's gonna rip it."

"Mace, sweetie ... let's calm down a little." Kelly wanted to go in the other room, lay down, and sleep until morning. And it was only two in the afternoon.

"Baby's flying." Macy stopped and sent Kelly a pleading look. "Please, Mama ... baby likes flying." Macy had talked well since before her second birthday last spring. With Molly as her role model, she did everything she could to keep up.

"Okay, but you can't fly your baby over Molly's picture." Kelly had no idea where her youngest had gotten such an idea. Flying babies. "Why's your baby flying, anyway?"

A smile lit up Macy's face. "To see Daddy!"

Kelly wasn't sure if it was the weariness in her soul or the way both her daughters clearly missed their father, but Macy's answer brought tears to her eyes. Tired, angry tears. Chase should've been home with them, not off chasing some crazy idea that was going to send them to financial ruin.

Molly looked at her and touched her fingertips to Kelly's cheek. "Are you sad, Mommy? Because of Daddy?"

"Yes, baby. I want him to come home, too." She had to find a way to lift the mood. Otherwise none of them were going to make it. "Okay, girls ... how 'bout some lemonade?"

The girls bounced in place and let out a string of happy cries and shouts.

"I'll take that as a yes." She owed it to her daughters to keep things as normal as possible, happy and centered around a routine. They still did devotions each morning and read storybooks about princesses at night. But after last night's talk with Chase, Kelly wasn't sure how much longer she could keep a happy face — even for the girls. She measured out three scoops of powdered lemonade mix in a plastic pitcher, and coughed a few times when the fine yellow powder filled her nose.

Molly spun around. "You're not getting sick, are you Mommy?"

"No, baby. I'm fine." She laughed despite the heartache she was feeling. Molly was the caretaker of the two, looking out not only for Macy, but for everyone in the family. If anyone sneezed or coughed or held their hand to their head, she wanted to know immediately if there was a problem.

They sipped lemonade while Molly moved on to another picture — this one for Kelly — and Macy continued to fly her baby doll through the living room. With every minute that passed, Kelly tried to convince herself she was fine, that this was only a phase in life, a season. One day soon Chase would come home and they would sort through the financial aftermath. Even if they went bankrupt over the failed movie, they would find their way to the surface again someday. That's what Christians did, right? As long as they had God and each other and the precious girls humming and drawing and playing around them, everything would be okay.

But today the convincing was an almost impossible struggle. Instead of joy and strength, Kelly felt filled with sorrow and emptiness, too tired to think of even one Bible verse that might dispel the gloom and give her hope for tomorrow. When the girls were down for their nap, she wandered into her bedroom and slid out a box of old letters and photo albums from beneath the bed. Maybe if she allowed herself to go back to the beginning she could remember why she had fallen in love with Chase in the first place.

They'd all been students at Cal State University Northridge, Kelly and Lisa Ellison taking classes for international studies degrees, and Chase and Keith working toward film production degrees. By then, Keith had spent years trying to make it as an actor. He earned bit parts and one small independent film project. But he and Lisa married and Andi came along, and God made it clear to Keith that he needed to pursue something else. That's when he went back to school to be a producer.

But along the way he and Lisa and Kelly took a mission trip to Indonesia. Everything about their dreams and goals changed in one week. Practically overnight Keith and Lisa were convinced they needed to move overseas and tell people about the salvation of Jesus Christ, teaching them to anchor their lives on God's eternal truth in the Bible.

The news was fantastic for Kelly. She'd gone into college with the idea of being a missionary, and now she had two friends who wanted to go with her. Chase entered the picture that next year. Even today Kelly wasn't sure if he really wanted to live in the jungle, or if he was simply that taken with her.

She ran her hand along the plastic box of memories. She could still hear Lisa's reaction when she heard the news that Chase was going to leave everything and join them in Indonesia. Lisa had laughed out loud, not a mocking laugh but one that said she was beyond amazed.

"Seriously? That guy would follow you to the ends of the earth." She let her shock show in her face. "He's such a pretty boy, Kelly. Are you sure he can handle Indonesia?"

Kelly had laughed then and often through that first year in the jungle. But the experience changed and matured Chase, and when he proposed to her a year later, her yes was nothing more than a formality. She was wholly and completely in love with Chase Ryan.

She sighed and just that effort alone felt wearying. For the third time that week she wondered if she was maybe depressed, if maybe she needed medication to find her way clear of the clouds.

But she dismissed the idea. She needed God and she needed Chase, and she needed to know they would still have a roof over their heads a year from now. As far as she knew, that combination wasn't something she could get with a prescription.

The plastic lid to the storage box had long since been tossed—too warped to fit. So the contents contained a fine layer of dust on the top items—including an oversized photo album that held pictures from their entire time overseas. She brushed her fingers along the beige cloth cover and in the afternoon sunlight she saw a small cloud of dust take to the air. She watched it dissipate and wondered. Maybe that was the problem with her life and her marriage. Even her faith. She'd let a layer of dust build up along the surface.

"You should be here, Chase," she whispered. Again tears blurred her vision, and she blinked a few times so she could see. When he finally came home, they could sit on the floor and look at these pictures together. That would have to give them a reason to feel strong again, right? She gazed out the window at the brilliant blue sky. *Give me strength, please God ... I can't encourage Chase when I feel like this.*

She waited, but again there was no answer. Just the subtle winds of sadness and discontent that blew across her barren heart. For ten minutes she looked through the book, through the chapters and years of their lives on the mission field. But no matter how hard she tried, she could barely recognize herself. It wasn't only that she was older, or that she could stand to lose twenty pounds. There was something in her expression, in the confident way she came across in every photo, that seemed foreign to her now.

"Who are you?" she brushed her fingers across the younger beaming happy face she'd had back then. "Who are you, Kelly Ryan ... missionary girl?" Her throat felt tight, and more tears filled her eyes. "And how did I lose you along the way?"

The memories were bright and brilliant, but they felt like they belonged to another person, another lifetime. She shut the book and set it to the side. The rest of the box had letters her parents had sent to them in Indonesia, an entire stack rubber-banded together. That had been the hardest part about their years away, how much her parents had missed. Her father had only recently retired from his job in LA, and they were making plans to move to San Jose so they could watch Molly and Macy grow up.

She set the stack of letters next to the photo album and sifted through an old velvet jewelry case with the broken necklace Chase had given her their first Christmas together. She opened the hinged box and moved her finger around the neglected pieces. She was always going to get it fixed. The necklace had a small white gold heart with a single tiny diamond. But the chain had broken three years ago or so and the pieces had stayed in this box beneath the bed ever since.

A single tear rolled down her cheek and landed on her forearm. She dabbed at the wet streak it left behind and sniffed once. Chase never had much money. It had taken him nearly a year to save up for that necklace, but he had wanted more than anything to give it to her. "One heart, one bright light," he had told her when she opened the gift. "That's what we share between us. This will always remind you."

Now there might never come a time when they could afford to have it fixed. She set the box to the side and peered down to the next layer of saved things. A small plastic frame jutted above the other envelopes of keepsakes. Kelly picked it up and dusted it against her jeans.

As soon as she turned it over, she knew immediately what it was, and her tears spilled down both cheeks. "Chase ... look at you." She rarely went through the contents of this box, but the last time she did, she'd somehow missed this picture. It was Chase, the summer of their first furlough back to the States, standing in the backyard of one of their supporting churches in Springfield, Missouri. The photo was faded around the edges, a close-up of Chase grinning in wide-eyed wonder. And in his hand—barely visible in the picture—was a glowing firefly. Until that trip, Chase had never been east of the Rockies.

But that wasn't the significance of the picture.

The moment came to life again as Kelly stared at the photograph. They'd had a wonderful Sunday service, welcomed by the staff and congregation at a small country church that had helped support them in their mission work. That evening the church had come together for a summer barbecue and picnic, with yard games and horseshoes and volleyball.

As the sun set, a couple dozen children scampered further out where the church property met up against a grove of trees. In the hot, humid August night, fireflies were out in full force, and the children began laughing and jumping, waving their hands trying to catch the tiny wonders.

Chase had been sitting at a folding table with Kelly and the pastor and his wife. "They're sure having a good time." He smiled, puzzled at the children's behavior. "What are they doing?"

"Catching fireflies." The pastor's wife looked wistfully toward the kids. "It never gets old for the little ones."

Chase lowered his brow. He looked from her to the pastor, and finally to Kelly. "You're kidding me, right? Just joking?"

"No." The pastor looked puzzled too. "That's really what they're doing. Catching fireflies."

"But," even in the dim light of the summer moon, they could all see the shock fill Chase's expression. "That's impossible." He shook his head. "Fireflies aren't real."

The pastor and his wife exchanged a slightly baffled look before the man turned to Chase again. "They're definitely real." He pointed to the back of the church property. "There are probably hundreds out right now."

"At least," Kelly chimed in. "Don't you see them, Chase? They look like twinkling lights because they turn on and off while they fly."

Chase was on his feet before she finished her sentence. "Come on," he took hold of her hand. "Unless I hold one in my hand I won't believe it." They moved quickly to the back of the property, but the closer they got to the laughing children, the slower Chase walked. "Those ... all those little lights in the air?" He looked at Kelly, sheer amazement in his eyes. "Those are fireflies?"

"Yes." She laughed from the joy of the moment. "I'll catch you one." She ran ahead and in no time she'd snagged one tiny firefly. She cupped her fingers loosely around it and carefully transferred it to Chase's hand. As she did, the firefly lit up for a few seconds, and then went dark again.

Chase was so shocked, he nearly dropped the little bug, but he held on, staring at it through the cracks between his fingers as it lit up again and again. He was so taken by the wonder and magic of the firefly, that his voice choked up. With the insect still in his hand he looked long and hard into Kelly's eyes. "Now ... now nothing's impossible. If God gave us fireflies ... if fireflies aren't just the stuff of fairytales and pixie dust, then ... then anything I might ever dream is possible."

Because they were meeting friends they'd never met and because Kelly wanted to remember them, she happened to have a disposable camera in her back pocket. She pulled it out and set the flash, and with the click of the button she captured a memory both of them would hold onto forever.

Many years had passed since then, but even now the wonder in Chase's eyes made her cry. God had used that moment time and again over the years in Indonesia. They'd be in an impossible situation, facing a complete lack of food or the death of one of the villagers, or a hostile faction of tribal people, and Chase would only have to look at her and say, "If fireflies are real... then God can get us through this."

Kelly held the picture with two hands and brought it closer, as if by looking intently into the long ago image, she could somehow find her way back to the days of easy wonder and disbelief, the days when nothing seemed impossible. A sudden beautiful realization filled her mind, and in a single heartbeat she knew what she needed to do.

Happy tears streamed down her face and she hugged the picture to her chest. *God... I hear You... I'll do what You say, I promise.*

"Mommy?" The tired voice came from behind her, and there was Molly, holding tight to her pink blankie. She padded closer and with tender care she brushed Kelly's bangs off her forehead. "Why are you crying?"

She couldn't talk, couldn't speak over the emotion falling like rain across her parched dry heart. She held up the picture. "See this?"

"Yes. It's Daddy." She brought her blanket to her face. "Why does that make you cry?"

"It's okay, baby." She set the photo back in the box and hugged her little daughter. "Mommy's not sad anymore, because I know what I have to do."

"Did Daddy tell you to do something?" Molly was still running her hand over Kelly's hair.

"No, baby... I think God did."

"Oh." Molly lowered her blanket, suddenly serious. "If God told you to do it, then you better do it."

"Right."

Molly yawned and gave Kelly another hug around her neck. "I'm gonna go find Macy, okay? So she can get up."

She had more control now. As Molly ran from the room calling for her sister, Kelly took a final look at the photo. But as she slid the box back beneath the bed, an idea stopped her. She took the picture from the box and set it on her nightstand. The afternoon suddenly held more promise than all the days of the past week combined. Not because she had any answers to their troubles, or because she missed Chase any less. But because for the first time since Chase started this movie business, she knew exactly what she was supposed to do. And she would do that thing no matter how much work it took.

Because this was something God told her to do.

Twenty-One

BAILEY SPENT ALL THE DAY SATURDAY with her brothers, watching Shawn, Justin, and BJ play soccer, and catching the last half of Ricky's flag football game. The boys played great, and Bailey loved sitting with her parents and Connor on the sidelines. He was in rehearsal for CKT's *Seven Brides for Seven Brothers*, but he was off this morning, so the two of them had the afternoon of sports together.

But even with all that distraction, Bailey couldn't get the image of Andi and Cody together out of her head. Even if twenty-four hours had passed. Neither of them knew she'd seen them talking in Andi's car, but she had. And the memory wouldn't fade.

They went to the five o'clock church service that night — a favorite with the family since the middle school class met then, and since their dad was busy most of Sunday helping coach the Colts. The message was from Romans 5, and Bailey felt like it was written specifically for her, like someone had called ahead on her behalf and given the pastor exactly what she needed.

Romans 5 taught that a person who loved and trusted Jesus didn't only have the guarantee of salvation, but a great deal of hope as well. Hope in eternity, hope in knowing God would always be there in the person of the Holy Spirit, and most hard to understand, hope in trials.

Bailey was well aware that compared with people starving in India or being persecuted in China, compared with a homeless man on a busy Los Angeles street or a cancer patient wasting away in a hospital—she had no trouble whatsoever. Not a single trial. But in light of what she'd seen last night, in that sermon she heard the words anew, like she'd never heard them before. The hope came in this: Suffering would eventually develop perseverance, and perseverance would in time create character. And character ... the knowing ... the knowledge that nothing could change your faith or belief or place with God ... that would then bring about hope.

Tim was with his family all day, and the two of them had texted only a few times. Still, last night had been full of laughter and good times. Back at her house after the game they played Catch Phrase and ordered pizza and laughed at BJ's pronouncement that he wanted some "sally" cream with his burrito. The boys might've been home from Haiti for seven years, but there were still times when BJ didn't quite have the right English phrase to describe what he wanted.

"All this time?" Their dad asked him, the laughter slipping out between his words. "All this time you thought it was sally cream?"

BJ only grinned and shrugged. "Sally cream ... sour cream ... whatever."

Bailey and Tim had been sitting by each other, and they laughed until Bailey could barely breathe. BJ had that effect on the family, and all of them loved it. Most of all BJ. So the night was good, and Tim's hug before he left was sweet and appropriate. He was sticking to his promise not to let things get physical on a regular basis. Kisses would be for special times, infrequent at best.

But all that good hadn't helped her sleep last night, and it hadn't stopped her from feeling secretly wounded all day. Not until they were back home did her mom find her and gently put her hand on her shoulder. "What's the matter, honey? You look upset."

A sad sound came from Bailey's throat. "You know me too well."

"I thought I picked up on it last night, but then ... you seemed pretty happy with Tim, so I thought maybe it had passed."

"The message tonight helped." Bailey closed her eyes and leaned into her mother's arms. "I just don't get it, Mom. I keep trying to let it go, but I don't know ... I feel betrayed I guess."

Her mom put her arms around Bailey's shoulders, and for a long moment Bailey returned to last night after the game. She was leaving the stadium, walking up the sloped path toward the parking lot wondering why Cody hadn't at least walked over to say hello, when up ahead she spotted Andi's blue Jetta. She was shivering from the cold night air, and she hugged herself as she realized what she was seeing.

Andi's car door was open and someone who looked a lot like Cody was stepping out, his attention still on Andi. She slowed her pace, and as the guy stood she sucked in a fast breath. He was definitely Cody, which meant what? Ever since Cody had left the stadium without talking to her, he'd been sitting here with Andi? Talking to her instead? She didn't want them to see her, so she blended better with the crowd and didn't look their way again.

Tim had been walking beside her. He picked up on her instant hurt, and leaned in close so she could hear. "What's wrong?"

"Nothing. Just a little cold." Bailey really was cold, but she could hardly tell her boyfriend the rest of what was wrong. That she was feeling hurt and betrayed because Cody had spent an hour or so with her roommate.

"You think she's interested in him?" Her mom drew back and with a light touch she lifted Bailey's chin so they could see each other. "Wouldn't Andi have told you?"

"I don't know." That's why for the rest of the night she had to hide her sorrow. It wouldn't have been fair to Tim to bring down the mood of the evening.

The boys had friends over in the next room, and their dad was reviewing plays for tomorrow. Her mom led her to the coat closet. "Put on something warm. Let's sit out front and talk."

Bailey loved this about her mother, how she was always willing to make time for her, no matter what was on Bailey's mind—whether it was nerves over an audition or a struggle in school, or something about a boy. Lately they'd had several talks about Cody, and always they reached the same conclusion. Cody cared for her, yes. But if he continued to tell Bailey that Tim was better for her, then he must not be very interested.

Bailey and her mom found the warmest coats in the closet, along with an old warm quilt and a pair of scarves. "This ought to keep us warm." Bailey giggled.

"Even if a blizzard comes up."

They both laughed as they headed outside and sat down on the first porch swing. Once they were bundled up, Bailey leaned her head on her mother's shoulder. "I like Tim. This isn't about that, you know?"

"Yes." Her mom put her arm around Bailey's shoulders. "Tim's a very nice boy. The two of you have always seemed right for each other. On paper, anyway."

"See, that's just it. Why on paper?" She straightened and looked into her mom's eyes. "Because that's the way I feel too. Like he's great in every way, but I'm still not sure I'm really in love with him."

"Being in love is a serious thing, honey. You've saved yourself physically; it's okay to save yourself emotionally, as well. That way when you commit yourself in love to a young man, it'll be incredibly special. You're still very young to have that forever kind of love."

Bailey liked the sound of that, and it made her feel less guilty about dating Tim, even though she wasn't ready to tell him she loved him, or to even feel in love with him. She liked him better this week than last, and the fact that he was opening up more about his feelings made things much nicer between them. She exhaled and set the swing gently in motion. "Which brings us to Cody."

"Ah, yes." Her mom's tone was full and pensive, because no one knew better than her mother what Cody meant to her. "I remember watching that boy come through the door on the Fourth of July, still on crutches, missing his lower left leg. I watched you register the fact, and then let it go."

"Because it didn't matter at all."

"I was upstairs near my bedroom door, so I saw the two of you talking before I went in my room. I thought to myself, No one has ever looked at Bailey like that." Her mom took a slow breath. "I told your dad that night that I thought Cody adored you, and both of us said we wouldn't be surprised if the two of you dated."

"I know. I thought that, too." Bailey was about to go into how Cody had practically ordered her to keep her feelings to nothing more than friendship. But as she went to explain that moment, her phone in her back pocket rang. She pulled it out and saw in the caller ID window that it was Andi. "Interesting timing," Bailey muttered. She made a face. "Hold on, okay? I wanna take this." She snapped open her phone and pressed it to her ear. "Hey, Andi."

"Hi!" She sounded a little too happy and upbeat. Probably because of her great night with Cody. "So where were you after the game?"

"We came home with the family." Bailey worked to keep her voice upbeat. "Did you end up going to the game?"

"Yeah. Got there after halftime, though, and guess who I saw?"

"Who?" She wanted to hear the entire story from Andi's perspective.

"Cody Coleman! He was just leaving as I was getting there, and he told me you had Tim with you." She stopped only long enough to grab another breath. "I didn't really have the best night, and I wanted to talk to you so bad. But I figured if you had Tim with you ..."

"I still would've talked. Tim isn't glued to my side."

"I know. But after I ran into Cody we started talking. He ended up sitting in my car through the rest of the game. At the end when people started coming out, we both looked but we never saw you or your brothers or your dad ... none of you."

Bailey chose her words carefully. She didn't want to make things awkward with her roommate, but she was dying to know. "What'd you guys talk about? Anything serious?"

"Sort of." Andi's tone gave her away; she was interested in Cody, no doubt. "We both shared long stories with each other. I told him about my night — which I still have to tell you — and then he told me his story — how come he lived with your family, and why you and he never had a thing."

Bailey's heart slammed into doubletime. Cody had talked with Andi about that? Again she didn't want to sound accusatory or rushed. When she'd allowed the right amount of hesitation, she laughed, as if to say the idea had never crossed her mind. "So, what did he say?"

"He said he's always been more like a brother to you." Everything about Andi's tone told Bailey she felt innocent of any wrongdoing, that her conversation with Cody felt — to Andi at least — like the most natural way to spend an hour on a Friday night.

But Bailey felt her heart crumble at the picture, Cody sharing his thoughts with Andi. She looked at her mom and shook her head, silently telling her that the conversation from Andi wasn't good. At least not for Bailey.

Andi was saying how they had a lot in common, how Cody knew what it was like to live dangerously, to experience life. "And

I told him how sometimes I want that life. You know, since I've been so sheltered."

Bailey rolled her eyes. "If I know Cody he didn't encourage that."

"No. Definitely not." She allowed the familiar confusion to enter her tone. "But I told him it's tough sometimes. Like my date with Jake. I told him you were in love with Tim and happy and enjoying life, but who did God have for me? Since there was no one, I figured I'd go out with Jake because, well ... why not? That's what I told him."

By now, Bailey really didn't want to hear about Andi's date with Jake. Everything about her actions Friday and her conversation with Cody felt like a ploy for attention, somehow. For the first time she wasn't sure she and Andi could be the best of friends — not if it meant Andi always getting in trouble and then using Cody to talk things over and find direction again. But Bailey couldn't be rude, so she listened anyway. She heard about the drive to the lake, and the strange feelings Andi had that maybe she was in danger, and the kiss, and Katy and Dayne. All of it.

"So, in some ways I guess I did what I set out to do. I had my first kiss with Jake Olson. But it obviously wasn't great, or I wouldn't have come looking for you." She paused. "Cody could tell I'd been crying. That's why we started talking in the first place."

Bailey's mom was watching her, so she stopped herself from rolling her eyes again. She had told her mom before that she hated when she started feeling bitter toward anyone. This was one of those times. The call didn't last much longer. Andi said she had homework to finish, and Bailey wanted alone-time with her mother.

"That didn't sound so good." Her mom's tone wasn't probing, just concerned. Again she put her arm over Bailey's shoulders.

"No. You should've heard her, Mom." As she went to close her phone, it vibrated and a text message came through. Bailey glanced at the small window on the front and saw it was from Tim. "Just a minute." She flipped open her phone and read the message on the bigger screen. *Just missing you, B . . . asking God to give you the hug I can't give you tonight.*

Bailey smiled and held it up for her mother to see. "You know how good it is to hear that right now?"

"Tim's matured a lot." Her mom smiled at the message and then at Bailey. "That was a very kind thing to say."

"Just that he's praying for me and he reaches out like that." She crossed her arms and settled back against the cushion of the chair swing. "Cody walked right past me yesterday at the game without saying a word."

"Well, now ..." her mom angled her head, a doubtful look on her face, "to be fair, you were with Tim. I saw him look at you as he left. I figured he probably felt uncomfortable coming over when you were with your boyfriend."

"But why?" Bailey would never understand Cody, not the way he was since he'd been home from Iraq. She tossed her hands and let them fall in her lap. "He's the one who's always talking about being friends, and what a great guy Tim is for me. If that's how he feels then he should be glad I'm with my boyfriend."

"Bailey." Her mom's tone said that she didn't for a minute believe that. "Come on, honey, that's not how Cody feels. I told you I saw the look in his eyes when he was here on the Fourth. He adores you, but maybe ..." her expression grew thoughtful and she looked out into the night, "maybe he doesn't think he's good enough for you. He still sees himself as having a lot of baggage."

"But he's overcome all that."

"He might not think so." She put her hand over Bailey's.

"He should." Bailey heard her voice rise some, and she worked to bring it down again. "He loves God now, and he doesn't drink.

He doesn't hang out with the kind of girls he went after in high school, and he survived being a prisoner in Iraq." Bailey wanted to believe that her mom was right, that Cody's strange behavior was all because his feelings for her were so deep. He'd sort of said that in his letter more than a week ago. But in person his words didn't make it seem like he was longing for her, thinking he wasn't good enough. She turned sad eyes to her mom. "He told Andi that he's always been like a brother to me."

Her mom's lips lifted in just the hint of a smile, as if she had much to help Bailey understand but she wasn't sure where to start. "Let's say I'm right. Let's say his deepest feelings are for you alone, okay?"

"Okay." It felt good to think about, even if it weren't true.

"He runs into your roommate and the two of them end up talking. If the subject of Tim came up—"

"Which it did." Bailey always wondered how her mother knew so much. She could almost predict how the conversation with Andi had gone, even though she hadn't heard any of it. She frowned. "Andi told Cody I was in love with Tim."

"See?" Her smile grew. "So there's Cody, and what's he supposed to say when Andi asks him to explain the two of you, how come you never got together? He certainly isn't going to tell a girl he barely knows that he's hoping someday soon you and Tim will break up, or that he has deeper feelings for you than he's let on. I mean, honey, if he won't tell you, he won't tell her."

Bailey breathed in slowly, letting the possibility take root in her heart. Her mother could be right, but there was one flaw in her reasoning. "When he's with me, he doesn't have to tell me he thinks Tim's better for me. He can be nice and everything, and respect the fact that I have a boyfriend, but if he has such deep feelings for me he should at least give me a hint."

"It would help, wouldn't it?" Her mom shivered a little. "It's getting colder."

"There's one more thing. Maybe Cody didn't say he had feelings for me because while he was sitting there with stunning Andi Ellison he began having feelings for her. Isn't that possible?"

Her mom seemed to weigh out the idea. "I guess."

"And meanwhile I have Tim sending me the sweetest messages and really being there for me, telling me he cares and he only wants to take things slow out of respect for me."

"I'll say this," her smile was full of pride. "Both guys in your life respect you. That's proof that you've really let your character shine for God, sweetie. Your dad and I couldn't be more proud of you."

Her heart warmed. "Thanks."

"What if you're right? How will that affect your friendship with Andi?"

"That's what I don't know. I mean, I hate the fact that she spent an hour talking with him, the two of them sitting in her car like that." She let some of her frustration fade. "But I don't have a right to be upset. I guess ... if you're wrong and he only sees me as a sister, then I should be happy for him. You know, if he ends up liking Andi."

Her mom winced. "That'd be tough."

"But it would be right."

"Yes." Her mom nodded slowly. "It would definitely be right."

"What if this ..." an idea began to take shape in her mind. "What if Cody was brought into our lives so we could help him get away from all the girls and partying, and so he could find God ... all so that one day he could meet the real love of his life, the girl God has set apart for him." She didn't want to finish her thought, but she had to get it out. "And what if that girl is Andi Ellison?" She felt sick at the thought. "How could I be mad at either of them or at God ... you know, if that's His plan?"

Her mom searched her eyes. "You amaze me, Bailey. You have wisdom beyond your years."

"But seriously, Mom. I mean, I couldn't fight that if it was God's plan all along."

"That doesn't mean it would be easy." She tapped Bailey's cell phone. "But then there's Tim. And here's the greatest part." She gave Bailey a long side hug. "God has it figured out. All you have to do is keep learning, keep loving Him, keep living the life you've been living."

"Right." Bailey felt the weight of the possibility heavy against her heart. As she and her mom gathered the blanket and headed inside she knew for certain she couldn't stay angry at either Andi or Cody. Even now she only wanted to give them both a hug and tell them she couldn't stay mad. She cared for both of them, and like Tim, she was absolutely sure God had put them in her life for a reason. If that reason included her actually cheering them on, happy for them if they fell for each other, then Bailey couldn't be upset about that either. She couldn't be mad at them. Not for spending an hour talking in the car, or for sharing secrets when Bailey wasn't around. Not even if they fell in love.

Even if she had no idea how she'd live with that hurt.

Twenty-Two

THE MONEY WAS RUNNING OUT. It was late into the third week of filming, and they had enough in the bank for another week or so, but that was all. Chase had sat down with Keith a number of times and gone over the books. No matter how they tried to cut corners or stretch the funds they were working with, the answer was always the same. Statistically, financially, it was impossible for them to finish the film without additional investor money coming in.

Keith even considered flying out to LA and trying to get a meeting with Ben Adams' assistant. Last time he'd called, the secretary had been short with him, telling him Ben was out of the country indefinitely. Other possibilities remained dried up.

It was late Thursday, and Chase wanted more than anything to stop thinking about the financial crisis at hand. Because the sad irony was this — the footage they were getting from their cast and crew continued to be amazing. If only they could find more investors, they would have a movie that might be accepted into the film festivals, a movie that studios would fight for the rights to distribute. *The Last Letter* could touch the lives of people everywhere and make them think again about faith and family and the future God had for them. If that happened, the investors would be paid back in spades, and they could take their moviemaking to the next level — reaching the world with a message of truth and hope and changed lives.

But without an immediate influx of cash from investors, none of it would happen at all.

Chase was walking back to base camp when the director of photography caught up with him. "You seeing this stuff, man? I mean the dailies must be keeping you up at night they're so good." He was a veteran, an expert with more than a hundred films to his credit. "Something special like this film only comes along once every few years." He gave Chase a hearty pat on the back. "This is that film, man. I mean it. This is that film."

The truth hung over everything Chase did. If something didn't happen soon — and their accountant and investment team had run out of options — then they would have one of the best movies never finished. Sure, they could pack up and return home to San Jose, and they could knock on the doors of every millionaire they knew looking for an extra hundred thousand. But time would pass and things would change. The actors would move on to the next project, and by the time Hollywood came to strike agreements, the crew would be back to work on other films or TV shows. Only one hope remained for them now. An investor would have to come through.

One bit of great news was that Chase had given an interview to an *Entertainment Tonight* reporter yesterday about the progress of the film. He'd done everything in talking with the reporter to hint that they needed financial help, without signaling disaster to the cast and crew and investors that would likely watch the program.

The DP had moved on, so while Chase walked across the street to the eating area, he let the interview play again in his mind, every line, analyzing his answers and assuring himself that he'd done and said what he could.

The reporter had been very upbeat and positive — something that wasn't always the case with people doing the interviews. He'd flown out the day before so he could watch some of the dailies and interview Jake Olson and Rita Reynolds.

For his talk with Chase, the guy set up with a scenic part of IU's campus in the background. "This is the first big picture you and Keith Ellison have worked on, and rumor on the street is that you have something very special on your hands." The reporter's smile would've told anyone watching that he, too, thought the film was special. "What's your secret out here in Bloomington?"

Chase had an easy way about him on film, so though Keith had more acting experience, they'd chosen Chase to be the point person for this interview. He smiled easily at the guy and kept his answer equally full of humility and intrigue. "We have an extremely talented cast and crew," he let his expression grow more serious. "The script is amazing, very powerful. All that and a lot of help from above."

The reporter didn't visibly chafe at that last part, but he furrowed his brow. "You mention help from above. I understand you and your co-producer were Christian missionaries several years ago, and that there was some confusion early in the filming that maybe this was a Christian movie, that the cast had been tricked into signing onto the project. Can you talk to that issue?"

"Yes," Chase laughed, his tone the same affable, slightly baffled one he would've had if the guy had asked him why the sky was blue. "We did have that conversation and it went quite well. Keith talked to everyone on the set and told them that while the two of us are Christians, and while we think the film packs a powerful message, it isn't being marketed as a Christian movie." Chase went on to explain that there had been some very well-received Christian movies in recent years, and that there was certainly a market for those films. "But our goal is to reach the masses, the people who might not line up to buy a ticket for a movie that's outspokenly Christian."

"Meaning your film is clean with no cussing or explicit sex scenes?"

"Definitely you won't see any of that in our movies." Chase brought his laughter down some and got serious again. "We want more than a clean film, though. We want a film that will literally change lives. That's why we're doing this."

The reporter nodded. "Impressive. I spoke with Jake Olson and Rita Reynolds, and they said the same thing. They were taken by the story of *The Last Letter* and they felt compelled to star in it." He gave a disbelieving shake of his head. "And you're doing it all on an independent budget of just a couple million, is that right?"

"Well, I can say this—we're always looking for investors. But yes," he felt his strength building as he spoke, "we feel very strongly about remaining independent through the making of the movie. That way we retain creative control, and the movie won't become something we never intended it to be."

"I've seen some of the dailies, and I have to agree with the rumors." He turned and faced the camera. "*The Last Letter* is a movie you won't want to miss, being made by a couple of producers who are doing it their way. You gotta admire that in today's world." He signed off and shook Chase's hand. "Seriously, you've got a special picture coming together here. The movie is Oak River Films' *The Last Letter*." He turned to Chase once more. "I wish you the best of luck."

Scoring the interview was no easy feat. The show had called a week ago with the possibility of a story, but only a remote one. They'd been praying about it since then with no word, and Chase and Keith were well aware of the victory in having the film recognized at all—especially this early in the process. But the reporter had been noncommittal about when the piece would air, and even whether it would air before the movie wrapped.

It was one more thing to pray for—that the piece would show up on national TV in time to catch the attention of that one investor who might then be drawn to the project. The interview was in many ways their last desperate hope at getting the money they needed. Otherwise they'd have to contact *Entertainment Tonight* and tell them to pull the story. No sense running a feature about a movie that never wrapped.

Chase grabbed a plate of chicken and baked beans from the food truck and took his place across from Keith and Lisa at the end of one of the tables. Most nights the cast and crew sat at separate tables, leaving distance between themselves and the producers. Tonight was no exception. As Chase sat down he realized the weight of the burden he was carrying, the fact that they were nearly out of money.

"Well," he slid forward and looked directly at Keith and his wife. They were far enough from the others that no one else could hear him. "I don't know if I can take much more of this." He smiled big, so that anyone watching might've believed his conversation was about the great-tasting chicken or the nice warm day they'd had. No matter what, he wouldn't let the others see him down. The actors and cameramen, the assistant director and DP, all of them took their cues from Chase and Keith. There were concerns working on such a tight budget, a sense of slight relief every time payday rolled around and they received their checks. It was that way with any independent film. Now, with the project in trouble, Chase didn't dare show his weariness or the fact that his fear was all but consuming him.

"We were just talking about it." Lisa took a bite of her beans and looked down. "Keith had another lead earlier today."

"But it fell through." Keith's expression was peaceful, steadfast. "We just got word an hour ago."

"Unbelievable." Chase focused on his chicken. He felt like they were talking almost in code, so careful not to let anyone else feel the gravity of their dialogue. "I keep thinking, I mean ... why would God lead us here only to let us fall?"

"We don't know we're going to fall." Keith's voice was barely above a whisper. "Something could happen. The feature story could run on *ET* and someone could come forward."

Chase finished chewing his chicken, his mind trying to find a realistic way of looking at the possibility. "I've been telling myself that same thing, how someone could see the feature and come looking for us." He lifted his eyes, and produced another smile for appearances. "But when I really think about it, I picture some possible investor sitting on his leather sofa flipping channels and coming across our story. He watches, but he's not really thinking anything more than how maybe he'd like to see this movie when it comes out. He has money, but he's worried about his foreign investments and his real estate holdings, and the instability of the stock market and the tax increases that seem to come every year or so." Chase kept the pleasant look, but he shook his head. "It's hard to picture the guy saying to himself, 'That gives me an idea. I should invest in a movie like that,' and then getting up and making a phone call to Oak River Films."

"Stranger things have happened." Keith's smile wasn't for the sake of anyone but Chase. Even with all that had happened and the alarming rate at which they were running out of money, Keith maintained his cool. "Besides, God brought us here. If He wants us to go home without a movie, then we take some time to ask Him where to go next."

"Yeah," Chase dragged his fork around his beans. "Like back to Indonesia."

"Right." Lisa's eyes were full of wisdom. "Indonesia was wonderful for all of us. If that's where God takes us again, I couldn't be anything but happy. I would go with a full heart."

Chase knew that was the right answer, but here—with the cast and crew depending on them—he couldn't catch the attitude of his friends. "You know what? I loved being a missionary in the jungle. I loved everything about it. You were both there to see the way God worked on me during those years." He leaned over his plate, his voice as quiet as it was intense. "But I don't want to go back to Indonesia. I want to make this film to the glory of God and get it out there for everyone to see." He straightened, his tone more resigned. "I guess I can't believe God brought us this far just to see us fail."

Keith and Lisa didn't try to say anything about that. Chase was about to go through the list of possible investors one more time, throwing out names and making sure that Keith had contacted everyone on the list one more time, when the director of photography walked up. "I need to talk to Jake and Rita about tomorrow's shoot." He removed his baseball cap and raked his fingers through his hair. "They haven't gotten rides back to the hotel, but I can't find 'em. Knocked on both their trailer doors, and they're nowhere. One of you wanna take a look for me? I can't finish up here until the three of us talk."

The chicken was good, but Chase's jangled nerves had cost him his appetite. He swung his leg out from the picnic table and stood. "I'll find them." He maneuvered his way between the tables, stopping along the way to pat a few of the minor actors on the back and to lean down and give Janetta Drake a hug.

"How's it going?" she always looked at him deeper than the others, because of all the cast, she alone knew the battle they were undertaking producing an independent film with a message of faith and hope.

"Good." He patted her arm and smiled. "It's fine, Janetta. Thanks for asking."

She looked at him a little while longer and shook her head. "It's not fine, Chase. I can see it in your eyes."

"What we're getting on film is beyond our highest expectations." He gave an easy shrug. "At least we've got that much."

"But what about the rest, the stuff producers deal with." The caring and concern in her eyes made him grateful once again that she was on the crew.

He could be honest with her, but only to a degree. The specifics about the impending financial crisis had to be confined to the production team alone. "Okay, here's what I'll tell you." He crouched down so he was at her level. "We could use your prayers. Let's just leave it at that."

She took hold of his hand and gave it a motherly squeeze. "You don't need to ask, Chase. I've been praying constantly since I arrived on set." She smiled and her eyes lit up like a child's. "God is doing something big here. He won't let you down. He told me."

"Good." Chase nodded, careful not to let the moment get too heavy. "Now I just wish He'd tell me."

After Janetta, Chase moved on with a few more hellos and compliments to his cast and crew. People needed compliments in order to give their best. Chase and Keith made it a point to praise the people they were working with as often as the chance presented itself. Finally he rounded the corner and walked across the street back to the set. They were working out of one of the classroom buildings on campus again, and he wondered if his two lead actors might've stayed on the set, going over blocking or lines.

But the area was dark and quiet, no sign of Jake or Rita. Chase lowered his brow, puzzled. *Strange*, he thought. Usually the two joined the rest of the cast for dinner. And since they hadn't gone back to the hotel they had to be here somewhere. He crossed the street again and walked between the rows of trailers to the one that belonged to Rita. It was twice the size of the others — another of her demands. She hadn't made an attempt to seduce him lately, but nothing would surprise him when it came to Rita Reynolds. Chase had a feeling there was a deeply insecure woman beneath the pretty façade that stepped in front of the camera each day.

"Rita?" he called out. "Jake?" The area between the trailers was very dark, and he walked in the shadows. He was nearly to the end of the row, almost to Rita's trailer, when her door opened and Jake took one step out onto the landing. He had Rita in his arms, and the two of them were caught in a makeout session that would've been well beyond PG-rated.

"Hey," he shouted at them as he walked closer. "Jake ... Rita ... what's going on?"

Jake jerked away, his surprise evident. A smile took over and he kissed Rita again, this time with blatant passion. When he pulled away from her, he shaded his eyes and peered out at Chase. "What's the problem? I'm just telling my co-star goodnight." His tone was both humorous and mocking, as if he wanted to convey the fact that Chase had no right to care if his two stars were kissing.

Rita looked embarrassed. She put up her hand to stop Jake from kissing her again. "Is something wrong, Chase?"

"Yes." He was seething mad as he walked up to them.

Jake released Rita and the two of them stood together, a not-quite-unified front. "You got a problem with us kissing?" He chuckled and turned to Rita. "We were just working on our chemistry, right?"

"Well," Rita couldn't say much. She was playing Jake's mother, after all. "I mean, it's no big deal, Chase. We're just letting off tension after a day on the set."

Chase raised one eyebrow. "This is my film, and it's my reputation on the line." He took a step closer, and he could feel the fire in his eyes. "The last thing we need is some on-the-set scandal to bring the paparazzi sniffing around."

"On-set romances happen all the time." Jake put his arm easily around Rita's shoulders. "We could kind of be like Ashton and Demi." He pulled Rita a little closer to his side. "Right, baby?"

Rita didn't seem to like the comparison. "I'm not that much older." She eased free of Jake's embrace. Her next words were layered in understanding. "I'm sorry, Chase. We didn't mean anything by it."

Her apology took Chase by surprise and eased some of his anger. "The thing is, you people are the stars of my picture. You're giving me performances that are way above the line, and I appreciate that." His voice was calmer, more even. "But I absolutely demand that what happens off-screen is above the line, as well. That we maintain a level of propriety while we're working that is impeccable—able to withstand whatever scrutiny comes our way."

"Okay... okay." Jake laughed and took a step back. He slid his hands in the pockets of his jeans and cocked his head back. "We were just having a little fun."

"Not on my dime." Chase hoped his look conveyed to Jake how serious he was. "Is that understood?"

"Fine." He straightened up and seemed to get suddenly repentant. "Our mistake, Chase. We'll be good little actors from now on."

"Thank you." Chase knew his star actor was mocking him, but he decided not to let on. "I appreciate that more than you know. By the way, the DP's looking for you. He wants to set up tomorrow's scenes."

Jake left, chuckling to himself, but Rita stayed. She put her hand on Chase's shoulder. "That shouldn't have happened. You're right."

Chase wanted to ask her how she could've let it happen, but he didn't want to have too deep a conversation with Rita Reynolds here in the dark spaces between the trailers. He nodded, keeping the walls in his eyes firmly in place. "Thanks for saying that. We need to keep it clean on the set."

"You're right." She still had her hand on his shoulder. "I guess ... I don't know, I still think every day about what we could be sharing. Not on the set, of course. But back at the hotel. A friendship," she massaged her fingers into his shoulder muscles. "Or something more."

A sigh rattled around in Chase's chest. "Rita, for the last time, I'm not interested." He was baffled at her determination.

"Maybe that's why I let Jake kiss me. At least he's not married."

"No. But he is your co-star, and for that reason, the two of you need to cool it until we wrap."

He took a step toward the eating area. "Come on, the DP wants to talk to you, too." He kept a few paces ahead of her, and once they were back with the others the gravity of what had just happened hit him fully. He walked back to Keith and Lisa and told them he couldn't take another minute on the set. "I need to get back. I'll see you in the morning."

"Seven o'clock call again."

"I know." He stopped himself from reciting the number of dollars that would fall from their bank balance once the clock started ticking in the morning. He needed some sleep or he would regret his poor attitude. "Thanks for your hard work, guys."

"You too." Keith stood and moved closer to him. "What was the deal with Jake and Rita? Where'd you find them?"

Chase barely had the energy to tell the story, so he stuck to the facts. He explained how he'd been walking toward Rita's trailer when Jake stepped out, the two of them caught in a passionate kiss. "I told them to quit it, and I asked them to keep their behavior above the line — the way they were supposed to be." Chase rubbed his hand into the back of his neck. He and Keith and Lisa could talk later about the problems an affair between the two co-stars could bring about. "Bottom line, they promised to lay low from now on, keep things clean on the set."

"Wow ... I mean, you ever wonder if there's anything else the enemy can throw at us to stop us from making this movie?"

"I try not to think about it." Chase felt the exhaustion in his smile. "See you later."

He left and as he drove back to the hotel he turned on the radio and heard Jeremy Camp's "I Will Walk by Faith." He turned up the volume and let the words fill his heart and soul. *I will walk by faith, even when I cannot see...* Chase let that phrase stay with him, let it work its way deep inside him. When the song ended he turned off the radio and stared blankly at the cars stopped at the light ahead of him. The citizens of Bloomington were good, hard-working family people, most of them going home at this hour to family dinners and homework sessions with their kids. The thought of it made him miss Kelly and the girls more than he had since he'd arrived in town.

God... everything is closing in around me. I can't see You in anything that's happening, and I'm not doing very well at walking by faith either. He remembered a scene from the great classic film, *It's a Wonderful Life.* When George Bailey was in trouble, his entire town came to his support and saved the day dropping fives and tens and twenties into a huge basket and sparing him a trip to jail in lieu of having Christmas with his family. That's what he needed, that kind of a miracle. *But, God, who's going to save our movie from failing?* He could hardly expect the townspeople to show up with tens and twenties. It was one thing for them to come together to pray, but this? *Father, I'm falling... I'm at the end of myself. We're almost out of money and then all of this will be for nothing—the investors' money wasted... the actors' time wasted... all of it a waste of time and energy.* He felt tears in his eyes, and he fought back his emotions. *I can't do this, Lord... I feel like I'm walking into a lion's den and taking the entire cast and crew with me.*

My son, I am with you... rejoice in your suffering. I will never leave you nor forsake you...

The answer wasn't clear or loud or definitive, but the verse filled his soul at just the right moment. God was with him, of that Chase could not doubt. God's Spirit lived in him and like Keith and Lisa said, if this wasn't the place where God wanted them, He would lead them to the next place. And since the verse that came to mind was about suffering, Chase had every reason to believe that's exactly what would happen. Oh, the cast and crew would be paid for every hour of their work—one way or another. The moment they ran out of money, he and Keith would have to face the group and tell them what had happened. Everyone would pack up and go their own ways and that would be that.

Failure beyond anything Chase ever imagined.

Even he and Kelly were struggling. She was worried frantic over what a failed movie would mean for their personal finances. She'd even said something about being homeless this time next year. He parked his car and walked heavy-hearted into the lobby past the fireplace. The old man at the check-in desk was friendly with all those from the movie staying at the hotel. He was a Christian, and Chase and Keith had talked to him a few times about the purpose of the film. In turn the man had promised to pray. Now he waved and gave Chase a big grin. "Long day on the set, my friend?"

"Very long." Chase smiled at the guy. "But God is good, right?"

"All the time!" The man handed Chase a fresh water bottle. "Tomorrow's a new day."

"Thanks. That means a lot." More than the man could possibly have known. Chase took the elevator up to his floor and trudged down the hallway to his room. As soon as he opened the door he saw someone move inside and he stepped back. When was Rita going to—

"Hi." The voice wasn't Rita's, it was Kelly's.

Chase walked inside and set his bag down, too shocked to move or speak or do anything but let the tears fill his eyes. "You ... how did you ...?"

"My parents bought me a ticket. I couldn't stay away." She was sitting at the table near his bed, the same one where Rita had been sitting that time. Chase had told Kelly about the incident, and now she smiled. "I was afraid you'd think I was Rita."

"I did." He was catching his breath, rebounding from the shock of seeing her. "Notice my first reaction was to back up into the hallway."

"I did notice." She stood and there were tears in her eyes too. She held out her arms. "I missed you."

He came to her, wrapped her into his arms, and held her close against his chest, clung to her as if she were the only friend he had in all the world. "You don't know how much I needed to see you tonight."

"I do know." She sniffed and leaned back enough to see him. "God told me to come, and so I couldn't stay away. You had to know that I believe in your dreams, Chase. I do." The tears ran unabashed down her cheeks and she lifted her face to his, kissing him in a way that took both their breath. The moment was laced with a desperate sort of passion and fear, a determination that they would walk together with God, wherever the path took them. In that embrace, in that moment of untamed love and longing for each other, one thing was desperately clear — whatever they faced, they wouldn't lose each other in the process.

When they eased back from each other, Kelly made a sound that was mostly laugh and partly cry. "I can't believe I'm here. It feels so good to see you."

"You too." He led her to the edge of the bed and they sat side-by-side. "I've never been more discouraged, Kelly. So much that I was afraid to call you." He looked down at his hands and absently twisted his wedding ring. "I hate making you worry."

"I'm done worrying."

The resolve and certainty in her voice caught him by surprise. "Nothing's better." He had to be honest with her. "No one's come forward, and if we don't find some money fast, we're finished."

"I know." Her smile was bathed in peace. She reached out and took his hand, lacing her fingers between his. "But if that happens, then God will get us from here to there."

"There?" He almost didn't recognize this new, completely confident Kelly. "Where's there?"

"Wherever He takes us." She turned toward him and hugged him once more, burying her head against his neck and staying that way a long time. "I forgot how important it was to dream, Chase. But God reminded me." She stood and went to her suitcase. From the outside pocket she pulled a padded envelope and brought it to him. "I found this the other day."

Chase had no idea what she might've found that could bring about this type of change in her, but he was grateful. After crying out to God the way he had earlier, he was certain her visit was God's way of encouraging him—even if encouragement couldn't pay the bills.

Kelly sat on the bed again and lifted a small plastic frame from inside the envelope. She turned it over and held it up for him to see. As soon as Chase realized what he was looking at, the tears he'd been fighting spilled onto his cheeks. Now he understood why she had come, why God had told her she needed to be here to remind Chase of his dreams. He studied the picture and he was there again, the hot, humid night air thick around him, realizing a wonderful miracle that until that day he hadn't believed was possible.

Chase looked up at his wife, and with his chin trembling he said the only thing he could think to say. "If fireflies are real ..." His voice cracked, and he couldn't finish the sentence. He framed her face with his hands, loving her more than ever before, and he tried again. "If fireflies are real ..."

She smiled at him through her own tears. "Then God can get us through this."

They hugged again and Chase had no words to thank her, no way of voicing what her visit and her reminder meant to him.

The light from the firefly in the photograph had said it all.

Twenty-Three

ANDI WAS BACK ON THE SET Friday afternoon for additional extra work, this time by herself. Bailey was no longer considered an extra because of her role as Jake's girlfriend, so they couldn't use her in scenes where she might be recognized walking along a campus path or sitting in a classroom. Andi missed having her camaraderie on the set, but she didn't mind the lack of scrutiny. Because she'd done something she told herself she wouldn't do.

She'd connected again with Jake Olson.

When she arrived at the set just before lunch, he came up to her and asked if she'd follow him to a grassy spot a ways from the tent. "Hey," he sounded disappointed in himself. "I'm sorry about last week."

At first Andi kept her guard up. "Don't worry about it." She started walking back toward the tent, but he touched her arm. The feeling shot electricity throughout her body, and she turned, flustered. "There's not much more to say." She gave him a look like this was wasting her time. "I have to go eat."

"Wait." He took a few steps and caught up to her. "I felt like a jerk that night. I mean it was so awkward—getting caught by Dayne and his wife that way."

"It was. I never should've let things go that far." She released an exasperated breath. "Look, Jake, I was okay with a kiss. One kiss and a nice walk around the lake. But that's not what you had in mind." Her smile was aloof, intended to dismiss him.

But again he stayed at her side. "Can I have another chance? I mean, I think I underestimated you."

His eyes pierced hers, and the feeling made her knees weak. "Underestimated me?"

"How good you are. In my business, there are almost no really good girls." He slipped his hands in his jeans and took on a look that seemed meant to garner her empathy. "A guy like me can get out of practice, forget how to handle a girl who's ... you know, really a treasure."

Andi felt herself falling again. After the hour she spent talking with Cody at last week's football game, she had no trouble forgetting Jake. All she wanted was a guy like Cody Coleman, a guy who would cherish her the way Tim Reed cherished Bailey. But here ... with Jake standing inches from her, she felt her resolve giving way like a sandcastle at high tide. "Really?" She crossed her arms, still trying to save face. "You're not just saying that?"

"Not at all." He motioned for her to follow him back to the tent. "It's Friday night. I just thought maybe we could hang out again, that's all."

"Not at Lake Monroe." Her answer was quick and laced with a teasing if reluctant laugh.

"No, not there." His grin was full of more apology. "How 'bout somewhere out in the open, with lots of people around. So you won't have to wonder about my motives."

The idea sounded better all the time. Andi tried to picture what it would feel like being seen with Jake Olson, the girl on his arm at some restaurant or party. Just then she remembered. "A guy in my math class told me about a frat party tonight. Right across from campus."

"That'd be great." His eyes danced and he looked less dangerous than before.

Andi wondered if she'd been too quick to write him off. Maybe he really was sorry for being such a jerk. Besides, after her talk with Bailey last Saturday she sensed her roommate wasn't really excited about Andi spending time with Cody. Not only that, but

Cody hadn't called or texted, so he couldn't have been too anxious to get to know her better.

But Jake ... Jake was very interested. The fact was more flattering than Andi wanted to admit. "I'm going to dinner with my parents, but I can head over to the party around eight."

"Perfect. Text me when you get there, and you can tell me where you are."

She flashed flirty eyes at him. "This is your last chance."

He produced a dramatic bow, like a renaissance man of old. "Your kindness and generosity overwhelm me, my princess."

"Jake!" she giggled. "You're crazy."

"About you." He made a few quick raises of his eyebrow and then he turned and headed toward the assistant director.

Andi went into the tent and served herself a scoop of tuna salad and a side of steamed vegetables. But she barely tasted any of it, because she couldn't believe the change in Jake, or the fact that tonight, for the first time in her life, she was going to a real party. At a frat house, no less. She'd seen those types of parties in the movies, and she figured this one would be the same—loud music, lots of laughter, and people drinking and hitting on each other.

She wasn't sure how much of the party she wanted to experience, but she was thrilled to be going. How could she understand what she was missing if she didn't at least try living the way other people lived? And with Jake there, she wouldn't have to worry about strange guys picking her up.

Throughout her day of extra work, whenever Jake was near her, their eyes would meet and she could feel his admiration to the core of her being. She was surprised that her parents hadn't noticed his attention, and she was grateful at the same time. The last thing she wanted was another lecture from her dad about the type of guy Jake Olson really was. Her dad meant well, but he didn't know. Jake was a good guy, she could tell that after their talk today. His explanation about not having much practice with "good" girls made perfect sense.

Throughout her day of filming, and on into dinner, her plans with Jake were all she could think about. She and her parents went to a steakhouse, and Chase and his wife joined them. Andi was glad about that too. The two couples kept getting into deep conversations about the filming and practically forgetting she was with them. Andi was glad because the talk kept the attention off of her.

Toward the end of the meal, her mom reached across the table and took hold of Andi's hand. "You doing okay, sweetie? You're quiet."

"I'm fine." Neither of them had found out about her date last Friday with Jake, and if things went well, they wouldn't find out about tonight either. "School's going great. My grades are almost all A's."

"Good for you, honey." Her dad's smile was kind and laced with approval. "You've been doing a great job on the set too." He didn't say that she'd handled well the disappointment of not getting the part she wanted. But that's what he meant, his tone told her that. "How are things with Bailey?"

"Fantastic." Andi smiled at the mention of her roommate. "She's doing great at rehearsals for *Scrooge*. She's the best Ghost of Christmas Past ever." Andi pictured the two of them at rehearsal the other day with Tim. He was amazing as Scrooge, and since Andi had to dance with him in the first act, the two of them were becoming better friends.

"I like Tim for you," Andi had told Bailey the other day after rehearsal. "You two are so much the same it's incredible. Like God made him just for you."

Bailey hadn't looked overjoyed at the comment, but she agreed all the same. "Tim is good for me. I see that a little more every day."

There were a few bumps here and there—like the hurt she felt from Bailey after Andi's talk with Cody that night. But that passed after a few days, and she and Bailey were becoming better friends all the time. Neither of them would've done anything to hurt the other, and they were opening up more about the deeper ways they thought about their faith and family, the guys in their lives. Bailey still worried about the way Andi was tempted to live a little on the edge.

"Rachel would have told you to stay away from Jake," Bailey told her this morning when they talked about their Friday night plans. Bailey was going home again, and she and Tim were seeing a movie. Andi mentioned the frat party, and Bailey had given her a doubtful look. "And she never would've gone to a party like that. You know it, Andi."

"Yeah," she gave a sad look at the picture that hung on her wall. "Look where it got her."

The conversation around the dinner table turned again to the movie, and Andi felt her phone vibrate in her purse beside her. She pulled it out and discretely—so she wouldn't be thought rude—she read the message. A thrill ran through her, the same thrill that always came when she saw his name. The message was from Jake. *Don't forget to text me when you get to the party. I'm sitting at the hotel... can't wait to hear from you.*

She checked the time on her phone. Seven thirty. She needed to get going. As they finished dinner, the women suggested dessert. "We haven't all been together like this in too long," Andi's mom said. "I could sit here catching up all night."

Andi took the statement as her cue. She spread her hand out on the table and leaned in, smiling at each of them. "I should probably get going. Still lots to do tonight."

"On a Friday?" Her mom looked disappointed again. "We love having you here."

"I know." She managed to sound practically heartbroken that she wasn't staying longer. "It's been a great dinner." She focused her attention on her mom. "We're still meeting for breakfast, right? That little place just off campus?"

"Definitely." Her mom gave a questioning look to the others. "You guys are in a meeting, right?"

"We'll be in meetings all day, phone conferences with our team back home." Her dad tried not to look worried, but his eyes showed his concern. "You girls should all go, all three of you."

"Great idea." Kelly looked prettier than she had in a long time. She'd done her hair and makeup and she and Chase seemed very in love. "What time should we meet?"

"Let's say ten. In case I'm up late studying." Normally Andi would've wanted the breakfast alone with just her mother and her, but in light of all she wasn't telling her parents, she welcomed the addition of Kelly to their breakfast date.

They all agreed that ten would work, and then Andi gave out hugs and goodbyes and headed for the parking lot. She texted Jake the minute she arrived at the party, even before she climbed out of her car. *I'm here ... it's the big yellow house on the east side of the street.*

Ten seconds passed and her phone rang. It was Jake. "Hey."

"Hi." Her mouth was suddenly dry, and she reached for a water bottle she had in the console between the two front seats. He'd said just one word, but his voice made her dizzy, overcome with anticipation for whatever fun the night held. "Did you get my text?"

"I did. I know the place." He had a way of making every conversation seem deeply personal, intimate. "I've passed it on the way back from the set a few times and seen kids hanging out there."

She laughed. "That's the place."

"Okay, well, hey ... so Rita stopped by for a minute. She wants to talk about our scenes for next week, run lines for a little while."

"Oh." She felt like a child whose birthday balloons had suddenly all gone flat. "So you're not coming?"

"No, no. Nothing like that." He sounded anxious to keep her happy. "I'll have the driver drop me off in an hour or so at the most. Then later on you can drive me home or I can walk. The hotel's only a few blocks away." His tone told her he felt terrible about the delay. "I'm sorry, Andi. It's business, you know?"

"Sure." She stared out the windshield at the crowd already gathering in front of the yellow frat house. "I don't really know anyone. Maybe I'll go back to my dorm and wait to hear from you."

"No, seriously, Andi. Go have fun." His concern for her was refreshing. "You'll see people you know. And I'll be there as soon as I can."

The idea sounded better than sitting in her dorm by herself. Adrenaline coursed through her at the thought of walking up to the kids and heading into the frat house not knowing a single person. Like something daring the old Andi never would've done. "Okay. I might do that."

"I have one question." Jake sounded like he was nervous to ask it. "Will there be drinking?"

"Drinking? You mean alcohol?" She was surprised. "Jake, come on. I mean, it's a frat party. Of course there'll be drinks."

"So ... will it ... offend you if I have a few beers?"

Again she was touched that he would think to ask. "Not at all. You can drink. I mean, you're old enough, and as long as you don't drive, I'm fine. You could just get a ride back from someone."

"True ... but I wanted you to be okay with it."

"Sure ... of course." Danger and intrigue mixed together in her gut and made her a little breathless. Would that be okay, really? Jake drinking when he was with her? What if after he started drinking he forgot about his promise to be more of a gentleman? She sucked in a nervous breath through her teeth. "I'll even pull you aside a few beers, so you'll have some in case they run out."

He chuckled and there was a fondness in his tone that didn't seem to want more than a nice night out with her this time. "What about you?"

"Me?"

"Yeah, are you going to drink? You could just walk back to your dorm."

She hadn't considered the idea. Drinking wasn't something she thought a lot about, but maybe this was the night to try it. Like he said, she didn't have to drive or get a ride with anyone. She could hang out, have a few beers, and then walk back to her dorm to sleep it off. Her heart raced the way it had the first time she had flying lessons from her dad in the small single-engine plane that took them in and out of the jungles of Indonesia.

"I'm not twenty-one."

"That's only if you're buying. Otherwise you can't get in trouble."

That didn't sound like the rule she'd heard before. Back in San Jose a group of kids got arrested and charged for being at a party where alcohol was being served to minors. "Only if you get caught."

"Right," he conceded. "Which you won't, because cops don't go to frat parties. I mean, I'm not telling you what to do, but I'd say live a little, Andi. Isn't that what you told me that first time we talked? That you were tired of being so sheltered?"

"All the time." What he was saying made sense. She felt goose bumps along her arms and again she stared at the growing crowd on the steps and front yard of the frat house. "Okay, maybe I'll go in and have a drink."

"Good." He laughed not in a mean way, but the way a big brother would laugh at his little sister's naiveté. "Don't be afraid of having two. A couple beers won't hurt you, and I'll be there as soon as I can get away."

There was the sound of a woman's voice in the background, and Jake muttered, "Just a minute. I'll be right off."

"Rita?" Andi could hear now that it was her voice.

"Yeah." He sounded bored. "We have to get some work done. You go have fun and I'll see you later."

"Text me when you get here. I'll come out and meet you."

He agreed and they hung up. As Andi got out of her car and locked the doors, she could imagine the stress of trying to memorize lines and act out a scene without hours of rehearsal. Her dad had told her that sometimes the actors barely have time to run the scene immediately prior to the shoot. Andi figured that would be the most difficult thing about being in front of a camera. No wonder Jake and Rita were turning in such great performances, if they were working after hours to run lines. His work ethic underlined what she'd already figured out at the set earlier.

That he was a nice guy after all.

Twenty-Four

ANDI CROSSED THE STREET AND AS she stepped up onto the lawn, she felt an almost electric rush. She was actually doing this, attending a frat party by herself. A number of guys turned around or looked over their shoulders to admire her, and the attention sent a rush through her. By the time she reached the door, two of them came up and introduced themselves.

"You're in my math class, right?" The guy was solidly built, well over six feet tall. He wore an Indiana football jersey and a baseball cap.

She couldn't remember seeing him before. "Uh ... a guy in my math class told me about the party, but ..."

"That was Ben!" The guy laughed loudly. He was holding a beer and he sloshed it in the direction of his buddy. "I told you Ben had more—" he seemed to catch himself. He held up his hand in her direction, "More nerve than the rest of us." He sloshed his beer again. "Good for ol' Ben, asking you over. He's inside. I can take you there if you want. I'm Lucas."

"What Lucas means is, I can take you." The second guy was black with a nice build and friendly eyes. "You don't want to waste your time on Lucas." He held out his hand to her. "I'm Sam. And I'm available—in case you wondered."

Andi giggled at the spectacle they were making of themselves. "That's okay." She took a few steps from them. "I'll say hi to Ben, and then I'll come back outside."

The guys seemed harmless, and when she moved on without them they didn't look too disappointed. It wasn't easy getting up the steps and into the house. The place was packed with people squeezing past each other in every direction. As she worked her way through the living room she spotted Ben in the kitchen. Suddenly she could feel everything about the situation filling her senses. The loud Chris Brown music pulsing through the house, the laughter and multiple conversations, and the sense that this ... this party and everything about it was what it meant to truly live.

She felt the heat from so many bodies, and halfway to the kitchen a guy tripped near her and spilled beer on her sweater. Andi only laughed and helped him gain his balance again. She'd never been around drunk people or drinking of any kind, but she didn't need experience to know that the guy was wasted.

"Sorry," he tried to touch her shoulder, but he missed and nearly fell again. "Wow, so sorry."

"Don't worry about it." She kept with the flow, and the drunk guy kept with his, moving toward the front door.

"Hey," he yelled at her when he was well out of reach. "You're beau'ful ... you know that?"

Andi didn't look back. She didn't want the whole room to know he was talking about her. When she reached Ben, he looked beyond thrilled to see her. "Andi Ellison, I never thought I'd see you here." He had to yell to be heard above the music and conversations.

"Me either." She looked over her shoulder at the packed house behind her. "A friend's meeting me here."

"Good ..." he put his arm around her and slowly led her to an enormous trash can filled with beer cans and ice. "This your first frat party, Andi?"

"How can you tell?" She grinned at him.

"You, uh ... you look a little lost." He snagged an icy can from the bin, popped the top, and handed it to her. "Here you go, beer's compliments of the frat guys."

She took it, her heart pounding. This was as close to bad as she'd come. This and her time with Jake the other night. Was she really doing this? Standing in the kitchen of a group of guys she didn't know, holding an open beer? She fought the urge to run from the house and throw the beer in the bushes on the way out.

"You're not rushing, are you?" Ben was still right beside her, still with his arm around her shoulders. But the way he had about himself he was only being friendly. At least that's how his attention felt.

"Rush? For a sorority, you mean?"

"Yeah, of course."

"No. I'm too busy. I do theater and acting, that kind of thing."

"Oh, right." He gave an exaggerated nod and took a long drink from his beer. "Your dad's that producer. He's in town making a movie. Someone in math told me about him."

"That's my dad." Andi would've bet the guy didn't know about her family's missionary background. And in this setting, she was okay with that. She wanted to turn the attention away from herself. "You're in this frat, then? Is that right?"

"For two years." He raised his beer and across the room a couple guys saw him and did the same. "Mayhem and madness, but somehow I've survived it." He pointed to her beer. "Your drink's getting warm."

"Oh," she looked around the room for a quick exit, but there was none. If she was going to drink, she wanted to do it on her terms, not because some guy was pushing her.

"It's good stuff," he grinned at her, still shouting to be heard. "If you don't want it, I'll take it."

Andi studied him, and she felt herself relax. Ben wasn't trying to harm her. He was only being friendly. It occurred to her that in the stuffy hot frat house she actually was thirsty. More thirsty than she'd realized. She'd come here to have fun, after all. Jake had told her she should have a drink, and she'd agreed. Otherwise right now she would be home in her dorm waiting for his call.

Besides, no one ever went to hell for drinking a beer, right? At least she didn't think so. She was young and single and these were supposed to be the times of her life. So what if she drank a few beers? She smiled at Ben. "I'll drink it. I was too busy talking."

"Good. We frat guys like to take care of the ladies."

Andi laughed because she didn't know what else to do. Her heart was thudding inside her chest, making her feel sick to her stomach with anxiety. What was she doing? She didn't need to drink beer just because she was at a frat party. Wasn't that what she'd always told her mom during her last two years of high school? A few times she'd been invited to a real party, one thrown by the kids of the local public high school. But every time her mom told her she couldn't go.

"Andi, there'll be drinking at those parties. Not only is that against the law, but bad things happen when kids get together and drink."

Always Andi would say the same thing in response. "Just because other people are drinking at a party doesn't mean I have to."

But here she was with an open beer in her hand. She looked down at the slightly foamy amber liquid sloshing around near the top of the can. What if it made her sick? What if she drank it and threw up right here in the kitchen? What if it was wonderful, instead? When she couldn't take the struggle another moment, she lifted the can to her lips and took a long sip. The liquid tasted awful and felt funny in her stomach. She waited a minute to see if she was going to suffer any strange side effects, but there was just one.

Her heart had settled down.

"Good stuff, huh?" Ben moved her away from the trash can of beer to a slightly quieter corner of the kitchen. "Tell me about your friend. Guy or girl?"

"Guy." She brought the can to her lips again and took two long sips this time. It didn't burn so badly as the first time, but the taste was enough to make her shudder. She was glad Ben didn't notice.

"Boyfriend?" Ben's attention was moving past friendly and into interested.

"You could say that." Andi liked having someone to talk to, but she wasn't interested in Ben. He had a sloppy beer belly and wild blonde hair. In a movie about frat houses, Ben would've been the rowdy, crazy one.

"New boyfriend?" he raised his brow hopefully.

She laughed and took another drink from her beer. "You could say that." What was the taste? There was something familiar about it, but she couldn't figure out what. She drank more, nearly finishing off the can, and it hit her. It tasted like the smell of dirty shoes. She shuddered again, but as she did, she noticed a warm feeling spreading through her veins. Not only was her heart relaxed, but her anxiety had faded completely. The room swayed a little and she steadied herself against Ben's arm. "Woooah ... sorry."

"Hold on there." Ben caught her and helped her find her balance again. "Don't tell me you're feeling one little can of beer?" He gave her a helpful look that said he'd take care of her. Then he lifted his can to his lips, tipped it completely upside down, and guzzled the contents in a single effort. He crumpled the can as he lowered it and then shot it across the kitchen into the sink. "Score!" He raised both hands, signaling a touchdown.

Andi didn't feel dizzy, not really. But everything about the party seemed easier, more enjoyable. "Hey, Ben ... could I have another?"

"Coming right up." He left her side, grabbed two beers, and by the time he was back at her side he had popped the tops of both. "There you go." He feigned a mock look of seriousness. "Now this new boyfriend of yours ... he's a loser right?"

She wasn't sure why, but the way Ben asked the question seemed funnier than anything Andi had heard in a long time. She started laughing and when she couldn't stop, she handed her open beer back to Ben. He put his arm around her again, patting her back in a teasing attempt to keep her from choking. She stood up slowly and leaned on Ben again. "Why ... why did you ask that?"

"Because," he handed her the beer back, and he moved in closer than before. "He let you come here alone."

Yeah. Andi hadn't thought about it that way. Sure he had to run lines, that was fine. But he shouldn't have wanted her to come to the party alone. What else could that mean except that he didn't care if she wound up in the arms of someone like Ben. She frowned. "I need to think about that."

He helped her lift her new beer to her lips. "You'll need this. Drinking and thinking are great friends."

Again she began to giggle, drinking long sips of beer between bouts of laughter. "How come you're not this fun in math, Ben?"

"Math?" He raised his beer up and again received a similar response from a number of guys around the kitchen and living room. "You can't drink brewskis in math. I mean, how much fun is that?"

"True." Andi almost didn't recognize her own voice. Had she really just told this guy that not much fun could happen without beer? She lifted the can and took another long drink. "Another thing is ... you don' laugh as much."

"Uh-oh." Ben covered his mouth with his hand, his alarm not in the least bit serious. "Someone's slurring their words."

"Me?" She hiccupped and began to laugh again. "Not yet." This time it was Andi who raised her beer. If Jake was going to be this late, then she could have fun with Ben. "This is only my secon' one. No slurring yet." She made a dramatic sweeping motion with her beer, like something she'd seen in a pirate movie once. But the action threw off her balance again and she wound up in Ben's arms. Before she could lose her beer on the floor, she drank down the rest of it and handed the empty can to him. "Yikes. Sorry 'bout that."

"No worries," Ben whispered the words near her ear, and while he was there he kissed the side of her neck. "I'll take care of you, Andi. You can trust me."

She struggled to right herself, and this time there was no doubt. The room was moving. She opened her eyes wide and blinked a few times. Had that really happened? Had Ben just kissed her? Whatever he'd done, it felt wonderful. She leaned against him, willing the room to stay in one place. She tapped on his beer can and grinned at him. "That stuff's stronger 'an it looks."

"You still thirsty?" He was closing in on her, and in all the room she could only hear his voice. "Just one more, and then you're done. Okay? We've got lots."

Andi had never felt this way before, but she knew what was happening and it both terrified her and thrilled her. She was drunk and Ben was taking advantage of her. She had expected that if she let herself get into a situation like this she would hate everything about it. The party, the drinking, and most of all herself. Instead, despite her deep fears, the entire experience was wonderful and overwhelming, filling her senses and making her wish the moment would never end. "Yes, Ben." She felt her eyes grow softer, more seductive. "One more. Jus' one."

He opened the beer and dumped some of it out, at least that's what it looked like. Then he grabbed a bottle of something and poured it into the little opening. Or maybe she was imagining that. Either way, he brought her the beer and as she was drinking it, he led her outside. The taste was different, but she couldn't figure out why. As they walked through the crowd, she managed to stay on her feet pretty well on her own. She leaned on Ben, but she wasn't falling down drunk. That wouldn't have been fun. Outside he led her to the edge of the crowd, where there was less noise and people. "This is better." He put one arm around her waist and pulled her close, so their bodies were touching. With the other hand he finished his beer and tossed the empty can onto the lawn.

Andi closed her eyes and rested her forehead against Ben's chest. "You can breathe better out here."

"You'll breathe even better when you finish this." Ben lifted her beer for her and with his help she drank down half of it.

"Hey! You lucky dog, Ben ... I knew you'd score her."

Andi opened her eyes and looked toward the voice, but the edges of things were blurry. Wait ... she remembered that guy. Lucas, right? Or was it Rufus? The guy who had talked to her when she first got here. For some reason she wasn't offended by what he said. She raised up her beer the way she'd seen Ben do, and she gave a happy shout to the guy. "Yep ... Ben's a lucky one!"

"Yeah ..." Rufus sounded disappointed. "You can say that again." A bunch of guys laughed and hit Rufus on the back and the group of them headed for the house.

"Here." Ben held her beer to her lips again and helped her finish it. "There you go." He threw the can behind him, and now that his hands were free, he slipped both of them around her. He was warm, and in the cool night it felt good to cuddle against him. For a little while it seemed like they were dancing, swaying beneath the late September stars.

Andi rested her head on his chest again. She was dizzier than before, glad Ben wasn't suggesting a fourth beer.

"Come on, I wanna show you something." He slipped his arm around her waist and led her across the street onto campus. At least it seemed like campus, but Andi wasn't sure because everything was moving, same way the house did earlier. They found a spot on the grass near some trees and he pulled her close again, his arms tight around her waist. "All we need is music." Ben whispered close to her ear.

She struggled to keep her eyes open. The fun feeling from before was fading, because now she didn't feel like laughing. She felt like sleeping and something wasn't quite right with her stomach. A queasiness was coming over her like a plastic bag. "Wha' happened to the party?"

"We don't need it." Ben's voice was kind.

"You're a nice guy, Ben ... thanks for lookin ou' for me."

"I told you I'd take care of you." He cupped the back of her head and brought his lips to hers just once. His kiss, his light touch, all of it felt nice and it took her mind off the dizziness. "I'll take care of you all night, Andi."

She wasn't keeping real good track of time, but pretty fast his kisses grew stronger, more urgent. "Hey ... slow down there. It was better when we were dancin'."

"I'll show you what's better." His voice was still kind, but he was rougher now. Before she could stop him or move away, he had his hands up the back of her sweater. He was holding her tighter than before, too tight.

"Stop it." She shouted the words, at least she thought she did. But he was breathing too hard to hear her. "Ben! I said ... stop it."

"Your boyfriend's not here, Andi ... just go with it. I can get you another beer if you want."

Another beer? The thought made her stomach tighten and convulse. She needed to be free of him, because what was he trying to do? He felt wild and reckless and out of control, and suddenly she was terrified. "Stop!"

But he kept kissing her, kept moving his hands against her, and at some point the wetness on her face wasn't only his kisses but her tears. "Please ... stop!"

There was the sound of feet on pavement and then someone shouted. "You okay over there?" The voice wasn't familiar, and Andi wondered what sort of scene they must've been making. She blinked and tried to focus. A guy and girl were standing there, and they both looked alarmed. Andi rubbed the palms of her hands beneath her eyes and bent over, trying to make herself breathe normally again.

Ben was angry, she could feel it in the way he was seething beside her. "Get lost, everything's fine." He took a step back and glared at the couple who had dared to interrupt them.

"She told you to stop, so stop already." The guy took a step closer to Ben. Then he turned to Andi. "You want him to leave you alone?"

Andi had stopped crying, but she was still wildly dizzy. She nodded and tried to answer, tried to say yes, of course she wanted Ben to go. But instead she swayed and braced herself against a tree, adjusting her sweater and trying to figure out ... what had just happened. Then before she could find the words, she felt her stomach convulse into a mass of knots, and without any other warning, she lurched forward and threw up across the grass and on Ben's shoes.

"Sick." Ben stepped away from her, wiping his feet on the damp ground.

A second wave of vomit followed and it knocked Andi down to her hands and knees. She gasped for breath, certain she was dying. She tried to call out for help, but again her stomach heaved and she could focus only on taking her next bit of air. She could barely lift her head, but she wanted to make sure Ben wasn't coming after her again.

She shouldn't have worried.

Ben was scowling at her, staring at the mess she'd made. "You're disgusting." He glared at the couple. "I'm leaving." He wiped his feet on the grass again. "You happy?" As he walked away toward the frat house, he yelled back over his shoulder. "Shoulda known you were only a tease, Andi Ellison."

Her body was trembling, her breathing still labored and shaky. She looked at the couple and felt her eyes fill with tears again.

"You okay?" The guy came a step closer. "Want us to call someone?"

Whether it was the vomiting or the harsh reality of what had just happened, Andi felt a slight sense of control returning. She sat up on her knees and squinted at the bright lights of the party across the street. Then she wiped her hand across her mouth and shook her head. "I can do it." She fumbled for her cell phone and found it in the back pocket of her jeans. The couple waited, hesitant. "Really ... it's okay. I'm fine."

After another minute of convincing them, the couple finally continued on their way. Andi sat up against the tree trunk and closed her eyes. Who could she call? Bailey would be so disappointed in her, and her parents ... there was no way she could call them. Then suddenly it occurred to her.

She could call Cody.

After what he'd told her the other night, he would understand about drinking. Him more than anyone else. She opened her eyes and tried to focus on her cell phone. After a few pathetic tries, she managed to dial his number. The nausea was coming back, so she tried to hurry.

"Hello?"

Shame and fear caught her breath, and for a few seconds she couldn't answer.

"Andi? Is that you?" Wherever Cody was the background was quiet. He'd probably been home studying — the way he said he usually spent his Friday nights. What would he think of her now?

She coughed twice and tried to clear her voice. "It's me. I ... I drank too much and I nee' your help."

"Where are you?" His tone was immediately serious and full of alarm.

"The ... yellow frat house. Across a' street." She was crying again, and she barely had time to hear Cody tell her he was on his way before she jerked forward and threw up one more time. When her body stopped convulsing, this time she lay on a clean patch of grass and waited. She wasn't sure how much time passed, but the next thing she knew, Cody was standing over her, his hand on her shoulder.

"Come on." He helped her to her feet. "We need to get you home." He slipped his arm around her waist and steadied her. "What in the world are you doing here, Andi?"

She wasn't sure if his voice was more disappointed or worried for her. "I ... I was supposa' meet Jake here."

"Jake Olson?" Cody was a strong support for her, keeping her moving. "I thought you learned your lesson about him last week."

"He said he was sorry." She wanted to look up at him, stare into those gorgeous eyes and see if he was real or an angel sent to rescue her. But she could barely keep her head up. Besides, she was too humiliated to look at him now. She wiped her hand across her mouth again and wondered if she'd gotten her sweater messy.

"So what happened? Did someone hurt you?"

"He was trying ... but I ... got sick on him ..."

Cody stopped every several steps and helped her find her balance again. "That's crazy, Andi. You could've been in big trouble."

"I ... I was in trouble ... Some couple came over or else ... he woulda ..." she started crying again. She stopped and put her arms around his waist. "Hold me, Cody ... I need you to hold me."

For a few seconds he let her cling to him that way, but then he tenderly removed her hands from his waist. "You need to get home."

"No ... I need you. A guy like you woul' never give me all that beer." Her shame knew no limits, because what was she saying? She was being moved along again, so she clung to his side. She didn't care how desperate she sounded. "I need you, Cody. You have to believe me."

He didn't slow, didn't show any signs of interest. "You need the Lord and a good night's sleep. We can talk about the rest later."

"We can?" She felt a flicker of hope. Maybe Cody was interested in her, after all. Even though she'd made a fool of herself tonight. "Where a' we going?"

"Keep walking. We're almost there."

They reached a set of stairs that looked vaguely familiar, but when Andi tried to open her eyes there seemed to be two of everything. And both sets were slipping about, refusing to stay still. "Yikes." She buried her head in his shoulder. "These stairs are tough." Her words ran together, no matter how hard she tried to articulate. She was embarrassed at herself. "I'm a real winner, hey Cody?"

"We'll talk about it later." He was stronger than she had thought. "Hold onto my neck, okay."

She did as he asked, and he swept her up into his arms. Then he carried her up the stairs and through the door. Once inside he set her down and helped her along like before until they reached a door. Her door. It all looked familiar again. Of course ... it was the door to her room.

"You have a key?" He waited.

A key? She padded her sweater pockets and then her jeans and finally she felt something. Her key ring. She took it from her pocket and held it out. "Not sure which one ..."

"I've got it." He opened her door in no time and helped her across the small floor to her bed. "Lay here."

She fell onto her bed and crooked her arm over her eyes. Even then the room was moving in giant circles and her stomach felt sicker than before. What a fool she'd made of herself. How could Cody ever look at her the same again. "Cody?"

"Just a minute." There was the sound of running water, and then he was at her side again. He had a cold damp washcloth and a bottle of water. "Sit up. See if you can drink this."

She could barely open her eyes, barely understand what he was doing. But when the cool water hit her lips, she figured it out. He was helping her, trying to ease her drunkenness.

"I'll leave the water here, okay?" He took the bottle, set it down, and came to her again. "Lay down and let's get this cloth on your head."

But Andi didn't want to lay down. She wanted Cody to hold her the way Ben and Jake had tried to hold her. It wouldn't be scary and rough with someone like Cody, and in that moment all she wanted was to be in his arms, to have him kiss her the way she wanted to be kissed. She slid to the edge of the bed and circled her arms around his waist. "Stay with me, Cody. Jus' lay with me for a while, okay?"

"Andi, you don't know what you're saying." He put his hand on her shoulder and gently tried to ease her back onto the bed. "Go to sleep. You won't remember any of this tomorrow."

"Yessa' will." She stood and tried to hug him, but her legs wouldn't hold her. "Stay, Cody. Bailey's gone for the weekend. She won't know."

At the mention of Bailey's name, Cody's resistance doubled. He took a step back, freeing himself from her embrace. Then he handed the wet cloth to her and moved for the door. "Sleep. I'll check on you tomorrow."

Andi was angry at him and humiliated, mad that he'd rejected her offer so easily and completely. But of course he had.

She had to look and smell pathetic after what she'd been through tonight. She didn't tell him goodbye or thank you or anything. Instead she flopped back down on the bed and put the cool cloth on her head. Fine. Let him go. She didn't need Cody to have a good time. She didn't need—

Before she could finish the thought, she felt her stomach kick into reverse again. She tried to run for the bathroom, but she fell to the floor and had to crawl there, instead. Her face barely found a spot over the water when she began throwing up. For what felt like an hour she sat there against the cold, damp toilet, her stomach convulsing every few minutes.

Somehow she made it back to her bed, but her heart was racing again and she was terrified about what she'd done. The list of terrible choices screamed at her, until she cried out loud for God to help her, for Him to forgive her. She never should've gone to the party, never should've drunk. How could she have let Ben treat her like that? And what had she said to Cody for that matter? How could she ever look him in the face again?

"I'm so bad." She cried out loud into the darkness. "Do you even love me anymore, God?"

Sometime after that she must've fallen asleep, because the next thing she was aware of it was daylight. The time on her clock read ten thirty, and she blinked a few times before the full force of her headache hit her. She pictured herself in the frat house kitchen, Ben from her math class all over her, and she felt disgusted with herself. How terrible she must've looked, how loose and cheap. Another image came to mind, Ben pouring something into her beer. She wouldn't have gotten so sick on three beers—even if she'd never drunk before. He must've poured hard liquor into her beer. That would explain how drunk she'd gotten.

She pictured him leading her to the lawn across from the frat house, and how quickly things had gotten out of control. Only then did she remember the couple interrupting them and her phone call to Cody. He had come without hesitating, because he was that kind of guy. She pressed her thumb and forefinger in against her temples and tried to stop the pounding there. Cody had walked her home, right? Which meant her car was still parked across from the frat house.

"Ughhh." She groaned as she tried to sit up. Then she remembered the breakfast date she'd had with her mom and Kelly. Her eyes flew to the clock again, but it was too late. She was supposed to be there at ten o'clock. "What have I done?" She slumped over her knees and held her head in her hand. She'd made a fool of herself in every possible way, going against her parents and her conscience, and most of all, her God.

She looked on the nightstand for her cell phone, but she found it still in the back pocket of her jeans. It was on silent mode, and sure enough, she'd missed three calls from her mother. She ran her tongue over her teeth and grimaced at the disgusting taste in her mouth. She'd been sick ... the memory was coming back now. The alcohol from last night still hung in her breath.

"How could this happen?" she muttered the question and covered her face once more. After a minute she reached into her nightstand drawer and pulled out Rachel Baugher's quote book. "You wouldn't recognize me, Rach." She flipped through the pages and came across one she hadn't noticed before. "Character is a long habit continued." Plutarch.

A long habit continued? What did that say about Andi, then? And what would Rachel say if she were here now, or Bailey for that matter? How could she ever look at her roommate again?

Suddenly she remembered her final question before she passed out the night before. After all she'd done in the past week, did God still really love her? At first she had no answers for herself, but then she leaned back against her pillow and there ...

there was the damp washcloth. She stared at it, and slowly the truth came to light. Yes, God did love her, even if she would never outlive the shame from what she'd done. God loved her because just when she was at her most desperate moment, He had sent her Cody Coleman.

What other proof did she need?

Twenty-Five

THEY WERE ALMOST OUT OF TIME, and soon Keith would have to sit down with Chase and come up with an exit plan, a way to address the cast and crew and thank them for their hard work, but at the same time to tell them that they couldn't finish the film. The last bit of hope they'd had—that *Entertainment Tonight* would air the special about their project sometime this weekend—had fallen through. The producer of the piece had left a message on Friday afternoon telling them that the story was finished, and that it would likely air sometime next month.

The call to *ET* was one more they would have to make in the days to come. If Keith's calculations were right, they could shoot the film the first half of Tuesday—in case some miracle came through. Unless that happened sometime between now and then, the dismissal talk would come during lunch that day.

They'd completed another full week of filming, and though Keith was concerned about Andi and the distance she had seemed to put between herself and her parents recently, there remained one very strong bit of light. The scenes they were capturing were still among the best work Keith or Chase or any of the film crew had ever seen. Clearly the cast and crew were passionate about *The Last Letter*, so if ever there was a way to finish it, they might still find a way to reach the world with the power of a moving picture.

But for now, Keith refused to borrow from the pain that was coming. He and Lisa and Chase were on their way to a Baxter Sunday dinner, something Dr. Baxter's daughters had been talking about with Lisa since the prayer meeting. None of the Baxters knew about the money problems the producers were facing, but Ashley had been back to the set a few times, and she'd asked Lisa how her family could continue to pray for the project.

If things went well today, Keith hoped to have the entire group of them pray. He reached out and took hold of his wife's hand, careful not to bump the vase of flowers she was holding. "I'm glad we're doing this."

"I've been looking forward to it." She looked more relaxed than she had all week, her eyes showed none of the stress she'd been carrying around. "Ashley's so nice. If we lived here, she and I would be best friends. All her sisters, really. And Katy, Dayne's wife. Their family is amazing."

From the backseat, Chase piped in. "It beats all-day meetings about money we don't have."

"Amen to that." Keith laughed and the feeling felt foreign enough that he chided himself. Today ... no matter what Tuesday held, he would love his wife and his new friends. He would engage in conversation about something other than the movie, and he would enjoy being part of a big family — even for just one day — and no matter what loomed ahead he would laugh.

He would definitely laugh.

As they pulled into the long driveway, the sun was just setting, casting brilliant light against the wraparound front porch and the trees that framed the property on either side. Keith had gotten the story from Lisa, that Dr. Baxter not too long ago had sold the old Baxter house, as they called it, to his daughter Ashley and her husband Landon.

"Wow." Lisa motioned for Keith to stop for a moment. "Look at this place. It's like the perfect family house. The porch and the windows, even from here it feels like the walls have seen a lifetime of love."

"It's how I pictured it." Keith leaned over the steering wheel and took in the place. "I can imagine the kids running across the big open grass and shooting baskets at the hoop out front."

"Looks like there's a creek behind the house. Probably perfect for frogs and snakes." Chase grinned. "But right now they probably think we're lost or something."

Keith laughed out loud this time. He parked near half a dozen other cars and they were met at the door by Ashley. She had her baby girl in her arms, her pretty dark hair tucked behind one ear. "Come on in. Everyone's here."

"I brought these." Lisa handed over the vase of wildflowers. "Thanks so much for including us."

"We're glad you came." As they walked through the entryway and down a hall she stopped at a painting on the wall. "This is mine." She gave an easy shrug with one shoulder. "It's what I do when Bailey babysits for me."

Keith, Lisa, and Chase all stopped and studied the piece of art. Lisa was first to comment. "This is beautiful. Before we go you have to show me your other paintings. Anything you have here."

Ashley laughed and continued down the hall. "The best artwork in this house are the faces around the table."

The thought was reassuring, a reminder to Keith and all of them that the movie wasn't the greatest thing at stake this week. People were vastly more important and the comment by Ashley reminded Keith that something was wrong with Andi. Keith and Lisa had known that since last weekend, but she wouldn't say more than a few words to them. Even today they'd asked her to come, but she'd refused. Too much homework. Her excuses were sounding like just that—excuses. Tomorrow he and Lisa were going to take her out to dinner and get to the bottom of whatever was troubling her. Until then, he would be grateful for the priorities Ashley had inadvertently helped bring back into focus.

They reached the main part of the house and the scene taking place through the kitchen and dining room was like something from a movie he'd love to make someday. Ashley got everyone's attention and introduced the three of them. "Now," she laughed, "don't worry if you don't remember everyone. There won't be a test."

"A test might help!" A blond boy came up and put his arm around her waist. He looked ten or eleven, and clearly he was her son.

"Thank you, Cole." Ashley lifted her eyebrows at him. "But we aren't going to make our new friends take a test."

"Okay." He gave a happy look as if to say the test thing was just an idea. Then he put his hand on his chest. "I'm Cole."

"I'm Maddie," a spunky little girl came up and stood next to him. The two of them caught each other's eyes and started giggling.

"Wait a minute!" John Baxter brushed his hands off on his jeans and waved at the group. "Everyone get with your immediate family. Then we'll do the introductions right."

Keith was laughing again. He put his arm around Lisa and didn't even try to keep a straight face while the Baxter family struggled for a way to even begin introducing their group.

"Okay ... let's start with Dayne, and move on, oldest to youngest. Everyone in your family."

Cole leaned close to the girl who must've been his cousin. "What's *intermediate* family?"

She made a face like she was trying to think of a good answer. "I guess the people you're sort of in the middle of. Like your mom and dad and stuff."

"Seriously, everyone." Ashley sent a somewhat stern look to Cole and his cousin. "Let's listen to Dayne. It's his turn."

Dayne took the lead, introducing himself, his wife, Katy, and their baby girl Sophie. Keith smiled to himself. As if Dayne Matthews and his family needed introductions.

After Dayne a tall, slender man waved in their direction. "I'm Peter." He grinned. "I married into this circus." He waited for the ripple of laughter and votes of agreement to pass. "I'm married to Brooke, and these are our daughters, Maddie and Hayley."

Maddie, the spunky one who'd been talking to Cole, raised her hand and then blurted out. "Just so you know, Hayley just learned to ride her bike." She looked to her mother for approval, that this detail was indeed noteworthy. She nodded. "I thought that was important for our intermediate family."

"*Immediate* family." Brooke put her finger to her lips. "Let's listen to everyone else."

Again Keith stifled a laugh. These people were great. He already felt the same way Lisa did, that if they moved here this would be where they'd come for Sunday dinner every week.

Next another young mom with a strong resemblance to Ashley jumped in. "I'm Kari, and this is my husband, Ryan. Our one-year-old Annie is out in the other room sleeping."

"We hope." Ryan brushed his hand across his forehead in a mock show of relief.

"Yes, we hope." Kari made a funny face. "And this is Jessie and our son, R. J."

Ashley went next. "You pretty much know me. I'm Ashley and this is Landon. Our kids are Cole, Devin, and little Janessa Faith."

Keith had the feeling as the introductions went on that each of these young couples had a unique and beautiful story, their reasons for falling in love and the journey that had brought them to this point. Someday he hoped to learn more about them than their names.

A quiet man went next. "I'm Sam, and this is my wife, Erin. We just moved back to town from Texas." He went on to introduce his four daughters, all of whom seemed sweet and polite, but more shy than their cousins.

Luke went last. "You know me."

"Yes." Chase gave a strong nod. "We could be family after how long we spent together battling the union."

Luke went on, "This is my wife, Reagan, and our children Tommy and Malin."

Both young children clung to their mother's leg, but Tommy stepped out from his hiding place long enough to hold up his hands claw-like and let out a long roar. "I'm not Tommy. I'm Tommy-saurus Rex!"

"Nice to meet you." Keith bit the inside of his cheek. Nothing could be more insulting to a dinosaur than to not be taken seriously.

"I'm John, the father of this wonderful group." He smiled at Keith and then spoke loud enough for the others to hear him. "Keith and I met over Jake Olson's stitches, in case everyone missed that part." He put his arm around a pretty woman with fashionable blonde-gray hair. "And this is my wife, Elaine."

"Whew." Chase pretended to be scribbling down the names on his hand. "I don't know about that test, Cole. I'll fail for sure."

"Yeah, but you got *my* name right!" he hurried over and high-fived Chase. "That's one-for-one!"

The dinner was something Keith would never forget. Two tables were set up in the dining room, and between them, everyone had a seat. And though eight different conversations were almost always taking place at once, somehow the feel and tone of each one seemed to blend perfectly with the adjacent one.

As if the music and rhythm of life for the Baxter family was always and beautifully on key.

Keith and Lisa sat near John and Elaine, and halfway through the meal John asked about Andi. "I thought she was coming."

"She was." Keith felt the unfamiliar ache in his heart where his daughter was concerned. "She's having a hard time right now

... confused between what she's been taught and what she thinks she is missing out on."

"We aren't sure she's being completely honest with us." Lisa linked arms with Keith and leaned in closer so John could hear her. "It's the first time we've gone through anything like this."

"I've been there." His eyes held a wisdom that was priceless, one that must've taken a number of trials to develop. He nodded at Luke sitting near Chase at the next table. "Luke went wild in college. There was a time when I honestly wasn't sure we'd get him back."

Keith was stunned at the admission. In the time they'd spent with Luke, he'd shown nothing but the strongest Christian character. In negotiations he'd been kind and patient, honest and forthright. To think of Luke as a rebellious college kid was not only shocking, it was comforting.

"They come around," John's smile brought with it a much-needed hope. "Train a child in the way he should go ..." his eyes held a look forged in pain. "They come around."

When the meal was over, and the dishes done, after dessert and coffee and after Ashley had shown Lisa several of her paintings, Keith looked at his watch and announced that the three of them needed to go. "We have a full day ahead of us."

"As long as we're all together," John motioned for the others to come closer. "Let's pray for our new friends."

The group was making its way into a circle, lifting kids onto their hips and giving the shush sign to the ones still in the family room. During the slight chaos, Dayne came up to Keith. "Still no investor?"

"No." Keith could feel the desperation in his smile. "We'll be out of money Tuesday. Just enough left to send everyone home."

Dayne grimaced. "That's just plain wrong. Someone out there has to be in the position to help." He thought for a moment and then shook his head. "We need to really pray. Not just tonight, but the way Cole likes to pray. Until something happens."

"We will. God's going to answer us one way or another. The fact that you're behind us means a lot. I wanted to tell you that." Keith gave Dayne a half hug. "And if He lets us keep making movies, I hope you'll consider coming out of retirement for one of our films."

Dayne's laugh was quick and easy. He shook Keith's hand and finally gave a slow nod. "I'll consider it. I can promise you that."

Everyone was finally in the circle, and hands were held all around. John led the prayer, his voice clear and strong. "Father, we come to You asking that You hear the needs of our new friends and the trials they're facing with their movie project. We don't know all the details, but You do, and so we pray that You'll go before Keith and Chase and let nothing—absolutely nothing—stand in the way of their decision to make films for You. The world of entertainment is an enormous mission field, Lord ... these two are willing to be workers there. So please ... be with them as they finish making their picture. Help them finish strong, in a way that brings You glory."

John paused, and in the silence a small voice popped up. "Please, Papa ... can I say a prayer?"

Keith opened his eyes and looked at the pixie blonde standing near Brooke and Peter. Keith remembered her because there was something special about her, an angelic innocence that made her somehow different.

"Yes, Hayley, you can pray." John smiled and nodded at his granddaughter.

"Dear Jesus," she paused a long while, maybe shy or maybe struggling for the right words. "Thank You for miracles."

The entire room fell silent, and after a few seconds, John allowed a kind-hearted chuckle. "Not much we can add to that. In Jesus' name, amen."

CHASE WAS TOUCHED DEEPLY BY THE Baxter family, their warm acceptance of virtual strangers in their midst, and their devotion to God and each other. Someday he would love nothing more than to share a night like this with Kelly and their grown family, the two girls they had now, and the children who might still be part of their family in years to come.

As the circle came apart, goodbyes and hugs were exchanged, and Keith, Lisa, and Chase headed out to their rental car and shut the front door behind them. Chase was just about to start his way down the front porch steps when his phone in his pocket rang. He pulled it out and smiled. It was Kelly. She'd gone home the day after her visit, and he missed her more than ever. He slid his finger across the lower screen and then pressed the phone to his ear. "Hey, baby."

"Chase! You were wonderful. You missed your calling, honey!" Her voice was shrill with excitement.

"Wait ... Kelly, slow down." His tone must've caught the attention of Keith and Lisa, because they stopped and turned toward him. "What do you mean, I was wonderful."

"On the interview!" She let out a joyful scream. "You missed your calling, babe. You should've been an actor."

"Wait." He leaned against the porch post and tried to make sense of what she was saying. "You're talking about my *Entertainment Tonight* interview?"

"Of course." She was so happy she was breathless. "You mean you didn't watch it?"

"They told me it wasn't going to air until next month."

"Well ... they were wrong. It just ended. I thought it was perfect."

"So it really ran?"

Keith came up to him and mouthed, "*ET?*"

Chase nodded, his world suddenly light with possibility. "I hope someone taped it."

"My parents did. They gave a preview, so I knew it was coming."

"I can't believe it. That means ..."

"It means there's still a chance." Kelly brought her voice down considerably and her love for him was something he could feel over the phone lines. "I know you're busy, but I had to tell you. I really believe God's up to something big here."

The call ended and Chase and his friends celebrated the news, amazed at the turn of events. "We really shouldn't be surprised. The little Baxter girl had the faith we all should have."

Chase kept hold of that thought all the way back to the hotel and as he was getting ready for bed. As he laid down for the night, he took stock of their situation. They had put everything they had into making this movie, but right now they stood on the brink of losing everything. The cast and crew would be furious and the news would hold them up as examples of radical Christians with no place in the entertainment industry. Yet even with all that, as he fell asleep he did what he knew God was calling him to do, the same thing he'd seen little Hayley do earlier that night.

He thanked God for miracles.

Twenty-Six

TUESDAY MORNING ARRIVED WITH NO SIGN of the miracle they needed, and in just a few hours the game would be up. Chase tried everything in his power and God's to focus only on the scene being shot, to believe that even still something could happen, a call could come through and they'd be in the black again. But once they broke for lunch, they would no longer have enough money to do anything but send the cast and crew home.

Other breakthroughs had come since their prayer time with the Baxters. Andi had stopped by the set Monday, apparently intent on talking to Jake Olson. But instead she'd caught him kissing Rita Reynolds. And while Chase still hated the idea that his two lead actors were having an affair, the news sent Andi running to the production trailer. Keith and Lisa spent two hours talking to her last night after the filming wrapped for the day, and Keith told him this morning that they'd reached an understanding.

"She told us she drank, and that she made some bad choices. She knows she's been rebellious and she's sorry." He looked sad, but genuinely relieved, as if the financial crisis hanging over them wasn't on his mind whatsoever. "She tells us Bailey helped her work through her mistakes and that her roommate is going to help her stay on track. For now, I feel like that's the answer we asked for. She's worried about the way her classmates are talking about her, but that's to be expected. She's making steps in the right direction."

That news had come over breakfast, and again Chase marveled that Keith and Lisa were able to eat. Especially Keith. He had volunteered to tell the cast and crew over lunch, and Chase only knew if he were in his friend's shoes, he would be somewhere quiet praying for strength.

He talked to Kelly at the mid-morning break, and even now—with their defeat hours away—she refused to give in to discouragement. "I believe in you," she told him. "And God loves you more than I ever could. So everything'll be fine one way or another."

She had promised to spend the day praying, and Lisa was meeting with several of her friends, doing the same thing. Every fifteen minutes or so, Chase would look up at the blue sky and try to see all the way to heaven. *Do you hear us God? We're almost out of time.* But the only answer was the ticking of the clock. The final two hours passed quickly, with Chase determined to finish well, to make certain that they captured the best acting, the highest quality lighting. So that what parts of the movie they did have were all equally brilliant. They hadn't compromised yet, and this was no time to start.

As noon drew near, the muscles in Chase's stomach tightened, until he wasn't sure he'd be able to walk upright to base camp. In less than an hour, they'd be humiliated, devastated in front of the entire cast and crew. Everyone was going to be upset, and some of them would be downright angry. They would demand to know why they weren't told sooner, and Chase wasn't sure what Keith would say.

They were hoping for a miracle from God, but He didn't come through. They didn't want to worry anyone, when they believed completely that God would save the film. What a terrible reflection of the Christian faith that would be. Chase was still trying to imagine the outcome of the rest of the day, when it reached lunchtime. He put his megaphone down on his director's chair and fought the heartache inside him. His eyes were damp as he turned away from the set one last time and walked over to Keith.

"It's time."

"I know."

"I don't understand it."

"Me either." Keith stood tall and looked beyond Chase to the majestic trees, the fall leaves fluttering in the unusually warm breeze. "We want to do something good here." He turned his eyes back to Chase. "But God won't let us." A sad laugh came from him. "I know He has a reason. But really ... I don't get it."

"Maybe it's because no one would've listened anyway." It was a possibility Chase had tossed around since the dinner with the Baxters. God could be saving us from a greater failure down the road. God did that sometimes, didn't He? Then again, maybe they'd never know the reason.

Chase checked his phone and saw that he had one message — from their team back in San Jose. He knew what it was, and he could listen to it later. He'd called their San Jose point person earlier in the morning and asked him to fax over the most recent bank account records. The call was probably just someone from the office letting him know the fax had been sent. It would be in the production trailer.

"You coming?" Keith swung his arm easily around Chase's shoulder as they headed toward the tent at base camp.

"I need to stop in at the production trailer. Grab the fax with the financials."

"All right, then." His look said he was at peace with where God had brought them. If the movie wasn't going to happen, it wasn't for a lack of prayer or because God wasn't good and right. It was only because this was God's will. And His will was perfect.

No matter how much heartache the next hour held.

BY THE TIME LUNCH WAS ALMOST over, a buzz was making its way through the men and women gathered beneath the food tent. Keith had a feeling some of them had figured out what was happening, why he had gone from table to table asking them to stay when they were done eating. Of course they were in some kind of trouble. Why else would a producer who had been pushing to use every minute of set time suddenly ask his entire cast and crew to stay after lunch for a meeting?

Keith pulled Lisa out back behind the tent, near the place where the food service guys hung out. Never mind if the food staff thought it strange, Keith needed a place to pray and he couldn't go far. His announcement would take place in just a few minutes.

They faced each other, hands joined, a few yards from the portable grill, still hot from the burgers Paul had served for lunch. Lisa's love and devotion shone from her eyes. "You okay?"

"I am." He shrugged with his whole body. "We did everything we could do. I have no regrets, nothing I would do over."

"This," her lip quivered, but she maintained her smile, "this failure is not a reflection on the quality of producer you are. I want you to know that. The movie would've been unforgettable. The people here these past four weeks all know that much."

He pulled her slowly to himself and hugged her. "Thank you." Then, one last time, he prayed about the movie and their ability to find their way from here. When he finished, he gave his wife a kiss. "We'll get through this."

"We will." She walked with him back into the tent, both of them ignoring the whispers between the food guys. Everyone would know soon enough.

In the tent, most people were finished eating, and the laughter and loud conversation that usually accompanied mealtime were replaced with anxious faces and whispers. All eyes were on Keith.

Lisa leaned in close to him. "Where's Chase?"

"I'm not sure. He went to the production trailer for a fax." He scanned the area beyond the tent. "He should be here by now."

A restlessness was adding to the feeling coming from the crowd, and after another minute of checking his watch and putting off the inevitable, he took a slow breath. "I guess Chase'll miss it." He exchanged a somber smile with his wife and moved in front of the small crowd, to the same place he'd stood when he explained to them the reason for this movie, the power it could have for people everywhere. That day, the cast and crew had gotten fired up with him, joining him in the purpose and passion for the project.

Today would be entirely different.

"Thank you for being here." Keith felt his emotions well inside him. He swallowed and stared at the ground for a few seconds, asking God for strength. When he could talk again, he looked up. "All of you know that *The Last Letter* is an independent film. That means Chase and I haven't accepted any funding from a studio, because to do so would mean to hand over creative control." He tried to smile, and wound up hoping his eyes would convey what his expression could not. Even now they would never consider letting a studio take over the project.

The people seated on benches and tables around him listened intently, a few shifting closer, in what looked like an attempt to hear every word.

"Creative control is very important to us. We believe this film has a message that could help people, bring them back to a relationship with God and their families. We aren't willing to put in this kind of time and energy only to have a studio change everything." He swallowed again. "So, we raised the money for the picture and we came here intent on sticking to that budget."

Again Keith quickly scanned the area outside the tent. Why wasn't Chase here? The two of them should be standing here together, giving everyone a united front. He wanted to fall to his knees and cry out to God, begging for a reason why He would let this happen. But all he could do now was get to the point.

"There have been long days and difficulties, and though each of you gave an effort beyond your best, we didn't plan for the shoot to last this long. All of that to say—" Keith looked up in time to see Chase hurry in through the front of the tent. His eyes were lit up and he shook his head vehemently, all the while waving a piece of paper in front of him.

The people had their backs to him, and they were too caught up in what Keith was saying to hear Chase's quiet entrance.

"What we've captured on film has been amazing." He tried to make eye contact with members of the group, but even so he was distracted by Chase, waving at him to do something ... but what? Stop talking? Bring him up? Get to the point? The document must've been the financials, but why would that be desperately important now? Keith cleared his throat, flustered. "You ... you are some of the most talented actors and crew I've ever known, by far the best I've worked with. So ..." Keith stumbled over a few more sentences, repeating what he'd said earlier, all while trying to understand what Chase was saying, why he was so frantic.

Finally Chase seemed to give up, as if he couldn't stand being misunderstood another minute. He walked through an aisle in the crowd and held his hand up to Keith, stopping him midsentence. "Sorry." His look said he would explain in a minute. "We'll finish this talk later." A smile started at the corners of his lips and grew until it filled his face. "Right now, since lunch is over, if you would all take your places. We're on a tight schedule today, so you know where you need to be." He raised his hand in a show of assurance that everything was okay. "Thank you."

For a few seconds the cast and crew looked at each other, confused by the sudden change in direction. But then Janetta Drake stood and motioned to the people around her. "Come on ... you heard him." She shot a pointed smile at Chase and Keith and then grinned at her cast mates. "Let's get this movie finished."

Keith watched them go, his pulse racing. Lisa joined him and they turned to Chase. Keith felt faint as he looked at his co-producer. "You just sent them back to work." He wasn't sure if Chase was gambling or losing his mind.

"I did." Chase peered over his shoulder, clearly making sure they were alone. "Here," he held the piece of paper to Chase. "Read this."

It was a fax but not from their team in San Jose. As Keith started reading, his legs began to shake. This wasn't the financials. The letter was long and detailed from an attorney, and Keith waved it back at Chase. He couldn't stand the suspense another moment. "Sum it up, will you? What happened?"

Chase's eyes glistened. "You ... me. We did it! God did it! We got the money." He looked straight up and let out a victory shout. "We got the money! We're back in business!"

"What ... I mean, now? At the last minute?" Lisa looked stunned. She was out of breath from disbelief.

"It was the interview." Chase took the paper and pointed to the second paragraph. "Remember Ben Adams? Turns out his daughter's a production assistant and she saw the piece on *Entertainment Tonight*. She called her dad and he connected the dots. All those messages you left, Keith, and now his daughter's excited about the film." He laughed and paced a few steps in each direction, clearly giddy with joy and disbelief. "Ben Adams is completely on board—whatever we need, he'll give us. Look at this," he pointed to a line near the bottom of the letter.

"Ben Adams 'would like to be invested in Oak River films at every level, every film. Whatever it takes to see this mission succeed. He'll be in contact with you later today.'"

Keith reached for Lisa and the two of them hung onto each other, fighting their tears, but losing. "Whatever it takes?"

"At every level?" Lisa's shock and joy came out as a relieved laugh. "Only God could've done this."

"Exactly." Chase beamed at them. "That's how He likes to do things—at the last minute, so we'll know for sure it wasn't our brilliance or our great plans or our hard work that brought about the miracle. It's Him."

Keith wasn't surprised, not deep inside. All along he'd believed God could bring them the money to finish the film, if that's what He wanted. No, the feeling overwhelming him now wasn't shock as much as it was gratitude. Their great and mighty God was giving the okay for them to move forward in a mission field desperate for truth, crying out for a reason to believe.

As he held onto his wife, he thought about what Chase had said, how maybe God was sparing them from a greater failure. *Thank You, Lord ... that You're not finished with us yet. That You'll still allow a couple of average guys like Chase and me to make a movie like this.*

I know the plans I have for you ... plans to prosper you and not to harm you, plans to give you hope and a future.

The verse flashed in his mind and Keith knew it was an answer, a direct answer from a God who could oversee the entire world and still have time to show his grace and mercy to a couple of small-time producers.

He held out his arms and clasped hands with Lisa and Chase. "Lord ... we are speechless, amazed at Your mighty power and the way that Your will was done here today. We promise You," he paused, his voice thick with emotion, "as sure as we stand here today that we will make this movie and any other film You let us create, and that we will not compromise the message of truth and faith and redemption. We will bring Your voice to the world as long as You allow us to do so. We thank You, God ... we celebrate Your sovereignty and we rejoice that You brought Ben Adams into our lives. In Jesus' name, amen."

Keith opened his eyes and grinned at his wife and his best friend. "Now, let's get out there and wrap this movie."

THE PARTY WAS HELD ON A lawn near the east side of campus, close to where the final scenes were shot, and not far from the place where earlier that day Chase picked up his megaphone and shouted the words he'd been longing to say from the first day he set foot on the set.

"That's a wrap!"

Now the cast and crew were celebrating with barbecued ribs and an enormous chocolate cake that read, "Congratulations to the amazing cast and crew of *The Last Letter*."

Chase was refilling his glass of iced tea when Janetta Drake walked up and gave him a side hug. "You did it."

"Come on, Janetta." Nothing could touch the great mood Chase was in. He grinned at his favorite actress. "You know better than that."

"You're right." She stepped back, her face practically glowing. "God did this." She angled her head as if she were weighing whether she should say the next part. "You were in big trouble a week ago, weren't you?"

He breathed in sharply and shook his head just once. "You have no idea."

"When you came up to Keith in the middle of the meeting... it was because God had given you a miracle, right?"

"Were you hiding in the production trailer?" He laughed, because he could. They could all laugh now that they were on this side of that crucial day.

"I was praying, like I told you. Every day. And that morning I woke up with the strongest sense that a very serious battle was taking place over the continuation of our movie. I figured something big was going to happen, and, well... we could all read the direction Keith was headed with his talk."

"You're right." He chuckled. "About everything. And yes, I got word that day about a new investor. He wants to do whatever he can to help us—not just with this movie, but with all of it."

Janetta's smile said she wasn't surprised. She hugged him once more. "We serve a mighty God."

"Yes, we do."

Chase would've loved for Kelly to be here, but it was Friday, and until yesterday they hadn't been sure they would wrap today. Now, though, he and Keith would spend one more day making sure everything was torn down and shipped to its proper place, and then they'd fly home. At this point, it made more sense for Kelly and the girls to wait there for him.

Keith and Lisa were talking with the DP, laughing about something and for a long moment Chase looked around the wrap party and soaked in every detail. Janetta had told them that a few of the minor actors had recommitted their lives to God because of what they'd experienced working on *The Last Letter*. The thought made Chase smile. God was letting lives be changed already.

There was a commotion near the edge of the field where it butted against the parking lot. Andi and Bailey had arrived for the party, the two of them grinning and happy. The girls walked over to Lisa and Keith, and it was easy to see that whatever struggles his friends were having with their daughter, they were working things out.

It was another victory, and Chase could feel God's presence moving powerfully among them. The dailies had continued to show footage that took their breath away, footage that most certainly when combined and edited would put them in the running for film festivals and awards.

The future was more than Chase could imagine, so here he would simply enjoy the celebration, the finish line they'd reached together. He was drinking his iced tea, leaning against one of the picnic tables brought in for the party, when he heard voices behind him.

He turned and though the sun was setting and darkness was falling around them, he saw two people approaching — one a kind-looking man in his sixties, the other a tall, leggy blonde with an aura of charisma that shone in her eyes and her smile. He hadn't seen either of them before, and at first he figured they must've been locals, residents of Bloomington come to check out the final day of filming. But as they came closer, Keith hurried over and introduced himself to them. Chase couldn't hear them, but his friend's body language said they were someone Keith was expecting, someone he was thrilled to be meeting. Chase stood and walked toward them.

"Hey ... there he is." Keith waved him over. "Come meet Ben Adams and his daughter, Kendall."

Chase tried not to show his surprise as he put the pieces together. This was Kendall Adams, the woman who had seen his feature story on *Entertainment Tonight*. Kendall reached out and shook his hand. "I loved your interview."

"Yes." Her father stepped up and did the same. "You were insightful about your purpose, and direct with your intentions. Very well done, young man." Ben seemed to realize that formal introductions hadn't been made. "Forgive me. I'm Ben, and this is my daughter, Kendall."

"I'm Chase Ryan, sir." He looked from Ben back to Kendall. "Nice to meet you both." He sent a half smile in Keith's direction. "I didn't realize you were coming."

Keith chuckled. "I wanted you to be surprised."

Chase raised his eyebrows. "It worked."

They all laughed and Keith led them across the grassy field to the table where Lisa was sitting. There were more introductions, and then Kendall looked at the group of them, her eyes dancing with what looked like some unspoken bit of news. "I'm glad you're all sitting."

Chase liked her already, her determination and the positive attitude that exuded from her.

"You'll have to get used to Kendall," her father patted her hand. "She's a doer. Around her I always say look out and expect the unexpected." He lowered his voice and leaned across the table toward Keith and Chase. "It's like she's got a direct line to God."

They had Chase's attention. He reminded himself to inhale as he waited for whatever was coming.

"Okay, so before I left the office, I took a call from a literary agent." She laughed. "I'm not sure how he heard about my father's connection with the two of you, but he told me that one of his novelists has a great story that's been sitting at the top of the *New York Times* Bestseller List for more than a month. The woman's had offers from producers interested in making her book into a movie, but she's turned them all down."

"Never from the right people, mind you." Ben smiled proudly at Kendall, his eyes full of anticipation.

"Anyway, the agent tells me his author would love to sign the rights over to the two of you. She saw the special on *ET* too, and she can't wait to work with you."

What? Chase worked to keep his mouth from falling open. Had she just said that? Of course, Chase knew the book, and he had no doubt that a film on the subject would have dramatic life-changing potential. He looked at Keith and all he knew for sure was that his friend was experiencing the same surprise and disbelief. Chase held onto the bench on either side of him so he wouldn't fall to the ground. "So now ... I mean, this is unbelievable because—"

"Wait!" Kendall laughed in delight. "There's more." She swapped a conspiratorial look with her father. "You want to tell them?"

"No, honey." He easily deferred to her. "This was your deal."

"As soon as I knew we could have the rights to the novel, I called a friend of mine—Brandon Paul." She hesitated, looking more like a little girl on Christmas morning than a powerful player in the world of show business.

Chase felt his head begin to spin. Brandon Paul? He was twenty-one, a hit Disney sensation, whose face and image were on everything from T-shirts to lunch boxes and key chains. Everything he touched turned to gold, and more than that he had a young generation of kids looking up to him, wanting to be just like him.

"So, here's the deal." Kendall kept her voice low, so the people at the table next to them couldn't hear what she was saying. "I told him about the book and the two of you, and ... no, he's not a Christian, but he likes his image clean. He's talking to his agent today, but he would love to play the lead."

Keith looked like he might pass out, and Chase understood how he was feeling. He tried to swallow, but his mouth was too dry. Instead he looked intently at Kendall. "You're serious? This all happened in the last few days?"

"Yes! Because God is with the two of you, I can feel it." She held her hands out to her sides, showing an exuberance that clearly couldn't be contained. "He owns the cattle on a thousand hills, right? This mission you're on, we have no idea how big it'll be."

They talked a little longer, and Ben moved the conversation back to his daughter. "Kendall likes her work as a production assistant," he stroked his chin, his eyes thoughtful, "but I think she'd be better suited working with the two of you. I mean, I'm invested either way, but I thought I'd mention it."

"Dad." She gave him a patient look that said he'd overstepped his bounds just a little. She turned to Chase and Keith. "I wasn't going to ask you just yet, but I'd like you to think about it. I can get you plenty of funds—not just from my dad, but from other investors I know." She hesitated and her excitement was like fresh air in a stuffy locker room. "I believe the same way you do about the power of film. I want to be a part of this if you'll let me."

Keith took the lead. "I like the idea. Chase and I can discuss it this next week."

She smiled. "Good enough."

Their conversation moved from the quality of footage Chase and Keith had gotten while on the Bloomington set, to the possibilities that lay ahead for their next project. Kendall and her father stayed only an hour and then left for the airport, a one-day turn-around trip to tell them the unbelievable news in person.

Gradually, the party wore down and the cast and crew exchanged hugs and phone numbers, photographs and promises to stay in touch. A warm humid weather front had moved into town, and the locals had been talking all weekend about this being their Indian summer, and how even August hadn't been this hot. Chase loved the change. The warm night air felt wonderful compared with the cold from a week ago. They were walking to the car when Chase stopped and stared at a cropping of bushes at the edge of the field. It couldn't be, but then ... he stared at the sight, and he felt goosebumps on his arms.

"What is it?" Keith followed his gaze. "What're you looking at?"

"Don't you see them, flashing their pretty lights near the bushes?" Lisa grinned, snuggling close to Keith. "They're fireflies. The last of the summer."

"Right." Chase was drawn to the sight, unable to look away. "Fireflies."

They climbed in the car and Chase thought about the little Baxter girl, the *ET* interview, and the faith of his wife and friends. He was reminded of God's provision and providence, his miracles and majesty. With what they had faced this past week, and the victories that had unfolded, of course there would be fireflies tonight. He could feel God near him, reminding him of His great and marvelous love.

Because if fireflies were real ... then God could get them through anything.

A Note from Karen

Dear Friends,

For months now I've been getting your letters, smiling when you ask me, "You're not really going to stop writing about Bailey and Cody, are you?" The answer was as easy for me as it's been for you. Bailey and Cody live on in my heart, where my imagination is watching them move into their college years, and into the lives God has for them. When a story is that strong in my heart, I have no choice but to write about it.

As much as I love writing every story God gives me, I must say there was a special joy bringing to life this first book in my new series. I had fun knowing that if my new characters needed a doctor, John Baxter wasn't far away, and that when legal troubles presented themselves, Luke Baxter was the natural attorney for the job. The idea that Ashley and her sisters would pray for my producers made this book special for two reasons — I love the new characters, but I can still check in with the old.

For those of you who don't know it, the Baxter family was the subject of my Redemption Series, Firstborn Series, and Sunrise Series — in that order. If you haven't read them, you miss nothing by staying with this new series. On the other hand, you can go back and read their stories and have a little more to smile about when you hear mention of Cole or Maddie, Tommy or Hayley.

Another reason I'm going to love this series is that I'll have the chance to take a hard look at some of the contemporary issues facing our society today, how it's easy to become confused and embrace whatever becomes popular with the culture, and how difficult it is to see real truth in anything we view in movies or on TV, anything we read about in the newspapers.

All that, and of course, Bailey and Cody. I love that they're on a college campus, where so much of our nation's moral crisis is rooted. This series will give me the chance to show through Bailey's character how hard it is to stand up for the truth in the face of today's free-for-all social climate. Mistakes will be made and consequences will take place, but through it all God's voice will be heard. The way His voice is always heard whether people are willing to listen or not.

In the books ahead, Bailey and Cody, Andi and her parents, Chase and Kelly, and Kendall Adams all will face great temptations and trials, and at the same time brilliant, tearful triumphs. As always, I'm grateful that you're starting this new journey with me, and I look forward to hearing your feedback. You can contact me at my website, www.KarenKingsbury.com.

Take a minute and visit my website where you can get to know other readers, and become part of a community that agrees there is life-changing power in something as simple as a story. On my website you can post prayer requests or you can stop by to pray for those in need. You can also send in a photo of your loved one serving our country, or let us know of a fallen soldier. Either way people will be praying for you and your family, grateful for your sacrifice to our country.

My website will also tell you about my ongoing contests including "Shared a Book," which encourages you to let me know when you've shared one of my books with someone in your life. Each time you let me know, you're entered for the chance to spend a summer weekend with my family. In addition, everyone signed up for my monthly newsletter is automatically entered into an ongoing once-a-month drawing for a free signed copy of my latest novel.

On my website you can find out which women's events I'll be speaking at next, and whether you might live close enough so we'd have the chance to meet in person, share a hug, or take a picture together. There are also links that will help you with matters that are important to you — faith and family, adoption, and ways to help others.

Also, you can find out a little more about me and my family, my Facebook and Youtube channel, and my Karen's Movie Monday — where I release a Youtube clip each Monday dealing with some aspect of my family and faith, and the wonderful world of Life-Changing Fiction™. Finally, if you gave your life over to God during the reading of this book, or if you found your way back to a faith you'd let grow cold, send me a letter at Office@KarenKingsbury.com and write, "New Life" in the subject line. I would encourage you to connect with a Bible-believing church in your area, and get hold of a Bible. If you can't find one, and can't afford one — include your address in your email and I'll send you one.

Again, thanks for traveling with me through the pages of this book. I can't wait to see you at the start of *Above the Line: Take Two*.

Until then, keep looking for fireflies.

In His light and love,
Karen Kingsbury
www.KarenKingsbury.com

Reader Study Guide

Please use the following questions for your book club, small group, or for personal reflection.

1. What drove Keith Ellison and Chase Ryan to leave Indonesia and move to California to make movies? Is there anything you feel that passionately about? Explain.
2. What does Keith mean when he says the culture has forgotten about truth? Can you give an example of this from your own community?
3. The producers see the world of entertainment as a vast mission field. What do they mean by this?
4. Do you agree with them? Why or why not?
5. Is it important for producers today to consider making films that favor faith and family? Give an example of a film you've seen lately that had a positive effect on your life. Explain.
6. Andi Ellison is troubled by the death of her friend, Rachel. Has there been something tragic in your life that defies an easy explanation? How have you learned to live with that situation?
7. Has your faith or the faith of someone you love been tested in recent years? Explain.
8. Andi talks about wanting to experience life. Have you lived through a time when you made wrong choices for the sake of experiencing life? Share your stories and how those choices affected your life.
9. Lisa Ellison spends nearly the entire shoot in Bloomington with her husband. She might've done other things with her time. What do you think motivated her to stay on the set?

Talk about an incident when you sacrificed your time and energy in support of someone else.

10. Kelly Ryan doubted her husband's ability to make a movie on such a limited budget, and she was right. Is it better to be encouraging or right when it comes to your input over the major decisions in the lives of people you love? Share an example of how you handled such a moment, and how the situation played out.

11. Time and again, Keith and Chase felt God was reminding them that persecution was something that came with being a Christian. Talk about a time when you suffered through persecution. Did it draw you closer to God and the people around you? Explain.

12. Read chapter one of James. How did the producers show a sense of joy even in the face of trials? How have you been able to show that kind of joy in your life?

13. Bailey Flanigan has a great relationship with her mother. What proof of this was there in the story? Do you have that type of relationship with your family members? Why or why not?

14. Andi allowed herself to compromise her beliefs several times. What compromises did she make? Has there been a time in your life when you compromised? How did you feel about yourself? How did you feel about your faith?

15. The Baxter family stands as a strong example to Keith and Chase as a beautiful picture of what a family should be like. What in this book demonstrated the closeness of the Baxters? In what ways is your family close and connected like the Baxters?

16. Bailey struggles at times in her honesty toward her roommate. How do you feel about that? Is it okay to keep private details to yourself when you first meet a friend?

17. Both Bailey and Andi experienced jealousy in the early weeks of their friendship. Have you had a friendship that was plagued with jealousy—one way or another? What was the outcome of that friendship?
18. Bailey finds herself in a situation where she must want the best for her roommate, Andi, even if that means accepting the fact that Andi might be interested in Cody Coleman. Have you ever had to accept some difficult situations as part of loving a friend or family member? Explain.
19. Hayley Baxter says a very short and eloquent prayer at the end of dinner the night everyone is gathered at the old Baxter house. She simply thanks God for His miracles. What miracles have you witnessed in your life or the life of someone you know? How did you feel about God after that?
20. Chase Ryan is amazed at the reality of fireflies. Because they exist, he believes God can do anything. What example of amazement exists in your life? How has it affected your faith?

Take Two

One

KENDALL ADAMS SAT ACROSS FROM HER father in the executive boardroom of his Los Angeles high-rise and stared at the rolling hills of Hollywood in the distance. October was always like this—brilliant blue skies and air as clear as a summer day in Montana. Kendall breathed deep, stood, and sauntered to the window.

"I'm still amazed—" She glanced over her shoulder at her dad. "—that you're doing this."

"It's my passion too." Her father smiled, and the warmth in his eyes belied his cunning business sense and high-profile international-billionaire status. "I've been looking for an investment opportunity like this for years."

Kendall looked down from twenty-three stories at a busy Melrose Boulevard. What would this venture bring, this decision to team up with Chase Ryan and Keith Ellison? Was filmmaking where she would find healing for her broken heart?

She watched a breeze dance through the palm trees that framed the constant traffic below.

"You're thinking about him again." Her father was on his feet, coming toward her. "I can feel it."

"No." She linked her arm through his as he came up alongside her. "About the movies. And whether or not this is when life finds its way back to normal again."

A tight-lipped sigh hung briefly on her dad's lips. "I wish I never would've introduced you to that ... that—"

"It's over." Her calm voice reflected none of the pain that still colored the edges of every moment. "I don't blame you or me. Or God. It's time for whatever's next."

A comfortable silence fell around them, tempered only by the distant sounds of telephones and office staff on the other side of the door.

"Will you tell them? The producers?"

"No." She didn't hesitate. "What happened was private. The media never really figured out the story, so no one else needs to."

Sympathy shadowed her father's expression. "Good call. You'll spend a lot of time with Chase and Keith, but it's better to ... well, you know, keep things on a business level."

Kendall studied her dad for a long moment. Times like this she still wondered if he merely offered fatherly advice or worried about saving face, about making sure no one knew how much she'd lost over the last year. How much they'd both lost.

A shiver ran down her spine. Maybe if she pretended it never happened, a time would come when she might go a whole day without feeling the pain.

The phone rang from the middle of the long table and her dad answered it. "Yes, fine. We're ready for them." He hung up and reached back to give her a hug. "It's a new day, Kendall. God's going to use this partnership. I have a great feeling about it."

Giving her father a smile, she ordered herself to set aside the memories of the past. Her dad was right. This was a new time for both of them.

She smoothed her blouse and stayed at her father's elbow as he moved to the door. His secretary knocked at about the same time and ushered in Chase and Keith. This was the first time the four of them had been together since the wrap party in Bloomington, Indiana, for *The Last Letter*, so the greetings between them took a little longer than usual.

As soon as they were seated at the table, Chase leaned back and gripped the armrests. "Keith and I truly appreciate you taking the time to meet with us." He looked at his friend and then back to Kendall and her father. "But with the economy the way it is, we don't want you to feel obligated to give us additional financial help. We wanted to get that out at the beginning."

Kendall felt like rushing around the table and giving the guy a hug. Did he know how rare his attitude was in Hollywood? The idea of looking out for someone else first?

She shared a smile with her dad and the look in his eyes told her to take the lead. She sat up a little straighter. "Actually, we're more committed to your movies now than ever."

"That's right. Kendall has great news about your next film—the one we talked about last time we were together." Her father looked elated. He had said once that his fortune brought him no joy whatsoever except when it could be used to share God's truth and light, and when it could help make other people's dreams come true. "And I'm certain you're needing more funds for the editing process, is that right?"

"Actually, we're okay." Keith opened a file he'd brought with him and handed copies of an accounting sheet to Kendall and her father. "The funds you provided at the end of the shoot have gone a long way. We'll get through the editing process okay. It's what happens after that."

"Publicity and advertising—or the P&A budget, as they call it." Kendall's father grinned. "Not a problem, guys. Count me in. We want this movie on the big screens."

Chase looked a little dizzy, and again something about him touched Kendall's heart. He was sincere and kind, genuine in his desire to make movies for the purpose of reaching people. With everything in her she hoped the movie business never changed him.

Once they moved past the initial budget issues for *The Last Letter*, Kendall took over. "The author of *Unlocked* is still very interested in giving you both the option for her book. It's been on the *New York Times* Best-Sellers List for ten weeks now."

"We know." Keith allowed the hint of a smile. "We figured she must've had a hundred offers by now."

"She has." Kendall felt her eyes begin to dance. Like her father, she loved this—watching the impossible become a reality for a couple of good guys like Keith and Chase. "But she wants to work with you." She pulled a notepad from her bag and checked the details. "Stephanie's on deadline for her next novel. She'll be busy the next month or so. Then she'd like to fly here and meet you. Get the option in ink." She looked up. "That should give you enough time to finish editing *The Last Letter* and submit the film to the festivals. Which I'd like to help with, by the way."

She could see Chase wrestling with a question. After a few seconds he lost the battle. "Brandon Paul? Is that still an option for *Unlocked*?"

Kendall laughed—the happy lighthearted laughter that had once marked her world. "He's more than an option. I talked to him yesterday. He's in. We only have to work out the details with his agent, pull together a screenplay and a director." She grinned at the men around her. "Monumental details like that."

Both Keith and Chase hesitated, but seeing Kendall and her father's confidence, they both chuckled and the mood relaxed. They spent the next few moments talking about their families, their wives and kids. Keith was worried about his college-aged daughter, Andi, away at school in Bloomington, and Chase was concerned his wife might get tired of running things back in San Jose. But for the most part, life was good for the producers, and Kendall was glad. They would need to be strong. If their experience was like hers, Hollywood life would test them sorely.

The meeting lasted another thirty minutes while they worked out specific details of the financing and repayment plan for *The Last Letter*. They discussed how Kendall would look for additional investors for *Unlocked* as well. The budget would be considerably higher because of Brandon Paul, but because of her father Kendall was very connected with Hollywood's wealthy elite—people looking for film projects to invest in. She knew she'd find someone.

When the guys left, everyone shared hugs. Kendall hugged Chase last, and not until she was in his arms did she realize with great alarm something that hadn't occurred to her before.

Chase's athletic build was the same as that of Kendall's ex-husband.

She drew back quickly, though not quickly enough to let on what she felt. Heat rushed to her cheeks, and she hurried through one last round of good-byes.

Even before the producers reached the end of the hall, Kendall's father kissed her cheek. "I have to check on another meeting down the hall. Will you be here?"

"No." She still felt flustered, dizzy almost. "I ... I have an appointment in Laguna Beach with an investor."

She bid him good-bye and walked to the elevator, grateful no one else found their way into her car as she made her way down. Why hadn't she seen it before, the physical resemblance between Jay Randolph and Chase Ryan?

She hurried through the lobby and into the parking structure, and when she was alone in her car she leaned back against the headrest and closed her eyes. *God ... let me get past this. Please.* She longed for a response. But there was none. And like that, the past played out again in her mind.

The car accident had been horrific, one of the worst in recent history. It had nearly killed Jay, and the details that followed had nearly killed Kendall. Jay had been driving Kendall's car. The head-on crash had taken place in a handful of seconds, long enough for a drunk driver in a work truck to cross the double yellow lines on Mulholland Drive and barrel head on into a speeding Jay. The mangled metal heaps that remained once the dust settled made it hard for rescue workers to know exactly how many victims they were working with.

At first media reports had it that Kendall had been killed in the wreck. But she was working with Compassion International in Costa Rica when the frantic text messages began popping up on her phone.

Are you alive?

Are you okay?

Thank God Jay's alive!

And dozens of promises to pray. She took a flight back that afternoon, and by the time her plane touched down everyone knew the truth.

The dead body in the passenger seat of Kendall's BMW was not Kendall, but rather the twenty-two-year-old model Jay had been secretly seeing. At almost the same time, another significant piece of information rose to the surface: the young woman had been eight months pregnant with Jay's son.

The story hit the news, of course, but to this day Kendall was grateful it hadn't blown up across the front pages. The media never made much of the fact that Jay was Ben Adams' son-in-law, and since the accident wasn't only Jay's fault, the media lost interest. The same couldn't be said for the lawyers in the case.

The parents of the dead pregnant model hired a team of attorneys days after her funeral. The victim had been the single mother of two little girls—neither fathered by Jay. But since the drunk driver had no insurance, and since Jay was cited with reckless driving for speeds in excess of eighty miles per hour, the lawyers came after Kendall's father—the registered owner of the BMW.

In court the truth about the woman came out. She had been a terrible mother, rarely visiting her children and leaving her own mother to raise them. At the time of the accident, the model hadn't spoken with her mother or her daughters for more than a year. Still, her mother contended that she could continue to raise her granddaughters, but she would need a great deal of money to pull it off. By the time the haggling and courtroom drama ended, the settlement for the woman's daughters had cost Kendall's father just under a million dollars.

The accident cost Kendall a lot more than that.

She talked to Jay just once afterwards, late at night during an unannounced visit to the hospital. She found him hooked to an IV, his legs in a pair of casts, bandages around his head. Even with that, he was watching TV as if he hadn't just been party to a fatal accident, as if his whole world hadn't fallen apart. She stood in the hospital doorway staring at him, seeing him the way he'd looked five years earlier, the night they met.

He must've heard her, because he turned his head, and when he saw her, his face fell. For a long while he held her gaze, then he turned off the TV and looked away. "I'm surprised you came."

"Me too." She moved slowly into his room, clutching her purse in front of her, as if keeping something between them might protect her heart from further damage. She reached the side of his bed and waited. Just waited, because she figured it wasn't her job to do the talking.

The silence quickly became unbearable and he rattled loose a long sigh. His eyes found hers again. "I was going to tell you." He brought his hand slowly to his face and pressed his fingers against his brow. "I just ... I hadn't figured out how."

Kendall could voice just one question. "Did you ... love her?"

He closed his eyes for a long time. When he opened them again he said something that had stayed with her ever since. "Everybody loves everybody in this business." His lips were dry and cracked. He ran his tongue over them, buying time. "It was my fault. I let it get out of hand."

"Out of hand?" She wanted to scream at him. His girlfriend had been about to deliver his baby. The baby Kendall hadn't been able to give him. "Were you planning to marry her?"

Again he hesitated. Then, "It doesn't matter."

Kendall thought of a dozen more questions, a hundred things she might say. But in the end she said nothing. The silence between them deafened her, the whir of machines and the sickly, antiseptic hospital smell filling her senses.

Finally he spoke. "My attorney is drawing up the papers. The divorce will be final before summer's over."

And like that, five years were finished.

The trouble was Kendall hadn't seen it coming. In the days since the accident she had relived every wonderful day of their relationship a thousand times. In all her life she'd never met anyone like Jay Randolph. He had a faith that made him larger than life, and a charisma that made him the center of attention wherever he went. Her father introduced them at an Academy Awards after-party. Kendall liked to say he swept her off her feet and stole her heart all in a single conversation.

Kendall credited the Lord with a pair of miracles in the months since that final meeting with Jay. First, she had survived with a determination to live—to truly live. Part of that came from her desire to help filmmakers like Keith and Chase make an impact in the entertainment industry.

The second miracle was this: her love for God lived still. She'd been tempted at first to walk away from her faith. That's what Jay had done. In Hollywood, Jay's beliefs had crumbled and fallen away until they were nothing more than a patch on his sleeve. They hadn't stopped him from having an affair, so why should Kendall think her faith could help her?

But that attitude had lasted only a few weeks before she literally felt herself wasting away inside.

Kendall grabbed a long breath and opened her eyes. The faith she'd seen in the eyes of Chase and Keith was real, genuine, and that was Kendall's greatest concern. She couldn't stand to see the movie business do to them what it had done to Jay. That's why she'd felt so alarmed by the strange feelings she'd had when she hugged Chase. She could never, ever develop feelings for him. Rather, the three of them needed to stick together, talk about their faith and their commitments, include God every step of the way.

Kendall's resolve grew as she started her car and pulled out of the parking complex. If they didn't keep God at the center of everything they did, the power of their films wouldn't really matter.

Because the next moral failure to hit Hollywood could be one of theirs.

Two

BAILEY FLANIGAN PULLED HER JACKET TIGHT around her shoulders and pressed hard into the wind as she crossed the Indiana University campus. The rain beat against her lined hood and she picked up her pace, hurrying toward the theater building and her rehearsal for the upcoming musical, *Scrooge*. The old ornate brick building was in sight when she felt her phone vibrate. Andi or Tim, she figured. No one else would text her in the middle of the day.

She pulled her phone from the pocket of her rain jacket, and what she saw caught her breath. Cody Coleman? They hadn't talked in nearly a month.

Bailey stared at his name as she slowed her steps. He was more Andi's friend now, ever since the homecoming game when he'd walked past her and Tim without stopping. That same night Cody had spent an hour sitting in the parking lot talking with Andi. Now Cody and Andi texted and talked often.

Though the situation hurt, Bailey hadn't shared her feelings with anyone except her mom. When they talked about it they agreed: Cody had moved on. Sure, they'd seen each other on campus — from a distance, usually — and they sat in the same Campus Crusade meeting every Thursday night, but other than a polite wave or a quick hello, he hadn't talked to her.

Bailey scrolled down to the message. She felt her heart rate pick up as she read it.

MISS YOU ... MORE THAN YOU KNOW.

She read it again. And a third time. The message was short, but it spoke straight to her soul. She could tell herself whatever she wanted about Cody. Whether he'd moved on or not, she still had feelings for him.

"Does he ever mention me?" she had asked Andi just that morning as they left their dorm.

"Not really." Andi frowned. "It's weird, I agree with you. I think it's because of Tim."

Bailey's mom thought the same thing. Ever since Tim Reed had become Bailey's boyfriend, Cody had backed off. Never mind his promise of friendship, he'd cut her off completely. There were times when she wanted to make the first move, call him and ask why he was being so ridiculous, staying away from her and her family. But she always figured if he really wanted to reconnect, he'd call first. After all, he was the one who had walked past her at the Clear Creek High football game a month ago with barely a glance in her direction.

It was raining harder, so she used her body to shelter her phone. Her fingers flew across the small keyboard as she tapped her response.

YEAH, CODY ... MISS YOU TOO.

She hit Send and slid her phone back into her pocket. Rehearsal for *Scrooge* was set to begin in half an hour, and she needed to go over her lines before things got started. She planned to find a quiet place in the auditorium and focus on her part. Andi and Tim were going to meet her there, since they also had lead parts in the upcoming show. This was no time to get into a conversation with Cody. She would need more than a few minutes to catch up with him, to find out why he'd been so distant.

She picked up her pace, adjusting her backpack a little higher on her shoulders, but before she walked another ten yards, her phone buzzed again. She released an audible sigh, and it hung in the cool, damp October air. "Don't do this, Cody," she whispered. "Don't mess with my heart."

She pulled out her phone once more. This time his message was much longer — so long it took two texts to get it across.

I KNOW ... YOU DON'T THINK I CARE BECAUSE WE HAVEN'T TALKED. I GET THAT FEELING WHEN ANDI AND I TEXT. YOU NEED TO KNOW I'M JUST LOOKING OUT FOR YOU. WELL ... OKAY, FOR BOTH OF US. YOU HAVE TIM, AND THINGS BETWEEN YOU TWO ARE MORE SERIOUS ALL THE TIME.

Bailey hated when he talked that way. She let her exasperation build as she scrolled to the second part of his message.

THERE'S NO ROOM IN YOUR LIFE FOR ME, AND THAT'S OKAY. I ACCEPT THE FACT. BUT PLEASE, BAILEY, DON'T THINK THIS IS THE WAY I WANT THINGS. LIKE I SAID, I MISS YOU MORE THAN YOU KNOW.

She read the messages once more, and tears stung her eyes. If he missed her, he should call her, maybe fight for their right to a friendship. Tim would understand. And besides, back before Cody went to Iraq, he'd had feelings for her that went beyond friendship. They both had.

Cody would be waiting for an answer. She started to tap out some of what she was feeling, but changed her mind. She was almost to the theater. Tim would pick up on her sad mood, and that wasn't fair. Besides, she was looking forward to rehearsal. Today they'd practice the scene all three of them were in — the scene from Scrooge's Christmas past.

She erased the few words she'd written and typed out a shorter message instead.

I WANNA TALK, BUT NOT NOW ... CALL ME LATER.

As soon as she sent it she felt a sense of satisfaction. If he really missed her, he'd call.

She reached the theater door and put thoughts of Cody out of her mind. *Scrooge* opened in four weeks, and she wanted to give the rehearsal time her best effort. This was her first college musical. Much was riding on her performance.

Andi was already sitting in the auditorium, but as their eyes met, she didn't look like her happy, lighthearted self.

"How's your day?" Bailey walked to a seat a few spots from her roommate and dumped her wet backpack on the chair between them. "The rain got you down?"

Andi shrugged. "Rainy days and Mondays. Never a good combination, I guess."

"What happened?" After more than a month of sharing a dorm together, she could read Andi like a sister. She gave her a half smile. "You bombed your math midterm?"

The question was intended as a joke, and Andi allowed a small laugh. But the defeat in her eyes and the way she held her shoulders remained. "Remember the guy I met at that frat party?"

Bailey winced. "Ben, right? The guy in your math class."

"Yeah, well. He told his friends about me ... about that night." Shame shadowed her expression. "One of his buddies invited me to a party this weekend. He said there was always room for girls like me." She looked deeply hurt by the remark. "'Girls like me'? Is that really my reputation? After one stupid party?"

"For a few guys, maybe. But it's not like everyone on campus thinks that."

Bailey and Andi had talked about Andi's horrible experience at the frat party. She'd drunk more than she intended and walked with Ben across the street, where something worse would've happened if some couple hadn't come along and started asking questions. Ben left in a huff and Andi — too sick and drunk to walk home — had called Cody, of all people.

Every detail of Andi's terrible night had come out the next day, so Bailey knew the whole story. Even how Andi had tried to throw herself at Cody that night, and how mortified she'd been that Cody turned her down.

Bailey had been secretly relieved to learn Cody hadn't taken advantage of the situation. Still, it was hard for her to comment on her roommate's trouble that night when every action had been her own fault.

Andi stared at the auditorium floor, her brow lowered in deep concern. "Not just a couple guys. Their friends too. They probably think that."

"Okay, so six guys on a campus of forty thousand students." Bailey reached over and touched her roommate's knee. "I think there's still time to rebuild your reputation."

Andi leaned on the arm of her chair and held her head a little higher. "I guess. I just hate that anyone sees me that way. It's so weird, because ... well, you know that's not really me."

Bailey reached into her backpack and pulled out her script. "Think of it this way: every time you tell them you're not interested, you'll basically be telling them it was a one-time thing, a crazy night you still regret."

"True." Andi nodded slowly. "You always make me feel better, Bailey." She opened her own script. "I hate that I got drunk that night, but I don't know ... I'm not sure if drinking itself is really wrong. Like, the kids that do that all the time—as long as they're not hurting anyone, does that mean they're not good people? I'm still confused, I guess."

Bailey resisted the urge to sigh. This had been Andi's line of thought off and on since they'd met. She was the daughter of missionary parents, and she'd spent most of her life in Indonesia. But now her dad was a producer and had finished his first film, and Andi felt like she needed to rid herself of the good-girl image. As if she was ashamed of being too sheltered, too clean-cut.

Bailey flipped to her scene in the script and lifted a look to her friend. "You know how I feel."

A wary half-smile tugged at Andi's lips. "Just because a person thinks they're doing well doesn't mean they are."

"Right. The only measuring stick we have is the Bible." She tried to sound matter-of-fact, not overly critical. "We can mess up, but we have to keep getting back on our feet and turning to Him. That's what it means to be a Christian."

Andi thought about that for a few seconds. "I guess. It's just not as clear as it used to be." She was flipping through the pages of her script when her phone rang. Whatever name appeared in the window, Andi's smile was quick to reach her eyes. She snapped her phone open and settled back in her chair. "Hey! I thought you weren't calling until later."

Bailey wanted to ask who it was, but she didn't want to seem nosy. She focused her attention on her script and did her best not to listen to Andi's end of the conversation. But a minute into the talk, Andi laughed out loud. "Cody, you're so funny!"

That was all Bailey needed to hear. She stood and set the script down, motioning to Andi that she was going out to wait for Tim. Outside she fought the tears that tried to form. As far as she could tell there was nothing more than friendship between Andi and Cody, but still ... They talked often, and whatever was happening between them seemed to be getting stronger. Even that would've been something Bailey could handle — if she and Cody were speaking to each other. In light of Andi's happy conversation, the pain of Bailey's lost friendship with Cody was more than she could take.

Not that she could talk about it with anyone but her mom. Tim wouldn't understand. If she was happy dating him — and she was — then why would it upset her so much that an old friend had lost touch with her? That would be his question and he'd have a right to it.

She would have no more answers for him than she had for herself.

The front steps of the auditorium were covered and dry, despite the damp air. She sat down and rested her elbows on her knees. At almost the same time she spotted Tim. He was walking toward her at his usual determined pace, red backpack slung over his shoulder. When he saw her, a smile filled his face and he waved. Bailey returned the wave and waited for him to walk up.

Dating Tim was easy, natural. The two of them had everything in common — their stage experience with Christian Kids Theater, their love for God, and the types of families they came from. Tim had no shady past, no troublesome background, no baggage. For years she had wanted nothing more than for Tim Reed to fall for her. And now he had.

He jogged up the stairs and took the spot beside her. "Hey." He put his arm around her shoulders and hugged her. "You look cute in a rain jacket."

"Thanks." She snuggled a little closer to him. "How were your classes?"

"Great." He reached for her hand and rubbed his thumb along her fingers. "You're cold. Here ..." In an act that was as thoughtful as it was romantic, he lifted her freezing hand close to his mouth and blew warm air against her skin. Once ... twice ... After the third time he rubbed her hand and grinned. "Better?"

"Better." She studied him, grateful. How many times had she dreamed of sharing a moment like this with him? "Tell me about your talk?" Tim was taking debate class and today they had staged a mock argument over Dr. Seuss's book *The Butter Battle*. Tim's side had argued in favor of buttering bread butter-side up.

He laughed and shook his head. "Craziest thing."

He launched into a story about how the other side came dressed with the backs of their shirts dyed yellow, and how his team had acted out a skit that ended up being mostly bloopers, especially after one of the girls got tongue-twisted and began fighting for the wrong side. Bailey enjoyed the story, loved the way it felt to sit here sheltered from the rain on the steps of the college theater with Tim warm beside her. She thought about the conversation Andi was having inside, and a pang of guilt pierced her heart. She had no right to be bothered by Cody's friendship with Andi. Neither of them meant to hurt anyone. Besides, for now it seemed possible that Tim was part of God's plans for her. That meant maybe Cody was part of God's plans for Andi. If that ended up being the case, Bailey could do nothing but embrace the situation. She was happy and content, and maybe this was only the beginning for her and Tim. Cody was simply a part of her past.

If she could only convince her heart.

Because no matter what logic said, she couldn't shake the hurt in her heart over losing him. Or the fear she lived with every day—that a part of her would always love Cody Coleman, the boy who'd played football for her father and lived with their family through his hardest years.

The once-in-a-lifetime guy she had fallen for when she was too young to know any better.

Three

THE RENTED SANTA MONICA STUDIO EDITING room was half the size of a single-wide trailer, with fewer frills. But that didn't matter to Keith. He and Chase sat in front of a computer control panel, their eyes glued to the spectacular images on the large screen overhead. Never mind the stuffy room. The picture drew them in so they were no longer in Santa Monica, but in Bloomington, Indiana, where *The Last Letter* had been filmed.

The editing equipment was state of the art, available for rent only in the Los Angeles area and provided by the earlier investment funds from Ben Adams. For the past few weeks Keith and Chase had spent Tuesday through Thursday working nearly around the clock to edit their film. Constantly during that time, they were reminded that a production team could capture tremendous acting on film, but the magic—the real magic—happened here.

In a ten-by-ten editing room.

"Mark that." Keith hit a button on the control panel, pushed back, and stood. He stretched and rubbed his weary eyes. "Dinner?"

Chase squinted up at the plastic black-and-white clock, the only decor in the room. "Seven thirty." He released a slow burst of stale air and hit another few buttons. The screen overhead went dark. "When did we eat lunch?"

"We didn't."

"Right." Chase chuckled, then yawned. "Late breakfast." He rose and rubbed the back of his neck. "The hours run together."

It was mid-November, and temperatures in Santa Monica hovered in the seventies, even at this hour. What little they'd seen of the day had been warm and blue and beautiful. Typical Southern California beach weather. Keith flipped off the light and locked the door behind them. Down a series of hallways and a flight of stairs and they were outside, a block away from Santa Monica's Third Street Promenade.

Keith drew a long breath. "The breeze feels good."

"It's called real life." Chase slipped his hands into his back pockets, his pace slow and thoughtful. "I keep forgetting it's out here."

They both laughed this time. Their editing hours were crazy—work through midnight, walk back to the Georgian Hotel on Ocean Boulevard, climb the stairs to the second-floor two-bedroom suite they were sharing, and crash for five, maybe six, hours. Then back at it by seven in the morning. With the price they were paying for the editing room, they had to keep this pace. Besides, they had a deadline. Kendall had entered the film in a number of independent film festivals, and if any of them bit, they'd need a finished product by the end of the year.

On top of that, they had a first-look deal with a major studio—something that guaranteed a DVD release, based on the actors the film had attracted. The problem with that deal was that the studio might not want a theatrical release. Putting a movie on the big screen cost millions, and rumor had it the studio was struggling. If the film didn't make it to the theaters, there was a chance Chase and Keith wouldn't recoup the money they'd spent making it. The investors would be repaid, but the producers would suffer the greatest financial loss.

So the pressure was on in a number of ways.

"The thing is—" Chase tilted his face toward the dusk sky overhead. "—even with all the madness, I love it." He looked straight at Keith. "I mean I absolutely love it."

Keith smiled. He loved that Chase shared his enthusiasm. "I never imagined ..."

"I know." Chase stopped for a red light. "It's like we're sitting on this amazing movie, and no one has any idea."

They walked north. In this part of the city, Third Street was blocked off, allowing tourists and locals the chance to shop and ogle at the artists stationed up and down the Promenade. Up ahead a man stood in the middle of the street, a makeshift spotlight shining up on him. Head to toe the guy was silver. Tinfoil around his clothes, silver spray paint covering his arms, hands, and face. He played a flute. Next to him, a cheap portable table held a glass jar containing a handful of bills.

"Makes you wonder." Keith watched a few seconds longer. "The guy just woke up one day and decided he wasn't happy flipping burgers?"

"At least he's out here." Chase grinned and started walking again. "Doing something."

"Using his talent." Keith picked up his pace. "Pizza work for you?"

"Absolutely."

They ordered by the slice—two each—at a small dive just off Third and ate the first piece back out on Third Street at a tiny worn-out table with uneven legs. The breeze was cooler, the sidewalk fringed with street people, everything they owned on their backs or smashed into a shopping cart. The salty ocean air pulsed with heavy rap music from a couple street dancers at the other end of the block, the sound blending with the occasional honking horn and rumbling truck heading east on Santa Monica Boulevard.

Conversation was too hard against the noise, so they boxed up their second slices. Back in their rented editing room, they finished the pizza as Keith reviewed their notes from the earlier session. It was eight o'clock. Four hours until they could call it a night.

Keith grabbed two cans of Diet Coke from the small refrigerator in the back corner of the room and handed one to Chase. "Okay." He popped the top of his can and took a swig. "I want this scene less than two minutes total. We're still at five and change. I have an idea, but let's look at it again." He sat down in front of the console.

Chase took the chair next to him and hit the Play button. Three seconds from the front of a clip, two from the back, a camera angle deleted. A half hour disappeared, every cut piece saved in a digital file in case they needed it again. When the scene was down to two minutes, fifteen seconds, Chase rubbed his eyes. "That's better. Let's move on."

Before Keith could advance the film, his phone rang. He didn't recognize the caller ID. The area code was Los Angeles, otherwise he wouldn't have answered it. "Hello?"

"Keith Ellison? Barry Gaynor here. Los Angeles Film Festival."

"Yes, Mr. Gaynor." His heart slammed into double rhythm. The deadline for entering the LA Film Festival was December 5, weeks away. Entry in the competition was one of the reasons they were hurrying with the edit. "This is Keith. How can I help you?"

"Well," the man chuckled. "First off, call me Barry." He allowed a dramatic pause, then dropped his voice a notch. "Don't usually make these calls, but I had to this time."

Chase stopped fiddling with the control panel. He turned and watched the conversation, his brows raised. "LA Film Festival?" he mouthed.

Keith nodded.

"Anyway ..." The laughter faded from Barry's voice. "I hear from my good friend Kendall Adams you've got yourself a hit film."

"Kendall called them," Keith mouthed to Chase. He swallowed hard and tried to focus. "We were happy with it. Everyone gave it their best."

"That's what I hear. Kendall can't stop talking about it."

"We're editing now, my coproducer and I."

"Good. Think you'll be finished by the fifth?"

Keith allowed a smile. "That's the goal."

"So you're entering our festival, right? Kendall promised me."

"Yes. Definitely."

"When you submit it, send it to my attention." There was a smile in Barry's voice. "I'll be waiting."

"Definitely. Will do." They made small talk for another minute and the conversation was over.

Keith had cautioned himself not to get overly thrilled at any stage along the way of movie making. Too many things could go wrong. But as he set his phone down he had to work to keep from shouting out loud.

"What'd he say?"

"Kendall's the real deal. I guess she's friends with the guy who heads up the festival. You won't believe this." Keith stared at his friend and released a single laugh. "He called to make sure we were submitting."

"Because of Kendall?" Chase leaned back in his seat. "That could be huge. I mean, that doesn't happen."

Keith's heart settled down some. "Except with God. He might be using Kendall, but none of this happens without Him." He nodded at the oversized screen above them. "Let's get back at it."

They worked until after midnight, then walked back to the hotel. Fewer street people were out, but they were offered cocaine from a guy in a trench coat, and halfway to the Georgian they passed a pair of interested call girls. Keith and Chase never made eye contact.

"Have you thought about where this could go? I mean with Ben Adams behind us, and if we get picked up by a few of the festivals?" Keith tempered his voice. The wind off the ocean was stronger now, and he had to talk loud to be heard.

"I try not to." Chase shrugged. "I mean, it's exciting. But almost none of it's in ink."

The conversation faded until they'd climbed the green-painted steps to the hotel and walked up to their suite on the second floor. "You aren't convinced it's going to happen, are you?" Keith tossed his things on the small table near the television set.

"I believe in contracts." Chase flopped onto the sofa with a long sigh. "Look, I'm not trying to be difficult. Kendall's full of great ideas. The LA festival director wants us to submit our film. Stephanie Fitzgerald wants us to produce *Unlocked*. Brandon Paul wants to star in it. I'm having a blast, and everything sounds great ... but none of it's in ink. We still have a long road ahead."

"Reminds me of something I heard a director say once."

"What's that?"

Keith smiled. "'Movies very badly do not want to be made. It's the nature of the business.'"

"Exactly."

"Either way we have a great film."

Chase took a paperback from his bag and tossed it onto the coffee table. *Unlocked: A Novel*, by Stephanie Fitzgerald. "See?" He grinned at Keith. "I think it could happen. With God all things are possible, right?"

"You're gonna love the book." *Unlocked* centered around an autistic boy miraculously changed by the power of music, a boy whose life changed everyone around him — especially his older teenaged brother. It was a story destined for the big screen. Keith had finished the book a week ago. "The whole time, I could see Brandon Paul as the boy's older brother."

"It'd be huge." Chase smiled, but he didn't look excited. "All we need is an option from the author, an A-list screenplay, a meeting with Brandon Paul's agent—vice president of the top talent agency in town—and about ten million in the bank."

"Right."

"Makes teaching jungle tribes about Jesus look like a picnic."

Keith laughed and fell into a chair adjacent to the sofa. "Same God."

He took the remote and flipped on the TV. On the way to ESPN a news story caught his eye and he stopped clicking. Ten high school kids caught on camera playing drinking games.

"This one's for YouTube," one of them shouted out as the shots were poured.

"Yeah, YouTube!" One of the guys grabbed a glass and raised it high. "Winner's gonna be famous."

The anchor cut in and explained that before the end of that night one of the kids had died, and another stopped breathing and suffered brain damage. When the first two teens passed out—with one kid's video camera still rolling—the other teens merely laughed and clanked their shot glasses toward the forms on the floor.

Keith pictured Andi, his precious daughter, getting drunk at a frat party last quarter, and he felt suddenly sick to his stomach. He clicked the Power button and turned to Chase. "Knocks the wind out of you."

Chase was still staring at the dark TV screen. After a few seconds he leaned back in his seat and exhaled hard. "Saddest story I've seen in a long time."

"Makes me think of Andi." Silence fell heavy between them, the story, the reality of it, hitting its mark. Andi still hadn't shared all the details of her drunken night, but what if that had been her? Stepping up to the challenge of her peers, downing one shot glass after another? The boys who had fallen to the floor didn't look like particularly bad kids. Just kids. Teens giving in to the culture around them.

"Sometimes I need to remember—" Chase leaned forward, his elbows on his knees. There was an intensity in his eyes that hadn't been there before. "—that's our audience, those kids. That's why we're doing this."

"It's why we'll be back at it tomorrow, why we have to stay with it and believe God's doing something big."

"You're right." The clouds of doubt cleared from Chase's eyes. "It's why we believe in Kendall Adams and Brandon Paul and every other detail along the way."

"Exactly." They were quiet again, and Keith turned his eyes to the window and the sheer curtains dancing in the ocean breeze. The pictures wouldn't leave his head. The teens gathered around someone's kitchen, the vodka bottles lining the counter. The shot glasses and the laughter. All the laughter, as if they were bullet proof. As if they wouldn't be attending a funeral a few days later.

What about the parents? How helpless had they felt seeing the video, watching their kids pass out, watching them collapse to the floor, desperately wanting a second chance to somehow be there, to call for an ambulance? How did any of them feel now?

Suddenly the images in Keith's mind changed, and he wasn't seeing the shot glasses or the liquor bottles or the dying teenagers.

He was seeing his daughter, bright-eyed and innocent, telling a circle of jungle women about the love of Jesus Christ. And he was seeing her as she was now—experimenting with drinking and guys and choices that went far outside the realms of her upbringing and faith.

That was it, really. The kids in the video were no different from Andi and every other young person. They faced temptations that came at them from every side. Pornography and homosexuality, drinking and drugs, and anything goes. A disdain for faith, and an overall hedonistic lure that had a way of changing even the most grounded kids. That's where the power of film could make a difference. The right movie could give a generation of young people a reason to stand firm, to believe again in the rewards of living right and holding fast to God's truth. That's all Andi needed right now. It's all any kids in this generation needed.

A reason to stand.

Keith could hardly wait for morning.

Four

KELLY RYAN SHUT THE BEDROOM DOOR where her girls were finally napping and walked silently down the hallway of their small ranch house to the kitchen. The girls had been up late last night, hoping for a call from their daddy.

A call that never came.

Two weeks remained before Thanksgiving, and again Chase and Keith were off in Los Angeles editing, working practically around the clock to finish the movie before the festival deadlines.

Kelly entered the kitchen and grabbed a handful of M&Ms from a bowl on the counter. She popped a couple in her mouth, and then a few more, so they'd last. Then she gave up and finished off the rest all at once.

Lately she'd been more overwhelmed than she wanted to admit. The M&Ms were proof. It was only two o'clock and she'd nearly finished off half a bag. Between that, the overdue electric bill, and the laundry piled taller than Macy on the living room sofa, rest was nowhere in sight.

Back in Indonesia, Kelly had eaten fish and vegetables, whole grains and beans, and little else. She'd been lean and full of energy, ready to handle whatever crisis or task the day brought. But with Chase gone, she felt frustrated and forgotten. Last night was like so many of those before it. She and the girls ate leftover macaroni and cheese and then stayed up waiting for Chase's call. When contact didn't come, Kelly faced a barrage of questions.

"But why, Mommy?" Molly's brow lowered. Not much slipped past her. "Doesn't he have his cell phone?"

"Yes, baby." Kelly had felt so weary she thought about crawling into bed next to her oldest daughter and forgetting the work that waited for her in the kitchen. "I'm sure he wanted to call."

Macy listened to every word, and the combination of the late night and the ache of missing her father finally caused her to burst into tears.

"I want my Daaaaddy."

"Okay, okay." Kelly lifted the covers up over Molly and then moved to Macy and did the same. She sat on the edge of Macy's bed. "Let's quiet down. Everything's going to be all right." She rubbed her hand over Macy's back, comforting her. "Let's pray and ask God to help Daddy get his work done quickly."

Kelly prayed out loud and sang songs about Jesus and God's promises until both girls fell asleep. Then she trudged back to the kitchen to a sink overflowing with dishes that hadn't been washed since breakfast. The old house didn't have a dishwasher, so when every last dish and pan was scrubbed clean and dripping dry, Kelly found the Baskin Robbins Rocky Road in the garage freezer and dished up a bowl. Companionship for a round of laundry and late-night infomercials. She didn't cut the lights in her bedroom until just before one a.m., setting herself up for another rushed morning with Molly and Macy scrambling into her room and jumping on her bed sometime before eight.

Molly was four, and Macy two, and neither of them attended preschool. Kelly taught them letters and numbers and a few times each week the three of them sat around their wobbly kitchen table and colored princess pictures or made crafts with bright card stock and water paints. But the rushed morning changed everything about the hours that followed, and today was no exception.

Kelly moved into the living room and grabbed the first threadbare towel from the mountain of laundry. When Chase was here, they'd have the girls in bed by eight-thirty and work on the laundry or bills together. Strange how in his absence the workload seemed to quadruple.

A sigh slipped from deep inside her. "I'm sorry, Lord. I hate this. I should have a better attitude."

If only she wasn't so tired. Her days as a missionary had been equally hard, but in a different way. There was manual labor—threshing wheat, grinding flour, baking with the village women, cleaning. She'd learned to sew and repair basic functional household items and cook, and every night at dusk activity wound down. Sleep came easily in Indonesia, the way it rarely did in San Jose—at least with Chase away.

She sighed and checked her reflection in the microwave hood above her gas stove. No shower, but she had at least brushed her hair and put on a light foundation. She had to at least look decent with company coming over. Today was the second Thursday of the month, which meant Laurie Weeks would be here any minute.

Laurie headed up the Monday-morning Bible study at San Jose Community Church. She had three kids, a constant stream of family photos on her Facebook, and a love for the beach—same as Kelly. A few months back when Bible study let out, Laurie asked if they could have lunch together. Over Caesar salads Laurie noted that Chase had been gone a lot. Kelly explained about the movie, about the mission of her husband and Keith, and over the next hour the two became fast friends. Kelly was grateful. She needed friends now more than ever.

Kelly grabbed another handful of M&Ms and slid them into her mouth. She hated this new habit, getting by on junk food. But when she was running on empty, the candy helped. The trouble was she was gaining weight because of it, which meant that any junk food in the house had to be hidden from Chase. The last thing she wanted was his scrutiny, him wondering why she wasn't eating right and taking note of her slightly bigger size. She wasn't hungry, of course. She was overwhelmed. Treading water in an endless sea of menial tasks and impossible debt, struggling to grab even a breath of air so she could keep at it one more day.

But not Chase. He couldn't see how she was drowning because his own happiness didn't allow it. He came home from the editing trips overflowing with excitement about the movie. What did he know about her life these days? The lawn mower was sputtering along on its last leg, and the vacuum needed replacing. Most of the time, Kelly felt like just one more broken-down machine, completely cut off from Chase's work and his exciting movie life.

When he was home, Kelly had a dozen questions, but the one that rose to the surface most often lately was about the movie's theatrical release. She had believed from the beginning that if they actually finished the film, if they found enough investor money to complete the project, then it would take only a matter of months before the picture hit the big screen. Especially now that the guys had connected with glamorous Kendall Adams and her father. Because of them, money for their film projects was much less of a concern.

But Keith and Chase had an attorney now—Dayne Matthews' brother, Luke Baxter. Luke had read Chase and Keith's contract and warned them that a theatrical release wasn't a guarantee—even with the right funding.

According to Luke, the contract with the studio was ironclad. Either the studio executives would view the final cut of the movie and give the okay for a theatrical release, or they wouldn't. The problem was this: even with the P&A budget covered, the studio would face a financial risk by putting the film in theaters. Very simply, it was a risk the execs might not want to take.

And if the film didn't make it to theaters, the guys would likely not make back their money.

Kelly had been horrified when she first understood the situation Chase and Keith faced. She talked to Keith's wife, Lisa, and the two agreed they needed to pray. Without a theatrical release, Keith and Chase could face bankruptcy and a complete loss of credibility as filmmakers. All their efforts could amount to little more than nothing.

Kelly filled the kettle with water, slipped it onto the front burner, and turned the flame up high. Laurie loved tea at their twice-monthly get-togethers. It would be the healthiest thing Kelly had placed in her mouth since Chase left for LA four days ago.

She leaned against the counter and stared at the dull linoleum floor. *Remember the fireflies*, she told herself. *Don't forget about the fireflies.* Years ago when Chase learned fireflies really existed, he determined anything was possible. It was a mantra they lived by. But Kelly was lonely and depressed. Money was tight, and there was no end in sight to the long days without her husband. She still wanted to believe in his movie career, but week after week without him had sapped her of every bit of excitement and enthusiasm.

"Stay positive," Chase told her two days ago, the last time they talked. "God's brought us this far. He'll work out the details."

Kelly wanted to believe him.

There was a light knock from the front room. She slid the bowl of M&Ms to the back edge of the counter and hurried to get the door.

An unusual rain had hit San Jose that morning, and the storm was blowing hard outside. Laurie shook the water from her windbreaker and stepped quickly inside. "It's nasty out there." She was breathless as Kelly shut the door behind them. "Feels like it could snow."

"Another ten degrees and it could."

The water had begun to boil in the other room. Kelly led the two of them into the kitchen, where she poured the tea. Apple-cinnamon, a reminder of the holidays right around the corner.

They sat at the table and Laurie caught her breath talking about her kids. Audrey wanted to take another mission trip, and Lucas was switching his major at San Jose State. Sam had won senior honors on his football team, and life was good. Good and fast and full.

A comfortable quiet filled in the spaces between them, and they sipped their tea, listening to the wind howl through the trees outside.

Laurie put her cup down. "Chase is still in Santa Monica?"

"He is." Kelly's face fell before she could stop herself.

"That's what I thought." Something in Laurie's eyes changed. "You look tired."

Tears came from nowhere. Kelly blinked them back and studied the teabag in her cup.

Laurie waited, patient and kind as ever. "Wanna talk about it?"

A sound more sob than laugh came from Kelly and she brought her fingers to her lips. "It's nothing, really. I mean ... things are okay with us."

"The movie?"

"I guess." A teardrop fell onto the table. Kelly dabbed at it, and then at her eyes. "The guys might not get a theatrical release for *The Last Letter*. If they don't ... the film could lose money, and ... Well, the actors will think the movie was a mistake." She found control again. "It could be their last picture."

Confusion clouded Laurie's eyes. "I thought they got some kind of good news a while back."

"They found funding, otherwise they wouldn't have had the money to finish the film. But now their attorney is telling them they're in an unbreakable deal with the studio, and the studio is struggling like everyone else. The theatrical release of an independent film is a risk, and so without a miracle, the movie will only release on DVD."

The rain picked up and pounded a steady rhythm on the roof and windows of the Ryan's three-bedroom ranch. Wind howled and a tree outside bent almost to breaking. When the gust let up, Laurie took another drink of her tea. "Is that it, then? The movie?"

Kelly didn't have to ask what she meant. "It gets old, I guess. Chase gone all the time." Frustration tightened her throat, and she whispered her next words. "We've maxed out our credit cards and taken out loans. We're living on barely anything. All this ... for what? How's the culture affected if the movie never makes it to theaters?"

"Honestly?" Laurie set her cup down. Her eyes radiated kindness. "I'm more worried about you and Chase than the movie. When's the last time you went out?"

"Alone?" Kelly tried to remember. "I can't remember."

"Okay, how about this. I'll take Molly and Macy one night this weekend so you and Chase can go to dinner."

"Really?"

"Of course. My kids love your girls." Laurie sat a little straighter, enthused about her idea. "We can play croquet out front. Sam's been into that lately. You and Chase pick a nice restaurant and take your time. Let's make it Saturday, so he won't be drained from the drive back."

Kelly didn't want to admit they didn't have enough money for dinner at a restaurant. Besides, she had no idea what she'd wear. Most of her clothes were too tight to look good. But so what? Chase loved her, anyway. Maybe they could eat at home and take a walk around the track at Mount Pleasant High School down the street. Just to get out together. The idea sounded better than any of the weekends they'd had lately. Chase coming home tired, desperate for sleep, and spending his waking hours watching football or on the phone with people connected to the movie.

"Saturday?"

"Saturday." Laurie laughed, her smile easy. "Say yes."

"Well ..." Suddenly the idea sounded wonderful. "Okay." She reached across the table and took hold of Laurie's hands. "Thanks, Laurie. We'd love it."

The conversation moved to matters at church—the current women's Bible study, which was nearly finished with Thessalonians. "Something in the middle of chapter 5 keeps staying with me." Laurie folded her hands around her mug. "'Be joyful always; pray continually; give thanks in all circumstances, for this is God's will for you in Christ Jesus.'"

Kelly looked outside. The wind and rain were just as bad as before, with no signs of letting up. *Be joyful always. Pray continually. Give thanks in all circumstances.* She hadn't done any of that lately. But then ... when she was on a downturn like this, she never did. Between the kids and keeping the house running, she didn't have a minute to herself. Besides, she couldn't spend the day grazing from one snack to another and praising God at the same time. With her, it was one or the other.

Laurie stayed until Molly padded down the hallway, holding her worn blanky and rubbing her blue eyes. She stopped short when she saw Kelly wasn't alone. "Hi, Miss Laurie."

"Hi, Molly." Laurie's eyes immediately softened. "You look just like my little girl did when she was your age."

Molly smiled, not sure what to say. She went to Kelly. "Time to get up?" She yawned.

"Yes, sweetie." Kelly held out her arms and Molly came to her, sliding up easily on her lap. Kelly kissed her blonde head. "Is Macy still sleeping?"

"Mm-hmm. She's more tired than me." Molly jumped down and shuffled to the sofa a few feet away in the den. She curled up at one end and brought her blanket to her face.

Laurie helped carry the mugs into the kitchen, and then hugged Kelly good-bye. "Call me if something changes. But really, Kelly. Saturday. I'm planning on it."

When her friend was gone, Kelly took the spot beside Molly and patted her lap. Molly climbed up and laid her head down on Kelly's shoulder. "I miss Daddy," she muttered into Kelly's sweatshirt.

"Me too." She stroked Molly's long hair. "He'll be home tomorrow."

From the other room, soft tired cries told them both that Macy was awake. "Sissy!" Molly was on her feet again, scrambling toward the bedroom she shared with her sister. She looked over her shoulder as she ran. "Let's do something fun, Mommy."

Kelly pulled herself up and caught a glimpse of her reflection in the mirror that hung on the wall next to the TV. She looked heavy and old and worn out. The rain was bringing her down, and she agreed with Molly. They needed something fun. Something to take the edge off the loneliness and uncertainty, the fears about the movie, and the long stretches of days without a call from Chase.

She grabbed another handful of M&Ms on the way to helping Macy up onto the toilet. Her youngest was dry, at least. A victory.

Back in the kitchen, Kelly took out a large mixing bowl and the bag of Nestlé chocolate chips she'd bought the day before. "I have an idea." She found a grin for her girls.

"Mmmm!" Molly jumped around and patted Macy on the head. "Yay, Macy, look! We're gonna make cookies!"

"Cookie!" Macy put her hands straight up and danced in a circle with her sister.

That's right, Kelly told herself. *Chocolate-chip cookies. Something to make us feel good.*

Rejoicing and praying could come later.

Today she would bake.

Five

THE THANKSGIVING DINNER PARTY TOOK PLACE at Katy and Dayne Matthew's house high above the shores of Lake Monroe in Bloomington, Indiana. Bailey was home for a few days—no classes or rehearsals—and Andi had used her parents' frequent flyer miles to fly to California and be with her parents. So at three o'clock on Thanksgiving Day Bailey found herself in the backseat of her family's Suburban headed for the lake. A light snow swirled through the air, and a layer of threatening clouds hung over the afternoon. Something by Carrie Underwood played in the background, but Bailey wasn't listening. She was working too hard trying to shake the loneliness that hung around her heart.

"Don't you think it's kinda weird?" Ricky was in the third seat, belted between Justin and Shawn.

"What's that, honey?" Their mom shifted so she could see Ricky from the front passenger seat.

"Having Thanksgiving dinner somewhere else? It feels weird."

"It does." Shawn nodded, and Justin and BJ agreed.

"I mean, it'll be fun," Ricky grinned. "I love looking for eagles off their back porch, especially in the snow. But still..."

Bailey agreed. She missed the routine and tradition of Thanksgiving at home, but she knew the reason.

"Like I told everyone a week ago ... Dad has a game tomorrow." Mom smiled. "Your father and I agreed we'd rather not spend the day cooking." She gave their dad a quick kiss on the cheek. "I think it was a great call."

"Nice of the Matthews to ask us." Dad looked in his rearview mirror at the six kids. "It'll be a good change."

"Yeah, except ..." Ricky shrugged. "It wasn't the same this morning without the turkey smell and the liver and neck and everything."

The other boys laughed, and after a few seconds Ricky did too. They were still laughing when they turned into the Matthews' long driveway. Bailey stared at the house and remembered a few years back when Dayne had been in the terrible car accident in Los Angeles. Back then he was the biggest movie star in Hollywood, and with paparazzi chasing him, he'd lost control and nearly been killed. During his recovery, Bailey and her family and everyone involved in Christian Kids Theater had come together and completely made over this lake house. When Katy and Dayne returned to Bloomington, the house and yard were filled with everyone who'd taken part in the work. The makeover had brought people together, and kids in CKT still talked about it.

They parked and piled out. Bailey took two of the four pumpkin pies — their contribution to the meal. Those and the bag of rolls Ricky carried. With the entire Baxter family expected for dinner, Bailey figured there would be thirty-four people eating turkey.

"Good thing the girls are bringing extra turkeys." Her mom stepped aside and let Shawn rush ahead to get the door. "We'll need them for this group."

"Yeah, for our group alone!" Ricky rubbed his stomach. "I could eat a whole drumstick."

"You usually do." Justin giggled and elbowed his younger brother.

"Okay, that's enough." Their dad came alongside Shawn as they knocked at the door. "No roughhousing today. Be Flanigans, and be helpful." He winked at them amid a host of "Yes, Dad" responses.

Now that she was older, Bailey loved watching her parents, the way they snuck kisses and hugs and still laughed every day, and the way they set a high bar for her and her brothers. It was the sort of marriage and family life she wanted someday down the road.

"The Flanigans!" Katy was the first to the door. She hugged Bailey's mom and welcomed everyone else. "The football game's on in the den!"

"Can we go out back and look for eagles?" Ricky was already one step in that direction. "And watch football after?"

"Of course." Katy laughed and led Ricky toward the back door.

"But don't track snow into the house." Their dad followed and lightly roughed up Ricky's blond hair. "And don't stay out too long. It's getting colder."

Dayne entered from the other room and grinned at the group. "It's not a party till the Flanigans are here, that's what I always say!" He gave their dad a solid hug with one arm. In the other he held a sleeping baby Sophie, who at five months was the perfect mix of Katy and Dayne. Bailey took in the sight of him and smiled to herself. Dayne Matthews might've been brilliant in the roles he played on the big screen. But no role had ever suited him as well as this one: husband and father.

Would that be her someday, married to an actor years after the two of them had lived out their onscreen dreams? Or would the man holding her baby be a former football player, like her daddy? Bailey couldn't picture what the future held, only the present. She and Tim were still seeing each other. He was supposed to stop by for dessert later — an invitation Katy had personally given him.

Bailey walked the pies into the kitchen where Ashley was placing potato pieces into a pot of boiling water. "Hey!" She looked up and blew at a wisp of her bangs. "Happy Thanksgiving!"

"You too." She set the pies down and moved closer. Out of all the Baxter sisters, Bailey was easily closest to Ashley. She babysat for her, and back during her CKT days, Ashley had been at many rehearsals painting backdrops and pitching in with the sets. "Where are the kids?"

"With Landon." Ashley took another handful of potatoes and set them into the water. "He's convinced Janessa loves football."

Bailey laughed. In the other room she could hear her parents talking to Kari and Ryan, and beyond them there were other voices. Luke and John Baxter's and the rest of them. She noticed the frozen bags of peas sitting alongside the kitchen sink. "Need help?"

"Not just yet. But stick around. I'm sure we'll think of something."

They talked for a few minutes about Ashley's painting schedule and Bailey's rehearsals. "I'll be pretty busy until the show closes mid-December."

"I love *Scrooge* as a musical." Ashley finished her job and put a lid on the pot. She turned to Bailey and wiped the back of her hand across her forehead. "We're all going. I think on opening night."

Bailey felt a wave of nervousness, but it quickly passed. She'd played to full houses at every CKT opening night. This wouldn't be much different. "Tim's doing great. I mean, sometimes I think he *is* Scrooge."

Ashley's eyes were kind, but they looked at her a little deeper than before. "How are things? You and Tim?"

"Good." Her answer came a little too quick. She could tell from her expression that Ashley wanted a different answer from the expected one. "It really is. I just wish ..."

"You could stop thinking about Cody?"

Bailey felt something sad fill her eyes. "Yeah. I haven't talked to him in weeks."

"Your mom was telling me that." A knowing look crossed her face. "You know why, right?"

"'Cause of Tim." She took in a slow breath. "Love's so complicated."

"Well said." Ashley's quiet laugh was that of someone who had been there. "Only by God's grace did Landon and I find our way together."

"I can't picture you two apart."

"We almost let it go." She looked out the window. Snow was falling harder now. "We would've regretted that the rest of our lives. But even still we almost didn't make it." She looked at Bailey again. "Sometimes the most difficult path is the very one we're supposed to be on."

"Hmmm." She could've been talking about Bailey and Cody, for sure. "I keep praying, asking God to show me."

"He will." Ashley put her hand on Bailey's shoulder. "In His time He'll show you just what you need to know. I would only add one piece of advice."

"What?"

"Be looking. Because the kind of love God wants for us, the kind I have with Landon … That sort of love rarely happens twice."

Bailey's mom, Katy, and Ashley's three sisters entered the kitchen ready to do their part to move the dinner along. Their chatter ended the quiet moment between Bailey and Ashley.

Bailey opened the cans of black olives and poured them into one of the serving dishes. She was tossing the cans into the garage recycling bin when from her back pocket she felt her cell phone buzz. Probably Tim texting her about what time he should stop by. She paused on the steps of the garage and checked.

But the text wasn't from Tim. Once again it was from Cody. Bailey felt her breath catch a little as she stared at the message on her screen.

HAVEN'T TALKED TO YOU IN A WHILE ... JUST WANTED TO WISH YOU AND YOUR FAMILY A HAPPY THANKSGIVING.

She hesitated, looking from his name to the message and back again. Andi had been talking to Cody almost daily, and she'd told Bailey that Cody was spending Thanksgiving with his mom. Just the two of them. Andi might be Cody's new friend, but Bailey knew him better. She understood how difficult spending time with his mother was for him. His father hadn't been in the picture since he was a baby, and his mom had introduced him to drinking games when he was just fourteen. By the time he reached his senior year in high school she was in prison on drug charges. She'd been out for several years now, deeply sorry for how she'd let Cody down during his growing-up years and clean from drugs and alcohol as far as Bailey knew. But it was still difficult. In the past Cody—and then in later years both he and his mom—had spent Thanksgiving with Bailey's family. Cody had less of a problem being with his mom when they were in a big group.

He had to feel lonely today, same as Bailey.

She exhaled and realized something: this must be the reason she'd felt down on the way to the Matthews' house. She was missing Cody. Whether she wanted to admit it or not, whether they had spoken only hours ago or not for the past few weeks ... she missed him.

The happy mix of voices continued on the other side of the garage door, but where Bailey was standing, a few feet from the trash and recycling bins, it was cold and quiet. She tapped out a quick response.

HAPPY THANKSGIVING TO YOU AND YOUR MOM TOO. WE MISS YOU.

She leaned against the cool garage wall and waited, reading his message and hers twice more before the next text came through.

HOW'S TIM?

Anger stirred the muddy waters in Bailey's soul. Couldn't he at least tell her he felt the same way, that he missed her as much as she missed him? The way he'd told her that day when she was on her way to rehearsal? He did miss her—he had to, otherwise he wouldn't have texted her.

She slid her phone shut in a rush and slipped it back into her pocket. They wouldn't have any friendship at all until he could see past her relationship with Tim. Cody had been her friend long before she started dating Tim. The fact that he continued to let Tim come between them meant only one thing.

He was okay with letting their friendship slip away.

Everyone was setting the table when she returned to the kitchen, and the dining area was a joyful chaos of little kids being seated at one of three tables and highchairs sliding into place. Bailey pitched in, setting bowls of sweet potatoes on the various tables and finally taking the place between her mom and Ricky. All around the dining room people talked and laughed, celebrating the time together and remarking about the look and smell of the food spread out before them.

But Bailey felt no hunger. She wanted to call Cody and tell him to quit being so distant, to get in his car and come over so they could walk down to the lake in the snow and find what they'd lost these last few months. The idea was ridiculous for a lot of reasons, not the least of which was that Tim would be here in an hour.

When everyone was seated, Dayne stood and prayed. "Father, we come to You this Thanksgiving Day with full hearts. Thank You for giving us eternal life, and for the people around this table. Thank You for long-lasting relationships, and for new life—" He paused, his voice rich and full. "—like baby Sophie and baby Janessa. We have so much to be grateful for, dear God. Bless this food to our bodies, and thank You for providing it. We love You, Lord. In Jesus' name, amen."

A round of amens echoed from around the room.

After everyone served their plates, Dayne asked them to share what they were most thankful for.

"One rule." Katy smiled at the group. "An answer can only be given once."

"I'm first!" Cole, Ashley's son, jumped up and raised his hand. Landon helped him back to his seat.

"Cole will go last." He put his arm around Cole.

"Ahh, Dad." Cole wasn't really that upset, because his eyes still danced. "All the good answers will be taken."

"You can be thankful for me, Coley!" Maddie, Brooke's oldest, cast a teasing look across the table at her cousin. "Unless that one's already taken."

Everyone laughed, and the round of thanks began. Bailey was glad for the distraction. People quickly moved from being thankful for God and family and friends and food to specific things—the success of the local crisis pregnancy center, the way the Colts were coming together for Bailey's dad, and her brother Shawn's *A* on a recent biology test. Bailey felt her phone receive another text message just as her turn arrived. She ignored it. "I'm thankful for my roommate, Andi. She's sort of like a sister, and I'm grateful for that."

Finally it was Cole's turn. He thought for a long moment, clearly struggling to think of an answer. Finally he threw his hands in the air. "Okay, fine. I'm thankful for Maddie."

"Thank you, Coley." Maddie folded her hands on the table and gave her cousin a satisfied smile. "I'm thankful for you too."

Again everyone laughed, and conversations broke out all around. Bailey poked her fork around in her peas and mashed potatoes, but all she could think about was the text waiting for her. Even during a regular dinner, her parents didn't like them texting. Today that would be especially true. She ate a few bites of turkey and set her fork down.

"You okay?" Her mom's smile was full of compassion.

As usual, she could read Bailey's heart and mind even though nothing had been said about the text messages. Bailey shrugged one shoulder. "Cody texted me."

"And?" With so many people talking around the room no one listened to them.

"Wished me a Happy Thanksgiving." She sighed. "I told him I missed him, and instead of saying he missed me, too, he just asked me how Tim was."

Her mom gave her a sympathetic smile. "Maybe he's being smart."

"How?"

"He's making you think about your decisions." She put her arm around Bailey's shoulders and gave her a gentle squeeze. "Look who you're sitting here thinking about."

Her mom had a point. But was Cody's silence really deliberate? With all the time he spent talking to Andi, it seemed like only a slight possibility. "Maybe he's interested in Andi. He doesn't want me missing him, when I'm supposed to be thinking about Tim. You know ..." She met her mom's eyes. "So I don't do something stupid like start liking him again."

"I don't think so." Her mom picked up her knife and fork and cut a bite of turkey.

"You seem so sure."

"I am sure." Confidence shone in her eyes. "I saw how he looked at you that day at our house. He adores you, Bailey. No matter what you decide, I think maybe he always will."

Bailey hung onto that thought.

When dinner was over, everyone worked together clearing the tables and loading Katy and Dayne's two dishwashers. Bailey was helping her mom and Ashley place ten pies along the granite kitchen bar when the doorbell rang. Dayne answered it, and Bailey watched from where she worked as Tim Reed stepped inside. He and Dayne talked for a minute, the way they always did when they saw each other. Tim had been one of the first CKT kids Dayne met, and the two shared a special friendship. Dayne was a sort of mentor for Tim, which was a great situation for a lot of reasons.

Their conversation gave Bailey the chance to watch Tim from a distance. He was taller than back in his CKT days, and handsome in a polished sort of way. He loved God and he fit in well with Bailey's friends and family. *Why, then,* she asked herself as she pulled three pie servers from a drawer and set them on a napkin, *aren't you head over heels for that guy?*

She had no answers.

Tim finished talking with Dayne and crossed the room to the kitchen. He smiled when he saw her, but she wasn't sure his eyes actually lit up. Not the way she would've liked. "Hey ... Happy Thanksgiving." He gave Bailey a quick hug as he studied the pies. "Looks like I got here just in time."

They compared notes about the day and ate pie and played a new board game—Eye to Eye—and when the night was over sometime after ten o'clock, he hugged her again and they went their separate ways. The ride back was quiet, with Ricky and BJ nodding off before they had gone far. The trip gave Bailey time to review her evening with Tim. They'd had fun, for sure. They laughed and enjoyed being together. But if she was painfully honest with herself, something was missing. Something in the way Tim looked at her.

She remembered her mom's words. *"I saw how he looked at you ... He adores you."*

Maybe that was it. Tim looked at her on a surface level. He smiled and seemed happy to see her. But when Cody looked at her, there were no layers left, nothing he didn't reveal, nothing he couldn't see. He didn't really look at her so much as he looked into her. To the deepest, most real, places in her heart and soul.

Her mom seemed to sense she needed alone time, so she didn't ask about Tim or how Bailey had felt seeing him. Good thing. Bailey didn't have an answer for herself, let alone her mother. Not until she was changing out of her jeans did she remember her phone and the text message she'd never read. She pulled it from her pocket and clicked a few buttons.

I MISS YOU TOO.

She was drawn into those four simple words as if he was standing right here beside her. Again her breath caught. Tears stung her eyes, and she blinked them back. She wasn't crying because she was sad. The tears were because maybe her mother was right. He must care more than he let on or he wouldn't have sent this text a full hour after his last one. Maybe he'd analyzed his message about Tim and how Bailey hadn't answered, and finally—after a very long time—he'd texted how he felt. How he really felt.

He missed her too.

As she finished getting ready for bed, her thoughts moved from the text message to her conversation with Ashley earlier that day. Love was complicated. That was true with Tim, and it was true with Cody—whatever sort of love she had for the two of them. Landon had been the difficult path for Ashley, and right now Cody was the difficult path for Bailey. So maybe Cody would be a bigger part of her life again someday. Or maybe they'd only be friends. Even that was more than they now shared.

She thought about Ashley's advice: to pray about Cody and Tim, of course, but also to look for the answers. *"That sort of love rarely happens twice."* Yes, that's what Ashley had said.

Bailey climbed into bed and lay still on her pillow, the darkness around her. *I'm looking, God. I want to hear You, but nothing seems very clear.*

I am here, my daughter. All things work to the good for those who love me. Remember that.

The answer came quickly and easily, the way it rarely did. The response was part of a Bible verse from Romans chapter 8. Something she'd read yesterday morning before class. But still ... it was sort of surreal to think God loved her enough to speak peace to her like that. That He loved her whether she heard His responses or not. He was here, with her, regardless.

She closed her eyes, wrapped in the Lord's arms, loved and cared for. Only one thought from the day remained as she drifted to sleep, and it made her smile, lying there in the darkness.

Cody missed her.

One more thing to be thankful for.

Six

THE DEADLINE TO FINISH EDITING THEIR movie was a living, breathing being, hounding them through every day and crawling into bed with them at night. Even still, Chase and Keith took Thanksgiving off. Their families deserved that much. Chase had pushed for dinner at their house, since that way they could put the girls to bed after dessert. But now the meal was behind them, he wondered if he'd made the wrong choice. Maybe pulling off a big dinner had been too much for Kelly, or maybe she was still upset with his schedule. Whatever it was, Chase hadn't been able to lighten her mood all day. It was late now, and they sat around the room with the Ellisons and their daughter, Andi, talking about the week ahead.

"You really think you'll finish before the fifth?" Lisa sat next to Keith, but the question was directed to Chase. He was the director, the one with the skill in the editing room.

"We have to do color correction and sound mixing. The principles are scheduled to meet us at the studio early next week for voice touch-ups. And we've hired someone to work on color. The guy's amazing."

"Is there money for that?" Kelly's question came out sharp, pointed. She sat across the room in a worn-out chair they'd gotten at a garage sale. One more sacrifice in the quest to make movies.

"We're still working with money Ben invested at the close of filming." Chase dug deep for an extra dose of understanding. He'd told her this before. "We can definitely get through the editing process."

"But if there's no theatrical release?" Kelly looked tired and anxious, the lines between her eyes deeper than usual. She didn't have to spell out the dire financial consequences. Not with Andi in the room.

"No one'll take you seriously if you go direct to DVD." Andi sat on the other side of her father. She'd been a great help with Molly and Macy today, and now they were asleep she seemed glad to be part of the adult conversation.

Andi was right. If she hadn't said it, Chase would have. The financial concerns were only part of the trouble they faced. They had to wrap up editing and submit to the film festivals Kendall had lined up. Then they needed to pray for a favorable response from the festival committees. If that happened, they'd have a good argument for a theatrical release when the studio screened the film. Not only so people would take them seriously, but so they would have a chance to earn back the money they'd spent.

"Luke Baxter is working on the studio contract, looking for a loophole. But he agrees that we need to pray. God's the great Counselor, after all."

Kelly raised a wary brow. "Lawyers don't work for free. It all costs so much."

"We've accounted for that, Kelly. Obviously." Chase immediately regretted his tone. Kelly had a right to feel nervous.

"I was just asking." Kelly tried to hide her hurt, but her eyes gave her away. She stood and headed for the kitchen, glancing first at Keith's wife. "More coffee?"

"Definitely." Lisa joined her, and they rounded the corner into the kitchen.

At the same time, Andi stood and headed to the back room to work on a paper for her English class. Once they were gone, Chase heard Kelly's defeated laugh. "This thing is going to break us all—you ever feel that way?"

Chase couldn't hear Lisa's answer, but his wife's lack of confidence made him feel suddenly tired—too tired to continue the conversation. He looked at Keith and saw his friend had also heard Kelly. He kept his voice low so the wives and Andi wouldn't hear him. "I thought we were past this. A few months ago she was nothing but supportive."

Keith was within arm's reach, and he put his hand on Chase's shoulder. "You can't blame her for being worried."

"Lisa's not."

"Of course she is." Keith's smile was layered with wisdom. "She doesn't talk about it the way Kelly does, but if we don't make our money back on this movie, we'll lose our house."

The news hit Chase with a cold wave of reality. "That bad?"

"Yes." Keith clasped his hands and stared for a moment at the place between his feet. "We took out a second mortgage on the house, and the payments are way beyond our comfort zone. Same as you."

Chase nodded, his mind drifting. He and Kelly rented the house they were in, so as long as he drew a salary from their work they wouldn't be homeless. But their credit cards were maxed out. If the money ran dry, and if the studio waited too long for a DVD release, Chase and Keith could reach a point where there would be no money even for a meager paycheck. He pictured himself talking to Kelly, explaining that she would need to get a job so they could pay their bills, and he shuddered. He'd quit making movies and clean toilets at a gas station before he'd ask Kelly to get a job. Especially if it was to support him while he followed his dreams. The sobering reality of that made him understand a little of what had Kelly feeling down.

After the next round of coffee, Keith, Lisa, and Andi went home. Keith promised to pick up Chase for the drive to LA first thing Sunday morning. They wanted half a day to discuss their plans and meet with Ben Adams one more time before they returned to the editing room to begin their most intense week yet.

When they were gone, Chase leaned against the closed door and locked eyes with his wife. "Is it the money? Is that what's eating you?"

"I'm not the problem." Kelly touched her fingers to her chest, her expression anchored in disbelief. "We can't walk around pretending we aren't in trouble." She paused, and raw fear flashed in her eyes. "What if the film doesn't break even?"

Chase didn't want to fight. He folded his arms and leaned his head against the cool wood door. His tone was quietly resigned. "It's Thanksgiving, Kelly. We're supposed to be thankful."

"I am. But I'm also realistic." She tossed her hands and exhaled her frustration. "We're running out of money, Chase. You've got a movie almost done, and that's great. But where do we go from here?"

"Do we have to know?" His anger rose a level. "Whatever happened to trusting God? Believing He has a plan for us?"

"Don't start with that." Kelly let her hands fall to her sides. The girls were asleep down the hall, and he watched her fight to keep her voice in check. "Of course God has a plan. That doesn't mean the plan is for you to make movies, right? Or did you get a memo from God and forget to tell me?"

Chase hated when she was sarcastic. Her eyebrows lowered and the lines deepened across her forehead. In moments like this she seemed a different person from the girl he'd married. As if the two of them had never laughed or loved at all.

He thought of all the responses he might give her. He could tell her sarcasm didn't become her, and he could remind her that before they left the mission field they had agreed God wanted them here, in California ... making movies. But again he was too tired for the battle. He brushed his hand in her direction. "Never mind."

"Wait..."

He didn't want to. Without looking back, he walked to the kitchen and surveyed the dishes still crowded around the sink. He rolled up his shirt sleeves and began scrubbing the sweet potatoes and dried-on stuffing. Four of the plates were already washed when Kelly came to him. She studied him for a minute, and then joined in, wrapping up the leftover pie and putting away spices and whipped cream left out from dessert. From the corner of his eye, Chase watched her linger near the spice cupboard, searching for something.

Then, almost abruptly, she straightened and with only the slightest hesitation she told him good night and she was gone. As she walked away, he saw something he hadn't noticed before. She was wearing stretch pants—the kind she wore when she struggled with her weight. He'd noticed she was a little heavier than usual, but the pants were a sure sign.

He dried his hands and stooped down near the spice cupboard. Far in the back, where he would never have otherwise noticed it, was a wadded-up plastic grocery bag. He reached back and pulled it out. Even before he opened it, he had an idea of what he'd found. This was Kelly's weakness—hiding food. Sneaking chocolate and cookies so that no one would know she struggled. He opened the bag and there was the proof. It held at least fifty Hershey's Kisses, and just as many empty wrappers.

Anger rattled his nerves once more. He stood and moved to the trashcan beneath the sink, but he stopped before slamming the bag into the trash. Instead he set the bag out on the counter in plain sight. If she wanted to eat candy, she could eat it. He would love her no matter what.

"Why, God?" The prayer felt as worn out as he did. Did their money troubles really have her that depressed?

He massaged his thumb and fingers into his temples and willed the tension there to ease. Compassion tempered his frustration. Kelly didn't want to eat like this. She was worried and discouraged, afraid of their money troubles and Chase's future as a filmmaker. He looked out the window again.

What can I do, God? How can I love her so that I'm all she needs?

Almost as soon as he'd laid the question before God, Chase knew the answer. He would never satisfy all Kelly's needs. Only the Lord could do that. And until she learned to turn to Him when she felt overwhelmed, the struggle would continue.

How long had she been discouraged this time? She'd come to the shoot and together they'd shared alone time—something rare for them. She'd been supportive and loving and sure that God would see them through. But after his second LA editing trip, he'd noticed something different about her. She seemed distant and short. Now he understood just how hopeless she must be feeling.

Please, God ... give her strength. I'm not sure how much I can help her.

No matter how he approached the subject, he couldn't win, couldn't help her. He finished the dishes, praying for her the entire time. Clearly the answer was the one God had placed on his heart moments ago: she needed Christ—His satisfaction, His fulfillment, His strength.

As he turned off the lights he no longer felt angry. Instead he was determined to do the one thing he could do: pray for her without ceasing, that she might find the strength to do the same.

Before her discouragement grew any worse.

SHE'D BEEN FOUND OUT.

Kelly knew it early Friday morning as soon as she saw the bag of candy on the counter. Her heart slid into a fast and frantic rhythm, because if Chase knew ... If he knew, then she wasn't sure how she could face him. He and the girls were asleep, but they'd wake up soon. Chase would give her that look, the one that said he was aware of her struggles and that he was disappointed in her. She would be forced to come clean about her eating, and she would feel like a fat failure in front of her husband. Too depressed to find her way to daylight.

Her heart found its regular beat again. Defiance muddied the stagnant water of her heart. If Chase knew, there was no point hiding the candy. She moved the bag back to the spice cupboard, right up front. She could eat what she wanted to eat, and if she gained weight, then so be it. She had to keep the house and yard up, pay the bills, and keep the family going on almost no money. She would find control later, after the New Year. Chase was never home anyway, gone running after a dream that seemed less and less likely.

The pans were still soaking in the sink. She studied them, defeated, and caught her reflection in the mirror. She stopped short and stared at herself, hating what she saw. The weight was piling on, and she could do nothing to hide the fact. Her face looked pasty and puffy, creased with concern and deceit.

She took a step closer. Rebelliousness didn't become her. When had her eyes lost the shine that marked them a few months ago when she went to Bloomington, Indiana, and declared to Chase her absolute support? Punch drunk, that's how she looked, battered by the abuse she wielded on her own body. Her blank eyes reminded her of someone lost somewhere in the middle rounds of a boxing match against depression. A match she was destined to lose.

A realization began to take root, and she felt conviction taking hold of her, shaking her and ordering her out of the ring. Life wasn't meant to be a web of lies, and only one reason could explain why Chase had found out about her recent mindless eating.

God wanted him to find out.

She hung her head and didn't try to stop the gathering tears. A long, slow sigh made its way from her, taking with it every argument she'd ever made in favor of hiding food and falling prey to a diet of chocolate and McDonald's. None of this was Chase's fault; it was her own. Chase loved her and cared for her and the girls in a way too great for words. His time away was a necessary part of the commitment of filmmaking—an adventure she'd agreed to and supported even as recently as her trip to Indiana.

Footsteps sounded in the hallway, and Kelly ran her fingertips beneath her eyes. She sniffed and looked at herself once more. *God, I need You. I can't do this without You.* The next few minutes were going to be humiliating, but if they were God's way of taking her out of the fight, then she had no choice but to go along. However awful she felt.

"Kelly?" Chase came up behind her and stopped a few feet away. "I didn't hear you get up."

"Sorry." She wasn't willing to look at her husband yet. She knew exactly what she'd find in his eyes. Disapproval, disgust, and disappointment. The three *D*s. "The pans needed washing."

She held her breath and turned, facing him. But as they looked at each other, Kelly found she could barely exhale. Chase's expression wasn't angry or suspicious. His light-brown eyes showed a vulnerability, a love and concern that melted Kelly and shattered her defenses.

"Can you come here?" His words were kind and without accusation. He made no attempt to come to her, almost as if he could sense her vulnerability and he wanted her to know he wasn't on the attack.

She came to him, her eyes never leaving his. He wasn't her accuser, he was her friend, the one who had stood by her regardless of her highs and lows. As she reached him, he held out his hands and she wove her fingers between his. The touch of his skin felt intoxicating, lightening her spirit more than anything hidden in the cupboards — as if the unspoken honesty between them resurrected an intimacy long buried in layers of guilt.

Her body came up against his and she rested her head on his chest. "I'm sorry." Looking at him was still too painful. "About the candy."

He kissed the top of her head, their hands still linked. "You don't have to hide from me, Kelly. You're under a lot of pressure here. I know that."

"But ..." She lifted her eyes to his again. "I'm turning to all the wrong things."

There was no need for him to say anything about that. "I'm here, Kel. If you need help, I'm here. I love you no matter what you eat, or how you look. I just want you to be happy."

The reference to her looks cut, and she winced a little. He'd have to be blind not to notice the weight she'd put on these past few months. At the same time, she believed he meant what he said — that he loved her whatever her size. But meaning it and living it out were two very different realities. If she didn't want their marriage to suffer, she had to find her way out of the darkness. "I've been so down, running everything here by myself."

"I'm sorry." His words were deeply sincere. "I hate being gone."

She released his hands and slid her arms around his waist. "I wish you weren't leaving so soon." If only he could stay this next week, take walks with her and shop with her, help her have a normal week. Maybe then she could make things right with herself and him, and even God.

"I love you, do you know that?" He leaned back enough to see her, study her. "You couldn't do anything to change that, Kel. I mean it. But don't hide things from me."

"I won't. Never again." Kelly laid her head against his chest once more and heard his heartbeat. The heartbeat of a man who loved her unconditionally. She tried to imagine telling Chase about surviving on candy and macaroni so she could find the energy to drag herself through a day of mowing the lawn and clipping coupons, washing dishes and doing laundry. All while trying to be both mother and father to their girls. No wonder she hid her stash of junk food. It was proof she was beyond discouraged and relying on all the wrong sources to survive.

Verses flooded her mind, Scriptures that ordered God's people to keep their deeds in the light, to avoid all darkness where sin could grow unchecked. Rather than flinch away from them, she embraced them, accepted them as truth. For another five minutes they stood there, clinging to each other, breathing to the beat of each other's heart, and believing that Kelly's secret, mindless eating was behind them. She would move ahead in honesty and light. She would tell him when she was tempted to spend an entire day eating ice cream bars and chocolate chip cookies. She wanted a fresh start now, so she could enjoy Christmas without the feelings of stomach pains and indigestion, without the oppressive guilt and weight gain. She was finished with it, once and for all. As soon as the moment passed, before anything could deter or distract her, Kelly would visit her hiding places and gather the garbage, taking it directly to the trashcan in the garage. And that would be that.

But before she could make a move, the girls woke up. They came down the hall holding hands, their flannel nightgowns covering all but their bare feet and fingers. When they reached the place where their parents stood hugging each other, the girls began to giggle.

The moment was suddenly over, and the girls clamored for breakfast and a trip to the park and piggy-back rides on Chase. There were eggs to make and dishes to wash and laundry to start, and in the mix of laughter and chaos that was their morning, Kelly never got around to throwing out the junk food, never made her way to her hiding spots.

She still intended to, of course. She would toss everything as soon as she had a chance, as soon as the morning allowed.

And for at least half the day, she actually believed that.

By noon, a compromise began to take shape. She wouldn't toss the food just yet, because what if the girls wanted a sweet snack? Money was tight, so it was practically sinful to throw out perfectly good cookies and candy. She could put them out when company came, the next time Laurie Weeks stopped by, maybe.

The compromise grew and swelled, and by nightfall she was already planning a trip to McDonald's with the girls as soon as Chase left for LA. They could eat cheaper from the dollar menu than anything she could cook, and at least she'd get one night without dishes. As for the other junk food, she wouldn't eat it now. She'd merely keep it around for a pick-me-up.

Just in case.

Seven

ANDI MET BAILEY FOR LUNCH THE day *Scrooge* opened at Indiana University's performance auditorium. She'd never been in a musical, and her stomach hadn't been right all day. She took a table in the midst of the confusion of the cafeteria and scanned the doorway for her roommate. She was still looking when a guy from her science class walked up.

He was biracial—white and Middle Eastern, maybe. Tall with a nice smile. Once in a while he'd asked her about lecture notes, but his name escaped her. "Waiting for someone?"

"My friend." Andi was careful not to seem interested. The guy was nice looking, and he seemed charming in his own way. But she'd already gotten into too much trouble with guys she didn't know. She smiled, but kept the walls up behind her eyes. "She'll be here any minute."

"That's okay." He sat down and put his backpack on the table. "I'm Taz. You've seen me in science class, but I'm also a film student. You're an actress, right?"

An actress. "I am." She liked the sound of it, even if so far she'd only been an extra in her dad's movie. "How'd you know?"

"You're gorgeous. Your dad's a producer—I saw you as an extra when he was filming on campus. And you're starring in *Scrooge*, which opens tonight." He winked at her. "I'll be there, by the way. Me and my roommates. They're film students too."

He pulled an envelope from a pocket in his backpack and slid it across the table. "This is for you. I didn't want to give it to you in class."

Andi's nerves were already on edge because in six hours she'd be slipping into the flowing gown that made up her costume for *Scrooge*, hoping she could still breathe when the curtain went up. She stared at the guy, now sitting in Bailey's seat. *A little pushy*, she thought. But something about his approach appealed to her. "You wrote me a letter?"

"Sort of. It's more of an offer." He leaned back and smiled, definitely satisfied with himself.

"Hmmm." Andi ignored the slight wave of anxiety his mention of opening night caused her. She felt her defenses fall. The film student stuff piqued her interest. "You're making a film? Is that what you're saying?"

"A short film. It's for a class, but I have connections. If I get the right people to star in it, we might win some awards." He stood, his eyes dancing. "It'd look great on your résumé."

A hint of a thrill ran down her spine. A short film with her as the star? That would be way better experience than extra work. Maybe then her dad would take her dreams of an acting career seriously. At least she would have something to show an agent or a director. She tossed her blonde hair over her shoulder and took the letter. "Thanks for thinking of me."

He laughed. "Are you kidding? You would be amazing."

The flattery felt good.

In the distance she saw Bailey make her way toward the table, so she hurried her next words. "How do I reach you?"

"Everything's in there," Taz nodded at the envelope. His smile was friendly, confident bordering on cocky. He gave her shoulder a quick, light touch, and his eyes connected with something in hers. "See you tonight." With that he was gone, moving through the crowd in the direction he'd come.

A few seconds later, Bailey reached the table and sat down, breathless from the cold air outside. Six inches of snow covered the Indiana campus, and another foot was forecast for the weekend. The perfect backdrop for *Scrooge*.

Bailey looked at Taz as he reached the cafeteria door. "Who was that?"

"Some guy in my science class." Andi still had the envelope in her hand. "I guess he's a film student." She lifted the envelope. "He gave me this."

"What is it?"

"An offer to star in a movie he's making."

"Really?" Bailey took off her coat and gloves and settled in closer to the table. Her eyes sparkled and she looked relaxed and comfortable. Not even a little nervous about opening night. "Well ... come on! Open it."

Andi shared everything with Bailey. Whatever the offer inside the envelope, she was glad her roommate was excited for her. She slipped her finger beneath the sealed flap and pulled out a single piece of paper, then slid her chair around the side of the table so she and Bailey could read it together.

"'Dear Andi,'" she read aloud. "'My name is Taz Bazzi, and I'm in your science class. I'm making a movie—a short film, really—and I'd like you to consider starring in it.'"

"Andi!" Bailey grabbed hold of Andi's wrist. "That's fantastic. Lots of actresses get their start in short films."

"Seriously?"

"Yes. For sure." Bailey looked back at the paper. "How'd he know you could act?"

"He saw me working on *The Last Letter* and he knows my dad's a producer. At least that's what he said." Andi continued reading. "'I've been looking for the perfect girl for the role, and for awhile now I've known it was you. So here's a little bit about my film. It's sort of a docudrama about a conflicted girl trapped by her parents' outdated rules and understanding.'"

Andi gave a nervous laugh. "That's a little close to home."

"Keep reading."

She found her place. "'The girl's parents think she's at college, but she takes a quarter off and finds her way to the streets. She tries a lot of dangerous and edgy things before realizing that her place is here, back on campus.'" That was the end of the summary. The rest was Taz's contact information.

"Does she ever work things out with her mom and dad?" Bailey sounded less enthusiastic than before.

"Doesn't say." Andi turned the paper over, but it was blank on the back. She flipped it again and found his contact information, and then for the first time saw a few lines in small print at the bottom of the page. It told her they could set up a screening time and that the shooting schedule could be worked around her availability. The very last line was something Andi couldn't bring herself to read out loud.

Some partial nudity required.

Bailey peered over Andi's shoulder and read the fine print at the same time. "Partial nudity?" Bailey pushed back from the table. "Creepy guy. Probably not even a film student. Just a porn freak."

Andi was bothered by the partial nudity thing, but she wasn't as upset as Bailey. Partial meant a few shots in her bra and underwear. Something like that. Besides, film was art. Wasn't that what the actors on her father's set had talked about? Sometimes compromise was necessary in order to get a message across ...

Her eyes moved to the bottom of the page where a website was listed. She folded the paper and put it back in the envelope. "At least he was upfront."

"Yeah." Bailey's laugh was filled with disbelief. "Because he wants a look at *your* front. Don't you get it? The guy's probably making a soft porn film and somehow I get the feeling you're flattered."

She was, but she didn't want to say so to Bailey. Her roommate had connections like megastar Dayne Matthews and his actress wife, Katy Hart Matthews. What did Andi have? A dad who was more missionary than moviemaker and whose first film might never find its way out of DVD Land. If she wanted to be an actress, Taz was right. She needed all the experience she could get.

She slipped the envelope through the opening at the top of her backpack and smiled at Bailey. "I'm scared to death about tonight."

"Wait." Bailey leaned forward, more intense than before. "You're not considering that? Tell me you'll throw it in the first trashcan."

"I wanna check out his website." Andi kept her tone even, as if her calmness might make Bailey see that she was overreacting. "I owe him that much."

Bailey's eyes flashed. "You don't owe him anything. Come on, Andi. Show up to read for a guy like that and you could be raped."

"Please." Andi managed a light-hearted laugh. "If I was going to do it, I wouldn't meet with just him. There'd be other people and it would have to be somewhere on campus."

Another shocked sound came from Bailey. "You can't be serious? You're actually considering this? Even with the nudity?"

"Partial nudity. Like in a bikini or bra or something."

"So you're going to do it?"

"Well ..." Andi hesitated. Only one right answer remained. "Of course not. I'm just saying I should respond to him. Let's drop it, okay?"

"Tell him no."

"All right, all right." Andi wanted to say that she'd tell him whatever she wanted and Bailey could just get used to the idea. But she was pretty sure she wouldn't take the job, anyway, so it didn't matter. "Talk about tonight. Are you scared?"

"No." Bailey looked like she was struggling to transition from her disapproval to the play they were about to star in. She busied herself with her gloves and then stopped and found the beginning of a smile. "You'll be great, Andi. You don't have to be afraid."

"So you're really not?"

"Not at all." Gradually Bailey softened, and the smile returned to her eyes. "There's nothing like opening night. The packed house, the buzz of anticipation backstage, the orchestra warming up for the first performance."

Andi felt her stomach tighten again. "What if I get out there and forget my lines?"

"You won't." Bailey laughed. "The adrenaline rush actually makes you think more clearly. Remember your audition?"

The two of them and Tim Reed had auditioned in a group, each performing in front of the creative team separately. "I was scared then too."

"And you were brilliant." Bailey shrugged. "You'll be brilliant tonight too."

Bailey's confidence was contagious. By the time they left the cafeteria, two things had happened. First, Andi's nervousness had faded to nothing more than excited energy. And second, Bailey had forgotten about Taz and his offer. At least it seemed that way. But after classes when Andi reached the dorm, Bailey was already there, sitting cross-legged on her bed reading her Bible.

"Hey." Andi tossed her backpack on the floor near her dresser. It was snowing again, and she dusted off the shoulders of her coat as she peeled it off and threw it on the end of her bed.

"Hey." Bailey looked up, but only briefly.

"What're you reading?"

"Romans 12. 'Do not conform any longer to the pattern of this world, but be transformed by the renewing of your mind.'" She closed the Bible and anchored her elbows on her knees. "That section."

Andi knew it well. "Why that?"

"I don't know." Bailey sighed. "Just thinking about that Taz guy and his crazy offer. It's weird how people think they can do anything as long as they label it 'art.' Anything at all."

The sentiment was something Andi's father had said in the weeks leading up to his decision to leave the mission field for a career as a producer. He wanted to redefine art, take things way above the line from where they were. Andi wasn't so sure. She could see merit in some of the movies her parents disliked. She was pretty sure she and Bailey wouldn't see eye to eye on this, so she said nothing. Instead she busied herself with removing her gloves and scarf and setting them on the edge of her desk.

Bailey watched her. After this long as roommates and friends, they kept few secrets from each other. "You're thinking about it, aren't you?"

"About what?" Andi forced herself to look innocent.

"You know what." Bailey hugged her knees. "The film. The one with the nudity."

"Partial nudity." Andi had run out of busy work. She dropped to the edge of her bed, her shoulders a notch lower than before. "I think maybe I disagree a little."

"Disagree?"

"About the whole 'art' thing." Andi had been honest about her unconventional feelings before. She couldn't stop now if she wanted to stay close with Bailey. "Sometimes partial nudity might be valid for the sake of art, don't you think?"

"Not at all." There was no anger in Bailey's voice. The intensity from earlier in the day was gone, and in its place was a peace, a glow that seemed to come from deep inside her soul. But there was no hesitation, either. "Our bodies are sacred to God, the temple of the Holy Spirit. We're supposed to treat them with respect."

The truth came straight from the Bible. Andi knew that much. She pushed her fingers through her hair and tried to find an explanation that would make sense. "The body is a beautiful thing. Maybe it's honoring it to put the body in a more visible light." She stretched out on her side and leaned up on one elbow. "Or maybe if a film shows the terrible things that can happen to someone who makes bad decisions, and if that film requires partial nudity to get the point across, then maybe that's honoring. Because maybe it'll teach some teenaged girl not to make those same bad choices."

"Come on, Andi." Bailey raised one eyebrow. "You must be kidding."

That was the trouble. She wasn't kidding. Not that she was ready to sign up as the lead in Taz's film. She needed more information, like where the film would be shot and who would be there and whether it was truly a class project and how much nudity and whether it was in full light or only silhouetted.

"See, that's what I thought. You're seriously considering it." Bailey sounded worried. "Andi, you know better than that. I could give you a hundred Bible verses that would prove making that film would be a mistake. Romans is a good place to start."

"That's just it." Andi sat up again. "The pattern of the world interests me. I'm just being honest. I'm not saying I don't want to be a Christian, but ... I don't know. I want to experience life. Not avoid it."

For a long while Bailey didn't say anything. Then she stood, crossed the room, and sat down next to Andi. They both turned so they were facing each other. "I'm not going to judge you, Andi. But let's at least pray, okay? There's a lot going on."

"Sure." Andi didn't mind praying. She still liked the idea that God was there, that He cared about what she did or didn't do. But that didn't change her desire to experience life — in a safe manner, anyway. All of life. Maybe not by getting drunk at frat parties or by putting herself in dangerous situations. But acting in the short film of a student at Indiana University? Actually starring in it? The idea sounded more attractive with every passing hour.

Bailey seemed to sense Andi had made up her mind, but she said nothing about it. Instead she took hold of Andi's hands and began talking to God in a way that was familiar and comforting. She prayed about their opening night, that they would remember the words, and that the audience would be packed with people. "Let them see the meaning in the story, Lord," she added. "The message of regret for people who don't make the most of every day they've been given."

Her prayer moved on then to the movie offer from Taz. "The world will always have what looks like a better offer." Her voice was kinder still, without a drop of accusation. "Help us see life through Your eyes, Father. So that we know when the world is trying to mislead us. We need Your help, or we'll be ... Well, we'll be like people without faith. And that would be a very sad loss, Lord. Thank You for listening. In Jesus' name, amen."

Andi appreciated the prayer and the way moments like this made her and Bailey closer. But she still wondered if Taz was serious, if he and his roommates were really going to be at the show tonight. And if they were, she wondered if they would wait for her afterward. If so, then maybe she could ask him her questions in person. At least then she'd have all the information.

They both turned their attention to getting ready. Their characters needed long, curled hair—so they stood in front of the small mirror and shared Bailey's curling iron, passing it back and forth and spritzing hairspray as they went. They were just putting on their coats and gloves again when Andi got a text. Her first thought was Taz. Maybe he'd gotten her number and now he was texting her, looking for her answer. But as she reached for her phone, she saw she was wrong. The text was from Cody.

HEY, ANDI. WANTED YOU TO KNOW I'LL BE THERE TONIGHT. I'M TAKING MY MOM. CAN'T WAIT TO SEE IT. BREAK A LEG!

She grinned at the phone and her heart soared. She hurried with her response.

YAY! I'M GLAD YOU'RE GOING, BUT DON'T LOOK AT ME DURING MY SONG. LOL. I MIGHT FORGET THE WORDS AND RUN DOWN TO JOIN YOU IN THE AUDIENCE.

Andi couldn't figure out Cody Coleman. Times like this she was almost certain he had feelings for her, which would be amazing. There was no one she'd rather date than Cody. He was the hottest guy she knew, but more than that he had a wisdom, a faith that was borne of real-life experience and a genuine need for God. The kind of faith Andi wished she had.

"Who're you texting?" Bailey wrapped her thick wool scarf around her neck and chin. The air temperature outside was already in the low teens.

"Cody." Andi tried not to feel guilty, but she did. Whenever she and Cody texted, things felt a little awkward with Bailey. "He'll be at the show."

Bailey's eyes flickered, proof that the news clearly registered somewhere inside her. But nothing in her expression told whether she felt grateful or upset by the fact. Bailey grabbed her bag and headed for the door. "Did he say anything else?"

"Yeah. He's coming with his mom."

For a second, Bailey stopped and looked over her shoulder. "You know Cody's mom?"

"No." Andi wrinkled her nose, confused by the question. "Why would I know her?"

Bailey shrugged. "Just seemed like he wouldn't tell you that unless you knew her."

"I know she's had a rough life. Been in prison, drugs, that sort of thing. Cody says he's trying to build a new relationship with her."

This time there was no mistaking the hurt in Bailey's eyes. "Great." She checked her watch. "We better go."

They decided to drive because the theater was on the other side of campus and even a five-minute walk wouldn't be easy in the freezing-cold snow and wind. On the way to the car, and then to the theater, Bailey talked about her costume and Tim's nervousness about playing Scrooge. She touched on how she might take a break from theater after this quarter and the struggle she was having in her harder classes. But Cody's name didn't come up again.

Andi tried to assess Bailey's response to Cody, her seeming lack of interest. All along she had told herself that Cody had feelings for Bailey, that the two of them were only kidding each other by keeping their distance and maintaining that they'd never seen each other as more than friends. Anyone around the two of them could feel the chemistry there. But watching her now, Andi wondered if she might have read Bailey wrong. Maybe Bailey really didn't have feelings for Cody. She was still dating Tim, after all.

They ran into the theater, using their backpacks to shield their curly hair from the snow, and Andi was suddenly overcome with a rush of joy and exhilaration. Life was actually going right for her. She was truly living—living in a way that she wished her friend Rachel Baugher might've lived. Rachel, who died in a car accident without ever realizing her dreams. That wouldn't be Andi. She was going to live here and now, without reservations.

She ran through the list of all that was right in her life. She was about to star in her first musical, and she was being asked to star in her first movie—and it was a movie. Short film or not. On top of all that, maybe Cody did like her after all. The possibility seemed so real she could almost see the two of them together, holding hands and laughing. Bailey wouldn't care. At least it seemed that way.

And for the first time every dream she'd ever had seemed within reach.

She could hardly wait for the curtain to go up.

Eight

BAILEY COULDN'T EXPLAIN THE HURT CONSUMING her heart.

This was opening night, and she wanted everything about it to be a celebration. She was sharing the stage with Tim, a guy she admired and respected. In the audience would be her parents and brothers, along with some of their friends. Katy and Dayne had bought a block of tickets in the center orchestra section, so they'd be there, along with Ashley and Landon and the boys and a few of the other Baxter sisters and their families. Everyone Bailey loved.

Even Cody Coleman.

She and Andi helped each other into their costumes and then moved into the greenroom where all cast members did their own stage makeup. They sat next to each other at a long row of tables. Each spot had a stand-up mirror, and as Bailey began applying her makeup, she was struck again by the sadness consuming her. Or was it jealousy?

This is all because of Cody, she told herself. *Dear God, I know he's not interested in me as anything more than friend. Help me stop thinking about him.* But the moment the quick prayer was over, his face was back in her mind again. Smiling at her, haunting her.

"You okay?" Andi dabbed white powder over her foundation. For the part of Isabelle, she needed to look paler than usual.

"Sure." She gave Andi an instant smile, almost too instant. "Just thinking about my lines."

"Oh." Andi resumed her dabbing. "Okay. You seem kinda quiet."

"Sorry. I'm like this before the first show." She smiled again at her friend. "I'm fine. Really."

Her hurt was something she would only share with God, at least until she had some alone time with her mom. Figuring out her feelings for Cody was hard enough without involving her roommate.

She took a cotton pad and lightly applied thick foundation across her cheeks. Why didn't he at least ask about her? Cody knew she was in the show, so he could have dropped her a quick text as easily as he'd texted Andi. The occasional random text, like on Thanksgiving, wasn't enough. Or was he really avoiding her because of Tim?

She began moving too fast, and her foundation streaked. *Slow down*, she told herself. So what if Cody's here tonight. The way he'd treated her lately, he was just another guy on a campus of tens of thousands of guys. But even so, she couldn't shake his image.

She applied another layer of makeup. She needed paler skin for the show. The Ghost of Christmas Past was supposed to have an otherworldly, ethereal look. When she finished, she stepped back. "Definitely ghostlike," she muttered.

"You look great." Andi put the finishing touches on her eye shadow. She was pale, but striking. The way Isabelle was supposed to look.

Bailey hadn't been jealous of her friend's part since the cast list went up, but here, knowing Cody would be in the audience ... For a brief moment she wished she could take the stage in the dress Andi was wearing instead of the velvet cloak assigned to the Ghost of Christmas Past.

They were both studying themselves when she saw Tim enter the room. At least she assumed the guy was Tim. The transformation was that dramatic. He had reported to the theater half an hour earlier to meet with a professional makeup artist, and now he looked sixty years old. His hair was streaked mostly gray and his face looked haggard and wrinkled.

She turned to face him. "That's amazing. You look totally different."

"I even talk different." A few of the other cast members stared at him as he crossed the greenroom. "They put some kind of tightening gel near my mouth so that I'll sound like an old man."

"It's working." Bailey took a step closer and studied his face. "Seriously, I almost didn't recognize you."

"I hope not." He tried to laugh, but it sounded strained with his tight mouth. "This isn't really the look I'm going for offstage."

Bailey giggled as Andi faced Tim too. "Definitely Scrooge." She put her hands on her hips and did a slow twirl. Her dress was pale blue with small white lines of satin. It clung to her upper body, while below her waist it billowed out in soft folds of blue that gracefully hit just below her ankles. With her blonde hair hanging down her back in curls, she was stunning. Any of them could've seen that. She grinned at Tim. "What do you think?"

Tim watched her. "Wow." His stage makeup couldn't hide the appreciation in his eyes. "Scrooge would've been a fool to walk away from you."

The compliment made Andi blush even through her pale powder. "Why, thank you, Ebenezer."

Bailey pulled her red velvet cloak around her shoulders and tried not to be bothered by the exchange. She couldn't blame Tim. His character was motivated largely by the regret he felt in walking away from the woman he'd loved as a young man. Scrooge needed an attraction to Isabelle for the audience to believe the story.

Still, the comment made her feel thick and unattractive. Her cloak came in tight around the neck, but otherwise she would remain shapeless on stage. The only thing that would make her performance stand out was the slight bit of sarcastic humor written into the script. Their director had told her to milk it for all it was worth.

But nothing about the role made her feel pretty.

Tim seemed to realize he hadn't shown her the same attention he'd shown Andi. He came to her and put his hands on her shoulders. "I like your hair that way, curled." He touched his fingers to the side of her face. "You're beautiful, Bailey. A vision."

"In a red velvet cloak?" She made a silly face. "That's okay. Thanks about my hair though. I like it this way too."

He gave her a side hug just as the director bounded into the room. "Okay, people. We've got a full house." He chuckled. "Oh, and Dayne Matthews is in the fourth row. This will be a first for my career directing plays at Indiana U." He made eye contact with Tim and a handful of the other leads. "Let's give it our best tonight."

They circled up and he gave them a few reminders. "All right." He sounded as nervous as any of them. "Everyone take their places."

Only Tim and the kid playing Bob Cratchet were needed for the first scene, but before he walked onto the stage, Tim looked into her eyes. "All day I kept thinking about you, how this was like CKT and ... I guess just how special it is that you're here." He kept his voice to a whisper. "That we're in this together."

"I guess I hadn't thought about that." For the first time since she'd met Andi for lunch, Bailey felt her mood lighten. She'd been consumed with Andi and the shady film offer, confused by how a girl raised by missionary parents could actually consider starring in a movie with nudity. Then there'd been the lack of texts from Cody. And the way her costume hung like heavy drapes.

But now, with Tim gazing at her—even though his eyes sagged with artificial wrinkles—she suddenly felt like a princess. A montage of memories from a dozen CKT shows played in her mind. From days when she had dreamed of dating Tim Reed.

And now here she was, Tim's girlfriend, the two of them about to take the stage at Indiana University for the first time. "You'll be amazing... just like always."

"You too." He looked like he wanted to kiss her, but it wasn't the time or place. Instead he gave her hand a quick squeeze and walked onstage. The orchestra was silent, ready for the cue from the conductor. He gave it and the music began in a beautiful rush of strings and horns, and like that, the air was filled with Christmas.

The opening scene was flawless. Tim was so believable that Bailey and the others couldn't help but watch from the wings. Bailey had to keep reminding herself that the guy in the counting shop on stage was her nineteen-year-old boyfriend and not the crotchety mean old man he pretended to be. He was that convincing. Tim seemed to pick up steam, getting better still as he was warned by his dead business partner that he would be visited by three additional ghosts.

Bailey and Andi stood in the wings and squeezed hands. "You'll be great," Bailey whispered.

"I think I'm sick." Andi's eyes were wide.

"You're not." Bailey heard her cue but suddenly all she could think about was Cody—where he was sitting and what he was thinking. Whether she would be able to see him from the stage. She pushed his image from her mind. "Gotta go."

She adjusted her cloak and walked on stage with a sort of floating, waltz-like step. Tim was on his knees looking under the bed for any sign of a ghost, grumbling about the warning being a bunch of nonsense. Before he could stand, Bailey tapped him on the shoulder.

His dramatic reaction received a loud bit of laughter from the audience. Bailey remained stoic, straight faced. She had to work to keep herself from listening for Cody's voice.

"Who are you?" Tim scowled at her, stood, and dusted himself off.

Bailey lifted her chin, proper and poised. "The ghost whose presence was foretold to you."

Their exchange was brief and well rehearsed. They'd worked on stage together too long to be anything but professional in a moment like this. She led Tim across the stage to where he could watch a scene from his childhood. After that, she ushered in another moment from Scrooge's past—the dance at Fezziweg's where Scrooge first falls in love with Isabelle. Andi entered the stage and there was almost a collective gasp at the vision she made. Truly she was stunning.

Andi danced with young Scrooge, and together they sang a perfect duet. Whatever anxiety Andi had felt about this scene, she was in her element now.

After watching the dance come to an end, Tim reached out toward Isabelle, who of course could not see him. Tim's expression, the longing in his body language, told everyone in the theater he wanted nothing more than a chance to go back in time, back to that moment with Isabelle. Just once more.

The way I feel about Cody, Bailey thought. Again she forced herself back into the scene. But distraction came easily. Bailey's part required her only to stand alongside Tim and watch the past play out. She had only a handful of words left before the end of her scene. Was Cody mesmerized by Andi the way the rest of the audience must be? She blinked. *Focus, Bailey ... God, please help me focus.*

Tim looked ready to cry as he watched young Scrooge bend on one knee, pull out an engagement ring, and hand it up to a thrilled Isabelle. At the same time, Tim slowly took hold of that same ring, now on a chain around his neck.

"Come." Bailey took his hand and led him to yet another spot on the stage. This time the scene was far sadder. The saddest in the entire play. Young Scrooge was in the counting house as Andi walked up, dressed the same but with a bonnet and a shawl over her shoulders.

"I'm leaving, Ebenezer." She delivered her lines like a pro.

For the first few seconds, young Scrooge barely looked up, still counting. But when Andi insisted that where she was going he would not see her anymore, he stopped. "Why? You were going to marry me."

Tim took a step closer to the action, desperate to stop the younger version of himself. "Don't let her leave ... you fool!"

But Andi tossed the engagement ring onto his counting scale, and with a final few words, she left. Again Bailey caught a glimpse of Tim as he reached out, longing for a way back to yesterday. Anyone would've believed he'd been in love with Andi, and that he'd never gotten over her.

The scene ended with another song — a duet between the two Scrooges, one where Andi returned to the stage in a lyrical dance intended to represent her moving farther from his life. Again she was graceful, a vision as she moved across the stage.

Bailey watched her, but she was thinking about Cody again. *He's probably falling in love with her right now*, she told herself. What guy wouldn't be? Her red cloak felt heavier, thicker than before. She must've looked like a set piece compared to Andi. A coat rack, maybe.

Tim glanced back at her, as if she could do something to undo the passing of time. Then he turned to Andi once more and launched into his final verse of the song. As it ended, as Andi danced offstage, Tim turned, anguished, to Bailey and took her hand. "Spirit, remove me from this place. I can bear it no more." The handhold was a plea, an urging from Scrooge, but Tim held her fingers a little longer than they'd rehearsed. His eyes locked onto hers, and though no one from the audience — not even the director — could've told he was breaking character in any way, he did. For a flicker in time, the longing in his eyes was as intense as it had been when he stared at Isabelle. Only this was real, Bailey had no doubt. And it was aimed at her.

The incident was over almost as soon as it began, but it left Bailey breathless. She wanted to smile, but she couldn't, because the Ghost of Christmas Past certainly did not smile. But inside she was giddy. Tim might as well have stopped the action and announced to all the room that Andi couldn't turn his head. Not when he was in love with Bailey.

She felt herself stand a little taller as the scene wound down and as she delivered her final lines — lines that warned Scrooge to love today, while time still allowed. "There is never enough time to say or do the things you want in this life, never enough time to love the way you want to love," she told him. "We are only here for a little while, Scrooge, and then we are gone."

With that, she took the same slow, otherworldly steps off the stage, ignoring Tim's pleas that she stay with him, that she allow him to live a little longer in the past. As soon as she stepped into the wings, she fell against the wall and remembered the moment with Tim again. Suddenly her own lines came back to her. *"Never enough time to love the way you want to love..."* So why was she wasting her time thinking about Cody? She was dating an amazing guy, one she'd looked up to all her life. He had none of Cody's crazy past. He'd never been drunk or slept with a girl, and on top of all that he cared enough to know exactly how she felt in the midst of their scene.

Whatever her feelings for Cody, however she'd been frustrated by him, none of that mattered. Tim was a great guy, and he'd proved that out there on the stage, not caring if anyone caught what he was doing or not. Her heart felt lighter than it had all day.

She removed her red cloak and listened as Tim and the Ghost of Christmas Present sang one of Bailey's favorite songs from the show. "I like life ... life likes me ... life and I fairly fully agree ..."

Bailey couldn't agree more. She worried about Andi's choices, and yes, if Cody fell for her there would be times when Bailey would hurt. But she had Tim, and in light of that sweet moment on stage, she couldn't be happier.

Tim was wonderful in the final scene of the first act, and Bailey watched his every move, silently cheering for him. As the curtain fell at the beginning of intermission, Bailey waited for him in the shadows.

He started to pass by, the area too dark to make out shapes or people. "Tim," she whispered as loud as she could without being heard on the other side of the curtain.

"Bailey?" He was out of breath, adrenaline and exhilaration no doubt racing through his veins.

"Here." She reached out and touched his arm. "You were amazing."

"You too."

They couldn't hang out in the wings for long. The director would expect them to report to the greenroom to hear his notes on the first act and to receive any last-minute direction for the second half of the show. But they had a few minutes at least.

"I mean, I kept believing you were really Scrooge."

He came nearer, facing her. Even this close and as their eyes adjusted to the darkness, he looked like an old man.

"I love this. I could perform in New York, you know?"

"You could."

"You too. Seriously, Bailey, you should've been Isabelle. You're so good."

She should've been Isabelle? Bailey opened her mouth to thank him, to tell him that was the exact thing she needed to hear, but the words got jumbled on the way up from her heart. Instead she slipped her arms around his neck and hugged him. Finally, when she was sure of her voice, she pulled back and searched his eyes. "Thank you."

Here was further proof that something was building between them, something that hadn't been there before. Tim didn't ask what Bailey was thanking him for. He didn't have to. Instead his voice softened. "I wanted you to know that my character might desire Isabelle—" He brushed his cheek against hers. "But I want you, Bailey. Only you."

Her heart responded by pounding in her chest, and she wanted more than anything to kiss him. A quick kiss wouldn't have violated any university theater rule, but again this wasn't the time. So she eased from his arms and grinned at him. "Come on. We need to get back."

Bailey played a townsperson in the second act, and everyone in the cast gave their all as the show ran down. In the final scene, when Tim sang about being ready to begin again, Bailey wanted to join him. If ever she'd been ready to truly move on it was here, tonight. Not until she was back on stage and staring at a standing ovation did she realize perhaps the most important thing about the night—something that hadn't happened since the moment Tim looked at her that way in the middle of their scene.

She hadn't thought about Cody once.

Nine

From his place in the back of the theater, Cody watched the actors take the stage for their curtain call. He could've been wrong, but he sensed a change in Bailey, something he couldn't pinpoint or put into words. Up until now, on the rare times when he and Bailey shared a few words or a conversation, he sensed she still had feelings for him.

Just not enough feelings to walk away from Tim Reed.

But now? There seemed to be some new and stronger chemistry between Bailey and Tim, and as the applause began to die down and the houselights came up, Cody watched Tim sling his arm around Bailey's shoulders, both of them laughing as they walked offstage with the cast.

He looked away. At the other side of the theater near the front were Bailey's parents and brothers, people who just a year or so ago had been his family. He thought about crossing the theater to say hello, but they would be looking for Tim now. Not him.

"I see you." His mother leaned in close. She was still clapping, but she made sure he could hear her voice over the noise of the audience.

Cody turned to her, his expression blank. "See what?"

"How you look at her."

"Andi?" Cody shifted and watched Andi saunter toward the edge of the stage. She was still waving at the crowd. He had told his mom that he and Andi were becoming better friends and that she'd asked him to her opening night. He nodded as his eyes found his mom's again. "She was beautiful. Perfect."

His mother had been absent for so much of his life, trapped by her demons and addictions. She had missed much, but not anymore. These days she was going to church with a few friends from her alcohol recovery class, and she'd been sober longer than he could ever remember. They were actually building a relationship for the first time.

She looked at him and raised a brow. "Not Andi." She held up her copy of the *Scrooge* program and pointed to a photo just inside the front cover. "Bailey Flanigan. You couldn't take your eyes off her."

With everything in him, Cody wanted her to be wrong. Bailey wasn't interested. She was dating Tim, and that was that. Especially tonight, when something very special seemed to linger between the two of them. Andi was striking, gorgeous as Isabelle. In his high school days, back when he was a jerk to just about every girl he came across, Cody wouldn't have had the ability to see past Andi Ellison.

His mom was still looking at him, and he felt something crack in his resistance. Finally he drew a long breath and admitted just enough. "I've cared about her longer." The crowd was filing out, moving past them, and Cody was in a hurry to talk about the play or where they were going afterwards for coffee. Anything else. Bailey and he were a thing of the past for lots of reasons. He wasn't comfortable having his mom look straight into his heart, not when he hadn't quite given her viewing privileges.

But they were at the end of their row, and before they could file out, she touched his arm and waited until he looked at her again. "It's okay, Cody. I've known for a long time."

"Known what?" He tried to sound neutral rather than frustrated.

Her voice grew nostalgic. "How you feel about that girl. How you've always felt."

"Mom." He forced an exhale. "No offense, but you weren't around when Bailey and I were friends. And that's all we were. We've never been anything more."

"I wasn't around much." Her eyes were heavy with the pain from years lost. "But when I got out, when I came home ... I saw the way you looked when you talked about her. I knew then." She had to look up to him, but she put her hand on his cheek. "And I know now."

"Mom." He didn't want to talk about Bailey. Not with his mom, anyway. He was trying to build something new with her, which meant he didn't want to look backward. Not regarding his mom, and certainly not regarding Bailey. When it came to the ins and outs of his heart, she was hardly a qualified expert. He smiled at her. "Can we talk about something else?"

"It's just—" She let her hand fall back to her side. Her face grew concerned, almost worried. "Cody ... I like the Flanigan family, but ... I don't want you to get hurt. You've been hurt enough."

He was suddenly aware of his prosthetic lower leg and his lonely afternoons and a lifetime of not knowing his mother—and, mixed together, he hated how it made him feel. "Mom, please." He was not a victim. Not because of his war injury or his past, or anything Bailey might mean to him. "I'm not hurt. I'm fine."

She ceded with a slight nod, and her eyes shifted to the sticky floor between them. "I'm sorry. I just ... I worry about you."

"Don't. I can take care of myself." He couldn't get angry with her. It was too late for that. He put his arm around her shoulders and gradually walked her down the aisle toward the door. She was trying, something he'd prayed for. His frustration gave way to kindness, confidence. In this, their new relationship, he was the leader, the stronger one. He had almost forgotten that. "So ... what'd you think of the show?"

"Good." Her smile was tentative, but she understood. The conversation about Bailey was over. "Very good, really. The guy playing Scrooge was amazing."

Tim Reed. Cody narrowed his eyes. "He's been acting for awhile. Just a freshman too."

"Really?" His mom seemed ready to move on, too, glad that Cody wasn't upset anymore. She put her arm around his waist and gave him a hug. "The show put me in a Christmas mood." She looked up at him. "I think we should put lights up this year. What do you think?"

The conversation felt easy again, the way Cody liked it. They were still talking about decorating for the holidays when they walked into the far end of the lobby. The crowd was spread throughout the space, and the cast mingled among them, everyone laughing and talking and taking pictures. His mom gave him a gentle elbow in the ribs. "There's your friend. She played Isabelle. What's her name?"

"Andi." He followed his mother's gaze, and there she was, looking as beautiful as she had on stage. "Andi Ellison." Cody watched her, the way she tilted her head and tossed her hair. She was talking to a couple of guys and clearly enjoying the attention. Andi knew she was beautiful. She would always know it.

"I like that girl." Her mom took a few steps. "I'll be in the restroom." She dropped her voice, as if anyone would hear her with the commotion around them. "Go talk to her. I saw her look over here."

"Thanks, Mom." He kept his tone light. When she was gone, he leaned against the far wall and slid his hands into his jean pockets. He wished he had feelings for Andi, wanted to be interested in her. His mom was right. Andi was into him. Cody had known that for a long time. Especially after she'd made a play for him that night when he'd helped her home after she got drunk at the frat party. But there were ten quick reasons why he wasn't interested. The biggest: Bailey Flanigan. He could hear her laugh from across the room. He sighed, and it felt like it came from the basement of his soul.

Cody studied the architecture along the windows and doorways. He read the posters that lined the wall leading into the theater. Anything so he wouldn't give in to his desire to find Bailey and at least stare into her eyes, tell her she'd done a great job. *Don't look for her*, he told himself. *She's with Tim. She'll be with him now.*

A minute passed before he lost the battle. Without being too obvious, he made a casual sweep of the room and saw her in the middle of a large group—her parents and brothers, three of the Baxter sisters and their families. She had her red cape slung over one arm, and even from this far away the sight of her took his breath.

Cody shifted a few inches for a better look, and Tim came into view. From the opposite end of the long room, he looked like an old man, still in costume like the rest of the cast.

His eyes easily found their way back to Bailey. Her long, light brown hair falling around her shoulders in layers of curls, her fine features and infectious laugh. How had he let her slip away? Their story was almost like the one that had played out on the stage. A story of lost chances and useless regret. If he could will it, he wouldn't be standing here alone, watching her live her life with some other guy. He would be back in her entryway, Fourth of July, holding her and telling her how much he'd missed her while he was gone. God could've taken him home after his capture, and he would've been okay with it except for one thing.

The memory and hope of Bailey Flanigan.

But instead of telling her exactly how he felt, instead of admitting he was in love with her, he'd done the opposite. He'd praised her for dating someone more her type, and he'd assured her that he wanted only to be her friend. For her sake. Because she deserved better.

But now ... now he wasn't the drunk guy who played with girls' hearts. He was a different person, a guy who loved God and wanted a future based on faith and family. He was the right kind of guy for her now. And no one would ever love her more.

Cody stood a little straighter and filled his lungs with a determined breath. All his life he'd been a fighter. He'd scrapped and scrounged to survive as a latchkey grade school kid when his mother's drinking left him without supervision, and he'd fought hard to find his place with the Flanigans—his only way of getting through high school. No one had worked harder on the football field, and when he was a prisoner of war, he had never, not once, given up.

So why had he given up so easily on Bailey?

The muscles in his jaw tightened, and he forced himself to look away. Maybe he was supposed to take to heart the message of the musical. It was almost the New Year, so this could be the time in his life when he stopped hiding in the shadows and actually tried a different tactic. Like talking to her and texting her, being the friend he'd promised to be. She wasn't married. Unless she asked him to stay away, he could certainly make himself more of a presence in her life.

The change of heart coming over him was so strong, he didn't see Andi until she was standing directly in front of him. She giggled and ran her hand along his forearm. "Hey ... you look like you're in another world."

He was. "Oh, hey, sorry. I didn't see you." He felt his guard go up. "You did great."

"Thanks." She crossed her arms in front of her and shivered a little. "I was scared to death. You have no idea."

"We couldn't tell."

Andi hesitated. "Oh ... your mom!" She glanced around. "Where is she?"

"Restroom. She'll be right back." Cody peered in the direction his mom had walked off in, and for the first time he realized she was taking a long time. He turned back to Andi. "How many shows in the run?"

"All this weekend—five shows—and then three midweek and another five next weekend. Thirteen altogether."

"That's a lot." He didn't want a long conversation with Andi. She was a nice girl, but he didn't want to lead her on. He pressed his back against the wall behind him again. "You and Bailey weren't at Cru this week." Cru was the Campus Crusade meeting each Thursday on campus. At the beginning of the semester they'd all gone together.

"Dress rehearsals." Andi wrinkled her nose in a cute girly sort of way. "This week we have a show, and then Christmas break. I guess we'll start up again in January."

"I guess." He looked down the hallway again for his mom. Maybe he should go after her, in case she'd fallen or something. He gave Andi a distracted glance. "You ready for finals?"

"Pretty much." She gasped. "I almost forgot to tell you. This guy in my science class is a film student. He's making an independent movie and he wants me to star in it! I was just talking to him! Isn't that great?"

"Yeah, great." Cody didn't want to be rude, but he was finished here. "Hey, listen. I gotta go find my mom." He hugged her. "Seriously. You were great tonight."

"Thanks." She seemed flustered, a little confused by his early exit. "I sorta thought maybe we could go out for coffee, you and your mom and me. I guess I could hang out with the film guy." She gave a disappointed shrug. "He asked, but ... I don't know. I wanted to hang out with you."

"Oh." He hesitated. She was sincere and kind, and a girl whose shaky faith could use all the right people surrounding her. What would it hurt if they included her for coffee? Bailey was obviously busy tonight. "Okay, sure. Let me go find my mom."

He held back from taking another look at Bailey as he walked the opposite direction down a hall toward the bathrooms. He wasn't sure whether to be worried about his mom or not. He'd lost track of time watching Bailey, so he wasn't sure how long she'd been gone. A few minutes? Five ... ten? He picked up his pace.

Just as he was about to turn the corner, she stepped into view, fiddling with something in her purse. She stopped short when she saw him. "Cody. What are you doing?"

"Looking for you." He dropped his gaze from her eyes down to her purse and back up again. Why was she acting guilty? Like she was hiding something? "What took so long?"

"I got a phone call." She slipped her purse up onto her shoulder and smoothed her coat, more confident than a few seconds ago. "Someone from my Bible study."

Cody hesitated. He'd seen his mother crash hard too many times to count, seen her spiral into the evil, clutching hands of her addiction and each time fall lower than the last. He studied her eyes and searched for a hint of deceit, for even the beginnings of the telltale signs — the shaking hands and slightly wild-eyed look. But there was nothing, no reason to doubt her. He breathed out. "Okay." He turned and fell in beside her. He wanted to believe her with everything in him. This was their time, their chance to be mother and son, like they'd never been before. He allowed his nerves to settle and again found a smile. "I ran into Andi. I told her she could join us for coffee."

"That's wonderful." She grinned at him, maybe a little too big. Maybe not. "Introduce me!"

They reached the foyer again and Andi was still there where he'd left her, talking to a few of her fellow cast mates. He couldn't tell if Bailey was still in the group at the far end of the room or not.

His mom leaned in as they drew nearer to Andi. "She's so pretty."

"Yes, Mom." Cody chuckled. He wasn't used to spending time with his mother, and her persistent efforts to set him up were almost comical. As if in these past few months she wanted badly—almost desperately—to become his friend and confidante.

They reached Andi, and Cody put his hand on her arm. "Mom, meet my friend Andi."

"Andi! Why you're absolutely adorable!" His mom still didn't have strong social graces. She was nervous, having spent so many years behind bars of one kind or another, and sometimes she made up for it by being a little overly dramatic, a little over the top. This was one of those times.

"Mrs. Coleman, ma'am." Andi nodded. "Nice to meet you."

"Aren't you sweet." She laughed awkwardly. "Call me Cassie. That's what my friends call me." She gave Andi an impulsive hug. "You're a perfect Isabelle."

"Thank you, ma'am." Andi's eyes danced. Awkward or not, she was eating up the attention.

Cody was ready to leave. Across the room, he noticed Bailey separate herself from the group and jog lightly toward them. He willed her to stay away, because already Bailey suspected he had feelings for Andi. And with his mom certain Bailey was going to break his heart, everything about the coming moment screamed disaster.

His mom didn't notice Bailey. She was still gushing over Andi in a way that was borderline embarrassing. "I'm sure Cody told you we thought you were brilliant tonight, just brilliant. Brilliant."

She was at the last "brilliant" when Bailey reached them. Bailey seemed to register that this might be a special moment and that maybe she shouldn't interrupt. Her last few steps were slower, tentative. "Hi. Sorry … I don't want to interrupt." She nodded at Cody and his mom and finally turned her attention to Andi. She was already taking a step back, retreating. "We're getting pizza. Wanna come?"

"Um …" Andi smiled at Cody. "I'm having coffee with Cody and his mom."

"Right." Bailey seemed to realize she might've been rude. "Hi, Mrs. Coleman, Cody. Thanks for being here."

"I was just telling Andi that she was brilliant tonight." His mom linked arms with Andi. If Andi thought the move was strange, she didn't act like it. His mom grinned widely. "The perfect Isabelle."

"Yes." Bailey seemed flustered, unsure of what to say. "Well, just wanted to see if you had plans. See you later."

"Okay." His mom waved good-bye to Bailey in a way that seemed almost sarcastic.

Cody was furious with his mother. She had intentionally lavished praise on Andi at Bailey's expense. Bailey had already turned around and was walking away. Cody's mind raced, looking for a way to salvage the moment. "Bailey … wait." He took a few hurried steps in her direction and then walked slowly beside her until they were out of earshot of his mom and Andi. He touched her elbow and she stopped and faced him.

"You better go." Her eyes were ice cold. "Don't want to make them wait."

"Bailey, please … don't be like this." He wanted to tell her she would've made a more believable Isabelle and that he'd had a revelation and he was going to be a much more present part of her life. But Andi and his mom were waiting, and there wasn't enough time to explain himself. "You were wonderful tonight."

She looked at him a little longer than necessary, but still the walls were up. "Thanks." She took another step away. "You and Andi... have fun tonight." With that she was gone, hurrying back to her family and Tim—none of whom seemed to have noticed the two of them talking, or even that Cody was there.

Cody wanted to put the entire last ten minutes into reverse. He should've gone to Bailey and complimented her sooner. Tim or no Tim. The trouble was he had a habit of keeping his distance. This new determination, this change of heart God had given him wasn't something he could act on immediately. He had to think things through first. But still—now he'd made things worse than before. Or his mom had.

He walked back slowly. His mom no longer had her arm linked with Andi's, but she was speaking with a great deal of animation, talking with her hands and telling Andi some long story about who knew what. Their coffee break brought more of the same. His mother dominated the conversation, talking fast and laughing at times that weren't always appropriate. Cody tried not to imagine that maybe she'd taken something in the bathroom, an upper of some kind. She was just making up for lost time, trying to be the best mother possible. That's what he told himself.

But more than that, as the night wore on and after he'd dropped off his mom and walked Andi home, after he'd given her a quick hug good night and told her once more how great she'd done in the play, and after he ignored her slightly wounded look because he didn't go with her into the common area of her dorm and talk for another hour, he became more convinced than ever about his next step, what the near future was going to hold. He was a fighter, and he had no reason to stop fighting now. He was going to do what he should've done a long time ago.

Fight for Bailey Flanigan as if his life depended on it.

Ten

THE LAST LETTER WAS DONE. THEY'D made their editing deadline with a few hours to spare and Chase could barely sort through the emotions consuming him. Exhaustion, relief, anticipation, and full-out heart-stopping exhilaration. He and Keith had looked forward to this day since they set out to be filmmakers. It was Friday, December 5, and they'd just sent off the first copy of their movie by courier service to arrive at the office of the Los Angeles Film Festival committee sometime before midnight. They'd called their wives with the great news, and now they were catching their breath, still hanging out in the rented Santa Monica editing room.

Chase leaned back in his chair and stretched his legs. "It's like a different movie—with the color fix and sound correction. The editing." His voice couldn't contain his enthusiasm. "Much better than I ever thought it would be. Even with the performances we got on set."

"Don't get too excited." Keith was standing, leaning against the console that contained the editing equipment. He wore old jeans, a rumpled T-shirt, and a weary smile. "We're not done yet."

"Ah, come on." Chase allowed a whine to color his voice. He didn't want to talk about the studio screening coming up or the possibility they wouldn't get a theatrical release. He couldn't stand to think of the meetings with Ben and Kendall or the work to be done in order to submit to Kendall's list of additional film festivals. Keith was right. The road ahead was long and precarious, but Chase didn't want to think about a single minute of it.

Not yet. He closed his eyes. "Can't we have a day to just be done?" He blinked his eyes open and sat up a little more. "Like maybe we could do something really unconventional and go celebrate. Get a couple Cokes and walk down to the pier."

"At nine-thirty?" Keith laughed. "I guess. You know what I want to do first?"

"Take a nap?" A yawn caught Chase mid-sentence.

"No. I want to pray." Keith moved to the chair opposite Chase.

"Yeah. I like that." Prayer. Because they never would've arrived at this place without the miraculous leading of God. Chase's mood was suddenly sober. "Go ahead."

Keith put his hand on Chase's shoulder and bowed his head. He waited for a few seconds. "Lord ..." His voice trembled. He sucked in a quick breath. They'd worked nonstop since five that morning to finish on time, and the moment was overwhelming for both of them. He tried again. "Lord God, we asked You to take us to Los Angeles and give us the chance to make movies for You. Well, here we are, one movie finished, and we are nothing short of awed. This editing room feels like hallowed ground, Father, because You met us here. None of this—" He took another quick breath, steadying himself. "None of it would be possible without Your provision, Your leading. So before we move from this place we wanted to say thanks. Thank You, dear God. For what You've done and what You'll yet do. Thank You. In Jesus' name, amen."

Chase was just adding his own amen when he felt his phone vibrate. He pulled it from his pocket as Keith slid his chair back in place and turned his attention to the editing console. They wanted at least ten master copies of the movie before they left the room. Eight were already made, and the ninth was ready to be popped out of the machine. Chase opened his phone and stared at the small screen. The text was from Kendall. She'd promised a meeting with Stephanie Fitzgerald and Brandon Paul, but so far nothing had come together. Chase smiled. They thanked God for what He was about to do and almost before they finished praying Kendall contacted them.

He held up his phone. "You won't believe this. Kendall's texting me."

Keith uttered a tired, knowing laugh. "I love how God works."

The message was brief.

SORRY WE'VE BEEN OUT OF TOUCH FOR AWHILE. MY DAD AND I HAD BUSINESS IN PORTUGAL. WE'RE BACK NOW AND I'M IN TOWN. ARE YOU IN SAN JOSE OR HERE?

Chase quickly texted back.

IN SANTA MONICA. JUST FINISHED EDITING THE LAST LETTER HALF AN HOUR AGO.

Her response was almost instantaneous.

CONGRATULATIONS. PERFECT TIMING, THEN. I'M CLOSE. THERE'S AN ALL-NIGHT DINER ON THIRD AND WILSHIRE. MEET ME THERE IN THIRTY MINUTES? WE NEED TO TALK.

"She wants to meet in half an hour." Chase was on his feet, his energy returning at a rapid rate. "Will we be done?"

"Should be." Keith checked the console again. "The last DVD will be ready in about ten minutes. That'll give us time to clean up and drop off the keys."

Chase began tapping on his phone's tiny keyboard again.

WE'LL BE THERE.

Her response was upbeat.

GOOD. CAN'T WAIT TO SEE YOU BOTH.

He closed his phone and slipped it back into his pocket. Then he raked his fingers through his hair and paced the length of the room. "The timing of this?" A single laugh came from him, a sound that was more grateful disbelief than mirth. "I mean, come on." He stopped and stared at his friend. "We've been calling them, what? Five times a day for a few weeks?"

Keith checked a few of the controls. "You sound surprised."

"I am." He laughed again. "I'm surprised I'm standing."

A calm filled Keith's eyes. "Aren't you the guy who worked beside me in the jungles of Indonesia? Didn't you see flood waters recede before our eyes without any explanation, and disease leave people who'd been sick for years?" His smile was warm. "Don't tell me you're surprised at this. God's got everything under control."

"Right." Chase allowed himself to relax a little. "Of course." In that instant he felt foolish for ever worrying, ever doubting they'd survive the process of making this first film—or that they'd connect with Kendall about the next one. He tried to imprint the moment upon his memory, how it felt knowing with absolute certainty that God was in control. He had a feeling he would need it as a reference point in the journey ahead.

The last DVD was ready, and they carefully loaded the original and ten master copies into a locked briefcase. Chase took a last look as they left. "I might even miss this place. It was starting to feel like home."

They both laughed as Chase hit the lights and they locked the doors behind them. Ten minutes later they walked through the door of the diner and scanned the place for Kendall. The smell of french fries and something sweet mixed in the warm air, and even in the somewhat dim light it didn't take long to see her. She was sitting with another woman, someone Chase recognized as the author of *Unlocked*. Her face had been on the cover of magazines and on talk shows since the book took off. He elbowed Keith, but his friend had clearly already noted the same thing. Kendall and the author here together could only mean one thing.

God was adding one more miracle to the list.

KEITH DIDN'T GET AS EMOTIONAL AS Chase, but still, he was working hard not to feel overwhelmed by what he saw.

"Two?" A teenage hostess approached them, bright pink hair and a pierced lip. She smacked her gum and grabbed a couple menus, waiting for their answer.

"Uh..." Keith saw Kendall notice them. "Actually, we're meeting someone."

"Fine." She handed them the menus. "Seat yourself. Your server'll be by in a minute."

Keith and Chase made their way to the table, and the women stood as they walked up. The author was black with stunning eyes, much prettier in person. Clearly she and Kendall were friends.

"Guys!" Kendall came around the table and shook first Keith's hand, then Chase's. "I'm so glad this worked out." She turned. "This is Stephanie Fitzgerald, author of *Unlocked*. She's a friend."

Introductions were made all around, and Keith marveled at the energy the two women shared. Stephanie had a glow about her. She had to be in her early forties, but she was tall and slender, and in her black dress pants and pale-blue silk blouse she didn't look a day over thirty.

They took their seats around the booth, and Stephanie leaned forward on her forearms, practically bursting. "Did Kendall tell you?" She looked at Keith. "I'm a huge fan of your work."

Keith resisted the urge to look over his shoulder, as if maybe she was talking to someone else. He took a sip of the water in front of him and stifled a nervous laugh. "She said something about it ... a few months ago."

"I know." Stephanie shared a frustrated look with Kendall. She talked fast, with a lyrical tone to her voice. "We're both so busy. I was on deadline for my next book, two of my six kids had birthdays. My husband and I celebrated twenty years. Just your average couple o' months at the Fitzgerald house." She grabbed a quick breath and launched into a story about how she'd stumbled onto a short film he'd made back in his college days and how she loved his sensitivity and the undeniable elements of faith.

"Everyone in town's asking for the rights to *Unlocked*." Kendall raised her brow in Keith and Chase's direction. "But Steph wants to work with you guys."

"Absolutely." Stephanie grinned at Chase. "I can't wait to see *The Last Letter*. There's buzz all over town." She included Keith. "Something special's happening with you two, and we know what it is." Her eyes shone with a light so genuine it warmed the space between them. "It's your faith in Christ. Same as it is for Kendall and me."

Keith couldn't have asked for a better start to the meeting if he'd scripted it himself. Stephanie Fitzgerald's books were mainstream — number one *New York Times* bestsellers. But they were gripping and inspirational, and Keith had heard that she was a Christian.

"Finally today I called Kendall and said if she couldn't set up a meeting tonight, I'd find you myself."

They all laughed, and Kendall patted Stephanie's hand. "Good thing I was in town. I didn't like thinking about her knocking on studio doors up and down Santa Monica Boulevard."

Keith didn't want to sound ignorant, especially after the praise and confidence Stephanie had just heaped on them. But he wanted to move things ahead. "An option, then, right? Isn't that what happens next?"

"Exactly." Stephanie pulled a two-page document from an oversized bag next to her. "I had my agent draw this up a week ago. He said it's pretty standard." She pointed to a line halfway down the first page. "Options usually cost around five thousand, sometimes more."

"But I told her you two hadn't made any money yet and you were working off investor funds." Kendall's smile filled her face as she turned to Stephanie. "So ..."

"So I asked my agent if we could take a zero off. Give you the option for five hundred instead." She looked completely at peace with the decision. Thrilled about it, even.

Under the table, Chase kicked his foot. Keith swallowed, not sure what to say. "That's … that's amazing."

"I want this to work for all of us." She leaned back, satisfied. "God's already told me it'll be bigger than any of us can imagine. Plenty of time for zeroes. It's all God's anyway."

"Yes." *Plenty of time for zeroes.* The author's faith seemed rock solid, and Keith silently breathed a prayer of thanks. Teamed up with Stephanie and Kendall, possibilities would become realities in a hurry.

"I want to tell you, Ms. Fitzgerald, *Unlocked* was amazing." Chase had been quiet until now. Probably trying not to pass out. "I couldn't put it down."

"Thank you. And call me Stephanie." She smiled at the group of them. "I think we'll make a wonderful team."

Kendall added to that. "Stephanie doesn't have time to be a part of every step of the process. She has two books to write next year, and she speaks at writer's conferences around the country. She wants a final look at the screenplay and a week or so on the set, but otherwise she's trusting us."

"I'm assuming Kendall will join you on the production team?" Stephanie's eyes were hopeful.

"Absolutely." Keith and Chase had talked about this at the last meeting with Ben and Kendall. She had experience at almost every level of filmmaking. They would be fortunate to have her on their team. "It's already a plan."

"She's the best." Stephanie gave Kendall a heartfelt hug. The waitress appeared then and they ordered a plate of nachos and four iced teas. When she left the table, Stephanie nudged Kendall. "Well, tell them already. I can't stand the suspense."

Kendall laughed. "I already did."

Next to him, Keith could feel Chase holding his breath again.

"But tell them about the phone call earlier today."

"Okay, okay." Kendall personified joy and optimism. She practically glowed as she continued. "Brandon Paul called me today. He's been filming his series with NTM Studios and finally came up for air today. He told me he's talked to his agent and he wants the lead in *Unlocked*. It's very important to him. So we're a step closer."

Keith wanted to ask why the picture mattered to the young megastar, but that would come later. The dizzy feeling had returned, and he steadied himself discreetly against the edge of the table. "I wasn't sure ... We didn't know if he was still interested."

"More than ever." Stephanie looked satisfied. "Brandon and I are friends. We met on the set of his series a year ago. I was doing research." Her smile dropped off just a bit. "He's not a believer, but I'm working on him. I think the faith element of *Unlocked* intrigues him."

"That and the fact that it's a brilliant story." Kendall's smile faded, and her tone became more serious. "God has a reason for bringing Brandon Paul our way. I've known him for a few years. He's a great kid with more demands on him than most people will know in a lifetime."

Keith could only imagine. Like most NTM stars through the decades, the guy's face was everywhere. Everything from billboards to pop cans, tween jewelry and pillowcases to Blockbuster gift cards. He could only imagine the headiness of such fame, and the difficulty navigating it. "We shot *The Last Letter* in Bloomington, Indiana. Dayne Matthews lives there now with his wife and baby daughter."

"That's right." Stephanie nodded. "I knew he'd pulled out of the Hollywood scene. I wasn't sure where he'd settled."

"Chase and I had dinner with him and his family while we were there. He's got a lot of wisdom about handling fame. You know about his car accident right?"

"The whole world knew." Kendall frowned. "Paparazzi will kill someone before something's done about the insanity."

"He might be a help to Brandon at some point." Chase exchanged a look with Keith. "He's a great guy. Strong in his faith. Not many other people know what Brandon's going through."

"That's important." Kendall exchanged a look with Stephanie. "We'll keep that in mind as we move into this project."

Stephanie pulled another copy of the option from her purse and slid both across the table. "Take these. I don't expect you to sign them here, but read them over. Have your attorney take a look."

The waitress brought their food, and while they ate they talked about the book Stephanie was working on and a few of the stories she was planning for the future.

"How do you keep it all straight?" Chase took a long swig of his iced tea. "Don't the characters get mixed up in your mind?"

"Never." Stephanie laughed again. "My books are like movies in my mind. Very separate and distinct from each other. When I sit down to write, I see the film, like I'm in it somehow. I never feel like I'm making the stuff up. It's more like taking dictation, trying to capture everything I'm seeing and hearing and feeling."

"Amazing." Keith always marveled at the vastly differing ways God dished out talent. Back in college, he'd struggled to write his fifteen-page senior paper. A whole novel? It would've been an impossibility. "What made you write *Unlocked*?"

The question seemed to hit a painful nerve. The subtle way she dropped her gaze to her plate for a few seconds told them that much. "My sister, Jasmine. She was autistic."

Keith noted the way Stephanie used the past tense, but he didn't want to ask.

"Steph's sister was hit by a car when she was nineteen." Kendall's voice softened appropriately. "She and their mom were shopping, and something frightened Jasmine. She panicked and ran straight into traffic before her mom could stop her. She died at the hospital that night."

Stephanie's eyes teared up. "Twenty-two years ago. Doesn't get any easier."

"I'm sorry." Keith reached across the table and covered the author's hand with his own for a moment. As he withdrew it he looked at Chase. "We saw the dedication to Jasmine and wondered."

"We shared a room." Stephanie's eyes were bright again, dimmed only by the strength of the memory. "The doctors used to tell us she was unreachable, that she lived alone in her own little world." She shook her head. "But I knew otherwise. When we were alone, I'd put on music ... Diana Ross or the Temptations. Lionel Richie, even Elvis. I would start dancing, and after a minute, she'd smile at me and join in. Music gave us a bridge. We danced across it often."

Keith was breathless from the word picture. "The same way it happens in *Unlocked*."

"Yes." A love both bright and intense burned in her eyes. "We need to rethink the way we view autistic people. They can be reached if we try."

Kendall gave her friend a sad smile. "Steph and I have talked about it. In some ways—until we find that life-saving faith in Christ—we're all autistic. Living in our own world, trapped by the smallness of our existence and needing something, anything, to pierce the silence and open our eyes to the reality around us. Music can be that for us too. Music can introduce people to God."

Suddenly the passion Keith felt for this future project magnified a hundred times. This was what they'd asked for, right? Films that could touch and change the world. He tried to imagine the power in a picture like *Unlocked*. The power in the movie's soundtrack. A chill ran down his arms and he swapped a look with Chase. His friend was feeling the same way, he was sure. "I have a feeling God's going to use this movie in amazing ways."

Stephanie smiled, and again her eyes grew watery. "That's why I'm here." She studied Keith and then Chase. "I believe you two can touch the world with this movie. The way Jasmine's life, her joy and light, so deeply touched me."

The woman was both beautiful and poetic. Keith hoped they had lots of time together during the process—even with her busy schedule.

They talked a little while longer, and then Stephanie had to get going. "My honey's waiting up for me." She held out her hand toward Keith and then laughed at herself. "What am I doing? Come around here and give me a hug. We're already family—we have the same Father."

Keith and Chase moved out from behind the table and took turns hugging Stephanie good-bye. She was still smiling when she left, her steps light and full of the same energy that had come from her throughout the meeting.

When she was gone, Keith and Chase sat back down with Kendall. Keith felt breathless from the brilliance of all that lay ahead. "She's wonderful."

"Isn't she?" Kendall grinned. "I knew you'd love her."

"She's mesmerizing." Chase leaned forward on his forearms. "Something very special's happening here."

"And getting there will be the ride of a lifetime." She pulled out a notebook. "Okay, we have a lot to cover in a short time." She started by bringing up the idea of the three of them forming an official production team. "I wanted to talk about that sooner, but there wasn't time."

"Chase and I love your enthusiasm and vision. The people you're bringing into this."

"Absolutely." Chase finished his iced tea, his eyes never leaving Kendall's. "God put us together for a reason."

"I think we need a new name, at least for this film. Oak River is good—but we need something that shows the world your vision."

Keith appreciated how she called it their vision. She wasn't taking over, just coming alongside them—helping out in whatever way she could. "We haven't thought about a new name. But I'm open to the idea."

Chase was too, and after a few minutes they came up with a name they all liked better: Jeremiah Productions. The name came from the Scripture from Jeremiah 29:11: *"For I know the plans I have for you,"* declares the Lord, *"plans to prosper you and not to harm you."*

"The goal," Keith said, "has always been that the world would find hope in Christ as a result of the movies we make. So the name is perfect."

Once they had that detail established, Kendall flipped open her planner and tapped her pen on one of the squares. "I've set up a meeting with Brandon Paul for this Monday morning. Ten o'clock, here at the diner. It's an easy meeting place, and they serve a great breakfast. Legend in this town. Then I'd like you to meet his agent in Studio City the next day around four. My dad wants to catch up with you too."

Keith winced. They had planned to drive home in the morning, and then he and Lisa had tickets to fly to Indiana on Monday. They'd planned to spend the week with Andi and see several performances of *Scrooge*.

"You're busy?" Kendall picked up on his hesitation.

"We aren't, are we?" Chase turned to him. He seemed anxious to make the meetings work.

Keith understood. In this business, a month could easily go by before everyone had a clear date on their calendars again. "We have Andi's play this week." He studied the calendar page. "I guess we could head out at the end of the week instead. Catch the weekend shows."

"Right." Chase nodded. "That would work."

"You're sure?" She looked cautious. "Family commitments are a priority. I understand that."

"No. It's okay, really." Keith was already imagining how he'd tell Lisa, and then Andi. Chase would have to talk to Kelly too. But she would understand. Everything would work out. The meetings were crucial if they were going to push ahead with the production of *Unlocked*. "Let's plan it."

Kendall wrapped up their meeting telling them that she had a feeling things were going to get pretty crazy for them and their families. "You've got the film festivals and the screenings for *The Last Letter*. Everyone's going to be talking about you, your vision and talent, and the fact that you snared a coup with the acquisition of *Unlocked*." She paused, her expression more sober than it had been all night. "We need to pray for your families, for your faith and your sanity. For all of us, that we'll keep our feet on the ground."

Agreement came from Keith and Chase, and before they parted ways, they held hands and thanked God for the amazing situation He'd placed them in, begging Him to go before them, to protect them and their families, and to keep them grounded in His truth along the way.

As they left the restaurant, Keith stopped cold and stared at Chase. "Did that just happen?" He uttered a disbelieving chuckle. "I mean, really? Did it seriously just happen?"

Chase laughed too. "I have a feeling we'll be reminding each other often—that this is really happening."

They talked about all that had transpired in the past hour. The meeting with Stephanie Fitzgerald and her passion for this project. Kendall's enthusiasm, the vision she had for the future. The involvement of Brandon Paul. They decided to wait until tomorrow to call their wives, and as they reached the Georgian Hotel Keith thought again how grateful he was for the prayer at the end—that they stay grounded throughout the process.

Because even now he could barely feel the street beneath his feet.

Eleven

THE SATURDAY MATINEE WAS OVER, ANOTHER memorable performance by the *Scrooge* cast, and Andi was about to head into the lobby to meet the audience when she noticed a voicemail message from her parents. She pushed a few buttons and listened.

"Hey, Andi, it's Dad. We're stuck at the Denver airport. They're clearing ice off the runway." He paused. "I'm sorry, baby. We'll get there as soon as we can. Sometime tonight for sure."

Andi snapped her phone shut and tried not to feel hurt. Her parents could do nothing about an ice storm, but still... they were supposed to be here all week. Her dad's LA meetings had made that impossible, so now they only had this weekend to see her show. As it was they were going to miss tonight's performance, which meant they'd only see tomorrow's matinee, since the night show was sold out.

Fine, Andi thought. If her dad could make filmmaking a priority, so could she. The offer from Taz looked better all the time.

She had a text waiting too, and she checked it. Cody's name popped onto the screen.

HEY, ANDI. I TOLD YOU I MIGHT BE THERE TODAY, BUT I HAVE TOO MUCH HOMEWORK. I'M SURE YOU'LL DO GREAT. SEE YOU LATER.

Disappointment painted heavy brush strokes across her heart. Cody was pulling away, she could feel it, and she didn't know why or what she'd done. He didn't have to want her to be his girlfriend, but still it was nice talking to him. This past week they'd barely even done that. And now he was too busy to show up.

"Everything okay?" Bailey sat next to her, checking her makeup.

"My parents." Andi slipped her phone back in her bag. "They're stuck in an ice storm."

"Oh. I'm sorry." Bailey looked like she understood. "My parents'll be here tonight. If yours don't make it, come over afterwards. We're playing Pictionary."

"Okay." Andi smiled. Bailey's invitation took the edge off her loneliness. She really wanted her parents to be here, but at least she didn't have to be by herself. She hugged her friend. "Thanks. That'd be great."

They walked out to the lobby with several other cast members. The director liked them to mingle with the audience for fifteen minutes before changing out of their costumes and taking their dinner break. Andi loved this part of performing, hearing the praise from complete strangers, realizing how deeply they'd been touched by the show. Mixing with the public was one of the most fun parts of being in the show.

The local newspaper had run a review on the musical in Monday's paper, and the writer singled her out. "Andi Ellison is a breath of fresh air in this old, often stodgy, story of a grouchy man and his transformation. If Scrooge could walk away from the beautiful, talented Ellison, then he must need a serious fix." She hadn't told her parents about the review because she wanted them to see it in person. But they'd had one delay after another.

Out in the lobby, people noticed them immediately. Bailey was called over by a group of kids from Cru, and Andi was called in another direction by people waving programs. She smiled and walked toward them, and for the next ten minutes she signed autographs, answered questions about the stage process, and smiled for two dozen pictures. Only then did she recognize Taz and his friend—the one she'd met on opening night. From the corner of her eye she watched the two guys discuss something, and then the friend smiled and waved and walked away, leaving Taz by himself.

As soon as he was alone, Taz turned toward her. He hung back, watching her, aware of the people still gathered around her. When her eyes met his, he smiled at her, and the connection between them was almost physical. Andi looked back at the little girl holding out a program for her to sign. She hoped no one could see the sudden heat in her cheeks.

What was she feeling? An attraction to Taz? She blinked, fighting a sudden weakness in her knees. Taz's offer of a starring role had caught her attention, of course. She was anxious to talk to him about the dates for shooting his independent film. But until now she hadn't felt a connection between them. She tried to focus, but it was impossible. From twenty feet away, she could feel his eyes on her as strongly as if he were touching her.

When the audience goers had moved on, Taz slowly walked up, his confidence a tangible force around him. He smiled, and again she felt his eyes looking deep into her soul. "Can we talk?"

She felt flustered, and it bothered her. She smoothed out the layers of her blue dress and gathered her composure. "I have to change. And we have another show in a few hours."

"I'll get you a coffee. We can talk outside when you're ready."

Andi's heart picked up speed. He wasn't exactly asking, and that bugged her too. But a thrill of attraction ran through her veins at breakneck speed. An attraction like she'd never felt before. She heard herself telling him that she'd take a grande soy latte and that she'd be out in fifteen minutes.

His grin was slow and lazy, and his eyes danced. "I'll be waiting."

Back in the dressing room, the director spent ten minutes talking to the cast about the townspeople scenes. "You're getting a little out of control." He frowned. "Too much milling about and animated conversations. It's distracting us from the main characters."

When the director was finished, Bailey came up to her, brows raised. "I saw you."

"What?" Andi didn't want to answer for what she was about to do. She hadn't done anything wrong, and Taz was different, interesting.

"You know what." Her tone wasn't condemning or unkind, but she sounded worried. "The film student. I don't like the way he looks at you."

"He's fine." Andi busied herself with her costume, unbuttoning the back and slipping out of the dress. What did Bailey know about meeting guys at school? She had Tim. And now that Cody was losing interest... "I like him." Andi tossed her hair. "We have a lot in common. Besides, we need to talk about the movie."

Instant disappointment colored Bailey's expression. "Andi, no. You're not taking the role."

"I might." She worked to sound confident and controlled. Like she had thought through this.

Bailey's face mirrored her skepticism.

"I know—the partial nudity." Andi lifted her hands and let them fall back to her sides. "The way I see it, sacrifices need to be made for the sake of art." She thought about her parents' trip delay. "That's true with everyone in filmmaking."

"Don't compromise." Bailey released an exasperated sigh. "Please, Andi. Be smart. You don't even know this guy."

"I don't need to. It's not like I'm interested in him," she lied. "He wants me to star in his film. He's intriguing. It's that simple."

Bailey hesitated, like she wanted to say more. "Tim's waiting for me. We're getting lunch and sitting on the wall out back. You should join us."

"Maybe later." Andi hung up her dress, removed her character dance shoes, and slipped into her jeans and turtleneck sweater. "Taz is getting me a coffee."

Another sigh. "Be careful."

"Thanks." Andi looked up long enough to give Bailey a hurried smile. "I will."

With Bailey gone, Andi slowed her frenzied pace. Just once she wished her roommate could be a little adventurous. They were in college, after all. What other time of their lives would an offer like this come along, the chance to star in a student film? This was what college was about.

She regained the calm she'd lost in the last five minutes. She wasn't going to sit in her dorm fearing the world or the God who'd made it. Life was nothing but an accumulation of experiences, and this would be one she remembered always.

She fixed her hair and checked her makeup. It was a little heavy, but she didn't want to reapply it before the next show. She put her jacket on, snatched her purse from the floor, and made sure she had her phone. Then, with a final look at herself, she walked back into the lobby. She wasn't sure Taz was serious, or—if he was—that he'd be back yet. But he was there, leaning against the door frame of the main entrance, a coffee cup in each hand. He locked eyes with her from the moment he saw her, and didn't break the connection once as she walked up.

"You're even better this weekend than last." He handed her a hot white cup. "One soy latte."

"Thank you." Her heart was doing it again, pounding like crazy, and she wished she'd asked for something without caffeine. This was crazy, this breathless way he made her feel. She'd seen him in her science class every day since school started. Why the attraction now? She stared at her coffee and tried not to look flustered. "Where should we go?"

"There's a bench out there a little ways. It's more private than staying here." He held open the door and walked beside her as they headed down the path. The cold air hit them like a freezing wall and took her breath away. At least she hoped it was the cold air.

Taz wore a nice jacket, something from Abercrombie, and mixed with the ice cold air she could smell his cologne. His pace was slow and easy, like his smile. "Do you always have the biggest crowd after a show?"

"No." She giggled and felt the compliment to her core. Especially today, with Cody canceling on her and her parents delayed in Denver. "Tim Reed barely has enough time to sign all the programs that come his way. He's been brilliant as Scrooge."

"Because his greatest regret was losing you." He looked down, and their eyes met again. "That would make any guy crazy."

Andi didn't know what to say, so she smiled at him and then faced straight ahead again. Snow was gathered a foot high on either side of the path, but the cement was cleared. They reached the bench and she sat down first. He took the opposite side, leaving ample space between them. Andi felt herself relax. Bailey didn't have to worry. The guy wasn't making a move on her. He was making a movie. There was a difference.

They sat in silence for nearly a minute, sipping their coffee and watching their breath make wispy shapes in the air between them. Finally he lowered his drink and narrowed his eyes, looking into hers with a kindness and depth she hadn't noticed before. "I've wanted to make movies as far back as I can remember."

He didn't seem to be looking for a response, so she stayed with her drink, watching him, waiting.

"Film is a special medium, powerful, encompassing." He shifted his look to the barren trees not far from where they sat. "Only through film can a person vicariously experience the thrill of espionage or the pain of prison bars, the satisfaction of revenge or the power of taking another life." He paused and his eyes found hers again. "Film can make a person know what love should be, what sexual love feels like. The experience can be that real." He drew a slow breath. "It's a medium bigger than ourselves."

Andi wanted to feel embarrassed by his blunt description, but she was drawn by it instead. He was right in many ways. Wasn't that why people went to the movies? So they could live the lives of the actors on screen, if only for a few hours from the dark privacy of their theater seats? She lowered her coffee to her lap. "Acting's that way too. Crawling into someone else's skin and bringing something to life you otherwise wouldn't have known."

He seemed pleasantly surprised by her description. "Hmmm. A girl who's as deep as she is beautiful." He tipped his head in her direction, and his eyes flirted mercilessly with her. "You're a rare find, Andi Ellison. How come some guy hasn't snatched you up and made you his?"

"I don't know." Her cheeks were hot again. "I've been out of the country most of my life."

"Tell me." He was in no hurry. It was a part of his charm.

For the first time she wished her story was more exotic, that she'd been the daughter of a great and powerful archaeologist and together her family had spent more than a decade on the site of a world-famous dig in Africa somewhere. But she had to be honest. No matter what his belief system, she was what she was. "My parents were missionaries." She gave him a weak smile. "I grew up in Indonesia."

"Christian missionaries?" He seemed interested, if maybe slightly amused. "I admire missionaries."

"You do?"

"Yes. They are committed to their dreams and beliefs. To live a life of service toward another people is admirable. Like anything else that resonates in the soul."

"*Resonates in the soul?*" Yes, that was it. The new ideas and thoughts she'd been feeling were ones that resonated in her soul. Andi felt her head begin to spin. This was the sort of conversation she'd longed to have with Bailey or Cody—anyone who would talk to her. But whenever the conversation veered out of the box of biblical truth, her friends took a hard stance. Things were either right or wrong. Andi had a feeling that wasn't the case for Taz.

He looked at her in a way that made it feel like he'd known her forever, like no one would ever know her better. "My parents were Muslims, but they sort of lost their fervor for the dogma when they moved to the U.S." He took a slow sip from his coffee. "I'm agnostic. A skeptic, I guess. I believe people are entitled to believe. Whatever their beliefs." He chuckled and put his arm along the back of the bench. His shoulder muscles showed through his coat. "How's that?"

She laughed too. "I like it."

They talked for half an hour about politics and peace, raving radicals and religion before he paused for a long moment. "About the film." He angled his head, and she fell into his eyes. "Have you thought about it?"

Her attraction to him was growing stronger with every passing minute. He was interesting and intelligent, and so far a perfect gentlemen. But somehow Andi felt stripped bare in his presence. Like he had a gift of seeing past the layers of formality and pretense. "I have. I'd like to see the script." She cupped her hands around her drink and hoped he couldn't read the truth—that her mind was made up. She was taking the role. She could hardly wait to work under his direction.

"I have a copy in my car. How much time do you have?"

She pulled her phone from her purse and checked it. "Ten minutes, maybe fifteen. We have an extra dance rehearsal before tonight's call. It's a full company number."

He looked at her a long time, and she felt herself react. His stare was like a physical caress, and after several seconds she looked down at her drink. *What is this feeling*, she asked herself. *I've never experienced this in all my life.*

"Andi." His voice was velvet.

She looked up again.

"I love watching you on stage. You act with your whole body, heart, and soul. That's important." He leaned forward and rested his elbows on his knees. "In the art of acting, our bodies are the colors. Our hearts the canvas. This sort of artwork is expressed through the soul—if we're gifted at it, anyway." He patted her knee. "You're gifted, Andi. When you act, you work your magic straight through me. No doubt about that." He stood. "I'll get the script." With an easy, loping jog he was off, headed for the parking lot.

Andi exhaled and sank into the back of the wooden bench. It was like he has some supernatural power, something that rendered her captive, caught in his spell. She sipped her coffee and tried to understand why she hadn't felt this way before around him. Now there was something about him that made her breath catch in her throat, her heart race out of control.

She steadied herself. *Get a grip, Andi. You're being ridiculous.* But even as she handed out instructions to herself, she could smell his cologne hanging in the frozen air, hear his voice. *"I love watching you on stage ... You're gifted ... You work your magic straight through me ..."*

She closed her eyes. This was crazy. She barely knew the guy. The script did matter, even if she hadn't thought so a minute ago. She would approach the next conversation with him differently, with her head in charge.

She sat straighter and took a few deep breaths, willing her head to clear. He jogged back up the path a moment later and sat beside her again, a little closer than before. Had he given himself another spritz of cologne, or were her senses really that aware of him? She blinked twice, focusing.

"Here." He handed her a thin, stapled document. It couldn't have been more than thirty, forty pages.

As the papers moved from his hand to hers, their fingers touched and a jolt of electric attraction ran through her veins, dropping her stomach to her knees and making her fight for her next breath. Her mouth went dry, and she ran her tongue along her lower lip. "Thank you."

Taz was sitting sideways, facing her straight on. "The entire film won't be longer than half an hour. But I'm looking for a tremendous amount of energy in that time, a very powerful message."

Andi wasn't sure she should ask, but her curiosity got the better of her. "You told me a little about the plot, but ... what's the theme?"

"It's about pushing limits, taking chances and being willing to experience the consequences." He looked away. "Consequences aren't always to be suffered, but to be experienced. Wholly—body and mind, heart and soul." He found her eyes again. "If we are willing to experience anything in honesty, then we can become more than ourselves." He grinned, and the philosopher was gone. "Besides ... whatever the message, it'll be unforgettable if you're the lead."

"Thank you." The wind was picking up, and Andi started to shiver. "I'll read it." She tucked her chin in and felt her look turn shy. "When do you need to know?"

"Take a week. You'll need time after the show wraps tomorrow."

She was flattered that he knew her schedule. "A week it is."

He angled his head, flirting with her for all he was worth. "But you know ... I was thinking something."

"What's that?" The chemistry between them made her forget being cold.

"I might need to add a line or two in the script. You know, since I'm the producer and director. And I'd have to ask your thoughts on it."

"True."

"So ..." His eyes became puppy-dog hopeful. "I was thinking — for the sake of the film — maybe I should get your number."

She tried to keep a straight face, but she couldn't. Laughter tickled her throat. She held out her hand. "Give me your phone."

He did, and she entered herself and her number as a new contact. "There." She gave it back to him. "In case you come up with an extra line or two."

"Right." He stood and helped her to her feet. Again the touch of his hand against hers spread an intoxicating sensation throughout her body. She let her fingers stay in his a few seconds longer than necessary, the whole time looking straight into his eyes.

"I hope you like the script." His voice was soft, his face just inches from hers.

"Me too." She didn't blink, didn't dare break the connection between them.

He gave her hand a final squeeze and then released it. "This could be interesting."

"Yes."

"Complicated, but interesting." He was so close he could've leaned down and kissed her. But instead he took a step back and led the way as they walked the path back to the theater. At the lobby doors, he stuck his hands into his pockets and shrugged, his eyes full of depth and kindness, and a power she didn't fully understand. "See you around, Andi."

"Yeah." She gave a slight wave. "See ya 'round."

She had five minutes to report for dance rehearsal, and after that the night show passed in a blur. Her parents didn't show up, but they left another message. Their plane would arrive sometime around midnight, and they'd see her in the morning — before the Sunday matinee. But even with that disappointment, as she and Bailey headed back to the Flanigan house for Pictionary, Andi was beyond happy. On the drive, Bailey asked about Taz, but she kept her answers short and evasive. She didn't want to talk about him, didn't want anyone judging her. "It's no big deal," she lied. "I probably won't do the film anyway."

"What'd you guys talk about?" Bailey's eyes were shadowed in suspicion. "You were out there a long time."

"Mostly filmmaking. A little bit about the script." She shrugged. "It was nothing."

Bailey dropped the subject, which was good for both of them. They played on the same Pictionary team with Bailey's mom, and they won easily.

"It's not fair." Bailey's brother Shawn slumped back in his chair after the game. "Girls just know each other better."

Everyone laughed, and the girls won another round before calling it a night. On the way back to the dorm, Andi was grateful Bailey didn't bring up Taz again. Instead they listened to Rascal Flatts, which was perfect. The break in conversation gave Andi the chance to privately relive the time with Taz. Enough so that as she got ready for bed, for the first time she didn't think once about grabbing her Bible or Rachel's journal. She had no conflicting thoughts or pangs of guilt. Only memories of Taz. His smile and his eyes, the way he thought differently than the other kids she knew. The way he made her feel. And as she fell asleep she realized she was not just intrigued by the film student from her science class.

She was head over heels.

Twelve

BAILEY WATCHED THE CLOCK ON THE wall in her Advanced Algebra class and willed the last five minutes to pass quickly. She was meeting Tim for lunch, and she could hardly wait to see him. Since Christmas, both their schedules had been too busy to spend much time together. Bailey had been so focused on her grades it was already late January, and the two of them hadn't been on a date in weeks. Not only that, but life was about to get busier. Tim and Andi had auditioned for the university's upcoming musical—*Robin Hood*. Bailey's current class schedule was too intense for theater, but she was taking private voice lessons with Katy Matthews, Dayne's wife, and dance classes at night on campus.

On top of that Bailey wanted to be more involved with Campus Crusade, which was organizing a late-summer mission trip to Costa Rica. The Cru meetings had taken on a pattern. She and Tim would sit near the front, while Cody sat in the back. Most Thursdays Andi found a reason not to go. As for Cody, Bailey felt so distant around him, it was like they'd never known each other. But rather than focus on Cody, Bailey was getting more involved with the ministry aspects of the group. She and several other Cru girls had started meeting once a week in the common area of Bailey's dorm, and she was grateful for the interaction. They'd met twice so far, and both times Andi had been too busy with schoolwork to join them.

Bailey had a feeling there was more to it than that. Her roommate was splitting her time between schoolwork and Taz, but whenever Bailey asked about the filmmaker, her roommate shut down. As difficult as it had been for Bailey to imagine Cody and Andi together, certainly Cody would have been better for her than Taz.

"What about his faith?" Bailey had asked a few weeks ago.

Andi had given her a tired look. "He thinks everyone should have a right to believe what they wish."

Bailey wanted to ask her what Bible verse that came from, but she didn't want to be sarcastic. Cynicism would only turn Andi further from the truth. Instead she nodded thoughtfully. "And what about him? What does he believe?"

"He's agnostic. A skeptic, as he likes to say." Andi was quick to follow up on the fact. "Which is why it's good he has someone like me in his life."

Bailey tapped her pencil on her math book and tried to focus. The professor droned on about integers and absolute values within the context of a proof. Bailey let her eyes wander to the window and the snow outside. She missed Tim, but the time apart for them wasn't all bad. Bailey and her family had been together more often, which gave her the chance to hang out with her youngest brother, Ricky. He'd been sick with winter colds lately — coughing a lot and feeling tired. When she was home, Bailey could play backgammon or the Wii with him — so he wouldn't notice the cough so much. Not that she was worried about him. Ricky had had successful heart surgery as a baby, and he was very healthy now. But every winter was a struggle.

At the front of the classroom, the professor checked the clock and smiled at the auditorium full of students. "That'll be all. Tomorrow's Friday. Come prepared for a quiz on chapter 2."

Bailey slung her backpack over her right shoulder and hurried out the back door. She scanned the distance from the math building to the cafeteria and saw Tim walk into view. This was their meeting spot on Thursdays, when their schedules allowed them time to share lunch. She smiled and waved, and he jogged to meet her, his backpack pulled tight around his shoulders. "Hey." He gave her a quick hug as they walked. "I can't believe how cold it is."

They'd had a record-breaking winter so far, more snow than any of the locals could remember. Classes had even been cancelled a few days last week. One of the students had tacked a note on the Math Building: "School closed — due to global warming."

Bailey pulled her coat more tightly around her shoulders. "I can't wait for warmer weather." She felt her eyes light up. "I almost forgot. My mom's taking us to New York City for spring break. She wants to meet up with one of her old friends." She grinned at him. "She said you could come with us."

"Really?" He stopped and dropped his backpack on the cement pathway. "Are you serious?"

Her laughter was light and easy. "Yes, I'm serious!"

"We're going to New York City!" He let out a celebratory hoot, picked her up, and swung her in a full circle. When he set her down he did another solo circle. "I can't believe this." He put his hand on his head, his expression dazed. "That's the most amazing thing ever!"

"I know." She laughed again. "Come on. We're making a scene." She linked arms with him and snuggled close to his side. "If we're going to live there someday and star on Broadway, you better at least learn your way around."

"I still can't believe it." He stopped again. "I better double my hours at the bookstore."

"Nah, silly." She gave him a gentle tug and they kept walking. "My mom's treating. You'll go as our guest."

"Now I'm really in shock." He ran ahead of her a few steps, turned and faced her, walking backwards. "You're serious?"

"Tim." She shook her head. "You're acting crazy."

"Okay, okay." He exhaled. "I'll try to believe I'm not dreaming."

Inside the cafeteria they got their lunches and found seats together in a quiet back corner. This time Tim controlled himself. "Will we see shows and everything?"

"Of course." Bailey giggled. She realized something that had been more obvious lately: Tim made her laugh. Everything about being with him was wonderful and getting better all the time. "Going to plays? That's the whole point."

"So ... I mean, I haven't ever really researched Broadway. What's playing there?"

"My mom said something about seeing *Mary Poppins*—which is amazing, because we've seen it before. Then maybe *Shrek, the Musical*—which would be funny and stars Sutton Foster, who is, like, the best Broadway actress ever."

They talked about the brilliant set design and music of *The Lion King*, and a new show called *In the Heights*, about life in the barrios of New York City.

"Too bad we don't have more time." Tim was eating a cheeseburger. A blob of ketchup smeared onto his cheek, but he didn't notice it. "We'll be there just a week."

Bailey pointed to her cheek, and Tim caught the message. He swiped a napkin over his face and grinned at her. "I'm too frozen to feel anything."

"Yeah, but anyway, the shows are every night except Monday. Two on Wednesday and two on the weekend days. We could pretty much see whatever we want. My mom loves Broadway plays."

"Wow." He seemed speechless. "Tell your parents thanks. I can't wait."

The topic changed and they talked about *Robin Hood*. "We'll find out tomorrow if we got cast."

"Of course you will." She rested her forearms on the table and leaned closer to him. "You're unbelievable on stage, Tim. You'll be Robin Hood, for sure. You and Andi will have a great time." She no longer worried about Tim being attracted to her friend. Andi was different these days, and she spent much of her time with Taz. The time away had hurt their friendship. At least it seemed that way. She said she hadn't committed to Taz's film. But Bailey thought her roommate might be lying to her. She actually hoped Andi would get a part opposite Tim, so he could help talk some sense into her.

"There was more competition this time." Tim glanced at her, but only as he hurried to finish his burger. "You glad you didn't try out?"

"Definitely. I need a break. Katy Matthews is giving me voice lessons and I added a few night dance classes. That'll help me more than being in a play right now." Bailey's strength was dance, but it didn't hurt to brush up. Especially if she was serious about getting an audition in New York City. "One more thing about New York. My mom's friend knows the casting director of *Wicked*. I guess he's going to introduce us to some people while we're there."

"That's crazy." Tim looked beyond thrilled. "That's so great. I mean, picture it. You and me performing on Broadway together! Living the dream."

"One day." She gave him a full-faced grin. "But for now ... we better eat. Class starts in ten."

They finished and said good-bye just outside the cafeteria and walked separate ways to their next class. Tim was fun, Bailey thought as she trudged down the sidewalk. Never mind that sometimes she wished he were a little more romantic, a little more like the guy who had held her hand on stage during *Scrooge* opening night. Since then she'd longed for those moments, but they rarely came. Tim didn't look at her long enough to give her a window to his soul. But that could come later, if the two of them stayed together. For now it was nice to have a great guy in her life, someone who shared her faith and wasn't about to let her down.

The way she'd been let down before.

Snow began to fall as she reached the English building, and after she'd walked down the hall and up a flight of stairs, she saw the note. English 102 was cancelled. The instructor was ill and not expected back until Monday. Bailey adjusted her backpack and pulled her coat tighter. The walk from English to her dorm was the longest of the day. As she stepped back outside, her hood helped take the edge off the biting wind, but it only allowed her a limited window of sight. She was halfway to her dorm when she felt someone come up beside her.

"Bailey." The voice was Cody's. No amount of time could remove the sound of it from her heart. "Didn't you hear me?"

"What?" Her heart pounded so loud she was sure he could hear it. She pulled her hood down so she could see him. The campus was quiet this time of day, only a few people out of class walking across the outdoor mall.

Cody's eyes were intense, full of questions. "I had to run to catch you."

"Oh." Her mouth went suddenly dry, and she wondered if her heart might burst from her chest. "My hood ... I can't hear anything with it up."

Snow fell softly around them, and Cody tried to catch his breath. "Did you get a new phone?"

"No." Bailey looked down and kicked at the loose snow gathering near their feet. She lifted her eyes to him. "I've been busy."

He looked like he was trying to process that. "Okay." He shrugged and for a long moment he seemed at a loss. The muscles in his jaw tightened and he exhaled hard. "I've called a bunch of times. You know that, right?"

"I guess I'm not sure why." She took a step back and folded her arms across her chest. A chill cut through her, one that came more from being so close to Cody than because of the winter wind. "You went months without calling, and now ... Now I don't get it."

"That's why I've been calling." He moved like he was going to take a step closer, but then changed his mind. He buried his fists in his coat pockets and held his ground. "During your show, it was like—" He hesitated, struggling, his eyes lifting to the slate-gray sky. After a few seconds he looked at her again, his eyes bathed in emotion. "I can't let you go, Bailey. It was my fault. I talked about being your friend, but I didn't act like one."

Bailey thought of all the times Cody had blatantly ignored her, the times when he'd talked to Andi but couldn't be bothered to call her. Tears poked at the corners of her eyes, but she held them back. "I was so mad at you." Her voice caught between heartbreaking sorrow and fighting mad. "You had Andi and it was like ... I didn't matter at all."

"You did." He released a frustrated breath. "You do. I wish you could know how much I miss you."

"You miss what we used to have." She took another half step back from him. A talk like this would get them nowhere. They had their own lives now. "You're all about Andi. She can be your friend."

"No!" His answer was sharp, and it caught them both by surprise. He worked to calm himself. "She and I are nothing."

"Okay." Bailey, too, fought for composure. "Then I'm in love with Tim."

"Are you?" He was breathing harder now, leaning toward her, his eyes intense. A couple of kids passed on a nearby sidewalk, and again he lowered his voice. "Are you really, Bailey? 'Cause I see you with him, and all I'm saying is other than on stage, I've never seen you look at him, the way ..."

"The way what?" She practically spat the words, and in that moment she didn't care if they hurt him. She almost wanted them to hurt, so he'd give up and walk away. She didn't need him to play with her heart now.

Tears blurred her vision and she couldn't tell where her anger stopped and her hurt began. "The way *I* looked at you? Back when I thought you had feelings for me?" She looked over her shoulder, planning her escape. "I was wrong, okay. I was younger then and ridiculous. You never saw me that way." She backed up again. "It's too late now. We've moved on."

He came a few steps closer. "Don't leave." But before he could say anything else her cell phone went off.

She pressed her fingers to her eyes and pulled the phone from her pocket. It was her parents. "It's home." She held up one finger and took the call. "Hello?"

"Honey, it's Mom. We're at the hospital. Ricky's having trouble with his heart." She sounded controlled but scared. "His doctor's not sure what's happening. They're trying to stabilize him."

"Mom, no ..." She put her hand to her face and turned from Cody. "He's okay, right? I mean, he's not in real danger?"

"The doctor isn't sure." There were tears in her mom's voice. "Can you please come?"

"I'll be right there." She snapped her phone shut.

"What happened?" Cody was at her side again, his eyes filled with concern.

"Ricky. His heart." She looked up at him, and fear paralyzed her for a moment. "He's in the hospital." She took a step in one direction, and then changed her mind and started in another. Her car was in the parking lot outside her dorm, but she couldn't remember which way to get there. "I need to go."

"Come on." He took hold of her hand and started running. "My car's close. I'll drive."

Bailey tried not to think about the feel of his hand around hers as she ran beside him, the discussion from seconds ago forgotten. Cody had lived with them, and he loved all the Flanigan boys as if they were his own brothers.

Cody didn't release her hand until they were in his car. On the way to the hospital they talked about Ricky's recent cold. "He's been more tired than usual." Bailey had knots in her stomach. "We all figured he was just growing or something."

"We need to pray." Again Cody reached for her hand, and he begged God to be with Ricky and to give the doctors wisdom to get him out of danger. When the prayer was over, Bailey pulled her hand back. Her mind was racing in a million different directions. What was happening with Ricky, and how come his heart was having trouble so many years after his heart surgery? And why ... why was her whole body trembling because of a single touch from Cody?

They reached the hospital and raced inside and up the elevator to the fifth floor—the cardiac unit. As soon as the elevator doors opened Bailey spotted her parents down the hall talking to a doctor. Her mom broke off from the group and met her halfway down the hallway. "He's stable." She pulled Bailey into a long hug. "Thank God, he's stable." She drew back and kissed Bailey's forehead. "You got here fast."

"Cody brought me." Bailey's knees shook and she shivered. "What happened?"

"Thank you." Her mom hugged Cody and then rested against the hospital wall. She looked pale and exhausted. "He was playing outside, shooting baskets."

"It's freezing out." Bailey felt faint. She leaned her shoulder into the wall, facing her mother.

"You know Ricky. He's never cold."

"I remember that." Cody moved in close to them, his voice low. "You couldn't get the kid to wear long pants even in the dead of winter."

Bailey wasn't sure why, but Cody's presence made her feel safe and warm and protected. She couldn't analyze the reasons right now. "Then what?"

"He came in and he was white as a sheet. He said his chest felt funny, so I checked his pulse." Her mom closed her eyes. When she opened them, there were tears in her lashes. "It was racing so fast, Bailey. So fast I couldn't count it."

"You brought him in?"

"I was about to, but he fainted." She gulped and a stream of tears slid down her cheeks. "I called 9–1–1 and I went with him in the ambulance. Your dad followed behind with the boys—they're in the waiting room."

Bailey's head spun. Her little brother passed out? Did that mean he'd come close to ... to ... She couldn't think about the horrible possibilities. "What was it? Do they know?"

Her mom nodded. "His heart went into an abnormal rhythm. Maybe from the cold or from his exertion, or maybe because something's wrong with the electrical part of his heart."

"Meaning it could happen again?"

"It could. They'll check a few things while we're here, and then Monday we'll go to Children's Hospital in Indianapolis. They can run the rest of the tests there."

"What's the worst case?" Bailey wasn't sure she wanted to ask. She pictured her blond little brother shooting free throws in the front yard near the family garage this past weekend. If he had to cut back on sports, he'd be devastated.

"He might need a pacemaker. Something to help make sure it doesn't happen again."

The idea sounded horrific. "He's so young."

"It's only a possibility. He's on a medicine for now, to keep his heartbeat controlled." Her mom straightened and put her arm around Bailey. With her free hand she wiped at her tears again, then reached out and put that arm around Cody's shoulders. "It was so scary."

"Is he awake?" Now that they weren't outside in the freezing air, Bailey could smell Cody's cologne. She hated how easily she responded to his presence, falling for him as if she didn't have a boyfriend, as if he'd never ignored her, never chosen to be friends with Andi over her. She bit her lip. "Can we see him?"

She drew a long breath and released the hold she had on them. "He's tired, but he'd love to see you." She looked at Cody. "You too." She paused, sincerity in her tone. "It's been a long time."

"Too long." Cody didn't break eye contact.

Her dad was still talking to the doctor, but as Bailey and Cody walked up he stopped and hugged them both. His eyes told them that he was as concerned about Ricky as her mom had been. "Things were very bad for a little while there."

"We prayed on the way here." Bailey kept her arm around her dad's waist. "I'm sure everyone was praying."

"At church too. I called on the way here. And the Colts team chaplain rallied the guys."

"I could feel the prayers the whole ride here." Her mom steadied herself against her dad.

Bailey felt herself relax a little. "At least he's okay."

"For now. They want to watch him tonight, and then he can come home in the morning if his heart rate stays steady." Her dad frowned. "The tests next week will tell us a lot."

"Jenny said something about a pacemaker." Cody shifted so that he was a little closer to Bailey.

"He could end up with another open-heart surgery."

A sick feeling ran through Bailey. She couldn't stand the thought of her brother having that kind of surgery. She shuddered slightly and moved toward the door of Ricky's room. "We wanna see him, okay?"

"Go ahead." Her dad gave them a weary smile.

Her parents stayed out in the hall, talking in hushed tones while Bailey and Cody went in to be with Ricky. He looked tired but happy, unaware of the danger he'd survived in the past few hours. "Hey, Cody, how'd you get here?"

"I brought your sister." Cody took the spot on one side of the bed, and Bailey moved to the other. "We were together when she heard about this."

"Yeah, kinda weird, huh?" Ricky made a face. "I think I just got a little too cold."

"It's definitely cold out there." Bailey ran her hand over his now matted pale hair. "How you feeling, bud?"

"Tired." He yawned. "But I can breathe better."

They talked for awhile, and eventually Bailey's parents and brothers joined them. After half an hour, Bailey and Cody had to get going. Both of them had homework, and Cru was that night. With Ricky out of immediate danger, there was no reason to stay longer. They said their good-byes, and her brother Connor gave Bailey an extra-long hug. "It was really bad," he whispered. "God saved him, Bailey. Seriously."

Again Bailey felt a sick feeling pass over her. *God, thank You for helping him.* She uttered the silent prayer as easily as she drew her next breath. "Text me if anything gets worse."

Connor agreed. "You're home for the weekend, right?"

"Definitely."

"Good." Connor was in the latest CKT play, but he didn't have practice this weekend, so they could have time together. Time to catch up and laugh about the latest funny videos on YouTube or the news at Clear Creek High, where Connor was a sophomore.

Before they parted, Connor raised an eyebrow. "What's with Cody?"

Bailey's heart fell flat. "Nothing. He was there when I got the call. That's it." She drew back and waved once more to Ricky and the others.

"Hey!" Ricky made an effort to sit up, but he seemed too tired to pull off the move. "Cody, you gotta come around more. I can throw a football thirty yards now."

Cody chuckled. He and Ricky had always shared a special connection because of football. "I definitely have to see that."

Exhaustion and relief made Bailey feel tired as she and Cody walked back to his car. His elbow brushed against her arm a few times, and she tried not to enjoy the sensation. This whole crazy afternoon was like something from a dream, like it had never happened. They were quiet on the ride home, but the time gave Bailey a chance to collect her thoughts, to find solid ground again.

When Cody dropped her off at the front door of her dorm, he got out and stood facing her. The awkwardness was back, now that they no longer had a reason to be together. The wind chaffed at their cheeks and the barren branches in the trees overhead clacked together with every light gust.

Cody found her eyes and held them. He had a way of looking straight to her heart, and this late afternoon was no different. Finally he took a slow breath. "I meant what I said."

"About?"

"Being friends. I'm not giving up." He seemed to gather himself, his frustrations from earlier in check. "I'll keep calling and texting until you trust me again."

Bailey felt like the air had been sucked from her lungs. Until she trusted him again? Did he really know her that well? After so much time had passed since they'd talked, could he be so exactly spot on about how she felt? She wasn't sure what to say, so she looked down again and studied the snow.

"That's it, right? I pulled a disappearing act, and now you don't trust me."

She wanted to tell him to stop, that he had no right reading her thoughts. But she was too touched by how well he still knew her. Even so, she had to be honest. "I have Tim, now ... and you ... you need to move on too."

He started to say something, but again he changed his mind. "I can't do that."

Bailey felt the sadness build and grow inside her. Because this was where he was wrong. "You can."

"I wanna talk about you and me, what we could—"

"There is no you and me, Cody." She steeled her heart against him, protecting herself. "You wanted me to date Tim, and that's what I'm doing."

"You're in love with him?"

"Yes." She couldn't help the hesitation that followed. "Sometimes I think I am."

For a few seconds she thought he was going to note that a person in love would think so all the time. Not sometimes. But instead he seemed to lose the will to fight her. His shoulders sank a little. "Okay, then." He drew her tenderly into a long hug. "I'm glad Ricky's okay."

"For now." She could barely draw a breath, her heart racing from the feel of his arms around her. She couldn't remember feeling this way in Tim's arms even once.

"Yes, for now." He was still hugging her. "It was good seeing you today. Nothing's felt so right in a long time."

She exhaled, and tried not to cry. "Thanks." She spoke the words against his neck. "For being there today." When she couldn't stand another moment being so close to him, she pulled back. She wanted to tell him how wonderful it felt seeing him, and how he'd made her feel safe and protected at a time when she was scared to death. But there was no point. She took a step toward her dorm. "See you at Cru."

A subtle disappointment shaded his eyes, but he smiled anyway. "Okay. See ya."

Bailey turned and took quick steps up the walkway and into the dorm. She didn't turn around and wave one last time even though a part of her wanted to steal one more look. The fact was she couldn't turn around. Not because she was afraid he'd see the tears finally streaming down her face, but because she didn't want him to see something far worse. Her eyes would no doubt give away the fact that no matter how she lied to him or to herself, the truth remained — Tim or no Tim.

She was still in love with Cody Coleman.

Thirteen

KELLY WANTED TO BE HAPPY FOR Chase, but no matter how hard she tried she couldn't work up anything but the familiar feeling of despair. She sat on the edge of their bed and watched her husband buzz around the room, packing his bag and practically bursting with the thrill of all the week held.

"I mean, really, Kelly, I was beginning to wonder if the whole *Unlocked* things was really going to happen, like maybe Kendall was just being optimistic, you know?"

Kelly's stomach hurt from the waffles she'd eaten that morning. She crossed her arms and nodded. "I wondered too."

"But this is just like God. Four weeks with nothing, not a hint that Kendall's news was going to pan out. I mean, Brandon Paul might've changed his mind or maybe the studios weren't as interested as before. And then—" He snapped his fingers. "Out of the blue a call like this. I mean, Kendall's the real deal. She can make things happen, I'll say that."

Kelly wondered if her husband could hear himself. "She must be really something."

"She is." Chase stopped, as if for the first time in the last five minutes he grasped how he was coming across. "As far as the industry goes."

They were at the end of February and the call had come in yesterday morning. Kendall had been working behind the scenes, apparently, and now she wanted Chase and Keith to come to LA for a week of meetings. Talk about making things happen. Kelly had never known jealousy before, but she understood it completely now. Her husband could barely stop talking about Kendall and the magic she could work in Hollywood.

The first meeting this week would be a private screening of *The Last Letter* at Kendall's house Monday evening. In attendance would be Kendall; her father, Ben; Stephanie; and NTM's very own Brandon Paul—teen sensation and easily one of America's most well-known superstars. She could understand Chase's excitement. If only Kendall didn't have to be such an integral part of it.

"I can't believe it." Chase's smile seemed permanently etched into his face. His tone hadn't come down once since Kendall's call. "All those powerful people in one room just to watch our movie."

"They have to see if you're legit." Kelly meant the comment to sound positive, but it felt flat as it left her lips. Again she pressed her arms hard against her aching stomach.

"Legit?" His smile faded a little. "They already know we're legit or they wouldn't come out for a screening." He gave a quick laugh, as if he had no time to waste being negative or distracted. A stack of shirts sat on one side of the bed. He lifted it and placed it into his open suitcase. "This is about Kendall showing off our work and getting everyone else excited so that we can start getting things lined up for *Unlocked*."

"That's what I meant." Kelly stood and sighed. She watched Chase put a stack of socks and then a few pairs of dark jeans into the suitcase, then she walked to the bedroom window and stared out at the house next to theirs. Times like this the houses felt so close together she could practically reach out and shake hands with the neighbors. She closed her eyes and thought about how lonely she would be once Chase was gone. Let him go and show off his movie to a bunch of Hollywood types. Where did that leave her?

Chase stopped and stared at her. "You okay?" He was still smiling, his eyes still lit up. But for the first time that evening concern flickered in his expression.

"It's hard when you're away."

"Babe." Chase came to her and put his hands on her shoulders. "This is temporary. God's opening so many doors. Kendall says it's only a matter of time before we can buy something closer to LA. Then I can be home every night."

"Kendall probably knows." A tired smile tugged at her lips. She didn't want to sound bitter or jaded. "I'd like that."

"I'd like it too." He leaned in and kissed her lips — one tender, lingering kiss. "We all would."

"What am I supposed to do until then?" She looked out the window. "You keep leaving me to take care of the girls, handle the finances, run the house." She turned to him again. "All by myself."

Chase still had his hand on her back, but he let it fall to his side. "I've been home most of February."

"I know." Again she gathered up the hint of a smile. "I'm sorry. It's just ... I feel removed from it, Chase."

"From what?"

"Everything you're doing. The excitement and the meetings, the connections with people in the industry. The screening at Kendall's house, the socializing with the likes of Stephanie Fitzgerald and Brandon Paul." She faced him. "Doesn't it ever feel a little surreal?"

Chase thought about that for a long moment. "Not really." He met her eyes. "We prayed for this, all of us. Remember that? Day after day, months at a time. Now that God's answering us, I guess I only feel grateful."

She nodded, but she could feel her smile drop off. He returned to packing, talking about the conversation he'd had with Kendall and Brandon Paul's agent and how excited the young actor was to star in *Unlocked*, and how Stephanie Fitzgerald had texted him. Actually texted him! And how she was thrilled for the chance to preview his work Monday night at Kendall's.

Kelly studied him as he talked and packed, moving about the room with the energy of someone setting off for a once-in-a-lifetime trip. Something about him seemed different, more confident maybe. Better than having him down and discouraged, wallowing in fear of defeat, she supposed. But still, there were moments when she felt like she was watching someone else's husband get ready to leave. The energy in his face, the speed in his steps, the enthusiasm in his voice. And the realization that she had no real part in his excitement.

Suddenly a handful of scenarios ran through her head. Chase arriving in Los Angeles and being seduced by the Hollywood lifestyle, wanting to stay longer than a week, and maybe renting a place so he wouldn't have to commute. She pictured him coming home and telling her that he was going to stay at Stephanie's house, or maybe Kendall's. He would call and tell her he'd had it with her discouragement and that he was frustrated at her weight gain. Maybe he and Brandon Paul would hit it off and Chase's photo would be in the next round of gossip rags.

"Kelly?" Chase was standing there, his lips slightly parted, a baffled look on his face. "I was talking to you."

"Sorry." She took another deep breath and found the energy to cross the room again. She dropped once more on the edge of the bed and looked at him. "What'd you say?"

"I asked if the girls had anything special going on this week."

Kelly stared at him, not sure if he was serious or not. "Other than Molly's fifth birthday on Friday, you mean?"

"Uh ..." Chase blinked and stuttered a bit. "Exactly. Other than that."

"You forgot."

"I did not." He turned back to the suitcase and sifted through what he'd already packed. "I was distracted, that's all."

"You forgot about your daughter's birthday, Chase. Just admit it." The anger building inside her was the first strong emotion she'd felt all day. It made her feel better, like she at least had control over this.

"I'm busy, okay." His happiness took a momentary backseat to his impatience. "Of course I know when Molly's birthday is. I just forgot it was already coming up this week, that's all."

"Well, it is." Kelly's enthusiasm for an argument died a quick death. "You'll be home by then. Don't worry about it, Chase. I'll make sure everything's set up. A few presents, balloons, a cake and ice cream. The works. All you have to do is be home from Hollywood."

"Thanks." He maintained his frown, clearly concerned with himself for losing track of the weeks. But after a few seconds, he motioned to the bedroom door. "I need a few things from the kitchen. I'll be right back."

For a panicky instant, she wondered if he'd find her cookie dough, but then she relaxed. Not where she hid it in the back of the refrigerator. No one would look there. She stood and walked to the mirror atop their secondhand bedroom dresser. One side of the oak-wood frame was scratched, but otherwise it served its purpose. Kelly could get a look at herself coming and going, marking each day how she got a little farther from her normal weight, a little more out of control. She stared at herself, at the way her sides had filled out and her hips had rounded from her waist.

Why am I doing this to myself, God? She looked into her own eyes and waited. But she heard no divine answers, nothing but the roar of shame and guilt that came with every day she delayed the turnaround. The strange thing was she really didn't want to eat the junk. Honestly, nothing she'd slipped into her mouth had tasted good enough to swap out her health and appearance. But she ate, regardless. Ate almost as if she wanted to kill herself with the food. Or at least kill something about herself. Because when she was bent on eating like this, there was never enough chocolate, enough cookie dough or ice cream bars to fill whatever cavernous hole she was trying to fill. She wasn't hungry, she was broken. Too discouraged to see the sunshine outside.

She heard Chase's returning, and she stepped away from the mirror. Better not to let him catch her looking. The moment might give him pause to reflect on how she'd changed. The lie she told herself was this: if she didn't attract attention to herself, then maybe he wouldn't notice what was happening. In a moment like this it was a lie she believed, so she moved away from the mirror just before he reached the bedroom door.

"Vitamins!" He held up a bottle of One A Days and then tossed it in his open suitcase. "Can't forget these!" He hummed as he grabbed a bag of deodorant and toothpaste from the bathroom.

How is he so happy? she asked herself. *Doesn't he see I'm falling apart?* She watched him, but he was again bouncing-off-the-ceiling happy, looking forward to seeing where God would take their filmmaking, thrilled about spending a week with Keith and Kendall and his new friends. Kelly and her insecurities, her doubts and discouragement, were nowhere on his radar. For that matter, neither were the girls.

Molly and Macy ran into the room, Macy chasing after her older sister and screaming for the doll in Molly's hands. "Mine!" Her voice pierced the air. "My baby!"

"It is not!" Molly held it high, just out of Macy's reach. "It's mine, Mommy. Everyone knows she's mine."

Chase seemed oblivious, packing his shaver into a carry case. Kelly sighed and stooped down to Macy's eye level. "You have the baby with the blue dress. Remember?"

Macy stuck out her lip. "I want that one!"

Kelly thought about how much she was like her youngest daughter, wanting the junk food she couldn't have. It was a problem as old as the Garden of Eden. She pulled Macy close and smoothed her blonde hair. "The pink baby belongs to Molly." She kept her voice calm, something she was working on with the girls. "Now let's go get your dolly, okay?"

With her options dwindling, Macy hesitated for only a few seconds. Then she slipped her hand in Kelly's and stuck out her chin at her sister. "I have Mommy."

Molly looked concerned until Kelly sighed. "You both have me, and I have both of you." She smiled at the girls and then walked Macy to their bedroom and found the blue baby doll. "See?" She held it out for Macy. "This one's best for you, because she's yours."

Macy clung to the doll and pressed it against her face. "Mine."

Kelly dropped to her daughter's bed and closed her eyes. These days her body rode a wild rollercoaster, full of energy one minute, followed by a crash so low she barely had energy to walk through the house. This was one of those moments. Molly skipped into the room, her doll clutched tight to her middle. "See, Macy, that baby's yours."

No longer intent on arguing, Macy only clung to her doll more tightly. "Mine," she said again.

"Girls." Kelly's eyes were open now. "Let's remember that we love each other. You girls are best friends, so let's treat each other that way. That's what Jesus would want." Kelly felt like a hypocrite even as the words passed between her lips. What Jesus would want? Had she even thought about such a thing these past few months? The real issue was her relationship with Chase. What if things did work out for the guys? The risk would shift from a financial struggle to a moral one. What if Chase became too friendly with the beautiful Kendall Adams? Or what if they were suddenly rolling in the money? How could they live a high-end Hollywood lifestyle and still care about the souls of people?

All of it scared Kelly, and drove her to bury her feelings rather than take her doubts to Chase, or even to God.

"Honey? I gotta go," Chase called to her from the kitchen.

"Come on, girls." Kelly felt a hundred years old as she rose to her feet. "Let's say good-bye to Daddy."

"But . . ." Molly's eyes grew wide with concern. "He can't leave. This week is my birthday."

"He'll be back by then." Kelly hoped her smile brought Molly the assurance she needed.

The three of them walked to the kitchen and exchanged a round of hugs with Chase. The buzz of excitement still emanated from him, as if he couldn't wait to get on the road.

"What's the plan for tonight?" Kelly faced him, her arms folded in front of her.

"We're going over the first draft of the screenplay for *Unlocked*. We won't get through it all, but we have most of tomorrow too. Then tomorrow night's the screening at Kendall's."

Kelly nodded slowly. She'd never met Kendall, but she'd googled her and seen pictures. The girl was young, blonde, and stunning—full of the enthusiasm Kelly couldn't quite muster. Everything about her seemed to represent the glitz of Hollywood and the lure of filmmaking. Kelly sighed and tentatively eased her arms around Chase's waist. "Drive safely."

"We will." He lifted her chin with his forefinger. "You okay?"

"Fine." She found the practiced smile, the one that always seemed to make him stop asking questions. "I'm happy for you."

"I want you to be happy for *us*. Me *and* you. If things keep going like this, a year from now we could be in LA. None of these trips."

Kelly tried to picture fitting in with the Hollywood set, starving herself into size-5 jeans and dying her hair blonde like

Kendall's. She would never fit in, and then what? How could she and Chase continue if he wanted that world and she felt alienated by it? She maintained her smile. "Whatever you want, Chase."

"Not me." He leaned in and kissed her softly. "It's what God wants. Every prayer we've lifted to Him, He's answering for us. You watch." His eyes shone. "We're going to do this, baby. We're going to change the world with the power of film. God's letting it happen."

"Then ... I'll keep praying." It was the one thing she could do, even when she didn't feel like talking to God. She would pray. And maybe tomorrow she would toss the junk and try to eat better — salmon and broccoli, egg whites and vegetables, yogurt and flaxseed. She knew the drill. Now she only had to want it badly enough to change.

Chase pulled his suitcase to the front door and gave them all another round of good-byes. "I'll call when we get in tonight."

"You're staying at the Georgian again?" Kelly swung Macy up onto her hip.

"Yes. Same place, same room. Our home away from home."

Turned out Ben Adams knew the owner of the Georgian, so now the guys were getting a much lower rate. A good thing, since their savings were gone and they still had another few months of screenings before a studio might reimburse them for the money they'd invested in *The Last Letter*. Chase hoped that if Brandon Paul liked the movie well enough, they'd get a screening with NTM's home entertainment division, and maybe the film giant would pick up the movie. It was one more area they were praying about.

Kelly, Molly, and Macy stood on the front step and waved as Chase drove away in his used four-door. The girls then wanted to go out back and play on the swings. "Push us, Mommy! Please!" Kelly opened the door for them and promised to be out in a few minutes. When she was alone, she pulled a bowl of M&Ms from the cupboard and set it on the counter. She needed energy if she was going to handle another week of single parenting. She grabbed a small handful of the candies and popped them in her mouth.

"Mommy!" Her girls squealed with delight as she came into view. The yard was small and boxy, the swing set a rusted leftover from the last tenant. But the girls didn't care. For them it was paradise, a playground within a few running steps of the back door. "Push us, Mommy!" Molly was trying to pump her little legs, but she wasn't getting very high.

"Push!" Macy was sitting in the swing next to her sister, clinging to the chains so she wouldn't fall off.

"Hey, not fair. It's my turn!" Molly whined and stuck out her lower lip.

"You'll each get turns." Kelly gave her oldest daughter a look. "You have to be patient with your sister." Kelly pushed Macy a minute or so, and then stepped to the side and pushed Molly. "See ... you each get turns."

While she pushed the girls, Kelly noticed that the yard was overgrown again. But the mower needed new blades or a tune-up. One more thing they couldn't afford. That, and both girls had dentist appointments tomorrow — which meant a fifteen-dollar copay each. She blinked back tears as she kept pushing. *Dear God, I feel so overwhelmed. Please, help me get through this. I can't do this by myself.*

Precious daughter, you're not alone. I am with you always.

The reminder rang clear and true across the lonely places in her heart. On the mission field she'd heard God's voice constantly. But here He was easily drowned out by the noise of merely living. Fresh peace cast light across the moment. *Thank You, Lord ... for seeing me here, for caring.*

"I'm swinging higher than you, Macy." Molly stuck her chin out and kicked her feet high into the air.

"Nah-uh! I'm higher too!"

"Time for a break." Kelly straightened and pressed her hand to her lower back. She hoped for another gentle whisper, but not over the bickering of her little daughters. "Let's go inside and color."

The girls hesitated, but then they grinned at each other, slid down off the swings, and ran laughing into the house, their petty arguments forgotten. Kelly raked her fingers through her shoulder-length dark hair and followed them.

Inside, Molly raced into the kitchen and immediately found the bowl of candy. "Hey!" She pointed to the bowl. "It's M-a-Ms." She giggled. "That's better than coloring, don't you think so?"

Heat rushed to Kelly's cheeks, but she recovered quickly. Molly didn't understand the idea of hiding food, so she wouldn't connect the fact that candy was out now that Daddy was gone. "Candy's for special times." She slid the bowl toward the back of the counter, partly behind a plant and definitely out of sight from the girls' heights. She wanted her girls to eat healthy, to grow up avoiding the junk food that had so often trapped Kelly. "Maybe a few pieces after lunch."

"Mommm." Molly's whine was quick and incessant. "Please, can we have some now?"

"Later." She put her hands on her hips. "And never if you keep whining like that."

Molly took a few seconds to transition, but then she found her happiest, sweetest smile. "Okay, Mommy. Sorry about the whining."

A half an hour of coloring and Kelly was settling the girls down in front of a rerun episode of *Bear in the Big Blue House* when the phone rang. Kelly spotted Chase's phone number on the caller ID, and she smiled. Of course. He would be calling to apologize for not realizing the sacrifices she was making. He was having all the fun, and she was doing the work. Certainly an hour on the road would've been long enough to realize his mistake.

"Hello?" Her voice was pleasant, understanding. "Chase?"

"I'm sorry, babe." He sounded more frustrated than repentant. "Kendall just called. She's arranged a meeting with Brandon and his agent for Friday—it's the only day they're both available."

Her blood ran cold. "Molly's birthday?"

"Yes." His sigh rattled across the phone line. "I'm so sorry. Let's celebrate it Sunday, after I get home."

"She's not two, Chase. She knows what day she turns five, and she'll know you missed it."

"What can I do?" His tone held an edge, as if he didn't expect an argument. "I'd be there if I could, you know that. It's not like—"

"What?"

"Come on, Kelly." A softness crept back into his voice. "I hate this as much as you do. It's a sacrifice we need to make."

"*We?*" The week ahead loomed like a series of cloudy, gray afternoons without the slightest chance of sunshine. "Fine, Chase. Whatever you have to do."

For a long while he didn't say anything. She could hear the rush of wind and traffic in the background, and finally he groaned quietly. "I'm doing my best, baby. You gotta believe that."

Molly and Macy were sitting in the living room, their arms around each other's necks, glued to the TV. The three of them would get through the week, and Kelly would have to come out whole on the other end. What choice did she have? She closed her eyes and pinched the bridge of her nose. "I believe you."

"Okay, then." He sounded relieved. "Let's talk later tonight."

The conversation ended, and Kelly felt the beginning of tears. How could she explain that she didn't want to run their home by herself, that she was tired of being a single mom so much of the time. With all the great news about *The Last Letter* and *Unlocked*, there were still no guarantees. And every step of the way seemed to take Chase further from her, further from the simple missionary life they'd once shared.

God ... are You there? Really? She sniffed and listened, but this time there was nothing. No response, no Bible verses to lend her wisdom or comfort or peace. Suddenly she felt like running—fast and far, somewhere away from the aging little house. She wanted to open up to Chase, but she wouldn't think of telling him about her spiraling battle with discouragement. Depression, even. He wouldn't want to come home at all. But that meant she had little to say. Not to him, and not to herself. She grabbed another fistful of M&Ms and downed them in a single motion. Then she walked to the back of the house, stared out the window, and cried. Not just because of the dark place she'd worked her way into.

But because she no longer knew how to find her way to the light.

KEITH WATCHED HIS FRIEND CLICK HIS cell phone shut and drop it back down on the console between the two seats. A ripple of alarm wrapped around his heart and tightened a little. "How's she doing?" Keith was driving this first leg of the trip. He glanced at Chase, studying his frustration.

"Not happy." Chase anchored his elbow on the window frame and let his head fall into his hands. "Sometimes I think she doesn't understand. The time away's hard on me too."

For a while, neither of them said anything. Then Keith took a long breath and stared at the road straight ahead. "My dad used to tell me life was like an uncooked pizza crust."

Chase gave him a side glance.

"Think about it." Keith sat back in his seat, one hand on the wheel. There was no traffic, and this far out of San Jose the afternoon was blue skies and mid-seventies. He adjusted his sunglasses. "You get one ball of dough for life, and you spend your days rolling it out, making it go as far as it can possibly go." He caught another look at Chase. "As you roll the dough, little cracks develop along the edges. Fix them right away, and there's no problem. But let them go and they'll rip right through the center of the crust."

"That's what your dad used to say?" Chase sounded tired.

"Smart man. Used to make homemade pizza for us once a week. Told the story just about every time." Keith pictured his father, rolling out the crust and stopping every minute or so to fix the edges. "Cracks are like that in pizza and in life. Catch them early, or lose everything you worked for."

Chase dropped his hands to his lap and narrowed his eyes. "Cracks." He angled himself so he could see Keith better. "Like the one between Kelly and me?"

"Exactly." Keith didn't want to make the moment too dramatic. Chase had been struggling in his relationship with Kelly for a while now, and always they seemed to work things out. But if a crack was developing, now was the time to fix it. His expression grew more serious. "Whatever you have to do, Chase, whatever it is, take care of the crack. You and Kelly, your marriage, your family. It's more important than the whole ball of dough. Know what I mean?"

Slowly, Chase nodded. He turned and looked out the side window and again there was quiet in the car. Keith was fine with the lack of conversation. Maybe God was giving Chase a picture in his mind: the pizza maker, rolling out the dough and stopping along the way to smooth out the cracks.

God, speak to him. Give him wisdom where Kelly is concerned. We've come too far to let this movie-making hurt things at home for either of us. Please, God.

I am with you, Son. I am the strong tower you can run to in troubled times. I am here.

The silent answer resonated in Keith's heart, the way it often did. He didn't care if Chase thought the analogy about the pizza crust a little hokey. It was a visual that worked, one that had stayed with Keith since his boyhood days. Keith wasn't truly worried about Chase's marriage. Not now. But that was the beauty of saying something early. Trouble had been splintering the edges for Chase and Kelly long enough. The time had come to do some mending, or watch something far worse develop.

A split that neither of them could repair.

Fourteen

CHASE HARDLY BREATHED DURING THE SCREENING. He could barely take in what was happening around him. He'd never been anywhere like Kendall's house—a plush, expansive tri-level with entire walls of glass, built into the Hollywood Hills. And sitting with him around the room were people he'd once only read about. Kendall and her father, Ben; Stephanie Fitzgerald; and Brandon Paul. Even Luke Baxter had flown in for the week of meetings, confident he could help on a number of levels.

Kelly had asked Chase if he ever felt like his life had become surreal. He'd told her no, that he wasn't overwhelmed by the glitz and glamour of everything happening around him. But here, every few seconds, Chase asked himself what in the world he was doing rubbing elbows with some of the most powerful people in the industry.

The Last Letter seemed to take twice as long to finish, and more than once Chase and Keith exchanged a look that said neither of them could wait for feedback from the people watching. Everything about their future with *Unlocked* hinged on the next few hours.

Chase tried to relax and enjoy the film, but it was impossible. *God, it's in Your hands. Let them love it, and give us success here. Please...*

In response, Chase remembered one of his favorite Bible verses, something from Philippians chapter 4. "Present your requests to God. And the peace of God, which transcends all understanding, will guard your hearts and your minds in Christ Jesus."

Yes, that was it. He needed to place all his questions and fears in the hands of Christ, so that the peace of God would rule over not only this moment but whatever other moments the night held. Success or not.

When the film finally ended, Chase noticed something he hadn't before. Stephanie was crying. She wiped her fingers beneath her eyes and for a long while the group sat in the dark, watching the credits and saying nothing. Stephanie found a tissue from the coffee table and blew her nose. Then she turned to Chase and Keith and grinned bigger than anything she'd given at their first meeting. "That—" She motioned with her elbow toward the large screen, "—was beautiful. Absolutely beautiful." She stood and went to Keith first, and then to Chase, hugging each of them and practically lifting them off the ground. "That's what I'm talking about! I knew you were the right guys. Everything I'd seen and read told me that—your skill and determination, your talent and your faith." She stepped back and let out a loud victory cry. "Thank you, Jesus! We got nothing but sunshine and clear skies ahead. *Unlocked* is going to be amazing!"

The others in the room chuckled at her excitement.

"Hey!" Stephanie spun around and pointed at Brandon. "Don't laugh at me!" She was teasing him, enjoying the moment. "Tell me you didn't get tears all backed up in those beautiful eyes of yours!"

"Okay, okay." Brandon breathed in deeply through his nose. "You're right. It was good."

"I was crying like a baby." Luke tossed his hands and grabbed a tissue.

The sight of their attorney acting as emotional as Stephanie made them laugh and added to the feeling of celebration. Chase listened to the exchange and prayed he wouldn't wake up, prayed he was really hearing this sort of feedback and not lost in the middle of a dream. Keith popped him on the shoulder and grinned. It wasn't a dream. The people gathered in Kendall's screening room loved *The Last Letter*.

"It's everything I knew it would be." Kendall stood and flipped on a light. "What do you think, Dad?"

"Amazing." He pulled himself to his feet and gave first Keith, then Chase a hearty handshake. "You've got my support. Like I said, I'll fund the P&A for a theatrical release on this film, and I'm good for half the money on *Unlocked*."

Chase couldn't breathe. He pressed his leg against the sofa behind him so he wouldn't fall to the floor. The P&A budget was five million dollars, and though Ben had hinted about footing the cost, this was an actual promise. Chase had the feeling he was going to whip out a legal document over chips and salsa later that night. Sure, they still needed to convince the studio executives that *The Last Letter* was worth the financial risk for a theatrical release. But with this sort of reaction, Chase suddenly wasn't worried.

But more than that, Ben's offer to fund half the Brandon Paul movie meant two things. First, they were ready to talk to a studio about the project. And second, they could retain creative control—since providing half the budget would give them that privilege.

Chase could hear people talking around him, but all he could think about was Kelly, how she'd doubted whether they could make movies at this level, at the Brandon Paul level. And how God had proved to all of them that they could.

They moved into the kitchen and then on to the formal dining room, where a housekeeper had set the table with a Mexican dinner. Once they were seated and the food served, Chase and Keith talked at length with the others. Luke Baxter was showing himself to be a skilled professional, an up-and-coming legend in entertainment law. He had already drawn up paperwork for the financials.

"I understand you're available tomorrow also?" Ben took three *taquitos* from the closest platter. "We need something in writing to add to the investment money I've already put in for *The Last Letter*, and of course we need to spell out our deal with Brandon."

"Absolutely." Luke was quick to answer. "I'm in town all week."

Brandon set his fork down. "My agent and attorney want to be in on that. I think we're meeting Friday." He scooped a blob of avocado dip onto his plate. "My agent's going to want a polished screenplay before we commit to anything with a studio."

So many pieces to the puzzle. Chase felt dizzy, and not the least bit hungry even as everyone around him dove into their meals. The conversation didn't turn back to movies again until after dinner.

"Brandon." Kendall was sitting on Chase's other side. "Why don't you tell the producers your story. The one most people don't know."

Chase was dying to know more about the kid. They were about to invest millions of dollars into the guy—that and their futures as filmmakers. He and Keith knew little about the actor, only what was common knowledge in the magazines. Brandon was twenty-two, but he could convincingly play a high school kid. He'd come onto the scene as part of an NTM series about a high school jock who was really the son of a European king. *Prince Jake* was the series, and it had blown away the expectations of NTM. Prince Jake's image was on everything from pop cans to pizza boxes, T-shirts to bath towels. Brandon Paul could sing, dance, and act, and he was a teen heartthrob like the country hadn't seen in three decades. The only black mark was Brandon's younger sister, Paisley, who was also in show business but who had occasional drug trouble, according to the tabloids. But Chase had never found out more than that.

Brandon's eyes revealed little emotion. He was comfortable with this story, but clearly he didn't enjoy telling it. "My parents don't agree with my acting career. They homeschooled us and hoped that my sister and I would attend Harvard, get doctorate degrees, and find a cure for cancer. I call and tell them how things are going, but they don't watch my stuff, and they don't take it seriously." He gave a single shrug. "It is what it is."

"Tell them about your sister." Kendall's tone was soft.

"Right." He exhaled slowly. "We used to be very close. My parents didn't approve of our acting, but at least we had each other. But that wasn't enough for Paisley. She wanted my parents' acceptance so badly." He exhaled and stared at his lap for a long minute. When he looked up, the pain was there for all of them to see. "She's a drug user. Heroin. She'll surface for a few months, stay clean, and get a commercial or an extra role in a movie. But then she's gone again. Living on the streets, sharing needles with strangers. She goes by a different last name. The press doesn't know the half of it."

Chase's heart broke for the guy, and all he and his sister had lost because of their parents' narrow-minded attitude.

Brandon squinted as if he could keep out some of the pain. "Funny how people think money's the answer. I'll never live long enough to spend mine, but it can't help Paisley. Not until she wants the help. Every job, every day I'm on set, I feel like I'm living for both of us. Like I owe it to her."

Chase thought for a moment. In some ways Brandon's story reminded him of Dayne Matthews. A young guy without the support of his parents. The only difference was that Dayne's adoptive parents had been killed when he was eighteen in a single-engine plane crash. Still, the two actors would have common ground. Brandon might really benefit from the strength and faith of someone like Dayne.

Kendall was explaining that Brandon wasn't actually a Christian. "Not yet, anyway." She patted Brandon's hand. "I'm working on him."

"I'm open. It's just ..." His eyes grew distant. "I'm not quite sure God believes in me. You know?"

There was a general sense of acknowledgment about how Brandon felt, and Keith admitted that he had been through a time like that during his final years of high school. "I'd been taught about God all my life, but those few years, I wasn't sure what I believed."

"Exactly." Brandon gave a slow nod. "I guess you could say I'm searching."

"For now." Kendall's smile toward Brandon was kind and full of warmth.

"Yes." He chuckled. "For now."

Keith took over the conversation, engaging both Brandon and Ben about the themes of *Unlocked* and how they would play out on the screen. But before the talk could get too serious, too focused, Ben stood and smiled at the group. "You know what we need?"

Chase had no idea.

"A good old-fashioned ping-pong tournament." He grinned at Kendall. "My daughter's just about unbeatable. And I find nothing gets the imagination going better than a few rounds of table tennis."

They all laughed, and Chase and Keith joined the others on a walk out back and down a sidewalk to an outbuilding — this one holding two ping-pong tables and a half a dozen sofas anchored to the perimeter of the room. "It used to be a storage place for my father's boats." Kendall smiled as they went inside. "A few years ago we turned it into a ping-pong room."

Chase had never seen anything like it. A dry-erase board hung on the wall near the closest table, and scribbled across it was a tally sheet of some kind. Kendall laughed again. "My dad's pretty competitive. We keep track of the games we play in a year."

"Because one of these years I'm gonna beat her, by golly." Ben searched a shelf near the entrance to the room and grabbed a red paddle. "This is my baby. I call it The Blade."

Chase loved this. Who would've thought that movie people at this level would spend their evenings playing ping-pong?

Stephanie grabbed a paddle similar to Ben's. "I'm not so bad myself." She twirled the paddle in her hand and aimed it at Kendall. "Let's see who's queen of this palace."

"We'll sit out the first round." Keith nodded at Chase and the two of them took the nearest sofa. "So we can size up the competition."

That left Kendall and Stephanie on one table and Ben and Brandon on the other. Kendall seemed to go easy on Stephanie, and halfway through the game, the author was up by two points. But then it was like Kendall found another gear. She began using a spin-type serve and slamming the ball instead of returning it.

"Oooh, girlfriend's got game." Stephanie raised her hands and did a little victory dance on behalf of Kendall's play. "I don't mind losing to someone with skill, no, sir."

On the other table, Ben was giving Brandon a fight. But youth had its advantage, and the game was leaning hard in Brandon's favor. Chase liked Brandon's style—all offense and risk. It was the way they'd been forced to play the game of movie-making.

But even still, he kept finding his attention turning to Kendall. She laughed as easily as she breathed, and besides being a skilled player she had an infectious confidence about her. As if she never really doubted the fact that she'd win the game, any more than she doubted the fact that the movies she wanted to make with Chase and Keith would be successful beyond their wildest dreams.

If only Kelly could be like that, Lord—confident and convinced. Believing in the work we have ahead of us.

As soon as the thought passed through his mind, Chase roped it back and chastised himself. He couldn't compare Kendall and Kelly, not now or ever. Kendall had been born into the world of wealth and movies, so of course she was calmer about the risks ahead, more certain. Kelly knew only that they'd run up their credit cards and borrowed money they couldn't afford to repay to help fund *The Last Letter*. She was alone with the girls too often, and she wasn't happy about it. That much was obvious from the strain between them.

If they were going to work with Kendall and her father, Chase couldn't for one minute nurture a growing interest in anything about Kendall. Period.

Keith worked in on the next round, taking on Brandon, while Ben matched up against Stephanie. That left Chase and Kendall.

"I'm thirsty." She motioned for Chase to follow her. "Help me bring in a flat of water bottles."

Once they were outside, Kendall's pace slowed. Her eyes danced in the moonlight as she looked at him. "You're the real deal, Chase Ryan. I admire you."

He tried not to feel overly flattered. "Why?"

"Because." Their conversation was easy, comfortable. "Your ambitions and dreams, your mission for making movies that will change lives." She breathed in slowly and gazed at the stars overhead. "It's all going to happen. I've prayed about this for a long time, and I can feel it."

Chase tried not to focus on her pretty face, her confidence. For a moment he looked straight ahead toward the house. But then his eyes met hers again. "Sometimes it's hard to believe."

"Well, believe it." Her smile worked its way through him. "One day soon all of Hollywood will want a part of this, of what you and Keith are starting right here."

Their pace slowed almost to a standstill. Chase had been curious about her, but there'd never been a time to ask until now. "What about you, Miss Kendall? What drives you to be a part of all this?"

She thought for a second, her long blonde hair blowing gently in the night breeze. "Redemption, I guess. I've seen a lot of heartache in this town." Her smile was laced with sorrow, an expression that seemed to hold more than she was willing to reveal. "I want my days in this business to matter, I guess. Just like you."

They reached the house, and Kendall punched in a code near the third garage door, causing it to open. She moved toward a stack of water pallets. Chase tried to reach it before her, so she wouldn't think about carrying it. But as he bent to take hold of the top box, his right hand touched hers.

"I've ... I've got it."

"I can help." She looked at him, locked eyes, and for the flicker of an instant Chase felt it. An attraction between them that terrified him. He adjusted his grip on the box and heaved it into his arms. "Don't be silly."

Kendall seemed to try to hide her alarm, but it was there. She moved quickly back to the open garage door. "Thanks. I ... didn't mean for you to carry it by yourself."

The walk back to the rec building passed much quicker. They talked about ping-pong and her father's determination to beat her. But not once then or at any time during the rest of the night did he see the vulnerability she'd revealed to him on their earlier walk.

When they were finished playing and after they'd all downed a number of water bottles, they went outside and looked at the lights from the Hollywood Hills. Chase stood next to Keith, but Kendall had positioned herself on his other side — some distance away. "It's pretty, isn't it?"

"Mmmm. Yes." Chase looked from her to his friend. He wanted to ask Kendall more about her earlier comments, about all she'd seen in Hollywood. But this wasn't the place. "What do you think, Keith? Beautiful up here, huh?"

"Definitely. The perfect Hollywood home."

After a few minutes, Brandon and Stephanie announced that they had to get going.

"Well, then ..." Ben held his arms out. "Let's pray." He waited while the others circled up around him.

By the time Chase realized who he was standing next to and what was about to happen, it was too late. He kept his gaze away from Kendall's as they linked hands, and once more he tried not to think about the way her fingers felt against his.

Ben bowed his head. "We have much to be thankful for, much to ask of our Mighty God. We never imagined we'd be here, on the verge of a making a movie that the world will want to see, a movie that has the power to bring new life to everyone who sees it."

His prayer went on another minute and it ended with Stephanie adding a few heartfelt words. "*Unlocked* is a movie that could change the way people think. It could send them running into Your arms if we do things right." She spent a few seconds thanking God, praising Him. "We come before You, ready to hear Your voice. Whatever You ask. In Jesus' name."

"Amen." Kendall clapped, immediately releasing Chase's hand. She grinned at the others. "The glory of God. That's the only reason we're all here."

Chase tried to forget the attraction he'd felt earlier. There could be nothing more than friendship and business between him and Kendall. They were going to do what they'd set out to do, taking Hollywood by storm. And along the way they would accomplish the only goal that really mattered.

The goal to change lives with the power of film.

THE NIGHT HAD GONE BETTER THAN Kendall ever imagined—with the exception of one thing. Her attraction to Chase. She'd already warned herself about him, but she had to be more careful. Not that there was any real danger. He was happily married, and she wouldn't consider crossing the line of friendship. Her faith and her past wouldn't allow even the hint of that. But still she needed to watch herself.

The movie had been amazing, of course, as she'd known it would be.

After Brandon and Stephanie left, Kendall's father took off too. That left Kendall, Keith, and Chase. Kendall wasn't ready to call it a night. They still had the first draft of the screenplay to look over. She led them into a softly lit den and produced three copies of the script, one for each of them. Before they got started, Keith excused himself so he could call home. Kendall thought about telling Chase that maybe he should call home too. After all, this was exactly the sort of alone moment with Chase she needed to avoid. But she didn't want to seem too personal, so she took the farthest seat from Chase.

As he looked over the script, Kendall studied him and realized again that he was very attractive. He would stand out in the industry once he and Keith made a name for themselves. His athletic build and chiseled face would become recognizable in no time, and there would be offers to stray. Dramatic offers. She knew because they'd come her way more than once. She bit her lip and felt compelled to pray for him.

Please, God, help him be strong when temptation comes. Help me too. We need to stay close to You.

She leaned on the arm of the sofa. "Tell me about your wife. She must be wonderful, holding down things at home while you're out here following your dream."

"She is." Chase hesitated, but only briefly. "She's my best friend. I hope someday soon we can move down here. Then she can come to meetings like this, and at the end of the day we can be home together." He looked more composed than earlier, when they went for the water in the garage. "I think you'd like her."

"Me too." Kendall ignored the hint of envy. "It's rare, being married to your best friend." Kendall wasn't sure now was the time to tell Chase about her own sad past. Maybe later, when Keith was with them. The guys would both benefit from hearing the story at some point. For now she only wanted Chase to know she supported his marriage. "Don't ever let this business get in the way of what matters. It happens too often."

He smiled, and determination resonated in his expression. "Keith calls it the pizza-crust philosophy. Fix the small breaks along the edges so you don't get a crack straight down the middle."

She laughed out loud and nodded. "Exactly."

Keith joined them again, and they reviewed the highlights of the screenplay. They talked another hour about the pacing of *Unlocked* and how crazy things were bound to get. But long after the guys left, Kendall continued to pray for them. She went outside and sat on her patio deck, staring at the stars overhead and begging God to protect them against the devil's schemes. They were playing with high stakes and there were bound to be pitfalls along the way. Disappointments and discouragement, distraction and temptations.

She peered up at the vast sky and felt the closeness of the Lord. "God, please help me make this experience one that glorifies You," she whispered. "Help me do my part to keep all of us walking the narrow path." Her own personal life might not have been a shining example of God's love and commitment. But she couldn't help that. What she could do was help her new friends stay the course.

Because it would do no good to win the world through the message of a movie only to lose themselves in the process.

Fifteen

ANOTHER MONTH HAD PASSED AND STILL Cody was getting nowhere with Bailey. He was stuck in the middle of a debate in his sociology class, and his leg ached where the prosthetic piece fit up against his flesh—a sign the weather was about to change. Last week's warm temperatures had dropped so that here, at the end of March, winter felt like it had never given an inch in its tug-of-war with spring.

"What I'm saying is I can't support our troops in a situation like the war in Iraq. Our nation is practically fascist the way it attacks other nations without reason." The student speaker was a wiry guy with glasses and a loud voice. He had short hair and a clean-cut look that defied his views. "It's not about patriotism, it's about common sense." He was on his feet, staring down anyone who dared differ with him. "No one forced those men and women to enlist. They knew what they were getting into when they signed up. A losing conflict, and an ill-fated attempt at tearing down a society because of nothing more than fear."

Cody rolled his eyes. Since the spring quarter had begun, the professor had little control of the class. Days that were earmarked for lectures often became all-out debates, typically on topics involving war or terrorism or the rights of Americans to express their dislike of the United States. The professor was a woman who liked to point out that half of Hollywood would've left the country if the wrong president had won the recent election. Nearly every debate was sparked by the guy with the glasses. Peter something. Cody couldn't remember his name.

"How about that, class?" The professor's political viewpoint could swing either way. She sat behind her desk, her hands folded. Outside a chill wind whistled against the windows of the classroom. "Anyone have a differing viewpoint?"

Cody preferred to think about Bailey, about finding a way to connect with her again. He didn't want the task of facing off with the radical kid in his class, but someone had to do it. He hadn't gone to Iraq and lost his leg so that he could take a backseat when his country's freedom was being discussed. "I was one of those guys who enlisted in the army after high school."

A hush fell over the class. Across the room, Peter slowly took his seat, one eyebrow raised suspiciously in Cody's direction. The professor nodded. "Go on, Cody."

"I enlisted because I believe in the United States of America, in her freedoms for all people, and in her strength as a nation of peace, prosperity, and human dignity." His voice took on a strength that built as he continued. "I enlisted because I was then, and I am now, willing to risk my life to defend this nation. Because this country will fall into enemy hands if our generation is not willing to take a stand."

"Rhetoric," Peter mumbled under his breath.

"No." Cody's voice sharpened. He stood and took a step toward his fellow classmate. "Not rhetoric. The battle for freedom is real, one that requires people to act on what's right."

"War in Iraq?" The kid didn't seem as sure of himself as before. "That's what you think is right?"

"No war is right, but sometimes ..." Cody shifted to take some of the pressure off his prosthetic leg. "Sometimes war is necessary. In order to defend the privileges and freedoms we have as Americans."

He paused, not sure if he should go on. Finally he decided he'd said enough, but even as he lowered himself to his seat, a few guys at the far end of the classroom stood and began to clap. A girl and another guy joined them, and then most of the front two rows. Ten seconds passed while one student after another rose to their feet and joined in the applause. Finally only Cody and Peter and the professor remained seated.

The outpouring was more than Cody had imagined, and it touched him deeply. Even so, by the time the class was over, Cody felt exhausted, drained from the emotional battle of defending himself and his decision to serve. He was finished with his classes for the day, and he needed fresh air to clear his head. Snow still clung to the ground in patches, but the grass showed through along the campus mall. He took the long way around, purposefully walking past the football stadium and the practice field. A group of guys dressed in sweats were throwing the ball, working with a couple of coaches near the fifty yardline.

Cody stopped and watched.

Wasn't it just yesterday that he'd been the guy throwing the ball? Before Iraq, before he lost his leg? Back then he and Bailey had been more like brother and sister, and he'd known for sure he'd play football at the college level somewhere. But the offers didn't come the way Cody had imagined, and with his home life a mess, enlisting seemed like the best option. It still seemed that way.

While he was in Iraq his existence had centered around surviving one day to the next. But now that he was home... his ideas about the future had shifted with every quarter. He'd thought about being a doctor, and then maybe a firefighter or a paramedic—if they'd take him with his prosthetic lower leg. He even considered going into law so he could help defend freedom in a different way.

But standing here facing the football field, he felt a certain familiarity, one that had filled him and consumed him more often lately. He wanted to be a football coach. Like Jim Flanigan, he wanted to spend his days around the game he loved, influencing kids so that a generation of young men would grow up understanding sacrifice, hard work, and dedication. The sorts of things that came through in the game of football.

Yes, that's what he wanted to do. He would teach high school history and coach football, and he would pray to be an influence for generations of kids like himself. Kids drawn to drinking and partying, kids with little or no family influence who would be lost without the coaches and role models in their lives.

His vision blurred and he could almost see himself working with the quarterbacks and receivers, teaching them how to look for the open man and throw a ball downfield.

Teaching them about life.

He kept walking and as he turned away from the football field, another image came to mind. The face of Bailey Flanigan. She had to be part of this future too. But she was still dating Tim, still barely returning his text messages, and rarely answering his calls. She had a wall up around her heart, and he didn't know how to tear it down. If he could convince her to trust him again, then he could figure out her relationship with Tim, whether she was really in love with him. A thought that terrified him.

He kept his eyes down as he walked the path to the parking lot and found his car. He needed time away from campus, away from his constant search for Bailey between classes. He had a new job at the grocery store in Clear Creek, bagging food and helping people out to their cars. It paid more than the last one and helped him keep up his end of the rent. But today he had four hours before his shift, so he took the turn to Lake Monroe.

The leaves were just starting to bud out on the trees that lined the two-lane highway. Spring wanted a chance, if only the cold temperatures would let up. He reached the water and parked in his favorite lot, the one near the footpath that circled the lake. For five minutes he walked hard and fast over the trail, ignoring the pain in his leg, until he reached an outcropping of rock, a place where he'd come before to think and talk to God. He walked out onto it and sat down on a smooth, flat area. A breeze blew across the water and stung at his eyes, but he didn't care.

God, I have so many questions. So many unknowns about tomorrow. He squinted against the wind and lifted his eyes to the clear blue beyond the lake. *Your Word says You have great plans for me, to give me a future and hope and not to harm me. But how do I know which way to turn?*

My son, do not be troubled ... Do not be afraid ...

The words whispered to him in the rustling of tree branches on either side of the rocky point. As if God were indeed here with him, holding him up and encouraging him.

Sometimes he wanted a new start, a new university a thousand miles away from Bailey and his life in Bloomington. A place where people wouldn't know him as the GI who came home without his lower left leg. Where he wouldn't have to look for Bailey every time he walked out of class. But then, he'd only miss her more.

She belongs to someone else, God. Why can't I get her out of my head?

Wait on me, my son. Remember the fruits of the Spirit.

Cody closed his eyes and the words came back to him, words Jenny Flanigan had drilled into the minds of her kids, including him when he lived with them. *Love, joy, peace, patience, goodness, kindness, gentleness, thoughtfulness, and self control.* "If you truly seek God's plans for your life," she would tell them every day or so, "then your life will show fruit." And she'd go into the list again. *Love, joy, peace ...*

Patience was one of the fruits, but Cody was tired of being patient. He had a few friends, guys he'd played football with at Clear Creek High, but most of the old team was into heavy partying now. He'd rather stay home and study. But today—today he wanted the friendship of Bailey and her family so intensely he could feel the ache with every breath.

Show me, God. I want to be her friend. I can't lose her now.

Again the fruits of the spirit flashed in his mind. *Love and joy, peace and patience, goodness and kindness...* Maybe that was it. If he was going to show those fruits to the world, then he needed to stop avoiding the Flanigans. He'd turned his back on the family as surely as he'd turned his back on Bailey. Regret surrounded him. Ricky's tests had shown he didn't need another open heart surgery. Not yet. But he might someday soon. How could Cody justify staying away when tomorrow wasn't guaranteed to any of them?

He stood and breathed in deeply. God was here with him; Cody could feel His presence. And at least now he had a plan. Bailey could be busy with Tim, but that didn't mean he had to stay away from her family.

They were his family, too, and they always would be.

He walked with determination back to his car and made just one stop on the way out to the Flanigans'—his mother's house. He parked out front and stood on the porch, knocking, waiting.

"Mom?" The door was unlocked, and when she didn't answer it he went inside. "You home?" He heard something in the back bedroom, but she still didn't answer. "Mom?"

He'd made a point of spending more time with her—especially since Christmas. Their trip to see *Scrooge* had been sort of a new beginning, but every time he came to see her he had his doubts that maybe she was using drugs again. She was an addict, same as him. That meant the temptation would always be there.

He walked past the kitchen and there on the counter was something that stopped him cold.

A small mirror, and in the stream of light from the window he could see the hint of white dust on it. He didn't want to think so, but the mirror had the distinct look of something someone had used for cocaine. He grabbed hold of it and glanced around the counter for a razor blade — which would pretty much guarantee his suspicions. But there was nothing. He carried the mirror toward the bedroom. "Mom?"

"Yes!" She sounded too cheerful. "I'm in here."

He followed her voice into the bedroom and found her bustling about, making her bed and straightening her pillows. "Sorry." She stopped and put her hands on her hips, breathing deeply. "I didn't hear you. Today's cleaning day."

The last thing he wanted was to ask about the mirror, but he had to. She needed to know that he was watching, checking her behavior. He held it out to her. "I found this on the counter."

She hesitated for half a second. "Oh, that. It goes in my bathroom. I set my perfumes on it." She took it from him. "I was going to spray it with Windex, and I got distracted."

He released it to her and studied her for another half a minute. "I never noticed it before."

"I've had it forever." She hustled the mirror into her bathroom and came back empty handed, brushing her palms against her jeans. "So much to do. The place was a mess."

Cody wanted to believe her. A mirror, in and of itself, was not proof that his mother was doing cocaine or any other drug. But he had reason to wonder. Every other time she'd been released from prison she went back to using. He had prayed this time would be different, and so far he believed it was. But she needed the strength of Christ, same as he did. "You going to church with me this weekend?"

"Of course." She laughed easily. "Church and Sunday school." She'd found one for recovering addicts, and combined with her midweek drug classes, she seemed more grounded than before.

But still Cody worried. "Okay, then." He came to her and kissed her cheek. "I was just driving by. Thought I'd check on you."

"I'm fine, silly, but thanks for stopping." She didn't mention the drugs. Neither of them liked talking about the possibility. "My neighbor Linda invited me for dinner, so I have to get my cleaning done before then. She's a widow, you know. The two of us keep each other company."

Cody hung around another few minutes before leaving. His mother's quick actions and rattling conversation worried him, but he hoped she was telling the truth.

As he left he checked the clock on his dashboard. He still had more than two hours before his work shift, and only one place he really wanted to go.

He pulled into the Flanigans' driveway ten minutes later, parked his car in the familiar place, and walked the length of the covered porch to the front door. Jim met him and the two hugged. "I've stayed away too long," Cody said as he stepped inside.

"Way too long." Jim welcomed him in. "Can you stay for dinner?"

"Maybe this weekend." He looked Jim straight into the eyes. "I miss you guys a lot."

Jenny met up with them in the kitchen. "Cody! I can't believe you're here."

At the sound of his name, the five Flanigan boys hurried into the kitchen and surrounded Cody with pats on the back and challenges for a football game or a square off in a game of 21 on the basketball court. Ricky looked happy and healthy, and a sense of deep gratitude filled Cody's heart.

They played a round of Wii Mario Kart, and when Ricky had soundly beaten all of them, they went out front and played three-on-three on the basketball court. Cody found his place among them as easily as he had the first time he set foot in their home. The Flanigans loved him. No matter how much time passed, they always would.

Not until he was on his way out the door to his work shift did Jenny ask if he'd talked to Bailey. Jenny, more than the others, seemed to understand the feelings Cody had for the only Flanigan daughter.

"She doesn't talk to me much." He smiled, but he could feel the sadness in his eyes. "I made the mistake of ignoring her for a while, trying to give her and Tim space." He made a face. "It backfired, though. Now she doesn't trust me."

Jenny was quiet for a moment. Finally she put her hand on Cody's shoulder and gave him an understanding smile. "I know my daughter, and I know how much she cares for you." She tilted her head, weighing her next words. "Be patient. You and Bailey are young. Don't give up on her friendship just yet."

Her words resonated deep inside his soul. On the way to work, he couldn't get past the theme of the afternoon. *Patience.* He wasn't sure how that would play out in the weeks and months ahead, but he was sure of one thing: if God wanted him to be patient, he would be patient because Bailey was worth the wait.

Even if all he had to look forward to was her friendship.

Sixteen

ANDI HAD KEPT HER CONVERSATIONS WITH her parents to a minimum. Dad was so busy and her mom had too many questions about whether she was going to church and what she was reading in her Bible and whether she was dating or not. How could she break it to her parents that she hadn't opened her Bible once since Christmas?

But this was the last day of March, her father's birthday, and as she sat in her dorm room alone she suddenly missed him more than she had in a long time. She called him and smiled when he picked up on the first ring. "Daddy!" She wasn't the girl she'd once been, but in this moment she sounded the same, like nothing had changed. "Happy birthday!"

"Andi! Thanks, sweetheart. I wondered if I'd hear from you today."

"Where are you?"

"At home. We've been back and forth to LA almost every week, taking meetings around town, making plans and getting details in place for the next film."

"So it's really going to happen?" Andi felt a thrill run down her spine. "Brandon Paul and the whole deal?"

Her dad laughed. "We're meeting with him and NTM tomorrow."

"What?" Andi was on her feet, pacing the small floor of her dorm room. "I wanna be there! Who's starring opposite him?"

He rattled off a list of NTM stars, girls with years of experience. "It'll be a known name, for sure."

Andi felt the disappointment. She'd read the book *Unlocked* twice, and she loved the storyline. Two brothers—one a high school football star, the other a young autistic boy who couldn't connect with anyone until his brother's friend—involved in musical theater—reached out. With the power of music, the doors of autism were unlocked and a bridge built between the two brothers. "Can I at least read for the part?"

"Honey." There was no budging in her father's voice. "This is an NTM film, with NTM stars. Everyone will be a household name."

"But how do you become a household name if no one gives you a break?" She didn't want to sound whiny, but what good was it for her father to make movies if she didn't at least get a try when it came to casting?

"You wait your turn. And in your case, you finish school first." He lightened his tone. "How's the quarter going?"

"Great. Rehearsals are about to begin for *Robin Hood*." She was Maid Marian—a bigger part even than her role as Isabelle in *Scrooge*. But Tim hadn't gotten the part of *Robin Hood*. He was one of the merry men instead, so she was working mostly with kids she didn't know. "My grades are good and I'm caught up."

"What about your social life? You told your mom you were sort of seeing someone?" Her dad sounded awkward now, as if he really didn't want to know.

"His name is Taz. He's a film student." She wasn't ready to be fully honest about Taz or her feelings for him. She definitely wasn't going to tell her dad about the student film she was about to shoot. "He's interesting. I like hanging out with him. Nothing serious."

The conversation lasted a little longer, and Andi wished him happy birthday again before hanging up. Only then did she exhale and sink back onto her bed. It was a lot of work, keeping up even this much of a facade for her parents. But she had no choice. If they knew about Taz's strange way of thinking or the role she was about to take in his film, they'd be on the first plane to Indianapolis. They'd probably pull her from school. No need to worry them. She was entitled to explore a little. That's what college was about.

She glanced at Bailey's side of the room and wondered what her friend was doing. It was Friday midday, and that evening in a small classroom on campus Andi would film her first few scenes for Taz. Bailey was probably out with Tim, talking about the book of Romans or sharing a latte at the coffee shop off campus. Later tonight Tim would probably take her to a movie or hang out with her at the Flanigan house. Good and wholesome, her sweet friend Bailey.

Andi wanted more out of life.

She'd thought Cody might be the guy for her. Following his lead would've been one way she could've stayed on the straight and narrow, believing in God and His plans and the same old lines she'd believed all her life. But Cody wasn't interested and she certainly wasn't going to stay in her room alone, reading her Bible.

She finished her homework in two hours and checked the time on her phone. She was supposed to meet Taz and his team in less than an hour. She changed her outfit and slipped into her tightest jeans, a tank top, and a pull-over sweater. The scene called for her to look rebellious, so she darkened her eye makeup and added three extra layers of mascara. Even when she was satisfied with her makeup, she put her cosmetics in a travel bag and slipped them into her backpack. Taz had said to bring them, just in case they needed more.

Her decision to make the film was an easy one, especially after she read the screenplay. Her character was a good girl who only wanted to experience more of life. More than her parents were willing to let her experience. If Andi could relate to any character right now it was the teenaged girl Taz had dreamed up for his student film. If that wasn't enough, Taz had shown her three of his previous student films, and Andi was blown away. The quality and depth of his movie-making was on the level of some of the top independent films around. She was honored to take the role, and Taz had promised her the partial nudity was nothing. A quick shot, necessary for the integrity of the film. Bra and jeans — so hardly any real nudity at all.

"You'd show more skin in a bathing suit," he'd told her.

Andi stared at the mirror. Her father's words came back to her. Wait her turn. Wait for the very chance he held in his hands — the chance to star opposite Brandon Paul. She felt the bitterness of her disappointment. Her own father wasn't willing to help her. Fine.

Details of the night ahead played in her mind. "Tonight's for me," she whispered at her reflection. "I'll show everyone."

What better way than to star in Taz's film. She could make a name for herself and get the recognition she obviously needed. Then maybe it would be her turn. She'd show NTM and the film industry and her father — all at the same time. She wanted to be like the real-life NTM princesses, the girls who snagged all the roles and were idolized by little girls all over the country.

Andi studied her features. She had the looks, right? But NTM stars had been auditioning in Hollywood since they were old enough to walk. Andi? She'd been stuck in the jungles. She felt her determination double. Never mind her late start. College would give her the chance to show the world she was a skilled actress even without the experience.

On her way out the door, Rachel Baugher's journal caught her eye. How long had it been since she'd flipped through the pages of her friend's final words? She hesitated and walked to her dresser. For a long time she stared at Rachel's photo on the front, the same one that hung on her wall. Poor Rachel, who'd never lived long enough to experience life. Andi felt the loss of her friend like she hadn't felt it in months. She opened the spiral-bound book to someplace in the middle and began to read.

"As a camel kneels before his master to have him remove his burden at the end of the day, so kneel each night and let the Master take your burden." The quote was written in Rachel's painstakingly neat printing, surrounded by white space above and below so that the words stuck out on the page. The idea was nice, and a few years ago Andi would've agreed. Kneel before God and He'll take your burdens.

But Andi's burdens were different now. She wanted to be a movie star. Most days she couldn't understand how college was getting her any closer to her goal, with the exception of one thing—the movie she was going to make with Taz. Film projects like that would give her experience and open doors that simple prayer could never open.

Andi was sure of it.

She closed Rachel's journal and set it back down on her dresser. But after a few seconds she slid it to the back of her top drawer, along with the framed photo of her friend. Rachel was gone. Looking at her face each day only confused her. And with the opportunity Taz was giving her, she couldn't afford to feel confused. She shut the drawer and hurried from her dorm out across campus to the theater building.

When she reached the door of the classroom Taz had reserved for the film project, she saw there was dark paper taped across the small window. She smiled. Taz had promised her privacy. She knocked, and he opened the door after only a few seconds. His smile warmed her heart. "You're early."

"In case you needed me." She felt suddenly breathless, excited about what lay ahead. The screenplay was truly cutting edge, relevant and honest. This would be her biggest role yet, and she wanted to prove she was up to the task.

Taz touched his fingers to her cheeks. "I always need you, Andi." His voice was low and smooth, for her alone. "Make no mistake about that." He ushered her into the room where several other people worked to set up the shoot. Two college kids assembled oversized lights near a quasi-set consisting of a bed, a nightstand, and a mirrored dresser. In another corner of the room a student worked on a sound panel, testing a wireless microphone.

Relief washed over Andi. In the back of her mind she hadn't quite dismissed Bailey's warning—that maybe Taz wasn't legitimate, that he was some kind of weirdo, wanting her to strip in a student film. Now Andi could see Bailey would've approved. Nothing shady about the shoot whatsoever.

"You feeling it?" Taz turned to her. He touched his fingers to her shoulders and ran them lightly down the length of her arms.

She felt her cheeks grow hot. She felt his presence like a physical force—if that's what he meant.

He grinned. "The character, I mean? Are you feeling the character?"

Again she relaxed. "Of course. I've studied the script ten times this week."

"Good." He came closer, looking her over. "A little more eyeliner." He walked around her, looking over her outfit. "I'd like to tease out your hair a little. It looks too clean-cut the way it is."

She nodded, quick to agree. "I wasn't sure how to change that."

"I can take care of it." He called to a female student working over a clipboard in another part of the room. "Norma, can you do some touch-up?"

"Of course." The girl gave Taz a flirty smile.

A sense of pride came over Andi as she watched Taz. He wasn't interested in the girl or anyone else. He only had eyes for her.

When Norma was satisfied with Andi's hair and makeup, the two of them returned to the classroom. The lighting guys notified Taz that they were ready and then hung back, lost in their own quiet dialogue. A sound-proof observing area adjoined the room, and Taz ordered the crew into that space. "Places." His voice was confident, methodical. Not a bark like most directors. "Quiet on the set."

Other scenes would be shot on campus in daylight. Two were set to be filmed in a Bloomington diner. But tonight's scenes would be the most intense, where Andi's character was melting down and making choices about leaving home. Andi could relate to the character a little more each day.

"Andi..." Taz came to her and again touched his fingers to her cheek. His gentle caress sent electricity down her arms and legs. "You ready, love?"

She swallowed. "I am." This was her break. She'd show everyone.

"Okay, take your place."

Andi stood and smoothed the wrinkles in her shirt. She caught her reflection in the mirror and held it for a moment. What was that look in her eyes? Guilt? Anger took the lead in her emotions. Guilt should be the last thing she was feeling. She wasn't doing anything wrong. She blinked and tried to work herself into character.

Only one other student remained in the room where the filming was taking place—the cameraman, already positioned behind the enormous lens.

"Now remember..." Taz stood a few feet away, his eyes locked on hers. "You've just had a falling out with your mother, and you're sick of her rules, sick of your life. You want to run away." Taz's words were slow and melodic, mesmerizing. "You're angry, trapped, ranting at your fate. But then slowly, gradually, you focus on your image in the mirror. For the first time you see that you're beautiful, and that maybe your body is your ticket out. You could model or act. As you study your reflection, you slowly start to remove your clothes. First the pullover, then the tank top ... until all that remains is your bra. Hold that pose until I cut."

Andi knew her lines and her character's motivation. She had read the part too many times to count, wrestling with whether she should do it before realizing she had no choice. These were the stepping stones actresses had to take if they were going to reach the top. Besides, the film was sensual, and the storyline demanded this scene. At least from an artsy point of view.

Taz took a few steps back, "Okay, tell us when you're ready."

Andi thought about the teenaged girl, the struggle she felt against her parents. They couldn't tell her how to live or when to be home. She wanted to make her own rules for once, to be someone of her own creating. She waited as the character came to life inside her, and she gave a nod to the camera.

"Quiet!" Taz held up his hand. "Three, two, one ... rolling. Action."

Andi stormed into her room and flopped down on her bed, her arm crooked over her eyes. After a few seconds she sat up, angry, trapped. She exhaled hard and looked around the room, searching for a way out. The corkboard with school photos tacked to it, the simplicity of the bedspread across the foot of her bed. Same old thing, every day. She stood and made a face at the walls around her, at the familiarity of it. Slowly she moved to the window and grabbed the faux windowsill. "I hate this," she seethed through clenched teeth. "I hate it more every day."

Like a caged animal, she paced back to her bed and picked up a notebook on her dresser. A few seconds of staring at it, and she threw it down on the bed. "I want out!" Her words were hard and sharp. She loved this, loved her character.

Then, from the corner of her eye, she caught her reflection in the mirror. Slowly, and with new appreciation, she walked to the mirror and stared at herself. Her expression told the story. This was the first time she'd seen her body as an asset, a tool that might lift her from the doldrums of the life she shared with her parents.

Gradually, sensually, she pulled the sweater over her head and tossed it on the bed. Standing there in just her tank top and jeans, she studied herself once more. She ran her hands over her arms and shoulders, down the lines of her sides and toward her narrow waist. She allowed a smoldering feeling to build inside her, a feeling that came easily. Then slowly she peeled her tank top off and stood there, her chest heaving, her body breathless as she imagined the possibilities. Andi could no longer tell where the character ended and she began. It was like she was truly seeing herself for the first time. She stared at the mirror, waiting.

"Cut." Taz breathed a quick laugh as he came to her side. He touched her arm—awkward since she was still in her bra. "That was amazing. Really, Andi. You're a natural. I have a feeling you won't have time for many more student films. Not with that talent."

His words spoke straight to her heart, to the place her parents had failed to recognize. If Taz saw the talent in her, then Hollywood agents and directors would see it. Taz moved to the bed and handed Andi her clothes. "Get dressed, and let's do it again." His voice spoke straight through her, like a spell over her. "You were brilliant the first time. I can't wait to see what you give me next."

She did the entire scene a second time, and then a third, and with each one Taz grew more thrilled with her performance. Almost as if her acting were exciting him in ways Andi didn't quite understand. When she finished, he had her get dressed a final time, and he told the rest of the crew they could go. They would film the campus scenes next week.

Finally only Andi and Taz remained in the room. "I've been thinking." He gathered his things, keeping an appropriate distance between them. "I might put myself in the film, after all. Toward the end."

At the end of the screenplay, Andi's character met up with a guy from the streets, and the two of them shared a kiss. Nothing more, but still the scene was passionate. She placed her cosmetics into her backpack and faced him, trying to understand what he meant. "You mean ... you'd play the guy ... ?"

"The guy you kiss." He set his things down so he could approach her unencumbered. "That scene's about chemistry." He took another few steps toward her, until he was so close she could smell the mint on his breath, smell the fresh scent of his shampoo. He lightly touched her chin. "You and I, we have chemistry."

She tried to hide a quick gulp. What was it about him that captured her and rendered her unable to think straight? "We definitely have chemistry."

"Maybe ... maybe we should make sure." His smile melted her and he closed the distance between them. He placed his hands tenderly on either side of her face and for the most delicious moment he kissed her—kissed her in a way that made her dizzy. Nothing Andi had experienced had felt anything like this, and she wished he would never pull away.

When Taz pulled back, his eyes smoldered with desire that was beyond intense. "Yeah." His voice was thick and smoky, his fingers still soft against her face. "We have chemistry."

She thought he was going to kiss her again, but he stepped back and grinned at her. "Let's talk between now and next week, okay?"

And with that, the session was over. Taz was a gentleman, walking her back to her dorm and giving her a quick, appropriate hug before saying good night. The kiss hadn't been a come on, any more than the scene in her bra had been some weird act to satisfy Taz's curiosity. He was simply being a filmmaker, testing the waters to see if the chemistry existed. Now the film would be stronger because of it.

She went inside and hurried down the hall to her dorm. Bailey wasn't back, but Andi wasn't surprised. She'd probably spend the weekend at home with her family. Maybe tomorrow Andi would join her. But for now she wanted to be alone so she could replay the night over and over again. So she could picture Taz's reaction to her acting and feel his kiss on her lips one more time. Her guilt from earlier was gone. The partial nudity was nothing, really, and now that part of the film was behind her. No big deal.

As she stepped into the bathroom to wash her face, she was surprised by her reflection. Not the way her hair had been slightly ratted for the scene, or even the heavy makeup around her eyes. But something in her expression. Whatever it was, Andi felt strange and a little frightened by it. Because in that moment she didn't look like Andi Ellison, daughter of missionaries, seeker of Hollywood fame, actress.

She looked like someone she no longer even recognized.

Seventeen

BAILEY COULD HARDLY WAIT TO GET into the city. They'd taken a flight from Indianapolis to La Guardia first thing that morning, and now they were being driven into Manhattan. They had three hours before the eight o'clock showing of *Mary Poppins*.

"I can't believe we're here." She stared out the window and tried to get a glimpse of the New York City skyline. But the car was stuck in traffic just short of the Midtown Tunnel. The view would have to wait.

"You?" Tim had been practically speechless since they landed. "I'm blown away and we haven't even crossed the East River."

"This is always the worst part. Getting through the tunnel." Connor sat on Bailey's other side, and their mother had the front seat next to the driver.

The tunnel was always sort of weird, cars moving at a snail's pace in stop-and-go traffic, but every car crammed in so close. At one point, their car sidled up to a full-sized bus. Bailey stared at it. "That's crazy. If you stick your hand out, you can easily touch the side of that thing."

"I'll keep my window up." Tim laughed. "Let's talk about something else."

"That reminds me …" Bailey's mom handed back a copy of their itinerary. "Here's a list of the shows we're seeing. Your dad was able to connect with friends of his down here. We have the best tickets at each of these shows."

"It's like a dream." Tim looked over the list. "I never thought I'd have a chance to see one of these shows, let alone all of them. It must be nice to live like this."

Tim's comment hit Bailey in a strange way. Most of the time she didn't think about her parents' wealth. Her dad had been an NFL player and now a coach. Her family gave away a lot. She knew because they'd always believed in sharing those details with the kids. But still they clearly had plenty to live on. More than most people could ever imagine. She glanced at the guy she was dating. Tim's mom was a nurse, his dad the manager of a hotel in Bloomington. Of course Tim hadn't been on a trip like this.

But that wasn't what bothered her.

In the last week, Tim had been more attentive than usual, almost overly so. He sometimes sounded like he was in awe of the Flanigan family's money and the fact that they could take a trip like this. Bailey had mentioned it to her mom. "It's kind of weird. I mean, does he like me more now because we can take him on the trip?"

Her mom's answer was wise. "Money can be a problem in relationships, one way or another." She hadn't taken sides beyond that. "I think it's something to watch."

She was right. Tim had known them all this time and never acted so impressed by their means. This was no time to start behaving different because of it. Money was a tool, but Bailey's family didn't need trips like this to have a good time. They had as much fun playing Apples to Apples around the game table on a Saturday night.

Bailey looked over the itinerary, and Tim peered over her shoulder. They were spending all of spring break week there, and in all they would see six Broadway shows.

"This is unbelievable." Tim put his hand on Bailey's mother's shoulder. "This must've cost a fortune."

Bailey's mom looked back and smiled at Tim. "God has provided us with some wonderful times together." She exchanged a quick look with Bailey, a look that said her mom, too, had registered his comment. "I'm sure this'll be one of them." Not only that, but her dad had contacted someone from the Giants, who was friends with a Broadway casting director. "They're auditioning for a number of ensembles this summer. Dad thinks the two of you might get a look."

Bailey forgot her concerns about Tim and squealed at the news. Her mother hadn't said a word about this until now. "Are you serious?"

"Yes. I wanted to wait until it was for sure, and it is. We'll definitely be meeting the guy after the show on Thursday night."

Behind them a taxi driver laid on his horn, and still there was no light at the end of the tunnel. But none of that mattered. They were going to meet a real-life Broadway casting director. Nothing could be better than that.

When the traffic let up enough so that they got through the tunnel, the driver took them on a series of shortcuts through lower Manhattan until finally they were at Broadway and 42nd Avenue at the DoubleTree — the hotel where Bailey and her mom and brother always stayed when they came to New York City. Her mom paid the driver, and in no time they were shooting up the elevator with their luggage, headed for adjoining suites on the twenty-second floor. Both rooms had views of Times Square, and again Tim was beside himself.

"From the first time I took the stage, I've dreamed about this, about standing here over Times Square and seeing real live Broadway theater." He turned to Bailey and took her hand. Connor and their mom were still unpacking, so the two of them were alone in the living room that adjoined the two bedrooms. "Standing here, it's like I can feel our dreams coming true."

Bailey smiled, but even here on the brink of an amazing week in New York City his words fell a little flat, and she wasn't sure why. This was her dream, right? To sing and dance in a Broadway show, and to live in New York with Tim somewhere nearby. That was the dream, wasn't it? She imagined the two of them heading off for call time each night, working hard for the director and bringing audiences to their feet every performance. Of course it was the dream. There was nothing she wanted to do more than be here, performing in front of a live audience nine times a week.

Her mom and Connor finally finished getting ready, and the four of them headed down to the street level and grabbed a quick salad across the street. Afterwards, they walked a few blocks to the New Amsterdam Theater, where *Mary Poppins* had been playing for more than a year. Bailey and her mom and brother had seen it already and been blown away. She could hardly wait for Tim's reaction.

They filed into the theater, and when the lights went down and the stage came to life, she could feel Tim hanging on every word, moving forward in his seat as if he wanted to be closer to the action so he wouldn't miss a single line. Bailey smiled to herself. How great that Tim understood her passion for theater. It was something they would always share, something she couldn't share with her dad or a guy like Cody. She redirected her thoughts and leaned in close to Tim. "What do you think?"

"I'm blown away." Tim reached for her hand, but he didn't work his fingers between hers. Rather he held it sort of loosely, the way her dad might.

The sentiment was something he shared again and again that week, even while Bailey continued to feel a strange disconnect. The show performances were still unbelievable, but the rest of New York City had somehow lost a little luster since the last time they were here. She caught herself noticing the dank smell of urine and trash that lingered around the city streets, and the constant stream of honking cabs and aggressive drivers made her long for Bloomington. Even the towering buildings didn't seem as awe inspiring, but rather like walls keeping out the sky, closing in on her.

Bailey didn't tell anyone about her feelings. *This is crazy, God. I'm grateful to be here.* But in lieu of a response she only noticed other details that chipped away at her longtime belief — that this was where she wanted to live.

The highlight was a stop at Ground Zero where the Twin Towers once stood. They visited St. Paul's Chapel, and Bailey explained to Tim that Ashley's husband, Landon, had been one of the firefighters who sifted rubble and remains after the collapse of the towers. Landon still had a strange cough because of his time at Ground Zero.

"It's still hard to believe." Their mom pulled Bailey and Connor close as they studied a timeline of photos tacked to a chain-link fence surrounding the site. "I mean, no one dreamed anything like that would ever happen."

Bailey suddenly remembered a long-ago conversation she'd had with Cody about the terrorist attacks. *"If I have anything to do with it, that'll never happen again. Not ever."*

Cody had made good on his word, a fact that made Bailey proud of him still.

On another day, the group of them walked to Central Park, but again the reality fell short of Bailey's recent memories. Instead of seeing the park as living and vibrant, an oasis in the middle of the city, she noticed the vacant-eyed faces of the people on the park benches and the dirty, stagnant look of the lake.

"This lake is so famous! It's been in more movies than most actors." Tim was constantly thrilled wherever they went.

Finally it was Thursday and they attended the evening performance of *West Side Story*. The singing and dancing were enough to take Bailey's breath, and she could tell that beside her Tim felt the same way. That and the fact that they could hardly wait for the show to be over because this was where they would meet the casting director.

"Come on." Their mom led the way when the show ended. "This way to the stage door. Our names will be on a list."

A young woman at the door checked off their names and led them down a hallway to an elevator. "One floor up takes you to the wings."

Bailey could hardly contain herself. The wings? Of an actual Broadway theater.

But when they stepped off the elevator Bailey was surprised. The area was smaller than she imagined. Still, the buzz of people around them was both familiar and exhilarating. Actors turned in costumes and props, while others took off makeup in front of a long row of mirrors, or yelled out good-byes as they headed out.

A thin man with a beret and an unforgettable smile approached them, his brow raised. "Flanigans?"

"Yes." Bailey's mom stepped forward and held out her hand. "I'm Jenny." She turned and pointed to the rest of them. "These are my kids, Bailey and Connor, and our friend, Tim Reed. Bailey and Tim are in theater at Indiana University."

"Very nice. I'm Sebastian." The man nodded, politely sizing up Bailey and then Tim. "I hear good things about their musical theater department."

"We were also part of Christian Kids Theater in Bloomington. We've been doing musicals for years." Bailey held out her hand and shook Sebastian's, and Tim did the same. "Our CKT is run by Katy Hart Matthews; you might have heard about it."

The man angled his head and gave an impressive nod. "I have indeed. She's the actress who married Dayne Matthews. I read a write-up on your theater group in *People* once."

"That's us." Tim grinned.

"Tell you what." Sebastian gestured to the stage wings. "Let's give you a tour."

Sebastian clearly loved his job. He was greeted by various cast members as they moved their way along the narrow passage behind the stage toward the sets area and the different dressing rooms.

Tim whispered as they walked, "Weird how the props bring a scene to life from the stage, but back here ..."

"Plain and ordinary."

"Definitely," Connor chimed in. "Also, the wings are smaller than the Bloomington Community Theater."

"Definitely smaller." Bailey whispered. She felt like Dorothy, seeing the Wizard for what he really was. Almost like it would've been better to skip the backstage and keep the magic.

Sebastian was going on about the stage being slightly slanted forward so that the audience could see everyone in the back row. "Come out and stand on it." He moved onto the wooden stage, and the rest of them followed.

"Wow." Connor bent his knees a little and found his balance. "It's more slanted than I thought."

"The cast gets used to it." Sebastian laughed. "But it takes awhile."

Bailey tried to imagine dancing in character shoes on the angled floor. No question it would be harder than it looked from the audience. Tim stood a little ahead of her, his eyes shining with excitement. He looked so caught up in the thrill of standing here that he'd forgotten she was a few feet away.

When they were finished with the tour, Sebastian took down names and contact information for Bailey and Tim, and gave Jenny his number. "We'll have open auditions in late June," he smiled. "Contact me before that and I'll get you in. You won't have to wait in line with the rest of the cattle." He laughed at his own joke. "The line can wrap around the block before ten in the morning."

Bailey felt her head spin as she tried to picture the audition. A line of actors wrapping around the building? "How many spots will you fill?"

"Two, maybe three." Sebastian made a face. "It's tough competition. We'll see a thousand dancers looking for one of those spots."

Dancers. He'd called them dancers because ensemble actors danced and provided a visual and vocal backdrop. Nothing more. Even still, the audition would be the chance of a lifetime. Especially now, before either of them actually graduated.

Jenny asked about the contract length for those who were chosen from the audition.

"Six months to a year. Depends on the dancer's schedule, and how much we like them."

Bailey knew what her mom was thinking. If they auditioned that summer, and if by some act of God they were chosen for the cast, they'd miss at least the first quarter of the next school year. Her mom looked concerned about the possibility.

When the meeting with Sebastian was over, they walked to Ellen's Stardust Diner at 51st and Broadway, in the heart of Times Square. The place was a fifties-style hamburger joint with homemade malts and the smell of fresh french fries cooking in the back. The best part was how the wait staff sang while they worked. The music to one favorite hit song after another filled the place as the waiters took turns belting out the lyrics.

They found a table near the middle of the room and were just opening their menus when one of the waiters walked by singing "Love Me Tender." The guy had dark hair and striking looks, and his voice was incredibly trained. Tim leaned in toward the others. "What's he doing here? He should be down the street at one of the theaters."

Jenny nodded. "He was. He played Danny's understudy in *Grease* last year when we were here. This is where a lot of them work between shows."

"Except him." Connor pointed to a tall, curly-haired guy flirting with a table of teenage girls. "He can sing like crazy, but he's been here every time we've come."

Bailey watched the guy and wondered about him. They'd talked to him last time they were here. He explained that he made pretty good money, enough to survive. "And I'm doing what I love. Singing on Broadway."

The thought made Bailey shudder then and now. It was one thing to perform on a stage at a famous theater in town, but to perform while serving burgers and fries? There had to be another way to stay involved with theater — teaching with Katy at CKT back home, maybe. She would never want to live here that badly.

"You know?" Tim grinned at them. "This is the first place I'll apply when I move here. If I never get a part, this would be great."

Bailey glanced at him and then lowered her gaze to her menu. Tim's comment confused her. Her main attraction to him had always been the number of views they'd shared in common. But now ... Was this really how he saw his future? Here in New York City no matter what? Even if it meant waiting tables for years after he got a degree? Bailey couldn't imagine living here more than a few years. After that she'd want a place like Bloomington, where she could marry and raise a family.

They were halfway back to the hotel when her phone vibrated in her coat pocket. She checked it and her heart skipped a beat. It was a text from Cody.

JUST THINKING ABOUT YOU. YOU STILL IN NEW YORK?

His message lifted her spirits more than anything all night. She thought about not texting him back, especially because she was with Tim. Or was she? She looked at him, again walking a little ahead of her, taking in the barrage of sights and sounds and barely aware of her. He wouldn't notice if she turned and walked the other way, let alone if she texted Cody back. She kept up with her mom and Connor and turned her attention to her phone.

YES. BUT IT'S NOT LIKE I REMEMBER IT. I'D RATHER BE THERE WITH YOU.

She sent the text and then felt her cheeks grow hot. There were a couple of ways he could take her message. She meant she'd rather not be in New York City at the moment. Not that she'd literally rather be with Cody. Right? She pushed back her guilt and lowered her phone to her side just as another text came in.

LET'S HANG OUT WHEN YOU GET BACK. I MISS YOU. I STILL WANT TO TALK.

Her mom slowed her pace a little so she was right next to Bailey. "Who're you texting?"

Another wave of guilt washed over her. Tim was still up ahead, talking to Connor. Even so, Bailey spoke barely loud enough for her mom to hear. "Cody."

Her mom didn't ask anything else. She only gave an understanding nod and slipped her arm around Bailey's shoulders, and the two of them kept walking.

Bailey thought about Cody's invitation. If she texted him back, he'd for sure think she meant she'd rather be with him. She pictured him, his phone in his hands, thinking about her and in as much time as it took her heart to skip a beat she knew exactly what she'd meant by her text. She swallowed hard. Again she lifted her phone so she could see it and she texted him one more time.

I'D LIKE THAT. I MISS YOU TOO.

She sent it before she could change her mind. Then she slipped her phone back in her purse. This was wrong, texting Cody while she was with Tim, and she ordered herself not to text him again tonight. But she felt lighthearted and giddy, unaware of the city sounds around her. Her guilt didn't come close to the thrill of what those few texts meant to her. Suddenly she couldn't wait for what lay ahead for her. Something she never thought would happen again.

The chance to hang out with Cody one more time.

Eighteen

THE NTM MEETING HAD BEEN POSTPONED five times, and now at the end of April they were finally being ushered down an impressive hallway to the office of Ace L. Rustin, VP in charge of theatrical development for the studio. Keith tried to maintain a calm exterior, but everything about the afternoon had been surreal—from the private parking that had been arranged for them ahead of time to the walk down the studio's Brandon Paul Avenue to the framed posters of one hit movie after another. All that and the actual meeting hadn't even started yet.

A secretary held open a door and led them into a boardroom with a table longer than any Keith had ever seen. *Give us peace, God. You opened this door. Let us walk through with Your confidence.* He felt himself relax a little.

Besides him, their group was made up of Chase, Kendall, Stephanie Fitzgerald, and Luke Baxter, the lawyer Dayne Matthews had suggested. The five of them took seats across from each other at the front end of the table.

"I can't believe we're here." Chase folded his hands and kept his voice to a whisper.

"Don't talk like that." Stephanie wagged a finger at him, chastising him even while her eyes sparkled. "God did this. You're a child of the King!"

Keith wanted to add his own disbelief. This was NTM Studios, which meant he and Chase were doing well to breathe, let alone sit upright. But he kept his comments to himself. It was important that they stay on their game. NTM executives would certainly be on theirs.

In fact, a detail bothered Keith—a detail he hadn't mentioned to anyone but Chase, and even then only in passing. The series of delays with NTM had raised red flags in Keith's mind. Not once had they expressed hesitation or uncertainty about meeting Keith and Chase.

"If Brandon's interested, we're interested," Ace had told Luke Baxter. "It's merely a matter of getting our schedules lined up."

If Luke had doubts, he hadn't said anything. But for Keith the whole set-up seemed a little too easy. NTM didn't need him and Chase. They had Brandon contracted for at least one more movie deal. It would be easier and more cost effective for them to find a fresh screenplay written by one of the writers in the NTM stable. In every possible way, it would be wiser for NTM to find a way around the producers, to convince Brandon to take another project, one where there were no authors or outside producers to slice up the pie with.

The door opened and Ace L. Rustin strode in. Keith had heard about the man, how he carried an aura that left people ready to agree with him. Now Keith would have to say his contacts had downplayed the reality. Ace was tailed by two assistants, men with clipboards and notebooks. They took seats on the far side of Keith and their group, while Ace moved to the head of the table.

He leaned forward and shook their hands, looking each member of their group in the eyes. Then he sat down and grinned. "Looks like we've got a lot to talk about."

"We do." Luke had a proposal in his notebook. He didn't bring it out just yet. "We have a project we want to develop, as you know."

"And Brandon wants nothing more than to star in it." Ace nodded confidently. "I'm well aware of the situation and excited to get things going." He raised his hands and let them drop back to the table. "I mean, how often does Stephanie Fitzgerald walk into your studio looking to make a movie deal?" He laughed a little too hard, a little too easily. He looked at the author. "How'd you hear about Brandon?"

"We're friends. Met on a set a while ago. Last thing I expected." Stephanie chuckled and launched into the story. Keith had heard the short version, but this time Steph drew out the details. The end result was a situation that felt nothing short of a miracle. Even to the typically jaded NTM folks.

The connection started when Stephanie was on the set of the first movie made of one of her novels. She was sitting on the tailgate of an electrical grip truck one evening, watching the crew film a scene in the driveway of the set house when she got a text from Brandon. "I like texting same as the next girl." Stephanie laughed again. "He'd already contacted me a few weeks before that and told me he loved my books. Now he was just saying hi."

I'M ON THE SET OF MY MOVIE, she texted back. THIS STUFF IS HARDER THAN IT LOOKS. MAKES ME APPRECIATE YOUR LIFE.

HEY, he responded, SOMEONE NEEDS TO MAKE *UNLOCKED* INTO A MOVIE.

"I remember smiling, because here was Brandon Paul knowing my books like they were his own." Stephanie enjoyed herself, telling the story for all it was worth. "I texted him that there was in fact a lot of interest in making *Unlocked* into a movie. His next message came almost immediately."

WHAT??? JUST REMEMBER THIS. I WANT TO STAR IN IT.

"I looked at that text and sort of shook my head. *Crazy kid*, I told myself. He probably had his future tied up to a dozen movies without starting in one of mine. But the next day Brandon's agent calls." She laughed. "Turns out he was serious. More than anything he wants to be in *Unlocked*."

Ace listened, smiling politely, engaged by the story. He looked at Keith. "Sorry, now ... How did you and Chase get involved?"

This was what Keith had feared. It was one thing that Brandon wanted to star in a movie based on a bestselling novel. But the fact that the novel was already optioned by a couple of no-name producers? What major studio would want a part of that scenario?

Chase cleared his throat. "We were contacted several months ago by Ben Adams and his daughter, Kendall." The two didn't need introducing in Hollywood. "We were told by Kendall that Stephanie wanted us to produce *Unlocked*."

"This was before Brandon came on the scene." Stephanie grinned at Chase and then Keith. "These two guys have talent and integrity beyond anything I've seen in the business. If *Unlocked* is going to be made, I want them to make it."

"I see." Ace nodded slowly, the smile still tugging at his lips. He sat taller in his seat and lay his hands palm down on the table. "So here we are. All the pieces in place."

"Right." Stephanie looked pleased with herself.

"And you'll be wanting control?" Ace looked at Chase, and then Keith. "Is that why Ben is involved?" Ace asked the question as if it was obvious Keith and Chase didn't have the money for a Brandon Paul movie.

"Yes." Kendall took the lead this time. "My dad is one of our primary investors. Because of him, we're prepared to provide half the money up front."

Luke was the only person in the room who appeared less than enthusiastic. "My clients will want creative control and a back-end deal."

"Very good." Ace allowed a slow nod and studied his notebook. When he looked up, he smiled at the group. "Well, it's pretty simple, then, straightforward. You need to produce a script everyone can sign off on—Brandon, his agent, and our team here at NTM. Then we set a date for filming and line up locations and cast. I have a few NTM actresses who would be perfect opposite Brandon. Something to think about, anyway."

"I like that." Kendall nodded at Ace and then the others. "Let's talk about which girls you have in mind."

"Great." Ace pushed back from the table. "Thank you for meeting with us." He shook hands with everyone at the table again and directed his final comments to Keith. "I'll shoot you an e-mail with some of our A-list screenwriters. I'm assuming you'll have the budget to float that until we have the okay from all parties."

Keith tried not to gulp. An A-list screenwriter would want half a million dollars to write a screenplay for a movie with Brandon Paul. The preliminary screenplay had been written by a friend of Keith's, a writer whose price tag wasn't even a tenth of that. They could talk about this detail later. Keith smiled, unwavering confidence and nerves of steel. "We're prepared for that, yes."

"Good." Ace moved to the door ahead of them. "Let's try to have a screenplay before summer. That way we can meet again and make some decisions." He waved. "Thanks again. My secretary will show you out." His two assistants stood and followed him, and like that he was gone.

Keith didn't want to comment on the meeting yet. They needed a place outside NTM's studio lot where they could talk about what had happened, and the fears tugging at him. "I'd like to meet." He looked around the room and his eyes settled on Luke's. "Not here, of course."

"There's a Starbucks down the street. Outdoor tables. Let's meet in ten."

When they were all there, Keith got right to the point. "I have a funny feeling about this."

"Why?" Chase had ordered a vanilla frappuccino and was fitting his straw through the lid. "That's the easiest meeting I've ever sat through."

"Too easy." Luke raised an eyebrow at Chase. "Your friend's right. I get the feeling NTM is stringing us along, keeping us happy so we don't take the project across town to another studio. In the meantime, I have to believe someone in creative is working on a competing project, something where NTM would write and produce the film and Brandon would be just as happy with the storyline. Why in the world would they be content to give up half their profits or half the control?"

Keith was glad their attorney was tracking with him. Chase's smile fell away and he set his drink down. "Brandon wants to do *Unlocked*. That's what matters."

"Not really." Luke frowned. "NTM has one more film with Brandon unless he renews his contract. As far as NTM is concerned, they can put him in an NTM original screenplay and force him to wait a few years before doing *Unlocked*. There's simply no financial incentive in teaming up with us."

"Other than the obvious." Kendall looked indignant. She was sitting next to Chase and she looked to him for support. "The film's going to be a huge hit. It camped out at number one on the *New York Times* list for six weeks. That has to count for something."

"She's right." Chase shrugged. "They have nothing without the book."

Luke anchored his elbows on the table. "Ace Rustin has played these games with me before. I won't let him throw us under the bus. But I can only control so much." He pulled out a sheet of notes. "Here's what we need to do." He glanced at the paper in front of him and explained his strategy.

First, they needed a signed contract from NTM stating they were—in good faith—interested in proceeding with the project. Chase and Keith couldn't spend half a million dollars on a screenplay without a commitment in writing from the studio. Second, they needed Brandon Paul and his agent to talk with Ace and the team at NTM. "There needs to be no misunderstanding that *Unlocked* is the only film Brandon's interested in doing."

They discussed other options, but at the end of the brief wrap-up, Luke gave them what seemed like the straightforward truth. "There's a risk here that NTM will steal the idea and run with it. No, it wouldn't be a movie based on the bestselling novel. But it would be a movie starring Brandon Paul. Honestly, that's enough. They could even offer *him* a back-end deal, or convince his agent that he'll make less money if he stars in *Unlocked* over something the studio comes up with."

Keith felt dizzy. They'd landed at the top of this strange Hollywood world, and now their attorney was telling them, basically, that they could be knocked back to the bottom with little recourse. Luke promised to work on it some more tomorrow and then he was on his way, headed back home to Indiana. The rest of them were still talking when Keith's phone rang. It was Lisa, and just seeing her name brought Keith a relief he hadn't felt all day.

He gave her a quick synopsis of the meeting and the concerns he and their attorney were feeling.

"I have another concern for you." Lisa's tone grew heavier than he'd heard it in a long time. "It's Kelly. She isn't doing well."

"How do you know?"

"She hasn't been to Bible study in four weeks, and every time I see her she makes some excuse about why she can't get together or talk. Even her friend Laurie hasn't gotten anywhere with her."

Keith hated this, hated the way nothing they did was easy. "What do you think's the problem?"

"Honestly? I think she's depressed. She hasn't been doing her hair or taking care of herself. It seems like she's withdrawing from everyone." Lisa hesitated. "Chase must know something's wrong."

"He's aware of it, but we're busy all the time. It's easy to forget the trouble back home." Keith massaged his brow. "We can't lose this movie deal with Brandon Paul."

"Well, he better start remembering Kelly." She sounded more worried than frustrated. "Otherwise he'll lose more than a movie deal."

"That bad?" Keith glanced over his shoulder at his friend. He was sitting next to Kendall, the two of them lost in some conversation that involved Stephanie and seemed to shut out the rest of the world.

"Yes. Talk to him, please. Maybe she needs counseling or medication. Something."

"I think she still worries about whether we can really make a living doing films."

"Of course she does. We all do." The calm was back in Lisa's voice. "It's just maybe Kelly worries more than the rest of us. She's taking care of two little girls by herself, living on a budget that's barely realistic."

Keith knew. He was worried about the movie situation too — both *The Last Letter* and *Unlocked*. But he'd walked by faith before, and he wouldn't stop now.

As he hung up with Lisa, he closed his eyes and lifted a silent prayer on behalf of Kelly Ryan. *She needs You, God. She needs a touch from You, a reminder. Because all of us need to walk by faith. It's just a matter of remembering that on a daily basis. So help her remember. In Jesus' name, amen.*

He returned to the table and the discussion, which was about supporting cast for *Unlocked*. He would pray with Chase later on — about the movie and the challenge of working with NTM, and about his home life.

Because if that fell apart, the rest would too.

Nineteen

KELLY WAS SICK AND TIRED OF feeling sick and tired. She was doing it to herself, she knew that, and still she couldn't stop. For the past ten years, every time she'd hit a low like this she could muscle her emotions around and order herself to get in line again. God would meet her in the moment and she'd wake up one morning with the strength to carry on, to right her ship before the whole thing capsized.

But none of that was true now.

She was sinking fast, taking on water at an alarming rate without any ability to find that fresh day, that new morning when she'd turn things around. She'd prayed, of course. Maybe not as often as she should have, but she prayed. And today she was doing something she should've done a month ago. She was meeting with Laurie. Four times she'd cancelled, but today was Friday and Kelly had the feeling that if she didn't meet with her friend, the weekend would be terrible. She'd slip into an even darker place, one that maybe she'd never find her way free of.

Laurie arrived after lunch, and the two hugged for a long time. "You're not okay, are you?" She searched Kelly's eyes.

"No. I'm not." She wasn't ready to admit her obsessive overeating—not that she needed to say anything. None of her old clothes fit at this point. The trouble was obvious to anyone looking. "I feel dead."

Laurie squeezed her hand and the two of them made iced tea in the kitchen. Spring was finally in the air after a long and mostly gloomy winter. Now it was late April and temperatures were already pushing eighty. Molly and Macy were practically desperate to get outside and try Molly's new bicycle, the one she'd gotten for her birthday. They'd waited until Chase was home for her to open it—partly because he'd needed to assemble it and partly because it made everyone feel like he hadn't missed Molly's birthday. But he'd missed it. Kelly was still frustrated about the fact.

They took their drinks outside to the small front porch. Macy laid a blanket out on the front yard, where she and her pink baby doll sat side by side. "Ready, Molly. Show me how!"

"'Kay, watch me!" Molly had walked her bike down to the driveway next door and now she was making her way toward them. The bike had training wheels, but they were adjusted high on the bike to give Molly as much a feel of a real ride as possible.

"The girls seem well." Laurie sat in the chair farthest from the sidewalk—in case Kelly needed to get to the girls quickly.

"They are." Kelly shrugged, hating the feeling strangling her heart. "They're doing great, completely unconcerned." She positioned her chair so the sun was on her face, and she slipped on a pair of sunglasses. "I guess this is our normal now."

"Life has a way of doing that, giving us a new normal just when we thought we had things all figured out." Laurie smiled. "The key to life isn't looking for a safe sameness with every passing season. It's learning to enjoy the ride, whatever the next turn in the road might bring. Believing that God's driving, and He'll get us home safely—however bumpy the trip."

Kelly played her friend's words over in her head again. "Hmmm. Sounds nice."

"Because it's true." Laurie took a drink of her iced tea. "Sometimes ... it isn't the circumstances, but us." She winced a little. "Know what I mean?"

Of course she did. Kelly managed a sad laugh. "It's definitely me this time. I'm eating all wrong, and telling myself the wrong things about my marriage. I haven't jogged or walked or done a sit-up in months. I can barely get out of bed. Every night I promise myself it'll be different tomorrow, but morning comes and it's the same old routine." Her voice cracked and she had to swallow a few times. "I can't see my way out."

"Have you talked to Chase?"

"He's in his own world. He doesn't know what it takes to run things all alone. Besides, he doesn't want to be bogged down with my troubles."

Molly was riding faster now. She was coming from the right, picking up speed and waving as she rode. "Hi, Mommy! Look!"

"That's great, sweetie. Thataway! We'll have those training wheels off in no time." Kelly could turn on her enthusiasm for the girls. Very few people knew that she was dying inside, and even here with Laurie, she didn't want to be entirely honest.

"My turn." Macy stood, her doll forgotten. She watched her sister ride past and then turn around. This time as Molly blazed down the sidewalk toward them, Macy ran out and used her body to create a roadblock. With her legs spread, arms out, she shouted at Molly. "Stop, now! My turn!"

But as good as Molly was at picking up speed, she had far less practice at stopping. "Macy! Move!"

Kelly saw the accident coming. "Macy!"

Her younger daughter looked toward the front porch just as Molly lost control of her bike. Rather than plow straight into her sister, Molly jerked the handlebars to the left and flipped her bike on top of herself. A shrill scream followed, the kind that told everyone something was seriously wrong. Macy knew instantly that the crash was her fault. She covered her mouth with both hands and gasped loud enough for all of them to hear — even above Molly's cries. "Molly ... sorry! Sorry, Molly."

Kelly and Laurie were both on their feet running toward Molly, but Kelly reached her first. With a strength she wasn't feeling, she lifted the bike from her daughter's crumpled body and tossed it on the grass. "Molly, baby! Are you okay?"

Molly rolled onto her back and some of her injuries were immediately transparent. She had a scraped cheek and a cut on her forearm.

"Her arm doesn't look right." Laurie pointed to Molly's right forearm. "See there, how it's at an angle?"

Kelly didn't have to look very hard. No question Molly's arm bone was positioned in a way that was grotesquely abnormal. Macy started crying, her hands still over her mouth. "Sorry, Molly!"

Molly's screams quieted, but she was still crying hard, her sobs shaking her small frame. "M-m-my arm!" She held out the word *arm*, letting it fill the air like a desperate plea. "It hur-r-r-ts!"

Kelly didn't have to ask Laurie if she thought her daughter's arm was broken. But Kelly wasn't sure what to do next—whether to take Molly inside or try to wrap the arm, and how she was going to calm down Macy in the meantime. Her breathing came faster, and pain gripped her chest. *Get a grip, Kelly.* But even as she ordered herself, she felt a layer of sweat building on her forehead. Why couldn't she breathe? Panic raced through her, flooding her veins.

"Kelly?" Laurie looked hard at her. "You're okay. Breathe out."

"I ... I can't."

"My arrrmmm!" Molly's sobs were growing loud again. "Mommy, make it stop!"

"Sorry, Molly!" Macy paced a few steps in either direction, her hands over her face.

She couldn't do this, couldn't handle it. Not another minute. "No." Kelly shook her head at Laurie. "I ... I can't ... breathe."

"You can." Laurie remained calm. She stared straight into Kelly's eyes and put a hand on her shoulder. "Exhale."

Another series of gasps and Kelly felt herself getting dizzy, losing consciousness. "I ... can't."

Laurie rubbed her hand along Kelly's back. "Breathe out. You're going to be fine. Come on. Purse your lips and push out the air." Laurie paused. "Dear Lord, we need You here. Please, give Kelly peace. Help her breathe."

Kelly did as she was told. She exhaled through pursed lips. At first only a small amount of air slipped through, but gradually, with each breath, she felt herself grow calmer. The whole time Laurie prayed, Molly waited for someone to help her, and Macy cried out her apologies.

With her breathing more normal, the panic subsided enough that Kelly could kneel by Molly and stroke her hair. "It's okay, baby. It'll be okay."

Laurie was the first one with a plan. "Why don't you take her to Emergency. I'll stay here with Macy."

The idea was the only one that made sense. Kelly tried to concentrate, but lately her mind had been a jumble of emotions that couldn't be captured or tamed. Life happened pretty much in a fog around her.

She ran inside, grabbed a spray bottle of hydrogen peroxide and some cotton pads and hurried back to Molly, still lying on the ground crying. "Here, baby. This won't hurt too much."

"Noooo." She thrashed about, making the blood on her cheek run halfway down her face. "Please, Mommy ... No more!"

In the background, Kelly could see Laurie take hold of Macy's hand and lead her into the house. Kelly stared at Molly, at the blood on her face and the strange angle of her forearm. *What am I doing? The doctor can clean up her cheek. I need to get her to the hospital.* She ran halfway to the house and then stopped and turned around again. She couldn't leave Molly here on the sidewalk. She dropped the spray bottle and cotton pads and held her hand out to Molly. "Baby, you have to get up. We need to go to the doctor's."

"My aaaarrrm." Molly was sobbing harder now. "It huurrrts."

"I know, sweetie. The doctor will help." She crouched down and took hold of Molly's left arm. Gently, carefully she eased her daughter to her feet. "Want me to carry you?"

"Y-y-y-es!"

Molly was still very light, but now Kelly wasn't sure she had the strength or energy to pick her up. She stooped down and tried her hardest to bounce Molly up onto her hip. But instead Molly slid back to the ground, still crying. Kelly's heart responded by racing into double-time. "Please, Mommy ... I can't walk!"

For a few seconds, Kelly once more felt nothing but sheer panic. If Chase were here he would sweep their daughter up into his arms and they'd already be on their way. "Okay, baby. Mommy's gonna try again."

This time Kelly swung Molly onto her hip, but as she stood and took a few steps, her heart slammed around in her chest. If she carried her daughter all the way to the car, she wondered if she might have a heart attack. She stopped, out of breath, and set Molly down. "I need you to walk, baby. Mommy doesn't feel good."

Something in Kelly's tone must've convinced Molly that she needed to do her part. Together they walked to the car and Kelly buckled Molly into her booster seat. Only then did she realize she didn't have her keys. "I'll be right back."

"No ... Nooooo, don't go!" Molly shrieked, straining against the belt. "My aaaarm!"

Kelly could still hear her screaming as she ran inside, grabbed her purse, and flew back out to the driver's seat. "I'm here now, baby. Mommy's back."

Molly was sobbing so hard she could barely breathe, and she didn't get any calmer the entire way to the hospital. The whole way Kelly fought from slipping into another full-blown panic attack. She parked and once they were inside a nurse met them in the lobby with a wheelchair.

"She ... she fell off her bike." Kelly felt like she was hyperventilating. This sometimes happened when she ate too many sweets in one day, but never in combination with an emergency. She wondered if she would pass out and fall to the ground right here in the emergency room lobby. "She ... she ..."

Kelly tried to breathe, but she couldn't. Her lungs wouldn't take in a full breath, and black spots were circling on the perimeter of her vision. The nurse seemed to sense Kelly was on the verge of hysteria. She motioned to someone behind the desk. "I need an examination room for the girl." Then she put her hand on Kelly's back. "Everything's going to be okay. I want you to exhale a few times nice and slow. Then you can tell me what happened."

Kelly felt like she was going to be sick. Whatever she'd eaten that day, it wasn't helping. She was winded and heavy and unable to handle the emergency playing out around her. What if it were worse? What if Molly had hit her head? Would Kelly be so disabled that she'd slip into cardiac arrest, unable to assist her daughter? *This is it, God. I can't live like this anymore. I've got to get control again—I'm finished with this craziness. I need You to help me be finished with it. I feel like I'm dying and I can't even think clearly.*

"Breathe out ..." The nurse sounded like she was losing patience. A second nurse joined them and carefully pushed Molly through the emergency room door.

"Mommmy!"

Kelly felt faint. *Help me, God ... I can't do this!* The nurse's voice was very near her face, and finally Kelly did the same thing she'd done before with Laurie, pursing her lips and forcing a few breaths. After the third, she felt herself begin to calm down—just enough so she could finally inhale. As soon as she wasn't worried about passing out, she tried to shake off her own panic and she took her place next to Molly. "It's okay, baby." She sounded weak, but she wasn't leaving her daughter again. "Mommy's here."

"It hurts." Molly stuck her lip out, her little chest still convulsing from the sobs.

They hurried into a room, and a doctor made a quick decision that Molly needed a spoonful of liquid acetaminophen for her pain and an X ray. Kelly walked with her to the room, but she had to stand back with the technician during the actual picture-taking. Her absence only made Molly cry harder, and in the distant places of her mind Kelly had a random thought. What was Chase doing right now? Sitting in some meeting at some major studio, wasn't that it? He would have no idea that his family was in the middle of a crisis.

She waited until the X ray was finished and she and Molly were alone in the examining room before she took the receiver off the wall and dialed Chase's cell. It rang two times, three, and after the fourth it went to his voicemail. Kelly waited for the beep. "Chase, it's me." She sounded exhausted and still a little panicky. "Molly fell off her bike and maybe broke her arm. Call me, okay? We're at the hospital."

The diagnosis didn't take long. By then, the emergency room doctor had stabilized Molly's arm in a loose splint, and she'd fallen asleep, exhausted from the pain and the sobbing. The doctor pulled up a chair opposite Kelly and checked the chart he was holding. "Molly has a severe fracture in her forearm. It's quite bad, actually. With something like this, there's really only one way to set it, and that's through surgery."

Surgery? Kelly felt her heartbeat pick up speed again. Molly needed surgery? With Chase gone? The black spots danced into view again and she tried to remember Laurie's advice. *Exhale. Force yourself to exhale. Please, God ... get me through this.*

I am with you, daughter ... through even this I am with you.

The answer rang clear in her heart even over the sound of the doctor's voice. Kelly blinked and tried to focus. God was with her. She could do this.

The doctor explained that with breaks like this, the sooner they could set it the better. "I've called in an expert pediatric orthopedist. He can operate this afternoon." He studied her. "Can your husband be here by then?"

"No." She felt sick again. "He won't be here until late tomorrow. He's in LA."

"I see." The doctor looked concerned. "Do you think you'll be okay? I'd like someone to be here with you."

He must've heard about her near-fainting episode in the waiting room. She racked her brain, thinking about what to tell him. Laurie was staying with Macy, and she would do so as long as Kelly needed her. Then she remembered. Lisa, of course. Lisa was home this week and she would come in a heartbeat. "I ... I have someone."

"Very well, then."

She nodded, fighting the panic that breathed terrifying possibilities into her heart and mind. The doctor excused himself, and again Kelly took the phone from the wall. Her first call was to Laurie, who was more than willing to look after Macy. "I'll be here as long as you need me," she said. "And I'll keep praying."

Next Kelly called Lisa, who promised to be there in twenty minutes.

Finally she tried Chase again. This time he answered on the third ring, his voice quiet and on edge. "What is it Kelly? Is this an emergency?" He obviously hadn't checked his messages. "We're almost finished."

For a single instant, Kelly wanted to hang up, tell him never mind. That certainly whatever was happening with the studio was bound to be more important than life back home. But instead she swallowed every sarcastic thought she might've voiced and in a tone almost devoid of emotion said only, "Molly broke her arm. We're at the hospital." She sighed. "She needs surgery in the next few hours to set it."

"What?" The alarm in Chase's voice brought with it some sense of satisfaction. "How serious is it?" He was still whispering.

"Serious, Chase. She needs surgery."

He released a frustrated sound. "Let me call you after the meeting. It's almost over."

Kelly felt the room tilt. Was he really saying he'd call her back? When his daughter was lying in a hospital facing surgery? She was furious with him. "Fine." She hung up without saying good-bye and did her best not to slam the phone back onto its place on the wall.

She stood and paced to the door and back again. No wonder she'd been eating everything in sight. How else was she supposed to cope with the stress, the feeling Chase had abandoned them in a quest that had evolved over the last few months? Now his days in LA seemed less about changing the world and more about chasing fame and money. Anything to keep Brandon Paul attached to the next picture.

Molly moaned and rolled a little on the hospital bed. The doctor said he'd give her something to sleep if she woke up. He didn't want her moving around very much until after the surgery; she could do further damage to her arm. For now, though, Kelly wanted something to help *herself* calm down. When she was sure Molly wasn't going to wake up, she took a couple of one-dollar bills from her wallet. Walking quietly so Molly wouldn't hear, she left the room and went to the nurse's station. "My daughter's alone in there. I'll be right back."

"I'll check her in a moment." The nurse pointed to a monitor. "I can see her from here; don't worry."

Kelly nodded and headed out into the hall. When she reached the lobby, she turned away from the front doors and kept walking until she saw the vending machine. She stopped and stared at the food inside. Snickers ... Reese's Pieces ... Rolos ... two oversized chocolate-chip cookies. Her hands shook as she slid the first dollar into the slot. She wanted every bit of comfort she could get, and she positioned her finger over the letter and number corresponding to the Snickers. She could start there. But just as she was about to push, she felt a physical force holding her back.

She gasped and turned around, expecting to see someone standing there, stopping her from making the purchase. But she was completely alone. She blinked and stared at the machine full of junk. What had stopped her from pushing the button, and how come she was shaking so hard? Then in a rush she remembered her quick prayer, the one she'd silently uttered while trying not to faint an hour ago. What had she said? That she couldn't do this anymore, and that she was ready to stop, right? Wasn't that it? She'd even begged God to help her be finished with the craziness.

And now ... now something or someone had stopped her.

She lowered her hand and stared at the Snickers bar. She didn't need candy; she needed a Savior, a strength that went beyond herself. Not tomorrow morning or some other day, but here. Now.

She stepped back from the machine and then, at the last second, she pushed a button and heard the clank of quarters as they fell into the change dish. All four quarters. She swept them into her hand and without hesitation dropped them, one at a time, into the next machine — the one that held only bottled water.

She took her bottle and walked as quickly as she could back to Molly's room. Whatever had happened back there, she couldn't stop to analyze it. Whether the hand of God had held her back, or whether she'd subconsciously stopped herself, she wasn't sure. The only thing she knew was this: God had answered her prayer. Her marriage was on the rocks, and her little girl was about to have surgery. They owed tens of thousands of dollars because of *The Last Letter* and they'd yet to see more than the slightest bit of repayment for the funds they'd invested. But now, as she headed back to Molly's side, she had reason to smile because she had found the one thing she desperately needed, the thing she'd lost sight of these last few months.

Her determination to live.

Twenty

THE MEETING WITH THE STUDIO WAS over, and Chase stood out front of a restaurant across the street, frantic to get hold of Kelly. He tried her cell phone a dozen times before finally calling the three hospitals in the area. On the third try he found her—sitting with Molly in her room. A male nurse patched him through.

"Hello?" Kelly sounded angry, but less tired.

"Honey, it's me." His relief was an almost physical force across the phone lines. He hoped Kelly could tell how badly he wanted to talk to her. "I've been calling you for fifteen minutes."

"We can't use cell phones." She kept her eyes on Molly.

He started to say that he hadn't even known which hospital they were at, but he stopped himself. None of that mattered now. "So what happened? Start at the beginning."

In a monotone Kelly explained the bike accident. "It could've been a lot worse."

"Where's Macy?" Chase raked his fingers through his hair and leaned against the car. Keith was already inside, waiting for him.

"Laurie's with her, and Lisa is on her way here."

"Good." He racked his brain. They had come out of the meeting and gone directly to the restaurant. Kendall was on the phone with her father, and Keith had called Lisa. Chase was outside where he'd been since he first started trying to reach Kelly. "They're sure she needs surgery?"

"The break's terrible, Chase. One of the worst the doctor's seen."

Pain sliced through Chase's gut. His little Molly suffering such a bad injury when he wasn't home to help her? The meeting had gone brilliantly, but Chase knew better than to say so now. He asked how Molly was doing, and what the time frame was. "I can be home tomorrow evening."

"Tomorrow?" Her single laugh sounded desperate. "What, Chase? What's so important that you can't get in your car and drive home now?"

He hesitated in disbelief. "I have more meetings, Kel. What do you want me to do, race home and then turn around and come back here?"

"Whatever." She didn't sound like she had the strength to fight him. "We'll be here until Sunday morning."

"I'll come straight there as soon as I'm in town."

"Okay." She didn't sound intentionally mean, just indifferent.

He settled into a white wrought iron chair on the sidewalk. "Kelly, what's with you?"

"What's with *you*? Your daughter's had a terrible accident and you can't take my call? Are you serious?"

"I'm sorry. I was wrong. It's just ... we were almost finished working out the details of an actual theatrical release with *The Last Letter*, and I didn't want to miss anything."

She took a long breath. "Look, I don't want to fight. We'll talk when you get here tomorrow."

She left him no room for further conversation. He felt his shoulders sink a few inches and he slumped over his knees, trying to focus. "If you talk to her before the surgery, will you tell her I'm praying for her?"

"Of course." She was terse and businesslike, as if she couldn't wait to get off the phone and tend to more important matters.

"I love you." He covered his free ear with his hand so he could hear the nuances of her voice, her mood. "I'm sorry I wasn't there."

"It's okay. We're used to it." She paused, maybe regretting her sarcasm. "See you tomorrow."

The phone went dead before Chase could question her again about her mood. Only then did he realize that she hadn't asked about the theatrical deal. It was what they'd been praying for with *The Last Letter*, and now they had it. But Kelly hadn't even noted it. He clicked his phone off and slid it back in the pocket of his jacket. Then hung his head for a full minute trying to figure out his wife. When he'd been home lately, he'd tried not to look too deeply at the way Kelly was treating him. She probably wasn't happy with him. At least that's what he had come to believe. But at least she made an effort when he was home.

But now ... now there was no question she was angry. It had come through loud and clear over the phone lines. Angry at what? That's what he wanted to know. Angry because he and Keith were following the dream God had placed in their hearts? Upset because he was gone so often? He clenched his teeth and pulled himself into a straight position again. Didn't she know this was the hardest part? One day soon they could move to LA and this phase would be something from the past. But they couldn't blame each other along the way.

He remembered the time during the filming last fall when she'd come to the set and spent a couple nights with him. She believed in him back then, but since Thanksgiving things had changed with her. Was it depression? Had she allowed herself to get so out of control that she couldn't feel anything but misery?

He was about to pray for her, to beg God to mend things between them so that tomorrow he could hold her hands and help her know how he felt about her, that he would do anything to help her. But the sound of the café door stopped him before he had the chance. "Chase?" It was Kendall.

He sighed and put on the familiar mask, the one that he wore around their new partner so she wouldn't think for a minute that

Chase's home life was anything but ideal. He flashed her a concerned smile. "Hey, sorry. It took forever to reach her."

"How's Molly?" Kendall had come outside by herself. Keith was still inside the restaurant.

"She needs surgery for sure. I guess Macy jumped in front of her. Molly didn't want to hit her with the bicycle, so she took the fall instead."

"Ahh, sweet girl." Kendall took the seat next to Chase. "Anything we can do?"

"Pray." It was what he and Kelly should've done. "I guess the operation's pretty straightforward. They've called in a specialist, but still ... It's scary stuff."

"Definitely. Plus she doesn't have the best daddy in the world there to help her through it."

Chase tried not to register the compliment. He and Kendall had only been working closely together for three months or so, and already a pattern was starting to develop. With Kelly, he could do nothing right, and with Kendall ... With Kendall he could do no wrong. He stared at the ground near his feet. "If I were that great, I guess I'd be there."

"Hey." Her voice was soft, a caress whether she intended it to be or not. "Don't beat yourself up. The reason you're here is because you care about your family's future. Not just your financial future and the welfare of your wife and girls." She waited until he looked up. "You care about the next generation of kids. That's why you want to make these movies, remember? So in the big picture, you're the best dad of all."

He looked away because he didn't want to linger on Kendall Adams' eyes. She was good and right and true, and her intentions were entirely pure—same as his. But even so, looking into her eyes was like looking into her soul. Too much of that and he'd be on dangerous ground in no time. He knew at least that much.

His mind found its way back to the studio meeting. "What's the consensus?"

"About the meeting?" She grinned and a giddy laugh sounded in her throat. "It was perfect, great that we had Luke Baxter tapped in from Indiana. His input was incredible. I mean, the studio execs offer you a theatrical deal and even agree to split the P&A budget? In this market, that's like hitting the lottery."

"I sort of figured." Chase smiled and wished he could've told Kelly the good news. Maybe it would've helped her mood a little. He gazed up at the Los Angeles sky, already hazy at the end of April. "What about Brandon?"

"Keith thinks today's meeting was good for that too. If NTM steps out of line, Brandon won't sign another deal with them. Worst-case scenario, Brandon finishes his contract with NTM — does the final film, something the studio comes up with. Then we move on and take *Unlocked* to the executives we met today. They'd pay Brandon more, and they'd understand the faith element. The studio's leading the way in that area right now, and no one's close."

Chase sort of liked the idea. "Maybe we should aim for that, since NTM's dragging its feet."

"We could." Kendall nodded thoughtfully. "My dad would be supportive no matter where *Unlocked* winds up."

Keith joined them then, carrying a bag of to-go salads. "We can eat back at the hotel room. I have to talk to Andi, and it could take a while." He didn't sit down. "Everything okay with Molly?"

"We'll know more later tonight. Her surgery's in about an hour."

"Ugh." Keith groaned and hung his head for a few seconds. "I'm sorry, man. That's terrible."

"It could've been worse." Kendall stood and reached her hand out to Chase.

Without thinking, he took it and allowed her to help him to his feet. The exchange didn't seem to draw any strange looks from Keith, and Chase told himself it was nothing out of the ordinary. A friend helping another friend up at a time when weariness ruled the moment.

They walked to Kendall's car, and Chase took the front passenger seat. The three of them talked about *The Last Letter* all the way back to the Georgian Hotel. "You know," Kendall said as she pulled up. "You guys could stay with my dad. He lives down the street from me, and he has half a dozen guestrooms. You'd be closer to the studios."

Chase had wondered that for some time, how they might approach such an idea without seeming presumptuous. Never mind the good rate they were getting, they were still spending a fortune on hotel bills.

From the back, Keith patted Kendall on her shoulder. "Tell your dad yes. We'd love that." He thanked her and stepped out of the car. When he saw that Chase wasn't making the same hurried move, he waved. "See you inside."

Chase nodded. He wasn't sure why he wasn't jumping out of the car too. It was a valet area, and in a minute or so one of the uniformed parking attendants would hurry Kendall on her way. But Chase wanted to thank her first. "About earlier, what you said. How I'm a good dad for trying to get these films done." He opened the car door and set one foot on the ground. For the slightest moment he allowed his eyes to look into hers. "Thanks for that. I needed to hear it."

"I know." She put her hand on his knee, but only briefly. "It can't be easy, being gone so much. I'm sure your wife misses you like crazy."

"She does." His answer was quick, the only answer he could give. "Anyway..." He couldn't look away. "Just wanted to thank you."

She smiled. "It's the truth. Oh, and I'll be praying for Molly this afternoon. Let me know how it goes."

"I will." He hesitated one last time before stepping out of her car. "You'll meet us here for breakfast tomorrow?"

"Of course. We have the meeting with Brandon's agent, and then lunch with Brandon. Lots to talk about now that we have a theatrical deal. Everyone in Brandon's camp should feel a lot better about you and Keith producing *Unlocked*."

"Good." His smile was the easiest thing that had happened that day. "I'll see you then."

The moment seemed to call for a hug—especially since she had lifted his spirits when he was at such a low point earlier that day. But with the two of them in the car, a hug would be awkward. Besides, hugging hadn't really been part of their working relationship. Instead he waved once more and thanked her for the ride, then stepped out and headed up the front steps of the Georgian and into the open-air lobby. He needed to find a quiet place where he could pray about Molly. Not just Molly, but Kelly and whatever struggles she faced. But for now, he was glad that at least one part of his life was going right.

And that God had been kind enough to pair them up with a young woman as wonderful as Kendall Adams.

KENDALL DROVE DOWN OCEAN AVENUE WITH one thought on her mind: the safety and complete healing of little Molly Ryan. She opened her car windows and breathed in the ocean breeze. The farther north she went, the less traffic, and the more easily she could concentrate on her prayer.

She begged God for wisdom on the part of the surgeon, and for complete healing for the child's arm. Beyond that she prayed for Chase's home life. Not because he'd mentioned that anything was wrong, but because she sensed trouble. Maybe he was just tense about not being home when he was needed. Whatever it was, she prayed, and when she was finished she thanked God for the answers that were certainly coming.

Before she reached the turnoff for her home, she added one last plea to God. She'd loved and lost once a long time ago, and since then no one had come along. No one with faith in Christ or the integrity she needed in a relationship centered in Hollywood. That was okay, she had told herself a thousand times. She could be single and alone and still serve God by helping make movies with a message.

But spending time with Chase had increased her longing for a guy, for a man she might marry and share her life with. Before connecting with Chase and Keith, she'd wondered if there were any men left who would meet her high standards. If not, then she would stick by her determination. She'd rather be single. But since meeting the young producers—especially Chase—she knew differently. There were good guys out there, and she finished her prayer asking God to send one her way. One who was handsome and kind, humble and loyal, a guy who loved his family more than life and who would be guided each day by his faith in God. "Please, Lord ... send me a guy like that."

She rested her head against the seat back and smiled at the late-afternoon sunshine. Somewhere out there her guy existed, a guy who wasn't already married. She concentrated on the road ahead and felt no shame in the way she'd prayed. God understood what she meant. She wasn't attracted to Chase, though she still wanted to be careful around him. His wedding ring almost always stopped her from feeling an attraction toward him. But it didn't stop her from praying that the guy she married wouldn't be some Hollywood phony, some high-ranking executive with money and power and prestige. She wasn't looking for that in a man, not anymore.

She was looking for a guy like Chase Ryan.

Twenty-One

BAILEY WALKED INTO THE CRU MEETING and wondered if she'd see Cody. Tim wasn't with her tonight. They'd been home from New York less than a week, and since they'd missed a day of classes, Tim didn't want to fall behind on homework. Andi hadn't come either. She was hanging out with Taz again.

Bailey was about to head down the aisle to her place near the front when she spotted Cody sitting by himself in a seat near the back row. He smiled at her with his usual enthusiasm and motioned for her. Bailey felt her heart leap. His text while she was in New York had said they should hang out some time. Now at least maybe they could talk about it.

She walked down the empty row of seats and took the one beside him. "Hey."

"Hey." He stood and hesitated. Then, as if he didn't want things to be awkward between them, he gave her a quick hug. "Where's Tim?"

"Studying."

They sat down next to each other, and the sound of his voice felt wonderful beside her. "What about you?"

"I'm caught up. I didn't do the spring play, so I guess I had more time."

They had five minutes before Cru began. Cody shifted so he could see her better. In the process, his knee brushed against hers. Bailey didn't shift away from him.

"I stopped by your parents' house a few times."

Once a week, Bailey wanted to say, because her family shared with her each time Cody came by. But she stopped herself. Her brothers loved seeing Cody, and her dad said he'd been talking to him about coaching. She felt her smile light her eyes, the way it so easily did when she was with him. "They love when you come over. You're part of the family."

"I feel that way."

Cody seemed uncomfortable with silence between them, so he told her about his mom, how she was doing better and staying sober. "I take her to church every weekend, and each time she's getting a little closer to God. It's amazing." He chuckled. "For the first time in my life I have a mom, only now it's more like the tables are turned and I'm the one taking care of her."

Bailey could picture that. Cody had walked away from alcohol and escaped a prisoner-of-war situation in Iraq. Back in the U.S., he'd learned how to walk on a prosthetic leg without any limp whatsoever. He even competed in local triathlons. Of course he could take care of his mother. He could take care of anyone.

"So you wanna coach? That's what my dad said." She looked at him, let herself get lost in his eyes. Not because she wanted to have feelings for him again, but because she missed the connection between them. Missed it more than she realized.

"Yeah, I think I'm made for it. I want to help kids and teach them football. It's an important time in a kid's life. Without your dad, I would've drunk myself to death by now. So that's my new goal. Be a guy like your dad for some kid like me. For a hundred kids like me."

The picture warmed Bailey's heart. "You'll be wonderful at it."

"I hope so. It means an extra year of schooling to get my teaching credential, but I don't mind. I'm taking a few summer classes, so I might finish early, anyway."

She nodded, and without meaning to she thought about Tim. The trip had changed something in Bailey. She still wanted to perform on Broadway, but the city had lost some of its glamour. Even if she won a starring role, she couldn't picture herself living in Manhattan for long. But Tim ... Tim could hardly wait to pack his bags and find an apartment.

Her mother's voice came to mind, something she'd said the afternoon of Bailey's eighth-grade graduation. All the other girls had boys who liked them, but Bailey had only friends. She had wondered if maybe something was wrong with her, since none of the boys had wanted to go out with her.

"You're too mature for them," her mom had told her. "They think you're pretty, but they don't dare say so. Because they know none of them is what you'll be looking for someday."

"What'll I be looking for when I'm ready?"

Her mother had smiled, a knowing look warming her eyes. "For someone like your daddy."

Bailey had never forgotten that conversation, and along the way she could look back and realize why guys she'd had crushes on in high school had never worked out, and why a guy like Bryan Smythe from CKT would never have been a match for her. Those guys were nothing like her dad. But then, more often lately, neither was Tim.

"What're you thinking about?" Cody nudged his knee against hers.

"Nothing." She didn't dare say. Especially not in the wake of their discussion about Cody's coaching dreams.

The Cru leader, Daniel, took his spot at the front of the classroom. He started by reading from Psalm 139 about how God had known them since before they were born, and how He'd knit them together inside their mothers' bodies, and how His plans for them had been destined since before the beginning of time.

When he finished taking questions about the Scripture passage, he moved onto the year-end events. First, they were planning a retreat on the far side of Lake Monroe. A church camp had been there for decades. A cluster of cabins and a mess hall, located in a place secluded from the rest of the lake. Perfect for time away, time to reflect.

The weekend sounded perfect to Bailey. She listened intently as Daniel continued.

"We'll be there the third weekend in May. There are no classes that Friday, so we'll have three days." He held up an orange flyer. "The details are here."

Finally he told them about a mission trip to Costa Rica set for August. Cody leaned close to her. "I think I'm going. What about you?"

Bailey wanted to go in the worst way, but she needed to talk to Tim. The two of them were planning a weekend trip to New York in June so they could audition for the opening ensemble roles. If they won parts, then the mission trip would have to wait. "I don't know," she whispered. "Maybe."

"What about the lake retreat?"

"Definitely."

After signing up for the May weekend and after Bailey connected with the girls in her Bible study, she and Cody walked out into the night. The week had been the warmest since winter, and now, after nine o'clock, the air still felt fairly warm.

They walked slowly, side by side, until they came to the place where a couple of main paths intersected. "Can I walk you back to the dorm?"

As much as Bailey worried about her heart, she was glad for his offer. She didn't want to walk alone, but even more she didn't want to say good night yet. Cody kept his pace slow and easy, and Bailey fell into his rhythm.

"Okay ..." Cody's voice rang with subtle teasing. "Is this my lucky day?"

"Your what?" She smiled at him. "Why do you say that?"

"Because here we are hanging out, and I keep thinking if I get lucky—I mean, really lucky—maybe you'll tell me why you pulled so far away. I mean, I apologized for my stupidity in staying away from you last fall, right?"

She stifled a giggle. "Okay. Right."

He made a funny face. "So maybe you think I have bubonic plague? Or maybe you're so blinded with love for Tim you forgot I'm alive." His eyes lit up and he pointed at her. "Or you fell and hit your head and now you have amnesia and you can't remember where you know me from." He shrugged. "Or if you know me."

She laughed again. "Cody ..." They were walking more slowly now, and once in awhile Bailey felt his arm brush against hers. She had missed this so much, this camaraderie with Cody. "You're crazy." She grinned at him. "I don't think you have the plague."

"You saw my picture in a post office on a Most Wanted poster, and you've convinced yourself I'm a felon?"

"Come on ..."

Cody was laughing now too. "Or you've got it in your mind that I'm not Cody Coleman at all, but some evil twin, and now you're afraid to talk to me?"

Bailey laughed harder, so much that she slowed to catch her breath. How long had it been since she'd felt this way? Her feelings took her back and made her long for another time. She poked her elbow at him. "You're ridiculous."

"Actually ..." He gradually came to a stop and faced her. "I don't want to be too serious, Bailey, but really, for the life of me, I can't understand it."

They were at a part of the path that lay out in the open, no seclusion whatsoever. Even still, Bailey felt like they were the only two people on campus. She wanted to look away, but she couldn't. She'd avoided him this long, so maybe he was right. Maybe it was time she gave him an answer. "Really, Cody?" Her voice was soft, the laughter gone for her too. "You want the truth?"

"I do." He looked so good in his gray Colts sweatshirt and jeans. For a moment he looked like he might hug her, or touch her face. But instead he slipped his hands in his back pockets and waited. His eyes never left hers for a single second. "Why do you stay away from me? I miss you more each day."

"Because ..." She didn't want to cry, not now and not ever around him. But her heart didn't know the rules, and tears built up anyway. "I know you're sorry. But you cut me out of your life for nearly three months. Like you didn't care at all, and something happened to me during that time." She raised the zipper on her sweater, but the extra warmth didn't touch the chill inside her.

"What?" He studied her eyes, her expression. "What happened, Bailey?"

A hot tear slid down her cheek, and she caught it with her shoulder. "It's like I told you before. I still can't trust you. I almost deleted your texts last week too."

He couldn't have looked more hurt if she'd told him she'd forgotten his name. "Then you don't understand me at all."

"Of course I do. When you came back from war you told me you weren't interested in me as more than a friend. You wanted me to date Tim Reed, and that's what I'm doing." She wished she sounded more enthusiastic about the fact. "But you promised me I'd at least have your friendship. Only then ..." Another tear fell. "Then school started and you started going after my roommate." Her voice was slightly louder than before. "How did you think I was going to take that?"

He exhaled hard and rubbed the back of his neck. Without saying anything, he turned and stared at the empty campus lawn. After a few seconds he looked at her again, his eyes full of a hurt deeper than any she'd seen in him before. "You really think I could replace you with Andi Ellison?" The sound that came from him was more a frustrated cry than a laugh. "She's nothing like you."

"But that's what you did." Bailey pressed her knuckles beneath her eyes and willed herself to find control. "You became her friend instead of mine."

"Because you had Tim."

"Of course I had Tim." She caught her voice this time, and dropped it to a frustrated whisper. "You wanted me to. Wasn't that what you said? He had more in common with me, and he was better for me. All to distract me from the real issue. Why *you* weren't interested. But I didn't think you'd turn your back on me."

He looked completely defeated, and for a long time he only stared at her. Then finally he allowed a sad laugh and a shake of his head. "You'll never understand. You were already with Tim when I came home. You were happy, I could see that. It wouldn't have been cool to call you and text you all the time when you already had Tim."

She wanted to tell him that they weren't all that serious, even now, and that Tim's dreams were starting to feel very different from hers. But that would feel like a betrayal to Tim. She loved Tim, and however long they stayed together, she could never talk bad about him behind his back. Not now or ever. He'd done nothing to deserve that.

Instead she swallowed hard and lifted her eyes to the trees up ahead. New leaves showed on their branches, proof that once more winter wouldn't have the final say.

"Tim and I are still serious." She gave him a conflicted look. "So why the effort these past few months, Cody? Why the texting and calling?"

"Because God made it clear to me that I was an idiot. I never should've backed off just because of Tim. I wasn't a threat to him, and by backing off I only confused you." He looked intently at her, past the surface and straight to her soul. "I never stopped thinking about you."

"So that's it, huh? You want to be my friend."

"Exactly." His eyes gradually took on the light they'd lost in the heat of their discussion. "Because really, Bailey, I don't have the plague. I promise you."

Her cheeks were dry, and she laughed even though she hadn't intended to. Maybe things hadn't changed as much between them as she'd thought. Not if he could still make her laugh at will. "Brat." She kicked at his feet, then paused for a long while, lost in his eyes. "So you're saying I can trust you this time, that you'll be a real friend."

"As long as Tim doesn't care."

"He doesn't." Her answer came quickly. "He trusts me."

The joy in Cody's eyes was enough to make her laugh again, and once she started, he joined in. "You're not worried I'm an evil twin?"

"A little. But I'll stop erasing your messages." They started walking once more and she felt her eyes dance as she gave him a side glance. "How would that be?"

"Wow. I feel like the luckiest guy on campus." He leaned his head back and shouted. "Bailey Flanigan's going to stop deleting my messages!" He took a long breath and grinned at her. "Definitely the luckiest guy."

She kept laughing. "Shhh. People will wonder."

"Yeah, well, that's not always a bad thing." His laugh fell to a quiet chuckle. They were almost back at her dorm. "Now here's what'll happen. You'll go into your dorm and put away your backpack and before you can even think about washing your face you'll get a text message." He held out his elbow and touched it lightly to hers. "It'll be from me, and then ... instead of erasing it or ignoring it or banning it from your phone the way you're used to doing, you'll sit down on the edge of your bed and text me back."

They were at her dorm now, and they stopped at the bottom of the steps. "That's what's going to happen?"

"Yes." His eyes glimmered. "Okay?"

"Mm-hmm." She lowered her chin, feeling a little sheepish. "I guess I've been sort of rude."

"No, no." He punctuated the night air with his forefinger. "The plague can be very contagious, and you had to look out for your health."

She allowed herself to get serious one more time. "Not for my health. For my heart. In my book, friends don't just stop talking to each other."

A long breath slid between his lips. "I know. It was my fault. I'm asking you again to forgive me, Bailey. So we can try one more time."

"Okay." Her heart hung on every word he said. "I forgive you." They were standing so close she could feel the warmth from his body. "And I need you to forgive me too."

He tapped his foot against hers. "For what?"

"For not talking about this with you sooner."

This time they needed no words. Slowly Cody wrapped his arms around her. The hug lasted a long time, and Bailey wished it would've gone on longer. Because against all the odds, she and Cody had finally done the impossible.

They'd found their way back to each other.

They whispered good-byes, and when Bailey was inside her dorm, before she had time to wash her face, her phone alerted her to a text message. She smiled and picked it up.

I'M TRYING TO FEEL THE GROUND BENEATH ME, BUT IT ISN'T EASY.

Bailey grinned and texted back her answer. ME TOO.

ACTUALLY, I'M THANKING GOD WITH EVERY STEP BECAUSE I WASN'T SURE WE'D EVER HAVE THIS AGAIN, AND NOW WE DO.

MORE THAN THAT, she tapped out her response, WE ALWAYS WILL.

It was the one thought that kept her company as she fell asleep. She and Cody had found their way back to each other, back to the friendship they'd almost lost. No matter what Andi was out doing tonight, or how her feelings for Tim were shifting, that was all that mattered.

She had Cody again, and all was right with the world.

Twenty-Two

ANDI WAS GLAD THE SPRING SHOW was over. She'd received much praise for her role as Maid Marian, but deep inside she knew she could've done better. Her focus was off—the way it had been off since she and Taz began spending time together. For the past month, ever since they'd shot the first scenes of Taz's movie, the two of them had been nearly inseparable. When they weren't together, they were texting or talking on the phone.

Taz told her she was his kindred spirit, his soul mate. In the past words like that would've seemed cliché or trite, but with Taz they took on new meaning, the way all of life did with him.

"What is it with this Taz guy?" Bailey asked every few days. "Come on, Andi. Be honest."

But Andi would only smile and shrug. "He's nice. We're not dating or anything." She was telling the truth, even if she was purposefully evasive. "Just getting to know each other."

Even so, Taz had become an obsession. Andi was grateful she was a strong student and that her grades hadn't suffered. Because when she wasn't in class, she was all about Taz.

I CAN FEEL US IN THE TREES, he'd told her yesterday over a text. NEW LIFE BURSTING THROUGH EVERY BRANCH AND PUSHING THROUGH OUR HEARTS AND SOULS. CAN YOU FEEL IT?

The crazy thing was she could. Even if she wasn't always sure exactly what he meant. With Taz she felt free and full of potential, not stuck in a box the way she'd felt before. Their talks never stalled in the bog of Christianity or the Bible or the existence of

God—topics Andi had spent a lifetime exhausting. Instead she and Taz laughed and talked about the pulse of a person's soul and the beauty in a blade of grass. The topics were endless with Taz, and once in a while they even dreamed about the future.

Taz had been careful not to kiss her again. He'd wound up playing the role of her character's love interest, but the kiss they shared on screen was purely professional, art at its best. When they'd finished filming it, he let his eyes hold hers a few seconds more. "Definite chemistry," he said. And that was all—then or since then.

There were times when she wanted to beg him to kiss her the way she was dying to be kissed. Other times she wanted to scream at him, "Okay, so are you falling for me or what?"

But always the question seemed pushy or forced. "We are like wind and rain," he'd told her last week. "Dancing over the earth the way two people are supposed to dance." Another time he touched her cheek and whispered, "We enjoy each other—hearts, minds, and souls." His eyes shone with a mesmerizing depth. "One day, maybe, we will enjoy more than that."

In the past she'd feared a physical relationship with a guy. She had promised God, herself, and her parents she'd stay pure until she was married. So when guys made moves on her earlier this year, the attempts felt like an affront. Something to stay away from.

But everything was different with Taz. Each time they were together, her desire and curiosity grew. The more he seemed almost uninterested in kissing her, the more she wanted to be kissed. Her wanting him only added to the other heightened sensations she felt whenever Taz was around.

Andi tuned out her psych professor, clicked a button on her phone, and smiled. Another text from him.

HEY, BEAUTIFUL, I NEED TO RESHOOT A FEW SCENES FOR THE MOVIE. I REALLY WANT AN A ON THIS THING,

AND I'M NOT SURE THE STUFF WE DID IN THE BEGINNING IS STRONG ENOUGH.

Andi's mind raced.

THE BEDROOM SCENES?

YES. I DON'T WANT TO TALK ABOUT IT OVER TEXT. LET'S MEET AFTER YOUR LAST CLASS TODAY.

She wasn't sure what he had in mind, but the idea of meeting him sounded wonderful. They had several places on campus where they often stole a few minutes together and she gave in to the dizzy way he made her feel. When class was over, she met him on a hilly path overlooking an ancient chapel, one of the few religious buildings on campus. Andi tried not to think about how long it had been since she'd set foot in a church.

He took her hand in his, eased his fingers between hers, and led her to the top of the hill, to a bench set back from the path and shaded by two enormous maple trees. "Your skin feels good." His pace was slow so he could look at her as they walked. "Enchanting. Like everything about you." He slid his fingers deeper between hers. "Can you feel it?"

Kiss me, she wanted to scream. But instead she focused her attention on the place where their fingers connected. "Mmm." She smiled at him. "I can."

"People are meant to experience physical connection. You and I—" His smile touched the center of her soul. "—we're all about real love."

"We are." It was back. The dizzy lightheadedness that always came when Taz neared her. She swallowed and tried to clear her mind. What were they supposed to be talking about? "The movie," she said out loud. "You wanted to talk about the bedroom scenes?"

Taz seemed careful not to break the bond between them. His hand, his eyes, remained connected to hers. "What we have on screen is good. You're a talented actress, because you allow yourself the privilege of feeling. I watched the bedroom scenes ten times yesterday and I feel everything about your character. But I wonder something."

She reminded herself to breathe. "What?"

"The character is a very bad girl. And you, Andi..." He let his eyes caress her for a moment. "You are very good. So innocent."

Andi wasn't sure where he was going.

"I was too careful when I wrote that scene, too worried that if I pushed too far, you'd run, you'd tell me no and I'd lose you as an actress." He ran his thumbs along the tops of her hands. "I'd lose all this."

Time seemed to stop, and with everything in her Andi wanted only to fall into his arms and kiss him, a kiss that would last half an hour or longer or forever, even. She blinked and tried to understand what he was getting at. "My character wasn't bad enough?"

"Not really." He furrowed his eyebrows, intent on his explanation. "She's a girl about to do the unthinkable. She'll model, sure. But she'd sell herself if that's what it takes for freedom." He didn't blink. "In that bedroom scene she's making a decision to run away and use her body as a means of survival." He angled his head, his tone thoughtful. "If I'm realistic and honest to the storyline, the character wouldn't stop at her bra. She would take off everything standing in the way of her old self and her body. So that she could fully realize the power of her nakedness."

Why hadn't Andi thought of that? Of course her character wouldn't have stopped at her bra. She wouldn't have been afraid to completely strip in front of a mirror. She would've taken everything off and studied herself, aware that from that point on she would use her body to rescue herself from her parents' control and captivity. "So, you want to reshoot that part?"

"I do." His look implored her to understand. "Like I said, I should've written the script that way from the beginning. But I didn't want to ask you to do anything you'd be uncomfortable with." He paused. "I wrote the script for you, Andi."

She tried to remember who she'd been back then, how she might've reacted if there'd been full nudity in the original screenplay. Taz was right. She would've run from the idea, turned him down flat. Now, though, a strange excitement began working through her and she practically buzzed with the thrill of redoing the scene. The film demanded honesty, and nudity was as honest as a person could get. She didn't need to fear her body. Taz had taught her that. He saw the body as art, which meant Andi had a pretty good idea he would be particularly taken with hers.

"When can we film it?"

"This afternoon, if that works for you." Taz was always gentle, never forcing anything. He cared about her as a person, the beauty of her from the inside out, as he'd often told her.

They made a plan, and Taz checked his phone calendar. "I have to go. Do me a favor." His voice deepened, his head near hers, the two of them swimming in a private sea of feelings and emotions. "Until then, be the character. Be the girl trying to break free and find independence from her controlling parents. I expect what you'll give me on film today will be some of your strongest work yet."

He didn't kiss her, but he didn't have to. His presence left a physical impression on her, and as she walked to the library, it was several minutes before her heartbeat returned to normal. *"Be the character,"* she told herself. And in her mind she allowed a deep and powerful resentment to build against her parents. How dare they tell her what to do and how to handle her life? They didn't understand art or real love or the desires of a young girl like herself. Their old-fashioned views would only keep her from experiencing life and emotion. It was time she broke free, whatever way she knew how.

She played the thoughts over and over in her mind, allowing herself to freefall into the psyche of the character. But as she did, she could feel the lines blur between fiction and reality. Her life wasn't much different from that of the character's, was it? Her father had called earlier, and all he'd done was ask questions. Who was she seeing? What was Taz's background? Was the guy a Christian? Maybe she should get more involved in Campus Crusade or a local church. She hung up after ten minutes, exhausted.

She walked faster. *"Be the character ... Be the character."* How dare they tell her what to do, and how to handle her life ... Their old-fashioned views would only keep her from experiencing life and emotion. It was time she ... How dare they ...

Over and over and over again she immersed herself in the character. By the time she finished with the library and walked back to her dorm, she could no longer tell for sure who she was talking about—the character in Taz's film or herself.

She met up with Taz in the same classroom fifteen minutes earlier than he'd requested. This time they were the only people in the room, and Taz explained that he'd operate the camera. So she'd have privacy. She could hardly wait to reshoot the scene, to show him that she was capable of using her body, capable of cutting-edge acting. He went over the blocking, the timing of the scene, and the feel of it. The first part would be the same as before, but as she stared at herself in her bra, the idea would take root in her heart and then filter through her eyes. Why wear a bra? She might have to dance topless or strip to make money. She couldn't find the true power of her body with a bra in the way.

"The scene will be more shadowy than last time. Better to show curves and silhouettes than too much nakedness," Taz told her. Even here he was nothing but professional, caring only for the integrity of the film. "You're okay with this?"

Andi didn't want to sound overly anxious, but with all the buildup throughout the day, she could hardly wait to shoot the scene. "Yes." She felt her heart beating hard against her chest. "I think you're right. The honesty of the film demands it."

He smiled, grateful for her understanding and proud of her at the same time. "Let's get going."

They ran the scene twice through to the place where she was supposed to take off her bra, and each time he cut it there. "More emotion, Andi. More anger and defiance." His voice was smooth against her soul, leading her, guiding her. "Let go of everything you've ever held onto or believed. Here there is only the character and her emotions. Let's try it again."

Finally, on the fourth time, when she reached the climactic moment, she was no longer Andi Ellison, missionary daughter. She was the character, body and soul. The emotions came like springs of muddied water, pushing through her hands and fingers, emanating from her eyes. In the distance, she thought she heard Taz's breathing change, faster maybe, more intense. Good. Let him see what she could do, what she had to offer. Slowly, and with raw defiance, she unhooked her bra and one at a time, she eased the shoulder straps down. Then with little effort, she let the bra fall to the floor.

Taz had told her the truth: the lighting was dark and shadowy. But now that she had done it — now that she was naked from the waist up — she had the strangest compulsion to keep going, to take the rest of her clothes off too. But Taz hadn't asked for that, not yet, anyway. She was still the character, still a living breathing creation of Taz's imagination. So instead she turned slowly one way and then the other, admiring herself in the mirror, imagining how she would use her body as a key to freedom.

Taz let her go, let the character take on a life of its own, acting from the organic place of character embodiment, as Taz called it. Finally, after a minute or so, he called out, "Cut!" and he was at her side. "That was beautiful. I believed every second." His eyes were wide with excitement, his breathing still faster than usual. "I could feel you, Andi. You're so very talented."

She was still without her bra or her top, but she didn't mind. It almost seemed like Taz had a right to see her this way, like he'd created this part of her and now she had nothing to hide. There was something else going on inside her, a sense of power she'd never felt around him. Taz's expression, his jagged breathing—all of it was a sign that her body hadn't only been a tool for the character, but for herself as well. She'd seemed to have gotten to him deeply, physically, and the truth in that was electrifying. Sure, Taz was touched by her acting ability. But was also clearly affected by her body, by the way she looked without clothes and the way she moved in front of the mirror.

When he was finished praising her, he stepped back so she could get dressed, and she did so without any sense of modesty or embarrassment. "You think you got what you were looking for?"

"Definitely. More than I ever imagined."

Andi smiled. She slipped into a light jacket and sized him up. Always in their friendship, Taz had seemed like the one in control, the one perfectly willing to wait for things to reach a more intense level. He was clearly attracted to her, but he was in no hurry to take it further. Drawn to her, but in no rush to date.

But here the tables felt dramatically turned. His cool confidence had been shaken and he seemed like a high school boy crushing on a college woman.

He walked her back to her dorm, and halfway there he took her hand in his again, his fingers between hers. His breathing was back to normal now, and most of his control was in place. "Andi, I was wondering." An easy laugh came from him and he stopped, facing her. "There's a jazz concert on campus next Saturday, and then afterwards, I should have my film edited by then. Maybe you can come back to my place and watch it."

Andi's heart soared, but she'd learned from him. So she refused to seem overly anxious. "I'd like that." She drew a long breath and let her eyes find his.

As she did, he put his free hand on his chest and looked suddenly startled. "Hey ... I felt that." His eyes danced with that familiar teasing she'd come to love.

"What?" She held back a ripple of laughter, playing up the mock drama of the moment. "You're having chest pains, Taz? Is that it?"

"No." He touched his fingers to her throat and then laid them again on his chest. "You breathed in." The laughter faded into sheer, unfiltered desire. "And I felt the air."

Her body trembled with the depth of his flattery. In all her life, she'd never known anyone like Taz, never imagined anyone like him. Night shadows hovered around them, and they were alone on the path. It was a moment when her body practically screamed for his touch, his kiss. But he took a step back and finished walking her to the dorm. Before he left, he complimented her again on her acting. Then he told her good-bye. "I'll be on Facebook later."

"Okay." The increasing distance between them felt like a physical blow. But she wouldn't make the first move, so she backed up to the steps of her dorm building. It was Friday and Bailey was spending the weekend at home again. Facebook would take the edge off Andi's loneliness. "See you there."

As she walked back into her dorm, a picture came to mind. A scene from her favorite musical, *Phantom of the Opera*. Midway through the play, the Phantom has seduced Christine so completely she no longer has a choice in the matter. She belongs to the Phantom, heart and mind, body and soul. In the past, Andi couldn't relate to the dark connection between the two, but that was no longer the case. Taz had that sort of control over her, and

Andi had given it to him willingly. She was not his angel of music, she was his angel of acting.

Never mind the promises she'd made as a young girl; she belonged to Taz now. Whatever he asked of her, she would give because like he said, love needed to be shared. Emotionally, intellectually, and physically. Especially physically.

She i-chatted with Taz for an hour before turning in and fell asleep dreaming of his kiss.

She could hardly wait for Saturday.

Twenty-Three

KEITH FINISHED PACKING EARLY AND FOLLOWED the smell of fresh-brewed Kenyan roast into the kitchen. Lisa was filling two tall mugs, and she glanced at him as he entered the room. "Two more weeks. I can't wait."

"Me either." Keith took one of the cups and held it under his chin. The hot steam felt good on his face. "We have a dozen meetings between now and then, but the festival has everyone talking. The guys at the studio think we could take top honors."

"I want a front-row seat." Lisa held her cup in both hands and leaned against the kitchen counter. "Have you talked to Andi? I'd like us all to be there."

"She wants to go." He slid up onto the kitchen island and let his legs dangle over the side. It was impossible to be entirely excited about their movie when the topic of Andi came up. "I'm worried about her."

"The boyfriend?"

"Whatever he is." Keith took a quick sip from his coffee. It was still too hot to drink. "His name comes up, but she gets defensive. She won't admit they're seeing each other."

"They're still working on his student film." Lisa's forehead lined with concern. "I got that much out of her. She dodges the question when I ask if he's a Christian. She said he's a spiritual person. Whatever that means."

"I don't like it. She's talking about staying on campus for the summer, working at the library and taking a few classes."

"Her grades are good. She said she'll get all As and one B for this last quarter." Lisa lifted the mug to her face and blew at the wisps of steam. "But I'm worried too. She seems different. She used to tell me everything, even her doubts. Now it's more of a 'Good, great, fine' sort of existence."

Good, great, fine. It was the way Keith and Lisa would describe most high school kids in their relationships with their parents. *How are you? Good. What about your friends? Great. And your classes? Fine. Good, great, fine.* They'd always been grateful that they shared a deeper connection with Andi, that she felt compelled to tell Lisa every detail of her high school life. But now ... Keith lowered his coffee cup and stared out the window into the gathering darkness. "What if this is worse than it seems?"

"I've been on her Facebook. She doesn't have a single picture of this Taz guy anywhere. And all the comments on her wall are from high school friends or Bailey Flanigan."

"I'm not sure that's proof." Keith still had a strong feeling something wasn't right. "She knows we're on her Facebook."

"True." Lisa looked more worried than before. "Maybe we should fly out and talk to her?"

Keith thought about that. "I'm not sure if she'd open up to both of us. Maybe you and she can take a day together before the film festival, take the car and go to the beach. You know, create an environment for conversation."

Lisa nodded. "I like that. We have to make time to talk." She thought for a few seconds. "I'm really not that worried. Andi knows the truth as well as anyone on that campus."

"That's what I keep telling myself." Keith pushed back his fears and concerns. Andi was a good girl. She knew the Bible, and right from wrong. Whoever this guy was, it couldn't be too serious. Andi was way too smart and levelheaded to fall that fast for a boy who didn't share her beliefs. At least that's what Keith had convinced himself. He let the subject pass. "I told you about NTM, right? We still haven't got anything in writing with them."

"Doesn't that worry Luke?"

"He's suspicious, same as me. But for now we're pressing ahead with *The Last Letter*. The studio agreed to a four-hundred-screen theatrical release, but they're willing to triple that if the movie does well at the festival."

"That's a miracle, really." She set her mug down on the counter and folded her arms. "Has Chase got a commitment from Kelly yet about the festival?"

"Last time I talked to him, she was planning to stay home. Same as before." The past month had been rocky for their friends, but Chase was committed to talking with Kelly, getting her to open up about her feelings. "She's seeing a doctor next week, a therapist. In case she's dealing with depression."

Lisa made a frustrated sound. "She doesn't need a doctor to tell her she's depressed. That's been obvious since Christmas." She threw her hands into the air, then dropped them. "Her husband's gone half the time, their finances are shaky, and Molly's still struggling to recover from her broken arm. That's enough to make the happiest person on earth depressed."

"She needs more time with God."

"Definitely." Lisa sounded defensive for her friend. "That's true with most of us, and especially for people battling depression. But she might need some kind of bridge between where she's at and where she needs to be with God."

"Bridge?"

"Right. Like an antidepressant." Lisa softened her tone. "Depression is truly a chemical imbalance in the brain. Sometimes medicine is the only way to set life right again."

Keith didn't want to argue about the issue. "Kelly needs help, we can agree on that."

They were quiet for a long moment, drinking their coffee, lost in their own thoughts. "A reviewer from *Variety* screened *The Last Letter* this past week. Loved it, absolutely raved about it. The story will run in a few weeks."

"Really?" Lisa's face lit up. "I'm so proud of you, Keith. I love you so much. Have I told you that lately?"

He slid back down to the floor, set his mug in the sink, and crossed to her. "All the time." He put his arms around her waist and pulled her close. "That's why I'm the most blessed man ever."

"I don't know about that. But I'm proud of you because you deserve it. You and Chase have worked hard, and now it's all about to pay off." She kissed him, clearly enjoying their closeness. "Tell me about the review."

"They compared the screenplay to something from Arthur Miller." He raised a brow and couldn't resist a single amazed chuckle. "Not only that, but they likened Jake Olson to a young Marlon Brando."

Lisa stared at him. Then she brought her hand to her mouth, a joyous laugh escaping through her fingers. "Are you serious? *Variety* hates everyone."

"Not us." Keith caught her face in his hands and kissed her—a kiss of joy and celebration despite the concerns they shared about Andi or Chase and Kelly. They were making movies for God, and if they were going to change the world with the power of film, they first needed to convince the gatekeepers.

The *Variety* review was proof the Lord had gone before them.

That would hopefully remain true in the week ahead. He and Chase were flying out first thing in the morning. They wouldn't need their car for this next round of meetings. Ben Adams had arranged for a driver to take them around in his Bentley. "At this level, it's better to make an impression," Ben had told them. In addition, they were staying at his place. Their car would only be in the way.

"I'm going to check our airline reservations. Make sure everything's in place."

"It is." Lisa's words held a deeper meaning. "It's more in place than either of us could begin to understand."

Keith was still smiling when he rounded the corner to the computer. He sat down, moved the mouse, and waited for the screen to come to life. It took just seconds to find their reservation and make sure there'd been no changes or scheduled delays. Weather was great. Keith didn't expect any trouble. He was about to sign off when he realized he hadn't checked the news — not in several days. It was always good to be aware of the issues as they headed into studio meetings.

He typed "Foxnews.com" in the search line and hit the enter button. The connection was quick, and almost instantly a list of stories appeared on his screen. One held the name of Brandon Paul.

"What?" he whispered to himself. Panic grabbed hold of his throat and tightened its grip. He desperately scanned the words, trying to make sense of them.

"Brandon Paul Agrees to NTM Movie Deal," the headline read.

Keith wanted to believe it was their movie the story was referring to, but it couldn't be. Luke would've told them if the studio had reached an agreement, if they were ready to make an announcement like this. He clicked the headline and the story came to life. Keith could barely focus as he read.

> Executives at NTM Studios announced today that Brandon Paul will star in an NTM original movie about a mentally challenged boy whose love for music gives him wings. The story comes from an NTM original screenplay, and is ex-

pected to be filmed later this year. "We are committed to maintaining and building our relationship with Brandon," said Ace L. Rustin, NTM VP of Development. "We're in the process of negotiating a new five-year deal and doing everything we can to keep him in the NTM family."

That was it, just a news brief. For anyone else checking the headlines at this hour, the story would be nothing more than a bleep on the screen of Hollywood life. Brandon Paul in another movie. Ho-hum. But for Keith and Chase—for them it meant that everything they'd worked on for the past six months was finished. Gone for good.

A fine layer of perspiration broke out across Keith's brow and he hung his head, trying to catch his breath.

So that was it? Brandon had signed a deal to make a movie almost exactly like *Unlocked*, without telling them or their attorney or Stephanie? This was Luke Baxter's worst nightmare coming true.

Keith gripped his knees. Were there no ethics in Hollywood whatsoever? He fought the desire to shout at the screen, to demand that Fox News pull the story because it couldn't be true. Brandon had promised them this movie.

But there it was in black and white. He lifted his eyes and let himself read the details one more time.

God, what's happening? What does this mean? We were so close to making a name for us and for You.

He wanted to run outside and raise his voice to the heavens, begging God for some kind of understanding. Despite their lawyer's fears, Keith had told himself this couldn't happen. Not with God on their side. But here they were.

He checked the time on the computer and saw it was after eight o'clock. Still early enough to call someone, but who? Should his first contact be with Chase or Luke? He was reaching for the phone, still figuring out what to do and who to call, when the phone rang.

He answered it on the first ring. "Hello?"

"Keith." The voice on the other end was serious. Dire, even. "Ben Adams here."

"Ben." Keith stood and paced from the computer to the far wall of windows that overlooked the backyard. Had Ben seen the news already? He decided to play ignorant, at least at first. "Our flight's set for tomorrow. The meetings are all still in order."

"I'm not calling about that." Ben exhaled, and the sound rattled across the phone lines. "Have you seen the news?"

"Actually, I was just checking it. The NTM story was a complete shock."

"For us too. I've got a call in to Luke Baxter. But the timing couldn't be worse."

Keith waited, his heart racing.

"I met with my financial team today, and my accounts aren't what they used to be." His voice sounded tired, deeply discouraged. "The whole market thing isn't of interest to me, not on a day-to-day basis. I've tried to look the other way. But the market crash has cost me half my net worth."

Half? Keith felt the floor beneath him shift. He gripped the windowsill and closed his eyes. Ben Adams was supposed to be worth a billion dollars. That meant the change in the market had cost him, what? Five hundred million? Keith couldn't begin to understand what losing that kind of money might mean to a guy like Ben. "I'm ... I'm sorry."

"We all are. The fact is I planned to sell a portion of my stock portfolio to finance *Unlocked.* Now I can't do that. No one would sell in this market." He drew a steady breath. "For that reason, my advisor is warning me not to invest in the film — and I guess that's especially true now, since it looks like you've lost your star and your studio."

Keith blinked his eyes open and stared at the still-darkening sky. Was this really happening? Was he really having this conversation with the man who had seemed so financially stable? "I guess I need to talk to Luke. The NTM announcement doesn't make sense."

"Either way, I have to pull out. Try to understand." Ben seemed to gather himself somewhat. "I told my advisor I still wanted to provide half the P&A budget for *The Last Letter*. He wasn't happy about it, but he agreed." There was a considerable silence. "These are the times that make a man, Keith. Especially a man of God. You'll be all right, and so will I. The markets will bounce back; I've seen it all before. But we must cling to the Lord, otherwise we'll lose more than our financial security. We'll lose hope. And we can't lose that."

They talked for a few more minutes, though later Keith wouldn't remember a word of it—nothing but the part about God and His direction. When they hung up, Keith returned to the computer and dropped, entranced, to the chair. They'd lost the Brandon Paul movie. They'd done everything they could. They had the actor and the author, the funding and the best lawyer in town. But they'd still lost it.

He needed to talk to Luke and Chase and Stephanie Fitzgerald. He needed to know whether Brandon was behind this. And if so, why he'd turned his back on them. But more than that, he needed to talk to the Lord.

With his face buried in his hands, he cried out to God about what had gone wrong and asked the Lord for wisdom and direction. With no hint of an answer, he asked anyway. He begged for peace and clarity, and most of all he asked God how it was even possible that they could lose everything they'd worked for—the promise the future held and the ability to influence a generation.

All in five crazy minutes.

Twenty-Four

THE GIRLS WERE BOTH IN BED when the phone rang at Chase's house. He was packing again, something he always seemed to be doing, but before he could answer it Kelly must've picked it up in the kitchen. The call was probably for her anyway. Laurie Weeks had been in touch a lot lately, making plans for a women's conference coming to town in a few days.

But after a minute or so, he heard her footsteps. Not until the last few months had he understood how discouraged a person's footsteps could sound. He could've picked out Kelly's in a room full of people.

"Chase." Her voice held a flicker of concern. "It's Keith. He doesn't sound right."

Chase frowned. Life in Hollywood and their roles as producers couldn't have been any better. He couldn't imagine why Keith would call—unless a problem had come up with their flights. He took the phone and turned toward the bedroom window. "Hey, what's up?"

A long pause filled the phone line before Keith finally spoke. "It's over, buddy."

Chase's heart hesitated, and then slammed into double time. "What do you mean, it's over?"

"It's over. We lost the Brandon Paul movie."

Chase sucked in a quick breath, overcome by disbelief. "That's crazy. Nothing's changed. If NTM doesn't want it we'll take it somewhere else. That's what the meetings are for this week."

"Get to your computer. Fox News will help you understand." Keith sounded weary, defeated. There wasn't even the hint of possibility in his voice.

Kelly still watched from the doorway. Now as he passed her, she whispered to him. "What is it? What happened?"

He held up his hand and gave her a look that implored her to be patient. With the receiver covered, he mouthed in her direction, "I'll tell you in a minute."

She hesitated, but then she returned to the kitchen, her body language proof she wasn't happy about being put off. Chase had no choice.

He went to the den, pulled out his laptop, and powered it up. He was on the Internet in seconds, tapping out the address to Fox News. All the while, Keith remained silent. Completely silent — as if there was nothing he could say that wouldn't be absolutely clear once the news page loaded.

Chase saw the headline about NTM and immediately called up the story. It took less than a minute for him to understand what had happened. "This is crazy! They can't steal our story!" Fury ripped through him and he clenched his fist. "Are you kidding, Keith? Nothing's over. Stephanie's agent won't stand for this, and neither will Luke. This is a bunch of garbage."

"I talked to Ben Adams. He says NTM can do pretty much what they want. They have teams of lawyers to cover their tracks." If Keith had been angry earlier, he wasn't now. "There's more."

A sick feeling grabbed hold of Chase. Had everyone lost their minds? Of course NTM couldn't do this. They'd sat down at six different meetings with Ace Rustin and his cronies. The proposal, the storyline, everything about the movie was already in place. They couldn't just recreate the plotline and go their own way now. He directed himself to focus, to listen to whatever else Keith had to tell him. "Go ahead."

"Ben talked to his accountants today, and his people have convinced him not to sell stocks in order to finance a movie. Not until the market improves."

The air seemed to leave the room. "That's not possible." Chase was on his feet again, his head hanging, knees trembling. He tried to grasp at the first question to surface. "He's still with us, right? He still wants to invest in our movies?"

"He can cover half the P&A, but that's it. Even if by some miracle we wind up with the Brandon Paul movie, he can't help us out."

The reality was immediately clear. Without investor money, what did Chase and Keith really bring to the table? Producers had to have money to work with, otherwise they weren't producers. Chase began to shake, shivering as if overtaken with a high fever. "So that's it; we have no movie."

"It doesn't look that way." Keith hadn't sounded this down in a long time, maybe ever. "We have *The Last Letter*, of course. But even if it does well, we won't have profits to reinvest for at least a year or eighteen months. By then *Unlocked* will be a thing of the past. One more movie that's already been done."

They talked for a few minutes, and Keith explained that they would still fly to LA in the morning, still take meetings around town. They still had rights to the novel, so if not NTM, other studios would still be interested. Even without Brandon Paul.

"What if the studios cancel? I mean, we no longer have the star."

"We have the book." Keith's tone showed some sense of rebounding. "Either way we need to meet with Luke and Kendall, then Stephanie and Brandon. We need to find out how this crazy announcement happened, and move on."

"That's it? We find out what's behind it and give up?"

"Of course not." Keith's intensity was back. "We're missionaries first, remember that?"

Chase felt the chastisement straight to the depths of his soul. It was the first time since the phone rang that he'd even thought about God. He sank into the living room sofa chair and stared at the ground. "I remember."

"Okay, so we pray. We remind ourselves that no ground is ever gained for Christ without great effort. It's a battle, not a land grab. The world owns the movie industry, so what makes us think anything about this job will be easy?"

Slowly Chase began to nod. "You're right." He wanted to cry out to Jesus, apologize for having such a human response instead of immediately turning to his faith. "You've already prayed about this, I take it?"

"For the past half hour. But I want to pray together. Back in the jungles of Indonesia, we prayed as often as we breathed. We would rather miss a meal than a chance to pray together for the people we were preaching to."

Chase could picture that old life, and suddenly he longed for it, for the simplicity of knowing that his job was clearly spelled out: tell people about Jesus, one after another, as long as he drew breath. This world, the world of Hollywood, was much more complicated. Especially in moments like this. In the back of his mind he wondered what he would tell Kelly. An anxious sigh filtered between his teeth. "You start."

Keith took a quick breath and began. "Lord, we are Your witnesses here on earth, Your missionaries. We left Indonesia to take the message of hope and faith to the world of Hollywood. We've felt Your presence every step of this journey, back when our actress was threatening to run and our food truck burned down, back when we were out of money and not sure how we would finish one film, let alone more. But we stood firm, believing in You then, and we stand firm, believing now. You know all things, and You know why NTM would make such an announcement, and how things with Brandon Paul fell apart. We ask You now for clarity and vision, for wisdom and direction. Without You, we don't know where to turn."

A moment of silence separated their cries for help, and then Chase began. "I'm sorry, Father. I heard this terrible news and all I could think about was myself. The work I've invested, the money and hope. All of it lost. But You're a God of miracles. We can only follow where You lead. So lead us now, dear God ... Lead us now. We ask this in Jesus' name, amen."

There wasn't much more to say. They made last-minute plans for the morning drive to the airport and ended the call. Chase could hear Kelly in the kitchen, putting away dishes. He wondered if there were visible weights on his shoulders, or if they just felt that way.

Be with me, God. Help her understand. Keith is right. There must be something great on the other side of this mountain, or the battle wouldn't be so fierce.

I am with you, Son ... I am your strong tower.

The verse was from something Chase had read the day before. He clung to it as he walked to the kitchen.

Kelly turned around, her eyes anxious. "Well? That didn't sound very good."

"It isn't." He leaned on the refrigerator, and the old machine groaned in response. He shifted his weight away from it and made himself look into Kelly's eyes. "We lost the Brandon Paul movie." He didn't wait for her questions, but rattled off everything he knew about the Fox News story and the similarities between *Unlocked* and the movie NTM was calling an original. Then, barely taking time for a breath, he told her about Ben Adams and the funding crisis.

Slowly she dried her hands on a nearby towel, never once even blinking as she stared at him. "Without funding, there's no movie anyway. Isn't that right?"

"I'm not sure which piece matters most—the NTM announcement or the realization by Ben that he could no longer invest in our film." Chase tried to sound as positive as possible, but his voice failed him. "Either way, we have to accept the obvious. We no longer have a Brandon Paul movie."

Chase expected Kelly to fall apart. She would start crying and rail on Chase for ever believing that God had called him and Keith to the mission field of Hollywood. Of all things. But none of that happened. Instead she straightened and for the first time in a long time, a tender smile tugged at her lips. "Everything's going to be okay. We still have our faith." She held her hands out to him. "We still have each other."

He went to her, trying to figure out where she was coming from. All along she'd been doubtful of their movie ventures. So then why now was she so calm, so sure that things would work out? He pulled her close and stroked her back. "You're not mad?" His voice was a tentative whisper. This Kelly was the one he'd fallen in love with, the one who had all but disappeared these past months.

"I'm heartbroken. But I'm not mad." She ran her hands over the back of his head and whispered close to his ear. "This means you can stop traveling and be home with us. You tried your best, Chase. What more could God ask of you?"

Gradually, he began to realize what was happening. Kelly wasn't mad because she thought he was giving up, wholly and completely. With this single closed door, she figured the game was over. No more movie-making, no more traveling. No more wondering whether they'd be in financial ruin a year from now. He could get a real job and they could find their way to normalcy.

He drew back, feeling the shock in his eyes as he studied her. But before he could set her straight, she brushed her fingertips against his face. "My dad called yesterday. He knows someone at the post office. Most branches are laying off, but this one's hiring.

Just a few miles from our house." The enthusiasm in her voice was new, something she hadn't allowed for a long time. "His friend promised to put in a good word for you. If you're interested."

Chase felt like he was being ripped apart, like the floor had become a deadly sea of knives. "Are you serious?" He pushed back from her, not wanting a single minute more of her pity or easy answers. "I'm not looking for a job at the post office." He spat the words like they were laced with poison. "Keith and I are flying to LA tomorrow, where we're taking meetings on *Unlocked*. Without Brandon Paul. We're moving ahead, believing with everything we are that God will clear up the details."

Kelly's calm, collected veneer shattered like a cheap piece of glass. "But you just said it was finished. There's no Brandon Paul movie, right? So that means you come home and get a real job." Her tone grew intense, her voice louder than before. "That's what fathers do — they provide for their families."

"And wives support their husbands." He scowled at her for a long moment and then rolled his eyes. "We're not finished making movies. If God closes this door, He'll open another one somewhere. It's our job to find it."

"What if the door is right here in your own house? Huh, Chase? What you're doing scares me to death. Did you ever think about that?"

"There's nothing to be afraid of, Kelly. I won't let you down." He stared at her, alternately hating her and longing for her understanding. Finally he brushed his hand in her direction. "Never mind." He turned around and headed back to his laptop.

The headline still screamed at him from his computer screen. *Brandon Paul Agrees to NTM Movie Deal.*

For almost an entire minute he stared at the words as doubts began to crowd in around him. What if Kelly was right? At what point did they wave the white flag and surrender their dreams of making movies in lieu of earning a regular living? If he was honest, this news scared him too. The announcement was strange and unexpected, and for that reason maybe it *was* a sign. Maybe God could use him better as a mail carrier.

He felt angry tears in his eyes and he slammed his laptop shut. No! Kelly was wrong. This wasn't a sign. It was a mountain. Nothing more, nothing less. If this were a sign to quit making movies, Keith would've felt that way, too, right? He would've said something about having a meeting, just the two of them, and deciding whether they should call it quits.

But that wasn't how Keith felt. During their conversation he had even reminded Chase of Jeremiah 29:11. Jeremiah Productions. God knew the plans He had for them, to give them a hope and a future. If they felt led to Hollywood, convinced God wanted them to make movies that mattered, then they would follow that dream until every door was closed and locked. He would mention Kelly's fears to Keith, but he could almost hear his friend's response.

Trust God. We have to trust.

The Brandon Paul movie was just one door. Keith had even said they should feel excited, that the battle was only fierce because God has something better for them in the long run. So why couldn't Kelly see that?

He clenched his fists again and released them. A mail carrier? Was she serious? He'd rather go back to Indonesia.

He needed to talk to someone—Luke or Stephanie, someone who believed in their projects. Certainly Stephanie would be furious when she saw the NTM announcement. She was an early riser who turned in each night around eight o'clock. Otherwise he'd call her right now. NTM could put Brandon in an original film, but the screenplay would have to, indeed, be original. A story about a mentally challenged boy finding freedom in music? It was almost exactly the same plot as *Unlocked*. NTM or not, they'd never get away with it.

Even so, he needed to talk. He thought about calling Keith back, but his friend was clearly exhausted, and they still had their early flight in the morning. He racked his brain, wondering if he could reach Luke at this hour, and then deciding against the idea of even trying. It was much later in Indiana, and Luke was a professional. They would talk at length tomorrow, Chase had no doubts. But tonight ...

The idea hit him in a rush. He could call Kendall. She would know about her father's financial trouble, and she'd have a sense of how things would go tomorrow at their first meeting. She was used to the highs and lows of Hollywood.

He pulled his cell phone from his pocket and dialed her number without stopping for a minute to consider whether doing so was right or wrong. She was their business partner, their teammate. They needed to talk now more than ever.

The call almost went to her voice recorder, but at the last moment she answered. "Chase ..." Her voice held compassion and understanding. "You saw the news?"

"That and the situation with your dad."

"I know. I talked to him." She sounded down, but not out. "I hate this part of movie-making, how quickly things can fall apart. But I know this—" Determination rang in her voice. "God is still on His throne, and He's still working miracles. He didn't bring us this far to let us down."

Chase closed his eyes and breathed in deeply through his nose. This was what he needed, a confident, trusting voice on the other end assuring him that they might have lost a round, but they were still in the fight. "What's the deal with NTM? Any ideas?"

"Some. I put a call into Brandon, but he must be out. I've seen a few recent paparazzi photos of him clubbing it up with Hollywood's wild-child crowd. I've been meaning to talk to him about it, but we've played phone tag." She exhaled. "Now this."

"So you think ..." Chase grabbed at straws, desperate for more of her positive spin on things. "You think maybe it's all a mistake?"

"That's possible. Brandon was dead-set on starring in *Unlocked*. I can't believe he'd sell out to NTM like that. Not for any kind of money." She went on to explain that even if NTM offered him more money for ditching the author and producers, to take their offer would be shortsighted. "We have studios lined up who will pay him more than NTM, with all of us involved. This can't be about money."

He nodded, grateful for any hope she could offer. "Keith and I want to press on, but I don't know. I mean, do you think maybe God's closing the door on all of it?"

"Not at all." She sounded outraged by the idea. "Chase, you listen to me. You and Keith are two of the most talented producers I've ever come across. Combined with your talent as a director, I believe with all my being you're about to break into this business with a vengeance. Brandon's lucky to work with you, and I think Stephanie's told him so."

In the wake of her words, hope suddenly had a heartbeat again. Brandon Paul wanted to work with them. Which meant they could most likely attract other investors. A single announcement by NTM didn't change that, no matter what the explanation. "We'll meet for lunch tomorrow after you fly in," she said as the conversation wound down. "Between now and then I'll talk to Luke and Brandon, and we can figure out where things really stand."

"Okay." Chase felt much better. The weights on his shoulders were gone, at least for now. "God's brought us this far, right?"

"Exactly." There was a smile in her voice, and it was contagious.

He felt his own weary smile fall into place. "We need to believe, that's all."

"Right. God wins, remember that. You and Keith are God's filmmakers. You keep on, and He'll meet you. Seriously, Chase. You have to keep believing."

He let her words roll around his heart for a minute, soothing the wounded edges. "Thank you."

"We're a team. When I'm down, you can remind me. This time it's my turn."

As the call ended, Chase returned to his packing. Calling Kendall had been just what he needed. She was right. Even with the disappointments from tonight, their movie-making was headed in the right direction. Ahead of them they had this week's meetings for *Unlocked* and *The Last Letter's* appearances at the film festivals. And there was the theatrical release. *The Last Letter* might be a huge box-office hit. It was all suddenly possible.

He reached the bedroom and stared at his wife. Kelly had apparently brushed her teeth in record time, because she was under the covers, softly snoring, not concerned whatsoever about the state of his heart or his confidence. *Fine*, he thought as he looked at her. *At least I have Kendall to believe in me.*

He finished packing and set his suitcase near the front door. Then he brushed his teeth, set his alarm, and turned in, careful to stay to his side of the bed so he wouldn't wake Kelly. So he wouldn't have to deal with her. He'd be gone before she woke up, which meant one more time of parting ways without finding common ground. One more time of leaving home feeling her disappointment like a chain around his ankles. But that couldn't be helped. He would press on without her and when they climbed over this mountain he would spend time on his marriage. Until then, he could survive without Kelly's support, the way he'd survived these past several months. He didn't need her praise and encouragement.

God had given him Keith and Kendall for that.

Twenty-Five

ANDI UNDERSTOOD THERE WAS A BATTLE going on—a battle for her heart and soul. But she didn't care. If the world was on one side and God and her faith on the other, Andi was cheering for the dizzying, intoxicating world. Everything about her life had grown more intense, more exciting, since she'd fallen for Taz. And if that meant stepping over the edge, she would do it. For now, at least. While she still had so much about life to experience, so many emotions to discover. She could always go back if things got too deep. What was the worst that could happen?

Her date with Taz to the jazz concert had been like a journey of brilliant reds and oranges, all the colors of a sunrise and sunset combined into one amazing night. They sat next to each other, the heat from the nearness of his body filling her senses. But even then, he didn't kiss her. They talked about physical love as they walked back to her dorm, and Taz said he wasn't a fan of free love. "Our bodies are instruments of art and love, all tied into one. If we share them too freely, we cheapen the art."

Andi loved that, the way he saw physical love as simply one more form of art. Until that night, she'd wondered why he was waiting to kiss her, why he hadn't acted when he was clearly taken by her, the same way she was taken by him. But after their talk on the way back to her dorm that night, she understood better. If physical love was art, then this time of waiting was a prelude, a way to heighten the beauty of whatever lay ahead.

It was the second week of May and finals were over. Andi had studied hard, and she had a good feeling about her grades. Taz hadn't been a distraction in that sense whatsoever. She filed out of her psych class, and across the campus she spotted Cody Coleman. He was walking with a group of guys, and for a moment she stopped and watched him.

How different she might feel about her faith if God had allowed her to have a relationship with a guy like Cody. Whatever his rocky past, he was completely sold out to Christ now, and Andi guessed he always would be.

She started walking again, making sure her path wouldn't cross his. Their friendship had fizzled, and she could live with that. She didn't need a lecture from Cody about how she spent her time. She had Bailey for that. Also, she was in a hurry. Taz planned to make her dinner at his apartment tonight. She didn't need an awkward conversation with Cody to make her feel guilty.

She remembered a time a few weeks ago when she'd run into him between classes. "Why so quiet?" she'd asked him. She kept her tone light, not wanting to sound like the poor victim in their friendship.

"School has me pretty busy." He raised an eyebrow. "And you seem busy with Taz Bazzi."

Andi had been surprised. "You know him?"

"He went to Clear Creek High. Hung out with the music types." Cody shrugged. "Had quite a reputation with the girls."

Something about Cody's tone offended Andi that day. She wanted to defend Taz and his beautiful heart, his unique way of looking at life. "That doesn't surprise me. He's very special."

Cody laughed. "Be careful, Andi. He had that 'special' thing going on back in high school too. Most of the girls figured him out pretty quick. He could say what he wanted to get his way with one of them, and then he moved on." He let his laughter fade. "If you were my sister, I'd forbid you from seeing him. Seriously."

If she were his sister ... Andi hated the way he said that. As if she could never be good for anything other than a close friendship. She wanted to scream at him and ask him what was wrong with her. What did Bailey Flanigan have that Andi didn't? But she wouldn't give him the chance to hurt her any more than he already had. She held her head high. "We must know different guys, then. The Taz I know is nothing like that."

The conversation ended, and Andi hadn't seen or heard from Cody since. But now his warning came back to her, and she was frustrated at herself for remembering it. Today was a perfect day, otherwise. The sun was out and the leaves and flowers were coming to life across campus. The temperature was already in the mid–eighties. Finals were behind her, and tonight she and Taz were going to celebrate. She didn't need Cody or anyone else putting a damper on her excitement.

She walked back to her dorm and caught Bailey just as she was leaving. "I'm having dinner with my parents and Tim." She beamed with happiness. "Doesn't it feel good to have finals over?" She let out a victory cry. "And all of summer stretched out before us."

"Yeah, it's amazing." Andi had been so busy with Taz and her classes that she and Bailey had grown somewhat distant. "Did you decide what you're doing? For the summer, I mean?"

"I've got the Cru retreat at Lake Monroe. But after that I'm definitely going to New York in August with Tim and my mom. We're auditioning for ensemble roles in three shows — sort of an open casting call. After that, I'm not sure. If I don't get a part, I'll be in Bloomington." She set her bag down on her bed and looked at Andi, her interest genuine. "What about you?"

"I'm not going on the retreat, and I'm not going home. I know that much." She laughed at the idea. "My parents would have me signed up as a church camp counselor in no time." Andi realized how she sounded, but it was too late. She managed a sad smile. "You know what I mean."

Bailey hesitated, as if there was much she wanted to say. But she only held Andi's gaze for a long while. "You can stay with my family any time over the summer. We have the apartment. If your parents don't want to pay for the dorm ..."

"Thanks." Andi imagined the freedom she'd have with Taz if she had their dorm room to herself. Taz had three roommates. It was a rare night when — like tonight — he had the place to himself. "Actually, I'll probably stay in the dorm. I'm taking a few classes. Nine units, maybe. I'd like to get ahead a little, so that means making up the time somewhere."

"Acting still, right?"

"Definitely. My dad's struggling with the Brandon Paul movie, but there'll be others. I wanna be ready next time the chance comes up."

Andi felt strange, the way the conversation with Bailey was going. When they started out as roommates last fall they were so much alike — two girls with a love for God and a determination to be pure. But now ... their differences made even a talk like this feel strained. Like there was far more they weren't saying. "I talked to the librarian. Looks like she has a part-time job for me over the summer recataloging the books."

"Sounds tedious." Bailey wrinkled her nose.

"I can listen to my iPod while I work." Andi gave a light shrug. "Sounds like a paycheck to me. And my parents won't let me stay unless I'm earning money."

Again Bailey seemed like she wanted to say something, and this time she dropped the chitchat about their summer plans. "How are things with Taz?"

"He's wonderful." Andi felt her whole face light up. "I wish you knew him better, Bailey."

"I knew him a little at Clear Creek. He was a year older, so I'd forgotten until Cody reminded me." She frowned with worry. "He didn't have the best reputation."

"He's changed. I've never met anyone like him."

"Hmmm." Bailey fiddled with her bedspread. She'd packed up most of her things, so her side of the room was pretty bare. "What do your parents think?"

"They don't know that much, really. Just that I'm seeing someone."

"But it's more than that, right?" Bailey didn't sound judgmental, just concerned. "You can be honest with me. You're falling for him, huh?"

"I guess." Andi walked over and sat on the bed next to Bailey. "He talks about love and then he talks about art and film and music, and the lines blur between all of it. I've never met anyone so romantic."

"What about ... what about the physical stuff. He's kissed you, right?"

"That's the weird thing." Andi was dying for someone to talk to about Taz. Until now she and Bailey had only said a few words in passing, both of them too busy to discuss in depth their lives outside school. And of course Andi didn't want to be reprimanded. "We spend all our free time together, but every time I think he's going to kiss me, he backs away. I mean, I feel like we're kissing every time because, I don't know, we're just that close. But he's a gentleman, Bailey. He doesn't want to do anything I'm not comfortable with."

Bailey looked relieved. "That's good." She bit her lip. "What about the movie? The film you made?"

"It's finished. He turned it in last week as part of his final. I guess the department gave out awards and his film took the top prize." There was something else, something Taz wanted to tell her tonight. But for now that's all Andi knew. Except that the short movie was the talk of the Indiana University film department. "I think it really grew me as an actress."

Bailey nodded. "You took off your shirt, right? Down to your bra?"

The conversation was going too well for Andi to ruin it now with the whole truth. She nodded. "Yes. The scene called for it."

"You'd better hope it doesn't get out on the Internet." Bailey put her hand on Andi's knee. "You know how easy it is to put things on YouTube or Facebook. If your parents saw it, they'd be freaked out for sure."

"For sure." Andi's stomach twisted at the thought. She hadn't considered the possibility, and now it was too late. She would talk to Taz about it later.

"And what about God?" Bailey seemed more relaxed now. Less worried about hitting a taboo topic. "How are things with you and Him?"

"Well..." She winced. "I haven't exactly been a good little Cru girl this quarter. Too busy with *Robin Hood* and my grades."

"And Taz."

"Yes, and Taz." She took a quick breath and tried to sound upbeat. "But there's always the fall quarter. It's easier to get involved then, anyway."

"Yeah, but I wasn't talking about Cru." Bailey's voice softened. She cared; Andi could feel her sincerity in a way she'd forgotten until now. "I was talking about God."

"God." Andi stood and wandered back to her side of the room. She opened her dresser drawer and glanced at Rachel's journal, tucked in near the back. She shut the drawer and leaned against the wall near her bed. "I still believe, if that's what you mean. I guess I just have to find my own way. You know, because God will always be there for me."

"But we won't always be here for God." Bailey lowered her eyes to the dresser where she must've known Rachel's journal was. "Your friend Rachel's life told us that much."

Andi understood the message. There was risk for the people who walked away from God, who believed that He'd be there waiting in the tomorrows of their lives, when they were tired of exploring the world, when they wanted the safety of His narrow path once again. What if tomorrow never came, the way it hadn't come for Rachel Baugher? "I don't know," Andi sighed. "I have to find my own way. That's all."

"Okay." Bailey's smile was sad. "But remember what the Bible says about life. Real life."

"That only God can give it?" Andi knew her Scriptures. That much hadn't changed.

"Exactly. And apart from Him, there is no life at all." Bailey stood and checked the time on her phone. "I have to get going. Wanna join us for dinner?"

"No, thanks." Andi met Bailey near the middle of the room. "Taz is taking me out. We're celebrating his film and the fact that finals are over. I get to see the finished movie for the first time tonight."

Bailey nodded slowly, her eyes never leaving Andi's. "Be careful, girl. And call me if you need me." The two of them hugged. "Let's get together early next week."

"Okay." Andi was glad they'd talked. It had been too long without a heart-to-heart, and even though they disagreed about life and the way to true happiness, they were still close. Closer than Andi had thought. Bailey wasn't going to write her off just because of her decisions. Andi was grateful, because someday—some very far-off day—she might want to be like Bailey again. And when that day came, if it came, Bailey would be her best friend ever. The way she couldn't really be right now, when they were so different.

Bailey left, and a few hours later Andi arrived at Taz's doorstep.

He stepped out onto the small landing and looked at her for a long time, his eyes taking in the length of her. "You're the most beautiful girl on campus, Andi. In person, and in front of the camera." He led her in, and she caught the smell of incense burning in another room. It was sweet and spicy, but not overpowering, and it mixed with something cooking in the oven. A Mexican dish of some kind. Andi took off her sweater and laid it over the back of the first chair they walked past. She wore skinny jeans and boots, a form-fitting navy-blue T-shirt and her best perfume. She hoped it would be enough to finally convince him to make a move and kiss her.

She looked around his apartment, at the way it felt like him. She'd only been here one other time, and then only to meet up with him before a movie.

Now, with his roommates gone and the place cleaned up, she took time to appreciate the place. Photos of partially nude women hung on the walls, each of them shot in dramatic black and white, a collection of art the way only Taz could appreciate it. He watched her. "I look at those photos, at the way they use their bodies to make a statement about love and nature." He gazed at a row of portraits, and then back at her. "And all I see is you, Andi. The way you would look in every picture. Every pose."

Her head spun, and her mouth went dry. He was falling for her, he had to be. If he didn't kiss her tonight, she would find a way to kiss him. She couldn't go another night without feeling his touch.

They moved into his living room, which consisted of an old leather sofa topped with a number of warm, fuzzy blankets. He came close to her, so close she could smell the freshness of his skin.

With the lightest brush of his fingers, he framed her face. "I thought we'd start with the film."

"Great." She felt a thrill of excitement run through her. "I can't wait."

He clicked on the TV and turned off the lights. But before he pushed the Play button, he sat on the sofa beside her and faced her. "You won best actress, Andi. I didn't want to tell you until now, so I could see your eyes."

Hope surged through her. "You're serious?" She wanted to get up and run around the room, but she threw her arms around his neck instead. "You know what this means?"

A soft chuckle came from him. "It means I was right." He pulled back and looked deeply into her eyes. "You have a gift."

"It means I can act! I can do this for a living, I know it!"

They looked at each other for a long time, and Andi wanted him to kiss her in the worst way. But just when it seemed like he might, he put his arm around her shoulders instead and eased her close against his side. "The film is amazing, and it's all you." He hit the Play button, and the movie began.

When they reached the scene where she strips down, Andi held her breath. But Taz had stayed true to his word. The scene was shadowy and sensual, and other than the moment when she looked at herself in the mirror, it would've been impossible to tell she was the actress.

"Beautiful," Taz whispered near her ear. His breath came faster again, the way it had when he filmed the scene. "You take my breath away, Andi."

He whispered to her again and again throughout the film, and when it was finished, when he hit the Stop button and powered down the television, Andi could feel his desire like a physical presence. Taz turned to her and lightly touched her forehead, her cheeks. "You're mine. You know that, right?"

"Yes." Andi didn't hesitate. Her whisper was breathy, revealing her own heightened sensuality. "I've belonged to you for a long time."

That was all he needed to hear. In a move that felt almost scripted, Taz kissed her. The feeling was like every wonderful thing Andi had ever experienced, all rolled into one brilliant rainbow of emotions. She wasn't sure when he eased her onto her back or how he moved from kissing her to touching her, to peeling away her clothing. But whatever was happening, Andi didn't want it to stop. She'd never felt like this in all her life.

Thirty minutes later, when she had given Taz everything she had to give and was getting dressed, she felt a flickering pang of regret. Her father's face flashed in her mind, and she imagined for an instant how disappointed he'd be, how this was a promise that could never be lived out after tonight. But even if her father knew, and if she were forced to defend herself and her actions, Andi would do so. Because nothing in all her life had ever made her feel the way Taz had this past half hour.

She wasn't just another college girl sleeping with any other college guy. She was in love, and Taz was everything she'd dreamed of. She would remind herself as often as the doubts might come. So what if she wasn't the sweet and innocent virgin she'd hoped to be. She was a grown woman, mature enough to make her own decisions. Never mind everything she'd been taught or the narrow path she'd read about in the Bible. Everything would be just fine. What she and Taz had shared wasn't sex or sin or anything of the sort.

It was art.

Breathtaking and beautiful.

LISA SAT STRAIGHT UP IN BED, gasping for air and clutching at the covers. A feeling of utter doom surrounded her like thick fog and she could do nothing to get away from it. It was Andi! Her daughter was in trouble.

Lisa shot a look at the bedside clock. Just after midnight, three in the morning in Bloomington. Keith was in LA so it was too late to call him, too late to call Andi. But that didn't change how she felt. She sat up straighter and realized her heart was pounding. Faster, louder, faster, louder.

God, what's happening?

Pray, my daughter. You must pray continually.

The answer came quickly and with it a vivid picture of Andi the way she'd looked in the jungles, wide-eyed and happy, telling the women about Jesus. Something had changed that, she was suddenly certain. Never mind if Andi's Facebook didn't give clues, and if Andi kept convincing her and Keith that everything was okay. It didn't matter that Andi had never given them a reason to doubt her. This was an emergency. The intensity of Lisa's fear and panic couldn't have been worse if she were watching her daughter fall off a cliff.

Andi was in deep, desperate trouble.

Pray. She had to pray. That's what God wanted and that's what she would do. She climbed out of bed, trembling, shivering. *Please, God ... be with her. Save her from whatever's happening. Please.*

Lisa fell to the floor, to her knees and then flat on her face, her nose and mouth pressed against the rough carpet fibers.

God, she's our girl, our only child. Please, help her. Give me a window to her life so I'll know how to intervene. Open the lines of communication and clear the deception. Please, God ...

Lisa prayed that way for twenty minutes, battling the darkness and fear, the certainty that Andi was in dire trouble. Finally the panic eased and she stood, weary, exhausted from the fight. Even then she prayed, because that's what God wanted from her. She could hardly wait for morning because this time she would press until she received real answers from her daughter. She would accept nothing less. Because if the intensity of her strange and sudden certainty was accurate, her precious daughter didn't face the sort of trouble that could be quickly fixed.

But the sort that could destroy her.

Twenty-Six

KELLY AGREED TO THE WOMEN'S CONFERENCE for one reason. She had never felt further from God and Chase in all her life, and she was scared to death. Scared about the road she was on and terrified about where it might lead. Besides, Laurie had raved about the speakers and the music, and she'd done something else that pushed Kelly over the edge.

She'd arranged a babysitter for Molly and Macy.

When the teenage leader of the church's youth group showed up at her house just after eight that Saturday morning, Kelly was ready. She showed the girl around the house and explained the meals for the day. "You don't mind cooking?"

"Not at all." The girl smiled easily. "I cook all the time for my little sisters."

Finally, when Kelly had introduced Molly and Macy to the teenager and when she was certain she'd left every possible emergency number, she set out for Laurie's house. She was running early, so she stopped at McDonald's and bought two orders of hotcakes and a sausage biscuit. That way she wouldn't be hungry for lunch. She ate on the way to Laurie's and carefully wadded up the wrappers and reached back to stick them in the pocket behind her seat.

Not that Laurie would be looking. Kelly was leaving her car at her friend's house so they could ride to the conference together. Besides, she'd told her friend she was doing better. Which she was. Most days. Especially since her appointment with the therapist. Sure enough, he'd diagnosed her with a moderate to severe case of depression. More severe now that Chase was refusing to give up his crumbling movie dreams and come home. The doctor had prescribed Prozac, which was supposed to help not only elevate her mood, but also cut her appetite. Kelly wasn't sure if it was working yet, but she did feel a little better.

Laurie lived just a few miles away, and soon the two were hugging before getting into Laurie's car. "I have a feeling about today," Laurie told her as they climbed inside. "God's up to something big."

Kelly hoped so, but she certainly didn't feel it. She'd spent less than an hour talking to God the entire month of May, and now she felt like a hypocrite wasting a day at a Christian women's conference when she could be home cleaning or reading to her girls.

The event was in downtown San Jose at the HP Pavilion. Once they found a parking place and filed in with thousands of other women, Kelly's doubts returned.

"It'll take a half hour to get out of here," she told Laurie. "I mean, if something goes wrong with the girls."

"It's raining outside." Laurie put her arm around Kelly's shoulders. "They'll be inside watching movies and coloring all day. Nothing's going to go wrong."

Kelly had to agree. The rainy weather did limit the possibility of injuries. But maybe that wasn't why she felt uneasy. Maybe it was because Chase had flown down to LA that day and now he was meeting with his Hollywood friends and trying to figure out what to do next. He wanted nothing to do with Kelly's more practical response, which was fine. He was bound to see soon that the optimism from his Hollywood friends wouldn't pay their bills.

All around them seats were filling up fast. "There have to be eight thousand people here." Laurie leaned close, in awe over the gathering. "Can you imagine, this many women in one place praising God? Like a glimpse of heaven."

Kelly felt completely and utterly detached from the reality happening around her. What had happened that she wasn't caught up in the excitement? Back in her Indonesian days, she would've loved nothing more than a day like this, surrounded by women worshiping the Creator. But here ... she had no right to be excited about worship. She was at odds with her husband and she could barely get up each morning. What good would worship do except remind her of her failings?

The music started, and a sharp, professional praise band started in with "Blessed Be Your Name," a beautiful number by Matt Redman. The music and words were familiar, but Kelly hadn't heard them in so long that the memory of them almost seemed to belong to someone else. Even still, there was power in the sound of thousands of women's voices singing the same song, believing the same message.

"Blessed be Your name, in the land that is plentiful ..."

Kelly was familiar with the first verse, the picture of joy and prosperity during times when it was relatively easy to worship God. She let herself be drawn by the music, by the ebb and flow of it. By the time the song reached the first chorus, ladies all around her were rising to their feet, hands raised in praise. Kelly moved her mouth, singing along even if she didn't feel the words.

The second verse kicked in and Kelly finally felt her heart engage.

The words seemed to hang on the screen longer than usual, and Kelly read over them again and again. Words about her being in the desert place. Wasn't that exactly where she was now? She and Chase barely spoke to each other, and she couldn't stop her cravings for more than a day or two, no matter how hard she prayed.

Suddenly it hit her that maybe there was a connection. It was times like this — when she was in a desert, in a wilderness — that she most needed to bless the name of the Lord.

She stood as the song played on, and she clasped her hands near her chest. Next to her, Laurie was already on her feet. God was here; Kelly could feel His presence. But what could He possibly want with her? She had no right to stand here with these other women, women who were better believers, more faithful followers.

The song built to a crescendo and Kelly was surprised to feel tears on her cheeks. She dabbed at them and remained standing as the next song blended with the last. It was a Hillsong praise number called "Mighty to Save," and in the stronger days of last fall it had been one of her favorites. *"Everyone needs compassion ... love that's never failing ..."* The music grew and built to the chorus and Kelly had the strong sense that the words, the melody, were for her alone.

After another few songs, the morning worship ended and a speaker took the stage. She talked about the battle of life and how in the end Christians had the privilege of knowing for certain that they win.

Kelly was knocked back in her seat by that simple truth. She hadn't thought about that realization for far too long. No matter how tiresome and weary she felt today, with Christ she was on the winning team. She wasn't supposed to grovel along, discouraged and depressed. She was supposed to draw strength from that one fact. Her team was going to win. Why couldn't she just believe God would take care of them when they had so much to look forward to? She felt terrible, like the worst possible wife, the worst Christian ever. If only she'd heard this six months ago, before things had gotten so out of control.

More music followed but Kelly couldn't sing along. She stared at her lap and let the tears fall. The second speaker talked about the struggles and disappointments of life and how wrong it was to drag them through each day when God called all people to trade them in.

"Give Him your ashes, and He'll give you a crown of beauty," the woman declared.

The entire auditorium burst into applause.

Kelly thought about that. How long had she walked around dragging a bag of ashes? And wasn't there a point in time when it was too late to trade it in for beauty? Certainly God had to be tired of her weak attempts at living a Christian life. Maybe ashes were all that was left for her now.

The next speaker talked how each of them needed to accept their place in life, because God was the One who had done the placing. When she was finished, the speaker invited ladies to the front if they wanted to ask Jesus into their lives for the first time. "He's calling you, my friends, calling you to a life of freedom and strength, peace and purpose. Come now; don't let anything hold you back."

Kelly fidgeted in her seat. She had fresh tears on her cheeks, but this wasn't the time to go up front. Besides, she already had Jesus. She'd believed in Him, and she'd been baptized. What more was there? Someone might see her and wonder why she was going up when she'd been a Christian all her life. She'd served as a missionary, after all.

But when the first wave of women reached the front, the speaker invited another group of people.

"Maybe you've been stuck in your faith, unable to hear God or feel His strength in your life. If that's you, then this is your day, your moment. Come and give Him your situation. Feel His loving arms holding you up, leading you to the front of the room where people can pray for you."

There was no one holding onto her, no one pulling her to her feet, and no one keeping her stuck to her chair. But Kelly felt the struggle as surely as she felt her next heartbeat. A tug-of-war was going on between the life she'd been living and the life God was calling her to. A tug-of-war where she, Kelly Ryan, was the rope.

She watched as one woman and then another, and then dozens of women made their way to the front. Emotions and heartache flowed freely and the floor of the HP Pavilion became wet with the tears of the women strong enough to accept the call.

But still Kelly sat. She hadn't come here to make a decision or find renewal in her walk with Christ. She was simply taking a break for herself, spending time with Laurie. She needed more time before making a decision like the one the women around her were making. If she went up front, that meant she was willing to give up her resentment of Chase's determination to make movies and find strength in Scripture — the way she used to find it.

Maybe tomorrow or next week, but not now. She remained seated, watching countless women find freedom. Next to her, Laurie leaned close and patted her knee. "Like I said, God's doing something here today."

No question. But it would take longer for Him to do something with Kelly. No amount of emotion or tears could change her life or the facts as they were. Chase had no patience for her concerns and he seemed to rush to get out the door and back to LA. She was overwhelmed most of the time and she would most likely remain so — even with the Prozac. If she went forward here and now, then what? That wouldn't make her into the nice, supportive wife or clear away the work she had in running their home by herself.

Not now, God. I can't surrender now ... I'm not sure about anything.

The pressure on the rope grew greater. She could feel it, feel the battle raging. But still she sat.

During lunch, Kelly excused herself to the restroom. But afterward, she stepped outside and sat on the edge of a cement block wall under an overhang, one of the few places outdoors that was still dry. She didn't care about eating; a boxed lunch wasn't interesting to her on a day like this, and there was no candy for sale inside—she'd checked.

"Okay, God ... What are You doing?"

She'd had her phone off all morning, but now she turned it on. She felt a sudden urge to talk to Chase. Even for a few minutes. She clicked his name and immediately the phone began to ring. She waited—two rings, three, but on the fourth the call went to his voicemail. Her mouth opened to leave him a message, an apology or a plea that he call her later so they could talk. But nothing seemed right, and she hung up. Better to talk to him in person.

The rain had let up, but still the sky remained a dark gray. In a moment like this it was hard to believe the sky would ever clear again, same as it was hard to believe that for her life.

Why, God? Why am I fighting You?

She pictured the prayer lifting all the way to heaven, but there was no answer. No sign that God cared about her sitting here, lost in her own little world of ashes and self-pity.

Inside the music started up again. Laurie would wonder where she'd gone and how come she'd passed on lunch. Kelly pulled herself up and worked her way through the crowd back to her seat. The song was another Hillsong number, "From the Inside Out," and they were halfway through the first verse when Kelly took her seat.

"Everything okay?" Laurie looked into her eyes, clearly trying to see the truth.

"Fine." Kelly covered with a quick smile. "I went out to call Chase."

"Oh." Her friend nodded. "Good."

She turned her attention to the praise band. No point telling Laurie she hadn't even gotten through to her husband. She'd needed time alone—even in this massive crowd. The music filled the air around them. *"Everlasting, Your light will shine when all else fades ... never ending, Your glory goes beyond all fame ..."*

The line seemed custom-made for Kelly. No matter what lay ahead, Christ's light would remain, beyond the darkness and valleys, beyond the deserts and wilderness. Beyond any fame — whether their future involved a movie deal with Brandon Paul or not. God was King of all, Lord of all.

Kelly could still feel something holding her back from breaking completely, from giving in to the Lord's calling. But the wall was crumbling.

Each word of the song seemed written for her, and she stood with the other women, joining her voice with the throng.

She wanted to believe the lyrics, wanted to let God have His way with her, but her shame and guilt were too great. What reason would the Lord have for wanting her? How many times had she given God control only to take it back the next morning — overwhelmed by worry and discouragement? She was stuck, but still she sang, and as she did she could feel her vision growing clearer, feel the Lord's love nearer than before.

Finally, at the end of the day, came a concert by Nicole C. Mullen. Back in the days when Kelly listened to Christian music morning to night, Nicole had been one of her favorites. Her songs "Redeemer" and "Call on Jesus" were songs that marked eras in her life, times when she was a new mom and doubting her ability to stay strong for everyone who needed her. Kelly hadn't known Nicole was closing out the day, and now her time here seemed ordained from God. As if the Lord Himself had arranged for this performance.

"I need a brainwash from my head to my soul ... I need a brainwash, bring it down to my toes ..." Nicole's voice rang out across the auditorium. She was young and fit, and she easily danced as well as any of the teenage dancers behind her on the stage, including her fourteen-year-old daughter. The audience was on its

feet singing along, enjoying the call to be of pure mind. Kelly swayed to the music, startled by the message.

The battle she was losing was in her mind. Each day she woke up overwhelmed only to wallow in self-pity the whole day—feeding the emptiness in her soul with comfort food. Only if she changed her mind, only if she gave God control over her thoughts, would she find freedom from her depression and mindless eating.

Nicole moved on to her hit songs, and all around her Kelly could hear the sniffling of women giving in to God's gentle prodding. "*I know ... my Redeemer lives ... I know, my Redeemer lives ...*" Kelly sang along, and for the first time that day she felt herself meaning every word. She was a failure, yes, and a sinner at the worst level. She'd ignored God and walked purposefully in a direction opposite the one He called her to. But still He lived, and He was hers. Her very own Redeemer. Even if she were the only one left on the face of earth.

The concert flew by, and toward the end, Kelly could feel tears on her cheeks again. She couldn't fight God much longer. It was a losing battle. No matter how much she'd let Him down, He wasn't giving up on her. She could feel the rope of her soul sliding in His direction.

Nicole ended her performance by introducing her last song with a brief story. "There was a woman in the Bible, desperate for healing. A woman who had been suffering for more than a decade. No one and nothing could heal her, but Jesus was passing by that day. There would be crowds of people, and hundreds more worthy of His attention than she could ever be." Nicole walked slowly to the edge of the stage. "But she knew. She absolutely knew that if she could only reach out and touch the hem of His garment, she would be healed. Her belief in Him and His power was that strong." She paused, letting the truth of the story sink in around the enormous room. "This song is called 'One Touch.'"

The music was pretty and lyrical, and Nicole started in with the first verse.

Then, as she sang, something dramatic began to happen. First her daughter, and then the other dancers moved stealthily out onto the stage. The girls wore flowing white dresses and black sweatshirts. On the back of each sweatshirt was a single, simple word: Shame ... Guilt ... Loneliness ... Doubt ... Addiction.

Nicole reached the chorus as her dancers formed an ominous half circle around her. Then with every bit of her energy, she clutched desperately at the air in front of her. *"If I could just touch the hem of His garment, I know I'd be made whole."* But as she reached out, the girls with Shame and Guilt and Addiction on their sweatshirts used all their energy to hold her back.

Nicole pushed against them.

The harder Nicole tried to press forward toward Jesus, the more Shame and Guilt, Loneliness and Doubt and Addiction held her back. The image was overwhelming and for the first time — the very first time — Kelly could see an actual picture of her life, the way Jesus saw her. She could try to touch the hem of His garment, she could beg Him for the scraps of His kindness, but something was holding her back. Something she had felt deep inside her for all these months.

Shame, guilt, loneliness, doubt, addiction.

The second verse began, and the story followed the one in the Bible. A crowd of people, a desperate attempt to press through to Jesus. Nicole's clear voice rang out. As she reached that part where Jesus looked back, every obstacle fighting for her soul stopped and stared.

Kelly began to cry, struck by the picture. That was how the battle went, wasn't it? If she would only get close enough to Jesus to touch the hem of His garment, she could hear His voice, and the things holding her back would hear it too.

One by one, the dancers representing Shame and Guilt and Loneliness and the rest fell in a heap to the floor. The message was as clear as it was powerful. No barrier could stand in the presence of Christ. *"If I could just touch the hem of His garment, I know I'd be made whole."*

As the song built, Kelly's tears came harder. That was her, reaching out to Jesus and letting her shame and addiction hold her back. But not anymore. *"Somehow He pressed His way through my madness,"* Nicole sang out, *"and His love has healed my soul."*

That was it, Kelly understood now. She needed to get close enough to Jesus to hear His voice, to touch the hem of His garment so she could be made whole again.

Laurie seemed to understand that something was happening with Kelly. She put her hand on Kelly's shoulder. "It's okay," she whispered. "Let God have His way."

Kelly nodded as the tears ran down her face and into her mouth. Salty and hot. *I'm sorry, Jesus. I don't want to fight anymore. I surrender. I surrender completely.* She didn't need more convincing. The picture of Nicole straining for Jesus and being held back was one that would stay with her forever. A picture of the battle. But the victory would also stay with her. She didn't need to fight against shame and guilt and depression. She only needed to stay close to Jesus, where the things that warred against her soul didn't stand a chance. Close enough to touch the hem of His garment.

The way she was standing now.

A Note from Karen

Dear Reader Friends,

More than any other book I've written, I was amazed at how life imitated art while I was writing *Take Two*. Midway through the book, and even after I'd written my outline, I had the privilege of attending the Palm Springs Film Festival, where my movie *Like Dandelion Dust* was one of the featured films. *Like Dandelion Dust* was selected as Best of the Festival and received much praise from local news and even a stunning review in *Variety*. In addition, it won Best Picture at a number of other film festivals.

But that is pretty much where the similarities ended.

The brothers who produced *Like Dandelion Dust* experienced some of the logistical distractions detailed in *Take One*, but here in *Take Two* fiction took over. There was no Kendall Adams or Ben Adams in the lives of the real producers. Even so, I believe the storyline of the fictional producers represents an important truth. In today's market, there is a great hunger for Christian films, for movies with a message and not merely a couple hours of mindless entertainment. That said, the struggle remains. The task of putting a movie onto the big screen is still daunting. I encourage you to pray for the many real-life producers like Chase Ryan and Keith Ellison who sacrifice much for the sake of changing the world with the power of film.

Also, I love that this series gives me the chance to follow Bailey and Cody and their group of friends. College life is very difficult for today's young people, with many distractions to faith and family and all that is right. It's important to see how differently a young Christian girl can meet those challenges and tests. Certainly as Andi goes her own way, the consequences will become clear. Likewise, as Bailey chooses God's will, though she may have heartache at times, she will find the plans God has for her.

In the books ahead Tim and Bailey and Cody, Andi and her parents, Chase and Kelly, and Kendall Adams all will face great temptations and trials, and at the same time brilliant, tearful triumphs. As always, I'm grateful you're continuing this new journey with me, and I look forward to hearing your feedback.

Take a minute and visit my website at www.KarenKingsbury.com, where you can get to know other readers and become part of a community that agrees there is life-changing power in something as simple as a story. On my website you can post prayer requests or pray for those in need. You can send in a photo of your loved one serving our country or let us know of a fallen soldier we can honor on our Fallen Heroes page.

My website will also tell you about my ongoing contests, including "Shared a Book," which encourages you to let me know when you've shared one of my books with someone in your life. Each time you let me know, you're entered for the chance to spend a summer weekend with my family. In addition, everyone signed up for my monthly newsletter is automatically entered into an ongoing once-a-month drawing for a free, signed copy of my latest novel.

Also on my website you can find out which women's conferences I'll speak at next and whether you might live close enough so we'll have the chance to meet, to share a hug, or take a picture together. In addition there are links that will help you with matters that are important to you — faith and family, adoption, and ways to help others.

Of course, on my site you can find out a little more about me and my family, my Facebook and YouTube channel, and my Karen's Movie Monday — where I release a YouTube clip each

Monday dealing with some aspect of my family and faith and the wonderful world of Life-Changing Fiction™.

Finally, if you gave your life over to God during the reading of this book, or if you found your way back to a faith you'd let grow cold, send me a letter at Office@KarenKingsbury.com and write "New Life" in the subject line. I would encourage you to connect with a Bible-believing church in your area, and to get hold of a Bible. If you can't afford a Bible—include your address in your e-mail and I'll send you one.

One more thing: I've started a program where I will donate a book to any high school or middle school librarian who makes a request. Check out my website for details.

Again, thanks for traveling with me through the pages of this book. I can't wait to see you next time. My next book will be a stand-alone called *Shades of Blue*. It's a book I've been longing to write for three years. After that, look for *Take Three*!

Until then, keep reaching for the hem of His garment.

In His light and love,
Karen Kingsbury

www.KarenKingsbury.com

Reader Study Guide

Please use the following questions for your book club, small group, or for personal reflection.

1. The editing process was long and tedious for Keith and Chase. What do you think drove them to put in such long hours? What have you been a part of in the past that required an amazing effort? What drove you in that effort?

2. What led to Kelly's discouragement and depression? Share about a time when you or someone you know was taken into a dark time because of a series of events.

3. Kelly struggled with mindless eating. Discuss what you know about this type of problem. What do you think led Kelly to struggle with this?

4. Thanksgiving Day at Katy and Dayne's was a chance for the Baxter family to be back together again. Tell about the times during the year when you and your family get together. What made this time special for the Baxters? What makes these times special for you and your family?

5. Discuss the importance of being thankful. What were the things Keith and Chase and their wives were thankful for? What are ten things you are thankful for?

6. What led Andi to be interested in the offer from the student filmmaker—Taz? Why is flattery from worldly sources such a dangerous thing in our walk with the Lord? Talk about a time when flattery led you to make a decision you regret.

7. Bailey felt a strain in her friendship with Cody through much of this story. What caused this strain? Share about a time when you experienced a strain with a close friend. What caused the strain, and what brought the friendship back around again?

8. For Keith and Chase, the first part of *Take Two* has them at a time in their professional careers when everything seems to be going right. What did the producers learn during this time? Have you learned more about your faith in good times, or in difficult times? Explain.

9. Cody wants desperately to help his mom stay on the right path, but still he worries about her. What does Cody do to show his mother he's there for her? What have you done to be supportive of someone you love? How has that support made a difference?

10. Explain Andi's series of compromises where Taz's movie was concerned. How did Taz convince her that these compromises were acceptable?

11. Talk about a time when you or someone you know made a series of compromises. How were those compromises justified?

12. Midway through the book, Keith began to experience red flags where the smooth and easy details of moviemaking were concerned. Why is it important to look closer when the details of life seem too easy? Talk about a time when the easy life suddenly became very difficult.

13. Bailey found much strength in her involvement with Campus Crusade. Why is it important for youth to be involved in a faith group of some kind? Why is it important for all Christians to belong to some sort of group of believers?

14. In what ways did Kelly make things worse in her relationship with her husband? What about her relationship with God? Talk about a time when you or someone you know made choices that harmed their relationships.

15. How could Kelly have helped her situation? Talk about how you or someone you know might find help in a troubling situation.

16. Kelly had the chance to attend a women's conference. Talk about a Christian conference you attended. Did you come away stronger because of it? Why or why not?

17. In what ways did God soften Kelly's heart during her day at the women's conference? Why was she reluctant to allow herself to be changed? Discuss Kelly's emotions that day.

18. Discuss how Nicole C. Mullen's song "One Touch" made a difference for Kelly. Explain how the visual illustration of the song connected with Kelly.

19. Have you ever imagined a spiritual battle as a literal force holding you back from Jesus? Talk about a time like that.

20. Cody and Taz are very different college guys. Talk about the differences, and what motivates each of these young men.

Read an Excerpt from the Next Book in the Above the Line Series: *Take Three*

Bailey arrived at the Lake Monroe retreat center lost in thoughts about her roommate. Their recent conversation had been good—for the first time in awhile. Maybe if they had more time together, Taz wouldn't be such an obsession in Andi's life. No matter what Andi thought about him, he was trouble. Bailey could feel it in her spirit. God didn't want Andi anywhere near the guy.

Still, convincing her would take a miracle at this point.

Bailey climbed out of her car and was met by a group of her Cru Bible study girls. Tim had had to cancel at the last minute—a case of strep throat—and Cody was spending the weekend with his mom, because of her birthday. At least that was the plan. But when she and the girls walked with their sleeping bags and pillows to their cabin, she heard Cody's voice.

She waited until she had her bed made before finding him with a few other guys near the fire pit. She caught his attention and he smiled. "I didn't think you were coming."

This wasn't the time for a serious conversation. But she had to know what had changed his mind.

"My mom had other plans." He grabbed an armful of wood and stacked it near the pit. "I'll tell you later."

While they ate, she could feel Cody's presence the way she could feel the presence of her family when they were in a crowd. A couple times she looked over her shoulder at him, and once she caught him looking too. He still hadn't explained what had happened with his mother, but there would be time for that later. Right now she needed to give her attention to the girls in her cabin. She'd asked God for closer friendships with them as a result of this retreat.

So far He was answering her prayers beyond anything she could've dreamed.

One of the guy cabins had cleanup that night, and Daniel dismissed the rest of the group for an hour of free time. A few of the girls wanted to make calls home, just to check in. Bailey waited until she was sure none of them were looking to talk to her, and then she wandered out the door and down the path toward Cody's cabin. She saw him long before she reached it, sitting outside on a tree stump, staring at the lake.

She stopped and watched him, the familiar way he held his head, the way the fading sun cast light over his shoulders. What was he thinking, sitting there like that? Was he worried about his mom, or a new girl in his life? Or maybe he was taking in God's beauty. She almost didn't want to disturb him, but then — as if he could read her mind — he looked her way and smiled. "Hey."

The path was smooth, but she watched her step anyway. Just in case some critter crossed in front of her. She was much more of a hotel girl, more comfortable at the Doubletree with samples of lotion and shampoo, than here in the woods. But she could appreciate both, and she was glad to be here. Especially now, with Cody a part of the retreat.

She reached him and grinned. "You looked lost in thought. I didn't want to interrupt."

For a second she thought he might tell her what he was thinking, but then he set his jaw, his smile guarded. "I'm glad you did."

He pointed at a path that led closer to the lake. "Wanna take a walk?"

"Sure." They set out side by side, and suddenly Bailey laughed out loud. "I just remembered something funny."

He slipped his hands into the pockets of his jeans and laughed a little too. The way he always did around her. "Which thing? There's lots to laugh at with you around."

"Hey." She pretended to be hurt. "I'm not sure that's a compliment."

"It is." His eyes danced. "Believe me, it is."

"Okay, well, remember when we were at the beach that time, on the other side of the lake? We took a walk and you challenged me to a race."

"Me?" He stopped and pointed to himself. "That was you, missy. You're the one who wanted to race."

"Anyway ..." She kept walking, undaunted. "I got about ten steps and I twisted my ankle. You had to practically carry me back to the picnic tables."

"That was the summer before I shipped out."

"Yeah, it was." She allowed her laughter to fade softly, mingling with the early summer breeze. They turned a corner and lost view of the campsite. The lake spread out before them, but still they walked on. Up ahead was a bench, and when they reached it, they sat together. Cody seemed careful to allow space between them.

"So what happened? I thought you were going to be with your mom this weekend."

"She met some guy." He frowned. "I'm not sure how good he is for her. I was sort of hoping she'd meet someone at church, but she met this one at the health club."

"She made plans with him?"

"Yeah. She said she didn't want me to miss a retreat on her account."

"That was nice."

"I guess." He breathed in slowly, deeply. "I still worry about her."

"I know. I can tell." She lifted her chin and filled her lungs with the sweet-smelling air. "I forget how great it feels to be out here, just us and God."

"That's why I came. I need time with God. To really think about this coaching idea and whatever else my future holds."

Despite the cool bench beneath her Bailey felt her heart warm inside her. Cody, whose life might've turned out so different, was doing better than any of them had dreamed. His life was a living miracle, every aspect of it. "I'm glad. I still pray for you all the time."

His expression grew deeper, the connection between them as close as she shared with any of her brothers. "The way I still pray for you." He faced the water again. "Speaking of which, what happened to Tim? I thought he was taking this trip for sure."

"He got sick. Strep throat."

"Oooh." Cody frowned. "That's too bad."

"Yeah. I told him I'd give him details when we get back on Monday."

Cody was quiet for a long moment. In the distance trilled the haunting sound of a blue heron, swooping low over the water. The sun had already set, and dusk was settling across the lake. "You and Tim," Cody said finally. "You're still very serious, aren't you?"

She sighed. He'd never quite understood that she had loved him first, that if he'd come back from Iraq and declared his love for her, she and Tim would've been nothing more than a passing fling. But Cody didn't have those feelings for her, and now she wished he wouldn't ask questions about Tim.

"Sorry." Cody faced her. "You don't have to answer."

"No, it's fine." She folded her arms in front of her and pulled one foot up onto the bench. "Things are the same."

"Your dad said you and Tim are auditioning in New York next week."

"We are." She shrugged. "It's something I've always wanted to do. But last time I was in the city it didn't have the same appeal as before. I don't know." She stared at the water, at the light reflecting across the center of the lake. "New York's crazy. All sorts of noise and smells and cramped living. You have to look straight up on some streets just to see the sky."

Cody made a face. "Not my style."

"Definitely not." She gave him a sad smile. If she wound up in New York, that would be the end for her and Cody. Distance would have the final say. "My dad can't stand it either."

The conversation flowed easily, without the walls she'd kept up around herself for so much of the last school year. It felt wonderful, being close to him again. "I guess I realized something this last time. When we go to New York, we stay at this nice hotel and see the top shows, sitting in the best seats. We stay three days and then we're out of there. But that's not how it would be if I lived there." She hugged her knee to her chest and looked at him. "I'd be commuting in on a bridge or a subway, walking fast and trying not to get accosted. I'd pay high rent to share a small apartment and have almost no fresh air."

The sky grew dusky, but in the dim light that remained an eagle floated in the distance and landed in a towering pine. A breeze brushed against her face and for a few seconds she closed her eyes. When she opened them, she smiled again. "No moments like this."

"What about Tim?" Cody seemed guarded when he talked about Tim. "How does he feel about the city?"

"He loves it. I think he could live there for the next five years and feel great about it. He really wants to perform."

"What about finding a church? Do they have anything like that in New York?"

"They do." She uttered a sad laugh. "But Broadway's a long way from the Bible Belt."

They talked for a few minutes about a church she'd heard about not far from Times Square. "If I lived there, I guess I'd become a part of that."

Again Cody was quiet. Their hour was almost up, and they would need to get back soon. Neither of them had brought a flashlight. "So you really think it could happen, huh? You and Tim, performing on Broadway, living in New York City?" He smiled. "I guess that would be a dream come true for both of you."

"I guess." Everything about the possibility sounded right, like something she'd longed for since her early days with Christian Kids Theater. But right now, with the fresh lake air all around them and Cody by her side, her dreams were no longer as clear as they'd once been. "What about you?" She hadn't asked for a long time, and now she wanted to know. Even if she was afraid of his answer. "You seeing anyone?"

"Me?" A quiet laugh rattled his chest. "Definitely not. God's still making me into the guy I need to be. I want that before I want a girlfriend."

His answer made her feel starry eyed. "She's a lucky girl, Cody."

"I'm saving my heart for her. Any sort of casual dating at this point in my life would only cheapen what I have to offer." He looked out at the water again. "Whoever she is."

For the craziest moment, Bailey wanted to tell him that he didn't need to wonder, that no other girl would ever love him the way she could love him. But she stopped herself before she said something and sounded like a crazy person. She had a boyfriend, after all. She could hardly confess her love to the friend beside her when she had just finished talking about building a life with Tim in New York City.

"What are you thinking?" Again Cody seemed to read her mind.

"Nothing." Her smile was shyer than before. "Nothing I can tell *you*, anyway." She put both her feet down on the ground and kicked at his tennis shoe. "I'd say let's race back, but I can't afford another sprained ankle. Not with my audition next week."

Again he laughed. "That's just one of the things I love about you, Bailey. You make me laugh."

"Same with you."

"Can I tell you something?" His knee brushed against hers, and just as quickly he eased back, keeping things between them appropriate and on the level.

"Yes. That's the deal now. We're friends." She tapped his foot again. "You can tell me anything."

"Okay, now, don't weird out on me or think I'm trying to get between you and Tim or anything."

She giggled. "Go on. At this rate you'll never spit it out."

"The truth is I thank God every day for you, Bailey. For your family and your friendship. For the way we've found each other again."

"Ahhh." She tilted her head and let her eyes get lost in his. The last remainder of daylight shone on his face and she knew without a doubt she'd remember this moment as long as she lived. Without wondering whether it was right or wrong, she put her arms around his neck and hugged him. "That means the world, Cody." The hug was quick, nothing she wouldn't give one of her brothers. "I'm glad you told me." She pulled back and felt her eyes start to dance. "Now it's my turn."

"Go on."

"I thank God for you too. I was so mad at you back in the fall, when you wouldn't talk to me." She made a face and wagged her fist at him. "I thought we'd never have a day like this again in all our lives."

"I was worried about it."

"But here we are." She held up her hands and let them fall lightly to her knees. "That's why God's so amazing. He knows how to fix things, even after we make a mess of them."

"Exactly." He stood and reached out his hand. "Come on, it'll be pitch dark in a few minutes."

She took his hand and felt the thrill of his touch all the way to her toes. Once she was standing she drew her fingers from his and kept the conversation light. She could hardly hold hands with Cody. First, it would only confuse things. And second, holding hands with Tim never sent a chill through her. And she wasn't ready to analyze what that meant or what it said about her relationship with Tim. Better to keep her distance where Cody was concerned. Besides, he was holding out body and soul for the girl of his dreams. She didn't want to get in the way of that, even if a part of her desperately wished she were that girl.

On the way back, Cody told her about a bear sighting in the woods not far from the campsite.

"Great." She was about to tell him the story of her little brother BJ and a northern copperhead he'd nearly stepped on when her foot settled on something soft and slithery. She screamed and fell all at the same time, her ankle giving way beneath her as she dropped. She had no idea how Cody moved so fast or how in the dark he was able to catch her, but the next thing she knew she was in his arms, clinging to his neck. She pointed down at the ground. "There's a snake, Cody! Be careful."

He set her down a few feet away and went back to the spot where she'd felt the snake. Using the toe of his shoe, he pressed around and came up with something long and bendable. "This, you mean?"

He brought it closer and she stifled another scream. "Don't, Cody! It could be poisonous. Shawn says there's copperheads all around this lake."

"Well..." He held his hands out so she could see exactly what had frightened her. "This branch is definitely not part of the copperhead family, I can promise you that much."

Bailey straightened and stared at the thing Cody was holding. "A branch? You've gotta be kidding. I could feel it moving."

"It's a young branch. A little more flexible than some." He tossed it off the path and grinned at her. "You probably scared it to death."

She tested her ankle, but it was fine, and suddenly she pictured herself stepping on the branch and practically jumping into Cody's arms. She burst into laughter again and had to hold onto Cody's waist as they walked. Otherwise she would've fallen to the ground, unable to breathe because she was giggling so hard.

The others already had flashlights out, and as they reached base camp, everyone wanted to know what was so funny. Bailey told her snake story, but when she reached the part about stepping on the branch, she cracked up once again. Cody had to finish the story.

It was like that throughout the weekend. She had hours of solitude with the Lord, times when she could pray about the direction God had for her life, and whether New York City was something she really wanted. Other hours she and the girls talked together, or she and Cody took long walks together. Always their time ended up in laughter, except for once — the last night of the retreat.

That night, with the moon little more than a thumbnail of light overhead, they sat by the fire until everyone else had turned in. They talked about Cody's mother and Bailey's wonderful family and Cody's dream to help kids the way Bailey's parents had helped him. They sat close together, neither of them seeming to mind when their knees touched a time or two.

Before they turned in, Cody held out his hands to her. "Pray with me, Bailey. Can you do that?"

She wasn't sure how smart it was, but she didn't hesitate. She slipped her fingers in his and together they bowed their heads. She started the prayer, the way she'd seen her mom and dad pray together so many times over the years. "Dear Lord, this time away has been so good for us, for the friendships that have grown stronger and for the way You feel closer than ever. Right now I want to thank You for Cody and his friendship. Please, Lord, keep him close to You always. And let him know how much he means to me."

It was Cody's turn, and he gave her fingers a subtle squeeze as he started. "God, You know how I feel about Bailey." He hesitated for a moment, as if his feelings for her weren't something he was willing to actually put into words. "I begged You for a second chance at her friendship, and now here we are. Copperhead snake branches and all." They both shared a couple seconds of quiet laughter, the sound of the fire crackling a few feet away. When he had control again, he finished. "Lord, I ask that You protect what we've found on the far side of Lake Monroe this weekend. I feel closer to Bailey than ever before, and I'm blessed for that fact.

"People could live all their lives and never have a friend like Bailey Flanigan. So thank You, Lord. And I pray for her audition coming up. If You want her to live in New York, to perform there and be part of a revival taking place in that city, then throw open the doors for her this next week. Let her stand out and let her get a role in a Broadway play." He paused, and there was no hiding the sadness that had crept into his voice. "But only if it's Your will, Father. Otherwise, shut the door. Then she'll know which way You're leading her."

He took a steadying breath. "Be with Tim, too, dear God. If these two are meant to be together, make that clear. Life is too short to waste on half-hearted connections and meaningless run-throughs. So let them know whether what they have is something that will last." He paused once more. "Most of all, let Bailey know how much I love her. How much I've always loved her. In Jesus' name, amen."

Bailey didn't want to let go of his hands, but slowly he let go first. She had lost her breath somewhere around the part about half-hearted connections and meaningless run-throughs, and when he asked God to let her know how much he loved her she felt her heart go into a rhythm she didn't recognize. She swallowed hard, trying to find a way to right her world back on its axis. He didn't mean the sort of love she'd always wanted from him. *It's only a friendship love*, she told herself. *Nothing more.*

But still, as they stood and shared a long hug, and as he walked her to her cabin and they said good night, Bailey had to remember to exhale. She lay in her bed in her sleeping bag for a long time, looking out the window at a brilliant spread of stars and replaying every word of Cody's prayer. He really did love her. That much was evident by the way he'd asked God to bless her audition, and in the way he'd prayed for her and Tim. When was the last time she and Tim had prayed like this, with such intensity about serious matters? She couldn't remember the last time they'd prayed together about anything.

She fell asleep certain that the one thing she didn't want was an existence of half-hearted connections and meaningless run-throughs. Never mind that Cody didn't see her as the girl of his dreams, the girl he was saving his love for. They had this between them, a wonderful bond that some people could spend their whole lives seeking.

Before she was fully asleep, she made up her mind about something: she would rather be alone than have a love that was less intimate than what she still shared with Cody Coleman. They had found something special these past few days. A deep friendship-love that had come to life once more amidst the presence of northern copperhead snake branches and laughter and God.

Most of all, God.

Coming Home

A Story of Unending Love and Eternal Promise

Karen Kingsbury, New York Times Bestselling Author

Coming Home is a novel about tremendous victory and unprecedented loss, a story of faith and a forever kind of love, love that will stay with you long after the last page. This stand-alone novel will serve as either a grand introduction or a beautiful conclusion in the saga of the Baxter Family.

The Baxters make plans to come together for a summer lakeside reunion, a celebration like they haven't had in years. But before the big day, the unthinkable happens. As the Baxter Family rallies together, memories come to light in the grief-stricken hours of waiting and praying, memories that bring healing and hope during a time when otherwise darkness might have the final word.

In a season that changes all of them, the brilliance of family love overshadows even the valley of heartache as the Baxters draw closer to God and each other. Along the way, secrets are revealed and the truth about the Baxter Family history is finally made known. Ultimately, in this portrait of family love, the Baxters cling to each other and to God's promise of forever.

Coming June 21, 2012

ZONDERVAN.com

BAILEY FLANIGAN SERIES

Leaving

Karen Kingsbury,
New York Times *Bestselling Author*

The Bailey Flanigan Series begins with Bailey leaving Bloomington for the adventure of a lifetime. She has won an audition for the ensemble of a Broadway musical in New York City. She's determined to take advantage of this once-in-a-lifetime opportunity, but is she really ready to leave family and friends for the loneliness of the city? And what of Cody? His disappearance has her worried about their future and praying that their love can survive.

In order to be closer to his mother in jail, Cody takes a coaching job in a small community outside Indianapolis. New friends, distance, and circumstances expose cracks in his relationship with Bailey Flanigan.

Love, loneliness, big opportunities, and even bigger decisions highlight the first book in the new Bailey Flanigan Series that features members of the popular Baxter family and finally completes the Bailey Flanigan/Cody Coleman story.

Available in stores and online!

ZONDERVAN
.com

BAILEY FLANIGAN SERIES

Learning

Karen Kingsbury,
New York Times *Bestselling Author*

Learning, book two in the Bailey Flanigan Series, picks up where *Leaving* ended. Bailey Flanigan and Cody Coleman are not only separated by physical distance, they are also faced with great emotional distance. While Bailey grows closer to her dream to be an actress and dancer in New York, Cody coaches a small high school football team ... on and off the field. But neither feels complete without the chance to share their dreams with one another.

Can distance truly make the heart grow fonder? Or will Cody learn to turn to others to share in his happiness? And in the face of tragedy, who will be there to provide comfort?

As Cody's past catches up with him, he must learn to reach out for help or risk withdrawing permanently inside himself. Both Bailey and Cody find themselves learning significant life lessons in this poignant love story, featuring members from Karen Kingsbury's popular Baxter family.

Available in stores and online!

ZONDERVAN
.com

BAILEY FLANIGAN SERIES

Longing

Karen Kingsbury, New York Times Bestselling Author

Longing, book three in the Bailey Flanigan Series, picks up where Learning ended. After a long and lonely silence from Cody Coleman, Bailey Flanigan becomes closer to her one-time Hollywood co-star, Brandon Paul. Nights on the town in New York City and long talks on the balcony of Brandon's Malibu Beach home make Bailey dizzy with new feelings and cause her to wonder if her days with Cody are over forever.

Meanwhile, Cody's work coaching a small-town football team has brought him and his players national attention. In the midst of the celebration and success, Cody finds himself much closer to a woman who seems to better understand him and his new life. Even so, never does much time go by without Bailey and Cody experiencing deep feelings of longing for each other, longing both for the past and for answers before they can move forward.

Will an unexpected loss be the turning point for Cody? Will Cody and Bailey find a way back together again for the first time in more than a year? And if they do, will their brief time together be enough to help them remember all they've been longing for?

Available in stores and online!

ZONDERVAN
.com

BAILEY FLANIGAN SERIES

Loving

Karen Kingsbury, New York Times Bestselling Author

The answers Bailey Flanigan once longed and prayed for are finally becoming clear.

In Loving, the fourth and final book in the Bailey Flanigan Series by New York Times bestselling author Karen Kingsbury, Bailey is planning a wedding and making decisions that will shape her future. Bailey enjoys the beginning of her new career and time spent with Brandon while Cody faithfully coaches his team on and off the field. Will she spend her life with Brandon Paul in Los Angeles, or will her heart draw her back to Bloomington, Indiana and Cody Coleman, her first love? Bailey has learned much and grown over the years, but the greatest challenges, the richest joys, and the deepest heartaches are still to come.

Featuring members from Karen Kingsbury's popular Baxter family, Loving completes Bailey and Cody's story — the finale thousands of fans have been waiting for.

Available in stores and online!

ZONDERVAN®
.com

Unlocked

A Love Story

Karen Kingsbury,
New York Times *Bestselling Author*

Before You Take a Stand...
You've Got to Take a Chance.

Holden Harris is an eighteen-year-old locked in a prison of autism. Despite his quiet ways and quirky behaviors, Holden is very happy and socially normal — on the inside, in a private world all his own. In reality, he is bullied at school by kids who only see that he is very different.

Ella Reynolds is part of the "in" crowd. Star of the high school drama production, her life seems perfect. When she catches Holden listening to her rehearse for the school play, she is drawn to him... the way he is drawn to the music. Then, Ella makes a dramatic discovery — she and Holden were best friends as children.

Frustrated by the way Holden is bullied, and horrified at the indifference of her peers, Ella decides to take a stand against the most privileged and popular kids at school. Including her boyfriend, Jake.

Ella believes miracles can happen in the unlikeliest places, and that just maybe an entire community might celebrate from the sidelines. But will Holden's praying mother and the efforts of Ella and a cast of theater kids be enough to unlock the prison that contains Holden?

This time, friendship, faith, and the power of a song must be strong enough to open the doors to the miracle Holden needs.

Available in stores and online!

ZONDERVAN
.com

Share Your Thoughts

With the Author: Your comments will be forwarded to the author when you send them to *zauthor@zondervan.com*.

With Zondervan: Submit your review of this book by writing to *zreview@zondervan.com*.

Free Online Resources at www.zondervan.com

Zondervan AuthorTracker: Be notified whenever your favorite authors publish new books, go on tour, or post an update about what's happening in their lives at www.zondervan.com/authortracker.

Daily Bible Verses and Devotions: Enrich your life with daily Bible verses or devotions that help you start every morning focused on God. Visit www.zondervan.com/newsletters.

Free Email Publications: Sign up for newsletters on Christian living, academic resources, church ministry, fiction, children's resources, and more. Visit www.zondervan.com/newsletters.

Zondervan Bible Search: Find and compare Bible passages in a variety of translations at www.zondervanbiblesearch.com.

Other Benefits: Register yourself to receive online benefits like coupons and special offers, or to participate in research.

ZONDERVAN®

ZONDERVAN.com/
AUTHORTRACKER
follow your favorite authors

KAREN KINGSBURY

NEW YORK TIMES BESTSELLING AUTHOR KAREN Kingsbury is America's favorite inspirational novelist, with nearly 20 million books in print. Her Life-Changing Fiction™ has produced multiple bestsellers, including *Unlocked, Leaving, Take One, Between Sundays, Even Now, One Tuesday Morning, Beyond Tuesday Morning,* and *Ever After,* which was named the 2007 Christian Book of the Year. An award-winning author and newly published songwriter, Karen has several movies optioned for production, and her novel *Like Dandelion Dust* was made into a major motion picture, now available on DVD. Karen is also a nationally known speaker with several women's groups including Women of Faith. She lives in Tennessee with her husband, Don, their daughter, and five sons, three of whom are adopted from Haiti.

Lightning Source UK Ltd.
Milton Keynes UK
UKHW040800100921
390264UK00001B/184